SAS
STORIES OF
HEROES V

DAVID MONNERY
SHAUN CLARKE

BLITZ EDITIONS

This edition published in 1995

Published by Blitz Editions
an imprint of Bookmart Limited
Registered Number 2372865
Trading at Bookmart Limited
Desford Road, Enderby
Leicester, LE9 5AD

ISBN 1 85605303 2

Typeset by Hewer Text Composition Services, Edinburgh
Printed in Great Britain by Cox and Wyman Limited, Reading

SOLDIER N: SAS

THE GAMBIAN BLUFF

SOLDIER N: SAS

THE GAMBIAN BLUFF

David Monnery

1

'This town is 'coming like a ghost town . . .'

The song seemed to float ominously out of every open door and window as Worrell Franklin walked slowly down Acre Lane.

'Do you remember the good old days before the ghost town?'

No, not really, he thought, although only a fool would deny that things were getting worse.

A Rasta walked past him, going up the hill, and the look he flashed Franklin was for his uniform, not his face. Or, to be precise, the combination of the two. The oppressor's uniform, the face of the oppressed. A black soldier in a white man's army.

Franklin was used to looks like that, and to the more subtle ones that blended hostility with respect, contempt with envy. He was someone who had got out, escaped. He was someone with a job, which these days felt more and more like a privilege in itself.

Normally he did not wear his uniform around Brixton – it was just easier not to – but this morning he had it on for a reason. The only reason around here. For impressing Whitey.

He turned left onto the High Road and walked north. A crowd of youths were outside the tube station, doing nothing, just waiting for something to ignite their interest. On his side of the road a crowd were gathered round a TV shop, watching the Royal Wedding on the dozen or so sets in the window. When Franklin had left his mum in their living room Lady Diana had been setting out from Clarence House in the ceremonial Glass Coach, looking like an upmarket Cinderella. Now she was walking up the steps of St Paul's, trailing an ivory-coloured dress which looked long enough to play cricket on.

The camera followed her into the cathedral, dwelling on a few famous faces in passing: Mrs T in a blue pillbox hat, Nancy Reagan in a nauseating pink, the Queen in aquamarine, looking like she usually did, as if she was trying hard not to notice that someone had farted nearby.

And then there was the King of Tonga, whose specially reinforced chair had been featured on the news that morning. It would hardly do to have the great fat git crashing through his pew in the middle of the ceremony.

Franklin tore himself away from the glorious nuptials and walked on under the railway bridges. The police station was another two hundred yards down on the right, across from the junction with Stockwell Road. Even from a distance it looked like a fortress, with its windows protected by wire mesh, and the building itself by iron railings.

He wove his way through the stopped traffic at the lights and walked in through the front door. The desk sergeant's face went through that series of expressions which Franklin could have painted from memory. First there was the instinctive mixture of contempt and hostility accorded any black face, second the unpleasant element of surprise which went with putting that face above the authority of a uniform. Then the observer's brain engaged, realized that it was a British Army uniform, and spread relief back through the limbs. Finally the question of a reason for his presence intruded, creating a wariness which was usually expressed through mock aggression.

It all took about five seconds.

'What can we do for you, John?' the sergeant asked. Behind him, from somewhere deep within the recesses of the station, the sounds of the Royal Wedding could be heard. Another two policemen were watching the exchange, both of them white. Where are the black policemen? Franklin wondered. Probably 'out in the community', trying to explain themselves.

This was why he had joined up, to get away from all this.

'My name is Worrell Franklin,' he said formally. 'I believe my brother Everton Franklin is in custody here.'

The desk sergeant's face went through another sequence, culminating in brisk correctness. He opened one of the ledgers in front of him and ran his finger down a list. 'That is correct, sir,' he said. 'He was remanded by the magistrates this morning.'

'I'd like to talk to someone about the circumstances of the arrest, and to see my brother if that's possible.'

'I don't know . . .'

'I only have a twenty-four-hour leave,' Franklin lied, 'so I would appreciate it if something could be arranged.' He wondered if anyone had recognized the winged-dagger badge, or whether he would have to spell out his membership of the SAS.

The desk sergeant glanced round at his two comrades, who stared blankly back at him. 'I'll see what I can do,' he said, adding 'have a seat, sir' as he disappeared through a door. The other two resumed their paperwork.

Franklin sat down on the long bench and picked up the copy of the *Sun* which someone had left behind. Opposite the tits on page three he read that the identity of the Toxteth hit-and-run policeman had still not been established. Surprise, surprise, he thought. And the constable who had been brained by the TV thrown from the high-rise walkway was still in critical condition. There were victims wherever you looked.

Too much fighting on the dance floor . . . The bloody song would not leave him alone.

The sergeant returned with a plain-clothes officer, who introduced himself as Detective-Sergeant Wilson. 'Like in *Dad's Army*,' he explained, most likely out of habit. 'Not often we see the SAS in Brixton,' he said. 'We could have used you a few times this year,' he added with a smile.

Someone had recognized the beret badge, then. Franklin politely returned the smile. 'Can you tell me the circumstances of my brother's arrest?' he asked.

'I can.' He opened the file he was carrying, and extracted a typed sheet. 'I'm afraid he's facing four charges – possession of an offensive weapon, assault, damaging a police vehicle and using threatening behaviour. This is the arresting officer's report,' he said, handing it across.

It was not exactly a literary masterpiece. Nor did it seem particularly precise where it needed to be. The gist of it was that two officers had been inside one of the small businesses in Spenser Road when someone had thought fit to roll a petrol bomb under their car. Several arrests had followed, including that of Everton Franklin. He had apparently put up rather more than token resistance, setting about a policeman with a cricket bat.

'There's nothing here to connect my brother with the torching of the vehicle,' Franklin murmured. Indeed there was nothing to suggest why the police had tried to arrest him in the first place.

'He was probably carrying the bat,' Wilson said, when confronted with this apparent oversight. 'More evidence must have been offered to the magistrates, or they wouldn't have remanded him.'

It didn't seem the time or place to push the issue. 'Can I see my brother?' he asked.

'If you wish, sir.' The detective waited for a reply, as if hoping for a change of mind.

'Yes, I would like to,' Franklin said patiently. He was depressingly aware that if he had not been wearing his uniform his chances of getting even this far would have been less than zero.

'Then come this way, sir.'

He was led down two corridors and ushered into what looked like an interview room. There was just a single table, with one chair either side of it, and two more against a wall. The two windows to the outside world were high enough to reveal only sky, the one in the door was small enough to remind Franklin of depressing prison films.

'It'll be a few minutes, sir,' Wilson said, and disappeared, closing the door behind him. Franklin could hear the TV coverage of the Royal Wedding through the ceiling.

The minutes stretched out. How long could it take to bring someone up from the cells? Franklin had a sudden sinking sensation in his stomach – what if Everton was one of the unlucky few who went into a police station and never came out again? It did not happen often, but it did happen. It would kill their mum. Except that she would kill him first. He had always been expected to look out for his younger brother, and he had, at least until he had left home for the Army. He could scarcely watch over him from Germany or Northern Ireland. Or even from Hereford. And Everton was nineteen now. He should be able to look after himself.

But try telling his mum that.

He was about to go looking for Wilson when the door opened to reveal Everton. 'Fifteen minutes, sir,' Wilson said from behind him, before closing the door on the two brothers.

'What you doin' here?' Everton asked wearily, sitting down at the table.

'It's good to see you, too,' Franklin said, holding up a palm in greeting.

Everton gave it a half-hearted slap with his own. His face, Franklin noticed, bore a couple of angry-looking bruises. 'How d'ya get those?' he asked.

'How d'ya think? I assaulted a policeman's boot with my head.'

Franklin said nothing.

'Don't you worry 'bout me, bro,' Everton said, more to break the silence than for any other reason. 'There's some Rastas here who pulled their own dreadlocks out to scourge the poor policemen with. By the roots,' he added.

'I read your arrest sheet,' Franklin said.

'Yeah? I bet that was a fine piece of fiction. They probably write poetry in their spare time, like that dickhead detective on telly.'

'What did happen?'

'You have to ask?'

'Yeah, I have to ask. If the police report is a fine piece of fiction then I need someone else to tell me some fine fact, right?'

Everton breathed out noisily. 'OK. I got no call to take it out on you.' He sighed. 'What happened was what always happens. Someone gives the police reason to freak, and they freak. Arrest anyone they can who's the right colour, fill up the cells, then retire to their easy chairs upstairs to square their stories . . .'

'What happened? Did a police car get petrol-bombed?'

Everton smiled. 'Yeah. It was a couple of dumb kids. They's probably halfway to Jamaica by now. They just roll this Coke can full of petrol with a bit of rag in it under the car. There's no one inside it – the cops are inside Dr Dread's, looking for some reason to bust him again. And the bomb goes off, but only like a firework – the car don't go up or nothing. I was right there, talking to Benjy, when it all happens, and we see these kids in the garden next door playing cricket so we run in and try and get 'em to move in case there's an explosion, right, but they ignore us, so we have to steal their bat. They come running after us, and the next thing I know about five policemen are jumping on top of me and throwing me in the back of a van. And they bring me here. And they make up a nice story for the magistrates, who all look at me like I should be grateful for not having been shot already.' He looked at his brother. 'That's the whole story,' he said.

'And they beat you up?'

'Not really. Just a couple of playful punches in the van. It was nothing much. I was lucky. Like I say, some of the Rastas really got treated bad.'

Franklin looked at the floor. Somewhere deep inside him, in that place he had learned to shut it away, his anger was straining for release. He suppressed the urge – where could it take him that he had not already been? He asked if Benjy had also been arrested.

'No. He must have picked the right road to run down. Or maybe he just not carrying a cricket bat . . .'

'So he can be a witness. Where's he live?'

'He won't want to make himself that conspicuous. He knows what happens if he does.'

'What happens?'

'You've been away too long, bro. His car gets stopped every time he goes out, his social security gets delayed, the sniffer dogs take a liking to his house . . . you know.'

'I'll talk to him anyway. And there must have been other witnesses.'

'Hundreds. And they all know they're on a hiding to nothing. Even if they speak out the judges take the word of the policeman. So why speak out?'

Franklin had no answer. 'You still looking for a job?' he asked Everton.

'Me and the rest of Brixton.'

'I'll get you out of here,' Franklin said.

'Oh yeah? Then I'll keep my eyes on the windows for when the big black man comes abseiling in.'

Franklin refused to be provoked. 'I'll talk to some people,' he said.

'Worrell,' his brother said, 'one thing I like to know. The next time Brixton goes up, and they need the Army to put out the fire, whose side you be on?'

'I go where my conscience say I should go,' Franklin said. 'I not on anyone's side,' he added, noticing that it only needed a few minutes with Everton and the old anger to have him talking like a Rasta again.

'Then I hope your conscience is in good shape, man,' Everton said, 'cos I think you're gonna need it to be.'

'Yeah. You worry about your own future,' Franklin said, getting up. 'And don't go assaulting no more policeman's boots with your head.'

'I'll try real hard to restrain myself.'

'Any message for Mum?'

'Tell her I'm OK. Not to worry.'

'OK. I'll be back.'

As if on cue, Detective-Sergeant Wilson opened the door.

'We're done,' Franklin said. He had already decided to make no complaint about the beating his brother had been given. It would serve no purpose, and it might conceivably get in the way of getting Everton released. 'I appreciate your help,' he told Wilson, catching a glimpse of his brother's disapproving face over the detective's shoulder.

Out on Brixton Road once more, he took a deep breath of fresh air and walked slowly back in the direction he had come. The crowd was still clustered around the bank of televisions, watching the now-married twosome leaving St Paul's. They looked happy enough, Franklin thought, but who could really tell? He wondered if they had made love yet, or if the royal dick was yet to be unveiled. Maybe the Queen Mother would cut a ribbon or something.

He remembered his own mother had asked him to pick up some chicken wings in the market. Her younger son might be in custody, but the older one still had to be fed. Franklin recrossed the road and walked down Electric Avenue to their usual butcher. A street party seemed to be getting under way, apparently in celebration of the royal event. Prince Charles was the most popular establishment figure in Brixton – in fact, he was the only popular establishment figure. People thought he cared, which in the summer of '81 was enough to make anyone look like a revolutionary.

The only big difference between this and a thousand other British neighbourhoods was the colour scheme – the flags and balloons were all red, yellow and green rather than red, white and blue. Even the kids milling on the street corners seemed to have smiles on their faces this morning, Franklin noticed. For a couple of hours it was just possible to believe there was only one Britain.

Unless, of course, you were locked up in one of the Brixton Police Station's remand cells for no better reason than being the wrong colour in the wrong place at the wrong time.

2

One of the many heads of state attending the Royal Wedding was Sir Dawda Jawara, President of the small West African state of The Gambia. In the colonial twilight of the early 1960s Jawara had led his nascent country's pro-independence movement, and ever since that heady, flag-exchanging day in 1965 he had presided over the government of the independent state. The Gambia was not exactly a huge pond – its population had only recently passed the half-million mark and its earnings were mostly derived from groundnuts and tourism – but there was no doubting who was the biggest fish.

The Wedding over, the embassy limousine swished President Jawara out of London and south down the M23 towards Haywards Heath, where he planned to spend a long weekend with an old college friend. With him he had one of his younger wives; the senior wife, Lady Chilel Jawara, had stayed at home to preside over the household and the well-being of his eight children.

That evening he watched reruns of the Wedding, and talked with his host about the next day's test match. It had always been one of Jawara's great disappointments that his country, unlike, say, Guyana, had not taken the Empire's game to its collective heart. The occasional unofficial test matches against Sierra Leone in the early 1960s had by now almost faded from the national memory.

Lately, though, there had been more serious causes for Gambian concern. The previous November a Libyan-backed coup had been foiled only with Senegalese help, and in the meantime the poor performance of the economy had led to food shortages, particularly in the volatile townships in and around the capital. That evening, sitting in his friend's living room, a pleasant night breeze wafting through the open french windows, Jawara might have felt momentarily at peace with the world, but not so his countrymen.

As *Newsnight* drew to a close in the Sussex living room, two lorry-loads of armed men were drawing up in front of The Gambia's only airport, at Yundum, some ten miles as the crow flies to the south-west of the capital, Banjul. The forty or so men, some in plain clothes, some in the uniform of the country's paramilitary Field Force – The Gambia had no Army as such – jumped down from the lorries and headed off in a variety of directions, in clear accordance with a previously decided plan. Those few members of the Field Force actually on duty at the airport had received no advance warning of any exercise, and were at first surprised and then alarmed, but the appearance of Colonel Junaidi Taal, the 500-strong Field Force's second in command, was enough to set their minds at rest, at least for the moment. Clearly this was official business.

Taal did not stop to explain matters. As his men fanned out to occupy all the relevant aircraft, offices and communication points, he headed straight through the departure area and into the office of the airport controller.

The last plane of the day – the 21.30 flight to Dakar – had long since departed, but the controller was still in his office, catching up on paperwork. As his door burst open he looked up in surprise. 'What is this ...' he started to say in Mandinka, his voice trailing away at the sight of the guns in the hands of the civilians flanking the Field Force officer.

11

'There has been a change of government,' Taal said bluntly in English.

The controller's mouth opened and closed, like a fish's.

'The airport will remain closed until you hear to the contrary,' Taal said. 'No planes will take off, and no planes will land. The runway is being blocked. You will inform all the necessary authorities that this is the case. Understood?'

The controller nodded vigorously. 'Yes, of course,' he said, wondering, but not daring to ask, how much more of the country these people – whoever they were – had under their control. 'What reason should I give the international authorities for the closure of the airport?'

'You don't need to give a reason. They will know soon enough.' He turned to one of the two men in civilian clothes. 'Bunja, you are in command here. I'll call you from the radio station.'

Banjul lies on the south-western side of the River Gambia's mouth and is separated from the rest of the southern half of the country – the major tourist beaches of Bakau and Fajara, the large township of Serekunda and the airport at Yundum – by a large area of mangrove swamp, which is itself intersected by numerous small watercourses and the much larger Oyster Creek. Anyone leaving or entering Banjul had to cross the creek by the Denton Bridge, a two-lane concrete structure two hundred yards long. At around two a.m. Taal and twenty rebels arrived to secure the bridge, left half a dozen of their number to set up checkpoints at either end, and roared on into Banjul.

The lorry drew up outside the darkened building in Buckle Street which was home to Radio Gambia. No one answered the thunderous knock on the door, so two

12

Field Force men broke it down, and the rebels surged into the building. They found only three people inside, one man in the small studio, sorting through records for the next day's playlist, and one of the engineers undressed and halfway to paradise with his equally naked girlfriend on the roof. The engineer was bustled downstairs, while the two remaining rebels handed his girlfriend her clothing bit by bit, snickering with pleasure at her embarrassment, and fighting the urge to succumb to their own lust. It was fortunate for the girl that the coup leaders had stressed the need for self-discipline – and the punishments reserved for those who fell short of this – to all of their men. The girl, tears streaming down her face, was eventually escorted downstairs, and left sitting in a room full of records.

The radio station now secure, Taal called Bunja at the airport and checked that nothing had gone amiss. Nothing had. Further calls confirmed that the Banjul ferry terminal and the main crossroads in Serekunda had been seized. Taal called the main Field Force depot in Bakau where the coup leader, Mamadou Jabang, was waiting for news.

'Yes?' Jabang asked, his voice almost humming with tension. 'Everything has gone according to plan?'

'So far,' Taal said. 'We'll move on to the Presidential Palace now. Are our men in position around the hotels yet?'

'They should be,' Jabang replied. 'The tourists never leave their hotels anyway,' he added sourly, 'so it hardly seems necessary to use our men to keep them in.'

'We don't want any of them wandering out and getting shot,' Taal reminded him. Their chances of success were thin enough, he thought, without bringing the wrath of the white world down on their heads.

'No, we don't,' Jabang agreed without much conviction. 'We're on our way, then. I'll see you at the radio station.'

Dr Sibou Cham yawned and rubbed her eyes, then sat for a moment with her hands held, as if in prayer, over her nose. You should pray for a decent hospital, she told herself, one with all the luxuries, like beds and medicines. She looked down at the pile of patients' records on her desk, and wondered if it was all worth it.

There was a muffled crack, like a gun being fired some way off. She got wearily to her feet and walked through the treatment room to the empty reception area, grateful for the excuse to leave her paperwork behind. The heavyweight concertina door, which would have seemed more at home in a loading dock than a hospital, was locked, as she had requested. Ever since the incident the previous May this had been done. Her attacker might be in prison, but there were others.

She put the chain on the door before unlocking it, then pulled it open a foot, letting in the balmy night air. Almost immediately there was another sound like gunfire, but then silence. It was a shot, she was sure of it. Perhaps a gang battle. She might be bandaging the victims before the night was over.

She closed the door again and sat down at the receptionist's desk. All the drawer knobs were missing, which seemed to sum up the state of the place. It was all of a piece with the peeling cream paint on the walls, the concrete-block partition which had been half-finished for six months, the gaping holes in the mosquito screens, and the maddening flicker of the fluorescent light. It went with a pharmacy which had fewer drugs than the sellers in the marketplace.

What was she doing here? Why did she stay? One person could not make all that much difference, and maybe the very fact that she was there, working herself into the ground day after day, took away any urgency the authorities might feel about improving the situation.

But where else could she go? Into private practice, of course. It would be easier, more lucrative. She might even get some sleep once in a while. But she could not do it. In The Gambia it was the poor who needed more doctors, not the rich. If money and an easy life was what she wanted, she could have stayed in England, got a job in a hospital there, even become a GP.

Most of the other Africans and Asians she had known at medical school had done just that. They had escaped from the Third World, so why on earth would they want to go back? They would bitch about the English weather, bitch about the racism, but they liked being able to shop at Sainsburys, watch the TV, give their children a good education. And she could hardly blame them. Their countries needed them back, but to go back would be a sacrifice for them, and why should they be the ones to pick up the tab for a world that was not fair?

She could hardly pretend it had been a sacrifice for her, because she had never been able to separate her feelings about the practice of medicine from the unfathomable desire she had always felt to serve humanity. A doctor went where a doctor was most needed, and it was hard to imagine a more needy country in this respect than her own.

But – lately there always seemed to be a 'but'. Since the attack on her there had been a sense of . . . loneliness, she supposed. She felt alone, there was no doubt about it. Her family lived in New York, and in any case could not understand why she had not used her obvious gifts to make more of her life. More, that is, in terms of houses, cars and clothes. The people she worked with were the usual mixed bunch – some nice, some not so nice – but she had little in common with any of them. There were no other women doctors at the Royal Victoria Hospital, and the male doctors all wished they were somewhere else.

The Englishman who had saved her that night had become almost a friend. Or something like that. He flirted a lot, and she supposed he would take any sexual favours that were offered, but he had a wife in England, and she guessed that he too was more than a little lonely. And he was at that age, around forty, when men started wondering whether they had made the right life for themselves, and whether it was too late to do something about it.

She was nearly thirty herself, and there seemed little chance of finding a husband in Banjul, even if she had wanted one. She was not sure what she did want. Not to be alone, she supposed. Just that.

It was a funny thing to be thinking in an empty hospital reception area in the middle of the night. She sighed. In the morning it would all look so . . .

The burst of gunfire seemed to explode all around her, almost making her jump out of her skin. For a moment she thought it had to be inside the room, but then a shadowy figure went racing past in the street outside, then another, and another. They were probably heading for the Presidential Palace, whose gates were only a hundred yards away, around the next corner.

It had to be another coup.

16

There was a loud series of knocks on the concertina door and shouts of 'open up'. She took a deep breath and went to unlock it. As she pulled it back a man half fell through the opening, wiping the blood from his head on her white coat as he did so. Behind him another man was holding a bloody side. 'We need help,' he groaned, somewhat unnecessarily.

Taal had walked down the radio station's stairs, and was just emerging onto Buckle Street when a distant burst of automatic fire crackled above the sound of the lorry's engine. It seemed to be coming from the direction of the Presidential Palace, half a mile or so to the north.

'Fuck,' he murmured to himself. He had hoped against hope that this could be a bloodless night, but the chances had always been slim. The men guarding the Palace had received enough personal perks from their employer over the last year to guarantee at least a few hours of stubborn resistance.

The last few bars of 'Don't Explain' faded into silence, or rather into the distant sound of the waves tugging at the beach beneath the Bakau cliffs. Lady Chilel Jawara had discovered Billie Holiday on a trip to New York several years before. Her husband had been attending the UN, and she had decided, on the spur of the moment, to visit an exhibition of photographs of Afro-American music stars. It was the singer's face she had first fallen in love with, before she'd heard a single note of her music. It was like her mother's, but that was not the only reason. It was the face of someone who knew what it was like to be a woman.

Not that Billie Holiday had ever been the senior wife of the president of a small African state. Lady Jawara had a lot to be thankful for, and she knew it. Her children

17

were sleeping between sheets, went to the best school, and ate when they were hungry. If they got ill a doctor was sent for.

As for herself, she enjoyed the role of senior wife. Her husband might rule the country but she ruled the household, and of the two administrations she suspected hers was both the more efficient and the less stressful. She hoped he had enjoyed the wedding in London, though she doubted it. Generally he was as bored by European ceremonies as she was.

She yawned and stretched her arms, wondering whether to listen to the other side of the record or go to bed. At that moment she heard the sound of a vehicle approaching.

Whoever it was, they were coming to the Presidential bungalow, for the road led nowhere else. She felt suddenly anxious. 'Bojang!' she called, walking to the living-room door.

'Yes, Lady,' he said, emerging from the kitchen just as a hammering started on the compound gate.

They both stood there listening, she uncertain what to do, he waiting for instructions. 'See who it is,' she said at last.

He let himself out, and she went in search of the gun she knew her husband kept somewhere in the house. The drawers of his desk in the study seemed the best bet, but two of them yielded no gun and the other two were locked. She was still looking for the key when an armed man appeared in the study doorway.

'Who are you? And what do you want in my house?' she asked.

'You are under arrest,' he said.

She laughed. 'By whose authority?'

'And your children,' the man added, looking round

with interest at the President's study. 'By the authority of the Revolutionary Council.'

'The what?'

Her contempt stung the man. 'Your days are over, bitch,' he said.

The firefight which began at the gates of the Presidential Palace soon after four a.m., and which continued intermittently across its gardens, up Marina Parade and down to the beach, for the next two hours, woke up most of those sleeping within a quarter of a mile of the Palace.

Opposite the new Atlantic Hotel in Marina Parade, Mustapha Diop was happily snoring his way through it all until his wife's anxiety forced her to wake him. The two of them sat up in bed listening to the gunfire, then went together to the window, where all they could see was a distant view of the moon on the surf and any number of palm fronds swaying gently in the night breeze.

Diop and his family were from Senegal, and had been in Banjul only a few weeks, since his appointment as secretary to the committee overseeing the proposed union between the two countries. Since a treaty already existed whereby either government would intervene to save the other from an armed take-over, Diop was already aware that he might prove an important bargaining card for any Gambian rebels. The sudden violent knocking on the door downstairs made it clear that the same thought had occurred to them.

Half a mile to the west, the gunfire was only audible, and barely so, when the breeze shifted in the right direction. Moussa Diba and Lamin Konko shared a north-east-facing cell in Banjul Prison, and Diba, prevented from sleeping as usual by the vengeful thoughts which circled his brain, was at first uncertain of what it was he could hear. The sound of lorries rolling past, headed into Banjul from the direction of the Denton Bridge, offered him another clue. Either there was a mother of an exercise going on – which seemed about as likely as an edible breakfast – or someone was trying to topple that little bastard Jawara. Diba smiled to himself in the gloom, and woke Konko with a jab of his foot.

His cellmate groaned. 'What is it?' he said sleepily.

'Listen.'

Konko listened. 'Gunfire,' he said. 'So what?'

'So nothing. I thought you'd enjoy some excitement.'

'I was having plenty in my sleep. There's this girl I used to know in my village. I'd forgotten all about her . . .'

He rambled on, making Diba think of Anja, and of what she was doubtless doing. The woman could not say no. Unfortunately, he could not say no for her, not while he was locked up in this cell.

Another burst of gunfire sounded, this time closer. So what? Diba's thoughts echoed his cellmate's. Whatever was happening out there was unlikely to help him in here.

Simon McGrath, awoken in his room on the fourth floor of the Carlton Hotel, thought for a moment he was back on the Jebel Dhofar in Oman, listening to the *firqats* firing off their rifles in jubilation at the successful capture of Sudh. The illusion was brief-lived. He had never had a bed in Oman, not even one as uncomfortable as the Carlton's. And it had been more than ten years since the men he had helped to train had taken Sudh and started rolling back the tide of the Dhofari rebels.

This was Banjul, The Gambia, and he was no longer

in the SAS. Still, he thought, swinging his legs to the floor and striding across to the window, the gunfire he was listening to was coming out of Kalashnikov barrels, and they were not standard issue with the Gambian Field Force. Out there on the capital's mean streets something not quite kosher seemed to be taking place.

The view from his window, which faced south across the shanty compounds towards the Great Mosque, was uninstructive. Nothing was lit, nothing moving. He tried the light switch, but as usual at this time of night, the hotel's electricity was off.

McGrath dressed in the dark, wondering what would be the prudent thing to do. Stay in bed, probably.

To hell with that.

He delved into his bag and extracted the holster and semi-automatic 9mm Browning High Power handgun which he had brought with him from England. Since McGrath was in The Gambia in a civilian capacity, seconded from the Royal Engineers to head a technical assistance team engaged in bridge-building and pipe-laying, his possession of the Browning was strictly illicit, but that hardly concerned him. The Third World, as he was fond of telling people who lived in more comfortable places, was like an overpopulated Wild West, and he had no intention of ending up with an arrow through his head. A little string-pulling among old contacts at Heathrow had eased the gun's passage onto the plane, and at Yundum no one had dreamed of checking his baggage.

He threaded the cross-draw holster to his belt, slipped on the lightweight jacket to hide the gun, and left his room. At first it seemed as if the rest of the hotel remained blissfully unaware of whatever it was that was happening outside, but as he went down the corridor he caught the murmur of whispered conversations.

He was about to start down the stairs when the benefits of a visit to the roof occurred to him. He walked up the two flights to the fifth floor, then one more to the flat roof. With the city showing its usual lack of illumination and the moon hiding behind clouds, it was little lighter outside than in, and for almost a minute McGrath waited in the open doorway, searching the shadows for anyone who had chosen to spend the night in the open air. Once satisfied the roof was empty, he threaded his way through the washing lines to the side overlooking Independence Drive.

As he reached this vantage point a lorry full of men swept past, heading down towards the centre of town. Several men were standing on the pavement opposite the hotel, outside the building housing the Legislative Assembly. A yellow glow came from inside the latter, as if from gas lamps or candles.

It looked like a coup, McGrath thought, and at that moment a fresh volley of shots resounded away to his right, from the direction of the Palace. There was a hint of lights through the trees – headlights, perhaps – but he could see nothing for certain, either in that direction or any other. Banjul might be surrounded on its three sides by river, sea and swamp, but at four in the morning they all looked like so many pieces of gloom.

The Royal Victoria Hospital, whose main entrance was little more than a hundred yards from the Palace gates, showed no more lights than anywhere else. McGrath wondered if Sibou was sleeping there that night, as she often did, or whether she had gone home for some of that rest she always seemed to need and never seemed to get.

He would go and have a look, he decided, one part of his mind commending him for his thoughtfulness, the other thanking his lucky stars that he had come up with a good excuse to go out in search of adventure.

It was almost six-thirty before Colonel Taal felt confident enough of the outcome of the fighting around the Presidential Palace to delegate its direction, and to head back down Buckle Street to the radio station for the prearranged meeting. Mamadou Jabang and his deputy, Sharif Sallah, had arrived in their commandeered taxi more than half an hour earlier, and the subsequent wait had done little to soothe their nerves.

'What is happening?' Jabang asked, when Taal was only halfway through the door. He and Sallah were sitting at either end of a table in the station's hospitality room. 'Has anything gone wrong?'

'Nothing.'

'The Palace is taken?' Sallah asked.

'The Palace is cordoned off,' Taal answered. 'Some of the guards have escaped, either down the beach or into the town, but that was expected.' He sat down and looked at the two of them: the wiry Jabang with his hooded eyes and heavy brow, Sallah with the face that always seemed to be smiling, even when it was not. Both men were sweating heavily, which perhaps owed something to the humidity, but was mostly nerves. Jabang in particular seemed exhausted by the combination of stress and tiredness, which did not exactly bode well for the new government's decision-making process. Nothing perverted the exercise of judgement like lack of sleep, and somehow or other all three of them would have to make sure they got enough in the days to come.

'It will be light in half an hour,' Jabang said.

'And the country will wake to a better government,' Sallah said, almost smugly.

Taal supposed he meant it. For some reason he could never quite put his finger on, he had always doubted Sallah's sincerity. Whereas Jabang was transparently honest and idealistic almost to a fault, Sallah's words and deeds invariably seemed to carry a taint of opportunism.

Maybe he was wrong, Taal thought. He hoped he was. Jabang trusted the man and there had to be easier ways to glory than taking part in the mounting of a coup like this one. Everyone knew their chances of lasting success were no better than even, and in the sanctum of his own thoughts Taal thought the odds considerably longer. Seizing control was one thing, holding on to it something else entirely.

McGrath had decided that even in the dark a stroll along Independence Drive might not prove wise, and had opted for the long way round, making use of Marina Parade. On this road there was less likely to be traffic or headlights, and the overarching trees made the darkness even more impenetrable. He worked his way along the southern side, ears alert for the sound of unwelcome company, and was almost level with the Atlantic Hotel when two headlights sprang to life some two hundred yards ahead of him, and rapidly started closing the distance. There was no time to run for better cover, and McGrath flattened himself against the wall, hoping to fall outside the vehicle's cone of illumination.

He need not have bothered. The lights swerved to the left, disappearing, as he immediately realized, into the forecourt of the Atlantic Hotel. He wondered what the rebels had in store for the hundred or so guests, most of them Brits, and all of whom had come to The Gambia on

24

package tours in search of a sunny beach, not the wrong end of a Kalashnikov.

He would worry about that later. For the moment he wanted to make sure Sibou was all right. Hurrying on past the Atlantic, he came to the doors of the Royal Victoria's Maternity Wing, and decided that it might be better to use them than attempt the front entrance. Ten minutes later, having threaded his way through the labyrinth of one-storey buildings and courtyards, he found himself looking across at the lit windows of the emergency department some twenty yards away. Several men were standing around inside, some of them bending down to talk to those who were presumably lying, out of sight, on the cubicle beds and waiting-room benches. One man was moaning continuously, almost forlornly, but otherwise there was virtual silence.

Then he saw Sibou, rising wearily into view after treating one of the prone casualties. Her dark eyes seemed even darker, the skin stretched a little tighter across the high cheekbones, the usually generous mouth pursed with tension and tiredness. McGrath worked his way round the perimeter of the yard to the open window of her private office and clambered over the sill. He opened the door a quarter of an inch and looked out through the crack. The corridor was empty.

Sooner or later she would come, and he settled down to wait, thinking about the first time they had met, a couple of months earlier, soon after he had arrived on his secondment. The circumstances could hardly have been more propitious for an intending Galahad. He had come to the Royal Victoria looking for the tetanus shot he should have had before leaving home, and found himself face to face with a room full of terrified Gambians, her half-naked on the floor and a man about to rape her at knife-point in full view of everyone else. All the old

training had come instantly into use, and before he had
had time to ponder the risks McGrath had used the
man's neck for a chopping board and his genitals for
a football.

The damsel in distress had been grateful enough to
have dinner with him, but he had foolishly allowed
himself to be a little too honest with her, and she had
declined to be anything more than a friend. That had
not been as difficult as he had expected, though he still
dreamed of covering her ebony body with his kisses, not
to mention her covering his with hers. But Sibou was
great company even fully clothed, and he had even found
himself wishing his wife and children could meet her.

He could not remember being so impressed by someone's dedication – in the face of such awe-inspiring odds
– for a long, long time. She could have had a doctor's job,
and a doctor's ample rewards, anywhere in the world,
but here she was, in this ramshackle office, struggling to
stretch always inadequate resources in the service of the
ordinary people who came in off the street, and offering
every one of them a smile almost beautiful enough to
die for.

McGrath looked at his watch. In twenty minutes it
would begin to get light: where did he want to be when
that happened? At the Atlantic, he decided, where there
would probably be a working telephone and some chance
of finding out what was happening. After all, now he had
found out that Sibou was all right, there had to be more
pressing things to do than watch her smile.

He was halfway out of the window when she came
in through the door. She jumped with surprise, then
burst out laughing. 'What are you doing, you crazy
Englishman?' she asked.

He pulled himself back into the room, wondering
how anyone could look so sexy in a white coat and

stethoscope. 'I've come to take you away from all this,' he said grandly.

'Through the window?'

'Well . . .'

'And anyway, I like all this. And I'm busy,' she added, rummaging around in her desk drawer for something.

'I just came to check you were OK,' he said.

She turned and smiled at him. 'Thank you.'

'What's happening out there?' he asked.

'Out in the city? Oh, another bunch of fools have decided to overthrow the government.'

'And are they succeeding?'

She shrugged. 'Who knows? Who cares?'

'I thought you didn't like Papa Jawara.'

'I don't. But playing musical chairs at the Palace is not going to get me the medicines I need. In fact I'm having to use the little I've got to patch up those toy soldiers in there.'

'How many of them?'

'About a dozen or so. We're already running out of blood. Look, I have to go . . .' She suddenly noticed the holstered gun inside his jacket. 'What are you wearing that for?' she demanded to know.

'Self-defence.'

'It will give them a reason to shoot you.'

'Yeah, well . . .'

She threw up her hands in disgust. 'You play what games you want,' she said, adding over her shoulder, 'and take care of yourself.'

'I'll come back later,' he called after her, although he was not sure if she had heard. 'What a woman,' he muttered to himself, and worked his body back out through the window. He retraced his steps through the sprawling grounds to the Maternity Wing entrance, crossed over the still-dark Marina Parade and scaled the wall of the grounds opposite. Five minutes and another wall later he was standing on the beach. Away to his right, over the far bank of the river mouth, the sky was beginning to lighten. He turned the other way, and walked a couple of hundred yards along the deserted sand to the hotel's beach entrance.

The kidney-shaped pool shone black in the artificial light, but its only occupant was an inflatable plastic monkey. McGrath walked through into the hotel building, hands in pockets to disguise the bulge of the Browning. In the lobby he could hear voices, and after a moment's thought decided to simply take a seat within earshot, and pretend he was just one more innocent tourist.

It was a fruitful decision. For five minutes he listened to two voices trying to explain to several others – the latter presumably the hotel's management – that there was a new government, that the foreign guests would not be allowed out of their hotels for at least a day, but that there was nothing to stop them enjoying the sun and the hotel beach and the swimming pool. It was up to the management to make these rules clear to the guests. And to point out that anyone attempting to leave the hotel grounds risked being shot.

3

'All authority now rests in the Revolutionary Council,' said the voice coming out of the speakers. Someone on the hotel staff had channelled the radio through the outdoor hi-fi system, and around a hundred staff and guests were sitting around the hotel pool, listening to the first proclamation of the new government.

'The Socialist and Revolutionary Labour Party, which was illegally suppressed during the regime of the tyrant Jawara, has contributed nine members to the new ruling Council. The other three members have been supplied by the Field Force, which has already proved itself overwhelmingly in support of the new government.'

Oh yeah? McGrath thought to himself. Some of the bastards must have been in on it, but he doubted if it had been a majority.

'The Jawara regime,' the voice went on, 'has always been a backward-looking regime. Nepotism has flourished, corruption has been rife, tribal differences have been exacerbated rather than healed. Economic incompetence has gone hand in hand with social injustice, and for the ordinary man the last few years have been an endless struggle. The recent severe food shortages offered proof that, if unchecked, the situation would only have grown worse. That is why the Council has now assumed control, so that all the necessary steps to reverse this trend can at once be taken.'

The voice paused for breath, or for inspiration. What was the magic panacea going to be this time round, McGrath asked himself.

'A dictatorship of the proletariat . . .'

McGrath burst out laughing.

'. . . a government of working people, led by the Socialist and Revolutionary Labour Party, will now be established to promote socialism and true democracy. This will, of course, take time, and the process itself will doubtless provoke opposition from the forces of reaction, particularly those remnants of the old regime who still occupy positions of authority throughout the country. In order to accelerate the process of national recovery certain short-term measures must be taken. Accordingly, the Council declares Parliament dissolved and the constitution temporarily suspended. The banks and courts will remain closed until further notice. All political parties are banned. A dusk-to-dawn curfew will be in force from this evening.

'Guests in our country are requested, for their own safety, not to leave their hotel compounds. The Council regrets the need for this temporary restriction, which has been taken with our guests' best interests in mind.'

McGrath looked round at the assembled holiday-makers, most of whom seemed more amused than upset by the news. There were a few nervous giggles, but no sign of any real fear.

'Oh well, we'll be going home the day after tomorrow,' one Lancastrian voice said a few yards away.

Maybe they would be, McGrath thought, but he would not bet on it. It all depended on how secure the new boys' control was. If it was either really firm or really shaky, then there was probably little to worry about. But if they were strong enough to keep some control yet not strong enough to make it stick, then these people around the pool might well become unwilling pawns in the struggle. Hostages, even. It could get nasty.

The voice was sinking deeper into generalities: '. . . their wholehearted support in the building of a fair and prosperous society. It wishes to stress that the change of government is an internal affair, and of practical concern only to the people of The Gambia. Any attempt at interference from outside the country's borders will be considered a hostile act. The Council hopes and expects a comradely response from our neighbours, particularly the people and government of Senegal, with whom we wish to pursue a policy of growing cooperation in all spheres . . .'

So that was it, McGrath thought. They were expecting Senegalese intervention. In which case, it should be all over in a few days. He did not know much about the Senegalese Army, but he had little doubt that they could roll over this bunch. And then it was just a matter of everyone keeping their heads down while the storm blew itself out.

'How did it sound?' Jabang asked as they settled into the back seat of the commandeered taxi. A few minutes earlier two Party members had arrived from Yundum with Jawara's personal limousine, assuming that Jabang would wish to use it. He had sent them packing with a lecture on the perils of the personality cult.

Which was all to the good, Taal thought. And maybe riding round Banjul in a rusty Peugeot behind a pair of furry dice was a suitably proletarian image for the new government. At least no one could accuse them of élitism.

'Junaidi, how did it sound?' Jabang repeated.

'Good, Mamadou, good,' Taal replied. Jabang looked feverish, he thought. 'We all need some sleep,' he said, 'or we won't know what we're doing.'

Jabang laughed. 'I could sleep for a week,' he said, 'but when will I get the chance?'

'After you've addressed the Council,' Taal said.

'Just take a few hours. We'll wake you if necessary.'

'And when will you sleep?' Jabang asked.

'Whenever I can.' But probably not for the rest of the day, he thought. Whatever. He should get his second wind soon.

The driver arrived with Sallah, who joined him in the front. The street seemed virtually empty, but that was not surprising. Today, Taal both hoped and expected, most people would stay home and listen to the radio.

'I must talk to the Senegalese envoy after the Council,' Jabang remembered out loud. 'Where is he at the moment?'

'In the house where he is staying,' Sallah said over his shoulder. 'He has only been told he cannot go out.'

'You will bring him to the Legislative Assembly?'

'Yes.'

'Good.' Jabang sat back as the taxi swung through the roundabout at McCarthy Square, his eyes darting this way and that as if searching for something to rest on.

Watching him, Taal felt a sudden sense of emptiness. He had known Mamadou Jabang for almost twenty-five years, since he was fourteen and the other man was seven. They had grown up in adjoining houses in Bakau, both sons of families well off by Gambian standards. Both had flirted with the religious vocation, both had been educated abroad, though on different sides of the Iron Curtain.

Taal had graduated from Sandhurst in England, while Jabang had received one of the many scholarships offered by Soviet embassies in Africa during the early 1970s. The former had worked his way effortlessly to his position in the Field Force, and only Jawara's unspoken but justified suspicion of Taal's political sympathies had prevented him holding the top job before he was forty.

Jabang, on the other hand, had become mired in politics, and had foolishly – as he himself admitted – allowed himself to overestimate Jawara's instinct for self-preservation. The SRLP had become too popular too quickly, particularly among the township youths and the younger members of the Field Force, and in the early summer of 1980 Jawara had seized on the random shooting of a policeman to ban the Party. With all the democratic channels closed, the SRLP had spent the succeeding year planning Jawara's overthrow by force.

And here they were, driving to the parliament building behind a pair of pink furry dice, the new leaders of their country, at least for today. Taal felt the enormity of it all – like burning bridges, as the English would say. If the Council could endure, then he and Mamadou would have the chance to transform their country, to do all the things they had dreamed of doing, to truly make a difference in the lives of their countrymen. If they failed, then Jawara would have them hanged.

The stakes could hardly be higher.

'Junaidi, we've arrived,' Jabang said, pulling him out of his reverie. Mamadou had a smile on his face – the first one Taal had seen that day. And why not, he thought, climbing out of the taxi in the forecourt of the Legislative Assembly. They had succeeded. For the moment at least, they had succeeded.

He followed Jabang in through the outer doors, across the anteroom and into the chamber, where the forty or fifty men who had been waiting for them burst into spontaneous applause.

Jabang raised a fist in salute, beamed at the assembly, and took a seat on the platform. Taal sat beside him and looked out across the faces, every one of which he knew. He had the sudden sinking feeling that this would be the high point, and that from this moment on things would only get worse.

Jabang was now on his feet, motioning for silence. 'Comrades,' he began, 'I will not take up much of your time – we all have duties to perform,' adding with a smile: 'And a country to run. I can tell you that we are in firm control of Banjul, Bakau, Fajara, Serekunda, Yundum and Soma. Three-quarters of the Field Force has joined us. I do not think we have anything to fear from inside the country. The main threat, as we all knew from the beginning, will come from outside, from the Senegalese. They have the treaty with Jawara, and if they judge it in their interests to uphold it then it is possible they will send troops. I still think it more likely that they will wait to judge the situation here, and act accordingly.

'So it is important that we offer no provocations, no excuse for intervention. At the moment we have no news of their intentions, but I will be asking their envoy here to talk to his government in Dakar this morning. And of course we shall be making the most of the friends we have in the international community.

'The Senegalese will not act without French approval, so we must also make sure that nothing tarnishes our image in the West. The last thing we need now is a dead white tourist.' He grinned owlishly.

'The Council will be in more or less permanent session from now on – and when any of us will get any sleep is anyone's guess. All security matters should be channelled through Junaidi here.'

Taal smiled at them all, reflecting that it was going to be a long day.

The British High Commission was situated on the road between Bakau and Fajara, some eight miles to the west of Banjul. McGrath finally got through on the phone around ten o'clock. The line had been jammed for the previous two hours, presumably with holiday-makers wondering what the British Government intended to do about the situation. As if there was anything they could do.

He asked to talk to Bill Myers, the all-purpose under-secretary whose roles included that of military attaché. Myers had helped smooth the path for McGrath on the ex-SAS man's arrival, and they had met several times since, mostly at gatherings of the expatriate community: Danes running an agricultural research station, Germans working on a solar-energy project, Brits like McGrath involved in infrastructural improvements. It was a small community, and depressingly male.

'Where are you?' was Myers's first question.

'At the Atlantic.'

'How are things there? No panic?'

'Well, there was one outbreak when someone claimed the hotel was running out of gin . . .'

'Ha ha . . .'

'No, no problems here. People are just vaguely pissed off that they can't go out. Not that many of them wanted to anyway, but they liked the idea that they could.'

Myers grunted. 'What about the town? Any idea what's going on?'

'Hey, I called you to find out what was going on – not the other way round.'

'Stuck out here we haven't got a clue,' Myers said equably. 'There seems to be a group of armed men out-side each of the main hotels, but there haven't been any incidents involving Europeans that we know of. There was some gunfire in Bakau last night, but we've no idea who got shot. And we listened to Chummy on the radio this morning. And that's about it. What about you?'

McGrath told him what he had heard and seen from

the Carlton roof, and at the hospital. 'It seems quiet enough for now,' he concluded. 'Looks like they made it stick, at least for the moment.'

'If you can find out anymore, we'd appreciate it,' Myers said. 'It's hard to give London any advice when we don't know any more than they do.'

'Right,' McGrath agreed. 'In exchange, can you let my wife know I'm OK?'

Myers took down the London number. 'But don't go taking any mad risks,' he said. 'I'm not taking a day trip to Banjul, not even for your funeral.'

'You're all heart,' McGrath said, and hung up. For a moment he stood in the hotel lobby, wondering what to do. The new government had only restricted the movement of 'guests', by which they presumably meant the three hundred or so lucky souls currently visiting The Gambia on package holidays. McGrath was not on holiday and not a guest, so the restrictions could hardly apply to him.

He wondered if the guards at the hotel gates would appreciate the distinction.

Probably not. He decided discretion was the better part of valour, and after moving the holstered Browning round into the small of his back, left the hotel the way he had come, through the beach entrance. Already twenty or so guests were sunning themselves as if nothing had happened, a couple of the women displaying bare breasts. McGrath supposed they were nice ones, and wondered why he always found topless beaches such a turn-off.

Better not to know, probably. At least there were no armed men guarding the beach: the new regime was either short on manpower or short on brains. He headed west, reckoning it was best to avoid the area of the Palace and cut back through to Independence Drive just above the Carlton. There was a heavy armed presence outside the Legislative Assembly, but no one challenged him as he walked down the opposite pavement and ducked into the Carlton's terrace.

The hotel seemed half-deserted. There were no messages for him and the telephone was dead. He decided to visit the office he had been given in Wellington Street, in the heart of town. If he was stopped, he was stopped; there was no point in behaving like a prisoner before he got caught.

Outside he tried hailing a taxi, more out of curiosity than because he really wanted one. The driver slowed, noticed the colour of his face, and accelerated away. McGrath started walking down Independence Drive, conscious of being stared at by those few Gambians who were out on the street. It was all a bit unnerving, and recognition of this added a swagger to his walk. He was damned if he was going to slink around the town in broad daylight.

The stares persisted, but no one spoke to him or tried to impede his passage. Once on Wellington Street he noticed that the Barra ferry was anchored in midstream: no one could escape in it, and no one could use it to launch an attack on Banjul. McGrath found himself admiring that piece of military logic. The rebel forces were obviously not entirely composed of fools, even if they did include the last person on earth who could use the phrase 'dictatorship of the proletariat' with a straight face.

The offices of the Ministry of Development, where he had been allotted a room, had obviously not been deemed of sufficient importance to warrant a rebel presence. McGrath simply walked through the front door and up to his room, which he half-expected to find as empty as the rest of the building. Instead he found the smiling face of Jobo Camara, the twenty-four-year-old Gambian who had been appointed his deputy.

'Mr McGrath!' Camara called out to him. 'What are you doing here?'

'I've come to work,' McGrath answered mildly.

'But . . . there is a revolution going on!'

'There's nothing happening at the moment. Why are you here?'

'I only live down the street. I thought I would make certain no one has come to the office who shouldn't have.'

'And has anyone?' McGrath asked, going over to the window and checking out the street.

'No . . .'

'Jobo, what's happening out there? I'm a foreigner – it's hard to read the signs in someone else's country. I mean, do these people have any support among the population?'

The young man considered the question. 'Some,' he said at last. 'It's hard to say how much. Today, I think, many people are still waiting to see how these people behave. They will give them the benefit of the doubt for a few days, maybe.' He shrugged. 'The government – the old government – was not popular. Not in Banjul, anyway.' He stopped and looked questioningly at McGrath, as if wanting to know if he had said too much.

'People don't like Jawara?' McGrath asked.

'He is just a little man with a big limousine, who gives all the good jobs to his family and friends. He is not a *bad* man. People don't hate him. But I don't think they will fight for him, either.'

'You think most people will just wait and see?'

'Of course. It is easier. As long as the new men don't behave too badly . . .'

'They seem to have the Field Force on their side.'

'Some of them. Maybe half. My uncle is in the Field Force in Fajara, and my mother wanted me to check on him, make sure he's all right. That was another reason I came to the office: to borrow the jeep,' he added, hopefully.

'Fine, I'll come with you,' McGrath said.

Franklin had been woken early by his mother setting off for the dawn shift at the South Western Hospital in Clapham, and then again by his sister leaving for school. When he finally surfaced it was gone eleven, and he ate a large bowl of cornflakes in front of the TV, watching the opening hour of the Third Test between England and Australia. The play hardly came up to West Indian standards, but the England batting did remind him of the last time they had faced Roberts and Holding. Boycott and Gower were both gone before he had finished his second cup of coffee.

With some reluctance he turned off the television, got dressed and left the house. He was wearing jeans and a T-shirt – the people he meant to see today would not be impressed by his uniform. In fact, they would probably use it for target practice if they thought they could get away with it.

The weather was much the same as it had been for the Royal Wedding, but the mood on the streets seemed less sunny, more like its usual sullen self. Franklin's first port of call was the address for Benjy which Everton had given him – a sixth-floor flat on a big estate in nearby Angell Town. Benjy, a thin young man with spiky hair and gold-rimmed glasses, was alone, watching the cricket.

'You know why I've come?' Franklin started.

'It's about Everton.'

'Yeah.'

He let Franklin in with some reluctance, but offered him a cup of tea. While he was making it Gooch was bowled out. England were doing their best to make the Australians feel at home.

'Did you see what happened?' Franklin asked, when Benjy came back with the tea.

'When?'

'When he was arrested.'

'No. I'm running too hard, you know. One moment the street is empty, the next the policemen are tripping over each other. I go straight down the alley by Dr Dread and over the wall and out through the yards. The last time I see Everton he is standing there with the cricket bat. I yelled at him to come, but he must have run the other way.'

'OK,' Franklin said. 'Did you know anyone else who was there, anyone who might have seen what happened?'

Benjy shook his head. 'They all got arrested. Or they didn't stop to watch and didn't see nothing. Like I and I. I's sorry, Worrell, but that's how it goes. Anyways, if the police all saying one thing, then nobody listen to nobody else.' He opened his palms in a gesture of resignation.

Franklin walked down the twelve flights of steps rather than face the smell of concentrated urine in the lift, and stopped for a moment on the pavement outside the building, giving the sunshine a chance to lighten his state of mind.

It did not work. He walked back towards the centre of Brixton, hyper-aware of the world around him. There were too many people on the streets, too many people not actually going anywhere. It felt like a football crowd before a game, a sense of expectation, a sense of looming catharsis. It felt ugly.

He walked up to Railton Road to the address his mum

had given him, where the local councillor held surgeries on a Thursday afternoon. Franklin did not know Peter Barrett very well, but his father had always had good things to say about the man, and even Everton had given him the benefit of the doubt.

The queue of people ahead of Franklin bore testimony to Barrett's popularity in the community. Or maybe just the number of problems people were facing. Franklin took out his Walkman and plugged himself into the Test Match commentary. It was still lunch, so he switched to Radio One and let his mind float to the music.

Around two it was his turn. Peter Barrett looked tired, and a lot older than Franklin remembered, but he managed a smile in greeting. Franklin explained why he was there, knowing as he did so that none of it was news to the councillor.

It turned out that Barrett had already been contacted by half a dozen relatives of those who had been arrested in Spenser Road. He was trying to get them and any witnesses they could find to a meeting on the following evening. Then they could discuss what was possible. If anything.

'Do you still live with your parents?' Barrett asked.

'No, I'm in the Army,' Franklin said, wondering what the reaction would be.

Barrett just gave him a single glance that seemed to speak volumes, before carrying on as if nothing had happened. But something had – Franklin had failed a loyalty test.

Walking back up Acre Lane he wondered if he had doomed himself to a life in permanent limbo – for ever denied full access to one world, and with no way back into the other.

In Banjul, Mustapha Diop had not had the most relaxing

of mornings. The rebel soldiers who had arrived at his front door in the hour before dawn were still there, albeit outside. He had been 'asked' not to leave the house – in the interests of his own safety, of course – and had been unable to derive any joy from the telephone. The radio broadcast had rendered his wife almost hysterical, which was unusual, and all morning the children had been driving him mad, which was not. He was lighting yet another cigarette when two men appeared in the gateway and started across the space towards his front door.

One of them was thin-faced, with dark-set eyes and hair cut to the scalp, the other had chubbier features and seemed to be smiling. Once inside they introduced themselves as Mamadou Jabang and Sharif Sallah, respectively the new President and Foreign Secretary of The Gambia.

'I will come directly to the point,' Jabang said. 'We wish you to contact your government, and to give them an accurate picture of what is happening here in Banjul . . .'

'How could I know – I have been kept a prisoner here!'

'You have not been ill-treated?' Sallah asked in a concerned voice.

'No, but . . .'

'It was merely necessary to ensure that you did not venture out while the streets were not safe,' Sallah said. 'The same precautions were taken with all the foreign embassies,' he added, less than truthfully.

'Yes, yes, I understand,' Diop said. 'But it is still the case that I know nothing of the situation outside.'

'We are here to change that,' Jabang said. 'We are going to take you on a tour of the city, so that you can see for yourself.'

42

'And if I refuse?'

'Why would you do that?' Jabang asked with a smile.

Diop could not think of a reason. He smiled back. 'I suppose you're right,' he said, and a few minutes later, having told his wife where he was going, he found himself seated next to the new President in the back of a taxi.

'Do you know the town well?' Jabang asked, as they set off down Marina Parade.

'Quite well.'

'Good. We will go down Wellington Street to the ferry terminal, and then back up Hagen Street. Yes?'

'Yes, of course.'

The taxi sped down the tree-lined avenue, then turned past the Royal Victoria Hospital onto Independence Drive. There seemed to be few people outdoors, though one group of youths gathered around a shop at the top of Buckle Street offered clenched-fist salutes to their passing vehicle.

'It looks peaceful, yes?' Sallah asked from the front seat.

'Yes,' Diop agreed. Actually, it looked dead. What were these people trying to prove?

'Is there anywhere in particular you'd like to see?' Sallah asked.

My home in the Rue Corniche in Dakar, Diop thought to himself. 'No, nowhere,' he answered.

They drove back up Independence Drive to the Legislative Assembly, where Diop was ushered through into a small office containing desk, chair and telephone. 'You can speak to your government from here,' Sallah told him. 'And tell them that the fighting is over and the new government in full control. Tell them what you saw on the streets.'

'I will tell them what I know,' Diop agreed.

At that moment someone else appeared and started talking excitedly to Sallah in Mandinka, in which Diop was less than fluent. The gist of what was being said, though, soon became clear. As Sallah turned back to him, Diop did his best to pretend he had not understood.

'There is a problem with the telephone connection,' the Gambian said. 'In the meantime you will be taken back to your house.'

'I . . .' Diop started to say, but Sallah had already gone, and two armed rebels were gesturing for Diop to follow them. He walked back to his house between them, pondering what he had heard – that all connections with Senegal had been cut by the Senegalese Government. That could only mean one thing as far as Diop could see – Senegal intended living up to its treaty with the ousted government, and troops would soon be on their way to dispose of this one. Where that left him and his family, Diop was afraid to think.

Moussa Diba turned away from the cell window and its unrelenting panorama of mangrove swamp. Lamin Konko was dozing fitfully on the half-shredded mattress they shared, his hand occasionally stabbing out at the fly which seemed intent on colonizing his forehead. It was the middle of the afternoon – normally the quiet time in Banjul Prison – but today was different. Today all sorts of noises seemed to be sounding elsewhere in the building: whispered conversations, hammering, even laughter. And more than that: all day there had been tension in the air. It was hard to put his finger on exactly how this had expressed itself, but Moussa Diba knew that something was happening outside his cell, or something had happened and the ripples were still spreading. He did not know why, but he had a feeling it was good news. Maybe he did have his grandmother's gifts as a future-teller, as she had always thought.

Time would tell.

His thoughts turned back to the Englishman, as they often did. The man had humiliated him, and he was still not sure how it had been done. One moment he had had the woman on the floor ready for him and enough drugs in his hand to live like a king for six months, and the next he was waking up in a police cell, on his way to this stinking cell for five years. If he ever got out of here, Anja would be his first stop, and the Englishman would be his second. And next time the boot would be on the other foot.

4

McGrath and Jobo Camara took the Bund Road route out of Banjul, to avoid the rebel activity on Independence Drive, but there was no way round the Denton Bridge. As they drove past the prison, its two watch-towers both apparently unmanned, McGrath could feel the reassuring pressure of the Browning in the centre of his back. Driving hell for leather along a tropical road in a jeep brought back more memories than he could count, most of them good ones, at least in retrospect.

They saw the first checkpoint from about a quarter of a mile away. A taxi was parked on either side of the entrance to the bridge, and four men were grouped around the one on the left. Two were leaning against the bonnet, the others standing a few yards away, silhouetted against the silver sheen of Oyster Creek. All four moved purposefully into the centre of the road as they saw the jeep approaching, rifles pointed at the ground. None of them was wearing a uniform.

McGrath pulled the jeep to a halt ten yards away from them, and got down to the ground, slowly, so as not to cause any alarm.

'Where are you going?' one man asked. He was wearing dark glasses, purple cotton trousers with a vivid batik pattern and a Def Leppard T-shirt.

'Serekunda,' McGrath said.

'Whites are confined to the hotels,' the man said.

'Not all whites,' Jobo said, standing at McGrath's shoulder. 'Only tourists.'

'I work for the Ministry of Development,' McGrath

added. 'We have business in Serekunda, checking out one of the generators.'

'Do you have permission?'

'No, but I'm sure the new government will not want all the lights to go out in Serekunda on its first day in office. But why don't you check with them?' McGrath bluffed. He was pretty sure that the checkpoint had no means of communicating with the outside world.

The rebel digested the situation. 'That will not be necessary,' he said eventually. 'You may pass.'

'Thank you,' McGrath said formally.

They motored across the long bridge. A couple of yachts were anchored in the creek, and McGrath wondered where their owners were – they seemed rather conspicuous examples of wealth to flaunt in the middle of a revolution. On the far side the road veered left through the savannah, the long summer grass dotted by giant baobab trees and tall palms.

Ten minutes later they were entering the sprawling outskirts of Serekunda, which housed as many people as Banjul, but lacked its extremes of affluence and shanty-town squalor. Jobo directed McGrath left at the main crossroads, down past the main mosque and then right down a dirt street for about a hundred yards. A dozen or so children gathered around the jeep, and Jobo appointed one of them its guardian, then led McGrath through the gate of the compound.

Mansa Camara was sitting on a wooden bench in the courtyard, his back against the concrete wall, his head shaded by the overhanging corrugated roof. He was dressed in a traditional African robe, not the western uniform of the Field Force.

His nephew made the introductions, and asked him what had happened.

'I resigned,' Mansa said shortly.

'Why?'

'It seemed like the right thing to do, boy. I'll give it to Taal – he was honest enough about it. "Join us or go home," he said, "and leave your gun behind." So I came home.'

'How many others did the same?' McGrath asked him.

'I do not wish to be rude,' Mansa asked, 'but what interest is this of yours?'

McGrath decided to tell the truth. 'I work here,' he said, 'so I'm interested in whether these people can hang on to what they've taken. Plus my embassy is worried about all the tourists, and wants all the information it can get.'

'No problem there,' Camara said. 'Not as long as the leaders are in control. They know better than to anger foreign governments for no reason.'

Jobo took out his cigarettes and offered them round. Mansa puffed appreciatively at the Marlboro for a moment, and then shouted into the house for tea. 'Jobo is a good boy,' he said, turning back to McGrath, and I know he likes to work with you. So I answer the question you ask.' He took another drag, the expression on his face a cigarette advertiser's dream. 'One-third is my guess,' he said. 'One-third say no, the other two-thirds go with Taal.'

'They really think they can win?' Jobo asked.

'Who will stop them?' Mansa asked. 'There is no other armed force inside the country.'

'So you think the British will come, or the Americans?'

Mansa laughed. 'No. The Senegalese may. But Jobo, I did not walk away because I think they will lose. I just did not want any part of it. My job is to keep the law, not to decide which government the country should have.'

He looked at McGrath. 'That is the civilized way, is it not? Politicians for politics, police for keeping the law, an army for defending the country.'

'That's how it's supposed to be,' McGrath agreed.

The tea arrived, strong and sweet in clay pots. Another cigarette followed, and then lunch was announced. By the time McGrath and Jobo climbed back aboard the jeep it was gone three.

'Did you like my uncle?' Jobo asked as they pulled out into Mosque Road.

'Yep, I liked him,' McGrath said.

Serekunda seemed more subdued than it had when they arrived, as if the news of the coup was finally sinking in. The road to Banjul, normally full of bush taxis and minibuses, was sparsely populated within the town and utterly empty outside it. In the three-mile approach to the Denton Bridge they met nothing and saw no one.

The personnel at the checkpoint had changed. The man in the purple batik trousers, along with his three less colourful companions, had been replaced by two men who seemed more inclined to take their work seriously. As McGrath drove slowly over the bridge they moved into the centre of the road. Both were wearing Field Force uniforms; one was holding a rifle, the other a handgun.

The one with the handgun signalled them to stop.

McGrath did so, and smiled at him. 'We're working . . .' he started to say.

'Get down,' the man growled. His partner, a younger man with a slight squint in his left eye, looked nervous.

Jobo recognized him. 'Jerry, it's me,' he said, and the man smiled briefly at him.

His partner was not impressed. 'Get down,' he repeated.

'Sure,' McGrath said, not liking the unsteadiness of

the hand holding the gun. He and Jobo got out of the jeep, the latter looking angry.

'What's this for?' he angrily asked the man with the handgun.

'Give me your papers,' the man demanded. 'And your passport,' he said to McGrath.

'Papers? I have no papers,' Jobo protested. 'This is stupid. What papers?'

'Everyone leaving or entering Banjul must have a pass, by order of the Council,' the man said, as if he was reciting something memorized. 'You are under arrest,' he added, waving the gun for emphasis.

It went off, sending a bullet between Jobo's shoulder and upper chest.

For a second all four men's faces seemed frozen with shock, and then the man with the handgun, whether consciously or not, turned it towards McGrath.

The ex-soldier was not taking any chances. In what seemed like a single motion he swept the Browning from the holster behind his back, dropped to one knee, and sent two bullets through the centre of the Gambian's head.

He then whirled round in search of the other man, who was simply standing there, transfixed by shock. There was a clatter as the rifle slipped from his hands and fell to the tarmac. McGrath flicked his wrist and the man took the hint; he covered the five yards to the edge of the bridge like a scared rabbit, and launched himself into the creek with a huge splash.

McGrath went across to where Jobo was struggling into a sitting position, looking with astonishment at the blood trickling out through his shirt and fingers. 'Let's get you to hospital,' McGrath said, and helped him into the jeep.

He then went back for the body of the man he had

killed. The only obvious bullet entry hole was through the bridge of the nose; the other round had gone through the man's open mouth. Between them they had taken a lot of brain out through the back of the head. At least it had been quick. McGrath dragged the corpse across to the rail and heaved it into the creek, where it swiftly sank from sight in the muddy water.

Colonel Taal replaced the telephone and sat back in the chair, his eyes closed. He rubbed them, wondering how long he could keep going without at least a couple of hours of sleep.

He found himself thinking about Admiral Yamamoto, whose biography he had read long ago at Sandhurst. In November 1941 Yamamoto had told his Emperor that he could give the Americans hell for six months, but that thereafter there was no hope of ultimate military victory. Even knowing that, he had still attacked Pearl Harbour.

Reading the biography Taal had found such a decision hard to understand, yet here in The Gambia he seemed to have taken one that was remarkably similar. They could take over the country, he had told the Party leadership, but if any outside forces were brought to bear their military chances were non-existent. Like the Japanese, their only hope lay in the rest of the world not being bothered enough to put things back the way they had been.

But the rest of the world, as he had just learned on the telephone, did seem bothered enough.

Should he wake Jabang? he wondered. Probably. But just as he was summoning the energy to do so, Jabang appeared in the doorway, also rubbing his eyes.

'I can't sleep,' the new President said, sinking into the office's other easy chair and yawning.

'I have bad news,' Taal said wearily.

'The Senegalese?' It was hardly even a question.

'They're sending troops tomorrow morning. I managed to get a connection through Abidjan,' he added in explanation.

'Shit!' Jabang ran a hand across his stubbled hair, and exhaled noisily. 'Shit,' he repeated quietly. 'How many?' he asked. 'And where to?'

'Don't know. I doubt if they've decided yet. As to where, I'd guess they'll drop some paratroops somewhere near the airport, try and capture that, and if they succeed then they can fly in more.'

Jabang considered this. 'But how many men can they drop?' he asked. 'Not many, surely?'

Taal shrugged. 'A few hundred, maybe five, but . . .'

'And if we stop them capturing the airport they can't bring any more in, right?'

'Theoretically, but . . .'

'Surely our five hundred men can stop their five hundred, Junaidi.'

Taal shook his head. 'These will be French-trained soldiers, professionals. Our men are not trained for that sort of fighting . . .'

'Yes, but an army with political purpose will always triumph over mere mercenaries, Junaidi. History is full of examples. Castro and Guevara started with only twelve men and they beat a professional army.' Jabang's eyes were fixed on Taal's, willing him to believe.

'I know, Mamadou. I know. But the circumstances were different. And anyway,' he added, overriding a potential interruption, 'if we send all our five hundred to defend the airport who will keep order elsewhere? We just do not have enough men.'

'So what are you proposing we do – nothing? Should

we head for the border, after being in power for just a few hours?'

'No.' It was tempting, Taal thought, but he would not be able to live with himself if they gave up this easily. 'No, we must resist as long as we can.'

Jabang grinned. 'Yes,' he said, 'yes!' and thumped his fist on the arm of his chair.

'What is it?' Sharif Sallah asked, coming into the room, a smile on his face.

The temptation to wipe the smile away was irresistible. 'The Senegalese are coming,' Taal said.

'What?'

'Sit down, Sharif,' Jabang said. 'And tell us how we can increase the number of our fighters in the next twelve hours.'

Sallah sat down, shaking his head. 'You are certain?' he asked, and received a nod in return. He sighed. 'Well, there is only one way to increase our numbers,' Sallah said. 'We will have to arm the men in Banjul Prison.'

It was Taal's turn to be surprised. 'You must be joking,' he said wearily.

Sallah shook his head. 'There are two hundred men in the prison, and many of them know how to use guns. If we let them out they will fight for us, because they will know that if Jawara wins he will put them back in the prison.'

'And what if they decide to use the weapons we give them to take what they want and just head for the border?' Taal asked. 'After having their revenge on whichever Field Force men put them in the prison.'

'We can keep them under control. In groups of ten or so, under twenty of our men. And in any case, they will know that Senegal offers no sanctuary for them. I tell you, they will fight for us because only we can offer them freedom.'

'And the moral question?' Taal wanted to know. 'These men are not in prison for cheating on their wives. They are murderers and thieves and . . .'

'Come on, Junaidi,' Jabang interrupted. 'There are only two murderers in Banjul Prison that I know of. But there are a lot of men who were caught stealing in order to feed themselves and their families.' He looked appealingly at Taal. 'Most crimes are political crimes – I can remember you saying so yourself.'

Yes, he had, Taal thought, but a long, long time ago. In the intervening years he had learned that not all evil could be so easily explained. 'I'm against it,' he said, 'except as a last resort.'

'You were just telling me this is the last resort,' Jabang insisted.

As soon as he could McGrath had pulled off the open road and examined Jobo's wound. It had already stopped bleeding, and seemed less serious than he had at first feared. Still, it would have to be looked at by a proper doctor, if only because there was no other obvious source of disinfectant.

He drove the jeep straight down Independence Drive, mentally daring anyone to try to stop him. No one did, and once at the hospital the two men found themselves in what looked like a scene from Florence Nightingale's life story. Somewhere or other there had been more fighting that day, because the reception area was full of reclining bodies, most of them with bullet wounds of varying degrees of seriousness. The woman receptionist, who must have weighed at least eighteen stone, and who would have looked enormous even in a country where overeating was commonplace, clambered with difficulty over the prone patients in pursuit of their names and details. Sibou Cham, who looked like grace personified in comparison, was forever moving hither and thither between the reception area and the treatment rooms as she ministered to the patients.

It was almost two hours before she got round to seeing Jobo.

'You look all in,' McGrath told her, with what he thought was a sympathetic smile.

'Yes, I know, you have a bed waiting for me.'

'I didn't mean that,' he said indignantly. 'Not that it's such a terrible idea,' he murmured, as an afterthought.

She ignored him and bent down to examine the wound. 'Did he really get shot by a sniper?' she asked.

'You don't want to know,' McGrath said. 'Is he going to be OK?'

'Yes, provided he keeps away from you for the next few days.'

'It was not Mr McGrath's fault,' Jobo blurted out. 'He saved us both . . .'

'She doesn't need to know,' McGrath interrupted.

Sibou gave him one cold, hard look and strode out of the office.

'I don't want to get her in trouble,' McGrath explained. 'The other guy – you called him Jerry – what do you think he'll do?'

Jobo thought. 'I don't know. He was always a scared kid when I knew him at school. And not very clever. He may worry that he'll get in trouble for letting his partner get shot or for running away. He may just go home and keep quiet, or even go up to the family village for a few days.'

'Or he may be telling his story to Comrade Jabang right this moment.'

'I don't think so.'

'Well, there's not a lot we can do about it if he

is. Except maybe send you to your village for a few days . . .'

'I come from Serekunda,' Jobo said indignantly.

'Oh, pity.'

The doctor came back with a bowl of disinfectant and a roll of new bandage. After carefully washing the entrance and exit wounds she applied a dressing, then the bandage, and told Jobo to take it easy for a few days. 'If it starts to smell, or it throbs, come back,' she told him. 'Otherwise just let it heal.'

'I'll take him home,' McGrath said. She was already on her way back to the reception area. 'When do you get off?' he called after her.

She laughed. 'In my dreams,' she said over her shoulder, and disappeared.

Outside the jeep was still there, much to McGrath's relief and somewhat to his surprise. Darkness was falling with its usual tropical swiftness. He helped Jobo aboard, climbed into the driving seat, and started off down the road into town.

The first thing that struck him was how dark it was. Banjul's lighting would have done credit to a vampire's dining room at the best of times, but on this night every plug in the city seemed to have been pulled, and McGrath's vision was restricted to what the jeep's headlights could show him.

The sounds of the city told him more than he wanted to know. The most prominent seemed to feature a never-ending cascade of glass, as if someone was breaking a long line of windows in sequence. Some evidence to support this theory came at one corner, where the jeep's headlights picked out a tableau of three shops, each with their glass fronts smashed, and fully laden silhouettes bearing goods away into the night.

The sound of tearing wood also seemed much in

evidence, offering proof, McGrath supposed, that in the Third World not many shops were fronted by glass. Banjul seemed to be in the process of being comprehensively looted.

And then there was the gunfire. Nothing steady, no long bursts, just single shots every minute or so, from wildly different directions, as if an endless series of individual murders was being committed all over the town.

It was eerie, and frightening. At Jobo's house his mother pulled him inside and shut the door almost in the same motion, as if afraid to let the contagion in. McGrath climbed back into the jeep and laid the Browning on the seat beside him, feeling the hairs rising on the nape of his neck. He engaged the gears and took off, hurtling back up the street faster than was prudent, but barely fast enough for his peace of mind.

It was only half a mile to the dim lights of McCarthy Square, only forty seconds or so, but it felt longer. At the square he slowed, wondering where to go. The Atlantic Hotel offered a whites-only haven, but there would be guards there, maybe guards who were looking for him, and he knew he would feel more restricted, more vulnerable, surrounded by fellow Europeans. Particularly if the rebels suddenly got trigger-happy with their tourist guests. No, he decided, the Carlton offered more freedom of movement, more ways out. And he could sleep on the roof.

The Party envoys, along with an armed guard of a dozen or so Field Force men, arrived at the prison soon after dark, and after a heated discussion with the warden, which ended with his being temporarily consigned to one of his own cells, they addressed the assembled prisoners in the dimly lit exercise yard.

Moussa Diba and Lamin Konko listened as attentively as everyone else.

There had been a change of government, the speaker told them, and all prisoners, with the exception of the two convicted murderers, were being offered amnesty in return for a month's enlistment in the service of the new government. They would not be asked to fight against fellow Gambians or workers, only against foreigners seeking to invade the country. If they chose not to enlist, that was up to them. They would simply be returned to their cells to serve out their sentences.

'What do you think?' Konko asked Diba.

'Sounds like a way out,' Diba said with a grin. He was still inwardly laughing at the exemption of the two murderers, whom everybody in the prison knew to be among the gentlest of those incarcerated there. Both had killed their wives in a fit of jealous rage, and now spent all their time asking God for forgiveness. Some of the thieves, on the other hand, would cut a throat for five dalasi. He would himself for ten.

'I've only got two years more in here,' Konko said. 'I'd rather do them than get killed defending a bunch of politicians.'

'We won't,' Diba insisted. 'Look, if they're coming here to get us out, they must be desperate. It must be all craziness out there in Banjul. We'll have no trouble slipping away from whatever they've got planned for us, and then we hide out for a while, see how the situation is, get hold of some money and get across into Senegal when it looks good. No problem. Right, brother?'

Konko sighed. 'OK,' he said with less than total conviction. 'I guess out there must be better than being in here.'

'There's women out there,' Diba said. Anja was out there. And with any luck he would have her tonight.

The two of them joined the queue of those waiting to accept the offer of amnesty. Since only three of the prison's two hundred and seventeen eligible inmates turned down the offer it was a long queue, and almost an hour had passed before the new recruits were drawn up in marching order on the road outside. They were kept standing there for several minutes, swatting at the mosquitoes drawn from the swamp by such a wealth of accessible blood in one spot, until one of the Party envoys addressed them again. They were being escorted to temporary barracks for the night, he told them. On the following morning they would be issued with their weapons.

The barracks in question turned out to be a large empty house in Marina Parade. There was no furniture, just floor space, and not enough of that. The overcrowding was worse than it had been in the prison, and, despite the protests of the guards, the sleeping quarters soon spilled out into the garden. There was no food, no entertainment, and after about an hour the sense of too much energy with nowhere to go was becoming overpowering. The guards, sensing the growing threat, started finding reasons to melt away, and with their disappearance an increasing number of the prisoners decided to go out for an evening stroll, some in search of their families, some in search of women, some simply in search of motion for its own sake.

Diba went looking for Anja.

Finding Independence Drive partially lit by a widely spaced string of log brazier fires, he slipped across the wide road and down the darker Mosque Road. It could not be much later than ten, he reckoned, but Banjul was obviously going to bed early these days. There were no shops open, no sounds of music, and few lights glowing through the compound doorways.

Occasionally the sounds of conversation would drift out across a wall, and often as not lapse abruptly into silence at his footfall.

Conscious that he had no weapon, Diba kept a lookout for anything which would serve for protection, and in one small patch of reflected light noticed a two-foot length of heavy cable which someone had found surplus to requirements and discarded. It felt satisfyingly heavy in his hands.

Some fifteen minutes after leaving Marina Parade he found himself at the gate to the compound where she had her room. Her husband's family had once occupied the whole compound, but both his parents had died young, he had been killed in a road accident in Senegal, and his brothers had gone back to their Wollof village. She had fought a losing battle against other adult orphans, and the compound had become a home to assorted con men and thieves.

To Diba's surprise the gate was padlocked on the inside. He climbed over without difficulty, proud of how fit he had managed to keep himself in prison, and stood for a moment, listening for any sounds of occupation. He heard none, but as his eyes became accustomed to the gloom they picked out a pile of identical cardboard boxes stacked against a wall. They were new stereo radio-cassette players. No wonder the gate had been locked. He walked gingerly down one arm of the L-shaped courtyard, and turned the corner. The first thing he noticed was the yellow glow seeping out under Anja's door, the second was the sound of her voice, moaning softly, rhythmically, with pleasure.

Maybe it's not her, he told himself, a knot of anger forming in his stomach. He silently advanced to the door, and placed an eye up against the gap between the window shutters.

A single candle burnt on the wooden table, illuminating the two naked people on the bed. She was underneath, her back slightly arched, eyes closed, hands behind her head, gripping the cast-iron rail of the bedstead. He was above her, supporting his upper body on two rigid arms as he thrust himself slowly this way and that. The two bodies glistened in the candlelight.

Anger surged through Diba's guts, but he fought it back. He took two deep breaths before walking through the curtained doorway into the room, the length of cable loose in his hand.

Though her eyes were closed she became aware of him first. Perhaps it was a draught from the door, or perhaps they really did have a telepathic connection, as she had always claimed. Her eyes opened, widened, and snapped shut again as he swung the cable in a vicious arc at the man's head.

Blood splattered, and the man seemed to sway, as if he was held upright only by his position inside her. She cried out and twisted, and he collapsed off the bed with a crash, falling onto the already crushed back of his head. Two thin streams of blood emerged from his nose and mouth, merged on his cheek, and abruptly ceased flowing.

Diba used a foot to roll the body into the shadows. Anja was just lying there, one hand still gripping the iron rail, the other covering her mouth, palm outwards. Her eyes were wide again, wide with shock. He reached down a hand and brushed a still-erect nipple with his palm.

She reached for the sheet to cover herself, but he ripped it away from her, and threw it on the floor.

He pulled his shirt over his head, tore off his trousers and stood over her, his dick swelling towards her face. For a moment he thought of thrusting it into her mouth, but the expression on her face was still unreadable, and he did not want it bitten off.

'Moussa,' she said.

He clambered astride her, and thrust himself into the warm wetness which the dead man had so recently vacated. She moaned and closed her eyes, but Diba was not fooled. He came in a sudden rush, spilling three months of prison frustration into her, and then abruptly pulled out, and rolled over onto his back.

For several moments the two of them lay there in silence.

'How did you get out?' she asked after a while, her voice sounding strange, as if she was trying too hard to sound normal.

'They let us all out to fight for the new Government,' he told her.

She risked moving, raising herself onto one elbow. 'Is he dead?' she asked.

'Looks like it,' Diba said coldly. It was funny – he would have expected to feel something after killing a man, but he felt nothing at all. Unless he counted being aware of the need to make sure he was not caught.

But he did remember how angry he had felt. 'Who was this man you were fucking?' he asked in a threatening voice.

'Just a customer,' she lied. It was her experience that men who got it for free did not usually feel jealous of those who had paid.

She was right. 'You been prostituting yourself?' he asked, with an anger that was less than convincing.

'While you're in the prison I have to eat,' she said, risking some self-assertion for the first time.

He reached out a hand and grabbed her by the plaited hair. 'You sounded like you were enjoying it,' he said.

'Men like that need to think they're making you feel good,' she said.

He grunted and let her go. He wanted to believe her –

he always had. 'OK,' he said. 'But you're all mine again now – got it? And we're getting out of this shit-hole.'

'Where to?'

'I haven't decided yet. You got anything to drink?'

'No, but I can get some beer from Winnie's. It'll take five minutes.'

He grabbed one of her cheeks in his hand and held her eyes. She was so fucking beautiful. 'You wouldn't disappear on me, would you?' he asked.

'I'll be five minutes.'

'I'd kill you, you know that.'

'Yes, I know that.'

'Right.' He let her go, watched her slip the dress over herself and head for the door, careful not to look at the prone body under the window.

He supposed he ought to do something about that.

He put his trousers back on, grabbed the corpse by the feet and dragged it out into the courtyard. Anja had left the gate open, so he carried on into the darkened street, his ears straining for other sounds above the scrape of the man's head in the dust. After fifty yards he decided he had gone far enough, and simply left the body in the middle of the road. With any luck they would think he had been hit by a taxi in the dark.

Back in her room Anja was engaged in opening one of three bottles of beer on the edge of the table. He took it from her and sprang the cap off, remembering doing the same thing at other times in the past, in that same candlelit room.

'Do you mean you're in the army now?' she asked.

He shrugged. 'They want us to defend their revolution,' he said. 'They're going to give us guns in the morning. And then ... I don't know. But I'm not going to get killed for a bunch of fucking politicians. I'll take their gun all right, but who I use it on is my business.' He smiled. 'And I've got a few ideas on that myself.'

'The Englishman who caught you,' she said, before stopping to think.

'How do you know about that?' he asked angrily.

'It was in the newspaper', she said. 'Someone showed it to me.'

'What was? What did it say?'

'That you were caught at the hospital by an Englishman, that's all,' she said. There had been more, but she reckoned he would not want to hear the details of his humiliation.

'It was bad luck,' he said. 'But yes, I owe him.' And the doctor too, he thought. He had had her naked once, and he would have her naked again, only next time she would not have the white bastard there to protect her. He would make her kneel for him.

He looked across at Anja, who was just as beautiful as the doctor, but had grown up as poor as he had. He felt the old desire mounting in his body. 'Take the dress off,' he said.

5

The column of five open lorries, each carrying twenty ex-prisoners, rumbled through Serekunda and south towards Yundum Airport. It had been light for only an hour or so, and the heat was not yet oppressive. Diba sat alongside Konko, the Kalashnikov leaning against his thigh, watching the countryside go by. He was not very happy with the situation. A town man, he felt much more confident of melting away into the scenery when it was composed of shanty compounds. Outside the town he felt too conspicuous.

Still, he had had no chance to get away again since returning to the temporary barracks an hour before dawn. Most of the other nocturnal absentees had also come back: like Diba they saw little hope of escaping the country under the present circumstances, and no hope of anything but longer prison terms from a returning Jawara. For the moment the new regime was their only friend – not to mention their only source of weaponry and ammunition.

The lorries with the Kalashnikovs had drawn up outside the barracks just as dawn was breaking, and the men had been told to claim their guns as they boarded. The new regime was obviously not composed entirely of fools.

Diba wondered if he really would find himself in a battle before the day was over. Not if he could help it, he told himself.

'Where do you think we're going?' Konko asked him.

'The airport,' Diba replied. It was a guess. There was

nothing else of any importance in this direction, only three hundred miles of villages. Unless of course the new government had decided to invade the rest of Africa.

He was right the first time, for the lorries swung off the road to Brikama, taking the airport turn-off. The land was flat savannah, dotted with the occasional tree, but otherwise offering no more cover than that provided by the long wet-season grass. For the first time the possibility of being attacked from the air occurred to Diba. He remembered the opening shot of the film he had seen just before his arrest – a wall of palm trees exploding into flames. It had been about Vietnam, but he could not remember the title.

Also for the first time, he wondered whether leaving the prison had been such a good idea. His mind went back over the previous night, and told him it had been. And there had to be some way to make use of this situation for his and Anja's benefit. He just had to be patient, and recognize the opening when it came.

The lorries were drawing up in front of the airport terminal. The tailgates were lowered, the men ordered down and divided into groups of ten by two uniformed Field Force men. From the looks on their faces the latter hardly seemed enamoured of their new reinforcements. And Diba had to admit that his fellow prisoners hardly looked like soldiers. All were still wearing the clothes they had been wearing in jail, which ranged in condition from rags to almost reasonable, from utterly filthy to merely soiled.

The groups of ten were led off at intervals through the airport's main doors. When Diba and Konko's turn came they found that the building was only a temporary port of call: after each man had been issued with a hunk of bread and a couple of bananas they were led out through other doors at the back and onto a wide expanse of tarmac, where several large planes were parked. None looked like it was expecting to fly.

Diba's group, accompanied by a roughly equal number of Field Force men and other rebels, headed north up the main runway to its end, and then pressed on another two hundred yards until they reached a row of landing lights, protruding from the grass like fetish poles. Spades were produced and the ex-prisoners took turns excavating trenches while the others scanned the sky, talking nervously among themselves and occasionally throwing a contemptuous glance at the diggers.

Within an hour the group of twenty was arranged in a semicircle of trenches, the airport behind them, empty savannah and sky in front of them. The sweating Diba and Konko shared the latter's last cigarette and hoped that the rest of the day would be as peaceful.

McGrath was woken by a loudly honking formation of geese flying low over the hotel roof. He had been having one of those lovely English dreams, sitting in the conservatory his wife had spent so much effort on, watching the sparrows eating from the bird table on the lawn outside. It had all been so peaceful.

He looked at the sun, then at his watch. It was gone eight already, and his back ached from the hardness of the roof, but he felt reluctant to get up. Dreams like that – and he seemed to have more of them with each trip abroad – always produced a vague aching in his heart, and made him wonder why, if he really missed her and the children so much, he spent so much of his time so far away from them.

I mean, he said to himself, what the fuck am I doing at my age sleeping out on an African hotel roof because it's not safe to sleep in my fucking room?

He reached for the transistor radio that he had

recovered from his room the night before and tuned in to Radio Gambia. And like the night before, the programming consisted of replays of the new leader's message to the world, sandwiched between bouts of Bob Marley. The rebels were still in control.

McGrath manoeuvred himself into a sitting position, his back against an air vent, and thought about what he should do. For all he knew, the entire rebel army was out looking for him, although it seemed unlikely. He had heard no commotion in the hotel below him, and he tended to trust Jobo's judgement in the matter of the boy who had thrown himself into the creek. Of course it would be prudent to assume the new authorities were looking for him, and to stay where he was until he knew otherwise, but the thought of sitting on the Carlton roof for the rest of the day did not seem very appealing.

His first job, he decided, was to talk to the High Commission, and find out what the hell was going on. For that he would need a telephone, and the roof seemed lamentably short of them.

He walked down to his room, listened at the door for a few moments to make sure no one was waiting inside, and then let himself in. The water was on and hot, so he treated himself to a shower and changed clothes before going downstairs. The lobby was empty, the telephone dead as a doornail. He would have to revisit the Atlantic.

From the lobby window the road outside also seemed devoid of people, as if it was a Sunday morning. But two guards were standing guard at the gates to the Legislative Assembly, and several more men in uniform were talking to each other just outside the doors. McGrath was about to step out into the street when the Carlton's manager hurried out of the dining room to intercept him.

'Mr McGrath,' he said breathlessly. 'I wanted to talk to you. To give you warning.'

'What of?' McGrath asked, surprised at such concern.

'I remember your arrest at the hospital,' the man said, as if in explanation.

'Yes?'

'They have let all the prisoners out,' the manager explained.

'They've what!' McGrath exclaimed. 'Why, for Christ's sake?'

The manager shrugged. 'To fight for them, of course. They've given them guns and driven them off somewhere. But I thought you should know. The man you arrested . . .'

'Ah.' Now he understood. 'I understand. Thank you. I will be careful.'

'Maybe you can arrest him again,' the man said with a smile.

'Maybe.'

The manager smiled and retreated into the bowels of the hotel. Still absorbing this new information, McGrath walked out through the terrace and down the side of the building to where he had parked the Ministry of Development jeep. He wondered if Sibou had heard the news. He would have to make sure she had.

He eased the jeep out into Independence Drive. The guards outside the Legislative Assembly stared at him, but neither did nor said any more. McGrath drove the hundred yards or so to where the side road cut through to Marina Parade and turned onto it. Halfway down he had to swerve to avoid two bodies lying in the middle of the road. He stopped the jeep, got out, and went back to look at them. Both were oldish men, and both had had their throats cut. More than a few hours ago, for the pools of blood had long since dried into a brown crust.

He went back to the jeep and drove on, turning right again onto Marina Parade, oblivious to the beauty of the trees that hung across the road. The crust of civilization was so thin, he thought. Take away the repressive hand of the law, and hey presto, there would be a queue of sickos waiting to prove that morality grew out of the barrel of a gun. Or the blade of a knife. Or whatever came to hand.

The Atlantic Hotel was an oasis of order. Black waiters in red shirts were still serving breakfast to fat Europeans, and smiling at them as if their lives depended on it. Or at least their tips. He must have got out on the wrong side of the roof this morning, McGrath told himself. The world seemed cast in shades of sourness.

Or maybe moving from slashed throats to croissant-guzzling tourists in under five minutes was a little too swift a transition. He got himself a cup of coffee and carried it through to the lobby.

At least the telephones were still working. He called the High Commission and drank most of the coffee while whoever it was that had answered went looking for Bill Myers.

'Simon,' a voice said eventually, 'glad you're still alive.'

'Just about,' McGrath said. 'Banjul is getting a bit hairy. You know . . .'

'Help is on the way,' Myers interrupted him. 'Senegalese Army should be arriving sometime today.'

'Arriving where?'

'No idea. But wherever it is, I don't suppose it'll take them long to clear this shower out.'

'Maybe,' McGrath said noncommittally. He supposed it was good news to him personally – instead of being arrested for shooting a rebel he would probably be given a medal. 'Did you know they've emptied the prison?' he asked Myers.

'Oh shit, they haven't.'

'So I'm told. And armed the prisoners.'

'That's bad news. And the other thing is – we've got no idea what they've done with the old Government – it's only Jawara who was out of the country. And then there's the little matter of his family, too. It could still get very messy.'

'Sounds like it. Anything you want me to do at this end.'

'No,' Myers said after a brief pause, 'just stay in touch. According to London there's a rumour that Jawara has asked the PM for help. Who knows, she may even ask your old mob to lend a hand. So you may yet become indispensable.'

'Thanks a bunch, Bill,' McGrath said. 'Remind me to send you my invoice for services rendered to the Crown.'

Myers laughed and hung up. McGrath put the receiver down and thought about what he had heard. The SAS in The Gambia – that would be one for the Regiment's scrapbook. And if a hostage situation did develop . . .

It would be interesting, to say the least. For the moment, though, he had other things to worry about. Like Sibou Cham. He drove down Marina Parade to the hospital, and parked right outside the entrance. Soon, if not already, the rebels would be too busy worrying about the Senegalese to worry about him.

Once inside, he walked straight through towards her office, but an orderly barred his way at the threshold. Dr Cham was sleeping, and not to be disturbed. Dr Cham had not slept for two days, he added, in case the message had not got through.

'OK,' McGrath said. 'I just want to leave her a message. But it's important she gets it,' he added firmly.

'What's so important?' Sibou's voice asked from inside the next room.

'You wake her,' the orderly said indignantly.

'It's OK, Cissé,' Sibou said. 'McGrath, come and tell me your important message.'

She was lying fully dressed on the treatment table, staring up at the ceiling. 'They've opened up the prison,' he said, watching for her reaction.

Her eyes closed once, and opened again. 'He's out,' she said.

'Yeah. So I thought maybe I would hang around here for a while, and keep you company.'

'That . . .' She stopped herself. 'There's no need,' she said eventually. 'He can't get to me here . . .'

'He did before.'

'That was different. These days this place is swarming with armed men. I can't get rid of them.' She looked up at him. 'Thank you,' she said, 'but I'll be careful. And so should you be. I think he has more of a grudge against you than against me.'

He shrugged. 'OK. But I'll drop by every now and then . . .'

'Thanks,' she said again.

He went back to the jeep, drove it back to the Carlton, and climbed back up to the roof, taking his binoculars with him. It was about twenty minutes later, soon after 10.30, that the first Mirage flew low over Banjul, shattering the calm and more than a few hopes.

Cecil Matheson walked up the gracefully curving stair-case to his first-floor sanctum in the Foreign Office. It had taken the chauffeur an hour to bring him the mile across London from his Pimlico home, and the *Times* crossword was proving unusually stubborn. All in all, he felt frustrated, and ready to take it out on the first available scapegoat.

Unfortunately, his first call of the morning, which arrived before he had even had time to re-order his desk, was from the Prime Minister.

'Cecil,' she began, without so much as a 'good morning', 'this business in The Gambia . . .'

'Yes, Prime Minister,' he said dutifully, wondering what the hell she was talking about. He had spent the previous day at home, watching the cricket and catching up between overs on the latest Argentinian claims to the Falklands. No one had thought to disturb him with news from The Gambia. Had the wretched little country left the Commonwealth, or banned the English cricket team, or stopped buying British? Maybe her son Mark had got himself lost again on some transcontinental rally devised exclusively for the idiot offspring of prominent world leaders.

'President Jawara called me late last night and asked if we could help,' she said.

Help with what? Matheson was thinking, when his eyes made contact with the relevant report. 'Exactly what does he have in mind?' he asked, scanning through the sheet in front of him.

'Just some military advice. The Senegalese are sending troops in this morning, but I think President Jawara would like some British help – The Gambia was a British colony, after all. And he was here in London for the Royal Wedding when it all happened.'

Matheson grunted to himself. According to the report he was reading, Jawara had been overthrown by an alliance of Marxist rebels and members of his own army. So he had had to ask for military help from his Senegalese neighbours. And now the crafty bastard wanted a counterbalance to his new allies. He did not want to clear out the criminals only to find that his house had been occupied by the police.

'So I thought a small advisory group,' the Prime Minister continued. 'The SAS would seem best qualified. And be a good advertisement for the country.'

'Yes, I'm sure they could undertake such a task,' Matheson agreed. The previous year's breaking of the Iranian Embassy siege had been efficient enough. Almost awesomely so. Yet it had not exactly quelled some doubts, particularly among the opposition, as to the Regiment's cut-throat methods. Over the five years of the SAS's deployment in Northern Ireland there had been rather a lot of fatal accidents involving terrorist suspects.

'Very well,' the Prime Minister was saying. 'I'll leave it with you to contact Hereford. Tell them we definitely want to offer the President some help, but it's up to them to suggest exactly what. You can arrange the necessary liaison with the Gambians.'

'Certainly . . .' Matheson started to say, but she had hung up. He made a face at the phone and read through the report properly. Reading between the lines, he doubted whether the Senegalese would have much trouble re-establishing Jawara's authority. But the large number of tourists did suggest an unpleasantly serious risk of hostages being taken. It could all become a bit of a mare's nest, he thought. Perhaps the SAS was not such a bad idea, after all.

First, though, he had better go through all the necessary international courtesies. The French first, he thought, and asked his secretary to connect him with his opposite number in the Quai d'Orsay. René Bonnard was one of God's more acceptable Frenchmen – on occasion Matheson even suspected he had a moral code. It was probably just a trick of the light.

'René,' he said warmly, once the connection had been established. 'I'd just like a few words about the Gambian situation,' he went on, fighting the usual losing battle with his French.

'Let us speak English,' Bonnard said. Pride in one's language was one thing, but it was just too painful listening to Matheson's version of it. 'I hope you don't think we're treading on your feet . . .'

'No, no, not at all. The treaty between Senegal and The Gambia was there for just such an eventuality. We have no problem with Senegalese intervention, quite the contrary. I'm calling to let you know that we shall in all probability be sending a small team of our own – and at Jawara's request, of course . . .'

'Of course,' Bonnard agreed wryly. 'Hedging his bets – is that the English phrase?'

Matheson laughed. 'Indeed it is.'

'Well, we will be happy to offer any assistance we can. I assume Jawara will set up any necessary liaison facilities between the Senegalese military and your men, but if we can do anything . . .'

'Since the Senegalese were trained by your people, it might be useful for our men to get some idea of who they'll be dealing with – the quality of the ally, so to speak . . .'

'I'm sure that can be arranged,' Bonnard agreed. 'At the moment I don't imagine there's any chance of your boys flying direct to Banjul, so they'd have to come through Paris anyway, *en route* to Dakar. I could set up a meeting at Charles de Gaulle easily enough.'

'Thank you, René. I'll be in touch.' Matheson replaced the phone, asked his secretary to get him the State Department, and sipped at the coffee which had just appeared on his desk. Tadeusz Lubanski was a very different proposition from René Bonnard. A 'tad obnoxious' as some Foreign Office wit had dubbed him.

The buzzer announced the call had been put through. 'Good morning, Mr Lubanski,' Matheson announced brightly. The reply was a sound between a grunt and groan. Matheson smiled to himself. 'Sorry to wake you up,' he went on, with the modicum of sincerity he could muster, 'but we're considering some military action, and I assume you would wish to be consulted before the fact, rather than after.'

'What are you going to do, Cecil? Invade China?'

'No, nor any other part of south-east Asia,' Matheson rejoined. 'We're just sending a few advisers to The Gambia – you know where that is?'

'Africa, by any chance?' Lubanski asked sarcastically. 'There's been a coup . . .'

'We do notice these things, Cecil.'

'Ah, of course. Well, the Senegalese Army is going in to put things back together and we're just sending in a few of our own men to lend them a helping hand.'

'Very commendable,' Lubanski said drily.

'So, the United States Government has no objections?'

'No, Cecil, I think I can say with some certainty that we don't. If you and the French want to play golden oldies down Africa way, then be our guests. Wear your pith helmets with pride.'

'Thank you,' Matheson said coldly.

'You're welcome. Now I'm going back to sleep.' There was a click as the line went dead.

'Bastard,' Matheson muttered. He took another gulp of coffee and asked for a number in Hereford.

Lieutenant-Colonel Bryan Weighell was sitting in his office at the Stirling Lines barracks of 22 SAS Regiment, thinking about his three children. Now that his ex-wife, Linda, had announced her imminent wedding to the idiot barrister he wondered what would happen to his relationship with Helen, Jenny and Stephen. As it was now, he only saw them for a few hours each Sunday, and presumably their moving to London would make things even more difficult. He supposed he could drive down from Hereford each weekend, but it would not be the same. He would always have to be *out* with them, at cinemas or zoos or McDonald's. And they would have new schools, new friends, new interests. And a new father.

He himself would become a more distant figure, and not just in miles. Maybe they had known him long enough for something to stick, something which could be brought back to life when they grew up, yet he was not at all sure of it. Helen, the eldest, was only twelve.

It was all profoundly depressing.

Like the state of the world, come to that. The Royal Wedding had been celebrated against a backdrop of cities torn by rioting, soaring unemployment, a new cold war. Something was up shit creek in the state of Denmark, Weighell told himself. Even his beloved SAS had been reduced to doing the dirty work in Northern Ireland. Shooting teenage joyriders in Armagh was not how he had seen the future of the Regiment.

Maybe he should take an early discharge and get a consultancy job – it would not be difficult. Maybe one in London to be near the kids. Or maybe one abroad, somewhere the kids could come and stay with him. A week of real contact would probably be worth a lot more than regular trips to McDonald's. And Linda would let them come, for she was determined to be civilized about it all.

Weighell glared savagely out of the window at the

sunlit yard, half-wishing she had given him more real justification for anger.

The telephone rang.

'Lieutenant-Colonel Weighell?' a vaguely familiar voice asked him.

'Speaking.'

'I'm Cecil Matheson. Junior Minister at the Foreign Office . . .'

Now Weighell recognized the voice. A tall, smarmy-looking man who always seemed to be staring down his nose at TV interviewers. Not that most of the interviewers deserved any better . . .

'The Prime Minister has asked me to call you,' Matheson was saying. 'Are you aware of what's been happening in The Gambia over the last two days?' he asked.

'Can't say I am.'

'It's on the front page of this morning's *Times*,' Matheson said curtly, neglecting to add that he had missed it himself in his eagerness to get to the crossword.

'I haven't seen the paper yet,' Weighell said, reaching across for the tabloid on his desk, and finding its front page devoted to the ins and outs, to coin a phrase, of the Royal Honeymoon.

Matheson briefly outlined the events of the previous forty-eight hours in The Gambia, and recounted the gist of his conversations with the Prime Minister and René Bonnard. 'She wants to know if you can – and I quote – make yourselves useful down there.'

'Doing what?'

'Advising the Senegalese, advising Jawara and his government.'

'Do the Senegalese *want* advice?'

'Probably not. But Jawara obviously wants some

sort of counterbalance to them. You know what these situations are like.'

'Unfortunately. But why's the PM going along?'

'General goodwill. Fellow member of the Commonwealth, etc. Plus she has a fondness for . . . well . . .'

'Sticking her oar in?'

'You could put it that way. And she has a great admiration for your regiment,' Matheson added, wondering whether he had allowed himself to become a little too obviously disloyal. 'After the Princes Gate siege she thinks you can do miracles,' he added, reverting to his usual tone of disdainful detachment.

Weighell thought for a moment. 'Let me get this straight,' he said. 'You want us to send a small party to The Gambia to act as advisers to the President . . .'

'Two or three men, to offer help where help is needed.'

'Including military action?'

'We'll have to consider that if and when the need arises. The role will be essentially advisory. A hostage situation may develop, in which case your experience will no doubt be invaluable to whoever's in charge.'

'Advisory or not, I can't send my men into such a situation completely unprotected. They'll need clearance to carry handguns, at the very least.'

'I'm sure that can be arranged. Look, for all we know at the moment, the whole business may be over by this afternoon. I'll call you back, say around five, with the latest information. In the meantime, if you can come up with a game-plan . . .'

'Will do.'

'Thank you, Lieutenant-Colonel,' Matheson said before replacing the receiver.

Weighell stared idly out of the window for a few seconds, and then summoned his adjutant. 'Get hold of Major Caskey,' he said, 'and tell him I want to see him. As soon as he can manage. And get me a cup of tea. And a copy of the wretched *Times*.'

He took a quick look through the tabloid, on the off-chance there was any real news in it, and then resumed staring out of the window, this time thinking about his second in command – and the current duty officer – Alan Caskey.

The two of them really ought to get on better than they did, Weighell thought. They had two important things in common – the SAS and fucked-up marriages. It was not as if he disliked Caskey – he just did not feel drawn to him. The man seemed to have lots of close friends in the Regiment, but Weighell wondered how deep the friendships were. Caskey had always struck him as an archetypal loner, a law unto himself offering others little hope of real contact. Or was he just describing himself, Weighell wondered. It was an unwelcome thought.

The tea arrived, along with the *Times*. He read the front page report of the coup, and found it somewhat deficient in precise timings. Today was Friday, but the report could not even make up its mind whether the coup had taken place on Wednesday or Thursday. There were hints of dubious foreign involvement – the ubiquitous Libyans and Cubans, of course – but precious little in the way of proof. It was also suggested that majorities of the local armed forces both supported and opposed the new government.

He had never much liked the *Times* anyway, though Linda had sworn by its absorbent properties when it came to changing the cat litter.

He looked across to the photograph of her and the children which still held pride of place above the map cabinet. He supposed it was somewhat inappropriate now. He would have to get a new one of just the children.

Or do what they had done in Stalin's Russia, and have her invisibly removed from the current photograph, and perhaps even replaced by someone new. First, though, he would have to find someone.

The two Mirages of the Senegalese Air Force had certainly made everyone jump when they first buzzed the airport, but no bombs had been dropped, no sticks of napalm unleashed, no missiles fired. For those in the trenches, like Moussa Diba, they represented a possible future threat, whose seriousness was completely unknown. Maybe all they were capable of was making a loud noise as they flew by.

On the other hand, the long lines of paratroops swinging down to earth from the giant transport planes a mile or so to the north looked like posing a depressingly immediate problem. It did not take a military genius to work out that their target had to be the airport. And once they had secured that, any number of troop-filled planes could land.

In the air control tower Junaidi Taal watched the descent of the airborne troops with a sinking feeling. There had to be at least five hundred, as many as he had available to face them, and the incoming Senegalese were trained soldiers, not a mixed bunch of policemen, Party activists and convicts who had been issued with rifles. At that moment, if Taal could have taken the coup back, he would have.

But he was not a man given to dwelling on what might have been. Their hopes might be fast receding, but they had not disappeared – not yet. He had an hour or so before the invaders got themselves organized enough to begin advancing on the airport. How could he use the time?

He picked up the phone which connected him with the

officer he had left in charge of the airport terminal. 'Have the explosives arrived yet?' he asked, knowing full well the answer would be no. The man would have phoned him if they had.

'No, sir, not yet.'

'Call me the moment they do,' Taal said.

'Of course, sir.'

It was truly ironic, Taal thought. Because The Gambia had never had an army, it had never had a central ordnance depot, and no stockpile of military explosives. And since the coup had seriously disrupted communications and shut down work on most official projects, it had proved extremely difficult to track down any civilian sources. The nearest one that Taal's subordinates had been able to find was in Soma, a hundred miles away, where explosives were being used to blast irrigation channels for rice cultivation. Plans to fetch a supply by helicopter had fallen through due to the lack of anyone capable of flying one of the several machines parked on the tarmac. Instead, a taxi had been dispatched along the pothole- and rut-strewn highway to the east. If the explosive was at all volatile then Taal would not have fancied being the driver making the return trip.

All in all, their chances of rendering the runway unusable before the Senegalese captured it seemed less than good. Like their chances overall. If Taal had been a betting man he would have put money on the Senegalese taking the airport by mid-afternoon, and Banjul by the following noon.

A mile to the north Diba's thoughts were more personally oriented. The flow of transport planes and parachutists had seemed depressingly relentless for a while, but the staunching of the flow, and the promise of imminent contact with armed troops made him wish for more planes.

He doubted whether those in charge on his own side had any idea of what they were doing. The big chief back at the airport was just a converted policeman, and the man in charge of this small company dug in behind the runway guide lights – a Wollof zealot named Jahumpa – seemed endowed with more enthusiasm than brains. In fact Jahumpa had the idiot eyes of someone who was willing to die for a cause, and Diba was fucked if he was going to join him for the ride.

'That cell of ours would look pretty good now,' Konko muttered beside him.

Diba was opening his mouth to reply when the silence was shattered by a swelling, high-pitched whooshing sound. A blinding flash and an exploding fountain of earth some forty yards behind them preceded, by a split second, the deafening crash of the explosion. Diba instinctively clasped his hands to his ears, which were already humming with the impact.

'Fuck,' he grunted, pulling himself as low as he could in the trench, just as another mortar landed in almost the same spot, providing a second white splash on his retinae and more whirring in his ears. He could just about hear Jahumpa, two trenches away, talking excitedly into the walkie-talkie.

Up in the air control tower Taal thought he could make out the Senegalese mortar positions a mile or so to the north. The enemy had no high ground and no air reconnaissance – not yet, at least – so it would be difficult for them to zero in on the defending positions, but that would slow them up rather than stop them. Already he could see groups of distant infantry on the move in wide flanking directions to either side of the airport. Even if the explosives arrived now he could see no hope of their being laid and detonated in time to cause any significant damage to the runway. The airport was a lost cause. And if he did not move fast the Senegalese would reach the Banjul road, and cut him and his men off from the capital.

'Pull them back,' he told his immediate subordinate. 'As quickly and as invisibly as you can. Then start moving them into the fall-back positions. I'm going to Banjul, but I'll be back in a couple of hours.' He turned to descend the spiral staircase, hesitated on the top step, then continued down. He had been about to order the destruction of all the aircraft on the tarmac, but had thought better of it. In the circumstances such an action would be little more than vandalism.

It was five past eleven, and the Australians had successfully survived the first over of the second day. The weather at Edgbaston looked much as it did outside Caskey's window – depressingly sunny. The English bowlers needed a few clouds, or the team as a whole would pay dearly for batting so ineptly on such a good wicket the day before.

Always assuming Botham did not provide another miracle.

It could hardly happen twice, Caskey thought. And anyway, once was enough. He would carry that innings at Headingley to his grave, smiling at the memory every time it surfaced.

He reached for the bottle of claret he had been allowing to breathe, and poured himself a small glass. It might be a dull time for the Regiment, and to describe his personal life as a disaster area might legitimately be considered an understatement, but there were still test matches which he could sink himself into, body and soul. There were still twenty-five days a year, rain permitting, when he could forget about the real world.

Cricket was like marijuana, as he had once explained

to a shocked New Zealander. It slowed everything down. Once you accepted cricket time and forgot real time, accustomed yourself to the new pace, it became as beautiful to the spectator as a Grateful Dead concert did to a dopehead. Needless to say, every West Indian he had ever met understood this instinctively.

He sipped appreciatively at the wine and willed the nightwatchman Bright to lose his concentration. Without success. He had a bad feeling about the coming day – he could see the Australians making four hundred on a wicket like this, and then skittling England out for half as much. Botham's innings at Headingley deserved better.

He had just put his feet up on the coffee table when the phone rang.

6

The knock on Lieutenant-Colonel Weighell's door was swiftly succeeded by the appearance of Caskey's willowy figure.

'Good morning, boss,' Caskey said, taking the proffered chair on the other side of his CO's desk.

'Good morning, Alan,' Weighell said. Somehow, Caskey's use of the SAS's customary 'boss' when addressing a superior officer always grated on him. Perhaps it just sounded too working-class for Caskey, whose background, unlike that of most men in the Regiment, was colonial and public school. 'I take it you've got nothing important on right now?' he asked.

'Nothing. What's up?' Caskey asked.

'Read this,' Weighell said, handing him the *Times* and pointing out the story.

Caskey read it through, and looked up quizzically.

Weighell explained the Prime Minister's request. 'And I thought with your African experience . . .' he concluded.

'I'd be delighted,' Caskey said. Even five days of cricket could hardly compete with a mission abroad, always supposing England's batsmen held out that long. It would put a distance between him and his wife, and between him and Liz. He could forget the whole damn business for a few precious days or weeks, and enjoy some real excitement while he was at it.

'The Foreign Office are ringing me back this afternoon. Can you dig up a third man for the party . . .'

'Third?'

'I've already picked a second. Trooper Franklin of G Squadron.'

'Because he's black?'

'Yes. I think putting three white faces into a situation like this might be less than diplomatic, don't you?'

'Did the Gambian Government request it?'

'No. I doubt if it occurred to them that the SAS might have black soldiers.'

'There are only two. West Indians, that is.'

'I know. And you know as well as I do that we've made no effort to increase the number, mostly because it would be hard to use West Indians in the sort of operations we've been involved in lately. They tend to be rather conspicuous in rural Fermanagh. But in Africa . . .'

'In Africa they give us credibility?'

Weighell grunted. 'Something like that. But Franklin's a damn fine soldier. If he wasn't, I wouldn't send him. The fact that he's black is just a bonus as far as this operation's concerned.'

'OK. I get the picture. And if he's as good as you say, I'll have no trouble with him.' He got to his feet. 'For the third man I'll see if I can find someone who's actually been to The Gambia.'

Joss Wynwood stretched his legs as silently as he could manage within the confines of the hedge. It was more than six hours now since dawn had rendered movement inadvisable. After all, who knew what Irish eyes might be smiling at him down the end of a sniper's 'scope?

Admittedly it was unlikely. From where he lay, half in the hedgerow, half in the long grass behind it, Wynwood could see empty country stretch away to the north, down to the distant glimmer of Lough Neagh some fifteen miles away. In the foreground, and not much more than twenty-five yards away, the road from Armagh to Newry ran from left to right. Parked off the road on his near side, and apparently changing a tyre on his Leyland van, a man in a blue woolly hat was happily whistling 'Danny Boy'.

It was a lovely day for an ambush. The sun shone intermittently, as fluffy white clouds sailed majestically across the blue sky, trailing their vast shadows across the green hills like a fleet of Zeppelins.

It all looked a lot more peaceful than Wynwood felt. He had been a badged member of the SAS for only a few months, and this was his first major action with the Regiment. His nerves were all on edge, from what felt like a tick in his eyelids to the prickling sensation on his skin. Every now and then he had to wipe the sweat from the stock of the Heckler & Koch MP5 sub-machine-gun he was holding.

He stole a glance to his right, where Trooper Davey Matthews – Stanley to his friends – seemed immune to such anxiety. He was probably fantasizing about the barmaid in Newry, Wynwood thought, for apart from football, Stanley's only interest in life seemed to be sex. Getting it, having it, talking about it, imagining it.

'What do you think the Pope does with an erection?' Stanley had asked him in the middle of the previous night. Wynwood had been too dumbstruck by the incongruity of the question to think up an answer. 'Takes it to confession,' Stanley had told him.

Wynwood smiled at the memory. Everyone in the SAS was fucking crazy, he thought. And he must be fucking crazy too.

When in Rome . . ., he thought. Making love with Susan had been wonderful from the very first time, half-pissed out of their skulls in her room at the training college. It had been wonderful in the back of his car, wonderful on that Gower beach with the moon coming up, wonderful in their Gambian honeymoon hotel, the fan whirring lazily above them.

Jesus, why does Stanley do this, he asked himself. What did he do with his own hard-ons?

Wynwood turned his attention back to the scene in front of him. The man in the woolly hat had now been changing his tyre for almost an hour, performing each task in the process with a speed that would have embarrassed a snail. Soon he would have no choice but to start changing the two tyres back again. His name was Martin Langan, and he was a corporal in the Regiment's B Squadron.

Watching him reminded Wynwood of how nice it felt to be cramped up in a hedge. It was always better to be the trap than the bait. Though this particular trap seemed unlikely to spring. If the Provos were coming, they should have come by now. Like all the old hands said: for every successful ambush you got ten that just end in premature arthritis.

The preparations for this one had taken a lot of time and effort. About a fortnight before, 14th Intelligence Company had got word from one of its informers that the IRA had plans to murder an ex-UDR officer. This man, William O'Connor, was now in the building trade, and currently engaged in a restoration job in Markethill, a small town halfway between Armagh and Newry. Each day he would drive there from his home in Armagh, in the Leyland van now sitting in front of Wynwood, wearing the blue woolly hat now clamped over Corporal Langan's head.

O'Connor had been persuaded by 14th Intelligence to keep to his usual pattern while they kept tabs on the local IRA brigade and mounted a round-the-clock observation at the already discovered site of their arms cache. Yesterday, one man had come to collect the guns in a Renault 4. Overnight, Wynwood, Stanley and a third man – Trooper Sansom, who was concealed in the derelict barn to Wynwood's left – had walked to the site of the intended ambush and concealed themselves. That morning O'Connor had happily surrendered his van and cap to Corporal Langan. It was now an hour and a quarter since the latter had faked his punctured tyre, and if the Nationalist grapevine worked half as well as everyone thought it did, the IRA men – lying in wait further up the road – should have known about it by now.

Out of the corner of his eye Wynwood saw Stanley pick up the walkie-talkie which connected them with Sansom. Maybe this was it. He waited while Stanley listened, watched the other man's face tighten with anger, heard the repressed frustration in his voice as he signed off.

'The useless bastards have lost them,' he hissed to Wynwood. 'So they may be on their way. They *were* in a blue Sierra, but Christ knows what they're in now.'

Langan went on tightening the bolts on the wheel, having presumably heard the same message from the walkie-talkie in the van's front seat. A car could be heard approaching from the right, which was the way they would come. Wynwood's grip on the MP5 perceptibly tightened. It was a Sierra, but red. And it went right past, the driver flashing a single sympathetic look in Langan's direction.

Wynwood did not envy Langan – that look could just as easily have been a gunshot.

Another car was approaching – it must be rush hour. This time it was a white Fiat, and as it slowed down Wynwood thought he saw the metallic gleam of a gun. Perhaps they had hoped to get a clear shot from the car, but Langan had arranged matters so that he was protected by the van from any but the most oblique angle.

The thought that it still might not be enough flashed through Wynwood's mind as the doors of the still-moving car swung open to eject two men in boiler suits, their heads covered by slitted balaclavas, gloved hands holding AK47 assault rifles. A third man was close behind them, dressed the same, but brandishing only a Webley revolver.

He was the first to fire, as Langan took a flying dive across the nearest wall. He might have been the first to die too, but it was hard to tell. All three Provos were shredded by fire from Stanley, Wynwood and Sansom before they had gone three paces. The driver of the car was still wrestling frantically with the gear lever when the windows of his vehicle were blown away by the redirected fire, and there was a momentary glimpse of something red collapsing out of sight.

A dreadful stillness settled on the scene.

Langan was already in the front seat of the van, talking on the radio, telling someone or other to seal off the road. 'They're all yours,' he was saying. 'We'll be out of here . . . yeah, well, we're all a bit shy, you know how it is . . .'

Sansom walked across, having examined the body in the car. 'His head would make a great pincushion,' he reported laconically. He looked down at the other three, spread-eagled across the grass verge. 'Looks like the Armagh Brigade will be needing some new recruits,' he added.

Wynwood forced himself to look at the men he had just helped to kill. He did not know their names, had never even seen their faces. He had an urge to tear off the balaclavas, and at least get some sense of who they were – who they had been – but he restrained himself.

It was partly, he admitted to himself, that he did not want to appear concerned in front of the others, but it was also partly because he knew it was unnecessary. He had no need to see their faces to know they had been human beings. He had just helped to kill four men – four terrorists who would have killed them with an equal lack of compunction. No matter what the fucking government in London said, this was a war. The IRA said it was, and the SAS believed them.

But Wynwood had never killed anyone before, and he was not quite sure what he was supposed to feel. It had been so quick. Ten hours of waiting and about ten seconds of death. He did not feel like throwing up – nor guilty, angry, excited or happy. If anything, he just felt sad. And maybe a little numb.

Stanley put a friendly hand on his shoulder. 'All part of death's rich pageant,' he said. Wynwood became aware of the sound of an approaching helicopter, and almost immediately a Lynx hove into sight above the hill behind them. The pilot put it down in the field behind the barn, and at Langan's signal the four SAS men trotted across to climb aboard.

Wynwood had one last glimpse of the shattered car and scattered corpses, before the pilot swung the Lynx away to the east.

Taal arrived at the Legislative Assembly in Banjul shortly before noon. The rest of the twelve-man Revolutionary Council was in session around the long table in the conference room, discussing the changes in educational policy they wanted to introduce. Taal felt a pang of sadness. It was with such intentions in mind that he had joined Jabang and the Socialist and Revolutionary Labour Party, and yet it was hard to imagine a less appropriate subject for discussion on this particular morning. Mamadou Jabang, he noticed, even had a smile on his face. Taal felt like a – what did the Americans call it? – a party pooper. In more ways than one.

'Comrade,' Jabang cut short the young man who was speaking, 'we must interrupt this discussion for a report from the Defence Minister. Junaidi?'

Taal thought about standing and decided not to waste his energy. 'I have not brought any good news,' he said shortly, and watched eleven faces react to the statement. 'As you no doubt know, the Senegalese have landed several hundred paratroops in the area to the north of the airport, around Kerewan. They are advancing on the airport, and will take it sometime within the next few hours . . .'

'What happened to our troops?' one voice asked, more in confusion than anger.

'They are fighting bravely,' Taal said, though since his departure they could, for all he knew, have scattered like rabbits. 'But they are outgunned and outnumbered. The enemy has mortars and air power, and the most we can hope for is to slow them down. They will take the airport, probably wait while they fly in more troops, and then they will start advancing along the road to Serekunda and . . .'

'How long do we have, Junaidi?' Jabang asked quietly.

'I would guess that they will be in Banjul by tomorrow morning,' Taal said. 'At the latest.'

Everyone seemed to start talking at once, and for almost a minute it seemed to Taal as if a collective panic was seizing hold of all those present.

But not Jabang. He got to his feet and stood there, not saying anything, reducing the rest to silence merely by the force of his personality. 'Comrades,' he said finally, 'we never believed this would be easy. And now we know for certain it will be hard. Jawara and his Senegalese friends have the military power – that is plain. There is no way that we can win on that battlefield. So . . .' He looked round at them all. 'What power do we have? What can we use? How do we stop their soldiers if not with soldiers of our own?'

There was a silence.

'What do we have?' Jabang said softly, as if he was asking himself. 'We have the support of the mass of the people, but that will mean nothing if we cannot hold onto power. We have our dedication, and our willingness to work for the regeneration of our country, but all this will mean nothing if we cannot retain power. You see, Jawara and the Senegalese put no value on what the people want, or on our dreams for the country. So what do we have that they do put a value on?'

'His wife and children,' Sharif Sallah said.

'The Senegalese envoy,' said another voice.

'And all the white tourists,' a third man added.

There was another silence, as the meeting contemplated such a step.

'They will call us terrorists,' someone said.

'They already call us that,' another replied.

'That is not the point,' Junaidi Taal said quietly. He now knew he had been expecting this moment, without realizing he was expecting it, ever since they had known that the Senegalese were on their way. 'Whether or not they call us terrorists or criminals is of no importance,' he went on. In any case, they had already crossed that line when they emptied Banjul Prison. 'What matters is whether it will *work*.'

'How will we know that unless we try?' someone asked.

Taal grimaced. 'What are we going to do – threaten

to kill Lady Chilel and the Senegalese envoy? In what circumstances? Does anyone really think the Senegalese will stop their army because of one man and his family? Or that Jawara will agree to give up the country in exchange for the life of one of his wives? And the fattest and ugliest one at that?' He allowed himself a smile, but there was no humour in it.

'Perhaps the white tourists would make better hostages,' Sallah suggested. Jawara and the Senegalese would not dare to go against the wishes of the English and French.'

'There are no French tourists,' Taal said. 'And it is the Senegalese we have to stop.'

'This is true,' Jabang agreed. 'And I think Junaidi may be right in this matter. But . . .' He paused, looking sadly at Taal. 'I'm afraid I can see no other course of action open to us. If threats do not work, we have not lost anything . . .' He smiled bleakly. 'Except for the good reputation we already lack. I recommend we put Mustapha Diop and Lady Jawara on the radio, and try to bluff them. At the very least it may win us some time. And who knows what can happen then? Perhaps the Senegalese opposition will come out for us, and make it more difficult for Diop to help Jawara.' He looked pointedly at Taal, as if asking for a response.

Taal was trying to remember another of those English phrases – his head seemed full of them today. Whistling in the dark – that was it. Highly appropriate in Banjul. 'No one will be happier than I will if we can stop the Senegalese with a bluff,' he said, getting to his feet. 'But in the meantime I must be getting back to Yundum.' And to the real world, he said to himself.

Alan Caskey made his way to Records, where he found the formidable figure of Sergeant Rainey with his feet up, a half-eaten ham roll in one huge paw, listening to the cricket on a small transistor radio. If Caskey had not already known it was a quiet time for the Regiment, the sight of Rainey taking it easy, even in his lunch hour, would have convinced him. Since his disablement in Oman, Rainey had set about duplicating the raw data of Regimental Records in his own mind, and of pursuing avenues of cross-checking of which no one had previously dreamed. It was rumoured that he occasionally went home to his wife, but no one could actually swear to seeing him leave the barracks.

'Any wickets yet?' Caskey asked, making himself a seat by moving a stack of files to the floor. He idly wondered how Rainey would adapt to the imminent computerization. Like a fish to water, probably.

'No, boss. Is this a business call?'

'Yep. But keep eating. I need someone who has been to The Gambia, preferably in the not too distant past.'

Rainey was silent for a while. 'I may be able to help you there,' he then said, carefully balancing the remains of his roll on the corner of a typewriter and getting up. He limped down the line of filing cabinets, opened the one at the end, and extracted a file. A quick glance inside it made him smile.

'Success?' Caskey asked rhetorically.

Rainey limped back and handed him the file. It belonged to one Trooper Joss Wynwood.

'Honeymoon,' Rainey said. 'Last year. And I think he's the only one, but I'll check.' He reached for one of several card-index boxes, and flicked through its contents. 'He's the only current member of the Regiment listed under The Gambia,' Rainey confirmed. 'But Simon McGrath – remember him?' he asked.

'I know of him, but we've never really met. I think our terms tended to alternate rather than overlap.'

'Well, he's out there now as head of a technical assistance team supplied by the Royal Engineers. In a civilian capacity, that is. Help with bridge-building, I think. Someone at REME HQ will know the details.'

'Do you have a file on him?'

'Of course.'

'OK, well I need to borrow his, Wynwood's here and Trooper Worrell Franklin's. And I promise to bring them all back.'

'You'd better,' Rainey said over his shoulder. 'Boss,' he added as an afterthought.

Sibou Cham was halfway through extracting a bullet from a child's forearm when the new Minister of Health arrived. The bullet's force must have been almost spent, because it had simply gouged itself an inch or so into the softer flesh, far enough to cause the girl excruciating pain but not far enough to do her any lasting damage. As it was, she was being a lot braver than Sibou could imagine herself being at such an age.

The new Health Minister did not seem impressed by this delay to his progress, and Lamin Mansebe, the Royal Victoria's chief administrator, was obviously keen to impress. 'Dr Cham, surely that can wait for a few minutes,' he said. 'Mr Sabally does not have much time to spare.'

She looked up at the two of them: Mansebe with his tinted glasses and Sabally, a tall, wide-browed man who was probably younger than she was. 'This will only take a few minutes more,' she said, and went back to her work.

'It is good to see there is still one place where ordinary people have equal access to health care,' Sabally said. 'We shall of course be expanding the state sector,' he added quietly, as if he might be guilty of betraying a confidence.

What with? Sibou wondered, as she placed the gauze across the girl's wound.

'Of course, the Royal Victoria has a long tradition of serving the whole community,' Mansebe said self-importantly.

And serving it badly, Sibou thought to herself.

'It will be the model for the new service,' Sabally said.

Sibou fastened the bandage and stood up. 'How can I help you?' she asked.

'In your office, Sibou,' Mansebe suggested.

She acquiesced, leading the way through the door and turning to find only Sabally had followed her. 'I have an infection,' he said, and started unzipping his trousers.

She considered pointing out that equal access to health care meant joining the queue of those still waiting for her attention outside. But she thought better of it. Mr Sabally might have the power to confiscate those stocks of blood and medicine which the black marketeers were hoarding. There was no point in offending him unnecessarily.

She was, perhaps, not quite as gentle as she usually was in her treatment of infections like his.

By the time Caskey got back to his quarters the teams had gone in for lunch, and after listening for the latest from The Gambia on the *One O'Clock News* – Senegalese troops had been airlifted in, though it was not clear exactly where to – he started looking through the three files he had borrowed from Records.

Joss Wynwood was twenty-four and, if appearances were anything to go by, seemed to be enjoying life. The smile that beamed out of his photograph seemed to say, this is fun. The eyes were slightly more watchful, the dark, tangled hair an anarchist's dream. So much for photographs, Caskey thought.

Wynwood was a Taff, born and raised in Pontardulais, where his father had been a miner. He had gone to the local grammar school while it still existed, which suggested a certain amount of intelligence, though not necessarily of the type that was useful in the SAS. After taking and failing two A levels he had joined the Welsh Guards, probably as the single sure way of avoiding life down the pit, and five years of service later had applied to the SAS. In both Selection and Continuation Training he had shown outstanding aptitude in those skills considered necessary in an SAS trooper. He had celebrated selection by getting married, and taking his wife on honeymoon to The Gambia.

Caskey thanked fate for dealing him such a good card. The lad sounded ideal material. With rather less optimism, he turned to the file on Worrell Franklin.

He too was twenty-four, and had arrived in the UK in 1957, as a baby. His father had worked as a guard on the London Underground until his death in an unspecified accident twenty years later. His mother still worked as a sister at the South Western Hospital in Clapham. Worrell was the oldest of three children, all of whom had attended the local comprehensive. He had gained two A levels – in History and Economics – before enlisting in the Royal Engineers. He had seen service in Northern Ireland, West Germany, and already, after only a year in the SAS, had proficiency marks in demolition and medicine. Like Wynwood he had almost sailed through Selection Training. Franklin had also, Caskey noticed in passing, been second in the British Army of the Rhine Championships 400 metres for two successive years.

The photograph showed a handsome West Indian face, wide-set eyes over high cheekbones and a straight nose.

The effect would have been almost ingenuous but for the mouth, which seemed set in defiance, as if daring the photographer to do his worst.

Another good card, Caskey thought. What had he done to deserve such luck?

Don't count your chickens, he told himself. First he had to find the two of them, preferably in Hereford and good health. He picked up the internal phone and dialled the operational roster desk number.

'Franklin's on a week's leave,' he was told. 'Due back Sunday night.'

'Where is he?' Caskey asked, half-afraid that the man would be up a mountain or down a pothole. He would be hard to spot down a pothole, Caskey thought. He hoped Franklin was not going to be unduly sensitive about such remarks.

'The contact number's a London one,' the adjutant told him. 'But Wynwood's more of a problem. He's on operational assignment in Armagh.'

'Bugger.' Caskey thought for a moment, and decided he could clear it with Weighell later. 'Get him back here, will you,' he said. 'ASAP. As in tonight at the latest.'

He hung up the phone just as the English team took to the field on his silent TV. Resisting the temptation to turn up the sound, he opened the file on Major Simon McGrath.

Beyond confirming what he suspected – that McGrath had served his two terms as an SAS officer in the gaps between Caskey's own three terms – the file told him next to nothing. The photograph showed a man with short, dark, curly hair and prominent eyebrows over dark eyes. He had a slightly upturned nose, a smallish mouth and the look of someone who had to shave twice a day. Despite this, he had a notably cheery expression on his face.

Caskey scratched his chin, realized he himself had not yet shaved that day, and wondered who could tell him more. The CO seemed a good place to start.

'Oh yes, I know McGrath,' Weighell told him, and suggested Caskey should come over for a cup of tea.

Both the tea and a suspicious-looking rock cake were waiting for him when he arrived at the CO's office for the second time that day. Ever since the day several years before when a shortfall in grenades had led to their substitution in a training exercise by the canteen's rock cakes, a vengeful kitchen staff had been devoting their not inconsiderable ingenuity to producing the hardest cakes in Britain, and perhaps the world. It had even been rumoured that they used cement.

Weighell, however, was a known devotee, claiming that the cakes reminded him of the boiled sweets of his childhood.

Caskey pushed his to one side and tried to ignore it.

'McGrath's a difficult man to describe,' Weighell said. 'But then a lot of our chaps are. He's . . . well, I suppose he's a bit of a Jekyll and Hyde . . . I don't mean he's two people, one good and one evil. More like . . . No, let me put it this way: he's a very gregarious man, gets on well with most people. He always says exactly what's on his mind and he seems to operate on a short fuse, but no one holds it against him because the outbursts never last more than a few minutes. He's unconventional to a fault. And he's had more women than I've had rock cakes.

'All of which might lead you to expect someone who always acts on the spur of the moment, and never stops to think before he acts. In short, a loose cannon. Which he is, at least to some extent. But he's also a devoted family man with three children – they live in Leominster – and a fanatical mountaineer. Note the mountaineering. That's a hobby for people who like taking risks, but it's also a hobby which demands real planning and precision. Then add the final piece of the puzzle – the man's an engineer, and a specialist in bomb disposal at that. You see what I mean?'

'Not exactly,' Caskey said.

'Well, what we have here is almost a definition of a good soldier: someone who's emotionally capable of taking risks, but has the sense to calculate them as well as he can.'

'Sounds like a good man to have around,' Caskey commented.

'Yes . . . I don't know whether I should say this or not,' Weighell went on, 'but I've never felt comfortable with the man, either on the job or off it.' He smiled. 'Which may just be a matter of two people who rub each other up the wrong way.'

'I see,' Caskey said, in a tone which suggested the opposite.

'Anyway, you'll probably get the chance to make up your own mind about him. If there's stuff going on all round him, I don't expect Simon McGrath has been sitting in his bungalow waiting for things to get back to normal. He'll be out there in the thick of it.'

Mustapha Diop had now been confined to the house on Marina Parade for almost thirty-six hours. He was sharing this confinement with his wife, their three children, and five of their children's friends from the embassy, who had been staying the night with them, and who had not been allowed to return home. All the Gambian staff had vanished, leaving his wife with all the cooking to do and the children in a state of near-permanent riot.

At first Diop had clung to the hope that things would blow over, that the new government would prove acceptable to everyone and that things would return to normal.

After being taken on the strange taxi ride through Banjul, he had reluctantly reached the conclusion that these were not the sort of people the international community was likely to welcome to its bosom. They were either idealists or madmen, two groups which Diop had always found hard to disentangle. The history of the twentieth century – not to mention the last quarter of a century in Africa – seemed to bear out his thesis: the only thing that ever really worked was doing things one step at a time. Grand ideas always seemed to end in someone's tears.

He hoped this particular grand idea was not going to end in his. There seemed little doubt that the planes he had been hearing all morning belonged to the Senegalese Air Force, for his government was holding to the Treaty and intervening on the overthrown Jawara's behalf. Diop hardly dared think about what the rebels were doing at this moment, or what their intentions might be towards him and his family. If they were looking for someone to take their frustrations out on, they could hardly find anyone more suitable.

The thought had no sooner escaped him than it took flesh, materializing in the form of three men walking towards his front door. One of them was the man called Sallah, who had been on the taxi ride with him and the coup leader, Jabang. The latter, Diop had to admit, had been reasonably personable for someone so intense, but Sallah had seemed neither likeable nor trustworthy. His heart sank.

They knocked on the door, which Diop thought had to be a good sign. He was not so sure when he opened it, and found two rifle barrels pointed at his stomach.

'You will come with us, please,' Sallah said.

'Where to?' Diop asked, not moving.

'The radio station. You are going to tell the world

what is happening here,' Sallah told him. 'And what might happen,' he added.

Diop did not like the sound of those last four words. 'May I tell my wife where I am going?' he asked with as much dignity as he could muster.

'There's no time,' he was told, and the rifle barrels twitched as if to emphasize the point. Diop followed Sallah out to the road, where the inevitable taxi was waiting. They got in the back with one of the armed men, who had to lay his rifle across all their legs. The other got in front with the driver.

No one spoke during the five-minute drive to the radio station. Once there, Sallah accompanied Diop up the stairs to the studio, where Jabang was already waiting with Jawara's senior wife, the Lady Chilel. To suggest that the atmosphere was cool would have been to vastly understate the situation: it was positively frigid.

'Lady Jawara,' Diop said, extending his hand in greeting before Sallah could say anything.

'Monsieur Diop,' she said graciously. 'I apologize for the behaviour of my countrymen.'

'Sit down and read this,' Sallah told Diop coldly, handing him a typewritten sheet of paper. 'You will be reading it over the air in a few minutes.'

Diop glanced through it. According to the text he demanded to be taken to meet the Senegalese commander, and wished to appeal to the Senegalese Red Cross, on behalf of the Gambian Red Cross, for medicine, food and vehicles. The text claimed he had seen people on the streets of Banjul making clenched-fist salutes in support of the revolution – well, he supposed he had seen one or two – and contained a personal plea from him to his own Government to negotiate a ceasefire with the newly formed Gambian Supreme Revolutionary Council.

Diop was pleasantly surprised. There were no threats

in the message, either to his own safety or anyone else's.

His relief was short-lived. Lady Jawara was the first to take the microphone, and she had a list of hostages to read out. It included herself, eight of her husband's children, seven members of his cabinet, and Diop himself, together with his wife and children. All would be killed if the Senegalese troops were not withdrawn by five o'clock that afternoon.

Since no one intervened to correct her, Lady Jawara had presumably read the text she had been given, but the tone in her voice – a mixture of contempt and disbelief – was one which Diop wished he could have emulated. Unfortunately the shock of having his life threatened – and with a deadline less than four hours away – had somewhat unnerved him, and his declaration sounded, to him at least, both nervous and hesitant. It was only when he had finished, and saw Sallah and Jabang exchanging smiles, that he realized that this was exactly what they had wanted.

The leader now took the microphone himself. There had already been a grievous loss of life, Jabang said, and no one could desire more. But, reluctantly, he felt compelled to announce himself ready to kill Jawara's family and cabinet if that was the price of preserving the revolution. 'The country is with us,' he claimed, and he had the power to execute the prisoners. Ultimately their fate lay not in his hands but in those of the Senegalese invaders. The latter had but to announce a withdrawal and the prisoners would all be freed.

Jabang stared at the microphone, as if willing it to believe him, and abruptly got up from the chair and walked to the window. Diop studied his face: the mouth pursed with anxiety, the skin drawn tight by tension across the forehead and cheeks, the eyes burning with their apparently inexhaustible intensity. Did the rebel leader mean it about killing all the prisoners? Diop asked himself. Did he have only a few hours of life left?

There was no way of knowing. Indeed, Diop suspected that Jabang himself had no clear idea of how far he was prepared to go.

7

It was four-thirty, and only thirty minutes remained until the expiry of the deadline. Nothing had been heard from the Senegalese forces or government – no radio broadcast, no telephone call, no visit from an intermediary, no white flag. And none of them was really expecting any, Taal thought. He had just returned once more from the front line, which was now located in the middle of the village of Lamin. The good news was that only one group of twenty fighters had been unable to escape from the Senegalese encirclement of the airport; the bad news was that several hundred more of the enemy had since been landed on the captured runway. If one thing was certain it was that the Senegalese were under no military pressure to negotiate.

The other eleven members of the Revolutionary Council had received Taal's report in the manner of condemned men hearing that their latest appeal had been denied. His suggestion that they relocate the government to Bakau, where the Field Force depot offered at least a defensible perimeter, had been voted on, and unanimously agreed, with a similar level of enthusiasm. Taal felt, but restrained himself from suggesting, that his fellow Council members would be better served getting out of this chamber and back among their Party comrades.

First, however, there was the business of the hostages to conclude. Or not to conclude. Taal fought back the temptation to say, 'I told you so.'

'We have here the classic dilemma,' Jabang said, as if he was discussing an interesting academic problem. 'If we do as we threatened, and kill them, then we will have no cards left in our hands at all . . .'

'And will not be able to expect any mercy from the victors,' Sallah interjected.

This amused Jabang. 'I am not expecting any now,' he said. 'As I was saying – if we kill them we have nothing left to bargain with. If we do not then we lose at least some of our credibility. Either way we lose. Of course, some' – he looked at Taal with a smile – 'might say we should never have made the threat in the first place, but we had to do something, or we would have lost the initiative entirely . . .'

'Why not kill one hostage?' one of the younger men asked. 'That would show we were serious, yet still leave something to bargain with.'

'That is true,' Jabang admitted.

But reluctantly, Taal thought, and that made him feel better. He did not like to think of his friend acceding to such a cold-blooded course of action. 'If we kill any of the prisoners,' he added in support, 'we will sacrifice any hope of receiving help from abroad.'

'Is there any such hope?' the younger man wanted to know.

'Our friends in Libya are trying to intercede with the Senegalese,' Jabang said, 'and through the Islamic Conference.'

'There is also another point,' Taal said. 'I don't want to sound too pessimistic,' he went on, thinking that would be difficult, 'but if this time we are defeated, we shall want the chance to fight again, and that means being accepted into exile in other countries. If we kill any of the prisoners – particularly Jawara's family or Diop's – no one in Africa or Europe will offer us safe haven.'

'I agree,' Jabang said, 'but I think we must continue

to give out the message that, in the last resort, we will have nothing to lose by killing them. Otherwise what is to stop the Senegalese from just rolling straight over us?'

'We can claim that the deadlines have been extended for humanitarian reasons,' Sallah suggested, which made Taal smile.

'That is agreed, then,' Jabang announced, looking round the table. 'Sharif, make the announcement on the radio. Jallow, see that all the prisoners are moved into the Field Force depot tonight. And if we're moving our men out of Banjul, we can put larger numbers outside the tourist hotels. The embassies in Bakau will get the message, and they'll see it gets passed on to the Senegalese. Which should give them something to worry about. And at least slow them down. And by the way, Junaidi,' he said, turning to Taal, 'we have information that an Englishman shot one of our people on the Denton Bridge. It was decided he should be arrested – as a sign that we are serious.'

It was on the stroke of five that the phone in Lieutenant-Colonel Weighell's office rang.

'Matheson,' the now familiar voice said curtly. 'Have you made any progress?'

'We're assembling a three-man team at the moment. They can be in London by eleven tomorrow morning. I assume you'll want to brief them before they go.'

'Someone will. We've just had news that hostages have been taken. We don't know how many, or who they are, except that one of the President's wives seems to be among them . . .'

'*One* of his wives?'

'He's a Muslim,' Matheson said drily. 'At least I assume he is. It seems unlikely that he'd be a Mormon.'

'I suppose not.'

'Very well,' Matheson said, his tone more business-like. If you can get your team to the MOD by eleven a.m. I'll have someone there to brief them on the situation.'

'And the context, Minister,' Weighell insisted. 'The more they know about the country they're going into the less chance there is of their making any major gaffes.'

'Understood,' Matheson said.

'One other thing I wanted to check with you,' Weighell said. 'Are my lads wearing uniform on this outing?'

'No. At least, assume not unless you hear to the contrary.'

After putting down the phone Weighell sat at his desk for a minute or so, letting his mind wander through tropical sunshine and palm trees. Maybe he should have gone himself, he thought.

He smiled to himself and called Caskey. 'You're on,' he told him. 'MOD, 1100 hours. Have you got hold of Wynwood yet?'

'He was still in debriefing when I called. I'll try again now, and give Franklin a call in London.'

'The FO says no uniforms, Alan,' Weighell told him, 'but they may change their minds.'

On the Yundum–Serekunda road there were some signs that the invaders were at least pausing for breath. Even so, crouched behind an overturned market stall, the Kalashnikov in his hands hot from firing, Moussa Diba was in no doubt that any such pause would only be temporary, and he was still looking for the perfect opportunity to wave his short military career goodbye. In the sky to the south-east he could see even more Senegalese planes coming in to land at the airport, carrying God knew what in the way of more men and weaponry. If this was not a lost war then he was Nelson Mandela.

A single bullet whistled above his head and embedded itself in the concrete colonnade of the abandoned Field Force station behind him. Fifty yards or so down the street a couple of Senegalese were inching their way forward from cover to cover. Diba fired a burst in their direction, and had the satisfaction of seeing them dive into the shelter of a building.

He wondered how they intended shifting the barricade which filled the street in front of him. Two taxis had been lined up nose to nose, several wooden carts and stalls from the marketplace piled up in front of them, and sundry other rubbish piled on top.

Maybe they would bypass it, he thought – just circle through the fields and meet up again on the other side. Or maybe not. In the distance a rumbling sound was growing louder, causing Diba to think the worst – a tank.

The source of the noise came into view. It turned out to be an armoured car, but that would be enough. It stopped about a hundred yards from the barricade, like a runner pausing to inspect a fence he intended to jump, then slowly gathered speed once more, crashing through the two taxi bonnets and coming to a triumphant halt on the rebels' side of the broken wall. Its machine-gun suddenly opened up, spitting fire in Diba's direction, sending splinters of wood flying from the upturned stall in front of him. One impaled itself in his cheek, causing blood to run.

He swore and looked round for Jahumpa, expecting the signal to retreat, but the idiot was firing impotently at the armoured car. Diba raised his Kalashnikov and took a sighting on Jahumpa's chest, but before he could pull the trigger his target picked up the walkie-talkie, said one word into it, and looked round, waving everyone back.

Diba forgot about him, and keeping the stall between

himself and the armoured car, crawled his way backwards into a gap between two houses. He then regained his feet and started running towards the open countryside.

He had just decided that this was the ideal moment to abandon his unit when he rounded the last house and practically ran into the rest of them. Their lorry was bumping its way across the savannah to pick them up.

Simon McGrath spent the afternoon on the roof of the Carlton, watching the increased traffic over the distant airport, and mentally following what he imagined would be the pace of the Senegalese advance. Most men would have gone mad with boredom after the first couple of hours, but a life in the military – and particularly his years in the SAS – had taught McGrath how to survive enforced inactivity with almost complete equanimity. At around five in the afternoon, with the sun sliding swiftly down towards the western horizon, it was hunger and thirst which drove him off the roof, not a restless mind.

His timing turned out to be extremely fortunate. A minute later and he would have walked straight into trouble; a minute earlier and it would probably have walked straight in on him. As it was, he was still descending the two flights of stairs to his room when he heard the clump of several booted feet on their way up from the lobby below.

He crouched down in the stairwell, just around the corner from the last flight down to his floor. The visitors seemed involved in a less than friendly conversation, and McGrath thought he recognized the hotel manager's voice among them. The language sounded like Wollof.

The bootsteps headed, as he had feared, for his room. There had to be at least four men, probably five. The bootsteps ceased, presumably outside his door, and further argument followed, this time in loud whispers. What the fuck are they doing? McGrath wondered.

A loud splintering noise provided his answer. They were breaking down the door, rushing into his room, and finding it empty. And now the manager was shouting at whoever had given the order to destroy his door.

McGrath smiled to himself, silently descended the flight of steps, and looked around. The third room along, in the opposite direction from his own, had its door open. He slid inside, careful to leave the door the same distance ajar, and waited, the Browning in his hand.

The party emerged from his room, still arguing, this time in English. The manager was demanding to know where he should send the bill for his door, while his adversary was accusing him of harbouring a terrorist.

That's me, McGrath thought with a grin.

The existence of the roof seemed to have escaped them, or perhaps the manager had convinced the visitors that McGrath must have gone out, because the whole party simply started back down the stairs. McGrath listened to their diminishing footfalls, and then headed down the corridor in search of a window overlooking the entrance. He found one just in time to see two men in Field Force uniform head back across the street towards the Legislative Assembly. Which presumably meant another pair were staked out in the lobby downstairs.

He went back to his room, stepping over the unhinged door and onto a floor covered with his personal possessions. He left them where they were, and stood at the window for a moment, staring out at the row of huge palms growing out of the corrugated sea, and the twin minarets of Banjul's Great Mosque rising behind them against the yellowing sky.

If they were after him, he thought, then they would also be after Jobo Camara. Always assuming that this was about the dead man on the Denton Bridge, and not the beginning of some pogrom against all the whites in Banjul.

The latter was not very likely. He would have to warn Jobo, and that meant getting out of the hotel.

He edged his way carefully down the three flights of stairs which led to the last bend above the lobby. The hotel seemed even emptier than the day before, which he supposed was hardly surprising. It was a favourite of Gambian businessmen, and Gambian business was presumably at a complete standstill. The businessmen would all be at home, waiting for the smoke to clear.

For a fleeting second McGrath felt the attraction of being at home himself, feet up in the music room, eyes closed, Bach filling the air. The moment passed. Even at the age of thirty-nine, he enjoyed this sort of thing too much.

He inched an eye round the corner of the wall. Two Field Force men, both carrying Kalashnikovs in their laps, were sitting on either side of the door which led out to the terrace and street.

McGrath went back up to the first floor, along to the back of the building, and down the fire-escape stairs. He carefully opened the door to the yard outside, but more out of habit than from any expectation of meeting anyone. The Field Force men were waiting for him to come back to the hotel, not trying to stop him leaving it.

The Ministry of Development jeep was still sitting where he had left it, temptingly available, but McGrath swiftly but reluctantly came to the realization that he would be a trifle conspicuous driving it round the streets of Banjul. It would take only ten minutes to walk to

Jobo's compound, and there was still enough light left to see where he was going.

He vaulted the wall separating the yard from Otto Road and started down it, keeping to the centre of the road, his eyes constantly searching the shadows on either side. After a moment's thought he took the Browning out from its holster and carried it openly in his hand – this was neither the time nor the place for false modesty. 'How can you tell me you are lonely?' he started to sing. 'Let me take you through the streets of Banjul . . . I will show you something that will make you change your mind . . .'

Ralph McTell, eat your heart out, he thought.

He got several strange looks, and one local even burst out laughing at the sight, shouting 'mad dogs and Englishmen' at him several times, despite the obvious lack of a midday sun. But no one tried to arrest him, mug him, or in any way interfere with his passage through the darkening city.

Jobo's compound in Anglesea Street seemed unusually full of light, though his knock on the gate seemed to diminish the illuminations somewhat. 'It's McGrath,' he shouted, hearing whispering and footsteps.

The gate opened, and the face of Jobo's uncle appeared.

'What you want?' he asked.

McGrath noticed that the man was wearing his Field Force uniform again, and hoped he had not walked out of one trap and into another. 'I've come to warn Jobo that the rebels may be coming for him,' he said, keeping the Browning behind his back.

'They have already come,' Mansa Camara said. 'Come inside.'

McGrath followed him across the compound yard, and into a large room on the ground floor of the colonial-period house which comprised the principal living quarters. Inside he found Jobo, smiling cheerfully despite the fact that he was still partly immobilized by his wound, and eight men in Field Force uniform. On closer inspection it became apparent that two of them were less than happy at being there.

'They came to arrest me,' Jobo explained, 'so we arrested them.'

'We have decided it is time to begin fighting back,' his uncle added. 'We are not sure what we can do, but we feel we want to do something.'

'Mr McGrath will know what is happening,' Jobo suggested.

Mansa raised a quizzical eye.

'The Senegalese will be in Banjul tomorrow,' McGrath told him.

'Then perhaps we can offer them some assistance,' Mansa said.

'They reckon another one's going to die tonight,' Wynwood said quietly. He and Stanley were halfway through their second pints in the base canteen they shared with the Armagh section of 14th Intelligence Company.

'Oh yeah. So how many's that?' Stanley asked, his thick Brummie accent offering an interesting counterpoint to Wynwood's soft Welsh lilt.

'He'll be number seven. Langan reckons it'll be a hot night in Belfast, what with that and our business this morning.'

'Probably. I suppose they're saying we gunned down four young innocents . . .'

'Something like that.'

'I suppose they were all on their way to a Mr Balaclava contest.'

Wynwood grunted. 'Probably. But . . . I don't know, Stanley . . . don't it make you wonder a bit, all these men willing to starve themselves to death. I mean, the TV's always calling the IRA a bunch of cowards, but from what I can see . . . well, they may be a bunch of psychos but they're not cowards.'

Stanley shrugged. 'My mother's got a martyr complex,' he said. 'Hard to imagine her on a hunger strike, though,' he added thoughtfully. 'They'd have to surgically separate her and the fridge.'

'Seriously.'

'What do you want me to say? That I admire the bastards? I think they're idiots. What are they dying for – so that Northern Ireland can be run by Catholic shitheads rather than Protestant shitheads? A, it won't happen. B, it wouldn't make any difference if it did. And C, they should realize what's important in life, like beer and women.'

'And football,' Wynwood volunteered.

'Exactly,' Stanley beamed. 'Now you're getting the hang of it. I'm sure going on hunger strike is a turn-on for all the Provo groupies, but actually dying seems a bit over the top.' He drained his glass and reached out a hand for Wynwood's. 'Same again?' he asked, somewhat unnecessarily.

Wynwood watched the ginger-haired Brummie walk up to the bar, and wondered if Stanley could be as straightforward as he seemed. There was certainly no indication to the contrary. Wynwood sighed. He liked the man, but he would not have wanted to be like him, even if he could. Beer, women and football – rugby football, that is – were necessities of life all right, but then so were eating and crapping. And when it came to what he did with his life, Wynwood liked reasons. Maybe some people could just follow their instincts, do whatever came naturally in any given circumstance and never look back, but he had inherited his father's tendency to reflect on things past and present, not to mention those in the future. His dad had always displayed a tendency to grow maudlin, usually about two-thirds of the way through his fifth pint, and it was a tendency which, according to his wife, Wynwood shared. But then she was English, and the bloody English thought emotion was something you reserved for gardening.

Where was I? Wynwood wondered, as Stanley accepted change from the barmaid, and said something which made her laugh. Reasons, that was where. Reasons for four men dead on a nice afternoon, reasons for men starving themselves to death. And not *political* reasons – he knew all that fucking crap ... So what kind of reasons did he want? He was buggered if he knew. And probably buggered if he didn't.

He had a sudden desire to see Susan, to hold her and be held by her, to feel her gentleness ...

'Great pair of tits on that one,' Stanley said, gesturing with his head back towards the bar.

Wynwood burst out laughing.

The credits for *It Ain't Half Hot Mum* were rolling up the screen when his mum asked, 'Are you happy, Franklin?'

'What do you mean?' he asked, startled.

'It's a simple enough question, boy.'

'Yes, I s'pose. Why do you ask?'

'Cos you wearing the longest face I ever seen for about three days now.'

'You want me to be laughing and singing when Everton's in jail?'

'No, of course not. But I don't think Everton's problems is all that's worrying you. Is your soldiering going OK?'

'Yeah. It's great.'

'And they don't treat you different cos you're a coloured?'

'No. Leastways, the system don't. There's always a few, but I can deal with that. And they know I'm there cos I can do the job. That's what the SAS is about, mum. Just doing things well.'

'So you tell me. I sometimes wonder what these things are you do so well, but I don't really want to know. I knows you're not a mean boy . . .'

'I'm not a boy, mum.'

'I knows that too. Have you got a girlfriend?'

Franklin hesitated. 'Not really.'

'I takes it from that she's white.'

Franklin burst out laughing. 'They'd have burned you as a witch,' he said.

'Ain't there no black girls in Hereford?'

He shook his head. 'Not really. It's a white town, through and through.'

'So what she like? What's her name?' his mother wanted to know.

'Miriam. She's a student teacher. She . . . What else do you want to know?'

'I want to know why she's after a black man.'

Franklin told himself to take a deep breath and count to ten. 'Maybe she's after me,' he said eventually. 'Maybe she's not as hung up on colour as some people.'

'Maybe,' his mum conceded. 'But it ain't common. And the ones like to think they colour-blind is often the ones using it to make themselves feel special.'

'I don't think she's like that.'

'You don't *think*?'

'I've only been out with her once.'

'OK, I say no more. You do what you want. You always did . . . no, I don't mean you selfish – you not

– I just mean you always like to find things out for yourself.' She smiled at him. 'So I still don't know why you so miserable.'

'I'm not. Not really.'

'There's an awful lot of "not reallys" coming out your mouth this evening.'

'Brixton's depressing.'

'Especially for us who have to live here.'

'I know. I lived here, remember. The whole country feels depressing, mum ... I ... I don't know. And anyway,' he said, looking at his watch, 'I got to get to this meeting Barrett arranged.' As he got to his feet there was a knock on the front door. 'Expecting anyone?' he asked her. She shook her head.

It was Everton.

'They released me,' he said eventually, after managing to free himself from his mother's embrace. 'They're dropping the charges.' He looked at Franklin, and it was not a look of gratitude. 'You pulled some strings, didn't you, bro?' he said.

'No.' Unless simply showing up in uniform had been enough. 'Didn't they tell you why you were being released?'

'They said it was insufficient evidence, but they didn't think that the day before. The magistrates didn't think that. And I was the only one released. You know how that gonna look, bro?'

'You's out and that's the main thing, Everton,' his mother said.

He ignored her. 'You know?' he asked Franklin again.

'Yeah, I know. But if I pulled any strings I didn't know I was doing it. I was just trying to get you out.'

'Like I asked him to,' his mother added.

Everton let his anger give way to sorrow. 'I know you

means well,' he told Franklin, 'but it just don't work any more, you looking out for me. Not wearing that uniform.'

'We're still brothers, Everton.'

'Yeah, I know.' He turned away. 'I need a bath, mum.'

'You knows where it is.'

Franklin and his mum were left standing at the bottom of the stairs.

'I think I'll go out for a drink,' he said, taking his jacket down from the hook.

'You don't want to take what Everton says to heart,' she said, but without any great conviction.

'I know,' he said, colluding in the self-deceit. 'But I could do with a drink.'

'Well you go and have one, then,' she said with forced cheerfulness. 'I'll make Everton some supper.'

Franklin let himself out and started walking. Maybe he would have a drink later, but his main aim had been just to get out of the house.

It was still light, and being Friday night the streets were full of people going out, people carrying booze home, music and ganja smoke floating out through the windows, as both smokers and loudspeakers limbered up for the night's parties. Down on Brixton Road the usual groups were gathered, wondering what would happen, wondering whether this would be one of the nights which exploded. There was no sense of inevitable violence, only of a general willingness to contemplate it if the moment seemed propitious.

Was this the Britain he had agreed to serve? Franklin walked away from it, up the hill towards Streatham, his long legs eating up the pavement. His mother's question would not leave him alone. Why was he unhappy?

It was simple really, but it was not something he could

explain to her. He loved being in the SAS, loved nearly every minute of it. He had even loved the selection procedure, and especially enjoyed scoring higher than the other entrants, all of whom had been white, in just about every test.

He loved mastering all the different skills involved, and facing so many different challenges. Even Northern Ireland had been a real eye-opener when it came to learning things about himself and what he could do. And there had been the jungle training in Borneo, and a month in Hong Kong as part of a training mission.

He had made friends too. White friends. A lot of the banter might be unconsciously racist, and occasionally it made him want to scream, but on most occasions there was no evil intent in it, and it had always seemed to Franklin – right through school and beyond – that picking fights over dumb or insensitive remarks proved nothing. If blacks took on the challenge and showed the whites that, on an even playing field, they could match them at anything, then the stupid remarks would start to die of their own accord.

That was why he had joined the white man's army and the white man's world. If enough other blacks did the same then maybe people could start forgetting about colour and getting down to the real problems – like poverty, unemployment and homelessness.

At least, that was how he had explained it to himself. The problem was, he was not sure he believed it any more. He loved his life in the SAS, but it only seemed to work within the cocoon of the Regiment. It did not work in Brixton, or within his family. It was like one of those relationships which could not be brought into the outside world, because the two people had nothing in common outside the love they shared.

Like him and Miriam probably. He hoped not, but he

would hardly be heartbroken if he never saw her again. And every time he went out with a white women there was this voice in his head reminding him how much easier it would be to find a black woman and have black kids and not have to deal with race all his life.

That was it in a nutshell. He did not want to deal with race. Nor be oppressed by it. It just got in the way of who he was. It was so stupid anyway, just a skin pigment, for fuck's sake. It should not matter. But it did. In Brixton Police Station he had been a black first, a human being second. Even to Everton, it sometimes seemed like he was a black first, a brother second. Only in the SAS had he felt respected for what he could *do*. Not for who he was, not yet. But for what *he* could *do*.

He stopped walking, and looked round to see where he had got to. He was at the crown of Brixton Hill, and it was finally getting dark. He no longer wanted a drink.

When he got home his mum had already gone to bed, and Everton had gone out. But there was a message from his brother on the kitchen table: 'Man named Major Caskey' – a phone number followed – 'wants you to call him back tonight. If you're gone before I get back – thanks.'

Franklin reached for the phone.

Caskey let himself into his top-floor flat in Cathedral Street shortly before eleven. Everything had been arranged for the next day, and he had even had time for a couple of pints in the Slug and Pellet on his way home. Solitary pints: usually you could count on at least half a dozen troopers propping up the Slug's bar, but tonight there had been nobody. Maybe there had been a party somewhere which no one had invited him to.

The flat looked no different from usual, yet somehow it seemed a little sadder tonight. In the photograph on the mantelpiece his wife looked a little more accusing, the kids a little more indifferent. He had thought of ringing Liz from the pub, but lately her husband had taken to answering the phone, and even he had to be getting a little suspicious at how many wrong numbers they were getting.

What a fucking mess. He was glad to be getting away, at least for a few days.

The *Radio Times* told him he had fifteen minutes before the test highlights, so he walked into the bedroom and started packing the small blue holdall he always used in such circumstances. It looked a little worn now, but he almost thought of it as a lucky charm.

Six pairs of underpants, six pairs of socks, six shirts, a spare pair of trousers. Compass, star chart, torch. Etc., etc., etc. Christ, after twenty years he knew the list off by heart.

The bag packed, he went back to the living room and poured himself a glass of the claret he had been forced to abandon earlier that day. The cricket was late as usual, but wonderfully restful, even in the ludicrous highlights formula. Cricket highlights – what a contradiction in terms! In cricket the moments only made sense in terms of the hours.

And it had been a bad few hours for England, with the Australians building a sixty-nine-run lead without ever looking more than merely competent. England had cut it to twenty by the close for the loss of only Brearley, which Caskey supposed was something. Throughout the day both sides had seemed in a thoroughly bad mood, and Richie Benaud was suitably disapproving.

For a few moments he sat there with the last quarter of an inch of claret, watching the BBC2 logo, knowing he was not ready for sleep. It was good to be going somewhere, he thought once more. It would change nothing, and the same mess would be waiting for him when he got back, but it was good to be going somewhere. Anywhere.

8

After several days of unseasonable dryness, the heavens opened in the early hours of Saturday 1 August. Moussa Diba's trench soon turned into a warm bath, and he was forced to sleep out on the open ground. An abandoned piece of corrugated-iron fence provided him with a hard, uncomfortable blanket. Still, at least it kept most of the water off him.

The rain stopped before dawn, and he had an hour or so of real sleep before Jahumpa did the rounds with his toecap, waking everyone up. The sun was already above the horizon, a large white disc behind a line of silhouetted palms, and the pools of rain on the road were beginning to evaporate, each forming its own private cloud of mist in the clear morning air.

There was no breakfast.

Diba washed his mouth out with some rainwater that had gathered in a fold of his iron blanket, and began baling out his trench, wondering what he should do. Or at least plan to do.

He supposed the Senegalese would be along in the not too distant future, though there was always the chance that they would head straight for Banjul. His company had been taken out of that line of march, and pulled back to form part of a defensive arc around the beach resort areas of Bakau and Fajara. Their current location lay astride the Serekunda–Fajara road, close to the village of Kololi, a mile or so from the coast. In front of them the road stretched arrow-straight for about a mile towards the outskirts of Serekunda. They would have no trouble seeing the bastards coming.

Diba wondered what was going on in the heads of the revolutionary leaders. Had they abandoned Banjul, or were they going to make a last stand somewhere? The Denton Bridge was the obvious place. If they could stop the Senegalese there, or blow it up, then Banjul could be held for a bit longer.

But what for? The rebels must know that they had lost. So what were they still fighting for? Because they could think of no alternative? Because they needed time to make a getaway? Who fucking cared anyway? He should be thinking about his own getaway.

Which was getting more and more complicated. If the Senegalese took Banjul – or even if they just got as far as the bridge – then they were between him and Anja, him and the Englishman, him and the doctor. That had occurred to him the previous night, but for one thing there had been no chance to slink away, and for another he was not at all sure Banjul would be a healthy place to be over the next couple of days. With the Senegalese in control, Jawara and his cronies would all be coming back, and they would be turning the town upside down, looking for the rebels, who they probably had no photographs of, and the released prisoners, whose mugshots they most certainly did have.

No, he would have to revisit Banjul before he headed for the border, but not just yet. For the moment Bakau seemed a safer bet. When the time came – and recognizing the right moment would be the difficult part – then he would do what he had to do. Steal enough money to buy a new life, kill the fucking Englishman, have a time to remember with the doctor, collect Anja and go. Guinea, the Ivory Coast, anywhere.

Four miles to the east, Colonel Taal's thoughts were running in similar channels whenever the exigencies of the situation allowed him the luxury of such reflection. It could all be summed up in one phrase, he thought: when do we cut our losses and run? And he suspected they would all have different answers. The Sallahs of this world would leave too early, the Jabangs would probably leave it too late. So they were both lucky to have him around, he thought with a sour smile.

He looked back along the bridge towards the Banjul end, but there was no sign of any vehicle approaching from that direction. It was hard to believe that there were no explosives in the entire western half of the country, but he was reluctantly coming to that conclusion. He supposed that when it came down to it, explosives were mostly used by armies and miners, and The Gambia had neither. But still . . .

It hardly seemed worth blowing up the bridge anyway. It might slow down the Senegalese, keep them out of Banjul for another day perhaps, but the Revolutionary Council had essentially abandoned the capital in any case, and there was always the argument that if they could not march into Banjul the Senegalese might just march all their forces straight into Bakau.

Taal could not help feeling he was wasting his time. There were nearly a hundred men dug in on either side of the bridge, and it would take the Senegalese a while to shift them, but he knew his side had lost both the battle and the war, and that now it was just a matter of how much they could salvage through the hostage negotiations. In which case, these hundred-odd men would be better served defending the Field Force depot in Bakau.

Jabang, however, had insisted on at least a token resistance to the enemy occupation of the capital. The longer they held Banjul, he said, the longer the radio station could continue broadcasting. How his leader had reached the conclusion that another two hours of broadcasting threats and demands were worth a hundred men, Taal could not say. But he did know he had come too far with Mamadou Jabang to start arguing with him at such a moment. It was, as the American military liked to say, a 'no-win situation'.

At the radio station Mustapha Diop was trying, without much success, to quell a slowly growing sense of panic. After his broadcast the previous afternoon, and the threats to kill him and his family at five p.m. if the rebels' demands were not met, he had been taken back to the house in Marina Parade. There he had agonized about whether or not to tell his wife, torn between a need to share his fear and an unwillingness to see her suffer. Instead, he had paced up and down for three hours, one eye on the window for the arrival of nemesis at his gates.

But five o'clock had passed without any visitors, and after another hour had passed Diop was beginning to let himself believe that the worst was over. When Sallah, accompanied by the same two 'comrades', did appear a few minutes later, Diop felt as if his stomach had dropped through the floor. The next thirty seconds were the worst of his life, and when Sallah coldly told him they only wished him to make another broadcast, he could have kissed the ugly bastard.

He had accompanied them to the radio station in the same taxi, by the same route. It would all have smacked of *déjà vu*, but this time there was to be no talk of prisoners or deadlines; they simply wanted him to politely ask his compatriots for two things: a ceasefire between the warring armies and negotiations between the rebels and the Senegalese Government.

Once he had done so Diop had expected to be driven

back to Marina Parade, but no such journey was forthcoming. They might need him again, Sallah had told him, and there seemed no point in making continual trips to and fro. And in any case his family were at this moment being moved to the Field Force depot in Bakau – for their own safety, of course. He would be joining them as soon as circumstances allowed.

A long evening had followed, during which Diop reached the unhappy conclusion that even a terrified man can experience numbing boredom. Sallah had left soon after dusk, and his other minders seemed disinclined to talk. The radio played either mindless Afro pop or repeats of his own broadcast, which sounded stranger and stranger as the evening wore on. Sleep, even the fitful kind in an upright chair, had proved a merciful release.

He woke with all the old fears and a few new ones, but soon found reasons for hope. To judge by the faces of his companions, he was no longer alone in feeling afraid. It seemed that at some point in the night they had belatedly come to the realization that theirs was likely to be the losing side. And one of the consequences of this realization was a desire to ingratiate themselves with him. He was allowed some privacy in the toilet, and even asked what he would like for breakfast.

It never arrived, of course, but it was nice to be asked. The rebel in charge, a Mandinka named Jimmy Gorang, spent most of his time on the telephone, presumably talking to his superiors. The look on his face just before eleven, when the connection was suddenly severed, would have been comic in any other situation. His mouth gaped open, he shook the receiver, then pressed a few times on the cut-off button. He then tried redialling, once, twice. Eventually it seemed to sink in that the line was dead.

His countrymen had taken the Denton Bridge, Diop guessed, and put a temporary block on all communications between Banjul and Bakau. The question was: how would his captors cope with their new isolation?

Caskey had told him to pack for the tropics, so Franklin just gathered together the most lightweight clothing he could and stuffed it into the somewhat battered suitcase his father had originally brought from Jamaica. His mum was already at work, his sister at school and his brother still in bed, so he ate breakfast alone and walked down to the tube. He changed onto the Piccadilly at Green Park and got off at Holborn, with almost an hour in hand for the ten-minute walk to the MOD building in Theobald's Road.

It being Saturday, the area seemed almost empty, and most of the cafés were closed. He eventually found an Italian sandwich bar open, bought coffee and a doughnut, and sat in the window watching the buses go by. Major Caskey had not told him much on the phone the night before – in fact all he knew was that three of them were going to Africa. Which was a big place. His first reaction had been to be thrilled by the news, and the fact that he had been selected. His second had been to wonder whether even his soldiering was now a hostage to his race. Had he been chosen for this mission simply because he was black? Franklin intended to ask Caskey precisely that question the first chance he got.

At least the third member of the party was not the Regiment's other West Indian.

'Joss Wynwood, B Squadron,' the man in the MOD hospitality room introduced himself, the chirpiness of the Welsh accent somehow made more apparent by the unruly shock of dark hair and wide grin which accompanied it. Franklin found himself taking an instant liking to the man.

'Worrell Franklin,' he replied, smiling back. 'G Squadron.'

'Any idea where we're going?' Wynwood asked.

'Africa was all the boss told me. What did he tell you?'

'Nothing. Which boss? All I know is that I was given a flight ticket to London and ordered to report here at eleven.'

'Where were you?'

'Armagh. But if it's Africa I can see a connection,' he added. 'I had my honeymoon in The Gambia last year, and I was just reading in the paper that there's been a coup there.'

'Dead right,' a voice said behind them. Caskey dropped the blue holdall, introduced himself and shook each man by the hand. They looked young, he thought. Both of them. Which was hardly surprising – when he was their age they would have just been starting primary school. 'We're on the second floor,' he said, picking up the holdall again.

They took the lift up, and the two troopers followed Caskey down a long corridor and into a large room. It made them think of school – rows of tables and chairs facing a blackboard and map easel. A thin man in a dark-blue suit was busy draping several maps over the latter. He looked about thirty, had black, sleeked-back hair, a cheery smile and a public-school accent.

'Be with you in a mo',' he said.

'From the Foreign Office,' Caskey explained. 'This is just the background briefing. We'll get a more detailed briefing on the current military situation from the French in Paris.'

Wynwood and Franklin exchanged impressed glances.

'Any chance of a night at the Folies Bergère?' Wynwood asked.

'A night in the Charles de Gaulle departure lounge if you're lucky,' Caskey said. 'Two if you're not.'

'And they said the SAS was the glamorous Regiment,' Wynwood lamented.

The FO man was clearing his throat. 'I'm not sure how much you need to know,' he began, 'so if it's too much or too little, just tell me.' He turned to the map. 'This is West Africa,' he said, and this uneven sausage shape is The Gambia. It's about two hundred miles long and between twenty and forty miles wide. The River Gambia runs down the middle of it and is the reason why it looks that way – the British just wanted control of the river for strategic reasons, and enough land on either side of it to make the territory viable. As you can also see, it is completely surrounded by Senegal, which was a French colony.

'In fact the two countries would make a lot more sense together than they do separately – the River Gambia would provide exactly the transport artery for a united country which Senegal lacks, and Senegal would provide the hinterland which the river lacks. And that's the main reason why the two countries have been moving towards a confederation – or at least they had been until the current crisis.

'But I'm getting ahead of the story. The population of The Gambia is about 600,000, of which about a quarter live in the towns at its western end. Here' – he pointed at the map with a ringed finger – 'is the capital, Banjul, which used to be called Bathurst. Business and government are still centred there, but it tends to be like the City of London: most of the people who work there don't actually live there. So by day you have business as usual in peeling colonial mansions, and by night it reverts to being a large shanty town.

'Here is where most of the middle class tends to live' – the finger pointed again – 'about eight miles away along the Atlantic coast. Bakau and Fajara are basically outer suburbs, much plusher, much less fraught. Most of the embassies are there, and that's where the big hotels are being put in for the European package tour trade.'

'Finally, here, forming the third corner of a triangle with them and Banjul, almost like a gateway to the rest of the country, is Serekunda, which is probably more populous than Banjul by now, but is basically just an African township. It's the place which looks most authentic to the tourists when they drive from the airport to their hotels. They can say they noticed Africa somewhere between the duty free and the beach.'

Wynwood smiled to himself at this. He remembered driving through Serekunda in the coach quite well, but had only a dim recollection of the beach – somehow the chalet had seemed a more appropriate setting for what Susan and he had in mind. It occurred to him that if he had been picked for this mission on account of his knowing The Gambia, then he was travelling on mostly false pretenses.

'The people,' the FO man was saying, 'are mostly Muslim – about ninety per cent. The largest tribal grouping are the Mandinka, who make up just under half the total, followed by the Wollof – about sixteen per cent – and then several other small minority groups. The tribal boundaries don't follow the national boundaries. For example, there's a lot more Wollofs over the border in Senegal. Generally though, tribalism has never been a serious problem in The Gambia. All the chiefs got their own patch to lord it over, and none of the minorities seems to feel any real grievance. All of them are represented – were represented, I should say – in the Government.'

'Is it a democracy?' Caskey asked.

The FO man smiled. 'Formally, yes. But Jawara has been in charge now for almost twenty years, since before independence, and – how should I put it? – well, he's always the one in the best position to win the elections. He's not a bad ruler, and not a very good one either. The Gambia is poor, make no mistake about that – the annual per capita income is about £100. It doesn't have anything much in the way of natural resources – peanuts and sunny beaches are the only things they have which anyone else wants, and Jawara's made a fair fist of encouraging tourism. But there are other things he could have done, which other small countries have done to earn revenue, like printing lots of stamps, or running lotteries, or setting up a free port . . . There hasn't been much imagination devoted to the country's problems, and the few major schemes which have been launched since independence have nearly all been ill conceived and incompetently handled. And in the last few years the economic chickens have started coming home to roost: there was widespread famine in 1978, and more shortages last year. Like I said, Jawara's not a bad ruler, and he's certainly not a half-baked psycho like Amin or Bokassa. He's more like an African Mr Average.'

'And what about the guys who mounted the coup?' Caskey asked.

'We don't know much about them. The Socialist and Revolutionary Labour Party seems in charge, and that goes back a few years. It was banned last year after a policeman was shot, although it was never clear whether that was the reason or the excuse. Ideologically, they spout the usual Marxist rubbish, which sounds even more comic coming out of a continent without any industry or workers than it does anywhere else. But that may just be window-dressing. A lot of their inspiration – and probably their weapons – comes from Gaddafi, who also likes the phraseology, but takes its meaning about as seriously as I do. And since it seems that over half the military – the Field Force as it's called – has supported the coup, it's obviously not just a matter of a small bunch of loonies seizing power. I'd guess that Jawara must be pretty unpopular outside the tourist areas.'

'Has it been a bloody coup?' Franklin asked.

'Hard to say. The reports we've had have only put deaths in the low hundreds, but the coup leaders have appealed for blood donors, so it may be more.'

'What's the latest news you have?' Caskey asked.

The FO man went back to his map. 'The Senegalese took the airport yesterday, and since then they've been advancing on Banjul up this road. I'd guess they'll take it sometime this morning.'

'That won't leave us much to do,' Wynwood complained.

'The rebels still seem to be in control of this area,' the FO man said, indicating the Bakau–Fajara coastal strip. 'That's where their main depot is, and that, I should imagine, is where they've taken their hostages.' He smiled. 'I'm sure they'll find something for you to do. Any questions?' There were none. 'Then good luck,' he said, removing the portfolio of maps from the easel and heading for the door.

Caskey turned to the other two. 'Here's the drill,' he said. 'Next stop is the Hospital of Tropical Medicines for our shots, then the Regent's Park barracks for kitting out and lunch. We've got a four o'clock flight from Heathrow to Paris, and then a five-hour wait for the Dakar flight . . .'

'Why Dakar?' Wynwood wanted to know.

'That's where Jawara is at the moment. He wants to see us, or at least me. And the only people flying into The Gambia at the moment are the Senegalese Air Force.'

The Denton Bridge was still in rebel hands, at least for the moment. The first Senegalese attempt to take it, using two armoured cars and a hundred or so infantry, had been an ignominious failure. The rebels' bullets had simply bounced off the cars, but without infantry support they could hold no ground, and the vulnerable foot soldiers had been forced back by well-directed fire. For the first time since the airborne landing, Taal had reason to feel proud of his men.

It could not last. The Senegalese were now simply waiting, and Taal could guess what for, long before he actually heard the sound of the approaching Mirages. There were two of them, and they streaked in across the waters of Oyster Creek, cannons firing. The rebels hunkered down into the shallow trenches they had dug in the soft earth of the flood plain, but to little avail. Both Mirages unleashed a cloud of small objects: anti-personnel bombs, designed to explode above the ground into a thousand deadly shards.

Suddenly the air was full of crying, screaming men, and those who had escaped were not about to give the planes a second chance. They were already running in all directions, most of them towards Banjul, but some into the mangrove swamps, and others straight into the dubious safety of the water.

Taal took a deep breath, and waited to see if the Mirages would return for a second strike. He could not see them, but at the swelling sound of their engines, he scrambled underneath the bridge.

The planes swooped in again, but either the pilots had shot their only bolt or their humanity prevailed, because no more splinters of death were cast across the fleeing soldiers. At the other end of the bridge Taal heard one of the armoured car engines pushed into gear.

It seemed like a good time to make his departure. He walked swiftly down to the water's edge and stepped aboard the President's speedboat, which had been liberated from the Palace moorings and brought around the coast with exactly this eventuality in mind. 'Go,' he told the driver, who needed no further encouragement to open the throttle and send them shooting out from under the cover of the bridge, with such force that Taal was almost thrown backwards over the stern. If anyone shot at them the sound was masked by the noise of the outboard, and within a minute they were out of range, the bridge receding behind them, the ocean filling the horizon in front.

Most of Banjul either saw or heard the two Mirages as they swooped low across the town after their attack on the rebel positions at the bridge. One of Diop's guards put his head out of the second-floor window at the radio station, and was spotted by most of the small group of men concealed in the building on the other side of Buckle Street, a deserted school.

'There's five of them out front,' Mansa Camara said. 'Maybe two inside, maybe more. But nothing we can't deal with. Those five outside look ready to jump out of their skins if someone farts at them.'

McGrath grinned. 'OK, but we don't know if they have any of the hostages inside,' he argued. 'If we get Jawara's senior wife shot, I don't reckon much on your chances of promotion.'

Mansa laughed. 'He'd probably make me head of the Field Force. It's the young wife he takes everywhere these days. But . . .' He turned to McGrath. 'How are you thinking we should do this?'

'Send a small party in the back,' McGrath said without hesitation. 'At a given time you call on the ones out front to surrender, which should flush out the ones inside.'

'I take it you would like to be the "small party" at the back,' Mansa said wryly.

'I'll take Kiti,' McGrath said, indicating another of the Field Force men, who grinned back at him.

'OK,' Mansa agreed. 'How long?' he asked.

'Give us fifteen minutes,' McGrath decided.

'Right.'

McGrath and Kiti left the school the way they had come in, over the back wall, and worked their way around in a large circle, crossing Buckle Street a hundred yards down from the station, and ending up in front of the building in Leman Street that backed onto it. They advanced carefully down the side of this structure, until the back windows of the radio station building came into view. Though they were partly hidden by a large mango tree, no one seemed to be keeping a watch from the windows. A back door looked similarly unguarded.

The two men stealthily crossed the intervening space, on the alert for any sign of danger, and McGrath gingerly tried the door handle. It was locked. But the window next to it was not. The shutters opened with only a slight creak, and a judicious insertion of McGrath's knife released the catch on the windows. He climbed in and stood motionless for a moment, listening for any relevant sounds, then gestured Kiti to follow.

Twelve minutes had passed. McGrath signalled Kiti to stay where he was, and went on a short tour of investigation. The next door led into a short corridor, which ended in a lobby. From this another open door led into a large empty room, and carpeted stairs led upwards.

He went up them two at a time. The next floor was also unoccupied, though all three rooms seemed in regular use. One was full of records and tapes, one a kitchen, the third a bathroom. On the floor above McGrath thought he could hear voices. Then he did hear the sound of someone beginning to pace up and down.

Almost fourteen minutes. He swiftly descended the stairs, crooked a finger at Kiti, and led him back up to the first floor. He put the Field Force man behind the bathroom door and himself behind the corner of the opening into the music library.

A loud voice suddenly boomed out: Mansa must have found a megaphone somewhere. Almost instantly guns opened up in the street below, though from inside the building it was impossible to tell whose they were. Nor did McGrath have time to think about it. A man came hurtling down the stairs from the floor above, tripped over the Englishman's extended foot, and smashed his head into the kitchen door jamb with a satisfying thud.

McGrath was halfway up the next flight of stairs when a face appeared briefly in the doorway above. By the time McGrath had reached the threshold of the studio, the man it belonged to was backing away, one hand gripping another African around the throat, the other holding a Luger to his head.

'I will kill him, I will kill him,' the man said, but his victim apparently had other ideas. With a look on his face that suggested the end of his tether had finally been reached, he kicked back like a mule at the rebel's shin.

The rebel shrieked, let go his grip and fired the gun, all in the same moment. As his prisoner fell away he tried in vain to re-aim it in McGrath's direction. Two bullets from the Browning knocked him backwards into the glass partition separating the engineer's room from the studio, and he slid slowly down to the floor with a bemused expression freezing on his face.

On the other side of the studio the other man was getting slowly to his feet.

'Are you OK?' McGrath asked.

'I think so,' Mustapha Diop said. It looked like his career as a radio star was over.

The three SAS men sat in the back of the London cab, Franklin and Caskey facing forward, Wynwood perched uneasily on one of the dicky seats facing back. He might be uncomfortable, but the long ride to Heathrow also offered him the first chance he had had to relax since his drink with Stanley in Armagh the previous night. It had been quite a day.

His arm was sore from the typhoid and yellow-fever jabs, his backside sore from the gamma-globulin jab against hepatitis. They had not had an immunization against being shot by African rebels, so at least he had been spared being sore somewhere else.

It was sunny outside, a lovely summer afternoon. London looked almost attractive. Wynwood had always felt vaguely intimidated by the British capital – its sense of . . . smugness was the word. Londoners thought they were the centre of the world, all of them, from the rich, chinless bastards in Kensington to the pink-haired punks in Camden Town.

Maybe they were right. He thought about Pontardulais and its people, living in their small goldfish-bowl world. He thought about Armagh, where everyone seemed to know everyone else, and even kneecappers seemed on first-name terms with the kneecapped. Maybe London was a network of villages like that, which strangers like him could not differentiate, but he doubted it.

He would have to ask Franklin sometime. Though maybe it was different for blacks.

Why did he think that? Because he associated black faces with villages? Wynwood realized for the first time that going to Africa would have a very different meaning for Franklin from the one it had for him. For him, the thought of 'Africa' was simply exciting. He had joked that the SAS was 'the glamorous Regiment', but before being badged he had at least half-believed it. Three months in Northern Ireland had cured him of such romanticism, and imbued in him the knowledge that even the most unglamorous jobs could still be well worth doing. But that did not mean he should not enjoy the glamorous assignments when they came. And being part of *the* SAS three-man team to The Gambia was glamorous by any standards. And definitely worth a sore arm and a sore bum.

In the seat opposite, Franklin was having similar thoughts, though in his case the pride in being selected for this job was tempered by the knowledge that the colour of his skin had played an important role in the selection. He had asked Caskey the direct question while Wynwood was receiving his injections, and the Major had not tried to sugar the pill.

'Yes,' was the reply. 'The CO's reasoning was that an all-white team would have less credibility in a black country. But if that upsets you, I can tell you that I would not have agreed to take you if I didn't think you were up to the job. Fair enough?'

'Yes, boss,' Franklin had said, knowing it was the best he could have expected. If it still did not feel quite right – and it did not – then that, he told himself, was too bad. He had to get over it. Whatever the reasons for his selection, he was going. To Africa, where everyone in his family had ultimately come from, and where none of them had ever been. That felt good, and, he had to admit, it also felt good just to be getting out of England. Away from all the problems.

The roads they were travelling down seemed festooned with the litter from the Royal Wedding celebrations, which somehow seemed to sum up the whole country. It was all so fucking inappropriate. All that money spent on a wedding while the cities were going up in flames. And even the unemployed were dancing in the streets for Lady Diana. The briefing on The Gambia had scarcely painted a picture of freedom and prosperity, but it would have to be pretty fucking dire to compete with this. He grunted, causing Wynwood to open his eyes and grin at him. He grinned back.

Next to Franklin, Caskey was still running through all the various tasks they should have completed, and praying that he had not forgotten anything important. Their clothing needs had been met by a combination of what each man had brought with him, a scavenging trip round the Regent's Park barracks and a quick collective trip to Lawrence Corner, the nearby Army and Navy surplus store. The jabs had all been administered, the course of malaria pills started, the water purification tablets procured. Each man had a Browning High Power in his bag, together with a supply of ammo, and a couple of stun grenades. They had some idea of where they were going and why.

He could understand Franklin's questioning of his selection, and hoped it was not the beginning of a problem. In all other respects both he and Wynwood seemed like ideal companions for this particular trip. Though he supposed he should have realized that honeymooners tended not to get out and about very much.

It was just past three o'clock, and they were getting close to Heathrow. At the airport he should be able to get the latest score from Edgbaston, though he doubted whether it would be good news. England had lost a couple of wickets before lunch, and there was not much reason to believe they had not lost another couple since. But it would be nice to know all the same. He would have to buy one of those new portable things with the funny name. Walkmans, that was it.

The taxi drew to a halt outside the terminal building. Caskey paid off the driver with MOD petty cash, added a generous tip and led the other two through the crowds milling around the check-ins to a small door marked 'Security'. He knocked and walked straight in, greeting the surprised uniformed men inside with: 'SAS – we're expected.'

Behind him Wynwood was thinking: a bit over the top, but impressive anyway.

The uniforms certainly jumped to attention, one of them standing nervously in front of them while the other went to get their superior. He was not so easily impressed. 'Major Caskey?' he asked, and on receiving verbal confirmation demanded to see their passports and order papers.

Once satisfied, the security man led them through a series of rooms and corridors, finally emerging through a door on the travelling side of the boarding gate. Wynwood had a brief glimpse of less privileged passengers waiting to board before he was ushered down the flexible loading corridor and into the first-class section of an empty plane. After exchanging a few words with the crew their guide departed. Their bags, and the weaponry they contained, were stowed in the overhead compartments.

A few minutes later the rest of the passengers began to board, and within twenty minutes the plane was airborne. They were over the Channel before Caskey remembered that he had forgotten to find out the test match score.

At Charles de Gaulle they were allowed off the plane before the other passengers and led by a French security official through a labyrinth of corridors and steps to a private lounge overlooking the airport. Here they were offered drinks while they waited for their French Army contact, Major Jules Mathieu.

He arrived about half an hour later, just as Wynwood and Franklin were starting on their second Pils. He looked liked anyone's idea of a French officer, thin-faced and dark, with a pencil moustache and meticulously pressed uniform. His English put their French to shame.

'*Bonjour, messieurs*,' he began. 'I have just checked your flight details for tonight. There seems to be no problem with the Dakar flight, despite all the activity down there.' He rubbed his hands together as if they were cold. 'And you will be escorted aboard, without the . . . er, inconvenience of customs clearance or an X-ray check. Yes? *Bon*. And in Dakar you will be met by people from your own embassy. So, I understand you require the latest information about the situation of the Senegalese forces in The Gambia?'

Caskey nodded.

Mathieu spread his arms in an unmistakably Gallic gesture. 'The Senegalese do not tell us everything,' he said, 'but . . . what they have told us . . .' He reached into his briefcase and extracted a photocopy of part of a 1:250,000 map of The Gambia. Someone had already drawn on it with a red felt-tipped pen.

He held it in front of him, so that all three SAS men could see it. 'They say they have secured the road from the airport here at Yundum all the way to Banjul, and placed a strong force here at the Denton Bridge. They claim to have cleared the rebels out of both Banjul and Serekunda during today, and they probably have, though whether that amounts to restoring order or simply retaking the main boulevards I don't know. You know the rebels emptied the prison two nights ago?'

'No. We hadn't heard that.'

'Ah. Well, they did. So there are also many armed criminals on the loose, which must be making the military job more difficult. And then there is the question of the hostages.' He paused to rub his moustache with the outside of his thumb. 'The rebels have made several threats to kill the President's family and the Senegalese envoy and his family – he was released today, by the way – but so far, we think they have not killed anyone. Still, the Senegalese are being very careful . . . You understand – Jawara is Diop's partner in making the confederation between the two countries, and he will be telling his commanders not to take any actions that might trigger off a desperate response. They would like to catch the rebels *and* free the hostages, but now that the coup is, how do you say? – fucked? – the big priority is getting the hostages back alive. And of course, your SAS is famous for the Iran Embassy siege . . .'

'Do you know what weaponry the rebels have?' Caskey asked.

'Kalashnikovs, *c'est tout*. Jawara says they got them from Libya and the Senegalese are saying they came from the Soviets.' He laughed. 'And Tass says the Gambian Government bought them years ago, which sounds the most likely.'

'Do you know any of the Senegalese commanders personally?' Caskey asked.

'Not the C-in-C, General N'Dor. But I was at St Cyr at the same time as his second in command, Aboubakar Ka. He is a good soldier.' Mathieu smiled at some memory. 'And good company,' he added.

There was a silence while Caskey tried to remember if there was anything else he needed to ask.

'If you have no more questions,' Mathieu said, 'perhaps you would enjoy a meal, yes? Because I can assure you the dinner on Air Afrique flights is nothing to look forward to.'

'I could eat a nice French dinner,' Caskey conceded.

'*Bon*. Then follow me.'

They walked down a few more empty corridors, through a security check on Mathieu's say-so, and up to what looked like an extremely expensive restaurant. Mathieu disappeared from view for a few moments, before returning to tell them their meal was on the French Army. 'And *bon appétit*', he told them.

Caskey went off to phone the test match scorecard and came back looking depressed. 'The bloody Aussies have got two days to score a hundred and forty-two,' he said gloomily. 'With nine wickets left on a batsman's pitch.'

But the food did something to restore his spirits, and the wine something more. When Wynwood, glass of Burgundy in one hand and forkful of succulent steak in the other, happily exclaimed that this was indeed the life, Caskey could hardly find it in himself to disagree.

9

Sibou Cham lay stretched out on the camp-bed in her office. She felt weary to the bone but sleep would not come – it was as if her mind had parted company with her body, the one racing madly along, the other abandoned for dead hours ago.

How many people had she treated in the last forty-eight hours? Eighty? A hundred? A hundred and fifty? She had no clear idea any more. The faces and the bodies were all jumbled up. This man's face went with this shattered thigh, that woman's face with that lacerated ear. Or vice versa. They all had red blood and fear-filled eyes and they were all praying to her, the goddess of healing.

Lying there, she felt more alone than ever. She wanted someone to share who she was, she wanted a body beside her that was not broken or bleeding, that needed no help to function but only love to make it feel whole. She wanted someone reaching out to her whom she could reach out to in return.

It was getting light outside, which did not seem right. Maybe she had slept for a couple of hours after all. She got up, walked to the window, and pulled the lever which opened the sheets of slatted glass. Outside two small grey lizards with yellow heads were chasing each other around a tree stump. On one of the mats which had been left to dry in the sun a small boy was curled up asleep, his bare legs caked with dust.

Africa, she thought. Who would care for Africa? It had nothing anyone wanted. Nothing to sell, nothing to bargain with. Only more and more people fighting over the same amount of land, more and more people angry at their inability to grab a foothold in that wonderful world of cars and TVs and hi-fi which the tourists parade before their eyes. African rulers had no power to transform the continent's fate: all they could do – even the cleverest and the most well-meaning ones – was to try to soften the blow. No wonder there were coups. And no wonder they amounted to nothing more than a game of musical chairs. Except of course for those whose blood had been given to the dust.

In medieval times they had tried to cure patients by bleeding them; nowadays it was countries.

The Field Force depot in Bakau had always reminded Junaidi Taal of the prisoner-of-war camps depicted in Hollywood films. It was partly a matter of illusion: the watch-tower, which contributed so much to the effect, was actually part of the fire station next door, but the large trees which were scattered around the two compounds and overhung the wall between them, made visual separation difficult. From the road all that was visible was an impression of one-storey offices and barracks receding into the foliage, and the single, blue-painted tower rising above it.

It had rained heavily throughout the night, and as dawn broke on Sunday heavy drops were still falling from the trees, beating a sporadic tattoo on the corrugated roofs. This sound was mingled with the swelling dawn chorus of the birds and, rather more incongruously, the measured tones of a Bush House announcer reading the World Service News.

Taal looked at his watch, sighed wearily, and climbed laboriously from his bunk. He was getting too old for this sort of life, he thought. The sort which involved only about four hours' sleep in each twenty-four.

He pulled on a shirt, draped a blanket round his shoulders against the chill of the dawn air, and walked out onto the verandah where, as he had expected, Mamadou Jabang was listening to the radio. One hundred and fifty yards away to the left the sentries at the gates seemed awake and reasonably alert. To the right a man was carrying what looked like a pail of eggs towards the kitchen.

Jabang looked up at Taal with what could charitably be described as a wry smile. 'We didn't even make the news this morning,' he said. 'As far as the world is concerned it's all over.'

'The BBC is not the world,' Taal said shortly, and sat down on the chair beside Jabang's.

'I know, I know.' Jabang gestured towards the map which had been spread across the table. 'Tell me the situation,' he said.

Taal got up again and leaned over the map. 'At midnight,' he began, 'we controlled the whole of this road, from the Sunwing Hotel north of Bakau to the Bakotu Hotel in Fajara. On these two roads' – he indicated the highways from Serekunda to Fajara and Banjul to Bakau, which made three sides of a square with the Bakau–Fajara road – 'we have positions about a mile inland which the Senegalese have not really tried to shift.'

'Why not?' Jabang asked, more for confirmation than because he did not know.

'Two reasons. One, they have been busy taking and securing Banjul. Two – and this is only guesswork – they haven't made up their minds whether or not to risk us killing the hostages. And I said midnight but I'm assuming that this is still the situation. No one woke me with bad news.'

'I heard no gunfire during the night,' Jabang agreed. 'What about our radio van?'

'Let's find out,' Taal suggested, reaching for the radio. A few seconds later Jabang's own voice was coming out of the speaker. It was the original proclamation of the new government, now somewhat outdated.

'Where are they?' Jabang asked.

'Somewhere in Banjul. With the Senegalese holding the Denton Bridge there's no way they can get out.'

'I'd love to have seen the Senegalese commander's face,' Jabang said. 'They take the radio station, think that's the last the people will hear from us, and like witch doctors there we are again. I don't suppose we can reach them with a new tape?'

Taal smiled. 'We would have to find them first . . .'

'If we could find someone with a recorder in Banjul then I could talk into it down the telephone.'

'Maybe . . .'

'No, you're right, it's not worth it.' He turned back to the map. 'Can we hold the position we have for a few days?'

Taal shrugged. 'We can try, but . . .'

'If they are hesitating because of the hostages, then perhaps we should encourage them to think the worst,' Jabang said, as much to himself as to Taal.

'More threats?'

'Why not? They . . .'

'But what happens when we fail to carry them out again?'

'They will think we don't know what we are doing.' Jabang smiled. 'You have read the books, Junaidi. The hardest thing for the authorities to cope with in a situation like this is not knowing how far the opposition is prepared to go.'

'That is true,' Taal agreed. It was significant, he thought, that Jabang was now calling the other side 'the authorities' again. Even in the leader's mind they had recrossed the divide which separated government from rebellion. 'But, I must ask you, Mamadou: what can we hope for in the few days such threats might buy us?'

Jabang's mouth seemed to set in an obstinate line, the way Taal remembered it had done when he was a child. 'I still believe Libya may send us some assistance,' he said. 'They sent troops into Chad,' he added, almost belligerently, as if defying Taal to argue.

'Have you heard anything new?' Taal asked.

'No. But our friends in New York will still be working for us.'

Taal scratched his eyebrow and stared out across the wakening camp.

'I know it is not likely,' Jabang admitted.

'It will serve no purpose for any of us – for you, in particular, Mamadou – to be put on trial and hanged by Jawara.'

'I know. I have not lost my reason, Junaidi. When it really is hopeless . . .' He waved a hand in the air. 'But that hour has not arrived. This morning I shall talk to the Senegalese commander, and give a good impersonation of a deranged terrorist who thinks nothing of killing Jawara's family and a hundred white tourists. Then maybe we can negotiate some sort of amnesty for our people. Yes?'

The SAS men's Air Afrique plane landed in Dakar soon after dawn. It seemed to taxi for ever before pulling up a good two hundred yards from the terminal building. Just like the old days, Caskey thought, as he walked bleary-eyed down the steps to the ground. Nowadays only the Pope ever touched the tarmac in modern airports, and that was just because he wanted to kiss it.

As it happened, the three of them were the only passengers who did not have to take the long walk. A man from the Gambian High Commission – resplendent in a Hawaiian shirt – was waiting for them at the bottom of the steps, his Renault parked a few yards away. After making sure they had no luggage other than what they were carrying, he ushered the SAS men inside the car and set off at a breakneck pace across the tarmac.

As at Heathrow and Charles de Gaulle the formalities were not so much dispensed with as trampled on. Here at Dakar's Yoff Airport, there was no need even to enter the building. The Renault was stopped at one gate, as much, Caskey reckoned, for the sake of Senegalese pride as anything else. A uniformed officer looked at all three of them in turn, as if checking their faces with the passports he had not seen, and waved them through.

Franklin, watching the exchange between him and their Gambian escort, felt suddenly aware that he was somewhere he had never been before in his adult life – in a country run by black men.

They roared out of the airport, past a scrum of orange taxis and a crowd of people scrambling to board a bus, and out onto a dual carriageway. In the distance, down at the end of long side-roads lined with rough-looking, one-storey dwellings, they could see the ocean. The sky was clear of clouds, but the blue was tainted with brown, and a patina of dust already seemed to hang in the morning air.

'How far is it?' Caskey asked the driver. Unlike the other two, he had found sleep hard to come by on the plane. It was a matter of age, he supposed.

'Twenty minutes, maybe,' the Gambian said.

From the back seats Franklin and Wynwood were getting their first impressions of Senegal. A large sports stadium loomed into view, bare concrete rising out of the yellow earth, its ugliness turned into something else by the profusion of brilliantly coloured bougainvillaea clinging to its lower walls. Elsewhere the ubiquitous concrete was unadorned, fashioned into block houses, turning the landscape into a sandpit for giants. In front of the houses old car tyres had been half-buried in the sand to provide seats.

They raced down an open stretch of highway, with electricity pylons marching overhead, sand verges littered with rubbish, sand hills spotted with scrub receding into the distance. Giant cigarette advertisements loomed out of the dust, as if on a mission to leave no lung unscathed.

'Pretty, it ain't,' Wynwood murmured.

They entered the inner suburbs, where large blocks of flats and relatively modern-looking shops lined the road, then turned down a long, tree-lined avenue between what looked like government buildings of one sort or another. At its end they had a glimpse of a market that sprawled down several narrow streets as far as the eye could see, but the Renault honked its way down another tree-lined avenue. This section looked like Paris, Caskey thought; a seedy, half-finished, tropical Paris.

The car pulled to a halt outside a nondescript building in a nondescript street. 'We are there,' the driver said, climbing out and gesturing them to follow. He seemed determined to do everything at a hundred miles an hour.

Caskey walked slowly after him, shouldering the blue

holdall. A brass plaque by the doorway announced the Gambian High Commission. Inside a flight of steps led upwards to a desk area. It reminded Caskey of the Inland Revenue offices in Hereford.

'Please,' the driver said, indicating a waiting area in which comfortable chairs surrounded a large conference table. Seated in the chairs the table's surface was at eye-level, which meant that holding a conversation with someone on the other side of the room required the talkers to either sit bolt upright or slouch.

Caskey closed his eyes. 'Wake me if anything happens,' he told the other two.

'The President will see you now,' a voice said from behind him.

It was a different Gambian from their chauffeur, this time one more formally attired, in a beige suit, white shirt and red tie. He escorted them down a short corridor and into a well-lit, pleasantly furnished room. A large African rug lay in the centre of the floor, and around it had been arranged several armchairs and two sofas. The President was sitting on one of the latter, a pile of papers by his side. He was not a large man, and although he was not particularly good-looking there was a friendliness in his expression which was appealing. He got swiftly to his feet and walked across to greet them, his right arm outstretched. After he had shaken each man's hand, and they had introduced themselves by name, he invited them to take a seat.

'I am very grateful to the British Government for sending you,' he began, smiling at each of them in turn. 'And of course to each of you for accepting such a mission.' He paused as if expecting a response.

Caskey nodded.

'I'm happy to say,' the President continued, 'that the situation in my country is improving by the hour. Our

Senegalese friends have secured the airport and the capital and the road between them. In fact, all the rebels now hold is a small strip of land along the coast.' He grimaced. 'Unfortunately they also hold a number of hostages, including my own wife and several of my children, so bringing the whole business to a successful conclusion will not be a straightforward matter. Which is where I hope your expertise will come into play. Tell me, did any of you take part in the Iranian Embassy business last year?'

'Yes, sir,' Caskey lied. He was afraid Jawara might feel he had been fobbed off with duds if he found out that none of them had been at Princes Gate.

'A wonderful piece of work,' the President said. 'But of course I hope we can resolve our problem less . . . less dramatically.' He paused again. 'What I really wanted to make clear to you – the main reason for wanting to see you before we all fly to my country – is that you are my personal advisers, and that you carry my authority. The Senegalese – how shall I say this? – they may be – I think "touchy" is the English word . . . I am sure their commanders will be more than willing to listen to any advice you may have, but they will not want to appear as if they are taking orders . . . You understand? It is one of the legacies of colonialism. In the old days a white man's orders were obeyed no matter how stupid, and to compensate for this there is a tendency nowadays to ignore a white man's advice, no matter how sensible.' He smiled at Franklin. 'And I'm afraid in this matter you will be seen as an honorary white man,' he said.

Franklin smiled politely back, but said nothing.

'Very well,' the President said. 'We can deal with any particular problem if and when one arises. Now, unless something extraordinary happens in the meantime, I plan to fly to Banjul this afternoon. There is room for

156

you on the same plane. We shall leave here at around four o'clock, and until then you can either rest in one of the rooms here or go sightseeing, whichever you wish.'

'I'd like some sleep,' Caskey said, getting up.

The President got up too, and shook each man's hand again. 'Until this afternoon,' he said.

The man in the beige suit was waiting outside to escort them to the next floor, where a large double bed shared a room with a single. Caskey annexed the latter, claiming privilege of rank.

'I'd like to go out for a look round, boss,' Franklin said.

'Me too,' Wynwood agreed.

Caskey looked at them. 'Bloody youngsters,' he said with a sigh. He reached inside his pocket for the CFAs Mathieu had given them at Charles de Gaulle. 'OK. But don't spend it all. And don't get lost and don't start a war. And don't touch anything. Particularly the women.'

'Did you get all that?' Wynwood asked Franklin.

'Yeah. We're not to spend it all on women.'

They left Caskey groaning and went downstairs.

'Any idea which way?' Wynwood asked Franklin as they emerged into the street.

'To where?' Franklin asked.

'To where we want to go' Wynwood said.

'Where do we want to go?'

'How the fuck should I know?'

Franklin decided. 'Well, let's try this way then,' he said, pointing east.

'Suits me.' Outside in the street the temperature was on the rise. Still, it was not as hot as Wynwood had expected – perhaps Dakar's situation on the coast kept things cool. It would have been nice to have had some time to find out something about the country before they arrived. 'Hey, Frankie,' he said, struggling to keep up with the other man's long stride, 'do you know anything about this place?'

'Not a thing. Used to be French, that's about it.'

'You mean they speak French here?'

'Yeah.'

Wynwood looked round. 'Who would have guessed?'

'The word "Aéroport" in letters twenty feet high was a clue,' Franklin told him.

'I thought they were just bad spellers,' Wynwood said.

They walked on, conscious of the stares they were getting from the locals. Franklin wondered whether he would have been as noticeable on his own, and decided he probably would have. His clothes were different, for one thing. The Senegalese seemed undecided whether to wear African robes or European suits, but none of them seemed to be wearing jeans and T-shirts.

The street they were on debouched into a large rectangular space surrounded by multi-storey buildings.

'The Place de l'Indépendance,' Wynwood read off a sign. 'You reckon this is the centre of town?'

'No idea,' Franklin admitted.

'Hello, hello,' a Senegalese greeted them.

'Hello, hello,' echoed Wynwood.

'You are American?' the Senegalese asked them both.

'English,' Franklin said.

'Welsh,' Wynwood corrected him.

'You are in Dakar how many days?'

'One hour.'

More questions followed, and somehow it came up that the Senegalese had a naming ceremony for his son the next day, and that it was customary for a man in such a situation to find a foreigner and offer him a gift. As chance would have it he had on his person such a gift, and here were two foreigners! What luck! He insisted that Wynwood accept the gift, a miniature drum on a thong. The Welshman took it reluctantly, thinking there must be a catch. There was. It turned out that it was also customary for the foreigner to give the baby a gift. Wynwood regretted that he had no gift to hand, but it then transpired that cash was the most appropriate gift of all. The two SAS men looked at each and burst out laughing.

'You're a real pro,' Wynwood said, and got out the money Caskey had handed him. 'What are these worth?' he asked Franklin, who shrugged.

'Well, a thousand seems a lot to me,' Wynwood said, and handed the man one.

It did not seem a lot to him. 'More, more,' he said.

'You want the drum back?' Wynwood asked.

'No, I want more CFAs.'

'Tough shit. Be seeing you, chum,' Wynwood said, and walked off. Both Franklin and the Senegalese followed, the one feeling vaguely disturbed by the whole episode, the other more than vaguely annoyed.

He stayed with them halfway round the square, and several blocks up Avenue Pompidou, which looked as close to a main street as any they had seen. Trees lined both sides, and many of the buildings were French in style, creating anew the impression of an African Paris. There were cafés as well, and of two distinct types: those with a primarily African clientele and those which seemed to cater mostly to the expatriate French population. The latter looked cleaner, more expensive and more likely to rid them of their Senegalese shadow.

Wynwood chose one, walked in and took a window seat. A beautiful Senegalese girl took their order of omelettes and coffee, but the Frenchwoman behind the bar was obviously in charge. It felt strange to both men. If they looked one way they could have been anywhere in the developed world. The customers' faces, with one exception, were white, and the fittings were modern, right down to an Elvis Presley clock on one wall, his hips swinging out the passing seconds. But if they looked out through the window there was no mistaking which continent it was. A group of men in long robes were crowded on a bench, smoking cigarettes and passing the time. A boy with two stunted legs was parked under a tree, hand extended with a cup to each passer-by. Buses packed beyond the worst nightmares of a sardine rumbled by, blowing dense black smoke from their exhausts into the dusty air.

Franklin sat there, savouring the delicious coffee, watching and wondering.

Wynwood asked a youngish-looking man at a nearby table if he spoke English.

'A little, yes,' the man said.

Wynwood explained that they had only a few hours in Dakar and no idea what might be worth seeing. Could the man suggest anything?

He shrugged. There was nothing special. The Île de Gorée, perhaps, but that was half an hour's ferry ride away, and they might have to wait an hour for the boat.

'What is it?' Franklin asked, feeling he had heard the name somewhere before.

'It's an island, two or three kilometres from the city. It's very pretty, with the old colonial houses and the fort. And of course the Maison des Esclaves, the Slave House.'

Now Franklin remembered. It was the place from where most of the West African slaves had been shipped. Maybe even his own ancestors.

Wynwood asked whether there were any beautiful buildings to see in the city.

160

'Maybe the railway station,' the Frenchman said dubiously. 'Dakar is not a beautiful city,' he added, somewhat superfluously.

Wynwood thanked him. 'Let's just walk around,' he suggested to Franklin.

For a couple of hours they simply wandered the streets together, soaking up the atmosphere, stopping for the occasional drink, and fending off the extraordinary number of men whose sons were being named the following day.

They did stumble across the railway station, which pleased Wynwood. He had always been drawn to the atmosphere they evoked, and this one, with its magical blend of French and Islamic architecture, seemed no exception. A train was in the platform, packed and apparently about to depart. He asked someone where it was going, and was told Bamako, the capital of Mali. The journey was supposed to take twenty-four hours, the man said with a knowing smile. Wynwood asked him how long it really took. Thirty-six, he said, and cackled.

A few minutes later the diesel blew its horn, and the train jerked its way out of the station along the uneven tracks. Franklin watched it disappear, thinking that here in Dakar they were simply standing on the edge of Africa, but that this train was headed out towards the continent's heart. A part of him wished he was on board.

'This is General N'Dor,' a voice said on the other end of the telephone line.

'At last,' Jabang said. He had needed to threaten the immediate killing of a hostage to get the Senegalese commander-in-chief to the phone, and it had made him angry.

'What is it you have such need to tell me?' N'Dor asked, wishing his English was better.

'Would you rather speak in Wollof?' Jabang asked in that language, as if he had read the General's mind.

'It would seem sensible to be sure we understand what each other is saying,' N'Dor replied in the same tongue. 'I understood you were Mandinka.'

'I am.' Jabang wondered whether the General would be impressed by the fact that he had taken the trouble to learn his country's other indigenous languages, and decided that it did not matter a jot.

'So what do you have to tell me?' N'Dor asked again.

'I have to tell you that unless your forces on the Banjul–Bakau road return to the positions they occupied this morning we shall be forced to begin executing the prisoners.'

There was silence at the other end for almost a minute, but Jabang resisted the temptation to speak again.

'The forces you speak of have only moved a few metres since this morning,' N'Dor said.

'We know that. Moving back those few metres would seem a small price to pay for a hostage's life.' Don't ask for much, Junaidi Taal had advised him, but make sure you get it. Somehow they had to establish a pattern whereby the enemy was prepared to reward them for not carrying out threats.

At the other end of the line General N'Dor was in an impossible position. His Government had warned him to take no risks with the hostages' lives, and the Gambian President would not be on hand to remove the restrictions until later that evening. The rebel leader might be bluffing, and N'Dor thought he probably was, but not with enough certainty to risk calling him on it. There was really nothing he could do for the moment other than concede what was being asked. It was only a few metres, after all.

'Very well,' he said finally. 'My men will be withdrawn to the position they occupied this morning. But no further. This is not an ongoing process. You understand that?'

'Perfectly,' Jabang said. 'Thank you, General. Now, I have here a list of the prisoners we currently hold, which I thought you might find useful. I am sure the families of the prisoners would like to know that they are safe.'

'I will bring someone in to write them down,' N'Dor agreed.

'Excellent. Before you do that, can we arrange to talk again tomorrow morning, say at eleven o'clock? I think it must be in everyone's interests that we keep talking.'

Certainly in yours, N'Dor thought. And until someone told him he could take the gloves off, it was probably in his as well. 'Very well,' he agreed. 'Eleven o'clock.'

Jabang passed the phone to Sallah, who was waiting with the list, and with a wide smile on his face turned to Taal. 'We're not finished yet,' he said exultantly.

The flight from Dakar to Yundum in the forty-four-seater took under an hour. There were only eleven passengers on board; the President and seven assorted advisers in the front seats, the three SAS men in the back. Most of the President's men seemed to be chain-smoking, and by the time the plane touched down at Yundum a thin fog separated the two parties.

Two Senegalese officers were waiting on the tarmac beside a line of four vehicles: the presidential limousine and three taxis. Without much preamble everyone climbed in, the SAS men in the rear taxi, and the convoy took off, sweeping out through the airport gates past arms-saluting soldiers and onto an empty highway.

And into Africa, Franklin thought, staring out through the windscreen. There was nothing European about this landscape. On either side of the road flat savannah stretched into the distance, dotted with trees that bore the continent's distinctive style: tapering down from a flat wide top. A little further on a host of palms shaped like giant thistles rose from a stretch of cultivated land on the outskirts of a village. Here the dwellings were all white and of one storey, including the impressive police station with its colonnaded patio.

Dirt tracks led away from the road, and down these, in the distance, Franklin could see people walking. But the main street seemed strangely deserted, as if the President's path had been swept clear of those he claimed to serve. One group of three women did emerge from a house just as they went by, each with a large plastic bowl balanced on the head, but they turned only blank stares to the swishing cars, as if they were looking into the blind side of a two-way mirror.

After ten minutes or so they entered a large town, which the driver told them was Serekunda. Here there were groups of Senegalese soldiers at the two main crossroads, but few civilians on the streets. Franklin asked the driver if that was because it was Sunday. He received a disbelieving smile in return.

'Not exactly coming out in droves to welcome the man home, are they?' Wynwood commented from the back seat.

The driver chortled, and said something under his breath.

'This town is 'coming like a ghost town' ran through Franklin's head.

Beyond Serekunda they traversed another couple of miles of open country, before motoring across the heavily guarded Denton Bridge and entering the outskirts of

Banjul. 'That must be the prison they emptied,' Caskey said, pointing out a white building on the right. The words 'Female Wing' had been painted on one wall in huge letters. 'I wonder if they let the women out too,' he said.

'No,' the driver volunteered.

'More discrimination,' Wynwood murmured. Susan's friends would have something to say about that.

The convoy drove down Independence Drive, passing a line of Senegalese armoured cars parked outside the Legislative Assembly, before turning left and then right through the gates of what looked, in the distance, like a miniature Buckingham Palace. A long drive ran straight to the doors through grounds bursting with luxuriant tropical vegetation.

'Nice garden,' Wynwood said, 'shame about the house.'

'Enough,' Caskey told him, but the grin on his face rather weakened the reprimand.

The four cars drew up in the gravelled forecourt and disgorged their cargo. The SAS men followed the President's party in through the front doors, where a posse of servants were doing their best to appear overjoyed by their master's return. One of his aides came over to Caskey and asked the SAS men to take a seat in the first reception room.

They sat there for ten minutes, sweating with the heat, wondering why ninety per cent of life in the Army was spent waiting for some wanker to get his finger out.

The aide returned and escorted them through to another room, where the President was sitting on a sofa with a Senegalese officer. The latter, whom Jawara introduced as General Hassan N'Dor, did not, Caskey thought, seem particularly pleased to see them. In fact, he seemed reluctant to even shake their hands.

Jawara was trying hard to be genial enough for both of them. 'I have been telling the General,' he said, 'that you have been loaned to my country by the British Government to serve as my personal military advisers until the present problem regarding the prisoners has been resolved. He is of course aware of your Regiment's experience and expertise in the matter of hostage situations.'

'We will be happy to offer any assistance,' Caskey told N'Dor diplomatically, 'but of course we don't want to tread on anyone's toes.'

N'Dor gave him a slight nod, as if in appreciation of the sentiment. 'My English is not so good,' he said, which made Caskey wonder if he had understood the sentiment.

'I have suggested,' the President said, 'that we set up a group to oversee the hostage situation. It would include someone to represent the Gambian Government – probably the Vice-President – General N'Dor and his second in command Colonel Ka, and you, Major Caskey. General N'Dor has offered a room at the Senegalese Embassy for the group's headquarters.'

I bet he has, Caskey thought. 'That sounds like an excellent idea,' he said. 'Of course,' he added, 'the first thing we shall need is some current intelligence of the situation on the ground in Bakau. And for that we shall need some form of written authority from both yourself and the General, which will give us the freedom to pass through the lines.'

'Of course,' the President said. 'I'm sure the General will have no objection to that.'

N'Dor's face said he had, but he acquiesced nevertheless. An aide was sent to type out appropriate papers for him and Jawara to both sign. While they waited Caskey asked the General for his opinion of the current situation.

'There is nothing difficult about it,' N'Dor said. 'We could destroy the rebels in a few hours . . .'

'The General spoke to the rebel leader on the telephone this morning,' Jawara volunteered.

N'Dor scowled at the memory. 'He threatened to kill a hostage if I did not withdraw my men to a position further in the rear. I have orders not to risk hostage lives, so I agree.' He shrugged. 'That is all.'

'What kind of man do you think this Jabang is?' Caskey asked, thinking that the General's English was not much worse than his own.

'Not right in the head,' N'Dor answered without hesitation.

It was not the sort of analysis Caskey had in mind, but it would probably have to do.

The aide returned with the written authorities, and a reminder to the President that he was scheduled to make a radio broadcast within the next half an hour. 'I am coming,' Jawara told him, before turning to the SAS men. 'Rooms have been made ready for you here,' he told them. 'Please ask Saiboa here' – he indicated the aide in question – 'for anything you need.'

He left, accompanied by the Senegalese commander.

'Ever get the feeling you're not wanted?' Wynwood asked.

'Yes,' Caskey said. He had also just realized that no time had been set for the first meeting of the new hostage crisis group. 'I think we're going to have to write our own agenda on this one, lads. Which is why I wanted these pieces of paper. Let's find out what's going on and make a plan. Then we can decide which part of the General's anatomy to shove it up.'

'Sounds good to me, boss,' Franklin agreed.

'You know, I've never lived in a palace,' Wynwood said.

10

'My fellow Gambians . . .'

The President's voice, never impressive at the best of times, sounded positively squeaky emerging from Lamin Konko's tiny transistor radio. Konko himself was snoring noisily in the upper bunk, which made it even harder for Moussa Diba to follow what the President was saying.

One thing seemed certain – he was not offering anyone anything. 'It's all over – get back to work' seemed to be the gist of his message. No mention of leniency for anyone who offered helpful information or switched sides, no mention of amnesty at all. Diba was not surprised, but he did feel vaguely disappointed. He really was going to have to leave the country. And probably for good.

Jawara was making a final plea for the rebels to surrender, but still not offering them any incentive to do so. It was just window-dressing, Diba thought. Just propaganda.

He wondered what he would do if he was in Jabang's shoes. Just empty out the bank in Bakau and run for it, probably. What else could they do – they could not make the hostage thing last for ever, and what else did they have to bargain with?

Diba turned the radio off and sat there listening to the snoring Konko, aware that time was running out.

It was an hour or more before Caskey got through to the British High Commission on the telephone. He asked for Bill Myers, whose name he had been given in London.

'You've arrived,' Myers said enthusiastically. 'I was beginning to think McGrath would have it all sorted out before you got here.'

'Why, what's he been doing?' Caskey asked, feeling distinctly envious.

'Oh, shooting his way through roadblocks, capturing radio stations, you know the sort of thing.'

Caskey laughed. 'So why wasn't he at the airport to meet us? Where is he?'

'No idea. He knows you're coming – I told him yesterday. He was staying at the Carlton Hotel. Probably still is.'

'Where's that?'

'Independence Drive. Where have they put you?'

'Where else? The Presidential Palace.'

Myers grunted. 'Jawara probably wants you on hand in case he suddenly needs some bodyguards,' he said. 'Has he given you any instructions?'

'We're supposed to be liaising with the Senegalese, but their CO doesn't seem any too keen on letting us in on the act. I don't think he's a glory-hogger. He's either someone who likes to keep command lines simple or he's one of those Africans with a chip on his shoulder when it comes to accepting any kind of help from the old colonial powers.'

'Bit of both, I'd say,' Myers observed. 'I met him at some reception or other. He seemed to improve with each glass of wine.'

'Your glasses or his?'

'Both, I think. It's hard to remember.'

Caskey laughed again. He was already growing fond of Bill Myers. 'How are things out there with you?' he asked. 'Aren't you only about half a mile from the Field Force depot?'

'Bit more. But yes, we're behind enemy lines all right.

There's usually a group of them outside the gate, and we often see lorry-loads going past. But they haven't knocked on the door yet. Or rather they haven't knocked again, since the first morning, when they warned us to keep inside the compound.'

'Have you? What about food?'

'We're OK. But no, we haven't stayed indoors. Several of us have tested the water, literally in fact. We've taken to using the beach instead of the road – they run more or less parallel, and only about fifty yards apart. That way we've been able to keep tabs on the situation in the hotels.'

'Which is?'

'Hunky-dory. Well, almost. The Sunwing seems to have run out of tinned sauerkraut, so the Germans are desperate, but generally speaking everyone has just been sitting round the pool and reading pulp fiction, like they always do. The only difference is that they don't know when they'll be allowed home.'

'And what do you make of the rebels?'

'Mmm. Hard to say. I mean, you'd think any intelligent group of revolutionaries would make sure they were in control of all the relevant communications, right? But the telephone has been operating more or less normally – erratically, in other words – throughout. You could probably phone up the Field Force depot now and talk to Jabang.' He paused. 'But having said that, there's clearly some intelligence at work. They slowed the Senegalese down long enough to secure their hostages, and now they've managed to force a temporary stalemate. There's even a mobile radio transmitter somewhere in Banjul which is irritating the hell out of the Senegalese. They were in the middle of patting themselves on the back for capturing the radio station – which in any case was down to McGrath and some loyal Gambians – when Jabang's voice comes jumping out of the ether at them. Bit of a slap in the face for your friend the General.'

'So we're not dealing with fools here?'

'Not in the usual sense of the word. Irresponsible, yes. Emptying the prison was a stupid thing to do. From what I've heard most of the killing in Banjul was done by ex-prisoners settling scores.'

'Any idea of casualties?'

'Not really. Ask N'Dor. Less than a thousand, I'd say, but it's only a rough guess.'

'OK. I'll keep you up to date with what we're doing . . .'

'Uh-huh. I know what that means – we'll be the first to know what you're planning, some time after the event. I've had dealings with the SAS before.'

Caskey smiled to himself. 'We understand each other then. Ah, one other thing,' he said hurriedly before Myers could hang up, 'you wouldn't know the test score by any chance?'

'Of course we know it,' Myers said. 'What's the diplomatic service for if not to keep Brits up to date with the cricket?'

'Well?'

'Well what?'

'What's the score?!?'

'Oh that. We won of course.'

'Won? They only had about a hundred to make on a pitch like a pudding!'

'You're forgetting Botham.'

'Again?'

'Again. He took five for one in twenty-six balls. They were all out for a hundred and twenty-one.

Caskey could hardly believe it. Lightning obviously did strike twice in the same place. 'Amazing,' he murmured, as much to himself as Myers.

'You said it.'

'We'll be in touch,' Caskey said, still shaking his head in disbelief.

'Good luck,' Myers said, and hung up.

Caskey went back upstairs to where Franklin and Wynwood had established camp, in a suite usually reserved for visiting royalty. Prince Charles had apparently used it once, a piece of information which had caused Wynwood to wonder out loud whether the royal honeymoon was proving a success. 'I mean, tell me, boyo,' he had asked Franklin, 'can you actually imagine the two of them at it? Can you?'

Franklin had tried and failed and gone to have a bath. He was just emerging as Caskey arrived back upstairs. 'Would you believe we won the test match?' he asked the two of them.

'Just about,' Franklin said.

'You know,' Wynwood confided in the West Indian, 'I had this dream that the three of us had been flown out to Africa on some mission or other . . .'

'All right, all right,' Caskey said with a grin. 'Business.' He told the other two the gist of his conversation with Myers.

'So what now, boss?' Wynwood asked.

Caskey looked across at the window, which showed a rapidly darkening sky. 'I think we should talk to McGrath before we decide anything,' he said, 'and I wouldn't object to some food. Or a drink.'

'Good thinking, boss,' Wynwood said encouragingly.

'I take it we're going armed,' Franklin said, replacing the Browning in the holster on his belt.

'You bet,' Caskey said.

Downstairs the aide who had been detailed to look after them had bad news. There was no food in the palace, for the rebels had stripped the storeroom before departing on the previous day. He recommended the Atlantic Hotel, which was just up the road. They could use the jeep which had been sent by the Senegalese for their use.

Caskey offered a mental apology to General N'Dor and asked the aide for directions to Independence Drive and the hotel. This was also apparently a short drive away, and, as it happened, an unnecessary one. Caskey had no sooner turned the jeep out of the gate than two figures were caught in the arc of its headlights. One was a black woman, the other the white man he had last seen in an SAS photograph.

Caskey pulled the jeep to a halt. 'Simon McGrath, I presume,' he said with a smile.

'And you must be the Three Musketeers,' McGrath replied.

They shook hands, and Caskey introduced the other two. McGrath ushered Sibou forward. 'This is Dr Cham,' he said. 'She would be The Gambia's Florence Nightingale, but Florence was only a nurse.'

She ignored him. 'My name is Sibou,' she said, offering her hand. Franklin could not remember ever meeting such a lovely woman.

'Where are you headed?' McGrath asked.

'To look for you, and then the Atlantic Hotel for dinner.'

'Which is where we're going,' McGrath said, offering a hand to help Sibou up into the back of the jeep.

Five minutes later they were entering a sparsely populated dining room, and being ushered to a large table by an army of waiters.

'The tourists from here went home today,' McGrath explained, 'and the next batch have been cancelled because of the situation. Which is why our friends

174

here' – he indicated the hovering waiters – 'all look like they're suffering from withdrawal symptoms.'

Once they had ordered two bottles of wine and several beers Caskey invited McGrath to tell the story of the last couple of days. 'And don't make too much up,' he added with a grin, 'I've already talked to Bill Myers.'

McGrath went through what had happened, leaving nothing out, not even the shooting on the Denton Bridge. He caught Sibou's eye as he recounted those moments, and found he could not read what she was thinking from her expression. Maybe she was not sure herself, he decided.

Franklin, who was sitting between Sibou and McGrath, thought he could feel the tension in her as McGrath told of shooting the rebel, but maybe he was imagining it. He found himself admiring this cynical white Englishman, but not sure whether he liked him very much. He wondered what the relationship between him and the doctor was.

As they ate he managed to share a few words with her, asking whether she was a Gambian and how long she had worked at the hospital. She seemed not to mind being asked, but offered only monosyllabic answers to his questions, and looked genuinely interested only once, when he told her that his mother was a ward sister in a London hospital. It gradually dawned on Franklin that she was tired. Really tired. Tired beyond tired.

Immediately they had finished eating Sibou announced that she had to get back to the hospital.

'You need to go home,' McGrath told her.

'I need ... you're right, I need to go home,' she agreed.

'I'll take you,' McGrath said, getting up.

'Go and see if there's a taxi,' she said. 'If there is I'll take it. And you can stay and talk to your friends.'

'I . . .'

'I'm not arguing with you,' she said.

McGrath was back a couple of minutes later. 'It's waiting for you,' he said.

'It was good to meet you all,' Sibou said. 'And don't let this idiot talk you into anything. I don't want our next meeting to be at the hospital. Unless you'd like to see what one looks like around here,' she added, looking at Franklin.

He watched her thread her away out through the tables, balanced like a dancer.

'Now,' McGrath said, 'how do you lads feel like a little exercise?'

In the Field Force depot's main office the Revolutionary Council was once again in session. One of the twelve members was sick and confined to his bunk, but the other eleven were all there, and, Taal noted, all looking reasonably smart. It was impressive, he thought. Ludicrous perhaps, but still impressive.

Outside the crickets were making their infernal noise, and tonight there was no sign of a downpour to shut them up. Taal wiped his brow with a saturated handkerchief and wondered how many of those present were going to end up hanging from the gibbet in Banjul Prison.

Snap out of it, he told himself. That was what the English said. 'Snap out of it.' What a strange expression.

He tried to keep his attention on what Mamadou Jabang was telling the Council, but it was hard to concentrate on something you already knew off by heart. He and Jabang had spent most of the afternoon and evening thinking through the new policy, and he did not really care what the rest of the Council thought of it. There was, after all, no alternative.

'We will keep what we have,' Jabang was saying, 'and negotiate from that position. We have the hostages as one bargaining card, and we have the prisoners as another.'

A murmur of surprise greeted this statement.

'I am prepared to admit that releasing them was an error,' Jabang said. 'An offer on our part to deliver them back into custody will show that we are negotiating in good faith.'

'Are we in any position to do that?' one man asked. 'They are all armed now . . .'

'There are only about eighty of them here,' Taal said. 'And more than four hundred of us. It will simply take some organization, that's all. And with any luck it will not be necessary. All that we must do is keep them here, which means trebling the security around the depot. No one should be going in or out without written authorization from this Council.'

There were a few moments of silence while everyone digested this. 'OK,' one man said eventually, 'but what do we want? What are we negotiating *for*?'

'Our freedom,' Jabang replied. 'Free passage out of the country.'

'To where?'

'That will depend on which countries are prepared to accept us,' Taal interjected. 'But in any case, first we have to establish the principle.'

'That is true,' Jabang conceded. 'And to establish that principle we must make Jawara fear the consequences of refusal.'

Diba stood in the shadows under the depot's water tower and watched the two men stop for a few words with the sentries on the gate, before starting another lap along the inside of the wall. A few moments earlier another patrol had passed by on the outside of the gate. They were presumably circling the outer wall.

And then there was the searchlight which had been installed in the fire-station tower that evening. Its operator was either minus a brain or very well instructed, because the search pattern was decidedly random, the wide beam slipping this way and that across the depot compound, spilling out onto the road in front and into the trees behind. A man could get across the wall and away, but he would need to be lucky. There was no way to be certain, and Diba was not yet desperate enough to chance his life on such a throw of the dice.

Besides, he thought, as he walked back towards his barracks, the leaders had promised women the following evening. There was no hurry. If the Senegalese attacked the depot there was no way they could capture all three hundred men – some were bound to escape. He just had to be sure that when the time came he was one of them. And that should not be a problem, because most of the rebels would be too busy playing the hero, and most of the ex-prisoners were too slow on the uptake to think of running.

McGrath brought the jeep to a halt on the side of the open road. 'We'd better walk from here,' he said. 'No point in giving the enemy the idea that anything's happening.'

The other three got out. A cool breeze seemed to be blowing in from the ocean, which by Caskey's reckoning was a mile or so ahead of them. The sky was clear, the stars of the summer triangle bright in the northern sky. To the west, the reddish Arcturus hung balefully above the horizon.

They were on the Serekunda–Fajara road, about a quarter of a mile inland from the Senegalese front line. All four men had spent several minutes in front of the mirror with the make-up kit, and their faces and hands were artistically streaked with camouflage cream.

The soldiers at both the Senegalese checkpoints they had passed through – one at the Denton Bridge, the other at the crossroads in Serekunda – had eyed them with a mixture of suspicion, awe and, it had to be admitted, amusement. Still, the authorizations signed by Jawara and N'Dor had granted them free passage, and after a certain amount of head-scratching they had been allowed just that. The Gambia was their oyster, as McGrath announced. 'Pity there's no pearl,' he had murmured to himself.

'Ready?' Caskey asked. He had made it clear to McGrath, in as friendly a manner as he could manage, that the SAS group in The Gambia had only one boss – himself. He was the one who was responsible to Bryan Weighell, and ultimately to the British Government. As long as McGrath understood and accepted that he was more than welcome to join the party.

'You're the boss,' McGrath had agreed, and only time would tell if he meant it.

'You take lead scout, Simon,' Caskey said, organizing the four men along standard SAS lines. 'Joss, Tail-end Charlie.' As leader he would take up the second position, with responsibility for the left flank. Franklin would come third, and cover the right. For the moment, while they were still supposedly in friendly territory, there was unlikely to be any danger, but it paid to be careful. He could tell from the dark silhouettes of the palms that this was hardly the Brecon Beacons.

They started off, walking at a reasonable pace, but not so fast that they lost their sensitivity to the rest of the world. On either side of the road open countryside dotted with trees and the occasional low building stretched away into the distance. Behind them a dim glow in the sky over Serekunda announced the imminent moonrise.

After about ten minutes McGrath slowly moved his right arm up and down to signal a slow-down. Caskey caught him up, and took a look through his binoculars. Two hundred yards ahead of them, where several buildings were clustered under a group of palms close to the road, a number of vehicles were parked. Between them Caskey could make out a neatly sandbagged emplacement, which probably contained a machine-gun. Some way off the road, and shielded by a house from the enemy's view, four men were sitting round a fire. As Caskey looked one of them dragged on his cigarette, turning it into a miniature flare.

He passed the binoculars to McGrath, who took a look. 'They're Senegalese, all right,' he whispered. 'Not much of a war zone, is it?'

'No point in spoiling their rest,' Caskey observed. 'Right or left, do you reckon?' he asked, looking first to one side, then the other.

McGrath tried to remember what the area looked like in daylight. 'Left,' he said finally. 'I don't know this area well, but I think they've put in a golf course just up ahead, and on the other side of that we should find the approach road to the Bakotu Hotel. From the back of the hotel there's a path leading down to the beach. If we go to the right it'll cut down the distance, but we'll probably end up scrambling over garden walls in Fajara.'

'Left it is. Lead on, MacDuff.'

They crossed an expanse of difficult broken ground. The huge orange moon now looming behind them offered little help, but did manage to throw an almost malevolent sheen over the landscape. In some areas the surface was decidedly swamp-like, and Wynwood found himself imagining strange creatures lurking in the ominous ooze.

It was with some relief that they emerged onto a beautifully cut green, complete with a flag announcing that it was the third hole.

'Fancy a quick round?' McGrath asked Caskey.

'On the way back, maybe.'

Wynwood and Franklin rolled their eyes up at each other. There was only one thing crazier than an SAS trooper, and that was an SAS officer. Or, as in McGrath's case, an ex-SAS officer.

They traversed the third fairway, crossed the low fence which separated the tee from a narrow road, and waited for a moment, ears straining to pick up any sounds not made by nature. There were none. In the distance they could now hear the murmur of the ocean.

A quarter of a mile or so away several pinpoints of light suggested habitation. 'The Bakotu,' McGrath said. 'It has its own generator.'

They followed the road in that direction, still strung out in a line some fifty yards from head to tail, and then closed up on McGrath's hand signal. The hotel was now about a hundred yards distant, and with the aid of the binoculars Caskey picked out two men with rifles on sentry duty. They were standing facing the main entrance, obviously considering it their job to keep the tourists in rather than anyone else out. Caskey forced himself to wait five minutes in case there were others patrolling the grounds, but none appeared. He nodded to McGrath to continue.

They skirted the outer edge of the hotel car park, all the time keeping an eye on the backs of the sentries. Even if they had turned round it was doubtful whether they could have seen the SAS patrol, but they did not. McGrath led the way through a gap between two outbuildings, cautiously opened a squeaky gate, and found himself skirting a swimming pool. A discarded bikini top was floating on the water – clearly someone was still enjoying their holiday.

An arched doorway at the rear led out onto the footpath he remembered, which wound steeply down through trees to the beach. Checking to see that the others were still with him, he started off down the slope.

The tide was out, which was fortunate. If it had been in, the beach would have been impassable in several places between there and their destination. McGrath felt momentarily disappointed in himself for not remembering such an important element at the planning stage, then brought his mind back to the job in hand.

The beach seemed empty in both directions. The half beneath the low cliffs was still in shadow, but the flat sands stretching down to the sea were bathed in moonlight. Walking would be easier down there, McGrath thought, but they would also be plainly visible to anyone watching from above. They would have to trudge through the shadows.

All four men hunkered down in a circle.

'We're about a mile and a half from the nearest point on the beach to the rebel HQ,' McGrath said.

'And how far from the beach is that?' Wynwood asked.

'Only a hundred yards or so. There's a line of buildings – hotels, restaurants, embassies – between the beach and the road, and then the Field Force depot is on the other side. It looks like an American children's camp – all cabins and trees – except that it's also surrounded by a high wall. There's a fire station next door with a high tower.'

'Any questions?' Caskey asked.

'Yes, boss,' Wynwood said. 'If we run into someone what's the policy?'

'Avoidance if possible,' Caskey said. 'We don't want anyone knowing that we've recced this route if we can help it.' He looked round at the others. 'Anything else?'

There were no questions. McGrath led off along the sand, using any firm ground at the foot of the cliffs he could find, and the rest of the patrol followed, making sure that the spaces between them were both wide enough and irregular.

As Tail-end Charlie, Wynwood would occasionally spin round on his heel to check the area behind them, but no one came into view. This beach was as empty as his own favourite stretch of sand would be in the depths of winter. Nearly every summer of his childhood Wynwood's family had taken their annual holiday in one of the caravan parks around Tremadoc Bay, and at least once each trip they had all walked the six miles across the sands from Criccieth to Portmadoc, getting up such an appetite that the fish-and-chip supper which invariably followed tasted as good as anything on earth.

He sighed at the memory. Somehow he was finding this trip hard to take seriously. They had been whisked away from Britain to live in a palace, had been served a sumptuous dinner by more attendants than Lady Di had had at the Wedding, and had then been treated to an exposition of McGrath's *Boy's Own* exploits. Now here they were walking down a moonlit beach with palms waving overhead. Wynwood half expected to see Biggles roar by in a bi-plane. It felt as if he had come a hell of a long way from Armagh in not much more than forty-eight hours.

Up ahead of him Franklin was keeping his eyes peeled on the clifftops to his right, thinking about Sibou Cham, and asking himself the same questions most people must have asked after meeting her. Like – what was a beautiful, talented girl like her doing in a place like this? He smiled to himself. He already knew the answer – she was making the best use of her talent. Not in terms of her own material gain, and probably not when it came to her own development as a doctor, but undeniably the best in terms of other people's needs. She had simply put herself where she could make a real difference to the largest number of lives.

He wondered whether she had a political axe to grind and decided probably not. She just wanted to do her job and do it well. Like he did. Race never got in the way of doing your best. He realized he wanted to talk to her about these things, that she might . . . not have an answer for him, exactly, but maybe some clues. Just a little wisdom, as his grandmother used to say whenever she was asked what she wanted for Christmas. Just a little wisdom.

Some twenty yards further forward the moonlit sands were also bringing out the philosopher in Caskey. Nights like this were the reason he had loved his military career – the sense of freedom, the sense of being on the edge, the overwhelming sense of being utterly alive. Nothing compared with it, nothing at all, not even the day's news that Botham had done it again. Certainly not sex, which always came with such distressing side-effects – like having to deal with someone else's emotions. The only downside of nights like this was that they cast everything else into their shadow. He would go back to England, continue his military career for a few more years, hang around in pubs reminiscing about old times, watch the cricket. There were many enjoyable ways to pass the time. The trouble was, that was all they did, just pass it. On a night like this, with life and death at stake, every moment had to matter. And did.

As lead scout, McGrath's responsibilities included

picking out their route and keeping an alert eye for any rebel presence up ahead. He was enjoying himself every bit as much as Caskey, and sharing in the same realization that for him this much-loved way of life would soon be over. He would be forty in a couple of months, and though he was as fit as he had ever been, he knew that time was running out for his legs and his reflexes alike. In this job anything less than the best was not good enough.

He was also feeling the pull of home, and knew that the arrival of the three men behind him had done something to make that pull real again. He missed his wife and children, but then he always had – this was something else, a feeling of being tired of places where he felt alone. Sure, he had made friends in The Gambia – he had made friends wherever he had been in the world – but no matter how much he liked people like Sibou Cham or the Camaras he knew a gulf lay between them, a gulf that prevented him or them from ever growing close enough to . . .

The fire leapt into view as he rounded the small headland, causing him to stop in his tracks and inch his way back over those few feet of sand which inertia had carried him across. No shout came after him, no bullets. He signalled Caskey to stop, and walked back to meet him, his mind recreating a picture of the scene around the corner.

The four men gathered in a circle once more, this time deep in the writhing shadows of trees which swayed on the cliff edge above them. 'There are two men – I think they're both in uniform – sitting by a fire in the middle of the beach. Sitting on upright chairs, I think.' McGrath held his arms out, palms upwards, in a gesture of apology. 'I only had a split-second glimpse.'

'Weapons?' Caskey asked.

'One was holding something. Something shiny. I'd guess a rifle, but only because that's all I've seen up to now. It could be an SMG.'

'Suggestions?' Caskey asked them all.

'Is there no way past them?' Franklin asked, looking up. The cliff, though only about fifteen feet high, was virtually sheer.

McGrath shook his head. 'Not that I know of. Not unless we go back a ways and risk the road. And they're bound to be patrolling that.'

'Frankie, how do you feel about impersonating a local?' Caskey asked. 'You could probably get close enough to get the drop on them.'

'He doesn't look like a local,' Wynwood said. 'He's too damn tall, for one thing. And the clothes are all wrong.'

'And if they ask me anything in Mandinka I'm finished,' Franklin said, trying to keep his voice level. He did not want to turn down Caskey's request, but there was something about it that he really resented.

'How about two of us impersonating a couple of tourists?' McGrath suggested. 'Drunken English tourists.'

'I do a convincing drunken Welsh tourist,' Wynwood said.

'No kidding,' McGrath said wryly.

'Why not three?' Caskey wanted to know.

'Two's better,' McGrath insisted. 'Three will look too threatening. We want to look friendly. Very friendly.'

'OK,' Caskey said, looking at him and Wynwood. 'The parts are yours.'

'Who dares wins,' McGrath murmured.

They made sure to start singing some way before they turned the corner. Wynwood opened with a heartfelt chorus of 'Land of My Fathers', but soon decided to join in McGrath's spirited rendition of Abba's 'Knowing Me,

Knowing You'. They rounded the end of the headland, two arms about each other's shoulders, two waving wildly at the sky. One of the latter contained a bottle which McGrath had found under the cliff.

'Knowing me, knowing you, AHAAAA, there is nothing we can DO! . . . We just have to face it this time – WE'RE THROUGH!' they bellowed in different keys.

The two uniformed Field Force men were on their feet, and yes, McGrath noticed, they had been sitting in the middle of a beach on two upright wooden chairs. One of them started shouting at the two drunken tourists; something about going back to their hotel.

Wynwood and McGrath staggered on, vocally reaching for the sky.

'In these old familiar rooms, children will play . . . Now there's only emptiness, nothing to say . . . KNOWING ME, KNOWING YOU!'

One of the Field Force men was now laughing at them, his Kalashnikov pointing at the ground, while the other continued to shout at them, brandishing his in their general direction.

'Constable!' McGrath boomed, waving the bottle. 'Have a drink!'

They were only a few feet away now. Wynwood disentangled his arm from around McGrath and put it over his face, as if suddenly stricken by a dizzy spell. Then he opened his mouth as if to yawn, all the time watching McGrath, who had the man with the upraised gun to deal with.

The Englishman did not bother with subtlety. One minute he seemed to be offering the bottle, the next it was crashing down on the African's head. The other Field Force man's eyes were still bulging with surprise when the edge of Wynwood's hand came down on the side of his neck. The eyes could apparently bulge no wider, and he slid to the ground.

'May the Field Force be with you,' Wynwood murmured.

'Nice work,' McGrath said, examining the two men. 'They'll both be out for a while,' he added. 'But let's ice the cake a little . . .' He took a hip-flask from his pocket and began easing small amounts of whisky down the unconscious men's throats. 'No one'll believe their story if they smell of booze,' he explained to the other three.

'Good one,' Caskey said. 'And then . . .'

A shout from behind turned all their heads round, and there, coming down a flight of steps that had been cut in the cliffs was a third Field Force man. He seemed to realize his mistake at almost the same instant, and for what felt like several seconds appeared to hang motionless, like a cartoon character who had just run off the edge of a cliff.

Then he managed to put himself in reverse, and started scooting back up the steps.

'Frankie,' Caskey said, turning to where the black trooper had been standing, but Franklin was already off, racing across the sand and leaping the bottom three steps in one bound before the Field Force man had regained the top. And as he hurled himself up the steps Franklin's mind seemed to be on automatic, asking and answering questions like a computer talking to itself. Did the man he was chasing have a gun? Yes, he did. What had the man seen on the beach? Three white men and himself standing over his two comrades. Looking sober. Looking like they knew what they were doing. Conclusion: this man should not be allowed to report what he had seen.

Franklin reached the top of the steps, from where a pathway led up through a grove of trees towards the road. The man was fifteen yards ahead, and not a good runner. Franklin knew he would catch him within fifty yards.

The African must have known it too from the swelling sound of Franklin's boots behind him. He stopped suddenly and turned, raising the Kalashnikov to his eye and firing wildly. Bullets seemed to zip past Franklin's face, and as one part of his mind was registering disbelief at the fact that he had not been hit, the other was pulling the Browning from his holster, making sure his legs were slightly bent, locking his arms, and pulling the trigger.

The man's knees buckled, and he sank to the ground without making a sound.

Franklin walked forward to where he was lying, suddenly hyper-aware of the sounds around him: the waves rippling on the beach below, the breeze in the palm fronds above, the footsteps behind him.

It was Wynwood, who looked down at the corpse thinking, this is real all right. This man is as dead as the men in that lane in Armagh.

'We'd better get him back down to the beach,' Franklin said. 'I can manage,' he added, and used a fireman's lift to get the body across his shoulder.

'I'll keep watch up here for five minutes,' Wynwood suggested, 'just in case somebody comes to investigate.' It was hard to believe that the burst of automatic fire had not alerted someone, but he had no clear idea how far they were from the rebel HQ. And the breeze now seemed to be blowing offshore, which could only help.

Down on the beach Caskey and McGrath were waiting. 'Nice work,' Caskey told Franklin grimly. 'I wonder . . .'

'The tide's out almost as far as it goes,' McGrath said. 'If we take him out another twenty feet, and weigh him down with a rock or two . . . He only needs to stay hidden for a couple of days.'

They did as he suggested, completing the task just as Wynwood came back down from the clifftop. 'Nothing,' he said.

Caskey breathed out noisily. 'Then let's get moving again,' he said.

They left the two unconscious Field Force men by their glowing fire. Caskey had wondered whether they should be killed as well, but decided against. It might not be the right decision in military terms, but killing men who were already unconscious did not seem like cricket. Even the way the Australians played it.

Ten minutes later they reached a point which McGrath judged was level with the rebel HQ, and he scrambled up the sloping cliff to check his bearings. Away above the trees in the distance a bright light could be seen shining. There was only one place it could be – in the fire-station tower. They were in the right place. He signalled the others to join him.

They found a narrow passage between walls which led in the direction of the road, and cautiously advanced along it. A pile of crates containing empty Coca-Cola bottles suggested they were outside a restaurant or a hotel, and when they were no more than twenty yards from the road an archway led off the passage into a thatch-covered area full of seats and tables. The wall between this and the road was composed of blocks arranged in a geometric pattern, through which the moonlight cast a chequer-board of shadows.

Through the spaces they could see the front gates of the Field Force depot, across the road and some twenty yards to their left. As far as outside movements were concerned it was an ideal observation spot, and for the next hour they used it to log the frequency of both the perimeter patrol and the jeep which seemed to be tracking backwards and forwards between the Sunwing and Bakotu ends of the road.

There was no need to spy out the layout inside the depot – there were loyal Field Force officers to provide such details, and probably architectural plans somewhere or other – but it would be more than useful to know in which particular building or buildings the hostages were located. Such information could only be obtained by either surreptitiously seizing control of the fire-station tower – which would probably prove impossible – or sending someone over the wall. Without any clear idea of the layout within, and with the two men on the beach liable to wake up within a few hours, Caskey reluctantly ruled out the latter option as far as this particular night was concerned.

They went back the way they had come, down to the beach and back along it, passing the unconscious men beside the dying fire. The tide had turned and the moon was now high in the sky, dimming the stars.

They met no one on the path up from the beach, heard nothing as they went past the sleeping Bakotu Hotel, and decided sleep was a more pressing priority than a round of nocturnal golf. The jeep was waiting where they had left it, the Senegalese checkpoints manned by the same soldiers, who seemed to have no curiosity as to where they had been.

Shortly before two in the morning they dropped McGrath off outside the Carlton Hotel and roared back down Independence Drive to their palace.

11

It was scarcely seven o'clock when Franklin woke up, and far from fully light outside. Wynwood was snoring contentedly in the other bed. Franklin turned over and tried to get back to sleep, but the dawn chorus of birds in the Palace grounds was even louder than Wynwood.

Make the most of it, a voice inside his head told him. He would probably only be in Africa for a few days.

By the time he had bathed, dressed and got himself downstairs, the new day had established itself. There was only a single uniformed guard beside the doors in the wide entrance hall. One of the benefits of a coup like this one, Franklin guessed, was that you knew where your enemies were. For a while, anyway.

The guard smiled at him but said nothing. Franklin walked out into the morning, and shielded his eyes against the sun piercing through the trees almost directly ahead of him. Where should he walk to? Did it really matter?

He strolled down the drive to the gates, where two Field Force men did bother to examine his authorization before offering friendly smiles. He asked them which way to the centre of town, was pointed in a vaguely southerly direction, and set off.

The hospital where Sibou worked already seemed open for business, and he thought of dropping in to see her as she had suggested, but on reflection decided that this probably was not the ideal time. He kept going, turning left onto Independence Drive and walking past a small building which claimed to house the National Museum and a medium-sized Christian church proclaiming itself a cathedral. Several people were on the street already, either just walking to work or busying themselves outside their premises on the other side of the street. It felt more normal than the day before, less like a ghost town.

For the first time that morning he let himself think about the man he had killed the night before. The man who was now rotting in the Atlantic surf. He had had no choice. None at all. Saying it, he felt like a character in a Western, but it really had been a case of 'him or me'.

He found himself wondering if the man had a wife or children, and then stood there for a moment, unclenching his fists, telling himself that he was being stupid. This was the sort of thing that happened in wars and revolutions. The dead man had put his own life on the line the moment he picked up the Kalashnikov.

Franklin sighed, and became aware of the world around him again. Two boys, neither of whom could have been more than six years old, were staring at him.

'Have you got a pen?' one of them asked.

Franklin's hand went automatically to his pocket, although he knew he did not have one. 'Sorry, no,' he said. 'What did you want to write?'

The child who had asked looked up at him as if he was mad. 'For school,' he said. 'A pen?'

Franklin held out his arms to indicate he had none.

'Give me something,' the other child asked.

The only thing Franklin had was money, and that only in notes that were worth a pound or more each. Why not, he thought. It was Her Majesty's money; or Jawara's – he was not sure which. He gave them both a note, and watched their faces go through a bewildering range of expressions, of which disbelief, contempt and joy seemed the most dominant.

They did not stop around for him to change his mind.

He watched them hurry back across the street and into the grassy area beyond, both clutching their notes for dear life. For all he knew he had launched two children on a lifelong career as beggars. Or maybe he had given their families food for a week. Who knew? Maybe the doctor could tell him.

He retraced his steps, walking slowly to savour the strange sights and sounds, and purchased a bag of what looked like pastries from a roadside vendor. Back at the Palace he found that Caskey and Wynwood were no longer in their suite. The guard in the entrance hall pointed him towards a plain door underneath the palatial stairs, from which a narrower staircase led down to the staff quarters.

He was standing at the bottom, wondering which way to go, when the sound of Wynwood's laugh provided him with the necessary directions. Three rooms down he found the Welshman and Major Caskey sitting on one side of a huge wooden table, talking with a large African woman in a gorgeous blue and white robe.

'Coffee?' she asked Franklin.

He nodded and produced his pastries.

'I think he'll do,' Wynwood said to Caskey.

'He brought the buns,' Caskey admitted, 'but it was us who found the coffee.'

'True.'

'The Morecambe and Wise of the SAS,' Franklin said, sitting down. 'I can hardly see the join,' he added, staring at Wynwood's hairline.

'This hair has been in my family for generations,' Wynwood said indignantly.

'Who was the last owner to comb it?' Caskey asked with interest.

Wynwood spluttered into his coffee.

'You are supposed to drink it,' the African woman

told him sternly, as she placed a steaming cup in front of Franklin.

'To business,' Caskey said, once she had gone. 'The first thing to say is that we don't seem to have received our invitations to the Senegalese Embassy. I have a feeling this is one of those parties we're going to have to crash.' He smiled. 'Fortunately, it may also be one of those where the host will be too embarrassed to throw us out once we've got our feet inside the front door. So I suggest we just turn up at the Embassy in . . .' – he looked at his watch – 'in an hour or so. Sound OK?'

'We all like parties, boss,' Wynwood said.

'Right. The next question is deciding what we want from the Senegalese. I did some thinking last night, while we were coming back from our stroll, and it seems to me that one of our squadrons could wrap this all up in an hour or so.'

The other two tried not to eye him too warily. Both troopers knew that Caskey had a reputation for taking big risks. Usually with considerable success.

'We don't have a squadron with us, boss,' Franklin observed.

'No, so we'll have to create one on the spot. Look, the route we took last night – it seems to me that there's no reason why sixty men couldn't arrive opposite that depot the same way we did. And if they kept going straight through the gates, then, provided we knew exactly where the hostages were, we could have them out of there while most of the bad guys were still wondering what woke them up.'

'Where do we get sixty men, boss?'

'We borrow them from the Senegalese.'

Wynwood and Franklin both looked doubtful. 'They're not . . .' Wynwood started to say.

Caskey had anticipated the objection. 'We'd have to

give them a rush training course,' he admitted, 'but they are professional soldiers. A few hours' instruction from ours truly, and . . .' He shrugged. 'We're not dealing with a professional enemy here. Think about it.'

The other two did just that. Caskey was the one with the experience, and he was probably right. There was no doubt his plan went to the heart of the matter.

'Will the Senegalese buy it?' Wynwood wondered out loud.

'Will Jawara?' Franklin asked. 'It's his family that's under the gun.'

'Let's ask them,' Caskey suggested.

It turned out that a meeting was scheduled for ten a.m., though whether they would have received any notification of it before the afternoon remained a moot point. As it was, the SAS men's arrival could have been taken as evidence of their possessing a thought-reading capability.

But if General N'Dor was surprised to see them he did not show it. He introduced the SAS men to his second in command, Colonel Aboubakar Ka. The younger man seemed happier to see the British soldiers, offering his hand to each of them with a wide smile. 'I have heard much about your Regiment,' he told Caskey.

Five minutes later Jawara's Vice-President arrived, and the meeting got under way. Colonel Ka confirmed that there had been no substantial change in the overnight situation, and the General then asked Caskey for any thoughts he might have.

'We have come up with a possible course of action,' Caskey said. He recounted the story of their reconnaissance mission the previous night, notably omitting any mention of their unexpected encounters on the beach, and then went through the plan he had already outlined to Wynwood and Franklin.

General N'Dor's face remained mask-like throughout, but Colonel Ka's seemed torn between enthusiasm and something less sympathetic. The Vice-President showed no sign that he was even listening.

'Let me understand this,' N'Dor said in his awkward English, and then aimed several sentences in French at Ka, who replied in kind. 'You wish to train sixty of my soldiers?'

Caskey was nodding, but Franklin saw what had happened, and jumped in. 'We wish to give them special training for this special operation,' he said.

The General looked at Ka, who again told him something in French. This seemed to mollify N'Dor somewhat.

Caskey had also caught on. 'This is not a comment on your troops, General. If they were regular British soldiers we would still want to give them special instruction for an operation like this.'

'*Alors*,' N'Dor said. 'Good.' He looked at them for a moment, then at the table, then at Ka. 'I think there is no problem with this,' he said at last. 'But you understand, the negotiations are Number One. If they fail, or if there is no progress for many days, then we will consider the action you suggest.' He turned to the Vice-President. 'This is acceptable?' he asked.

'The President does not want any action taken which will unnecessarily put the hostages at risk,' he said, as if reciting a line he had learned off by heart.

It was what N'Dor wanted to hear, at least in so far as the three Englishmen were concerned. If anyone was going to take decisive action he wanted it to be his own men, led by his own officers.

He looked at his watch. 'I shall be talking to the

terrorist leader in ten minutes,' he said. 'He may have something new to offer.'

In the Field Force depot's command room Jabang was receiving a report from Taal.

'They made no attempt to advance during the night,' Taal said. 'And there is no sign of any this morning.'

Jabang's eyes lit up. 'Stalemate,' he said contentedly. 'So.' He got up and started pacing to and fro across the bare wooden floor. 'Do we try and force them back?'

'Not unless you want to start killing the prisoners,' Taal said.

'Not unless I have to,' Jabang muttered, as if to himself. 'So what do I tell this General? And how do we know that Jawara will accept any deal the Senegalese make?'

Taal shrugged. 'We get him to make a public announcement. And we've already agreed what to ask them for . . .'

'No deadline?' Jabang asked.

'No.'

'OK.' He took a deep breath and picked up the phone. 'Get me the number now,' he told their man at the Bakau exchange.

It rang almost immediately – once, twice, three times. Jabang was beginning to think the idiot had got him a wrong number when someone at the other end answered, and the gruff tones of General N'Dor barked 'yes!?' in Wollof – '*waaw*!?'

'*Jamanga fanaan*, General,' Jabang said.

'Good morning,' N'Dor echoed, with an equal lack of sincerity.

'I would like to commend you on moving your troops back as we requested,' Jabang said.

N'Dor said nothing.

'Let me be completely honest with you, General,'

Jabang continued. 'Our coup has failed. Not because the people of The Gambia wanted it to fail, but because the leader they do not want had already arranged to have a foreign army on hand to put him back in power. I . . .'

'I am not interested in political speeches,' N'Dor interrupted him.

'Of course not,' Jabang agreed sardonically. 'What soldier can afford to be? The point I am making is that we are realists here, not starry-eyed idealists who wish to die in a blaze of glory. We accept that this time we have failed.'

'We can agree on that much.'

Jabang ignored the sarcasm. 'We would like transport for three hundred men,' he said. 'However many planes that requires. And of course free passage to the airport. If this is arranged then we will release all the hostages – with the exception of Lady Jawara and the wife of the Senegalese envoy – at the airport. Lady Jawara and Madame Diop will be released when we reach our destination.'

'Which is?'

'That has not yet been finalized. But the planes must carry enough fuel for a four-thousand-mile journey.'

Cuba rather than Libya, N'Dor thought. 'Is that all?' he asked.

'That is all,' Jabang agreed.

'Then I will pass on your demands to my government, and to the government of The Gambia. I would guess they will have decided their reply by this time tomorrow.'

Jabang said nothing for a moment, wondering whether to challenge the length of time. No, he decided. 'We shall be waiting,' he said, but could not resist adding: 'and the hostages too.'

There was a click at the other end as N'Dor hung up.

'When?' Taal wanted to know.

'This time tomorrow. Do you think they will buy it, Junaidi? Surely the man wants his children alive more than he wants us dead?'

Taal shook his head. 'I don't know,' he said. 'I don't know.'

Some six miles to the west N'Dor was recounting the conversation to Ka, the Vice-President and the three SAS men. Caskey had originally asked if he could listen in on the other line, so as to get some idea of what sort of man they were dealing with, but N'Dor had refused, ostensibly because there was no point in an Englishman listening in to a conversation in Wollof.

'There were no new threats?' Caskey asked.

'They still threaten to kill the hostages,' N'Dor said.

'But there are no new deadlines?'

'No.'

'And no deadline for providing them with their planes?'

'No.'

'They are bluffing,' Caskey said.

'Why do you say so?' Ka wanted to know.

'If they had any intention of really killing the hostages then they would be tying themselves to deadlines, and killing one each time we failed to deliver. They are deliberately not putting themselves into a corner where they have to kill somebody. Because they don't want to.'

'You are not suggesting these are model citizens?' Ka asked with a smile, translating his remark into French for the General.

'Of course not. They may have just worked out that a dead hostage is no use to anyone, including them. As long as they don't do anything too barbaric,' he went on, 'they are giving us the chance to say – well, they're not so bad, why not let them go?'

'You may be right,' N'Dor interjected. 'And if you are, then it seems less risky for the hostages to continue the negotiation, *n'est-ce pas*? If we follow your plan to attack the depot they may start killing in the panic.'

'I think we could have the hostages safe before there was any chance of that,' Caskey insisted.

'Maybe,' N'Dor said in a tone that implied the opposite. He stood up to indicate the meeting was over. 'Colonel Ka will give you the men you need for this special training,' he said. '*Pour l'éventualité*. But I do not think we will need this operation.'

An hour later four lorries containing sixty-four Senegalese troops rolled up outside the Victoria Sports Ground, which Caskey had chosen as the only available piece of open ground in the immediate neighbourhood. While waiting for the Senegalese to arrive, however, he had become more aware of its primary disadvantage – openness to the public eye. Too many people seemed to be hanging around its edges wondering what the Englishmen were doing.

'You're a runner, Frankie,' Caskey said as the Senegalese disembarked. 'How about taking this lot for a run while Joss and I find somewhere more private for the training? We need some idea of how fit they are.'

'OK, boss. A couple of miles enough?'

'Perfect. Take them on a tour of sunny Banjul.'

Caskey gathered together the NCOs, explained what was happening, and handed them over to Franklin. He led them off at a jogging pace, down Leman Street towards the centre of the town. The streets still seemed half-deserted, but those Gambians who were up and

about all stopped to stare at the sight of a man in
civilian clothes leading sixty-four African soldiers down
the middle of the road.

He took them down about three-quarters of a mile,
cut through to the river, and led them back up Wellington
Street. Several men were breathing pretty heavily, but it
was a hot and humid morning. No one had collapsed
with exhaustion or fallen far behind. They were fitter
than Franklin had expected.

Back at the Sports Ground, Caskey had disappeared
and Wynwood was busy loading two tins of paint, one
red and one orange, into the cab of one of the lorries.
'Let's get them all aboard,' he told Franklin. 'It's prison
for them,' he added with a straight face.

Caskey returned, and they set off in convoy for Banjul
Prison, which he had managed to borrow from the
authorities for their training ground. On the way he
explained what he had in mind. 'This has to be a
belt-and-braces op,' he began, 'because that's about
all we've got. Guns and half a dozen stun grenades.
We didn't bring anything fancy with us, and there's
sod-all chance of finding anything around here. So . . .
that's the bad news. The good news is that the enemy is
probably no better off. We're not likely to be worrying
about remote detonations or anything like that. It'll just
be in and at 'em.' He paused for breath. 'Now as you
two youngsters probably know, the most likely way to
get shot in these situations is by your own side. And that
goes for the hostages too – they're more likely to get shot
by one of their rescuers than they are by the terrorists.
So what we need to do with this lot is just concentrate
on making them aware of what they should be shooting
at and how. With the aid of those tins of paint we can
turn one of the cell blocks here into a rough copy of the
Killing House back home. No fancy mirrors of course,

and no live targets either, but it should give them an idea. OK?'

'Yes, boss,' the other two said in unison. Both were secretly impressed.

They arrived at the prison, met and overcame the warden's expected resistance to their plans – 'but who will pay to have the cells redecorated?' – temporarily transferred the two murderers to the female wing, and lined up the Senegalese for Caskey to explain the morning's activities. He had to do this twice, since none of the Senegalese admitted to not understanding his French until after he had finished. The second time round one of the NCOs translated, although exactly how well no one was sure.

In the meantime Franklin and Wynwood had been busy painting figure outlines on cell walls in both red and orange, the idea being that the red ones represented the enemy, while the orange ones stood for the hostages. The Senegalese would be expected to fire bullets into the trunk of each rebel without injuring any of their captives. Since the two colours were not that dissimilar, particularly in light conditions which varied from cell to cell, it would not be an easy task.

The Senegalese seemed to enjoy it though, and by the afternoon had shown a substantial improvement. The morning's training had decimated the hostages, but in the session after lunch – which arrived by Senegalese mess lorry, and which proved considerably less tasty than the meals-on-wheels Wynwood's grandmother received – only two were killed.

Shortly after lunch the architectural plans Caskey had been waiting for arrived by motorcycle, and he used one cell wall and the remainder of the paint to copy out a large diagram of the Field Force depot layout. Through the afternoon groups of Senegalese were brought in to familiarize themselves with the basic layout, so that when more detailed information became available it would be easier to assimilate.

By five o'clock Caskey was well satisfied with the day's work. He reckoned that these men were capable of doing the job that was required of them, and was pleased to find that both Wynwood and Franklin agreed with him. The problem, he already knew, would be persuading General N'Dor to let them try.

Night had almost fallen by the time Franklin had washed all the dust out of his body and hair. He stood at the palace window rubbing himself with a large towel, watching the last vestiges of the tropical sunset being consumed by the darkness. Having put on his last set of clean clothes, he looked around the bathroom for something to wash the others with, thinking that in a palace there should be someone to do the laundry for him. 'And just who did you have in mind, boy?' he could hear his mother say.

He smiled to himself and used the hand soap to wash out some underwear, socks and a T-shirt.

Caskey had gone off to fill in McGrath on the day's events, and God only knew what the two of them would be getting up to. Franklin would not put it past them to invade Senegal, replace the Government, and have the new lot recall N'Dor, just so they could lead the charge on the Field Force depot.

And why not? Franklin asked himself.

As for Wynwood, he had gone off to the Atlantic Hotel to try and ring his wife. An exercise which would probably take up all of his evening and half the night.

Franklin rinsed out the washed clothes, hung them on the shower rail and went back to the window, wondering what to do. Who was he kidding? He had spoken to only two other people in The Gambia, and he had no desire to drop in on General N'Dor. Still, the thought of visiting the doctor made him unusually nervous.

She probably would not be there, he decided, as he walked out through the palace gates and across the road to the hospital entrance. But she was, and even flashed him a quick smile over the heads of the half-dozen or so patients waiting for her attention. He settled down in the reception area to wait – something for which the Army had trained him well.

After about fifteen minutes she suddenly appeared at his shoulder, and sat down beside him, smelling faintly of disinfectant. 'I can't talk for more than a moment,' she said. 'We seem to be having a busy evening, though . . .'

'Can I help at all?' he asked.

She gave him a doubtful glance.

'We each have an area of expertise,' he said. 'Mine's medicine. I mean, I'm not a doctor, or anything, but I can do basic tasks . . .'

'I never turn down offers of help,' she said. 'If you're sure . . .?

'A soldier's life is nine-tenths boredom,' he said. 'I'd be happy to.'

'You can read vital signs?'

'Yep.'

'Then follow me.'

For the next two hours he took temperatures, read pulses and checked blood pressures on all the new arrivals, and when required helped with the application of dressings. Most of the patients had the sort of complaints that a GP might have dealt with in England, but there were also several real emergency cases, like a woman who had just bloodily miscarried and a man who seemed to have had a mild stroke. The only evidence of the political emergency still in progress came from a man with a three-day-old bullet wound that had become infected.

While he worked Franklin observed the way Sibou dealt with the patients, watched her rummage for drugs in an impossibly disorganized cupboard, and listened in on her end of conversations with other parts of the hospital. One of the latter would long stick in his mind: she was saying that yes, she knew there were no beds available, but that this new patient – the woman who had miscarried – had to have one, and that so-and-so, who was going to be released on the following day in any case, would just to have to spend the night in 'the chair with arms'.

It was gone nine o'clock when the last patient had been dealt with, and the concertina door pulled shut.

'What happens between now and morning?' Franklin asked. 'If there's an emergency?'

'You mean, if an ambulance brings someone in from one of the villages?' she asked.

'Yes . . . oh, I see what you mean.'

'If someone rich cuts his finger off by accident then he takes a taxi to his private doctor. He'd never use this hospital anyway. And in a country with no ambulances and not many telephones someone poor who can manage to get himself to this hospital in the middle of the night either lives just round the corner or probably doesn't need treatment that badly. There are people here who can deal with the exceptions, but it only happens about twice a year.'

'Like the last few days.'

'Fortunately we don't have that many coups,' she said, taking off her white coat and hanging it on the back of her office door. Underneath it she was wearing brightly tie-dyed African trousers and a dark-blue shirt.

'I haven't eaten,' Franklin said. 'Would you like . . .?'

'I have my supper,' she said, indicating a plastic box. But she did not feel like dispensing with his company, not for a while anyway. 'I'll share it with you,' she said.

'What, here?'

'We can take it to the beach. It's only a five-minute walk.'

It took even less. The moon had not yet risen, and the horizon between sea and sky was black meeting black. The only light came from the stars, with the Milky Way hanging directly above them like a dim but particularly beautiful fluorescent tube.

'Do you often come out here?' he asked, as they sat down side by side in the sand, facing in the direction of the dark sea.

'In the daytime. I bring my lunch out here when I can. After dark it's not so safe any more.'

'Was it ever?'

'Oh yes,' she said, surprised that he should ask. She handed him something which was similar in size and consistency to a vegetable samosa. 'This was an incredibly peaceful country until recently,' she said. 'There was hardly any crime at all.'

'What changed it?' Franklin asked between bites. Whatever it was, it tasted good.

'Who knows? Most of the world seems to be going the same way. Maybe it's just that more people are aware of what they haven't got, and can see no good reason why other people have. I don't know . . . Frankie is your name, isn't it?'

'That's just a nickname. Worrell is my real name.'

'Where do you come from, Worrell?'

'Brixton. In south London.'

'I know it. I was a medical student at Guy's, near London Bridge.' As she said it, she wondered what

207

had made this man want to be a soldier. He seemed too gentle in some ways – in fact, if his work that evening was anything to go by, he would have made a fine doctor. She found herself wondering what his touch would be like, and scolded herself. This was just loneliness talking, a voice in her head said. Then let it talk, another replied.

He broke the silence. 'I want to ask why you came back here,' he said, 'but I think I know the answer.'

'You do?' She flashed a challenging smile in the darkness.

'You can do more good here.'

'Maybe that's part of it,' she said. 'Maybe a big part. I guess I'd like to think so. But it's not everything. I am a Gambian, an African. This is my home. It may not be a very rich or rewarding home in some ways, but it still feels like one. And in any case we can't all be born in London or Paris.'

'I was born in Jamaica,' Franklin said.

'Do you want to go back there?' she asked.

'I left it when I was three. England is my home.'

'You don't sound very enthusiastic.'

'You've lived there – you know what it's like.'

'You mean the racism? I guess I've forgotten. Or maybe I was lucky. Medical students live in a world of their own, and they come in all colours. What about the Army? You seem to get on all right with the others . . .'

'I only just met them, but yes, the Army's OK, most of the time. How long have you known Simon McGrath?'

'A couple of months. He saved me from an attack. Do you know the story?'

'No.'

'I was in the hospital one evening, and this man came in with a knife. He came to steal drugs, but he was high on

something and he made a spur-of-the-moment decision
that he wanted me too.' Her voice was almost playful,
but Franklin could hear the tension beneath. 'Well, he
hit me a couple of times in the face, and started tearing
off my clothes . . . there were patients watching, but he
told them if they interfered he'd cut my throat. And he
enjoyed the fact that they were watching. Simon came
in at just the right moment, and simply took the knife
away from the man. It was miraculous really. He just
made it look so easy.'

'What happened to the man?'

'He was given five years in prison. But . . .'

'Was he one of the men the rebels released?'

'They released everyone, I think. Yes, he's out there
somewhere. And I can't say it makes me feel very good,'
she added, grasping both arms around her knees and
hugging herself.

He thought about putting an arm around her, but
decided not to. 'I'm not surprised,' he murmured, and
tried to think of another subject.

'Shall we walk for a bit?' she asked.

'Yeah, why not.'

She led the way down to the water's edge, and they
walked along beside it in the direction of the Atlantic
Hotel beach. The two boys from that morning came
into his mind, and he told her the history of the entire
encounter, right up to his over-generous donation. 'I
thought afterwards it was a bad thing to do, but . . .'

'A pen is better,' she said, but the look on her face
seemed to say that he had done the right thing.

'Do you have a boyfriend?' he asked.

'No,' she said. 'I . . .'

'Could I kiss you?' he asked suddenly, surprising even
himself.

'I don't see why not,' she said, and turned into his arms,

laying both of hers across his shoulders and turning her face up to his. In the dim light her loveliness almost took his breath away, and as they kissed the absurd notion went through his mind that he had finally come home.

The kiss stretched out, feeding their mutual hunger for company, sex, love, each other. Franklin felt himself hardening, and for the first time since he was sixteen felt embarrassed by it. He tried to pull himself gently away, but she dropped her hands to his haunches and pulled him back.

And then they were kneeling in front of each other and removing their shirts, kissing some more, and finally sinking onto the sand and kicking their trousers away.

12

General N'Dor arrived fifteen minutes early at the Senegalese Embassy in Cameron Street, lit a cigarette and began pacing up and down the carpeted room. He never seemed to get a moment to himself at the military HQ in Serekunda, and he felt the need of some space to think in. The Embassy staff, unlike his own, seemed prepared to leave him alone.

He was not looking forward to another conversation with Comrade Jabang. 'Never take responsibility for something without first securing the necessary control,' he recited to himself. Where had his memory dragged that up from?

It was certainly pertinent. Here he was, with the responsibility for bringing these negotiations to a successful conclusion, but none of the necessary control. On the contrary, he was being given contradictory 'advice' from all over the place. The Gambian President, not surprisingly, wanted him to be patient, to take no risks with the hostages. Meanwhile his own Government was being pressured by the French, who in turn were probably being urged on by the British, to do something. The European tourists had been deprived of their European comforts for a few more days than they had expected, and wanted to go home. After all he had the famous SAS at his disposal, so why not use them? They had got the hostages out at the Iranian Embassy in London. All but one of them, anyway.

N'Dor asked himself whether he was being unreasonable. The thought of two white men leading sixty black Senegalese into battle seemed so redolent of the past,

211

such an insult to his country, that he found it hard to consider the matter in a purely practical manner. But there were other, less emotional reasons for opposing the Englishmen's plan. This was not London, there had not been three hundred armed men in the Iranian Embassy, and one of them had not been the Prime Minister's wife. Such an assault simply left too much to chance.

He told himself he had to keep an open mind. There probably was no course of action which did not carry serious risks. He simply had to keep a cool head, listen and evaluate.

N'Dor stubbed out his cigarette with a feeling of having reached some sort of conclusion.

The illusion lasted through the arrival of Caskey and the Vice-President, and almost a minute into their meeting. Then the Vice-President announced that he had brought with him the President's counter-offer to the terrorists. Provided that they laid down their arms and returned the hostages unharmed, the President promised a maximum of five years in prison for all former members of the Field Force. He was also prepared to agree a secret deal whereby the twelve members of the Revolutionary Council would be flown into permanent exile.

'Divide and rule,' Caskey murmured to himself. Jawara must have been educated in England.

'What is your opinion, Major?' N'Dor asked him.

'It's hard to say without more information about who we're dealing with. As I said yesterday, my instinct is that they're bluffing. In which case, offering them less makes sense. But, General, your people must have talked to the envoy who was rescued at the radio station – I forget his name. What were his opinions of the rebels?'

'His name is Mustapha Diop,' N'Dor said. 'And it was Colonel Ka who spoke to him.'

'Monsieur Diop seems unable to make up his mind

about them,' Ka said drily. 'They took him on a ride around Banjul to show him how much support their revolution had, and there was no one on the streets. He laughed when he told me the story. But it was not happy laughter, you understand. I think they frightened him a lot. Not so much with their threats, but because he never knew what they would do next. He seems to think they didn't know themselves, but from what we've seen I'm not sure he is correct in that. He is very concerned about his wife and children, of course.'

'Not much help there,' Caskey said. 'There is one thing we should ask for,' he went on, 'an expression of good faith on their part. The release of the children would seem a reasonable request in the circumstances.'

'I am sure the President would wish such a request to be made,' the Vice-President agreed.

'A good idea,' N'Dor said, thinking of his own children back in Dakar.

'It is almost eleven o'clock,' Ka said, looking at his watch.

N'Dor reached for the telephone, thinking that Jawara's offer had at least removed some of the responsibility from his own shoulders. If the rebels responded by shooting the Gambian President's wife, then no one could blame the Senegalese Army.

The phone rang several times before Jabang picked it up. 'You are early,' he said in response to N'Dor's good morning.

'I will call again,' N'Dor said shortly.

'No, it doesn't matter.' There was a momentary pause. 'Do you have the President's answer to our ultimatum?'

'We were not aware that it was an ultimatum,' N'Dor said. Jabang sounded on edge this morning, which was hardly a good sign. 'We consider this a negotiating process,' he added, 'a bargaining process without a fixed time limit.'

'We are in no hurry,' Jabang said, more coolly. 'Call it what you like. What is the answer?'

'The answer to the first demand is no, as it always is in a bargaining process,' N'Dor said calmly. 'But . . .'

'We are not discussing the purchase of a piece of cloth,' Jabang interjected coldly.

'Of course not. There are many lives at stake – those of the hostages you hold, yourselves and your men, my own men. I am not treating this matter lightly, Mr Jabang.'

There was silence at the other end.

N'Dor decided to continue. 'President Jawara is prepared to allow the twelve members of your Council free passage out of the country, and a maximum term of five years' imprisonment for all former members of the Field Force. All this depends on the unconditional surrender of all weapons and the absolute safety of the hostages. We would also like you to demonstrate your good faith by releasing all the children under the age of fourteen.'

The silence at the other end continued for what seemed an age, but was probably no more than fifteen seconds. 'I will call you back in an hour,' Jabang said, and hung up.

McGrath had spent the morning nursing a hangover and continuing his reluctant readjustment to civilian life. On the previous day, while the three current members of the SAS had been introducing the Senegalese to the joys of continuation training, he had been trying to gather information on how much damage had been wreaked on The Gambia's infrastructure by a week of political turmoil.

Not a lot, apparently. There might be well over a thousand dead according to the latest unofficial reckoning, but only two bridges and one electricity line were down. Another triumph for underdevelopment, he thought sourly.

His thoughts slipped back to two nights before, and the reconnaissance mission behind the rebel lines. It might have been a thousand times as dangerous as sitting behind a desk, but it had not felt half so much like work. He shook his head, which turned out to be a mistake.

'More coffee,' he muttered to himself, and was busy spooning Nescafé into a chipped mug when Jobo Camara came through the office door.

'Wasn't expecting you until next week,' McGrath said.

'I'm not here to work,' Jobo said with a grin. 'But my shoulder is OK, and I will be in tomorrow. Today is just a social visit – I came to see how the English hero of the radio station is doing.'

'I've become a legend in my own time, have I?' McGrath asked wryly.

'Don't worry about it,' Jobo told him, 'there are no plans for a statue. Not yet, anyway.'

McGrath laughed. 'They should put up one of that Senegalese with the wicked back-heel. It would make an interesting tableau.'

'My uncle told me about that. I'm going to see him now, at the police station. Want to come along?'

McGrath looked down. Whatever Mansa Camara was doing, it was bound to be more interesting than the stuff lying on the desk in front of him. 'Sure,' he said, 'I'll give you a lift.'

During the two-minute drive Jobo filled in McGrath on his uncle's sudden elevation to the position of Field Force commander in the capital. 'It must have been the radio station capture,' Jobo said, 'though I guess my uncle had a good reputation before the coup. Anyway, the President just promoted him on the spot.'

It was unlikely to be a long-lasting position though, as Mansa himself explained over coffee in his new office. 'That is the worst of this business,' he said. 'The Gambia has never had an army, but now we will have one. So that the next time this happens the President will be able to use his own troops rather than the Senegalese.' He grimaced. 'Always assuming that next time it is not his own army mounting the coup.'

'Uncle!' Jobo protested.

'What, boy?' Mansa asked. 'You expect me to forget about truth because the President gives me a good job? I'd rather go back to the village.'

'The Gambia will still need a police force,' McGrath interjected diplomatically.

'Yes, of course. But something good has ended. Maybe . . .'

There was a knock on the door, and a Field Force officer burst in, excitedly clenching his fists in front of him. 'It has been seen,' he cried. 'Sir,' he added as an afterthought.

Mansa was halfway out of his seat. 'Where?' he asked.

'In the Albert Market.'

Mansa was reaching for his uniform jacket.

'What has been seen?' McGrath asked.

'The mobile radio van that the rebels have been broadcasting from. We have been looking for it since Saturday.' He was on his way out of the door. 'Mr McGrath, I'm sorry to leave so suddenly but . . .'

They followed him down the stairs to where five men were waiting, all carrying Kalashnikovs. Mansa strode out through the door, beckoning the three men after him.

McGrath followed at a more leisurely pace, sorry to be missing out on whatever excitement was about to take place. He need not have worried — this was obviously the week for his guardian angel to keep him in the thick of things.

On the other side of the door he found Mansa waiting patiently for someone to bring a vehicle round. A few seconds later an officer emerged at a run from around the building. 'All the cars are out,' he told Mansa, who stood there looking like he could not believe it for a good ten seconds.

'You can borrow the Ministry jeep,' McGrath offered, 'provided you also borrow the driver.'

Mansa rolled his eyes at the sky. 'Yes, yes,' he said.

A minute later they were careering north along Wellington Street, McGrath and Mansa in front, three men in the back, and two more clinging to the sides.

'What does it look like?' McGrath shouted.

'Just a small Leyland truck. It has Radio Gambia written on the side, or at least used to have. If it's transmitting there will be an aerial . . .'

McGrath took the left fork onto Russell Street on two wheels, narrowly missing a lorry going in the opposite direction. There was no aerial, no Radio Gambia on the side, but it did look as though it had been recently painted, and it was a Leyland. He slowed sufficiently to make a U-turn without losing his passengers.

'What are you doing?' Mansa asked in surprise.

McGrath pointed at the truck, which was now about a hundred yards ahead of them. 'That's them,' he said, hoping to God he was right.

'Are you sure?'

'Ninety per cent,' he said, 'but there's one easy way to find out.' He rammed his foot on the accelerator and simultaneously sounded the jeep's horn. The driver in front took a sudden right turn, and then left at the next crossroads, before accelerating up Buckle Street past the fire station.

McGrath was now only fifty yards adrift. Both vehicles were doing about sixty, which was quite a speed for a main street that was only about half a mile long.

The van slowed dramatically to turn, shrinking the distance between them and giving McGrath a glimpse of two worried African faces in its back windows, then accelerated away. A rifle went off almost in McGrath's ear – one of the Field Force men had got overexcited and shot out a shop window. Mansa shouted at the man to sit down, and McGrath had a mental memory of Keystone Kops films he had seen as a child.

The van turned again, and again. This chase could go on indefinitely, McGrath thought, or at least until one of them ran out of petrol or misjudged a corner. And sooner or later some hapless civilian was going to step out onto the wrong street at the wrong time.

And then the driver in front made his mistake. Maybe he did not know Banjul as well as he thought he did, or maybe he just lost concentration at the wrong moment, but what he expected to be an open street turned out to be full of market stalls, with only a narrow, tunnel-like space between them. He negotiated this with aplomb, scattering pedestrians and bringing down at least two stalls in his wake, but the lack of an obvious path out of the area was his undoing. Reaching open ground he instinctively accelerated, only to find that the street in question ended about twenty yards later, on the ramp that led onto the River Gambia ferry.

Since, by order of the Senegalese authorities, the ferry was still anchored in midstream, the driver of the Leyland van had only his brakes to stop him. These squealed furiously but in vain, and the van skidded over the edge of the ramp and into the water with a mighty splash.

McGrath pulled the jeep up some ten feet short of the edge, and its occupants leapt out to scan the river for the van's occupants. Three at least had managed to get out, and were swimming sheepishly towards the waiting arms of the law.

The van itself was no longer visible, unless one counted the series of large bubbles it was sending to the surface.

Rebel Radio had gone off the air with a vengeance.

In the command room of the Field Force depot the atmosphere was a strange mixture of the electric and the funereal. Eleven men were sitting round the room while the twelfth kept guard at the door. No doubt some of their men could have been trusted to overhear the Council debate Jawara's latest offer, but no one could be certain of knowing which they were.

Jabang had decided to hear the opinions of the other Council members before expressing his own, a decision which he now realized had been a mistake. Three men had so far spoken, and all of them were for at least considering the offer, subject to various safeguards. As one of them said: if they handed back the hostages and laid down their arms, what was to stop the President simply having them all shot? He wanted the children as a token of faith, but what was he offering in return?

For the first time since the business had started Jabang felt a sense of despair gnawing at his heart. 'Junaidi,' he broke in, before a fourth man could counsel surrender, 'what do you think?'

Taal sighed and ran a hand through his thinning hair. 'We cannot accept such an offer,' he said straightforwardly, 'and retain any dignity. Or any political credibility.'

'What choice do we have?' Sallah asked him.

'We have several,' Taal answered him. 'We can fight and die for what we believe. We can attempt to escape without first betraying the men under our command. Or we can continue negotiating – I do not believe they can expect us to accept a deal like this.'

'Is there . . .' Jabang began.

'One last thing,' Taal said. 'We should keep all our people informed as to what the other side is offering. Because the other side may tell them anyway.'

'How could they?' Jabang asked, surprised.

'There are radios in the camp,' Taal said. Sometimes he wondered how someone as clever as Jabang could also be so obtuse. 'Of course, we could confiscate them, but that would look like we don't trust our own men.'

'We don't,' someone pointed out. 'Not all of them. And certainly not the prisoners.'

'We should never have released the prisoners,' Taal said quietly. 'I am not blaming anyone,' he added, 'I agreed to the decision at the time.' He paused. 'I have a suggestion. Let us accept the offer of free passage for ourselves, but only on condition that a general amnesty is granted for all those who have been involved. Except for the prisoners. Look at it from Jawara's point of view – he'll have us in exile, and the prisoners to take out his rage on. Which is hardly unjust, for they were responsible for ninety-nine per cent of the killing in Banjul.'

'And if he agrees we can immediately release the children,' Jabang added.

Twenty minutes later only he and Taal remained in the command room for the call to General N'Dor.

'As in any bargaining process,' Jabang began ironically, 'the first counter-offer is also refused. We are prepared to accept the offer of free passage, provided that a full amnesty is granted to all members of the Socialist and Revolutionary Labour Party. In return, we will release all our hostages and take all the former inmates of Banjul Prison back into custody. If you wish to accept these terms, then have the offers of free passage and amnesty announced on the radio at ten a.m. tomorrow, and we will release all the children at midday.'

'You don't wish us to mention the rearrest of the prisoners?' N'Dor asked, managing to keep most of the sarcasm out of his tone.

'That would not be in our interest or yours,' Jabang said coldly. 'Do you have any questions?'

'No, that seems clear,' N'Dor said. He did not suppose for a moment that Jawara would accept such terms, but they were certainly clear.

'Ten a.m. tomorrow,' Jabang repeated, and hung up.

After the unsatisfactory discussion with N'Dor, Caskey had returned to the prison, where Wynwood and Franklin were still attempting to hone the skills of the Senegalese. Some had taken to the course like fish to water, while others had proved more resistant to developing a capacity for instant decision-making. Rank seemed to play little part in this, and the two SAS troopers were busy trying to gather together their best students in the first assault teams without ruffling any feathers.

'No joy?' Wynwood asked, seeing the look on Caskey's face.

'No. I have a feeling the bastard would rather have all the hostages shot than accept any help from us.'

'He hasn't called it off?'

'No,' Caskey admitted. 'But he might as well. How are they doing?' he asked, meaning the Senegalese.

OK, Wynwood thought. 'If the General gave them the chance I think he'd probably end up feeling proud of them.'

Caskey sighed. 'Well, let's keep them at it. We've got nothing better to do.'

For the next two hours they continued with the simulated assaults, noting a steady improvement in their trainees' reflexes when it came to distinguishing hostages from jailers. Caskey was about to call it a day, and wondering whether to try using praise of his troops to change N'Dor's mind, when one of the prison guards – all of whom had greatly enjoyed watching the exercises – came up to tell him that an Englishman was at the gate asking for him.

Not surprisingly it was McGrath. 'Thought you'd like to know,' McGrath started without preamble, 'one of the rebel leaders has been arrested. Apparently just walked across no man's land and gave himself up.'

'Where is he?'

'At N'Dor's HQ in Serekunda. I imagine he's spilling a lot of useful information about his comrades' state of mind, not to mention the layout inside the Bakau depot and the exact location of the hostages.'

'You're not kidding,' Caskey agreed. 'How on earth did you find out – have you got spies everywhere?'

'I have,' McGrath said modestly. 'No, his name's Sharif Sallah, and he used to be number two in the Banjul Field Force unit, so someone at Serekunda must have phoned the Banjul police station with the news. That's where I heard about it.'

'And what were you doing in the Banjul Police Station?'

'Oh, just coming back from fishing Radio Gambia out of the river.'

'What?'

'It's a long story. And I've got to get back. I'll tell you later.'

He disappeared back through the gate. Caskey called over Wynwood and Franklin, told them the news, and announced that he was off to pay General N'Dor a visit.

'Good luck,' Franklin said.

'Be tactful,' Wynwood advised.

Caskey considered this advice as he drove the jeep across the Denton Bridge, and decided to hell with it. If the defector, whatever his name was, had any information which made it either easier or more imperative to launch their operation then he was going to tell General N'Dor so. And if the General did not like it, he could stick it up his Senegalese arse. And Caskey would take it straight to Jawara.

Diplomacy was for the diplomats.

At the Serekunda HQ General N'Dor was less than pleased to see Caskey, and angry that someone should have informed the Englishmen of the rebel defection without express sanction from himself, but he remained as politely dour as ever.

'Colonel Ka is interrogating him now,' he told Caskey, who immediately asked if he could join the interrogation team.

The General could think of no good reason for saying no, and a minute later Caskey was being escorted by an NCO out into the yard behind the building, where Colonel Ka was sitting behind a collapsible table in the shadow of a huge baobab tree. A few yards in front of him, and sweating profusely in the fierce sun, the defector perched uneasily on an upright wooden chair.

Things were not going quite the way Sharif Sallah had wanted. He realized now that he had acted somewhat precipitately, but sitting there in the Field Force depot command room, listening to Jabang and Taal throw away what seemed like their last chance of escaping retribution, he had inwardly succumbed to panic. If they would not accept Jawara's offer, he had reasoned to himself, then that was their affair. There was no reason why he should have to pay for their determination to martyr themselves. Why should he not simply accept the offer for himself?

He had waited half an hour and then simply asked one of the drivers to take him to the front line. The man had not thought to question him, for he was, after all, one of the leaders. And the rebel soldiers at the front had accepted his story that he was delivering a message to the enemy under a flag of truce. He had marched down the road with the white shirt held over his head and surrendered himself.

Once he had been driven to Serekunda, Sallah was told in no uncertain terms that no deal had been struck, and in rather vaguer ones that an unpleasant choice between jail and the noose was still his to make. If he cooperated fully, it was hinted, he might live to enjoy a life in Banjul Prison.

Sallah had not been prepared for this, and, rather than think things through, he had found himself entangled in the coils of self-justification. Since he could not admit to betraying his friends merely to save his own skin, he found it necessary to paint a highly exaggerated picture of his fellow Council members as confused, dangerous and unpredictable. If the negotiations failed, he said, they would undoubtedly kill both the hostages and themselves. He could not be part of such actions, he said. He was and ever had been a revolutionary, he emphasized, but history had always shown that revolutionary change could not be bought at the price of killing women and children.

He was going through this story again when Caskey arrived, and by the second time it had gained something in the telling. Caskey realized Sallah was trying to save his own hide, and thought him despicable on account of it, but he had no reason to doubt the traitor's description of the rebels' state of mind as a mixture of the desperate and the resigned.

'There's no knowing when they'll blow a fuse,' Caskey told N'Dor.

The General did not understand Caskey's meaning, but he had a shrewd idea of what was being said from the Englishman's red face and aggressive tone.

'We have finished the training programme,' Caskey went on. 'They are excellent soldiers,' he added diplomatically. 'All we need to mount the operation tonight is your say-so.'

'That is not possible,' N'Dor said.

'Why not, for Christ's sake?' Caskey asked, rapidly losing the battle to keep his temper in check.

N'Dor eyed him coldly. 'For one reason, *I* am not convinced that yours is the best plan for the situation. And *I* am the man responsible for the conduct of operations, for the lives of my troops and the lives of the hostages.'

Caskey stared back at him. 'Did you ever have any intention of allowing this operation?' he asked.

'It is one of the options,' N'Dor said. 'And that is all.'

Caskey drove back to the prison, where Wynwood and

Franklin had ordered a break in the training programme. 'They've had enough,' Wynwood told Caskey.

'Then send 'em back,' Caskey said. 'It doesn't look like we'll be needing them.' He told them what Sharif Sallah had said, and what N'Dor's reaction had been.

'He wants to do it his way,' Wynwood muttered.

'You can see his point,' Franklin said. 'Even if he's wrong,' he added in response to a glare from Caskey.

Wynwood and Franklin informed the Senegalese NCOs that the day's training was over, and watched them load their charges into the three lorries for the trip back to their camp near the airport. Then they joined Caskey, who was sitting motionless in the jeep's driving seat, apparently watching the sun go down across the distant sea.

'So what now, boss?' Wynwood asked.

'That's what I've been wondering,' Caskey said, making no attempt to start the engine. 'Any ideas?'

The three men sat in silence for a minute or more, each going over the situation in his mind.

'There's no way we could get any of the hostages out without raising the alarm,' Wynwood said. 'Especially children.'

'I have an idea,' Franklin said.

'Go on,' Caskey encouraged him.

'I was talking to Sibou – to Dr Cham . . .'

'I should think a lot of people have had that idea,' Wynwood commented.

Franklin ignored him. 'She told me there's another hospital about a quarter of a mile up the road from the Field Force depot. It's called the Medical Research Centre, and it's part-research establishment, part-hospital. It's run with British Government money, and there are about five doctors from England working there. If we could get some of the hostages – say, Lady Chilel and her children – to pretend they were sick enough to need a doctor, then maybe the rebels would take them to the hospital . . .'

'Why would they not just bring the doctor to the depot?' Caskey asked.

'The doctors could refuse. They'd have to be in on it.'

'If they're English doctors they probably drink like fish,' Caskey conceded, 'in which case Simon will probably know them all.'

'Why would the rebels take the risk, though?' Wynwood wanted to know.

'It won't seem like a risk,' Franklin said. 'This place is behind their lines, so they won't be expecting any trouble.'

'Makes sense,' Wynwood agreed. 'So all we've got to do is call Lady Chilel on the phone and get her to poison her children.'

'All we have to do,' Franklin explained patiently, 'is get to within whispering distance of her and pass over a few laxatives.'

'You mean someone will have to go over the wall?' Caskey said. It was not really a question. 'And the ideal candidate is you, Frankie,' he said. 'You'll be less conspicuous than either of us.'

'I thought he looked like an escaped prisoner the first time I saw him,' Wynwood admitted.

'Mr President,' Caskey began. It had taken an hour and a half's wait, but he had finally secured an audience with the man himself. 'I presume you know what has been going on. We have trained sixty Senegalese troops for a surprise attack on the rebel camp, believing that it is the best way to secure the release of the hostages unharmed. But . . . well, not to beat around the bush, General N'Dor refuses to sanction the operation . . .'

'I have no authority over General N'Dor's troops,' Jawara interjected.

'No, I realize that. And we realize that the operation we planned is a no-go. But given that, we still believe that an attempt could and should be made as quickly as possible to free at least some of the hostages, in particular Lady Chilel and your children. We have another plan which we would like you to consider.'

'This plan does not involve the use of Senegalese troops?'

'No.'

Jawara looked interested. 'Then tell me what you intend,' he said.

13

The three men set out at three in the morning, and the moon was already riding high above the ocean as their jeep sped across the Denton Bridge. The men at the Senegalese checkpoints passed bleary eyes over their authorizations, and wearily waved them on. The walk across the broken ground to the golf course proved a lot easier by the full light of a risen moon.

Down on the beach the sands were being shrunken by the incoming tide, but this time they planned to use the top of the cliffs for at least a part of their journey up the coastline. Phone calls to several of the hotels and embassies which were situated between the road and the sea had confirmed that a broken path did indeed exist, and would offer a way past any sentries on the beach itself.

Predictably enough, there were none. As they skirted the stretch of beach where Wynwood and McGrath had done their Björn and Benny impersonation, only sea and empty sands were visible below. They passed by the foot of the path which led up into the tunnel of foliage where Franklin had shot dead the rebel. He was presumably still anchored beneath the waves, Franklin thought, and blacked out the mental picture which came to mind.

Once installed in the restaurant's covered terrace, the main gate of the Field Force depot filling the view through Caskey's binoculars, the three men set out to construct a timetable for the patrols covering the inner and outer walls. They had an excellent map of the depot's layout, copied from architectural drawings in the Ministry of the Interior's files, and what they hoped was up to the minute information as to who was in which building at that precise time.

Sharif Sallah might have lied to them but Caskey doubted it. The rebel leaders might have decided to move everyone around once they knew of Sallah's defection, but there was only one block of prison cells, and no other obvious place to keep the hostages. With any luck they would still be where Sallah said they were.

Caskey wondered whether General N'Dor had suspected that they were planning something. Probably, he decided. If they had only wanted Sallah's information for the mass assault contingency plan then it could have waited until the next morning, and N'Dor was not stupid. He just did not want white men leading black men into battle.

'There's the inside mob again,' Wynwood whispered. He wrote the time down, made several calculations in the margins of the map, and turned to the other two. 'Not counting the searchlight,' he said, 'there's a four to five-minute window of opportunity along our wall. The next one begins at four-seventeen – which we couldn't make. The one after that should be at four-thirty-one – which we can.'

'Are they that regular?' Caskey asked.

'Within a couple of minutes, so far.'

Caskey turned to Franklin. 'All set?'

'I can hardly wait.'

Wynwood grinned at him. 'At least if you get constipated you'll have some laxatives with you,' he said.

'Yeah,' Franklin said. 'Whose crazy idea was this?' he muttered to himself.

'Good luck,' Caskey said.

'Thanks, boss,' Franklin replied, and was gone, back down the passage to the beach and along behind several buildings to a point where he could approach the road, out of the sight of both the sentries on the gate and the men in the fire-station tower.

He waited a full minute, checking for any movement that might have escaped their attention, and then silently loped across the road and into the shadows of the trees on the other side. He worked his way towards the depot, slipping across the entrance to the fire station, and stopped where he had planned, in the dark niche between the wall and a drunken-looking palm, some thirty yards from the corner of the Field Force depot.

He looked at his watch – another two minutes and the outer patrol should be rounding the corner. The seconds ticked away, past the appointed time by ten, twenty . . . Then he could hear the footfalls above the breeze in the foliage, and the low murmur of conversation. The two men rounded the corner and walked away from him, the down-pointed barrels of their Kalashnikovs gleaming dully in the moonlight.

Franklin moved forward carefully, more intent on silence than speed, and turned away from the road down the side of the outer wall, conscious that for the first time he was in danger of being picked out by the searchlight. Fortunately its current operator seemed intent on drawing lazy patterns across the area, rather than flashing from space to space in the manner of two nights before.

The SAS man counted his paces as he went, and after one hundred and fifteen he stopped, arranged himself behind the trunk of a convenient tree, and waited again. After a minute or so the searchlight beam snaked past him, catching the top of the eight-foot wall, and then swiftly retraced its path, as if the operator had seen something. Franklin tried harder to make himself as thin as the trunk which shielded him, but it proved to be a false alarm. He took a deep breath and carried on waiting.

The patrol on the inner wall were also later than the schedule dictated – almost a minute later. He listened to the sound of their feet grow and fade, gave himself another thirty seconds for luck, and then swung himself athletically up onto the top of the wall. He barely had time to drop down into the depot grounds before the searchlight beam swept past him once more.

The building almost immediately in front of him was, according to the defector, a storeroom. The one behind it should be the barrack block which had been converted into police cells. Sallah had said it did not have exterior guards of its own, but Franklin took no chances, watching and listening from a position behind the corner of the storeroom for a good two minutes.

The patrols apart, the camp seemed to be mostly asleep. He thought he saw a cigarette flare in the distant gloom, and definitely heard someone laugh away to his right, but the cell block seemed devoid of life. Franklin stepped out across the space, hoping that this did not mean the hostages had already been shot.

The cell at the end was supposed to hold Lady Jawara and four of the President's children. Sallah had not known whether it had a window, but the general opinion had been that it should have, and Franklin dearly hoped the general opinion was right.

There was a window, though it was not the one he had imagined. It occurred to him that he had been expecting a space with bars across it, like a jail window in a Western. He had only to pull out a stick of dynamite, light it from his cheroot, throw it through the bars and grin at the camera. Which film was that in? One of Clint Eastwood's ... He smiled to himself in the gloom and examined the real window. It had horizontal bars across the outside, slatted glass shutters on the inside, and a mosquito screen full of holes in between the two. Inside he could hear someone snoring.

He took out his knife and used it to beat a gentle tattoo on the slatted glass. Thinking he heard someone stir he chanced a loud whisper of 'come to the window', but no one came. He tried a little louder with the knife, praying that anyone outside would think it was something caught in the wind.

'Who is it?' a frightened voice asked. One of the children.

'A friend,' Franklin whispered. 'Come to the window so that I can talk to you,' he went on. 'But be very quiet.'

The child came into view – a little girl of no more than five, her lovely large eyes brimming with apprehension and curiosity.

'I have come from your father,' Franklin said softly, 'to give a message to your mother. Can you wake her up for me?'

The girl examined his face, as if she was searching for honesty. 'My father is the President,' she said.

'I know,' he told her. 'I have a message from him for your mother. Can you wake her up?'

'OK,' she said, and disappeared again.

Franklin could hear the child talking to someone, heard someone else groan and mutter angrily, then a loud 'sssshhhh', followed by 'don't you sssshhhh me, girl!' The child's voice started again, and half a minute later the face of Lady Chilel Jawara appeared in front of Franklin. 'Who are you and what is all this?' she asked in a haughty whisper.

'I am a British soldier,' Franklin said. 'Here's a letter from your husband to prove that I'm genuine.' He passed it through the window. 'Read it after I'm gone – I don't have much time. First thing tomorrow morning we want

you to ask them to let your children see a doctor –
Dr Greenwell at the Medical Research Centre up the
road. Tell the people in charge here that he's their usual
doctor. He will refuse to come here, so then you must
demand that yourself and the children be taken up there
to see him. Under guard, of course. Then leave the rest
to us.' He fished in his pocket for the vial of pills. 'These
will give you all diarrhoea and a slight fever,' he said,
'without doing you any permanent harm.'

'After five days of rice and water we already have
diarrhoea,' she said, then shook her head as if unable
to quite believe what was going on.

'Any questions?' he asked, looking at his watch. He
had two minutes to get back across the wall.

She thought for a good ten seconds. 'No,' she said.

'See you in the morning, then,' he said and turned
away. The coast seemed to be clear, and he slipped
back across the open space between the cell block and
the storeroom.

Suddenly a voice called out a challenge. Franklin sank
down onto his haunches and searched the darkness for
its owner. Whoever it was, he neither repeated the
question nor seemed to be moving. He might just be
standing there, waiting to see if Franklin would give
himself away.

He waited, conscious that seconds were ticking, and
that the inside patrol could arrive at any moment.

The voice cursed, and a cigarette end arced across the
darkness, landing some six feet from Franklin. Footsteps
faded into the distance.

The SAS man moved as fast and as silently as he
could to the wall, and was just swinging himself up
when he heard the sounds of an approaching patrol.
His instinct told him it was the one inside the wall,
but he had no sooner reached the top than it became

obvious that instinct had played him false. The two men of the outer patrol were ambling towards him, deep in conversation.

Franklin lay stretched out along the top of the wall, wishing he could become as thin as one of those cartoon characters who had just been run over by a steamroller.

At some punchline the guards snorted with laughter, almost directly under Franklin's perch, stopping momentarily before walking on towards the road. The SAS man found himself offering heartfelt thanks to whatever it was that had amused them. And then, incongruously, he remembered making love on the beach with Sibou Cham. Not now, boy, he told himself. He lowered himself quietly to the ground and followed the patrol towards the road. Ten minutes later he was rejoining Wynwood and Caskey, and giving a mute thumbs-up to the latter's raised eyebrow.

Two hours later Jabang was sitting outside his room, staring blankly up at the mosaic of foliage above his head, dimly aware of the birds singing around him. He had not slept well, and the thought of Sallah's betrayal was still like an ache in his heart. I'd like to wake up now, he told himself, and discover that this has all been a bad dream.

Mansa Nouma, one of the younger men whom he had once thought of as his disciples, suddenly appeared beside him on the verandah. 'Lady Jawara is demanding to see you,' Nouma said apologetically.

Jabang looked at his watch. 'At this hour?' he asked disbelievingly.

'She says her children are dying, and need a doctor.'

Jabang grunted in amusement. 'A likely story.'

'I thought, since the Council may decide on releasing the children . . .' the young man said hesitantly.

'What's this?' Taal said, coming onto the verandah. Nouma repeated himself.

'Let's go and see,' Taal suggested.

They threaded their way between the various barracks to the cell block, and in through the open front doors. At the end of the central corridor a shouting match was already in progress, between two men in Field Force uniform and the redoubtable figure of Lady Jawara.

'My children could be dying,' she shouted, catching sight of Jabang and turning the full force of her wrath on him, 'and these idiots who call you leader say they cannot see a doctor. What kind of men are you that take out your hatred on children? What kind of a revolution did you think you were going to have here, eh? I thought better of you, Mamadou Jabang. Not much better, but better than this. Using children as a shield.' The last words she spat out contemptuously.

Jabang refused to take the bait. 'So you think your children are dying,' he said unsympathetically. 'A third of the children born in the villages don't live to see their fifth birthday. But I don't suppose that comes up very often in palace conversation.'

'Is that a reason to punish my children?' she asked.

Jabang stood there looking at the ground, torn between his lifelong anger and his better self.

'Come in and see them,' Lady Jawara said simply. 'Please.'

The two leaders followed her into the cell, and were immediately set back on their heels by the stench. Two pails seemed almost brimful of diarrhoea. On the floor, two to each mattress, four pale children were laid out.

'Is this how you want your revolution to be remembered?' she asked them quietly.

Jabang turned on his heel and walked back out of the cell.

Taal caught up with him. 'We can't bargain with dead children,' he said.

'No,' Jabang agreed. 'We've got a doctor here, haven't we?'

'Not at the moment,' Nouma told them. 'Two were brought here from the tourist hotels when we had all the casualties, but they've both disappeared since. In any case she wants to see their usual doctor at the Medical Research Centre up the road. An Englishman. She says either he can come here or she will carry the children up to the Centre herself.'

Jabang sighed. 'An Englishman,' he murmured to himself. 'I suppose an outsider might be preferable. Call the Centre and tell – what's his name?' he asked her.

'Dr Greenwell.'

'Tell him ... no ... let me think.' Did they want outside eyes inside the camp? Did they have anything to hide? No ... And then it suddenly occurred to him that it might all be a trick to get someone in, to spy out the land for a possible assault.

He turned to Nouma once more. 'You can escort Lady Jawara and the children to the Research Centre,' he said. 'Take a couple of men with you,' he added. 'And be sure to have everyone back here by eleven.' That was when he was due to speak to the Senegalese commander again.

'Thank you,' Lady Jawara said quietly.

He gave her an ironic bow.

Some four hundred yards to the south, on the Fajara road, the Medical Research Centre had roughly the same number of buildings as the Field Force depot, but in an area about five times as large. Modern one-storey cream and white buildings were arranged around large areas of open grass, with cultivated flowerbeds marking the boundaries between them. It made Franklin think of the TV series *The Jewel in the Crown*. This, he thought, was what the British Empire had looked like.

He was sitting out in front of the building which housed the two wards comprising the hospital section of the research centre. He was wearing a doctor's white coat and stethoscope, listening to a flock of crows cawing in the trees around him, and keeping watch on the distant entrance for any sign of the expected visitors.

He was also thinking that maybe less British money should be going into places like this, and more into places like the Royal Victoria. But what did he know?

The large lizard which had been clinging motionless to the nearby tree stump suddenly scuttled away across the grass, almost making him jump. And at that moment a taxi emerged from the trees around the entrance and headed down the road to his right.

The driver turned left and came to a halt in front of the hospital doors, a few yards from Franklin. Two men climbed out of the front seats, both of them carrying Kalashnikovs. One wore a red T-shirt and black trousers, the other, Mansa Nouma, was dressed in an ordinary blue shirt and jeans. Franklin thought they both looked about twenty.

'Is this the place for Dr Greenwell?' Nouma asked Franklin.

He nodded.

Red Shirt opened one of the taxi's back doors to let out Lady Jawara and the four children.

'Go and find him for us,' Nouma asked Franklin, airily waving the gun's barrel to reinforce his request.

Franklin walked past them and through the doors into the entrance lobby. From there doors to left and right led into the two wards, while straight ahead there was a single large office for the sisters in charge. Dr Greenwell, as Franklin well knew, was waiting in that office. He knocked, went in and gave the doctor the prearranged signal.

By this time the two rebels had brought Lady Jawara and the four children into the lobby. Red Shirt was checking the window onto the men's ward, while Nouma was looking back through the open doors at the grounds outside.

'What can I do for you?' Dr Greenwell asked cheerily.

'She will tell you,' Nouma told him, gesturing with the gun towards Lady Jawara.

'I'm sorry,' Dr Greenwell said, 'but exactly who is it who is sick?'

'All my children. And myself,' Lady Jawara said.

'Then you must come this way,' the doctor said smoothly, gesturing them towards the women's ward.

The two rebels started to follow.

'No, no,' he said firmly. 'You cannot bring weapons through here. You will frighten the patients to death.'

'These are our prisoners,' Nouma said angrily.

'They will still be your prisoners,' the doctor said. 'We are only going to walk through a room full of sick women. Please, either wait here with your guns, or come with us and leave your guns behind. They will still be here when you get back.'

Nouma hesitated, then shrugged his acquiescence. It had been a masterful performance by the doctor, Franklin thought, but maybe they were also getting some help from a lack of confidence in the rebel camp.

The party walked down through the women's ward, Dr Greenwell in the lead, Lady Jawara behind carrying one child, the three other children and finally Nouma and Red Shirt, who seemed unsure of what to do with the hands that no longer held the Kalashnikovs.

At the end of the ward twin doors led through to another corridor, which ran between a series of offices and a line of curtained cubicles. Dr Greenwell opened one of the office doors and ushered in Lady Jawara and the children. Nouma was about to follow when the door closed gently in his face.

'Surprise, surprise,' Wynwood said, as he and Caskey emerged from behind the curtains, Brownings in hand. The two rebels looked round for escape, and found Franklin's Browning also pointed their way.

The day had started badly for Mamadou Jabang, and it did not seem to get any better. He ate the breakfast that was placed in front of him, but not because he had any appetite – his mind was too busy racing through unpleasant possibilities to consider his body's needs. The thought that Jawara might refuse their terms gnawed at him mercilessly, because he could think of no other solution which gave him the chance of life with honour. They could certainly fight and die, as Taal had said, but it seemed such a waste. They could kill the hostages as they had threatened, but he had no real appetite for that either.

After two hours of chasing the same unwelcome thoughts around his brain it suddenly occurred to Jabang that no one had notified him of Lady Jawara's return. With a sinking feeling in his stomach he sent someone to the gates to find out if Nouma and the hostages had indeed come back.

The answer was no. He sat there for a moment, palms together across his nose, wondering how he could have been so stupid. 'Get me the Medical Research Centre on the phone,' he told the messenger.

Making the connection proved easy enough, but Jabang had to threaten sending an armed unit before anyone would admit to knowing anything. Finally a doctor told him that, yes, they had been expecting Lady Jawara and her children for several hours – where were they?

'Are you telling me they never arrived?' Jabang asked coldly.

'That is correct,' the doctor said, with the kind of patronizing English accent that made Jabang want to throttle him.

Instead he simply hung up, and spent an angry few seconds wondering whether to send a lorry-load of men to search the Centre. It would be a waste of time, he knew that. They would not find Lady Jawara. The fat bitch had escaped.

The sound of distant gunfire startled him out of his unpleasant reverie. It seemed to be coming from the direction of Fajara, though it was hard to tell. Another burst seemed to come from the opposite direction, and closer. What the fuck was happening?

Right on cue, Taal appeared through the screen door, buckling the holster over the Field Force uniform he still insisted on wearing.

'What is it?' Jabang asked.

'No idea,' Taal replied, 'and no one seems to be reporting in. I'm going to find out. Why don't you come along? The men would appreciate seeing you.'

That made Jabang smile, partly with genuine pleasure, partly at the irony of it. 'I have to talk to General N'Dor,' he said.

'OK,' Taal said. He nodded his head in the direction of the latest gunfire. 'Though that may be N'Dor talking to us now.'

* * *

It was, albeit with a certain lack of eloquence. After being informed, soon after eight a.m., of the successful SAS swoop to release Lady Jawara and the four children, the General had spent half an hour letting his rage gradually subside. How dare they mount such an operation without his approval? Who knew what might happen to the other hostages in retribution for Lady Jawara's escape?

He knew he was overreacting, and guessed that President Jawara must have sanctioned the operation in person. It was his country, after all, and he had the right to employ whatever foreign help he felt he needed. That, N'Dor realized, was what really hurt – that Jawara had felt he needed more than the Senegalese. And the General knew that this resentment was also irrational. The English had centuries of military tradition, money to burn on training and weaponry, and far more experience of this sort of thing than his own troops could ever hope to have. Even so . . .

The General lit a cigarette and walked outside into the yard, where the giant baobab tree loomed over him like Africa incarnate. It was time to do something, he thought, and the English had at least removed the main obstacle to military action. There might still be thirty or so hostages in the depot, but none as prominent as Lady Jawara. It was time to take a small risk, to give the rebels a push and see what happened. They might fight back one way or another, in which case he could stop pushing. Or they might simply collapse, in which case his Senegalese troops would be the heroes of the hour. Africans sorting out an African problem.

He walked inside to his office, telephoned Colonel Ka, and issued the code-word to activate the contingency plan. Senegalese units would advance on and around the two major roadblocks, and into the area behind them. Flanking forces would liberate the Sunwing and

Bakotu hotels at either end of the Bakau–Fajara road, where over a hundred Europeans had been luxuriously trapped for almost a week.

He went back out to sit in the shadow of the baobab and lit another cigarette. Almost immediately the first sounds of battle drifted in from the north on the warm breeze.

He had been there about half an hour when an aide emerged from the doorway to tell him that the terrorist leader was on the line. N'Dor looked at his watch as he walked in – it was only ten-thirty-five.

'Good morning,' he said in Wollof.

'Who is firing those guns?' Jabang half-shouted at him.

'I don't know,' N'Dor lied. 'Whoever it is sounds nearer to you than to me,' he added disingenuously.

'If it is your troops it will mean an end to all negotiation.'

'If it is my troops, they will be firing in self-defence,' N'Dor said. 'Or without my sanction. You will have no reason to withdraw from the negotiations.'

'I already have one,' Jabang said. 'Lady Jawara was taken to the Medical Research Centre under a flag of truce, and this was violated. What more reason do I need?'

N'Dor resisted the temptation to blame the English. 'Your soldiers drove her straight to an embassy,' he said, 'where they released Lady Jawara and then asked for political asylum for themselves.'

'I don't believe you,' Jabang said automatically. He did find it hard to believe that Nouma would betray him, but then he had felt the same about Sallah. 'Which embassy did they drive to?'

'I can't tell you that,' N'Dor said. 'For obvious reasons. You could simply march in and take Lady Jawara back.'

'I could march into all the embassies,' Jabang retorted.

'You could. But that would damn you in the eyes of the entire international community, so you won't.'

There was a silence at the other end, in which the sound of several muffled voices could be heard.

'Can you please wait a minute?' Jabang suddenly asked with a courtesy that N'Dor found utterly incongruous. He lit another cigarette and waited.

In the Field Force depot command room Jabang, his hand over the mouthpiece, was hearing a report from Taal. 'It's impossible to tell if it was a coordinated attack,' Taal was saying, his eyes shining with excitement, 'but if it was they made an utter balls-up of it. At both roadblocks our men fired a few shots at the Senegalese, more to slow them down than stop them, but on the Fajara road the Senegalese simply retreated to their original positions and on the Banjul road they just turned tail and ran. Another unit which tried to outflank us on the Banjul road was attacked by a pack of dogs. I tell you, Mamadou, it's a farce out there.'

'But why?' Jabang wanted to know. He had never dreamed of news this good.

'They're just disorganized, that's all.'

'So it won't last. You're not saying we have any chance of victory?'

'Oh, no, none at all,' Taal said, crushing the hope that Jabang already knew was ridiculous. 'But it must improve our negotiating position.'

'Yes,' Jabang agreed. He took his hand away from the mouthpiece. 'General,' he said, 'your attack on our positions has apparently failed. You have obviously not been negotiating in good faith, but I am prepared to give you one last chance. I would have asked you to remove your troops to their previous positions, but my fighters seem to have done that for you.'

'I have not . . .'

'Just listen, General,' Jabang said contemptuously. 'I expect to hear President Jawara publicly accept our terms on the radio at ten o'clock tomorrow morning. If this happens, then all the children will be released immediately. If it does not, I shall begin executing the hostages until it does. Have I made myself clear, General?'

'Very,' General N'Dor said. 'But I . . .'

There was a click as the line went dead.

After having delivered Lady Jawara and the children to the British High Commission, the three SAS men had shared a celebratory drink with Bill Myers on the back verandah, and then retraced their path southwards along the beach. They had arrived at the back door of the Bakotu Hotel just as the Senegalese troops arrived at the front. The rebel guards had already vanished. Seventy tourists who had spent a nerve-racking week around the swimming pool reading thrillers were informed that they would soon be able to go home.

All three SAS men were dog-tired, but from what Lady Jawara had told them Caskey thought it more important than ever that General N'Dor sanction the much-postponed assault on the depot. The rebels were disorganized enough for it to work, and maybe desperate enough to do something stupid if left to their own devices.

Caskey was also keen to find out exactly what it was the Senegalese were doing. The officer in charge of liberating the Bakotu seemed oblivious to any other operations taking place, but the sound of gunfire to the north told a different story. Caskey only hoped that N'Dor had not decided simply to storm the depot with troops who had no clear idea of what they were doing.

'I've got a lift with the Senegalese to Serekunda,' he told the other two. 'You two stay here, get a couple of hours' sleep if you can. I'm going to try and persuade N'Dor to give us a green light for tonight.'

'Good luck,' Wynwood said drily.

Colonel Ka arrived back at General N'Dor's HQ with all the enthusiasm of a Spanish Armada admiral returning to Spain. On the ride over from the outskirts of Bakau his memory had served up just about every childhood and adult humiliation it contained, and now, standing on the threshold of the General's operations room, he had to muster up all his courage to simply walk on in.

N'Dor looked up, sighed, and gestured Ka to a chair.

He took it, wondering why the tongue-lashing had not yet begun. A scene from one of those absurd James Bond films came to mind – the one in which the head villain dispatched one of his underlings, chair and all, into a pool full of piranhas. The Colonel found himself involuntarily searching the floor for signs of a trapdoor.

'What happened?' N'Dor asked, his voice more resigned than angry.

'We have taken the Bakotu and the Sunwing,' Ka said. 'So most of the Europeans who were in the rebel-held zone have now been released. But the advance in the centre was frustrated.' He paused, wondering how to explain it.

'By the rebels or ourselves?' N'Dor asked.

'Both,' Ka said. 'But mostly ourselves,' he admitted. 'Either the instructions given were not clear enough, or individual officers failed to follow them correctly. There seems to have been hardly any attempt on the ground to coordinate the various moves.' He sat up straighter in the seat. 'But whatever the reason, the responsibility is mine, and I . . .'

'No, it isn't,' N'Dor snapped. 'It's mine. And if we don't take immediate steps to improve the situation, I shall no doubt pay the price of failure.'

Ka decided it was wisest to say nothing.

'Time also seems to be running out as far as the hostages are concerned,' the General added, and gave Ka a blow-by-blow account of his conversation with Jabang.

'Then we will have to move before ten o'clock tomorrow morning,' Ka said. He hesitated for a moment. 'May I offer a suggestion?' he asked eventually.

N'Dor nodded.

'Our unit which was detailed to take the Sunwing ran into some resistance just outside the hotel. In the forecourt and among the gardens to one side. There was an exchange of fire which lasted something like ten minutes before the rebels made a run for it towards the beach . . .'

'The point?'

'About halfway through this fire-fight two tourists carrying tennis rackets suddenly appeared in the middle of the no man's land between the two forces. I've no idea how or why, but that's not important. The point is that everyone stopped firing, just like that. Our men and the rebels. These two white men walked calmly across the forecourt and two groups of Africans waited until they had gone before restarting their battle.'

'I am sorry, Colonel,' N'Dor said, 'but this does not surprise me.'

'No, sir, but that is not my point. It seems likely to me that the rebel soldiers, like our own, are under strict instructions to avoid any European casualties . . .'

'Probably.'

'General, if we let the three SAS men lead the assault on the Field Force depot it will probably prove successful.

If it isn't, it's their failure. But if it is, we can say that we allowed white men to lead our attack because we knew that the presence of their white faces was likely to reduce casualties among our own soldiers.'

The General looked at him for several seconds with what could only be described as an inscrutable smile, and then suddenly burst out laughing.

N'Dor was still smiling twenty minutes later when Caskey arrived. 'As you no doubt know,' he told the Englishman, 'our offensive has run into some difficulties. I believe the time has come to launch the operation for which you trained my men.'

'Wonderful,' Caskey said, as pleased as he was surprised.

'One request,' N'Dor said, in a tone which made it clear that he was not asking. 'I should like the operation to take place soon after dawn tomorrow – in daylight, that is – as part of a general offensive against all the rebel positions. My regular troops are not equipped for night fighting,' he added in explanation.

'Very well,' Caskey agreed, not wishing to push his luck. In any case, he thought, there were also advantages in conducting their operation in daylight. It would certainly make it easier to tell friend from foe once they were inside the depot.

It did not occur to him that daylight would also make it easier to distinguish black faces from white.

14

Wynwood stopped suddenly, thinking he had heard a sound off to their right. 'Hear anything?' he asked in a whisper.

Franklin shook his head. The twelve Senegalese behind him were bumping into each other like trucks on a braking goods train.

It had probably been a representative of the local wildlife. Wynwood started forward again, moving their line of march in a long arc towards the rear of the enemy position. They had not seen anyone moving for some time, around either the barricade in the road or the houses the rebels were using as their camp, but that did not necessarily mean a thing. For all Wynwood knew the bastards were watching them through binoculars right now, and just waiting until they came into SMG range.

It was not likely though. It had rained for an hour or so in the middle of the night, the ground was soft, the moonlight dulled by high cloud cover. Conditions for a silent approach were almost perfect. And as far as they had been able to tell from observation the rebels had no binoculars.

Wynwood was twenty yards from the first building now, with the rest of the party strung out across the open ground behind him. He passed through the deep shadow of a mango tree, savouring its sweet scent but hoping that a ripe fruit would not drop onto his head.

As planned, the last two Senegalese in line were left by the door of the first building, and the two then bringing up the rear at the next. By the time they reached the back of the house which was being used by the officer in charge of the roadblock, only Wynwood, Franklin and four of the Senegalese remained. Two were left at the back door.

Wynwood reached the front corner of the house and put an eye around it. Four men were sitting round a smoky fire, two in uniform and two not, each with a gun within reach. Two of these were Kalashnikovs, the other two Sterling sub-machine-guns. The Welshman withdrew his head and used a finger to spell out SMGs on the wall. Franklin nodded in understanding. Silence might be a priority but not if it involved looking down the barrel of an SMG. The rebels would not be given any second chances.

'OK?' Wynwood mouthed silently. Franklin nodded again, the two Senegalese simply looked nervous.

The four men walked out into the open space, so naturally that it took the rebels a full three seconds to realize that they were not on the same side. And by that time they had also become aware of the four guns aimed in their direction.

'Stand up and put your hands above your heads,' Franklin said softly but with deliberate clarity, hoping that all four spoke English. Apparently they did. 'Now walk this way and lie flat on the ground. On your stomachs.' They did as they were told.

Wynwood went to pick up the Sterlings, gave one to Franklin, and indicated to the two Senegalese that they should keep their guns on the four prone rebels. Then the two Englishmen took up position at the front door of the HQ house, and Wynwood shouted 'now!' with all the power in his lungs.

There was the sound of doors being pushed open, shouldered open, kicked open, the sound of surprised voices woken from sleep, one crash of broken glass, one drawn-out groan, but not a single shot was fired. Ten

minutes later thirty-five rebels were being led in single
file up the road in the direction of Serekunda, with six
of the Senegalese soldiers in attendance.

If four of the prisoners looked somewhat underdressed
for their night-time stroll it was because Franklin and
three of the Senegalese were now sitting around the fire
in the clothes they had been wearing. Twenty minutes
later, when the four men of the regular rebel road patrol
arrived in their jeep, even the growing light of dawn
was not enough to expose the deception. All four were
arrested without a fight, and sent on down the road after
their comrades. As the first glow of the sun emerged from
the distant ocean horizon one route to the rebel HQ was
wide open.

A mile and a half away, at almost the same moment,
Diba awoke with a start. He lay there for a few moments,
wondering what had woken him, but could hear only
the birds in the tree canopy that covered the depot. His
mouth was dry from the booze, and maybe his brain
was a little fuzzy from the dope. He could still smell the
women on him, which made him feel good. A feeling
spread through him, as strong as it was unreasoned, that
this would be an important day in his life.

It was time to get away from the depot – even
with the sort of entertainment that had been provided
on the previous evening, the place was beginning
to feel more and more like a prison. There was
little doubt that Comrade Jabang and his revolution were doomed, and who knew what the crazy
bastards might do with their backs against the wall.
This lot might be more interested in looking good
and ordering people around than anything else, but
Diba had a sneaking suspicion that they *thought*
they were trying to help humanity, and anyone who

even thought something like that needed their brains washing out.

It was definitely time to put some distance between himself and the comrades, and get started on his own programme. The first thing was to get hold of a decent gun. A Kalashnikov was probably a great weapon for fighting wars, or even hijacking planes, but it did not fit snugly in the waistband of his trousers.

The sun was now clear of the sea, the sky beginning to clear. Caskey, standing up in the turret of the armoured car, looked back along the column of vehicles stretched out on the Serekunda road. Directly behind his vehicle were the four lorries containing their sixty-four Senegalese troopers, and behind them more armoured cars and lorries loaded with several hundred more soldiers. If N'Dor had got his act together a similar force would be launching an attack along the Bakau road in precisely twenty-five minutes.

Feeling a little like Ward Bond in *Wagon Train*, Caskey raised his arm and gestured the column forward. The armoured car jerked forward, almost throwing him off balance, and then settled into a satisfyingly smooth rumble. Caskey grinned to himself. The sun was shining, there was a breeze in his face, gorgeous palm trees waving him by, and he was off to war again. In moments like this he could understand the Sioux going into battle crying out that it was a good day to die.

Not that he expected to die in The Gambia. There would probably be a lot of sound and fury in the next half-hour or so – in fact he was counting on it – but Caskey did not really expect the terrorists to put up much of a show. It would be like sex, he thought – arriving was nice enough but it was the journey which provided most of the excitement.

Two lorries back Franklin was also thinking about sex. Or perhaps love – who could tell? He had not seen Sibou for more than two days, since escorting her home on the night they had made love. On the following afternoon the three SAS men had come across to Bakau for their appointment with Lady Jawara, and they had not been back to Banjul since. He wondered whether she was angry that he had not made contact. Or pleased. Maybe she would rather forget the whole business. After all, what could come of it – with him a soldier in Hereford and her a doctor in The Gambia?

He tried to put it all out of his mind. The Senegalese soldiers packed alongside him were mostly sitting in silence, some of them nervously chewing their lower lips or breathing deeply. A couple of the men who had taken part in the pre-dawn capture of the roadblock unit were in his lorry, and they seemed more relaxed than the others. It was all about confidence, as his athletics coach had told him over and over again.

They had been travelling for several minutes now; they had to be near the disembarkation point. Right on cue, the lorry started slowing down, and then turned right through the familiar gates of the Medical Research Centre. If the rebels had heard the approaching vehicles, then with any luck they would assume that they were on hospital business.

The Senegalese troops dismounted, and formed up in a column of pairs behind Caskey, Franklin and Wynwood. There was a lot of nervous grinning now, a clutching of amulets and the odd bow in what was presumably the direction of Mecca. At Caskey's signal the column started off, with the Englishman at the front maintaining a steady jogging pace along the stretch of bare earth which adjoined the right-hand side of the road. They had about four hundred yards to go, which at this pace translated into not much more than two minutes.

It felt longer. The trees which leant across their path offered some cover, particularly if the Field Force depot sentries were in their usual position just inside the gates, and the sound of a hundred and thirty-four feet was more muted than Caskey would have believed possible, but sooner or later someone was bound to become aware of their approach.

They were more than halfway now, and he was beginning to feel the pace a little. By this time the armoured cars should be on the move behind them, the plan being that they should become audible at exactly the same moment as the first assault team became visible. 'Hit 'em with everything at once,' was Caskey's motto, and preferably at speed.

The gates were only a hundred yards away now, and the fire-station tower leapt into view above the trees, but still no shots or cries of alarm rose up from the rebel stronghold. And then suddenly one of the sentries ambled out across the road and into view, looking as if he had not a care in the world. For several seconds he seemed engrossed in rolling a cigarette, but either the movement or the sound of the runners must have caught his attention, because his head jerked round and his mouth dropped open. The cigarette slipped from his grasp, he looked around wildly as if in search of somewhere to hide, and then half-ran, half-scrambled his way back towards the gates.

Through the entire pantomime not a sound escaped his lips. It was his fellow-sentry who raised the alarm, letting out a blood-curdling shout at the same time as he opened fire with his Kalashnikov, apparently at the trees across the street.

The moment the alarm went up, Caskey had told his

men, make as much noise as an entire fucking army. They now obliged, firing their Kalashnikovs and SMGs into the air with wild abandon, and shrieking like a bunch of hyperactive banshees. The drumming of their feet on the road suddenly seemed three times as loud, as if someone had accidentally knocked the volume control.

The ambling sentry had already disappeared, the one with the gun took one appalled look at what was coming towards him and bolted out of sight through the gates. Caskey was about twenty yards behind him, shooting through the open gateway in a half-crouching run, braced for the impact of whatever it was the rebels had to throw at him.

There seemed to be nothing. Figures were visible in the distance, some already running for cover, some foolishly just standing there, curiosity getting the better of their survival instincts. Thanking their lucky stars, the SAS men and the Senegalese troops spread out in the prearranged pattern, still running, with the leading twenty men heading straight for the last-known location of the hostages.

Jabang had, as usual, been sitting on the command office verandah when the first shot rang out. Instinctively, he knew what was happening, even before the sudden, tumultuous outburst of gunfire and shouting which came on the first shot's heels.

He walked quickly inside and picked up the light sub-machine-gun which Taal had got for him, and stood there for a few seconds, holding the gun and staring blankly into space. Then he strode purposefully through the command room and out of the building's front door. About a hundred yards away he could see men in uniform running in what looked like all directions. The Senegalese.

He became conscious that several of his own men were standing around him, all carrying guns, all looking at him and waiting for his orders.

He did not know what to tell them.

There was a loud explosion away to his right, in the direction of the cell block. The hostages were being released! Jabang started off instinctively in that direction, his men dutifully following him, but almost immediately found himself face to face with Taal.

The military commander, who had neither shirt nor shoes on, was carrying only an automatic pistol. 'Get to the back gate,' he told Jabang, 'it's the only way out.'

Jabang looked at him as if he was a creature from Mars.

'Go!' Taal shouted at him.

Jabang went, collecting more and more men as he went. The mad burst of gunfire which had started the attack now seemed reduced to the occasional shot, and at the gate Jabang could see many of his men already hightailing it into the distance across the stretch of mostly open countryside. He took one last look back, wondering where Taal was, and then started running for his life down the dirt lane and through the knee-high grass.

For all his determination to be ready when the time came, Diba had the misfortune to be in the middle of his morning shower when the assault team came through the gates. He struggled back into his clothes, grabbed the rifle which he had had the sense to keep with him, and cautiously poked his head out of the washroom barracks, just in time to see two white men race past him, followed by a bunch of Senegalese soldiers.

He pulled his head quickly back, waited five seconds, and tried again. The soldiers were gone. He stepped out, turned a corner and started running like everyone else towards the rear of the depot, swivelling his eyes to left and right for any sign of immediate danger. The parade ground in the centre seemed empty at first, but as Diba loped across it he saw a man emerge from the command offices on the far side, carefully buttoning his Field Force uniform shirt, as if this was the day of all days for being smartly turned out.

The man was carrying an automatic pistol, Diba realized, and he slowed his pace to a fast walk as Taal came towards him, then pulled up the Kalashnikov and blew a bloody hole in the neatly buttoned shirt. Hardly breaking step, Diba let the rifle drop and stooped to pick up the pistol. Now he had a weapon for the outside world.

Not far away Wynwood and Franklin were taking turns smashing the cell locks, and telling the hostages they were safe. Most of them looked undernourished and generally the worse for wear, but it seemed that none had been tortured or killed. In a world like this one, Wynwood thought, be thankful for such mercies.

Outside Caskey was experiencing a mix of emotions. The operation seemed to have been a complete success when it came to safely rescuing the hostages, but most of the rebels had probably escaped, because it had been planned that they should. The normal procedure for an op like this was to have assault and perimeter teams, the latter mopping up what the former flushed out. But this time Jawara and N'Dor between them had vetoed the encirclement of the depot, on the grounds that the terrorists were more likely to harm the hostages if they had no means of escape. Caskey had argued that the assault team would be moving so fast that the terrorists would have no time to realize they even had such options, but he had been overruled.

Still, he thought, looking round at the Senegalese

troops now swarming through the depot grounds, the rebellion was over. They had done what they had come to do. The Gambia belonged to President Jawara once more.

Two hours later General N'Dor gave a press conference under the baobab tree behind his HQ. He confirmed the strong rumour that two British Army advisers had taken part in the attack on the Field Force depot. 'We knew that the rebels did not shoot at white men,' he explained, 'because we had seen white men going and coming even in areas we considered dangerous. The rebels didn't shoot at them because they wouldn't know whether they were diplomats or other personnel, injury to whom could bring down outside intervention on their heads.' The General nodded here, as if he saw the rebels' point. 'Lives have been saved,' he went on, 'and that's what matters. Whether they were saved by white, blue or green men is to us unimportant.'

He offered no explanation as to why the rebels, seeing their last stronghold being overrun, should still be worrying about outside intervention.

By this time the three SAS men had been given a lift by the Senegalese back to the Presidential Palace, where they found the red carpet conspicuous by its absence. The President had apparently removed himself to his bungalow in Bakau, and the SAS men were politely informed that rooms had been reserved for them at the Atlantic Hotel. Their belongings had already been packed and taken across.

'I've heard of overstaying a welcome, but this is ridiculous,' Caskey said.

'At least our bags weren't taken to the airport,' Wynwood said.

Worse was to come for Caskey. From the Atlantic he phoned Bill Myers, who told him that direct communications with London had been established, and that the Foreign Office was less than ecstatic about the SAS unit's elastic interpretation of 'military advice'. They were also wondering why Caskey had not sent back a single report since their departure from London.

'Because we've been too damn busy doing the job we were sent to do,' Caskey said angrily. 'Sorry, Bill,' he added, 'it's not you I should be yelling at.'

'Don't worry about it,' Myers said. 'And your real boss sent you all a "well done".'

'Well, that's something.'

'And he's given you all a week's immediate leave.'

Caskey went back upstairs to tell the others, but both men were stretched out in their rooms, fast asleep. He went to his own room and sat down on the edge of the bed, feeling the familiar flatness of a mission completed.

It was early afternoon before Radio Gambia announced the routing of the terrorists and 'the restoration of democracy and order'. Those few rebels and criminals still at large in the Bakau–Fajara area would soon be captured, the announcer said. All those people who had not yet returned to their work should do so without delay.

Sibou Cham listened to the broadcast in the nurses' common room at the Royal Victoria, and wondered whether Moussa Diba was dead, captured, or one of the 'few still at large'. The odds were on his having been taken, but she had no intention of taking any risks until she knew for certain.

She wondered whether the news on the radio meant she would see Worrell Franklin that evening. It was always possible that she had completely misread him,

259

and that he had no intention of ever making contact with her again, but she did not think so. It had been so wonderful that night on the beach, and she found it hard to believe that he would not be as willing to repeat the experience as she was.

Two hundred or more rebels and ex-prisoners had managed to swarm out through the Field Force depot's back gate, but for most of them it proved to be no more than a temporary reprieve. There were only three ways out of the Bakau area: by sea, across open country, or by road. Few of the rebels had any experience with boats, the open savannah made them sitting targets, and all traffic on the few roads and tracks out of the area was subject to stop and search by the authorities. Not surprisingly, more than half of the escapees had been captured by midday, and a majority of the rest before the daylight faded.

Diba was not one of them. He had immediately realized that the suburbs of Bakau offered a better chance of avoiding detection than open country, and once he had gained the relative safety of populated streets Diba did not make either of the two mistakes most popular with his ex-comrades. Instead of beginning to believe in his own invisibility or instantly seeking out a ride to the haven of the poorer townships, he worked his way across the suburbs and out the other side, to where the mangrove swamps around Cape Creek offered a multitude of hiding places.

Through the rest of the daylight hours he waited, daydreaming of possible futures far from Banjul, and occasionally slipping into sleep for a few blissful minutes. He would wake with hunger gnawing at his stomach, limbs cramped from their confinement within the mangrove roots, and the sun apparently no further across the sky.

At long last night began to fall, and as soon as he judged it dark enough Diba started off on the three-mile walk which would bring him to the Denton Bridge. Working his way along the strip of broken country which lay between the ocean and the road was neither easy nor fast, but this route did keep him clear of checkpoints or patrols, and after less than an hour's walking he found himself looking out over Oyster Creek, the bridge a hundred yards or so away to his right. Beyond it, on the same bank, were the tourist-boat moorings.

He made his way down to the water's edge and began following it towards the bridge, keeping a careful eye on the Senegalese checkpoint at its near end. As luck would have it, a minibus had just arrived, and the soldiers had their work cut out examining the passengers and their luggage. As Diba passed under the bridge he could hear a heated argument start up on the road above — something to do with a chicken, though he had no way of knowing what.

There was no light on the small wooden jetty, and it was difficult to choose between the dozen or so dug-out canoes tied up against it. Diba had never been particularly comfortable in boats, but he was not much of a swimmer, and in Oyster Creek there was always the chance of meeting an undernourished crocodile. He untied the mooring rope of the best-looking craft, climbed gingerly aboard, and managed to sit down without tipping the boat over and himself into the water. Though the argument around the brightly lit bus on the bridge was still filling the evening air, he focused all his concentration on making no sound with the paddle until he was at least halfway across the wide creek.

In midstream he crossed under the bridge, so as to reach the shore on the ocean side of the road. There was no checkpoint on the Banjul end, and he decided to risk walking straight down the unlit road into town. An hour later he was making a wide loop round a checkpoint outside the Banjul High School, crossing Box Bar Road and ducking into the backstreets of Portuguese Town. Another ten minutes and he was slipping through the gate of Anja's compound.

Her room was in darkness, so Diba simply let himself in, anger rising at the thought of finding her with someone else. But she was not there, and neither were any of her things. The room had been stripped bare of everything but the bedstead.

He went in search of neighbours, and found two young men sharing some ganja in one of the other rooms. They looked at him blankly when he asked about Anja, so he dragged one of them across the yard by the ear to jog his memory. It worked, but not in the way he had wanted. Anja, it seemed, had moved out several days ago. And had not given anyone any idea where she was going. She had been frightened of someone, one of the young men volunteered, before realizing that he was probably talking to the frightener.

Diba gave him a contemptuous look and went back to Anja's old room to think. He had been savouring this moment for days, and now it had all been snatched away from him. He needed a woman, he needed to . . . to show someone who he was.

He told himself to calm down and think. His clothes had survived the day without getting too soiled, which was good. His first need was money – enough of it to get clear of the country.

He knew exactly where to go. Halfway down Jones Street, just by the intersection with Spalding, was the home of a money-changer who went by the name of The Christian. Diba had no idea what his real name was, but he did know the man kept his money at home, because he had once tailed him there from his pitch opposite the tourist market. In those days his ambitions had not extended beyond Banjul, and the fear of being identified had held him back from going ahead with a robbery, but now he was on his way out of the country. And in any case, no one was ever identified by a dead man.

He arrived outside The Christian's house, saw a light burning inside, and knocked on the door. The man himself answered it, his eyes growing rounder as he saw the automatic pointing at his chest.

'Get in,' Diba growled.

The man backed away. 'What do you want?' he pleaded.

'What do you think?' Diba sneered, closing the door behind him and bringing the gun up to within an inch of his terrified face. 'I want all the money you keep here, and it had better be a good sum. Or I'll just blow your head all over the wall.'

The man looked into his eyes, and did not like what he saw. 'OK, OK,' he said, 'it's in here, come, I'll give it to you, all of it.'

The money – a thick wad containing assorted denominations of dalasis, CFAs, English pounds, French francs and US dollars – was in a padlocked metal box under the table.

Diba's mouth watered at the sight. 'How much is there here?' he asked softly.

'About two thousand five hundred dalasis – that's almost a thousand dollars . . .'

It was a fortune. 'Turn round,' said Diba.

The man opened his mouth to speak, but decided not to. He turned round, and Diba swung the automatic against the side of his skull with all the force he could muster. After gathering up the money he put an ear against the man's chest to see if the heart was still beating. It seemed not to be, but just to make sure he hit him again in the same place.

He let himself back out into the night, feeling the adrenalin flowing through his veins, a faint throbbing in his head. A woman cast a doubtful glance in his direction as she walked by, and his smile in return only served to hasten her steps.

He needed a woman, he thought. And soon.

McGrath heard a later airing of the same news broadcast as Sibou, and immediately telephoned Mansa Camara's office to find out whether Diba was on the list of those killed or captured. The Field Force man was not there, but one of his subordinates told McGrath that he would try to get him the information. Ten minutes later he called back with the news that Diba had so far not been found, either alive or dead.

McGrath packed up work for the day and drove the ministry jeep up to the Royal Victoria. The reception area was empty and she was sitting in her office, feet up on the desk, apparently deep in thought. She looked up with a start, and he caught a flash of disappointment where he had expected fear. 'Waiting for someone?' he asked.

'No,' she said. 'How are you?'

'As well as can be expected.' He sat down on the edge of her desk. 'He may still be out there,' he told her bluntly.

'I know.'

'So I've come to take you home.'

She smiled at him. 'That's very kind,' she said, 'but – I don't know – I feel restless this evening . . .'

'Then let's paint the town red – what's left of it.'

'Oh . . . I don't know . . . what have your English friends been doing?'

'I don't know the details, but they've been over in

Bakau for the last couple of days. And probably running the whole show, if Caskey had anything to do with it.'

'And now it's over they'll be going back, I suppose?' she said, a little too obviously.

McGrath's face split into a grin. 'I get it,' he said. 'So which one is it? No, don't tell me ... Wynwood's happily married and Caskey's older than I am. It must be our Mr Franklin.'

She rolled her eyes at the ceiling. 'I like him, OK?'

He laughed. 'It's great,' he said. 'I was beginning to get worried about you.'

'You're impossible,' she said.

'So my wife tells me. Anyway, they're staying at the Atlantic Hotel now ...'

'Since when?'

'Since this afternoon. I'm meeting Caskey up there in an hour or so. Want to come? Or would you like me to take your boyfriend a message?'

'He's not ... And I can deliver my own messages, thank you.' She smiled at him. 'But you could drive me home, wait while I have a shower and change, and then drive me over to the hotel.'

'Uh-huh. And what's in it for me.'

'A double whisky?'

'You could have had me for a single.'

'I know.'

Diba could not believe his luck. Not only had the doctor emerged with the Englishman McGrath, but he was able to flag down a passing taxi in time to follow them back to the house in Wellington Street. He saw them enter the front door as his cab went by, and by the time he had paid off the driver and walked back the fifty yards someone had turned on the second-floor lights.

It was an old building from colonial days, and as far

as Diba could tell its bottom two floors were occupied by a daytime business. Certainly there was no sign of life through their shuttered windows, and generally speaking this was a commercial rather than a residential area.

He thought about simply knocking on the door and having one of them open it onto his gun. The trouble was, it might be the woman, and then he would have to find a way to deal with the Englishman. He knew from experience that was not likely to be easy. No, this time he had to be certain, and not give the bastard the slightest chance of a comeback.

Fifteen minutes they had been up there now, and the only reason he had for supposing they were coming down again was the slapdash way the Englishman had parked the jeep, slewed halfway across the road. Diba examined the columned porch, and decided that it would be an ideal spot for an ambush if they did come down again.

He went back into the road, looked up at the lights, and wondered if they were fucking at that moment. It made him feel hot thinking about it.

One light went out, and then another. Diba hurried back into the shadows of the porch and waited for the hoped-for sound of feet on the stairs inside. The seconds stretched out until he was almost convinced that they had gone to bed, and then he heard her voice, sounding almost insultingly happy, and the door swung open. She came out first, and he caught a glimpse of her body profile as she walked past him. The Englishman followed, almost too quickly, but in one motion Diba took a single step forward and brought the automatic swinging down on the side of his head. Not as hard as he had hit the money-changer – he wanted this victim alive, at least for a while.

Franklin examined himself in the mirror, took one last

admiring look at the batik trousers he had just purchased in the hotel shop, and left the room. 'See you later,' he told Wynwood through the Welshman's open door.

'Not if you're wearing those trousers,' Wynwood said. 'Have fun,' he yelled after him.

Franklin smiled to himself as he walked down the stairs. He could get to really like Wynwood, he thought. The Welshman did not get serious very often, but when he did it counted. He knew where the line was between being real and playing games, and in the work they were in it was a good thing to know.

He left the hotel and briskly walked the few hundred yards which separated it from the entrance to the Royal Victoria emergency department. There he received his first shock – it was in darkness. He looked at his watch, which told him it was half-past eight. Somehow he had assumed she would still be working, as she had been on the other days. Why, he asked himself, had he not thought to phone her earlier?

She must have gone home, he decided. He did not have her home telephone number, and he had no certain knowledge of the address, only a visual memory of where the taxi had stopped that night when he took her home. She had not wanted him to come up, and in the street he had been too busy kissing her goodnight to take much note of the surroundings.

But he did remember the name of the street.

Franklin walked down to Independence Drive, still cursing himself for his stupidity, and managed to find a taxi.

He climbed into the front seat. 'Wellington Street,' he told the driver.

'What number?' the man asked.

'I don't know. Just start at one end and drive slowly down.'

The driver gave him an odd look and pulled away. In not much more than a minute they were at the head of the street in question, and about half a mile down Franklin spotted the tell-tale clue – McGrath's Ministry of Development jeep. It was possible that the Ministry had more than one jeep, but highly unlikely that they employed two men with such indifferent parking skills.

It was now about twenty minutes since Diba had knocked McGrath unconscious and pressed the barrel of his automatic between Sibou's lips. Pulling the Englishman up two long flights of stairs had taken up quite a time – the man was heavy and Diba could only use one hand, since the other was needed for keeping the gun on the doctor.

She was worried that McGrath might be dying, but Diba would not let her examine him. In any case, it probably did not matter, she told herself, because the maniac was going to kill them both anyway. She fought back the rising tide of panic which accompanied this realization, and a second – that Diba had been so humiliated at their first meeting that the likelihood of him making any mistake at all was extremely slim.

But he might, she told herself, he might. And if he did she had to be calm enough to make the most of it.

They finally reached her flat on the second floor. After she had turned on the lights he dragged McGrath to the middle of the carpeted floor and then went back to lock the door, all the time keeping the gun pointed at her.

'Nice place,' he said, walking to the open window and looking out. The sky was full of twinkling stars, and the lights of Barra, two miles away across the river, seemed dead by comparison. Tomorrow he would get a taxi from there to the Senegalese border, and try and find some way round the border post. But that was tomorrow . . . He turned back to her.

'The house belongs to my father,' she said, thinking that any conversation was better than none.

'And where is he?'

'He lives in New York. He used to own the business downstairs.'

'And he gave his little rich-girl daughter all these rooms just for herself.'

'There are only two.'

'Two is a lot,' he muttered. His eyes were darting to and fro, as if looking for something. 'Find something to tie him up with,' he told her.

'I don't have anything.'

'Take off that dress and tear it into strips,' he said, grinning.

'I have another dress,' she said, turning away.

'That one,' he said, 'or I kill him now.'

She gave him a contemptuous look, pushed the straps from her shoulders and stepped out of the dress. She was shaking inside but trying hard not to show it.

'I thought about your body such a lot in prison,' he told her.

'It's only a body,' she said, wondering how long it would be before he asked her to remove her underwear.

He tore the dress up himself, and braided several strips until they were strong enough to hold McGrath's wrists together behind his back. Then he used the Englishman's belt to loop his tied wrists to the leg of a heavy wooden table. 'Now you can take a look at him,' he said. 'And bring him back to life. I want him to be able to see it all.'

She knelt down to examine the head wound. It was not as bad as she'd feared . . .

The bell rang in the hallway outside. Someone had pulled the rope at the front door.

'What's that?' Diba hissed.

'Someone at the door,' she said. She could only think of one person it would be, and the sudden feeling of hope almost overwhelmed her.

He stood there, uncertain what to do.

'They'll have seen the lights,' she said.

'Who is it?' he asked.

'I don't know.'

He slapped her with the back of his hand, almost knocking her off her feet. 'I don't know!' she half-shouted.

'Come with me,' he said, grabbing her by the arm and pulling her alongside him out through the door and down the stairs, just as the bell rang again above them.

He stopped and swung her round at the first-floor landing, intending to say how he expected her to get rid of the caller at the door, and remembered she was almost naked. 'Fuck!' he muttered violently. 'OK, you'll get behind the door,' he hissed. 'And if you make a single sound both you and whoever it is out there are dead.'

Franklin had spent a few minutes wondering what to do. Sibou had told him that McGrath was only a friend, and he had believed her, but standing out there in the street, the man's jeep in front of her house, he had begun to fear the worst.

You're being stupid, he told himself. Go and knock on the door.

He found an old-fashioned bell-pull and tugged on it, causing a bell to ring somewhere high in the house. For what seemed like an age nothing happened, so he pulled again, and then footsteps could be heard, which seemed to stop and start again, bringing all his suspicions back to life.

And then the door opened and an African face appeared, that of a man in his mid or late twenties, with a smile on his face and eyes that seemed not to match it.

Franklin had never seen Diba, never heard him described, but in that moment he knew that this was the man who had attacked her, the man whom McGrath had disarmed, and that he was holding a gun in the hand hidden from view behind the door.

Diba, for his part, had opened the door not only prepared for trouble, but also assuming that it would wear a white face. The sight of a man with a black face and batik trousers instantly eased his mind. 'What do you want?' he asked.

'Taxi,' the Englishman said creatively, making a fair stab at delivering both syllables with a Gambian accent. He looked at Diba, waiting expectantly. 'Woman called,' he added helpfully.

'She changed her mind,' Diba said, digging in his pocket and coming up with a five-dalasi note. 'Take this,' he said, and began to close the door.

The other hand was still out of view, and Franklin could not risk setting off the gun by launching himself forward. The door clicked shut, but no footsteps sounded inside. The man was waiting for him to leave before he moved back upstairs.

Franklin walked back down the steps, and turned left up the street, continuing on until he knew he was out of sight of the house. What should he do? The idea of going for the police was quickly abandoned: it would take hours and Sibou might only have minutes. She might already be dead. The thought cut through his mind like a knife.

There was only one thing for it – he had to get into the house, and now. It would have to be the back. He found a way between the next two houses down and stumbled his way through the dark backyard of the one which stood next to Sibou's building. The ground behind the latter was overgrown, the only back door seemed both locked and rusted shut, and the windows were barred as well as shuttered. The verandah on the first floor looked more promising, but it was fifteen feet up, and the wall seemed to offer no help to a would-be climber.

Inside the house Sibou was holding on to the hope that the man at the door had been Franklin. The voice had not sounded like his, but she could not think who else it could have been. She wondered for a moment if McGrath might have phoned for a taxi while she was in the shower, but there would have been no reason – they had his jeep. And anyway, she suddenly remembered, the man had said it was a woman who called.

It had to be Franklin. He would get help or something. She just had to stay alive long enough for it to arrive.

All these thoughts ran through her head as Diba dragged her back up the stairs. At the top he pushed her into the flat and again locked the door behind him.

Franklin, or whoever he went for, would have to come through that door, she thought. There was no other entrance. She would have to distract Diba somehow, make noises to cover any that her rescuers might make. One thought came into her mind and caused her to shudder. She would sooner die, she thought, and then realized she would rather not.

'Wake him up,' Diba said, waving the gun in the direction of McGrath. She dutifully leant over the Englishman and took his pulse, which was surprisingly strong. 'He'll come round in a little while,' she said, and at that moment an almost inaudible groan escaped from his lips.

Franklin had already wasted several minutes looking for something to help him onto the verandah when he discovered the line of iron rungs just round the corner of the building. Silently cursing himself, he started to clamber up as fast as the need for silence would allow, until one rung came half out of the wall and nearly sent him tumbling thirty feet down to the ground.

Moving more cautiously, he reached the level of the top-floor windows. Craning his neck round the corner of the house, he could see dim light coming from both, which suggested that light was filtering through from the room at the front. But he could see no way of reaching the windows from the ladder of iron rungs, and for a few moments he could see no reason whatsoever why the rungs had been placed where they had. Then he realized: the newer bricks to his right were blocking up what had once been a doorway.

He carried on up to the flat roof, pulled himself over the edge and lay still for a second, listening for any sounds that might be coming through from below. There were none. He got carefully to his feet and tiptoed over to the front edge, almost strangling himself on a half-invisible washing line. Here he could hear a voice – the man's – but not what he was saying. And then Sibou, who replied more clearly: 'You'll kill him!'

Putting his head over the edge, Franklin could see the lighted windows below. The shutters were open, and he guessed that the glass windows were too, but there was probably a mosquito screen. The top of the window was about five feet below the level of the roof. He had no harness, but there was little choice.

He went back for the washing line, decided it was

strong enough, and spent a few minutes knotting foot and hand holds at one end. Then he tied the other through one of the holes in the parapet where the water drained off the roof.

He stood there for a moment, thinking that he should have called the police, or someone, before coming up to the roof. If he fucked this up then there would be no help for her or McGrath.

But it was too late to think about that. Just don't fuck up, he told himself, and everything will be fine.

He lowered himself over the edge, walking his feet down the wall inch by inch as he let the rope out through his hands. When he was level with the window he paused, and wondered how many years' wages he would give for one stun grenade. Then he took a deep breath, bent at the knees, and pushed himself off the wall and out into space.

Sibou had told Diba that McGrath needed water, and he had accompanied her into the kitchen while she filled a cup from the tap. She noticed he had an erection, and wondered how long his desire for an audience would dampen his desire for her. Back in the living room she applied water to McGrath's lips and forehead, and was just opening the top button on his shirt when her ears, already straining for any sound from beyond the locked door, picked up the slightest of scraping noises from outside the open window.

She managed not to look at Diba, instead rising to her feet as noisily as she could manage. 'He can see now,' she said aggressively, walking away from McGrath. 'Let's get it over with,' she went on, moving towards the couch, pulling Diba's eyes away from the direction of the window. To hold them on her she reached back to unhook her bra, flicking it off her shoulders and letting her breasts fall free, just as Franklin came hurtling feet first through the open window.

Diba whirled around, tried to raise the arm that held the gun, but found both her hands wrapped around it. He slashed out with his other hand, sending her flying, and turned in time for a final glimpse of the taxi driver from downstairs, perched on his knees, both hands around the butt of an automatic that was aimed between his eyes.

Darkness fell swift as a camera shutter, eclipsing his world.

Epilogue

Caskey and Wynwood set foot again on British soil the following Sunday afternoon, having flown from the reopened Yundum Airport to Luton with a plane full of complaining package tourists. Despite assurances to the contrary from the High Commission in Bakau, their passage through customs and immigration was neither smooth nor speedy. No one at Luton had been given any advance warning of two returning SAS men bearing semi-automatic handguns, and the ensuing phone calls took much longer than the process under way in the main hall, that of relieving the tourists of their duty-free excesses.

Caskey had been half-expecting a posse of journalists, but not even a single newshound was waiting to dog their steps, and the two men ended up boarding the bus for the railway station like any pair of returning holiday-makers. A newspaper left lying on one of the seats gave no clue that The Gambia existed, let alone that anything newsworthy had happened there.

They sat on Luton Station, waiting for the delayed train to London, eyeing their fellow travellers as if they were from another planet. 'We've been gone almost exactly eight days,' Wynwood murmured, 'and it seems like a couple of months.'

'It always feels like that,' Caskey said. 'This time next week it'll feel like three months since we came back.'

The train finally arrived, and while Caskey read the paper Wynwood stared out of the window at the darkening countryside and suburbs, mentally comparing the silhouettes of oaks and poplars with palms and mango trees. Caskey was right, he thought, already Africa was turning into a dream.

In London the MOD had arranged for a taxi to whisk them across town in time to catch the last connecting train from Paddington to Hereford. Wynwood had time to call Susan before it left, and found himself, wholly unexpectedly, almost in tears simply from hearing the sound of her voice.

She brought the car to Hereford Station, and they gave Caskey a lift back to his flat in the centre of town. 'It was a pleasure working with you,' the Major told Wynwood as he climbed out of the back seat.

'It was mutual, boss,' Wynwood said.

Caskey walked slowly upstairs, feeling faintly envious of Wynwood's youth, not to mention the Welshman's obvious joy in being in love. He let himself into the flat, poured himself a generous drink, and sat down on the sofa. The previous Saturday's paper was still sitting on the coffee table, its back page headlining the news of England's inevitable defeat.

He leaned back in the chair and smiled. What a summer it had been!

Late that night Mamadou Jabang and three of his young acolytes arrived in the small town of Cacheu on the river of the same name. After a day holed up in a terrified supporter's house in Bakau they had travelled south in the President's speedboat, which Junaidi Taal had used for his escape from the Denton Bridge a week before, and which the Senegalese had not thought to either guard or remove from the beach beneath the African Village Hotel. The fuel had soon run out, but two days of drifting on the prevailing southerly current, the second without water, had brought them, bedraggled but hopefully

safe, to this estuary town in the small republic of
Guinea-Bissau.

What the next twenty-fours hours held in store none
of them could know. They had no money, and no way
of sending for any. The local authorities might simply
return them to The Gambia, or they might agree to
give them political asylum. Most likely of all, if Jabang
knew anything about his fellow African politicians, they
would choose to do neither. Letting revolutionaries stay
in one's country invited trouble, and sending them back
reminded your own people how oppressive your regime
had become. No, the local authorities would simply find
some way to pass on the problem to someone else.

Through such means, sooner or later, Jabang hoped
to find himself back among friends willing and able to
support him in a second attempt at rescuing The Gambia
from international capitalism.

Next time, though, he would steel himself to be
harder.

Arriving at his office that Monday morning, Cecil
Matheson found a full report waiting for him on the
events of the past two weeks in The Gambia. The *status
quo ante* had been satisfactorily restored, thanks in large
part to the efforts of the three SAS military advisers.

By this account – and by most others that Matheson
had picked up on the Whitehall grapevine – they had
somewhat exceeded their authority. Questions were
also being asked about the activities of a fourth man,
apparently an ex-SAS officer, who had not even had any
authority to exceed.

Still ... Matheson smiled to himself and closed the
folder. Perhaps he should send his American counterpart
a copy, he thought. After the farcical mess they had made
of trying to rescue their hostages from Iran the previous

year, Lubanski and the Pentagon could do with some professional advice.

That same morning McGrath dropped in on Mansa Camara at his home in Serekunda. McGrath still had headaches, but the Medical Research Centre had given him a clean bill of health, provided he agreed to avoid excitement for a fortnight. Chance would be a fine thing, he thought, as he parked the jeep. His SAS friends were gone, and Sibou would not be back for a few days yet.

He found Mansa in cheerful mood, despite the announcement that The Gambia was now to have an official army of its own. 'It's either that or risk the Senegalese Army marching across the border every time there's any trouble,' the ex-Field Force officer said. 'Sooner or later they might just decide it would be easier to keep their troops here on a permanent basis. And if we have to have an army I'd rather it was made up of Gambians. No country deserves an army that speaks another language.'

'So the Field Force is being abolished?'

'Yes.' Mansa grunted. 'Too many officers ended up on the wrong side. Some of them good men,' he added, as if surprised by his own readiness to admit such a thing. 'And there is one good thing about an army. It means the police force can be just that, and not get itself mixed up in politics.'

'Maybe,' McGrath agreed. 'I've been an Army man since I left school, but I was kind of getting used to being in a country where there wasn't one.'

'I noticed,' Mansa said wryly. 'Yes, well . . . Jabang and the comrades wanted to bring about change, and in that at least they were successful – The Gambia will never be the same again.' He shrugged. 'But in the long run I expect all the tourism will change us even more, and not for the better.'

McGrath thought about that as he drove back to Banjul. Mansa was probably right, but there seemed to be very few other ways that the country could earn the money to pay for all those consumer goods which most of its people seemed to want. It was sad, he thought. From what he had seen, the African people deserved better.

It had taken Franklin two days to sum up the courage to talk to Sibou about their relationship, and when he finally did so it came out much more negatively than he intended. 'I know you can't give up what you do,' he said, 'and I can't give up what I do. How can we keep anything alive when we live and work three thousand miles apart?'

She had looked at him for a moment. 'Do you want to keep it alive?'

'Yes, but . . .'

'There are things called planes,' she said. 'If you're coming from England, The Gambia is the cheapest place to get to in Africa. And that works both ways.' She had taken him by the shoulders. 'It won't be easy, and it may be impossible, but we can try. What have we got to lose?'

He had her to lose, he thought that afternoon, as they sat together on a stone wall overlooking the ocean. They had come to the Île de Gorée, the island off Dakar which the man in the French café had recommended to him and Wynwood, and which she had visited and loved several years before. Most tourists came over on the ferry, visited the famous Slave House, shopped for souvenirs, walked along the bougainvillaea-covered lanes, and returned to Dakar a few hours later, but there was one hotel on the island, with three high-ceilinged rooms and shuttered windows that opened onto a view across the beach and jetty.

Now they were sitting at the rear of the red-stoned Slave House, above the cells where hundreds of thousands had waited in suffocating squalor for a voyage to the New World. Here was where their two lives divided. His ancestors had been taken, and hers had not.

'Did you read that report,' she asked, 'the Senegalese General saying that he only let your friends lead the assault because the rebels would not shoot at white faces?'

'Yeah,' Franklin said. 'And all the reports I've seen only mention two SAS men, or two British soldiers.' He laughed. 'I might as well have been invisible.'

'Doesn't that make you angry?' she asked.

'Two weeks ago it would have,' he said. 'And I guess if I think about it then it still does . . .' He looked at her. 'But if I hadn't had a black face when I came to your door that night, Diba would have killed me, and probably you and McGrath as well . . .' He opened his palms in a gesture of resignation, and smiled at her.

'I like *your* face,' she said.

SOLDIER O: SAS

THE BOSNIAN INFERNO

SOLDIER O: SAS

THE BOSNIAN INFERNO

David Monnery

Prelude

Zavik, 17 July 1992

The knock on the door was loud enough to wake the dead, and John Reeve had little doubt what it meant. 'I have to go now,' he told his son, putting the book to one side. The boy must have read the seriousness of the situation on his father's face because he didn't object. Reeve kissed him lightly on the forehead and hurried down the new wooden staircase he'd just finished installing in his parents-in-law's house.

Ekrem Abdic had already opened the door to admit the others. There were four of them: Tijanic, Bobetko, Cehajic and Filipovic. One Serb, one Croat and two Muslims. Reeve knew which was which, but only because he had talked to them, visited their homes. If he had met them as strangers on the street, wearing the same jeans and T-shirts they were wearing now, he would have had no idea. The dark Tijanic looked more like a stereotypical Muslim than the blond Filipovic, whose father taught children the Koran at the town's mosque.

'They're here,' Tijanic said without preamble.

As if to verify the statement, a gunshot sounded in the distance, and then another.

'How many of them are there?' Reeve asked, reclaiming the Kalashnikov from where it had been hanging on the wall, out of reach of the children.

'I counted twenty-seven, so far. One transit van and three cars, all jammed full.'

1

'Let's go,' Reeve said. He stopped in the doorway. 'No partisan heroics,' he told his seventy-year-old father-in-law. 'If it looks like we've failed, just take the kids and head for Zilovice.'

The old man nodded. 'Good luck,' he said.

The four men emerged into the early dusk, the town of Zavik spread beneath them. The sun had fallen behind the far wall of the valley, but the light it had left behind cast a meagre glow across the steep, terracotta-tiled roofs. The thought of the kids and their grandparents struggling up the mountain behind the town produced a sinking feeling in Reeve's stomach.

At least it was summer. A light breeze was blowing down the valley but the day's heat still clung to the narrow streets. In the distance they could hear a man shouting through a megaphone.

'They are all in the town square,' Cehajic told Reeve.

'How many townspeople have gone over to them?'

'The five who disappeared this morning, but no more that we know of.'

They were only about a hundred yards from the square now, and Reeve led them down the darker side of the street in single file. The voice grew louder, more hectoring. The leader of the intruders was demanding that all weapons and cars be brought to the square immediately, and that anyone found defying this order would have their house burnt to the ground.

Reeve smiled grimly at the reference to weapons. As far as he knew there had been only about seven working guns in the town before the Serbs arrived, and his group was carrying five of them. Two others were in the hands of Muslim ex-partisans like his father-in-law, and they intended defending their own homes and families to the death.

The five men reached the rear of the building earmarked for their observation post, and filed in across the yard and up the rickety steps at the back. The old couple who lived there waved them through to the front room, where latticed windows overlooked the town square. Once this room would have housed a harem, and its windows had been designed so that the women could look out without being seen. As such, they served Reeve's current purpose admirably.

Several hundred people were gathered in the square, most of them looking up at the man with the megaphone, who was standing on the roof of the transit van. He wore a broad-brimmed hat, sunglasses and camouflage fatigues. A long, straggly beard hung down his chest.

On the ground in front of him two bodies lay side by side. Reeve recognized one as the town's mayor, a Muslim named Sulejman. The other looked like his brother.

Across to one side of the square, in front of the Catholic church, the irregulars' cars were parked in a line. All were Lada Nivas, and one had the word 'massacre' spray-painted along its side. Some of the invaders were leaning up against these cars, while others stood between them and the transit van, staring contemptuously at the crowd. Most were dressed like their apparent leader, though a couple had nylon stockings pulled bank-robber-style across their heads, and several were sporting Chetnik 'Freedom or Death' T-shirts, the words interwoven through skull and crossbones.

Their leader had finished addressing the crowd, and

was now talking to one of his cronies. Both men glanced across at the two corpses on the ground and then called over one of the men wearing a nylon mask. 'It's Cosic,' Tijanic said, recognizing the local man by his walk.

The man listened to the irregulars' leader and then pointed to one of the streets leading off the square.

'He's telling them where Sulejman lived,' Reeve said. He turned to Filipovic. 'You keep watch. One of us will be back as soon as we can.'

The other four hurried back through the house, down the steps and into the empty street. Sulejman's house was halfway up the hill to the ruined castle, and they reached it in minutes.

The big house was deserted – either Sulejman had had the sense to move his family away, or they had witnessed his death in the square. Reeve and his men walked in through the unlocked front door and took up positions behind the colonnaded partition between hallway and living-room.

The Serbs arrived about five minutes later. There were three of them, and they sounded in a good mood, laughing and singing as they kicked their way in through the door. Several were now carrying open bottles, and not much caring how much they slopped on the floor.

'I expect the women are hiding upstairs,' one man said.

'Come on down, darlings!' another shouted out.

Reeve and the others stepped out together, firing the Kalashnikovs from the hip, and the three Serbs did a frantic dance of death as their bottles smashed on the wooden floor.

THE BOSNIAN INFERNO

Tijanic walked forward and extracted the weapons from their grasp. 'I'll get these to Zukic and his boys,' he said.

'Three down,' Reeve said. 'Twenty-four to go.'

1

'Daddy, help me!' Marie insisted.

Her plea brought Jamie Docherty's attention back to the matter in hand. His six-year-old daughter was busy trying to wrap up the present she had chosen for her younger brother, and in danger of completely immobilizing herself in holly-patterned sticky tape.

'OK,' he said, smiling at her and beginning the task of disentanglement. His mind had been on his wife, who at that moment was upstairs going through the same process with four-year-old Ricardo. Christmas was never a good time for Isabel, or at least not for the past eighteen years. She had spent the 1975 festive season incarcerated in the cells and torture chambers of the Naval Mechanical School outside Buenos Aires, and though the physical scars had almost faded, the mental ones still came back to haunt her.

His mind went back to their first meeting, in the hotel lobby in Rio Gallegos. It had been at the height of the Falklands War, on the evening of the day the troops went ashore at San Carlos. He had been leading an SAS intelligence-gathering patrol on Argentinian soil, and she had been a British agent, drawn to betray her country by hatred of the junta which had killed and tortured her friends, and driven her into exile. Together they had fought and driven and walked their way across the mountains to Chile.

More than ten years had passed since that day, and they had been married for almost as long. At first

6

Docherty had thought that their mutual love had exorcized her memories, as it had exorcized his pain at the sudden loss of his first wife, but gradually it had become clear to him that, much as she loved him and the children, something inside her had been damaged beyond repair. Most of the time she could turn it off, but she would never be free of the memories, or of what she had learned of what human beings could do to one another.

Docherty had talked to his old friend Liam McCall about it; he had even, unknown to Isabel, had several conversations with the SAS's resident counsellor. Both the retired priest and his secular colleague had told him that talking about it might help, but that he had to accept that some wounds never healed.

He had tried talking to her. After all, he had told himself, he had seen enough of death and cruelty in his army career: from Oman to Guatemala to the Falls Road. That wasn't the same, she'd said. Nature was full of death and what looked like cruelty. What she had seen was something altogether more human – the face of evil. And he had not, and she hoped he never would.

Somehow this had created a distance between them. Not a rift – there was no conflict involved – but a distance. He felt that he had failed her in some way. That was ridiculous, and he knew it. But still he felt it.

'Daddy!' Marie cried out in exasperation. 'Pay attention!'

Docherty grinned at her. 'Sorry,' he said. 'I was thinking about Mummy,' he explained.

His daughter considered this, her blue eyes looking as extraordinary as ever against the rich skin tone she'd inherited from her mother. 'You can think about her when I've gone to bed,' Marie decided.

'Right,' Docherty agreed, and for the next ten minutes he gave her his full attention, completing the wrapping of Ricardo's present and conferring parental approval on Marie's suggested alterations to his positioning of the silver balls and tinsel on the tree. And then it was bedtime, and his turn to read to Ricardo. When he had finished he stood for a moment in the doorway to Marie's room, listening to Isabel reading, the bedside lamp making a corona around his wife's dark head as she bent over the book.

He walked downstairs, blessing his luck for finding her. Few men, he reckoned, found one such woman in their lives, and he had found two. True, with both there had been a price. Chrissie had been killed in a road accident only months after their marriage, sending him into a downward spiral of drunkenness and self-pity which had almost cost him his career and self-respect. Like Margaret Thatcher, he had been saved by the Falklands War, and in the middle of that conflict fate had led him to Isabel, who came complete with a hurt he longed in vain to heal. But he wasn't complaining – now, at the grand old age of forty-two, Jamie Docherty would not have swapped places with any man.

He went through to the kitchen, opened a can of beer and poured it into the half-pint mug he had liberated from an officers' mess in Dhofar nearly twenty years before.

'How about one for me?' Isabel asked him from the doorway, a smile on her face.

He smiled back and reached for another can.

She sat down on the other side of the kitchen table,

and they shared the silence for a few moments. Her smile had gone, he noticed.

'What is worrying you?' she asked suddenly.

You, he thought. 'Nothing really,' he said, 'maybe the future. I've never been retired before. It's a strange feeling.' He grinned suddenly. 'Let's face it, we haven't even decided which continent we're going to live in.'

'There's no hurry,' she said. 'Let's get Christmas out of the way first.' She put down her half-empty glass. 'You still want fish and chips?' she asked.

'Yeah, I'll go and get them.'

'You stay with the children. I feel like some fresh air.'

And some time on your own, Docherty thought. 'You sure?' he asked.

'*Sí, noes problema.*'

Docherty continued sipping his beer, wondering how many other households there were in Glasgow where all four occupants often moved back and forth between English and Spanish without even noticing they had done so. He had become fluent in the latter during the half year's compassionate leave he had spent travelling in Mexico after Chrissie's death. Isabel had acquired her bilingual skills before meeting him, during the seven years of her enforced exile in England.

Still, their linguistic habits were hardly the strangest thing about their relationship. When they had met he had been a ten-year veteran of the SAS and she one of the few surviving members of an Argentinian urban guerrilla group. If the *Sun* had got hold of the story their marriage would have made the front page – something along the lines of 'SAS Hero Weds Argie Red'.

In the public mind, and particularly on the liberal left,

the Regiment was assumed to be a highly trained bunch of right-wing stormtroopers. There was some truth in this impression, particularly since the large influx during the eighties of gung-ho paras – but only some. Men like Docherty, who came from families imbued with the old labour traditions, were also well represented among the older hands, and among the new intake of younger men the SAS emphasis on intelligence and self-reliance tended to militate against the rightist bias implicit in any military organization.

On returning from the Falklands, conscious of Isabel's opinions, Docherty had thought long and hard about whether to continue in the Army. Up to that time, he decided, none of the tasks allotted him by successive British governments had seriously troubled his conscience. When one arrived that did, then that would be the time to hand in his cards.

So, for most of the past ten years he and Isabel had lived just outside Hereford. Her cover during the mission in Argentina had been as a travel-guide writer, and a couple of enquiries were enough to confirm that the market in such books was expanding at enormous speed. She never finished the one she was supposedly researching in southern Argentina, but an offer to become one third of a team covering Chile was happily accepted, and this led to two other books on Central American countries. It meant her being away for weeks at a time, but Docherty was also often abroad for extended periods, particularly after his attachment to the SAS Training Wing. Whenever possible they joined each other, and Docherty was able to continue and deepen the love affair with Latin America which he had begun in Mexico.

Then Marie had arrived, and Ricardo two years later.

Isabel had been forced to take a more editorial role, which, while more rewarding financially, often seemed considerably less fulfilling. Now with Ricardo approaching school age, and Docherty one week into retirement from the Army, they had big decisions to take. What was he going to do for a living? Did they want to live in Scotland or somewhere in Latin America? As Isabel had said, there was no urgency. She had recently inherited – somewhat to her surprise – a few thousand pounds from her mother, and the house they were now staying in had been virtually a gift from Liam McCall. The priest had inherited a cottage on Harris in the Outer Hebrides, decided to retire there, and offered the Dochertys an indefinite free loan of his Glasgow house.

No urgency, perhaps, but much as Docherty loved having more time with Isabel and the children, he wasn't used to doing nothing. The military life was full of dead periods, but there was always the chance that the next day you would be swept across the world to face a challenge that stretched mind, body and soul to the limit. Docherty knew he had to find himself a new challenge, somehow, somewhere.

He got up to collect plates, salt, ketchup and vinegar. Just in time, for the ever-wonderful smell of fish and chips wafted in through the door ahead of his wife.

'Cod for you, haddock for me,' she said, placing the two bundles on the empty plates. 'And I bought a bottle of wine,' she added, pulling it out of the coat pocket. 'I thought . . .'

The telephone started ringing in the living-room.

'Who can that be?' she asked, walking towards it.

Docherty had unwrapped one bundle when she returned. 'It's your old CO,' she said, like any English military wife. 'Barney Davies. And he sounds like he's calling from a pub.'

'Maybe they've realized my pension should have been twice as much,' Docherty joked, wondering what in God's name Davies wanted with him.

He soon found out.

'Docherty? I'm sorry to call you at this hour, but I'd appreciate a meeting,' Davies said.

Docherty raised his eyebrows. It did sound like a pub in the background. He tried to remember which of Hereford's hostelries Barney Davies favoured. 'OK. What about? Can it wait till after Christmas?'

'Tonight would be better.'

'Where are you?' Docherty asked.

'In the bar at Central Station.'

The CO was in Glasgow. Had maybe even come to Glasgow just to see him. What the fuck was this about?

'I'm sorry about the short notice, but . . .'

'No problem. In an hour, say, at nine.'

'Wonderful. Can you suggest somewhere better than this?'

'Aye, the Slug & Sporran in Brennan Street. It's about a ten-minute walk, or you can take a cab . . .'

'I'll walk.'

'OK. Just go straight down the road opposite the station entrance, then left into Sauchiehall Street and Brennan Street's about three hundred yards down on the right. The pub's about halfway down, opposite a pool hall.'

'Roger.'

The phone clicked dead. Docherty stood there for a minute, a sinking heart and a rising sense of excitement competing for his soul, and then went back to his fish and chips. He removed the plate which Isabel had used to keep them warm. 'He wants to see me,' he said, in as offhand a voice as he could muster. 'Tonight.'

She looked up, her eyes anxious. '*Por qué?*' she asked.

'He didn't say.'

Lieutenant-Colonel Barney Davies, Commanding Officer 22 SAS Regiment, found the Slug & Sporran without much difficulty, and could immediately see why Docherty had recommended it. Unlike most British pubs it was neither a yuppified monstrosity nor a noisy pigsty. The wooden beams on the ceiling were real, and the polished wooden booths looked old enough to remember another century. There were no amusement machines in sight, no jukebox music loud enough to drown any conversation – just the more comforting sound of darts burying themselves in a dartboard. The TV set was turned off.

Davies bought himself a double malt, surveyed the available seating, and laid claim to the empty booth which seemed to offer the most privacy. At the nearest table a group of youngsters sporting punk hairstyles were arguing about someone he'd never heard of – someone called 'Fooco'. Listening to them, Davies found it impossible to decide whether the man was a footballer, a philosopher or a film director. They looked so young, he thought.

It was ten to nine. Davies started trying to work out what he was going to say to Docherty, but soon gave up the attempt. It would be better not to sound rehearsed, to just be natural. This was not a job he wanted to offer anybody, least of all someone like Docherty, who had children to think about and a wife to leave behind.

There was no choice though. He had to ask him. Maybe Docherty would have the sense to refuse.

But he doubted it. He himself wouldn't have had the sense, back when he still had a wife and children who lived with him.

'Hello, boss,' Docherty said, appearing at his shoulder and slipping back into the habit of using the usual SAS term for a superior officer. 'Want another?'

'No, but this is my round,' Davies said, getting up. 'What would you like?'

'A pint of Guinness would probably hit the spot,' Docherty said. He sat down and let his eyes wander round the half-empty pub, feeling more expectant than he wanted to be. Why had he suggested this pub, he asked himself. That was the TV on which he'd watched the Task Force sail out of Portsmouth Harbour. That was the bar at which he'd picked up his first tart after getting back from Mexico. The place always boded ill. The booth in the corner was where he and Liam had comprehensively drowned their sorrows the day Dalglish left for Liverpool.

Davies was returning with the black nectar. Docherty had always respected the man as a soldier and, what was rarer, felt drawn to him as a man. There was a sadness about Davies which made him appealingly human.

'So what's brought you all the way to Glasgow?' Docherty asked.

Davies grimaced. 'Duty, I'm afraid.' He took a sip of the malt. 'I don't suppose there's any point in beating about the bush. When did you last hear from John Reeve?'

'Almost a year ago, I think. He sent us a Christmas card from Zimbabwe – that must have been about a month after he got there – and then a short letter, but nothing since. Neither of us is much good at writing letters, but usually Nena and Isabel manage to write . . . What's John . . .'

'You were best man at their wedding, weren't you?'

'And he was at mine. What's this about?'

'John Reeve's not been in Zimbabwe for eight months now – he's been in Bosnia.'

Docherty placed his pint down carefully and waited for Davies to continue.

'This is what we think happened,' the CO began. 'Reeve and his wife seem to have hit a bad patch while he was working in Zimbabwe. Or maybe it was just a break-up waiting to happen,' he added, with all the feeling of someone who had shared the experience. 'Whatever. She left him there and headed back to where she came from, which, as you know, was Yugoslavia. How did they meet – do you know?'

'In Germany,' Docherty said. 'Nena was a guest-worker in Osnabrück, where Reeve was stationed. She was working as a nurse while she trained to be a doctor.' He could see her in his mind's eye, a tall blonde with high Slavic cheekbones and cornflower-blue eyes. Her family was nominally Muslim, but as for many Bosnians it was more a matter of culture than religion. She had never professed any faith in Docherty's hearing.

He felt saddened by the news that they had split up. 'Did she take the children with her?' he asked.

'Yes. To the small town where she grew up. Place

called Zavik. It's up in the mountains a long way from anywhere.'

'Her parents still lived there, last I knew.'

'Ah. Well all this was just before the shit hit the fan in Bosnia, and you can imagine what Reeve must have thought. I don't know what Zimbabwean TV's like, but I imagine those pictures were pretty hard to escape last spring wherever you were in the world. Maybe not. For all we know he was already on his way. He seems to have arrived early in April, but this is where our information peters out. We think Nena Reeve used the opportunity of his visit to Zavik to make one of her own to Sarajevo, either because he could babysit the children or just as a way of avoiding him – who knows? Either way she chose the wrong time. All hell broke loose in Sarajevo and the Serbs started lobbing artillery shells at anything that moved and their snipers started picking off children playing football in the street. And she either couldn't get out or didn't want to . . .'

'Doctors must be pretty thin on the ground in Sarajevo,' Docherty thought out loud.

Davies grunted his agreement. 'As far as we know, she's still there. But Reeve – well, this is mostly guesswork. We got a letter from him early in June, explaining why he'd not returned to Zimbabwe, and that as long as he feared for the safety of his children he'd stay in Zavik . . .'

'I never heard anything about it,' Docherty said.

'No one did,' Davies said. 'An SAS soldier on the active list stuck in the middle of Bosnia wasn't something we wanted to advertise. For any number of reasons, his own safety included. Anyway, it seems that the town wasn't as safe as Reeve's wife had thought, and sometime in

July it found itself with some unwelcome visitors – a large group of Serbian irregulars. We've no idea what happened, but we do know that the Serbs were sent packing . . .'

'You think Reeve helped organize a defence?'

Davies shrugged. 'It would hardly be out of character, would it? But we don't know. All we have since then is six months of silence, followed by two months of rumours.'

'Rumours of what?'

'Atrocities of one kind and another.'

'Reeve? I don't believe it.'

'Neither do I, but . . . We're guessing that Reeve – or someone else with the same sort of skills – managed to turn Zavik into a town that was too well defended to be worth attacking. Which would work fine until the winter came, when the town would start running short of food and fuel and God knows what else, and either have to freeze and starve or take the offensive and go after what it needed. And that's what seems to have happened. They've been absolutely even-handed: they've stolen from everyone – Muslims, Serbs and Croats. And since none of these groups, with the partial exception of the Muslims, likes admitting that somewhere there's a town in which all three groups are fighting alongside each other against the tribal armies, you can guess who they're all choosing to concentrate their anger against.'

'Us?'

'In a nutshell. According to the Serbs and the Croats there's this renegade Englishman holed up in central Bosnia like Marlon Brando in *Apocalypse Now*, launching raids against anyone and everyone, delighting in slaughter and madness, and probably waiting to mutter "the horror, the horror" to the man who arrives intent on terminating him with extreme prejudice.'

'I take it our political masters are embarrassed,' Docherty said drily.

'Not only that – they're angry. They like touting the Regiment as an example of British excellence, and since the cold war ended they've begun to home in on the idea of selling our troops as mercenaries to the UN. All for a good cause, of course, and what the hell else do we have to sell any more? The Army top brass are all for it – it's their only real argument for keeping the sort of resource allocations they're used to. Finding out that one of their élite soldiers is running riot in the middle of the media's War of the Moment is not their idea of good advertising.'

Docherty smiled grimly. 'Surprise, surprise,' he said, and emptied his glass. He could see now where this conversation was leading. 'Same again?' he asked.

'Thanks.'

Docherty gave his order to the barman and stood there thinking about John Reeve. They'd known each other almost twenty years, since they'd been thrown into the deep end together in Oman. Reeve had been pretty wild back then, and he hadn't noticeably calmed down with age, but Docherty had thought that if anyone could turn down the fire without extinguishing it altogether then Nena was the one.

What would Isabel say about his going to Bosnia? he asked himself. She'd probably shoot him herself.

Back at the booth he asked Davies the obvious question: 'What do you want me to do?'

'I have no right to ask you to do anything,' Davies

answered. 'You're no longer a member of the Regiment, and you've already done more than your bit.'

'Aye,' Docherty agreed, 'but what do you want me to do?'

'Someone has to get into Zavik and talk Reeve into getting out. I don't imagine either is going to be easy, but he's more likely to listen to you than anyone else.'

'Maybe.' Reeve had never been very good at listening to anyone, at least until Nena came along. 'How would I get to Zavik?' he asked. 'And where is it, come to that?'

'About fifty miles west of Sarajevo. But we haven't even thought about access yet. We can start thinking about the hows if and when you decide . . .'

'If you should choose to accept this mission . . .' Docherty quoted ironically.

'. . . the tape will self-destruct in ten seconds,' Davies completed for him. Clearly both men had wasted their youth watching crap like *Mission Impossible*.

'I'll need to talk with my wife,' Docherty said. 'What sort of time-frame are we talking about?' It occurred to him, absurdly, that he was willing to go and risk his life in Bosnia, but only if he could first enjoy this Christmas with his family.

'It's not a day-on-day situation,' Davies said. 'Not as far as we know, anyway. But we want to send a team out early next week.'

'The condemned men ate a hearty Christmas dinner,' Docherty murmured.

'I hope not,' Davies said. 'This is not a suicide mission. If it looks like you can't get to Zavik, you can't. I'm not sacrificing good men just to put a smile on the faces of the Army's accountants.'

'Who dares wins,' Docherty said with a smile.

'That's probably what they told Icarus,' Davies observed.

'Don't you want me to go?' Docherty asked, only half-seriously.

'To be completely honest,' Davies said, 'I don't know. Have you been following what's happening in Bosnia?'

'Not as much as I should have. My wife probably knows more about it than I do.'

'It's a nightmare,' Davies said, 'and I'm not using the word loosely. All the intelligence we're getting tells us that humans are doing things to each other in Bosnia that haven't been seen in Europe since the religious wars of the seventeenth century, with the possible exception of the Russian Front in the last war. We're talking about mass shootings, whole villages herded into churches and burnt alive, rape on a scale so widespread that it must be a coordinated policy, torture and mutilation for no other reason than pleasure, war without any moral or human restraint . . .'

'A heart of darkness,' Docherty murmured, and felt a shiver run down his spine, sitting there in his favourite pub, in the city of his birth.

After giving Davies a lift to his hotel Docherty drove slowly home, thinking about what the CO had told him. Part of him wanted to go, part of him wasn't so sure. Did he feel the tug of loyalty, or was his brain just using that as a cover for the tug of adventure? And in any case, didn't his wife and children have first claim on his loyalty now? He wasn't even in the Army any more.

She was watching *Newsnight* on TV, already in her dressing-gown, a glass of wine in her hand. The anxiety

20

seemed to have left her eyes, but there was a hint of coldness there instead, as if she was already protecting herself against his desertion.

Ironically, the item she was watching concerned the war in Bosnia, and the refugee problem which had developed as a result. An immaculately groomed Conservative minister was explaining how, alas, Britain had no more room for these tragic victims. After all, the UK had already taken more than Liechtenstein. Docherty wished he could use the *Enterprise*'s transporter system to beam the bastard into the middle of Tuzla, or Srebenica, or wherever it was this week that he had the best chance of being shredded by reality.

He poured himself what remained of the wine, and found Isabel's dark eyes boring into him. 'Well?' she asked. 'What did he want?'

'He wants me to go and collect John Reeve from there,' he said, gesturing at the screen.

'But they're in Zimbabwe . . .'

'Not any more.' He told her the story that Davies had told him.

When he was finished she examined the bottom of her glass for a few seconds, then lifted her eyes to his. 'They just want you to go and talk to him?'

'They want to know what's really happening.'

'What do they expect you to say to him?'

'They don't know. That will depend on whatever it is he's doing out there.'

She thought about that for a moment. 'But he's your friend,' she said, 'your comrade. Don't you trust him? Don't you believe that, whatever he's doing, he has a good reason for doing it.'

It was Docherty's turn to consider. 'No,' he said

eventually. 'I didn't become his friend because I thought he had flawless judgement. If I agree with whatever it is he's doing, I shall say so. To him and Barney Davies. And if I don't, the same applies.'

'Are they sending you in alone?'

'I don't know. And that's *if* I agree to go.'

'You mean, once I give you my blessing.'

'No, no, I don't. That's not what I mean at all. I'm out of the Army, out of the Regiment. I can choose.'

There was both amusement and sadness in her smile. 'They've still got you for this one,' she said. 'Duty and loyalty to a friend would have been enough in any case, but they've even given you a mystery to solve.'

He smiled ruefully back at her.

She got up and came to sit beside him on the sofa. He put an arm round her shoulder and pulled her in. 'If it wasn't for the *niños* I'd come with you,' she said. 'You'll probably need someone good to watch your back.'

'I'll find someone,' he said, kissing her on the forehead. For a minute or more they sat there in silence.

'How dangerous will it be?' she asked at last.

He shrugged. 'I'm not sure there's any way of knowing before we get there. There are UN troops there now, but I don't know where in relation to where Reeve is. The fact that it's winter will help – there won't be as many amateur psychopaths running around if the snow's six feet deep. But a war zone is a war zone. It won't be a picnic.'

'Who dares had better damn well come home,' she said.

'I will,' he said softly.

22

2

Nena Reeve pressed the spoon down on the tea-bag, trying to drain from it what little strength remained without bursting it. She wondered what they were drinking in Zavik. Probably melted snow.

Her holdall was packed and ready to go, sitting on the narrow bed. The room, one of many which had been abandoned in the old nurses' dormitory, was about six feet by eight, with one small window. It was hardly a generous space for living, but since Nena usually arrived back from the hospital with nothing more than sleep in mind, this didn't greatly concern her.

Through the window she had a view across the roofs below and the slopes rising up on the other side of the Miljacka valley. In the square to the right there had once been a mosque surrounded by acacias, its slim minaret reaching hopefully towards heaven, but citizens hungry for fuel had taken the trees and a Serbian shell had cut the graceful tower in half.

There was a rap on the door, and Nena walked across to let in her friend Hajrija Mejra.

'Ready?' Hajrija asked, flopping down on the bed. She was wearing a thick, somewhat worn coat over camouflage fatigue trousers, army boots and a green woollen scarf. Her long, black hair was bundled up beneath a black woolly cap, but strands were escaping on all sides. Hajrija's face, which Nena had always thought so beautiful, looked as gaunt as her own these days: the dark eyes were sunken, the high cheekbones sharp enough to cast deep shadows.

Well, Hajrija was still in her twenties. There was nothing wrong with either of them that less stress and more food wouldn't put right. The miracle wasn't how ill they looked – it was how the city's 300,000 people were still coping at all.

She put on her own coat, hoping that two sweaters, thermal long johns and jeans would be warm enough, and picked up the bag. 'I'm ready,' she said reluctantly.

Hajrija pulled herself upright, took a deep breath and stood up. 'I don't suppose there's any point in trying to persuade you not to go?'

'None,' Nena said, holding the door open for her friend.

'Tell me again what this Englishman said to you,' Hajrija said as they descended the first flight of stairs. The lift had been out of operation for months. 'He came to the hospital, right?'

'Yes. He didn't say much . . .'

'Did he tell you his name?'

'Yes. Thornton, I think. He said he came from the British Consulate . . .'

'I didn't know there was a British Consulate.'

'There isn't – I checked.'

'So where did he come from?'

'Who knows? He didn't tell me anything, he just asked questions about John and what I knew about what was happening in Zavik. I said, "Nothing. What *is* happening in Zavik?" He said that's what *he* wanted to know. It was like a conversation in one of those Hungarian movies. You know, two peasants swapping cryptic comments in the middle of an endless cornfield . . .'

'Only you weren't in a cornfield.'

'No, I was trying to deal with about a dozen bullet and shrapnel wounds.'

They reached the bottom of the stairs and cautiously approached the doors. It had only been light for about half an hour, and the Serb snipers in the high-rise buildings across the river were probably deep in drunken sleep, but there was no point in taking chances. The fifty yards of open ground between the dormitory doors and the shelter of the old medieval walls was the most dangerous stretch of their journey. Over the last six months more than a dozen people had been shot attempting it, three fatally.

'Ready?' Hajrija asked.

'I guess.'

The two women flung themselves through the door and ran as fast as they could, zigzagging across the open space. Burdened down by the holdall, Nena was soon behind, and she could feel her stomach clenching with the tension, her body braced for the bullet. Thirty metres more, twenty metres, ten . . .

She sank into the old Ottoman stone, gasping for breath.

'You're out of shape,' Hajrija said, only half-joking.

'Whole bloody world's out of shape,' Nena said. 'Let's get going.'

They walked along the narrow street, confident that they were hidden from snipers' eyes. There was no one about, and the silence seemed eerily complete. Usually by this time the first shells of the daily bombardment had landed.

It was amazing how they had all got used to the bombardment, Nena thought. Was it a tribute to human resilience, or just a stubborn refusal to face up to reality? Probably a bit of both. She remembered the queue in front of the Orthodox Cathedral when the first food supplies had come in by air. A sniper had cut down one of the people in the line, but only a few people had run for cover. There were probably a thousand people in the queue, and like participants in a dangerous sport each was prepared to accept the odds against being the next victim. Such a deadening of the nerve-ends brought a chill to her spine, but she understood it well enough. How many times had she made that sprint from the dormitory doors? A hundred? Two hundred?

'Even if you're right,' Hajrija said, 'even if Reeve has got himself involved somehow, I don't see how you can help by rushing out there. You do know how unsafe it is, don't you? There's no guarantee you'll even get there . . .'

Nena stopped in mid-stride. 'Please, Rija,' she said, 'don't make it any more difficult. I'm already scared enough, not to mention full of guilt for leaving the hospital in the lurch. But if Reeve is playing the local warlord while he's supposed to be looking after the children, then . . .' She shook her head violently. 'I have to find out.'

'Then let me come with you. At least you'll have some protection.'

'No, your place is here.'

'But . . .'

'No argument.'

Sometimes Nena still found it hard to believe that her friend, who six months before had been a journalism student paying her way through college as a part-time nurse, was now a valued member of an élite anti-sniper unit. Someone who had killed several men, and yet still seemed the same person she had always been. Sometimes Nena worried that there was no way Hajrija had not been changed by the experiences, and that it would be healthier if these changes showed on the surface, but at others she simply put it down to the madness that was all around them both. Maybe the fact that they were *all* going through this utter craziness would be their salvation.

Maybe they had all gone to hell, but no one had bothered to make it official.

'I'll be all right,' she said.

Hajrija looked at her with exasperated eyes.

'Well, if I'm not, I certainly don't want to know I've dragged you down with me.'

'I know.'

They continued on down the Marsala Tita, sprinting across two dangerously open intersections. There were more people on the street now, all of them keeping as close to the buildings as possible, all with skin stretched tight across the bones of their scarf-enfolded faces.

It was almost eight when they reached the Holiday Inn, wending their way swiftly through the Muslim gun emplacements in and around the old forecourt. The hotel itself looked like Beirut on a bad day, its walls pock-marked with bullet holes and cratered by mortar shells. Most of its windows had long since been broken, but it was still accommodating guests, albeit a restricted clientele of foreign journalists and ominous-looking 'military delegations'.

'He's not here yet,' Hajrija said, looking round the lobby.

Nena followed her friend's gaze, and noticed an AK47 resting symbolically on the receptionist's desk.

'Here he is,' Hajrija said, and Nena turned to see a handsome young American walking towards them. Dwight Bailey was a journalist, and several weeks earlier he had followed the well-beaten path to Hajrija's unit in search of a story. She was not the only woman involved in such activities, but she was probably, Nena guessed, one of the more photogenic. Bailey had not been the first to request follow-up interviews in a more intimate atmosphere. Like his bed at the Holiday Inn, for example. So far, or at least as far as Nena knew, Hajrija had resisted any temptation.

Bailey offered the two women a boyish smile full of perfect American teeth, and asked Hajrija about the other members of her unit. He seemed genuinely interested in how they were, Nena thought. If age made all journalists cynical, he was still young.

And somewhat hyperactive. 'Dmitri's late,' he announced, hopping from one foot to the other. 'He and Viktor are our bodyguards,' he told Nena. 'Russian journalists. Good guys. The Serbs don't mess with the Russians if they can help it,' he explained. 'The Russians are about the only friends they have left.'

He said this with absolute seriousness, as if he could hardly believe it.

'Hey, here they are,' he called out as the two Russians came into view on the stairs. Both men had classically flat Russian faces beneath the fur hats; both were either bear-shaped or wearing enough undergarments to survive a cold day in Siberia. In fact the only obvious way of distinguishing one from the other was by their eyebrows: Viktor's were fair and almost invisible, Dmitri's bushy and black enough for him to enter a Brezhnev-lookalike contest. Both seemed highly affable, as if they'd drunk half a pint of vodka for breakfast.

The two women embraced each other. 'Be careful,' Hajrija insisted. 'And don't take any risks. And come back as soon as you can.' She turned to the American. 'And you take care of my friend,' she ordered him.

He tipped his head and bowed.

The four travellers threaded their way out through the hotel's kitchens to where a black Toyota was parked out of sight of snipers. The two Russians climbed into the front, and Nena and Bailey into the back.

Two distant explosions, one following closely on the other, signalled the beginning of the daily bombardment. The shells had fallen at least two kilometres away, Nena judged, but that didn't mean the next ones wouldn't fall on the Toyota's roof.

Viktor started up the car and pulled it out of the car park, accelerating all the while. The most dangerous stretch of road ran between the Holiday Inn and the airport, and they were doing more than sixty miles per hour by the time the car hit open ground. Viktor had obviously passed this way more than once, for as he zigzagged wildly to and fro, past the burnt-out hulks of previous failed attempts, he was casually lighting up an evil-smelling cigarette from the dashboard lighter.

Nena resisted the temptation to squeeze herself down into the space behind the driver's seat, and was rewarded with a glimpse of an old woman searching for dandelion leaves in the partially snow-covered verge, oblivious to their car as it hurtled past.

Thirty seconds later and they were through 'Murder Mile', and slowing for the first in a series of checkpoints.

This one was manned by Bosnian police, who waved them through without even bothering to examine the three men's journalistic accreditation. Half a mile further, they were waved down by a Serb unit on the outskirts of Ilidza, a Serb-held suburb. The men here wore uniforms identifying them as members of the Yugoslav National Army. They were courteous almost to a fault.

'Hard to believe they come from Mordor,' Bailey said with a grin.

It was, Nena thought. Sometimes it was just too easy to think all Serbs were monsters, to forget that there were still 80,000 of them in Sarajevo, undergoing much the same hardships and traumas as everyone else. And then it became hard to understand how the men on the hills above Sarajevo could deliberately target their big guns on the hospitals below, and how the snipers in the burnt-out tower blocks could deliberately blow away children barely old enough to start school.

They passed safely through another Serb checkpoint and, as the two Russians pumped Bailey about their chances of emigration to the USA, the road ran up out of the valley, the railway track climbing to its left, the rushing river falling back towards the city on its right. Stretches of dark conifers alternated with broad swathes of snow-blanketed moorland as they crested a pass and followed the sweeping curves of the road down into Sanjic. Here a minaret still rose above the roofs of the small town nestling in its valley, and as they drove through its streets Nena could see that the Christian churches had not paid the price for the mosque's survival. Sanjic had somehow escaped the war, at least for the moment. She hoped Zavik had fared as well.

'This must have been what all of Bosnia was like before the war,' Bailey said beside her. There was a genuine sadness in his voice which made her wonder if she had underestimated him.

'How long have you been here?' she asked.

'I came in early November,' he said.

'Who do you work for?'

'No one specific. I'm a freelance.'

She looked out of the window. 'If you get the chance,' she said, 'and if this war ever ends, you should come in the spring, when the trees are in blossom. It can look like an enchanted land at that time of year.'

'I'd love to,' he said. 'I ... I thought I knew quite a lot of the world before I came here,' he said. 'I've been all over Europe, all over the States of course, to Australia and Singapore ... But I feel like I've never been anywhere like this. And I don't mean the war,' he said hurriedly, 'though maybe that's what makes everything more vivid. I don't know ...'

She smiled at him, and felt almost like patting his hand.

The road was climbing again now, a range of snow-covered mountains looming on their left. She remembered the trip across the mountains to Umtali while they were in Africa. The children had been bored in the back seat and she'd been short-tempered with them. Reeve, though, had for once been an exemplary father, painstakingly prising them out of their sulk. But he'd always been a good father, much to her surprise. She'd expected a great husband and a poor father, and ended up with the opposite.

No, that was harsh.

She wondered again what she would find in Zavik,

always assuming she got there. The three journalists were only taking her as far as Bugojno, and from there she would probably still have a problem making it up into the mountains. The roads might be open, might be closed – at this time of the year the chances were about fifty-fifty.

The car began slowing down and she looked up to see a block on the road ahead. A tractor and a car had been positioned nose to nose at an angle, and beside them four men were standing waiting. Two of them were wearing broad-brimmed hats. 'Chetniks,' one of the Russians said, and she could see the straggling beards sported by three of the four. The other man, it soon became clear, wasn't old enough to grow one.

From the first moment Nena had a bad feeling about the situation. The Russians' *bonhomie* was ignored, their papers checked with a mixture of insolence and sarcasm by the tall Serb who seemed to be in charge. 'Don't you think Yeltsin is a useless wanker?' he asked Viktor, who agreed vociferously with him, and said that in his opinion Russia could declare itself in favour of a Greater Serbia. The Chetnik just laughed at him, and moved on to Bailey. 'You like Guns N' Roses?' he asked him in English.

'Who?' Bailey asked.

'Rock 'n' roll,' the Chetnik said. 'American.'

'Sorry,' Bailey said.

'It's OK,' the Chetnik said magnanimously, and looked at Nena. His pupils seemed dilated, probably by drugs of some kind or another. 'Leave the woman behind,' he told the Russians in Serbo-Croat.

The Russians started arguing – not, Nena thought, with any great conviction.

'What's going on?' Bailey wanted to know.

32

She told him.

'But they can't do that!' he exclaimed, and before Nena could stop him he was opening the door and climbing out on to the road. 'Look . . .' he started to say, and the Chetnik's machine pistol cracked. The American slid back into Nena's view, a gaping hole where an eye had been.

The Russians in the front seat seemed suddenly frozen into statues.

'We just want the woman,' the Chetnik was telling them.

Viktor turned round to face her, his eyes wide with fear. 'I think . . .'

She shifted across the back seat and climbed out of the same door the American had used. She started bending down to examine him, but was yanked away by one of the Chetniks. The leader grabbed the dead man by the feet and unceremoniously dragged him away through the light snow and slush to the roadside verge. There he gave the body one sharp kick. 'Guns N' Roses,' he muttered to himself.

The Russians had turned the Toyota around as ordered, and were anxiously awaiting permission to leave. Both were making certain they avoided any eye contact with her.

'Get the fuck out of here,' the leader said contemptuously, and the car accelerated away, bullets flying above it from the guns of the grinning Chetniks.

She stood there, waiting for them to do whatever they were going to do.

The CO's office looked much as Docherty remembered it: the inevitable mug of tea perched on a pile of papers, the maps and framed photographs on the wall, the glimpse through the window of bare trees lining the parade ground, and beyond them the faint silhouette of the distant Black Mountains. The only obvious change concerned the photograph on Barney Davies's desk: his children were now a year older, and his wife was nowhere to be seen.

'Bring in a cup of tea,' the CO was saying into the intercom. 'And a rock cake?' he asked Docherty.

'Why not,' Docherty said. He might as well get used to living dangerously again. There were some at the SAS's Stirling Lines barracks who claimed that the Regiment had lost more men to the Mess's rock cakes than to international terrorism. It was a vicious lie, of course – the rock cakes were disabling rather than lethal.

'Is there any news of Reeve?' Docherty asked.

'None, but his wife's still in Sarajevo, working at the hospital as far as we know.'

'Where's the information coming from?'

'MI6 has a man in the city. Don't ask me why. The Foreign Office has got him digging around for us.'

Docherty's tea arrived, together with an ominous-looking rock cake. 'I'm hoping to take her with me,' he told Davies. 'Even if they've separated I still think he's more likely to listen to her than anyone else.'

'Well, you can ask her when you get there . . .'

'Sarajevo?' Docherty asked, his mouth half full of what tasted like an actual rock. Sweet perhaps, but hard and gritty all the same.

'It's not been a very good year for them,' Davies said, observing the expression on Docherty's face, and causing the Scot to wonder whether the CO had racks of the damn things in his cellar, each bearing their vintage.

'Sarajevo looks like the best place to begin,' Davies continued. 'Nena Reeve is there, and your MI6 contact. His name's Thornton, by the way. There must be people from Zavik who can fill you in on the town and its surroundings. Plus, there's the UN command and a lot of journalists. You should be able to pick up a good idea of what the best access route is, and what to expect on the way. Always assuming we can get you into the damn city, of course.'

'I thought the airport was closed.'

'Opened again a couple of days ago for relief flights, but there's no certainty it will still be open tomorrow. If it's not the Serbs lobbing shells from the hilltops it's the Muslims and Serbs exchanging fire across the damn runway, and even if they're all on their best behaviour it's probably only because there's a blizzard.'

'Lots of package tours, are there?' Docherty asked.

'The more I know about this war the less I'm looking forward to seeing any of my men involved in it,' Davies said.

Docherty took a gulp of tea, which at least scoured his mouth of cake. 'How many men am I taking in?' he asked.

'It's up to you, within reason. But I'd stick with a four-man patrol . . .'

'So would I. Are Razor Wilkinson and Ben Nevis available?' Darren Wilkinson and Stewart Nevis were two of the three men who had been landed on the Argentinian mainland with him during the Falklands – the third, Nick Wacknadze, had left the SAS – and Docherty had found both to be near-perfect comrades-in-arms.

'Nevis is in plaster, I'm afraid. He and his wife went skiing over Christmas – French Alps, I think – and he broke a leg. Sergeant Wilkinson is around, though. And I think he'll probably jump at the chance to get away from mothering the new boys up on the Beacons.'

'Good. I've missed his appalling cockney sense of humour.'

'Any other ideas?'

Docherty thought for a moment. 'I'm out of touch, boss . . .'

'Do you remember the Colombian business?' Davies asked.

'Who could forget it?'

Back in 1989 an SAS instructor on loan to the Colombian Army Anti-Narcotics Unit had been kidnapped, along with a prominent local politician, by one of the cocaine cartels. A four-man team had been inserted under cover to provide reconnaissance, and then an entire squadron parachuted in to assist with the rescue. One of the helicopters sent in to extract everyone was destroyed by sabotage and the original four-man patrol, plus the instructor, had been forced to flee Colombia on foot. In the process two of them had been killed, but the patrol's crossing of a 10,000-foot mountain range, pursued all the way by agents of the cartel, had acquired almost legendary status in Special Forces circles.

'Wynwood's in Hong Kong,' Davies said, 'but how about Corporals Martinson and Robson? They've proved they can walk across mountains, and it seems Yugoslavia — or whatever we have to call it these days — is full of them. And' — the CO's face suffused with sudden enthusiasm — 'I have a feeling Martinson has another useful qualification.' He reached for the intercom. 'Get me Corporal Martinson's service record,' he told the orderly.

Docherty sipped his tea, allowing Davies his moment of drama.

The file arrived, Davies skimmed through it, and stabbed a finger at the last page. 'Serbo-Croat,' he said triumphantly.

'What?' Docherty exclaimed. He could hardly believe there was a Serbo-Croat speaker in the Regiment.

'You know what it's like,' Davies said. 'The chances for action are few and far between these days, so the moment some part of the world looks like going bad the keen ones pick that language to learn, just in case. If nothing happens, any new language is still a plus on their record, and if by chance we get involved, they're first in the queue.'

'Looks like Martinson's won the jackpot this time,' Docherty said, reaching for the file to examine the photograph. 'He even looks like a Slav,' he added.

'He's a medic, like Wilkinson, but that might well come in useful where you're going. And he's a twitcher, too. A bird-watcher,' Davies explained, seeing the expression on Docherty's face. 'Bosnia's probably knee-deep in rare species.'

'I'll keep my eyes open,' Docherty said drily. He had never been able to understand the fascination some people had with birds. 'What about Robson?'

'He's an explosives man, and a crack shot with a sniper rifle. Which leaves you without a signals specialist, but I imagine you can fill in there yourself.'

'Those PRC 319s work themselves,' Docherty replied, 'and anyway, who will we have to send signals to?'

'Well, you might need to make contact with one of the British units who are serving with the UN.'

'But they wouldn't be able to get involved with this mission?'

'No, and in any case you won't be in uniform. This mission is about as official as Kim Philby's.'

'So when it comes down to it we're just a bunch of Brits dropping in to help out a mate.'

Davies opened his mouth to object, and closed it again. 'I suppose you are,' he agreed.

A little more than twenty miles to the south, Chris Martinson was moving stealthily, trying not to step on any of the twigs spread across the forest floor. He halted for a moment, ears straining, and right on cue heard the 'yah-yah-yah' laughing sound. It was nearer now, but he still couldn't see the bird. And then, suddenly, it seemed to be flying straight towards him down an avenue between the bare trees, its red crown, black face and green-gold back looking almost tropical in the winter forest. It seemed to see him at the last moment, and veered away to the left, into a stand of conifers.

The green woodpecker wasn't a rare bird, but it was one of Martinson's favourites, and, since a day trip from Hereford to the Forest of Dean never seemed quite complete if he didn't see one, there was a smile on his face as he continued his walk.

Another quarter of a mile brought him to the crown of a small hill giving a view out across the top of the trees towards the Severn Estuary. Some kind soul had arranged for a wrought-iron seat to be placed there, and Chris gratefully sat himself down, putting his binoculars to one side and unwrapping the packed lunch he had brought with him. As he bit into the first tuna roll a flock of white-faced geese flew overhead towards the estuary.

It had been a good idea to come out for the day, Chris decided. The older he got the more claustrophobic the barracks seemed to get. He supposed it was time he got a place of his own, but somehow he had always resisted the idea. Flats were hard to find and you had all the hassle of dealing with a landlord, and as for buying somewhere . . . well, it would only be a millstone round his neck when he eventually left the Regiment and did some serious travelling.

He had turned thirty that year, and the time for decision couldn't be that far off. And, he had to admit, he was getting bored with the same old routines – routines that only seemed to be interrupted these days by a few hairy weeks in sun-soaked Armagh or exotic Crossmaglen. Even the birds in Northern Ireland seemed depressed by the weather.

He ran a hand through his spiky hair. His life was in a rut, he thought. Not an unpleasant one – in fact quite a comfortable one – but a rut nevertheless. He hadn't really made any close friends in the Regiment since Eddie Wilshaw, and the man from Hackney had died in Colombia three years before. And he hadn't had anything approaching a relationship with a woman for almost as long. The last one he'd gone out with had told him he seemed to be living on a separate planet from the rest of humanity.

He smiled good-naturedly at the memory. She was probably right, and it was no doubt time he started reaching out to people a bit more, but . . .

A robin landed in a tree across the clearing and began making its 'tick' calling sound. Chris sat there watching it, feeling full of nature's wonder, thinking that life on your own planet had its compensations.

3

Docherty could hear the familiar London accent before
he was halfway down the corridor.

'. . . and in hot climates there's one last resort when
it comes to infected wounds. Any ideas?'

'A day on the beach, boss?' a northern voice asked.

'Several rum and cokes?'

'I can see you've all read the book. The answer is
maggots. Since they only eat dead tissue they act as
cleaning agents in any open wound . . .'

'But boss, if I've just been cut open by some guerrilla
psycho with a machete I'm probably going to be a long
way from the local fishing tackle shop . . .'

'No problem, Ripley. Once the wound gets infected
you can just sit yourself down somewhere and ooze pus.
The maggots will come to you. Especially you. Right.
Yesterday you were all given five minutes to write down
the basic rules of dealing with dog bites, snake bites and
bee stings. Most of you managed to survive all three.
Trooper Dawson, however,' – a collective groan was
audible through the room's open skylight – 'used the
opportunity to attempt suicide. He didn't report the dog
bite, so he may have rabies by now. It's true that in this
country he'd need to be very unlucky, but the Regiment
does occasionally venture abroad. And it doesn't really
matter in any case because the snake got him. He not only
wasted time trying to suck out the venom, but managed
to lose an arm or a leg by applying a tourniquet instead of
a simple bandage. Of course he probably didn't notice the

limb dropping off because of the pain from the bee sting, which he'd made worse by squeezing the poison sac.'

In his mind's eye Docherty could see the expression on Razor's face.

'Well done, Dawson,' Razor concluded. 'Your only worry now is whether your mates will bother to bury you. Any questions from those of you still in the land of the almost-living?'

'What do you do about a lovebite from a beautiful enemy agent?' a Welsh voice asked.

'In your case, Edwards, dream of getting one. Class dismissed. And read the fucking book.'

The Continuation Training class filed out, looking as young and fit as Docherty remembered being twenty years before. When the last man had emerged he could see Darren Wilkinson bent over a ring binder of notes on the instructor's desk. Razor looked, like Docherty himself, as wiry as ever, but there was a seriousness of expression on the face which Docherty didn't remember seeing very often in the past. Maybe life in the Training Wing was calming him down.

Razor looked up suddenly, conscious of someone's eyes on him, and his face slowly split open in the familiar grin. 'Boss. What are you doing here? If you've not retired I want my twenty pee back.'

'Which twenty pee might that be?'

'The one I gave to your passing-out collection.'

Docherty sat down in the front row and eyed him tolerantly. 'I'm recruiting,' he said.

'What for?'

'A journey into hell by all accounts.'

'Forget it. I'm not going to watch Arsenal for anybody.'

'How about Red Star Sarajevo?'

Razor lifted himself on to the edge of the desk. 'Tell me about it,' he said.

'Do you know John Reeve?' Docherty asked.

'To say hello to. Not well. I never did an op with him.'

'I did,' Docherty said. 'Several of them. We may not have actually saved each other's lives in Oman, but we probably saved each other from dying of boredom. We became good mates, and though we never fought together again, we stayed that way, you know the way some friends are – you only need to see them once a year, or even every five years, and it's still always like you've never been apart.'

He paused, obviously remembering something. 'Reeve was one of the people who helped me through my first wife's death. In fact if he hadn't persuaded me to get compassionate leave rather than simply go AWOL I'd have been out of this Regiment long ago ... Anyway, I was best man at his wedding, and he was at mine. And we both married foreigners, which sort of further cemented the friendship. You know my wife – you were there when we met ...'

'Almost. I was there when you had your first argument. About which way we should be running, I think.'

'Aye, well, we've had a few since, but ...' Docherty smiled inwardly. 'Reeve married a Yugoslav, a Bosnian Muslim as it turns out, though no one seemed too bothered by such things back in 1984. He and Nena had two children, a girl first and then a boy, just like me and Isabel. Nena seemed happy enough living in England, and then about eighteen months ago Reeve got an advisory secondment to the Zimbabwean Army.

I haven't seen him since, and I hadn't heard anything since last Christmas, which should have worried me, but, you know how it is . . . Then last week, two days before Christmas, the CO comes to visit me in Glasgow.'

'Barney Davies? He just turned up?'

'Aye, he did.'

'With news of Reeve?'

'Aye.'

Docherty told Razor the story as Davies had told it to him, ending with the CO's request for him to lead in a four-man team.

'And it looks like you said yes.'

'Aye, eventually. Christ knows why.'

'Have they reinstated you?'

'Temporarily. But since the team won't be wearing uniform, and will have no access whatsoever to any military back-up it doesn't seem particularly relevant.'

Razor stared at him. 'Let me get this straight,' he said eventually. 'They want us to fight our way across a war zone so we can have a friendly chat with your friend Reeve, either slap his wrist or not when we hear his side of the story, and then fight our way back across the same war zone. And we start off by visiting the one city in the world which no one can get into or out of.'

Docherty grinned at him. 'You're in, then?'

'Of course I'm fucking in. You think I like teaching first aid to ex-paras for a living?'

'I now pronounce you man and wife,' the vicar said, and perhaps it was the familiarity of the words which jolted Damien Robson out of his reverie. The Dame, as he was known to all his regimental comrades, cast a guilty glance around him, but no one seemed

to have noticed his mental absence from the pro-
ceedings.

'You may kiss the bride,' the vicar added with a smile,
and the Dame's sister, Evie, duly uplifted her face to meet
the lips of her new husband. She then turned round to
find the Dame, and gave him an affectionate kiss on the
cheek. 'Thank you for giving me away,' she said, her
eyes shining.

'My pleasure,' he told her. She seemed as happy as he'd
ever seen her, he thought, and hoped to God it would last.
David Cross wasn't the man he would have chosen for
her, but he didn't actually have anything specific against
him. Yet.

The newly-weds were led off to sign the register, and
the Dame walked out of the church with the best man
to check that the photographer was ready. He was.

'We haven't seen you lately,' a voice said in his ear.

He turned to find the vicar looking at him with
that expression of pained concern which the Dame
had always associated with people who were paid to
care. 'No, 'fraid not,' he replied. 'The call of duty,' he
explained with a smile.

The vicar examined the uniform which Evie had
insisted her brother wear, his eyes coming to rest on
the beige beret and its winged-dagger badge. 'Well, I
hope we see you again soon,' he said.

The Dame nodded, and watched the man walk over
to talk with his and Evie's sister, Rosemary. A couple
of years before, after the Colombian operation, he had
started attending church regularly, this one here in
Sunderland when he was at home, and another on the
outskirts of Hereford during tours of duty. He could have
used the Regimental chapel, but, without being quite sure

why, had chosen to keep his devotions a secret from his comrades. It wasn't that he feared they'd take the piss – though they undoubtedly would – it was just that he felt none of it had anything to do with anyone else.

He soon realized that this feeling encompassed vicars and other practising Christians, and in effect the Church itself. He stopped attending services, and started looking for other ways of expressing a yearning inside him which he could hardly begin to explain to himself, let alone to others. He wasn't even sure it had anything to do with God – at least as other people seemed to understand the concept. The best he could manage by way of explanation was a feeling of being simultaneously drawn to something bigger than himself, something spiritual he supposed, and increasingly detached from the people around him.

The latter feeling was much in evidence at the wedding reception. It was good to see so many old friends: lads he'd been to school with, played football with, but none of them seemed to have much to say to him, and he couldn't find much to say to them. A few old memories, a couple of jokes about Sunderland – town and football team – and that was about it. Most of them seemed bored with their jobs and, if they were married, bored with that too. They seemed more interested in one another's wives than their own. The Dame hoped his sister . . . well, if David Cross cheated on her then the bastard would have him to deal with.

The time eventually arrived for the honeymooners' departure, their hired car trailing its retinue of rattling tin cans. Soon after that, feeling increasingly oppressed by the reception's accelerating descent into a drunken wife-swap, the Dame started off across the town, intent on enjoying the solitude of a twilight walk along the seafront.

It was a beautiful day still: cold but crystal-clear, gulls circling in the deepening blue sky, above the blue-grey waters of the North Sea. He walked for a couple of miles, up on to the cliffs outside the town, not really thinking about anything, letting the wind sweep the turmoil of other people from his mind.

He got back home to find his mother and Rosemary asleep in front of the TV, the living-room still littered with the debris of Christmas. On the table by the telephone there was a message for him to ring Hereford.

She sat with her knees pulled up to her chest, her head bowed down, on the stinking mattress in the slowly lightening room. The first night was over, she thought, but the first of how many?

The left side of her face still ached from where he had hit her, and the pain between her legs showed no signs of easing. She longed to be able to wash herself, and knew the longing was as much psychological as it was physical. Either way, she doubted if they would allow it.

This time yesterday, she thought, I was waiting for Hajrija in the nurses' dormitory.

The previous morning, after the two Russians had been sent running back towards Sarajevo with their tails between their legs, the four Chetniks had simply abandoned their roadblock, as if it had accomplished its purpose. They had casually left the young American's body by the side of the road, bundled her into the back seat of their Fiat Uno, and driven on down the valley to the next village. Here she could see no signs of the local population, either alive or dead, and only one blackened

46

hulk of a barn bore testimony to recent conflict. As they pulled up in the centre of the village another group of Chetnik irregulars, a dozen or so strong, was preparing to leave in a convoy of cars.

The leader of her group exchanged a few pleasantries with the leader of the outgoing troops, and she was led into a nearby house, which, though stripped of all personal or religious items, had obviously once belonged to a Muslim family. Since their departure it had apparently served as a billet for pigs. The Chetniks' idea of eating seemed to be to throw food at one another in the vain hope some of it went in through the mouth. Their idea of bathing was non-existent. The house stank.

What remained of the furniture was waiting to be burnt on the fire. And there was a large bloodstain on the rug in the main room which didn't seem that old.

Nena was led through to a small room at the back, which was empty save for a soiled mattress and empty bucket. The only light filtered round the edges of the shutters on the single window.

'I need to wash,' she told her escort. They were the first words she had spoken since her abduction.

'Later,' he said. 'There's no need now,' he added, and closed the door.

She had spent the rest of the day trying not to panic, trying to prepare herself for what she knew was coming. She wanted to survive, she kept telling herself, like a litany. If they were going to kill her anyway then there was nothing she could do about it, but she mustn't give them an excuse to kill her in a fit of anger. She should keep her mouth shut, say as little as possible. Perhaps tell them she was a doctor – they might decide she could be of use to them.

The afternoon passed by, and the light faded outside. No one brought her food or water, but even above the sound of the wind she could hear people in the house and even smell something cooking. Eventually she heard the clink of bottles, and guessed that they had begun drinking. It was about an hour later that the first man appeared in the doorway.

In the dim light she could see he had a gun in one hand. 'Take off the trousers,' he said abruptly. She swallowed once and did as he said.

'And the knickers.'

She pulled them off.

'Now lie down, darling,' he ordered.

She did so, and he was looming above her, dropping his jungle fatigues and long johns down to his knees, and thrusting his swollen penis between her legs.

'Wider,' he said, taking his finger off the gun's safety-catch only inches from her ear.

He pushed himself inside her, and started pumping. He made no attempt to feel her breasts, let alone kiss her, and out of nowhere she found herself remembering her father's dog, and its habit of trying to fuck the large cushion which someone had made for it to lie on. Now she was the cushion and this Serb was the dog. As smelly, as inhuman, as any dog.

He came with a furious rush, and almost leapt off her, as if she was suddenly contagious.

The second man was much the same, except for the fact that he didn't utter a single word between entering the room and leaving it. Then there was a respite of ten minutes or so, before the group's leader came in. He stripped from the waist down, grabbed a handful of her hair and lifted up her face to meet his own, as

48

if determined to impress on her exactly who it was she was submitting to.

She let out an involuntary sob, and that seemed to satisfy him. He pushed inside her quickly, but then took his time, savouring the moment with slow, methodical strokes, stopping himself several times as he approached a climax, before finally letting himself slip over the edge.

The young one was last, and the other three brought him in like a bull being brought to a heifer. He couldn't have been more than fourteen and he looked almost as nervous as he did excited. 'Come on,' the others said, 'show her what you've got.' He unveiled his penis almost shyly. It was already erect, quivering with anticipation.

'I think he's ready,' the leader joked, and the other two grabbed hold of Nena and pushed her back across the mattress, legs hanging out across the floor. Then they pulled them wide. 'That's where you aim for, Sergei,' one of them said, running a finger down her bloodied vulva. 'We've got her nice and lubricated for you.'

He came when he was only halfway inside her, to the drunken jeers of his companions.

After that they retired to the room next door, leaving her lying, rolled up in a ball. She tried to ignore the pain, wondering how they could let her live after what they had done. Did they think the war would last for ever, that law and decency would never return, that they were immune to any retribution?

They probably did. She hoped they did, because what other reason could they have for leaving her alive to tell the story?

And if they did make that mistake . . . She lay there trying to fix all the details in her mind: the place, the faces, the tattoos, the names they had called each other, the individual smells . . .

She could hear them talking in the next room, and laughing too. She started to cry, silently at first, then in great, wracking sobs which seemed to go on and on and on.

Exhaustion must have driven her to sleep for a few moments, because she suddenly woke to find the group's leader standing over her once more.

'You're in luck,' he told her. 'The rest of the lads haven't come back, so you've had an easy night. But I thought I'd come for dessert.'

He pulled down his trousers and stood there, his cock hanging in front of her face. She could smell it, smell herself on it. 'Make it grow,' he said with a leer, and she took hold of it, trying to imagine she was back in the hospital, examining someone. And in his case, hoping to find something seriously wrong.

It swelled in her hand.

'Now suck,' he said, looking down at her.

She didn't say no, but there must have been something in her eyes, because he abruptly changed his mind, pushing her back across the mattress, roughly pulling off her jeans, and rolling her over. 'You'd bite it off, wouldn't you?' he hissed into her ear, and thrust himself into her anus. She cried out involuntarily, which seemed only to increase his ardour. After a minute of energetic pumping he pulled himself out rolled her back over, wedged her legs open with his own, and rammed himself into her vagina, this time coming almost instantly.

He exhaled noisily and lifted himself up, looking down at her. 'You enjoy it really, don't you. All you Muslim whores enjoy it.'

She said nothing, but she couldn't control the look in her eyes, and he hit her once, as hard as she had ever imagined being hit, across the side of the face.

Perhaps she had blacked out for a few seconds, because her next conscious thought was of the door closing behind him. And then she had lain awake for what seemed like hours, feeling that a stain had been etched into her soul, and that nothing would ever be the same again. And when the morning light had appeared around the edge of the shutter it had seemed the greyest of lights.

Now she sat there, hugging herself around the knees, waiting to find out which fate awaited her – death or more nights like the last.

They were awake in the room next door, and this morning she could hear them talking, as the wind outside had died down.

'I like blondes,' one man was saying. 'Fucking a blonde is ... it's sort of cleaner, know what I mean? Dark women feel dirtier somehow ...'

'Why can't we keep her?' a younger voice asked.

'Listen to the kid. Thinks he's a stud already.'

'But why can't we keep her?' an older voice asked. 'They expect us to look after the area, freeze our balls off on that road. We only get down to Stovic about once a month.'

There were a few moments of silence, moments in which Nena tried not to wonder what the alternative was to being kept.

'We're not keeping her,' the group leader said. 'Keep a woman here permanently and we have to feed her, watch her, keep her clean ...'

'What for?'

'Because they don't feel as nice if they've been rolling around in their own shit,' the leader said.

'She could do the cooking,' someone objected.

'Yeah? The moment you let her out of that room she needs a guard, right? Which means one of us will have to stay here. It's not worth it. She's not that great a fuck, anyway. All bones. She's old enough to be Koca's grandmother. She's going to Vogosca.'

Those last four words caused Nena to almost gasp with relief. Vogosca was a small, predominantly Serb town about four miles north of Sarajevo, and though she didn't know what awaited her there it had to be better than dying in this mountain village whose name she didn't even know.

Hold on, she told herself, hold on. She put her coat on and waited.

One of the men came to get her an hour or so later – the one who had not said a word as he raped her. 'You have to get washed,' he said, and he prodded her out through the house's back door. The clouds were almost touching the ground, the mountains completely obscured from view, but the snow still seemed dazzling to her eyes. 'You can clean yourself with that,' he said, pointing at the nearest snowdrift.

She looked at it. 'What kind of men are you?' she asked before she could stop herself.

He wasn't offended by the question. 'We are Serbs,' he replied. 'Your men are taking our women just the same way.'

She walked across to the snowdrift, took down the bloody jeans and squatted in such a way that she could wash between her legs. The snow made the abrasions sting, but somehow that seemed almost a blessing.

After she had finished he took her round the outside of the house to where the Fiat was parked and told her to get inside. She sat alone in the car for about ten minutes, and then he returned, climbed in and started the car.

'Where are we going?' she asked.

'Not far,' he said. Once they were outside the village he lit a cigarette, and, after a moment's hesitation, offered her one.

'I don't smoke,' she said. 'I'm a doctor,' she added, without thinking.

'Yeah?' he said, interested. 'I've got a pain in my chest right here,' he said, tapping it with the hand that held the cigarette and giving her an enquiring glance.

'That could be a lot of things,' she said. Hopefully lung cancer, she thought.

'You think it could be serious?' he asked anxiously.

'It could. Why not just stop smoking,' she said coldly.

'After the war's over,' he said. 'It's too fucking nerve-racking without cigarettes.'

After the war's over you'll be on trial for rape and murder, she thought.

Another ten minutes and they had reached a larger village. In its centre both Serb irregulars and uniformed Yugoslav Army troops were in evidence. A tank sat to one side, its gun barrel depressed towards the slushy ground, and on the other side of the road two empty armoured personnel carriers were tilted against the verge. Beyond the tank a civilian bus was parked. The indicator board still announced Travnik as its destination, but the driver was wearing military uniform, and the passengers were exclusively female.

Nena's abductor pulled her out of the car and pushed her on to the bus.

'Only one this week?' the driver asked sarcastically.

Nena was surveying her fellow-passengers. There were about a dozen of them, and they all seemed to be Muslims, ranging in age from the mid-forties to just past puberty. Every one of them appeared to be in a state of semi-shock, as if the worst had already happened but they didn't yet know what it was.

'Where are you from?' Nena asked the woman nearest the front.

'No talking,' the driver screamed at her.

The two women's eyes met in shared resignation, and Nena sat down across the aisle from her.

At least three hours went by before a couple of uni-formed soldiers came on board, and the journey began. Nena was growing increasingly conscious of how thirsty she was – one handful of snow in twenty-four hours was nowhere near enough to satisfy anyone. Hunger was less of a problem. She realized that living in Sarajevo for the last few months, she had grown accustomed to life on an empty stomach.

The afternoon dragged on, the bus coughing its way up hills and rattling its way down them. It was growing dark as they finally entered Vogosca. Nena had driven through the small town many times, but couldn't remember ever stopping. The bus drew up outside the Partisan Sports Hall, and the twelve women and girls were ordered off. A Serb irregular sporting the badge of the White Eagles gestured them in through the front doors, and once inside another man pointed them through a further pair of twin doors.

It was dark inside the room, but as Nena's eyes grew accustomed to the gloom it became apparent that they were in a gymnasium; one, moreover, that was already home to other women. All around the walls they sat or lay, thirty or forty of them, and as yet not one of them had uttered a word.

'What is this?' Nena asked, her voice echoing in the cavernous space. As if in response someone started to cry.

'It's the shop window of a brothel,' a dry voice said.

4

Chris Martinson pulled the jeep into the car park of Hereford Station and looked at his watch. The Dame's connection from Worcester was not due for another five minutes, which probably meant a twenty-minute wait. A ferocious rain was beating a tattoo on the jeep's convertible roof, and almost visibly deepening the puddles in the car park, but at least it was relatively warm for the time of year. Chris decided to stay where he was until the train came into view under the bridge.

Sergeant Docherty had called him with the request to pick the Dame up at the station, and though Chris had not had much to do with Docherty during his eight years in the SAS – the older man had left B Squadron for the Training Wing before Chris won his badge – he had managed to piece together an impression of him from what others had said. It would have been hard not to, for Docherty was something of a legend – the man who had almost succumbed to personal tragedy, and then come home the hard way from Argentina during the Falklands War, walking out across the Andes with a new wife.

Chris had a good idea how hard that must have been, having been involved in something similar himself in Colombia. Only he had neglected to bring a wife.

Docherty was not just known for his toughness though. He was supposed to be something close to the old SAS ideal, a thinking soldier. There were many in the Regiment who lamented the shift in selection policy over the last decade, which seemed to put a lower premium on thought and a higher one on physical and emotional strength. Others, of course, said it was just a sign of the times. The Dochertys of this world, like the George Bests, were becoming extinct. Their breeding grounds had been overrun by progress.

It suddenly dawned on Chris why Docherty had sent him to collect the Dame. The Scot had thought it would be a good idea for the two of them to talk before being confronted with whatever it was they were about to be confronted with. To psych each other up. Chris smiled to himself. A thinking soldier indeed.

A two-tone horn announced the arrival of the train, seconds before the diesel's yellow nose appeared beneath the bridge. Chris jumped down from the jeep and made a run for the ticket hall, his boots sending water flying up from the puddles.

The Dame was one of the last to reach the barrier, his dark face set, as usual, in an almost otherworldly seriousness, as if he was deeply involved in pondering some abstruse philosophical puzzle.

The face broke into a smile when he saw Chris.

'Your humble chauffeur awaits,' the latter said.

'I suppose the birds aren't flying today,' the Dame said, eyeing the torrential rain from the station entrance. 'How many miles away have you parked?'

Chris pointed out the jeep. 'Do you think you can manage twenty yards?'

The two men dashed madly through the half-flooded car park and scrambled into the jeep.

'What's this all about?' the Dame half-shouted above the din of rain on the roof.

'No idea,' Chris said, starting up the engine. 'But we're

about to find out – the briefing's due to begin in about twenty-five minutes.'

'You don't even know where we're going?'

'Nope. They're playing it really close to the chest. All I know is that it's a four-man op.'

'Who are the other two?'

'Sergeant Docherty and . . .'

'I thought he'd retired.'

'He had. He's been reinstated, presumably just for this one show.'

'Christ, he must be about forty-five by now. It can't be anything too strenuous.'

Chris laughed. 'I shouldn't say anything like that when he's around. He didn't look too decrepit the last time I saw him.'

'Maybe. Who's Number Four?'

'Sergeant Wilkinson. Training Wing.'

'I know him. At least, I've played football with him. He must be about thirty-five . . .'

'Hey, I've turned thirty, you know. Someone obviously decided they needed experience for this one, and you were just included to provide some mindless energy.'

'Probably,' the Dame said equably. 'Wilkinson always reminds me a bit of Eddie. London to the bone. A joker. He's even a Tottenham supporter.'

'Yeah, well,' Chris said, and both men were silent for a few moments, thinking of their old comrade, who had died in the village by the jungle river in Colombia. Probably with some witty rejoinder frozen on his lips.

'How was your Christmas?' the Dame asked eventually.

'Fine,' Chris said, though he'd spent most evenings desperately bored. 'Yours?'

'It was great. My sister got married yesterday, and I had to give her away. It was great,' he said again, as if he was trying to convince himself.

Chris looked at his watch as he turned the jeep in through the gates of the Stirling Lines barracks. 'Time for a brew,' he said.

The water-buffalo's head which reigned over 'the Kremlin's' briefing room – a memento of the Regiment's Malayan days – seemed to be leaning slightly to one side, as if it was trying to hear some distant mating call. Forget it, Docherty thought, you don't have a body any more.

He knew the feeling, after the previous night's evening in the pub with old friends. The good news was that he and Isabel couldn't be drinking as much as they thought they were – not if his head felt like this after only half a dozen pints and chasers.

'Bad news,' Barney Davies said, as he came in through the door. 'Nena Reeve seems to have gone missing. She's not been to work at the hospital for the last couple of days. Of course, things being the way they are in Sarajevo, she may just be at home with the flu and unable to phone in. Or she may have been wounded by a sniper, or be looking after a friend who was. They're trying to find out.'

'MI6?'

'Presumably. Did Robson get here all right?'

'Yes, boss,' a voice with a Wearside accent said from behind him. The Dame and Chris filed in, swiftly followed by Razor Wilkinson.

Docherty got to his feet, shook hands with the new arrivals, and then took up a position half-sitting on the table at the front, while the other four arranged themselves in a semicircle of upright chairs.

He began by introducing everyone. 'You two have been recommended to me by the CO,' he told Chris and the Dame. 'Though you may wish he hadn't by the time we're finished. We're going to Bosnia, gentlemen,' he added, almost as an afterthought.

He went through the whole story from the beginning, all the while keeping a careful watch on the two new men's faces. The mere mention of Bosnia seemed to have brought a gleam into the eyes of the lad from Sunderland, and as Docherty talked he could almost feel the Dame's intense eagerness to get started.

The Essex lad was a different type altogether: very cool and collected, very self-contained, almost as if he was in some sort of reverie. There were a couple of moments when Docherty wasn't even sure he was listening, but once he'd finished his outline it was Chris who came up with the first question, and one that went straight to the heart of the matter.

'What are we going in as, boss?' he asked.

'That's a good question,' Barney Davies said. 'You'll be flying into Split on the coast of Croatia, and while you're there waiting for transport to Sarajevo – which may be a few hours, may be a few days – your cover will be as supervisory staff attached to the Sarajevo civilian supply line. Once you're in Sarajevo ... well, not to put too fine a point on it, you'll just be one more bunch of irregulars in a situation which is not too far from anarchy.'

'But we have troops there, right?' the Dame asked. 'The Cheshires and the Royal Irish.'

'One battalion from each,' Davies confirmed, 'and

a squadron of Lancers, but they're under UN control, and that means they can only fire off weapons in self-defence. Their own, not yours. You should get some useful intelligence from our people out there, but don't expect anything more. The whole point of this op, at least as far as our political masters are concerned, is to restore our reputation as peace-keepers, with the least possible publicity . . .'

'You make it sound like the Regiment has a different priority, boss,' Razor said, surprising Docherty.

'I think it might be fairer to say we have an additional priority,' Davies said. 'Looking after our own. John Reeve has been an outstanding soldier for the Regiment, and he deserves whatever help we can give him.'

There was a rap on the door, and an adjutant poked his head around it. 'The man from the Foreign Office is here, boss,' he told Davies.

'Bring him through,' the CO ordered. 'He's going to brief you on the local background,' he told the four men.

A suited young man, carrying a briefcase in one hand and what appeared to be a large wad of maps in the other, walked confidently into the room. He had longish, curly hair, circular, black-framed spectacles, and the overall look of an anorexic Malcolm Rifkind.

'This is Mr Castle, from the Foreign Office's Balkan Section,' Davies said formally, as he walked across to make sure the door was firmly closed. Docherty suddenly realized how unusual it was for the CO to introduce a briefing. He wondered how many other members of the Regiment knew of this mission. If any.

'He is going to give you a basic introduction to what the newspapers now like to call "the former

Yugoslavia", the CO went on. 'I know you all read the *Sun* voraciously,' he added with a broad smile, 'so most of what he has to say may be only too familiar, but just in case you've missed the odd page of detailed analysis . . . Mr Castle.'

The man from the Foreign Office was still struggling to fix his unwieldy pile of maps to the Kremlin's antique easel. Chris gave him a hand.

'Good morning,' Castle said finally, in a voice that was mercifully dissimilar to Malcolm Rifkind's. 'Despite your CO's testimonial to your reading habits, I'm going to assume you know nothing.'

'Good assumption,' Razor agreed.

Castle grinned. 'Right. Well, Yugoslavia, roughly translated, means Land of the Southern Slavs, and these Slavs originally came south to populate the area more than a thousand years ago. The peoples we now call the Croats, Serbs, Slovenes, Montenegrins, Bosnian Muslims are all descendants of these Slavs. They are not separate races, any more than Yorkshiremen are a separate race from Brummies, no matter what Geoff Boycott might tell you. If you visited an imaginary nudist colony in Bosnia you wouldn't be able to tell a Bosnian Muslim from a Slovene, or a Serb from a Croat.'

He paused for breath, and smiled at them. 'What these peoples don't have in common is history. I'm simplifying a lot, but for most of the last five hundred years, up to the beginning of this century, the area has been divided into three, with each third dominated by a different culture. The Austrians and sometimes the Italians were dominant in Slovenia, Croatia and along the coast, imposing a West European, Catholic culture. In the mountains of Bosnia and Hercegovina – here,' he said, pointing at the map, 'there was a continuous Turkish occupation for several centuries, and many of the Slavs were converted to Islam. In the east, in Serbia and to a lesser extent in Montenegro, the Eastern Orthodox Church, with its mostly Russian cultural outlook, managed to survive the more sporadic periods of Turkish domination. In fact, fighting the Turks was probably what gave the Serbs their exaggerated sense of identity.

'So, by the time we reach the twentieth century we have a reasonably homogenous racial group divided into three cultural camps. Rather like what Northern Ireland might be like if a large group of Arabs had been settled there in the seventeenth century, at the same time as the Protestants.'

'Christ almighty,' Razor muttered.

'A fair comment,' Castle agreed. He seemed to be enjoying himself. 'The problem with people who only have cultures to identify themselves is that the cultures tend to get rabid. Since much of the last millennium in the Balkans has been a matter of Muslim versus Christian there's plenty of fertile ground for raking up old Muslim–Croat and Muslim–Serb quarrels. And in both world wars the Russians fought the Austrians, which meant Serbs against Croats. In World War Two this relationship reached a real nadir – the Croats were allowed their own little state by the Nazis, managed to find home-grown Nazis to run it – Ustashi they were called – and took the chance to butcher a large number of Serbs. No one knows how many, but hundreds of thousands.

'But I'm getting a bit ahead of the story. Yugoslavia was formed after World War One, partly as a recognition that these peoples did have a lot in common, and partly as a way of containing their differences for everyone else's sake. After all, the war had been triggered by a Bosnian Serb assassinating an Austrian archduke in the mainly Muslim city of Sarajevo.'

Castle checked to see if they were awake, found no one had glazed eyes yet, and turned back to the map. 'There are a few other minor divisions I should mention. The Albanians – who are a different racial group – have large minorities in the Serbian region of Kosovo and in Macedonia. Macedonians are not a separate ethnic group, and their territory has been variously claimed by Bulgaria – which claims that Macedonians are just confused Bulgars – and Greece, which claims etc., etc.' He grinned owlishly at them.

'It's a right fucking mess, then,' Razor observed.

'But all their own,' Chris murmured.

'At the end of the last war a temporary solution appeared – communism. It was the communists, under Tito, who led the guerrilla war against the Germans, and after the war they took over the government. The ethnic tensions were basically put on ice. Each major group was given its own state in what was nominally a federal system, but Tito and the Party took all the important decisions. The hope was that the new secular religion of communism would see the withering away of the old national-religious identities – everyone would have a house and a car and a TV and be like every other consumer.

'But when Tito died in 1980 there was no one of the same stature to hold it all together. The system just about stumbled along through the eighties, with the Party bosses holding it all together between them, but when communism collapsed everywhere else in eastern Europe, the rug got pulled out from under their feet.

'What was left was an economy not doing that badly, at least by other communist standards, but a country with nothing to bind it together, and of course all the accumulated grievances came pouring out. Under Tito the richer areas like Slovenia and Croatia had been forced to subsidize the poorer ones, but they hadn't been given much of anything in return. The Serbs, who dominated the Party and the federal institutions – and particularly the national army – had no interest in changing things, and the power to stop those who had. Not surprisingly the Slovenes and Croats decided to opt out.

'Slovenia presented no great problems, except that it set a precedent – if Slovenia could go, then why not Croatia? The trouble was that Croatia had a large Serb minority, and the Croat leaders made no effort whatsoever to reassure it.

'By this time everyone was acting very badly, like a bunch of mad prima donnas. The Croats decided to secede from Yugoslavia, and their Serb minority areas decided to secede from Croatia. That was a year and a half ago, the summer of 1991, and both secessions have stuck, so to speak. Croatia has been recognized as an independent state, but since the cease-fire at the beginning of this year the Serb areas are nominally "UN-protected" – in other words under Serb military control. There's no foreseeable hope of Croatia taking them back.

'Which brings us to Bosnia – your destination. The most enthusiastic Yugoslavs always thought of this as the heart of the federation. It was the most ethnically mixed area, the one where mutual tolerance, and even mutual

65

enjoyment, of the separate cultural traditions seemed most deep-rooted. It's mostly mountainous country, full of deep valleys and high passes, with towns clustered in the hollows. I travelled there several years ago, and found it beautiful. Most people do.' He grimaced. 'But an awful lot has been destroyed in the last six months.

'Anyway, once Croatia and Slovenia opted out, the Bosnian Government had an impossible choice to make – either accept a subsidiary position in a Serb-dominated mini-Yugoslavia or try opting out themselves, with the Yugoslav Army already encamped in their country and the Serb minority committed to opposing Bosnian independence by force of arms. They chose the latter, no doubt hoping that the international community would come to their aid. No such luck.

'I should say one more thing about Bosnia-Hercegovina. Each of the three peoples – Croats, Serbs, Muslims – have areas in which they are the majority, but there is intermingling everywhere. There was no way, a year ago, that you could have divided Bosnia tidily along ethnic grounds. Small villages were split two ways, sometimes even three ways – let alone regions.

'But of course the moment the international community started talking partition – quite mistakenly in my view – the rush was on. If a particular town had forty per cent Serbs, forty per cent Croats and twenty per cent Muslims, then the Serbs' chance of including it in a Greater Serbia would be much improved if the other sixty per cent could be persuaded to move on. And if two towns like that were separated by an area eighty per cent Muslim or Croat, then strategic necessity dictated that they be moved on too. This pattern is being repeated everywhere. Since no one's too sure of what is theirs, they're grabbing it anyway.'

'Is this what they call ethnic cleansing?' the Dame asked.

'Yes. Wonderful phrase, isn't it? The lucky ones are being simply moved on, but it looks like an enormous number of men have been killed, and an equally vast number of women have been raped, with the dual aim of humiliating them and making them pregnant. In both cases the Serbs seem the guiltiest party, by quite a considerable degree.'

'Isn't that like comparing Genghis Khan to Attila the Hun?' Barney Davies asked.

'No,' Castle answered immediately. 'At least, there doesn't seem to be that sort of equivalence. Why should there be? The Serbs in World War Two came nowhere near to matching the record of the Croat Ustashi for atrocities. And in this war, though individual groups of Croat and Muslim soldiers have undoubtedly been guilty of rape, the widespread reports of mass rape in Serb-dominated areas suggest that there is a systematic policy being coordinated from the top.'

'Jesus,' Chris muttered.

'At the moment,' Castle continued, turning round to flip over another map, 'this is the overall military situation on the ground. The Croats and Muslims have this' – he traced an area with an index finger – 'and the Serbs this. But of course the Muslim–Croat alliance is stronger in some areas than others . . .'

'Where's Zavik?' Docherty asked. He had looked it up in an atlas, but he wanted to see where it was in terms of the military situation.

'Here,' Castle said, pointing to a spot about twelve miles behind Serb lines.

'What sort of military units are we dealing with here?' Docherty asked. 'Regular Army divisions?'

'A good question. Everything from regular units down to gangs of bandits, with all the various possibilities in between. The official Bosnian Army is mostly Muslim but also includes Serbs and Croats. There are also various exclusively Muslim militias, and even volunteer units made up from Islamic veterans of Beirut, Iran, Afghanistan, etc.'

'Wonderful,' Chris murmured sarcastically.

'The Croatian Army has regular units in Bosnia, the Bosnian Croats have their own army, and there are also private militias. The worst of them are basically reborn Ustashi – they dress like designer stormtroopers and behave even worse. It's basically the same story on the Serbian side, with the old Federal Army now basically the Serbian Army, a Serbian Army of Bosnia, the Serbian Police of Bosnia, and any number of militias. The most famous are the Arkanovci, who are led by a man who calls himself Arkan and is wanted in about five European countries for armed robbery. Then there's the White Eagles and the Chetniks. Croats and Muslims, by the way, call all Serb irregulars Chetniks, after the nationalist guerrillas from World War Two, and they do tend to look alike – the fashion here is broad-brimmed hats and long beards, so they look like psychotic Australian Rasputins. By the same token, all Croat militiamen are called Ustashi, after the World War Two fascists.'

'What are these bands of merry men armed with?' Razor asked. Even he seemed subdued by Castle's account, Docherty thought.

'And how many men are we talking about?' Chris wanted to know.

'Serbs – about 70,000 fighters; 50,000 Croats; maybe 40,000 Muslims. They all have APCs for moving men around, and the usual automatic weapons. The Serbs have some Soviet tanks, and as much heavy artillery as they need, up to 155mm. Plus, probably twenty combat aircraft – Super Galebs and Oraos. Between thirty and forty helicopters – Gazelles, for the most part. The Croats and the Muslims have no planes, no tanks and, in the Muslims' case, not much artillery to speak of.'

'No wonder they need their fedayeen,' Docherty observed.

'Well, they can't get any weapons from outside because of the arms embargo,' Castle said. 'Any other questions?'

'Will it all have a happy ending?' Razor asked.

'I doubt it,' Castle said simply.

When he had gone, one question was uppermost in the Dame's mind. 'What weaponry are we taking in?' he wanted to know.

'Whatever we can carry without looking too much like an Action Team,' Docherty said. 'Certainly MP5s and High Powers. Any particular requests?'

'An Accuracy International,' the Dame said.

'Good idea,' Docherty agreed, remembering the Dame's reported prowess with a sniper rifle.

'How about a Chieftain tank?' Razor asked.

'If you can carry it, you can bring it,' Docherty shot back.

5

The plane touched down at Split airport soon after ten a.m. on Thursday 30 December 1992, and the bright sunshine and English summer temperature which greeted them at the open door was a welcome change from the freezing drizzle they had left behind in Oxfordshire.

In years gone by, Docherty reminded himself, thousands of Brits had arrived here on package tours for a week of Mediterranean winter warmth, armed with trashy novels and suntan lotion rather than Heckler & Koch MP5 sub-machine-guns.

A quarter of a mile or so across the tarmac a long line of Hercules C-130 transport planes were parked wing-tip to wing-tip, each bearing the UN logo. Behind them the Dalmatian mountains rose up from the coastal plain into a clear blue sky.

A tall, clean-shaven RAF officer sporting a pale-blue UN beret was waiting for them at the bottom of the mobile stairway. 'Flight-Lieutenant Frobisher,' he introduced himself, offering his hand to each of the foursome in turn. 'Which are the bags containing the winter clothing and the you-know-what?'

'Those two,' Docherty said, indicating the two large canvas holdalls Chris and the Dame were carrying. They'd been warned before leaving to pack the Arctic clothing and the weaponry separately from the rest of the equipment.

'I'll take care of them,' Frobisher said, and carried the bags across to where another RAF officer was talking to the pilot, dumped them at his feet, and exchanged a few words. Then he rejoined the SAS men, and gestured them towards a white jeep parked a few yards away.

Docherty clambered into the front seat, while the other three squeezed themselves into the back.

'The stuff will be kept here for you until you leave,' Frobisher explained. 'On one of those,' he added, indicating the distant line of transport planes, 'but when that will be depends very much on weather conditions. Oh, it's lovely down here,' he agreed, seeing their surprised faces, 'but up in the mountains it's a different kettle of fish altogether. Go thirty miles east of here and the temperature will drop about twenty degrees – Celsius, that is. Sarajevo's in the middle of a blizzard right now, with ground visibility down to about six inches. So don't expect an imminent departure. But don't not expect one either. If a window opens up we want you ready to go.'

'So we're not staying out here?' Docherty asked.

'There isn't anywhere, unless you fancy kipping down for a week in a C-130. In any case, the Croats watch what's happening at this airport like hawks, and the town's only twelve miles away. We thought you'd be a bit less noticeable there, so we booked you into one of the hotels. As you can imagine there's quite a lot of vacancies this year.' He looked at Docherty, as if expecting formal approval of the arrangements.

'Sounds good,' the Scot said.

'Is there room service?' Razor asked.

'I don't know,' Frobisher said doubtfully, as if uncertain whether the question was serious. It seemed unlikely that he'd ever had dealings with the SAS before.

Docherty had been expecting at least some formalities

to mark their official arrival in a foreign country, but Frobisher simply drove the jeep around the end of the forlorn-looking terminal building, through an open gate and out on to a wide highway that ran along parallel to the coast, at times almost directly above the breaking waves. In the distance silhouetted islands loomed abruptly out of the shining Adriatic, giving Docherty the impression of a warmer west coast of Scotland. On the other side of the highway sunlit slopes tumbled down almost to the verge. An almost idyllic setting, it was hardly what they had been expecting.

'It doesn't look like the war's reached here,' Chris observed.

'Not really,' Frobisher agreed. 'There's no argument about whose territory this is. Still, having said that, Split is home to some of the nastier Croat groups, and there has been trouble. There was a lot of intimidation against the minorities in the town a year or so back, people being fired from their jobs, scared out of their houses, a lot of beatings, a few deaths. Most of the Serbs and Muslims upped and left, though God knows where they went. The place doesn't have a nice feeling to it – at least I don't think so. Looks nice, though,' he added, then, pointing forward and to the right, said: 'That's it over there, on the peninsula.'

It did look nice, too nice for beatings and deaths. A lighthouse sat on the end of the headland, and behind it the ground rose in a high, wooded hill, which seemed to stand guard over the town nestling beneath it.

'One of the Roman Emperors built his retirement palace here,' Frobisher said.

'Tottenham played Hadjuk Split in the UEFA Cup once,' Razor added.

'Well, that's the last two thousand years taken care of, then,' Chris said.

Ten minutes later they were entering the outskirts of the town, climbing up and across the peninsula's spine, and motoring down towards the sea on its southern side. Their hotel, which bore the unpronounceable name of the Prenociste Slavija, was on one of the narrow side-streets inside the walls of the old Roman palace. Its interior was less impressive than its location, but all of them had stayed in worse.

'The rooms are booked for a week,' Frobisher told them. 'There's no chance you'll be going in today, but if tomorrow looks like a possibility I'll come by tonight and tell you. The telephones are not what you'd call reliable,' he added cryptically. 'Anything else? Ah yes,' he answered himself, pulling something from his pocket. 'This is a map of the town in case you need it. The hotel is here' – he pointed to the spot – 'and there's a decent enough restaurant here, just inside the East Gate. You've got money, I take it.'

'Aye. Dinars and dollars.'

'I should forget the dinars. Anything else?'

'How can we get hold of you?' Docherty asked.

'Just take a taxi out to the airport. The UN Operations HQ is on the second floor of the terminal building.'

When Frobisher had gone, Docherty turned to find the other three looking at him expectantly.

'Food, boss?' Razor asked.

'Sounds good. And then I think we'll go for a run, get used to the altitude.'

The others groaned in unison.

An hour and a half later, as the four men toiled their way up towards the summit of Marjan Hill for the third time, the Dame was beginning to revise his opinions about Docherty's readiness for retirement. A few yards behind him Chris was wondering whether Docherty had planned this demonstration with just such an aim in mind. Was the Patrol Commander intent on dispelling any doubts the younger men might have about his fitness? If so, he had succeeded.

Bringing up the rear, Razor was breathing heavily but still smiling to himself. Running up and down a hill in the sunshine sure beat teaching Continuation Training classes, he decided.

'That'll do,' Docherty told them at the summit. 'I don't want to wear you out before we get there.' He looked at his watch. 'OK, it's just gone four. We'll eat at seven. So you've got three hours to lie in the bath, write a classical symphony or take a look around. And we'll meet up in the same restaurant.'

The others nodded.

'I'll write the symphony,' Razor said. 'Wilkinson's Fourth.'

'Let's pray it's Unfinished,' Chris muttered.

Docherty eyed them fondly. There was nothing quite like bullshit for cementing the relationships in a four-man patrol.

Docherty took a quick shower, dressed and went out on his own. For half an hour or so he wandered through the narrow streets of the old town, inspecting the buildings with a slightly jaundiced eye. As a lover of Islamic and Spanish architecture – the legacy of time spent on active service in Oman and off duty in Mexico – he found Graeco-Roman styles too brutal and the later Renaissance architecture too florid by half. He was looking forward to seeing the minarets of Sarajevo, always assuming there were any left.

He knew that most people would think it wrong to lament the loss of an architectural heritage when so many people of all ages were being killed every day, but, as his friend Liam McCall had pointed out, there was no God-given limit on how many different things a man could lament at the same time.

And the Serbs weren't destroying those buildings by accident. Representing a thousand years of a culture's history, they were the visual embodiment of the lives of countless generations of Bosnian Muslims. Destroy them, and the books and the pictures they contained, and it was like erasing a people's memory.

He sighed. Maybe he was getting too old for this game after all.

He emerged on to Titova Obala, the seafront promenade. A couple of hundred yards to his left he could see Razor and Chris walking in the opposite direction, and smiled hopefully to himself. A friendship between those two could only strengthen the chemistry of the patrol, which Docherty already considered as good as any he'd known.

He crossed the wide street and turned right along the sea wall, looking out across the myriad boats lying at anchor across the harbour. Many seemed neglected, even dilapidated, and there was a sad air about the whole scene, as there was about the town as a whole. It was a Sleeping Beauty town, he decided, waiting for peace to kiss it awake.

A tousle-haired man in a thick woollen sweater was leaning against the harbour wall, staring out to where the sun was rapidly sinking behind an arm of the harbour.

To Docherty's surprise he had a copy of that day's *Daily Mirror* sticking out of the back pocket of his jeans. It had to have arrived on the same plane as they had.

'Good evening,' he said, wondering whether he'd get an English response.

'My God, the Scots have arrived,' the man said with a smile and a Midlands accent. He was younger than Docherty, probably in his mid-thirties.

'We understand what it's like being an oppressed minority,' Docherty said, 'so they called us in to sort things out. My name's Jamie, by the way.'

'Jim,' the man said, offering his hand. 'And what are you really doing here?'

'Admin work for the UN,' Docherty lied. 'How about you?'

'I'm on the lorries. The supply run to Sarajevo,' he explained. 'Got back this morning, and I'll probably be going back Saturday.'

'What's the situation like there?' Docherty asked.

'Bloody terrible. Imagine how bad it could get, and then imagine it being ten times worse – that's Sarajevo. The people there – the ordinary people – are bloody amazing, but . . . there seem to be more dyed-in-the-wool bastards per square foot in this country than you'd find anywhere outside a Conservative Party conference. I hope you're not a Tory, mate.'

Docherty grinned. 'No. How about the journey – no trouble on the road from irregulars? Or regulars, come to that?'

Jim shrugged. 'We have UN troops riding shotgun, for what it's worth. There's a lot of hassle, you know, having to get free passage agreed each time, and being stopped every few miles to have our papers looked at and the loads checked . . .' He shrugged again. 'But by God it's worth it when you see the faces at the other end.'

Docherty found himself envying the man. 'It must be,' he said.

'You know,' Jim said, turning to face him, 'I spent most of the last ten years delivering fitted bathrooms to people who didn't really need them. Can you imagine what that's like – spending your life doing something completely unnecessary? And then I saw this job advertised, and I just had to take it. My wife thought I was nuts, at least in the beginning, and maybe I am, but for the first time in my life I'm delivering something that people really need, and Christ it feels good.'

Walking back towards the hotel Docherty wondered, not for the first time, how the same species could accommodate the utter meanness which targeted minarets and the generosity of spirit which made a man like Jim risk everything because helping people felt so good. He would have liked to talk to Liam McCall about it – they could have shared each other's incomprehension.

The restaurant was not so empty as it had been at lunchtime: three other tables were already occupied, and two more had 'reserved' signs on them. A family of four was seated at one of the occupied tables, but the others contained only men, and young men at that. None of them was wearing uniform, and it might have been Docherty's imagination, but there seemed a hint of latent aggression in the air. It smelt of what Isabel liked to call a 'testosterone overload situation'.

Once again Chris translated the menu for them. He and Docherty settled for *brodet* – mixed fish stewed with rice – while the Dame opted for a seafood platter and Razor for an anchovy pizza. Four small glasses of plum brandy served as aperitifs, and they ordered a large carafe of Riesling to complement the meal. 'Here's to the taxpayer, who's paying for it all,' Razor said, raising his glass.

'In Sarajevo they're eating dandelion leaves,' Chris said soberly.

'Christ, I hate greens,' Razor complained, just as the door opened to admit another group of four men. The words 'designer stormtroopers' went through all four SAS minds at the same moment. Each of the newcomers had hair cut close-to-stubble short and clean-shaven faces. Each was wearing a jet-black uniform, black boots and black leather mittens with silver studs. Two of them were sporting Ray-Ban Aviator shades, and one had a black sweatband around his head, presumably to keep his non-existent hair out of his eyes.

Docherty's first impulse was to laugh out loud, but he restrained himself. For five reasons. One was their need to remain as anonymous as possible, the other four rested in low-slung holsters on each man's thigh – black, Czech-made Scorpion machine pistols.

'Jesus,' Razor muttered under his breath.

'More like Hell's Angels,' Docherty murmured. He remembered gangs of leather-clad rockers in the sixties who had walked into Glasgow cafés and pubs with exactly the same cold-hearted swagger. They had only been carrying bicycle chains and knives, and they had scared the shit out of him. Not so much because they were stronger, or because there were more of them, but because their only means of communication with each other was through finding strangers to victimize.

The new arrivals took a table about fifteen feet away from the SAS men.

'Keep the talk down and avoid eye contact,' Docherty softly told the others. 'We'll just enjoy our meal and get the hell out of here.'

The food arrived sooner than expected, as if the waiter was also keen to see them on their way as quickly as possible. As far as Docherty could remember, he was the only man who had heard them speaking English, and another waiter was dealing with the black-clad irregulars. Maybe there wouldn't be a problem.

Or maybe there would.

'You can tell how a man is by his friends,' a voice said loudly in English.

'A friend of Serbs is a pig,' one of his companions agreed. Docherty could feel the eyes boring into the side of his head, and fought the temptation to turn towards them.

'It is like they say – there are two peoples in Europe who do not like to wash – the Serbs and the English,' the first voice continued conversationally. Someone else laughed, and the other two followed his cue, like an echo. Presumably they didn't know enough English to join in the baiting.

It was all so ludicrously childish, Docherty thought, like a thousand scenes in a thousand bad Westerns. Sure, there were bullies everywhere in real life, but they usually had a better script than this. He placed a forkful of fish in his mouth; it tasted sourer than it should have.

He looked round at the others. Razor was smiling to himself, revelling in the luxury of having his back to the taunters. Chris was managing to look indifferent, but the Dame's mouth was set in a grim and angry line.

'We took an English nurse in Knin,' the voice said. 'She said she was a virgin.' He laughed. 'Not now. Now she has a hundred men to remember.'

Docherty took a deep breath. He was confident they could cope with any amount of bullshit, but could the shitheads in black cope with being ignored much longer? And if they couldn't then what form would the escalation take? And how the hell could they defuse the situation?

'*De dónde viene este vino?*' Razor asked suddenly, picking up the bottle and examining it with great interest. It had occurred to him that all four of them were both semi-fluent in Spanish and relatively dark-complexioned.

'Dalmatia,' Chris said. '*Es bueno, sí?*'

'*Sí,*' Razor agreed.

Docherty smiled inwardly and said he had always liked Yugoslavian wines.

The four SAS men launched into an enthusiastic discussion, in Spanish, of the relative merits of different wines. All of them were speaking the Latin-American variant, but Docherty doubted whether the Croats would know the difference. They had reverted to their own language, he realized with relief.

'They're talking about their plans for tomorrow,' Chris explained in Spanish, as if reading Docherty's mind.

'I hope they include a run-in with the fashion police,' Razor said.

They walked back to their hotel along the darkened street feeling good.

'Jesus, I'm ready for a bed,' Docherty said, as they walked in through the front door, only to find Flight-Lieutenant Frobisher rising out of the single, threadbare armchair to greet them.

'The weathermen say there may be a window around dawn tomorrow,' he said, 'so you'd better wait out at the airport.'

Ten minutes later they were back in Frobisher's jeep, motoring out through the empty streets of the port and on to the coast highway. The day's clear sky had given way to heavy, rolling clouds, with a hint of rain in the air. Their beds for the night turned out to be sackfuls of rice in the belly of a Hercules C-130.

6

Dawn was still half an hour away when the transport plane rattled off the runway and into the dark sky. Docherty stared at the solid wall of the fuselage and remembered the view they had enjoyed coming in to Split the previous morning, the islands scattered across the deep-blue sea.

The RAF pilots had both seemed cheerful enough, and the younger of the two had even relished telling them they were in for a 'Khe Sanh' landing at Sarajevo. Docherty had not spoiled the other three's flight by passing on everything he had heard about such landings from Americans who'd served in Vietnam. Just so long as they were all well strapped in when the time came . . .

They were in their full Arctic gear now: thermal vests and long johns, quilted under-trousers and jackets, thick woollen socks, gloves and high-neck combat boots, the latter a great improvement on their Falklands-era predecessors. As the quartermaster had told them: 'You might get shot dead but you won't get trench foot.'

Gore-tex jackets normally completed the outfit, but for this trip they were also wearing flak-jackets. Both Serbs and Muslims had reportedly acquired the nasty habit of using Sarajevo's runway for target practice.

Docherty leaned his head back against the plane's metal skin and closed his eyes, his mind reaching forward towards their arrival in the Bosnian capital. What would it be like? Would they find Nena Reeve? And if they did, would she agree to come with them?

He wondered again if this chosen course of action hadn't been a mistake. A C-130 like this one could have dropped the four of them within easy reach of Zavik. Granted, they would never have got clearance for a flight out of Split, but these planes had a range of close on 3000 miles. The whole mission could have been mounted from the UK.

Too much chance of political hassle, perhaps. And there was always a lot to be said for a thorough acclimatization. The town of Zavik, the immediate vicinity, the military situation in the area – all were complete unknowns. The chances of dropping a team into the heart of a battle zone might not be high, but it hardly seemed a risk worth taking.

Against that, they now had to countenance a landing in Sarajevo and an overland odyssey to Zavik. If the latest reports were correct then most of the journey would be through Muslim-held territory, but even with snow on the ground the military situation seemed alarmingly fluid. If all four of them came through this without a serious scratch, Docherty thought to himself, then he'd retire once more a happy man.

He glanced round at the other three. Chris was sitting opposite him, squinting in the dim light at the book he was studying – *Birds of Southern Europe*. His face even seemed relaxed when he was concentrating, which boded well. Already, after knowing the man less than forty-eight hours, Docherty had almost complete confidence in him.

The Dame was another matter. He had stopped reading his novel – some thriller about submarines – and was staring blankly into space. His expression was usually as serene as Chris's, but the similarity,

Docherty thought, was at least partly superficial. Both men seemed supremely self-sufficient – most SAS men were – but Docherty sensed that for Chris there was little or no struggle involved in the process. The Wearsider, by contrast, had mastered the art of retreating into himself, and of functioning effectively in the world outside, but the self he retreated into seemed a troubled one.

Which might bode ill for the patrol as a whole, or might have no effect whatsoever on the way the Dame handled himself. But it was something worth watching out for, that was certain. Like any decent football team, an SAS patrol had to grow into more than the sum of its parts. And it was up to the PC, the Patrol Commander, to make sure it did. He need not have been trained as a clinical psychiatrist, but he did need some idea of how to read other men.

'How much longer, boss?' Razor asked.

Docherty looked at his watch. 'Pilot said fifty-odd minutes, and we've been airborne forty-one. They'll tell us when they come to make sure we're strapped in.'

'It's that bad, is it, this Khe Sanh business?'

'No worse than taking off in the Space Shuttle, so I'm told.'

'Christ. Still, whatever it is, it'll beat being dropped in the fucking sea.'

Docherty smiled, remembering the look of blissful relief on Razor's face when, ten years before, the boat had picked him out of the Atlantic swell. On that mission the Londoner had spent much of his time thinking up 'mixed proverbs'; 'time waits for an old fool' had been Docherty's personal favourite. Razor still seemed full of jokes, but there was something else there now, something more sombre underneath. Maybe he was just growing up, in the best sense of the phrase. He'd certainly lost none of his sharpness – the switch into Spanish in the restaurant had been brilliant . . .

'Time to make your wills, gentlemen,' the pilot said, appearing between the rows of crated foodstuffs. 'Are you all strapped in like good lads? We don't want you flying around inside the plane getting blood on everything. Good.' He turned to go. 'We'll be on the ground in about five minutes,' he said over his shoulder, 'one way or another.'

'I love the fucking RAF,' Razor growled.

'Don't be surprised if the bottom of your stomach starts pressing up against the top of your head,' Docherty told them, and the words were hardly out of his mouth before they came true. With a gut-wrenching suddenness the plane seemed to stop flying and start falling, as if a wing had snapped off or all four engines had chosen the same moment to die. Within seconds the SAS men could feel the pull of gravity weaken, and what Docherty could only describe as a breathlessness inside his head. So this is what space travel is like, he thought, and then, just as his body was adapting to its presence within a plummeting shell, the plane seemed to rear up like a bucking bronco, dropping his stomach down to his feet. For what seemed like a very long couple of seconds he felt on the verge of blacking out.

The brakes slammed on, and with a great jolt the wheels hit the runway. A few moments later they were taxiing along at a speed which would have had them arrested for speeding on the M40, the Hercules seemingly on the verge of shaking itself into a heap of scrap metal.

From outside the plane there was the sound of a

loud blast in the distance. And then another, much closer.

They looked at each other.

'Welcome to Bosnia,' Razor said.

For another two or three minutes they sat in the belly of the taxiing plane, the sounds of shell fire audible above the noise of their passage. They had no way of seeing out, no real idea of how close the shells were landing, and there was nothing they could have done about it anyway.

'Everyone OK?' Docherty asked. He felt like he'd been picked up by a giant and given a thorough shaking.

They all said they were.

The Hercules rumbled to a standstill, and the pilot's head popped up between the line of crates. 'Journey's end,' he announced, in what for him seemed an almost funereal tone. 'I don't suppose you lads feel like helping us unload this beauty,' he said, setting in motion the slow descent of the tail ramp.

'Sorry, prior commitments,' Docherty said drily, as he watched the wall of an airport building coming into view. The ground had only a light covering of snow, but shovelled mounds of the stuff offered evidence of previous falls. The air seemed as damp as it did cold.

'That's the international arrivals door,' the RAF man said sardonically, pointing out a single red door marked 'No Exit' in English.

'Thanks for the ride,' Docherty said, and led the other three down the ramp. Once clear of the plane he could see, across the tarmac, the control tower with all of its windows boarded up. On both sides of the airfield slopes seemed to climb steeply away from the valley, their heights lost in cloud. It might have been one of the South Wales valleys on a bad day, if not for the occasional thump of artillery fire.

They were halfway to the building when two UN soldiers emerged from it, demanding in rapid-fire French to see their identification. Docherty produced the UN accreditations. The two soldiers inspected each SAS man's face with a thoroughness which any beautician would have envied, and then allowed them to pass.

Inside the building they found a vast expanse of floor littered with broken glass and spent cartridge cases, and another UN soldier hurrying across the debris to meet them, plastic bag in hand, as if he was on his way home from the shops. 'Sergeant Docherty?' he asked tersely, while he was still some ten yards away.

Docherty nodded. The officer was a Brit, a major in the Cheshires. He was wearing a flak-jacket under his greatcoat.

'Good. My name's Brindley.' He looked round the vast building. 'I'm just here to escort you to your hotel. Strictly against UN rules, but what the hell. Here' – he delved into the plastic bag and pulled out four pale-blue berets – 'just for the trip. We'll have to pass through a few checkpoints, and it's always better if they think they know who you are.' He looked round at them. 'OK. Let's go. The earlier in the day you make this ride the better it usually is. Most of the snipers seem to sleep until mid-morning.'

Chris and the Dame raised their eyebrows at each other.

In what had once been an elegant semicircular fore-court yet another jeep was waiting for them. This one was armoured, more like the vehicles they'd all used at various times in Northern Ireland. The level of respect accorded the UN was apparent in the line of bullet scars which stretched across the two large letters on the jeep's flank.

'Tighten your safety belts,' Brindley advised. 'And let me do the talking at the checkpoints.'

They started off at a steady twenty-five miles per hour, with Major Brindley carefully negotiating the threefold problem of treacherous winter conditions, potholes and shell craters. Visibility seemed to be getting worse rather than better as the morning advanced, which Docherty supposed was good news. Nevertheless he felt an absurd pang of regret at being denied a better view of the countryside surrounding the city.

They reached the first checkpoint within five minutes. It was manned by several Serbs in uniform, one of whom seemed on friendly terms with Brindley.

'Yugoslav National Army uniforms,' the major explained as they drove on. 'They're the most disciplined of the Serb forces. By a long way,' he added as an afterthought.

The next checkpoint was also manned by Serbs, but here only one was in uniform, and though he was clearly in charge, and coldly courteous in his examination of their credentials, the SAS men were more struck by the demeanour of the irregulars behind him. On their faces an overweening contempt was not masked by any obvious sign of intelligence. This, Docherty thought, was the rural version of the black-uniformed thugs they had seen in the Split restaurant.

'See that?' Brindley gestured with his head.

The SAS men craned their necks. 'Welcome to Hell' the sign by the side of the road read in bloody red letters.

'"Murder Mile" begins around that corner,' Brindley

went on conversationally, pointing ahead. 'Though I doubt if we'll have any trouble this morning.'

He accelerated the jeep, as if uncertain of his own prophetic powers, and they were soon barrelling down a stretch of straight road between two expanses of open ground, the jeep lurching from side to side as Brindley wove his way round the shell craters. They could see nothing through the mist to either left or right, but somewhere out there someone was tracking the noise of their passage, because a bullet suddenly pinged viciously off the outside of the jeep just above Razor's window.

'Fuck a pig!' he exclaimed. 'How the fuck can they see us in this?'

No one answered him, but Brindley trod down again, causing the jeep to lurch even more wildly. A dark shape loomed out of the mist – the burnt-out hulk of a car which hadn't made it – and Brindley sent the jeep careering past it. For a moment the wheels seemed to lose their grip on the packed snow, but somehow they righted themselves, just as another bullet bounced off the back of the vehicle.

'Almost there,' Brindley said, and within seconds they were entering the relative safety of a street lined with industrial premises. The collective sigh of relief was still clouding the air when the jeep pulled into the forecourt of an apparently wrecked hotel. The sign still claimed it was the Holiday Inn, but there were gun emplacements in the garden and the face of the building had clearly been ravaged by shell fire. At least half the windows had been boarded over, and half the remainder offered mosaics of broken glass.

'You'll be staying here,' Brindley said. 'It looks better inside,' he added, noticing their horrified expressions.

SOLDIER O: SAS

'It could hardly look worse,' Chris said.

'Who stays here?' Docherty wanted to know.

Brindley eased the jeep round the building and into what seemed a reasonably sheltered parking space. 'Only about a quarter of the rooms are full,' he went on, switching off the engine. 'With journalists mostly, though you'll see the odd group of Croatians doing a passable imitation of Nazis. They tend to drink too much and start waving their guns around.'

'We met some of them in Split,' Docherty said.

'Just ignore them,' Brindley advised. 'You'll also notice lots of men huddling in corners, pretending they're bona fide Balkans conspirators. They look more like fictional agents than real ones, and for all I know they're residents of a local mental hospital that the Bosnian Government has sent back into the community. I always get the feeling that they've all read a chapter of *The Mask of Dimitrios* in their rooms before coming down to the bar to try out the gestures.'

Docherty grinned. He was beginning to like Brindley.

'And they'll have a field day trying to work out who you lot are,' the major added. 'Four tough-looking Brit bastards with bergens full of God knows what. Maybe you'd better keep the berets for a while. I don't suppose the UN will miss them.'

They entered the hotel by a back entrance, and walked down a short corridor to the reception area. There were indeed several seedy-looking men in trilbies with the collars of their coats turned up. History repeats itself once as tragedy, and then again as farce, Docherty remembered. Who had said that?

Brindley was dealing with the receptionist, a young man with an impudent smile and what looked like the barrel of an AK47 protruding out from under his counter. 'Don't stand in front of any open windows,' the youth said, with all the animation of an air hostess demonstrating safety regulations, 'we have lost several guests that way already.'

'Room service with a bullet,' Razor murmured.

'Fourth floor,' Brindley told them. 'It could be worse.' He led the way to the bottom of the stairs. 'The bar and restaurant are on the mezzanine and first floors, gentlemen.'

'What's the food like?' Chris asked.

'Not bad, considering half the city are surviving on a diet of dandelion soup and dog biscuits.'

They started up the stairs.

'Someone found a spent bullet in their pizza the other day,' Brindley added conversationally.

'I didn't really think it was possible to feel homesick for Walthamstow,' Razor muttered.

Eight flights of stairs latter they found themselves outside rooms 417 and 418. Both had curtains drawn across boarded-up windows and single bare light-bulbs for illumination.

'I'm glad we're not staying in a dump,' Razor said, testing out one of the beds. 'Not bad,' he admitted.

Docherty was examining the view though a narrow slit between board and window frame. The mist seemed to be lifting gradually, revealing snow-covered slopes on the other side of the valley.

'I'd better fill you in on the local geography,' Brindley said, as he unfolded a large-scale map of the Sarajevo area and spread it across the floor. The four SAS men gathered around it.

'The city is more or less surrounded,' Brindley began.

'Basically, the Serbs hold the high ground, which includes not only these mountains but the upper reaches of the valleys to the north, east and south. The lower valley to the west is still contested territory; you could say the Serbs have a cork in the bottle, but it's not a very tight-fitting affair.'

'As the bishop said to the actress,' Razor murmured.

Brindley eyed him with what might have been affection. 'There are a few complications in the general picture,' he went on.

'Dobrinja, which we skirted round after leaving the airport, is a Serb enclave in Muslim territory, a siege within the siege. There are a couple of others like it, and since the roads wind in and out of the two sides' territories you can find yourself being stopped at checkpoints every mile or so. Which is more than a pain in the rear, incidentally – it drastically increases your chances of meeting some trigger-happy irregular who's full of the wrong sort of pills.'

'Where do they get them?' Docherty asked.

'God knows. But we know some of the militia leaders were heavies in the Belgrade underworld not so long ago, and there's no reason why they shouldn't have kept up their contacts with their old buddies. This isn't such a big country, you know – it just seems like one. We're not much more than a hundred miles from Belgrade as the crow flies.'

By 'this country', Docherty realized, Brindley meant Yugoslavia. 'What about here in the city?' he asked. 'Are there any safe areas?'

'Everything's in range of the Serb artillery, if that's what you mean. The shelling is sporadic these days – the visibility's often poor – but if you're above ground there's always the chance. Snipers are more of a problem. Most of the high-rises have been deserted by the people who lived in them, and the snipers have taken up residence instead. They shoot at anything that moves, small children included.' He looked up, a mixture of disbelief and tired outrage in his eyes. 'It's hard to credit. Still, at least you can take precautions against them. Once you're outside you'll soon get a good idea of which places are safe and which aren't. Nothing overlooks the narrow streets of the old town, for example, but any wide street intersection is probably in someone's sights. But don't just take your cue from the locals – some of them have become incredibly blasé. You get the feeling that they've been playing Russian roulette so long that they've almost begun to enjoy it.' He shook his head, as if he was trying to shake such lunacy out. 'So, where you see a local run, you run, but when you see one walking along with a big smile on his face, take a look around anyway. He may be sniper-happy.'

'Christ, what a place,' Razor exclaimed softly.

'These days it's about as far from Christ as you can get,' Brindley replied. 'But I don't want to give you the wrong impression. Some kind of normal life still goes on here, despite everything. The shelling stops for fifteen minutes, and it's like a rainstorm has stopped anywhere else – people come out. You see women walking past all smartly dressed with their handbags, people in cafés arguing about politics, people looking round the shops – those that have anything to sell. The last supermarket I went in had only razors and champagne.'

'Nice combination,' Chris said grimly.

'What about after dark?' Razor asked. 'I take it the night-life is a bit on the thin side?'

'You could say that. There's a curfew from ten p.m. to six a.m., and the whole city's basically blacked out. But nowhere's safe any time after dark. There's no civilian reason for anyone to be on the street, so anyone out there is considered fair game.'

'Kind of puts Belfast in perspective, doesn't it?' Chris said.

Brindley grunted. 'By the way,' he added, pointing at the map, 'this is where the British UN staff HQ is. If you need anything in the way of equipment there's no harm in asking.' He looked round. 'Anything else you can think of?'

'I don't think so,' Docherty said. 'The first thing we have to do is find a woman. A particular woman,' he added, in response to Brindley's raised eyebrow. He explained about Nena Reeve. 'But the FO already have someone working on that for us.'

'OK,' Brindley said, getting up.

'We appreciate the help,' Docherty told him.

'You're welcome. I wish we could do more, but soldiering for the UN — well, it's all in a great cause but it's like soldiering with both hands tied behind your back.' He smiled ruefully. 'Any idea how long you'll be staying?'

'None.'

'There is one piece of good news, gentlemen,' Brindley said. 'The bar here hasn't run dry once.' He reached for the door, just as someone rapped on it.

Brindley again raised his eyebrows at Docherty, who shrugged.

'Thornton,' a voice said through the door.

'The FO man,' Docherty said. He opened the door to reveal a man of medium height with short, curly hair and the sort of dissolute face favoured by producers of epic serials when casting young wastrels and cads.

'God, that's a lot of stairs to climb,' he said, coming in and flopping himself down on the edge of a bed.

'Good luck, lads,' Brindley told the SAS men, and shut the door behind him.

Thornton seemed to be recovering his breath; enough at least to fish in his pocket for a cigarette. He lit up with a Zippo lighter and blew smoke at the ceiling. Docherty, who had grown to dislike the man intensely in something under a minute, restrained himself from tearing the cigarette out of his mouth. After all, with the amount of cold draught that was blowing in around the boarded-up window, they were more likely to die of hypothermia than passive smoking.

'Welcome to Sarajevo,' the MI6 man said. 'Have you got a drink up here by any chance? No? Pity. How was the flight in? A bit on the bumpy side?'

'Have you got some information for us?' Docherty asked him.

'No, not really. But I do have the names of several people in the city who know Zavik well. They should be able to fill you in . . .'

'What about Nena Reeve?'

Thornton took a drag on his cigarette and looked round for an ashtray. Razor reached for the one on the bedside table and handed it to him.

'Thanks,' he said, nearly missing it with his ash. 'The woman has vanished into thin air. I went up to the hospital and talked to her boss and some of her colleagues, but none of them have a clue. I looked round her room – on the quiet, of course – but there's nothing there to suggest where she's gone. Oh, and I checked out the morgue, just in case. No joy.'

Docherty looked at him thoughtfully. 'How do you rate our chances of getting to Zavik?' he asked.

Thornton shrugged. 'I've got no information on the situation there . . .'

'I'm more interested in how we get ourselves out of Sarajevo.'

'Yes, I'm working on that. One of the Muslim militia leaders might be prepared to help out, if we can strike a decent deal. They'll probably want a few SMGs, something like that. I was supposed to see him this morning, but my translator didn't show up . . .'

'You don't speak Serbo-Croat?' Docherty interrupted, trying to keep the disbelief out of his voice.

If Thornton noticed, he didn't seem perturbed. 'No need in the old days – all the people who mattered spoke English. But don't worry, I'll get hold of him tomorrow.'

'Good,' Docherty said. 'Is there any news of Reeve himself.'

'Nothing lately. You know the stories, I suppose. The Croats say the Serbs burned all their people alive in Zavik, in their church of course. The Serbs say they know for certain he had a party of their irregulars shot in cold blood, and that his men have raped and killed their way through several villages in Serb-held territory. The Muslims claim he razed the mosque in Zavik and forced their children to eat pork. It's all the usual stories rolled into one.'

'Have there been no refugees from Zavik?'

'None that we've found, either at the coast or in Zagreb. Whatever's happening up there, it looks like the locals either can't or won't leave.'

'That's it?'

'That's it. There's no telephone link, of course, and the place is off the beaten track, way up in the mountains. Since it's inside territory the Serbs say they control, they presumably have it surrounded, or at least cut off. But no one knows for certain. There are rumours that the missing American – you hear about him? – ah, well, he disappeared about a week ago somewhere out there, and the story was that he was trying to get to Zavik.'

'What was his name?'

'Bailey, I think. The other Americans here can tell you about him.'

Thornton reached for another cigarette, and found his packet was empty. 'I'll get hold of Muftic tomorrow,' he said, getting up to leave and scratching his neck. 'I'll be in the bar downstairs tonight.'

'How about eight o'clock?' Docherty asked.

'Sure, I'll be there all evening.'

'I bet you will,' Docherty muttered as the MI6 man's footsteps receded down the hallway.

'What a wanker,' the Dame murmured.

'The Cheshires can't help, and this tosspot won't,' Razor said. 'I think we're on our own for this one, boss.'

Docherty smiled. 'Looks like it. But here's the good news. If he only talked to the members of the hospital staff who can speak fluent English then there's a good chance Chris can pick up something he didn't.'

It was approaching noon when Docherty and Chris left the hotel. Grey clouds still hung above the city, but they were higher now, and the crests of the hills on either side of the valley were visible. No shells had fallen on the city for a couple of hours.

The hospital where Nena Reeve had worked was in the old town, a mile or so along the valley to the east. Docherty and Chris made their way up the gently sloping Marsala Tita, keeping as close to the walls as possible, hurrying from doorway to doorway on what looked vulnerable stretches, and sprinting like mad across the wide intersections.

Docherty was taken back to his Glasgow childhood, of going shopping with his mother, and the two of them alternating walking and running between pairs of lampposts. Doing something similar on the streets of Sarajevo, at the grand old age of forty-two, it all felt a bit unreal, right up to the moment the sniper's bullet whistled past his head and dug a large chunk out of the kerb across the street.

He scuttled on across the intersection and looked up to find an old woman grinning toothlessly at him from a half-boarded window. She said something in Serbo-Croat which Chris translated as 'that was a close one'. Docherty wondered if the intersection she lived by had replaced TV as her prime source of entertainment.

The two men continued on their erratically paced way, leaving Docherty's feelings of unreality at the crossroads, and both felt a deep sense of relief as they entered the old town, with its narrow, sheltered streets.

Using Brindley's map, they found the hospital with no difficulty. Its walls and windows had fared even worse than the Holiday Inn's, and the main entrance was as littered with broken glass as the airport building's. Uniformed Bosnian Government soldiers were much in evidence, though exactly what they thought they were guarding seemed hard to fathom. Most of them simply stood there stony-faced as a steady stream of weeping visitors passed in and out.

The UN accreditations got Docherty and Chris inside, and the latter's linguistic skills won them directions to the chief administrator's office. She sat behind a desk overflowing with paper, eyes red-rimmed in a gaunt face. They should see Dr Raznatovic, she said; he had been Dr Reeve's boss.

A young orderly – he couldn't have been more than fifteen – escorted them through the maze, past patients lying in corridors, some of them with what looked simple fractures, some with gaping wounds and pain-racked faces, others with the serene expression of the dead. One corridor was slippery with blood, as if someone had been dragged along it.

Dr Raznatovic was between operations, and clearly torn between impatience at having to answer Docherty's questions and a wish to be helpful for Nena Reeve's sake. He spoke perfect English, so it seemed unlikely that they would learn any more from him than Thornton had.

'I don't know her well,' he said, banging a tap in the hope of inducing it to deliver some water. 'But she's a good doctor, and she stayed when many left. I talked to her sometimes when we worked together, but that was all. Sarajevo is not the sort of place you go out for a drink after work,' he added with a half-smile.

Docherty asked if Raznatovic knew of any closer friends that Nena had had in the hospital. He didn't, but suggested they try a sister on one of the wards, Sister Rodzic.

The young orderly, who had listened to their questions with profound fascination in his dark eyes, escorted them on another trip through the corridors. They found Sister

Rodzic almost asleep on her feet, and only too pleased to be given the excuse for a few moments in a chair.

She didn't speak English, which was a good sign. Still, it didn't seem as if she could tell them anything useful either, until, as the two men got up to go, she suddenly remembered something. 'There's a nurse in the emergency department,' she said. 'Dzeilana Begovic. I think Nena used to play squash with her sometimes. There are courts in the basement.'

The orderly took them back down, leading them through a children's ward where row upon row of pitifully thin children watched them pass with doleful eyes.

They found Dzeilana Begovic literally up to her elbows in blood. She was having slightly more luck than Raznatovic with a tap, coaxing a thin trickle of water from the pipes. 'Yes, I know Nena Reeve,' she agreed, 'but I have no time to talk.'

'It's important,' Chris said, realizing how thin the words must sound to someone engaged in work like hers.

She frowned, leaning forward on her arms against the wash-basin. 'OK,' she said after several seconds, and looked at her watch. 'I'm off in an hour. I will meet you in the Princip Café as soon as I can. It's on Boscarsija,' she added, and was gone.

'Where now?' the orderly asked in Serbo-Croat.

'The mortuary, I suppose,' Docherty said reluctantly. He had seen his share of war casualties, of blood and pain, but he still felt almost stunned by what he had seen in this hospital.

'This way,' the orderly announced, after Chris had translated their destination. He led them up two flights of stairs, along a long corridor and across a bridge between two buildings which had lost all of its windows.

They could smell the mortuary before they reached it, and the pungent whiff of plum brandy on the attendant's breath was something of a relief. 'We get twenty a day dead on arrival,' the attendant told them proudly, 'and the ground's too damn hard to bury them, even if you can find someone mad enough to show himself in the cemetery. The Serb snipers like shooting at funeral parties,' he explained.

'We just want to check that a friend of ours isn't here,' Chris said.

'Be my guests.'

'Stay here,' Docherty told Chris. There was no need for both of them to do it.

He walked slowly down the aisles, between the ranks of corpses. In some of the wounds there was movement, and Docherty remembered Razor's lesson about maggots – they only ate dead flesh. Well, that was the only kind of flesh on offer here. If they sealed the doors would the maggots consume it all?

He walked back down the other aisle. Nena Reeve was not there. He supposed it was something to be grateful for, that someone else's friend had died instead of his. He wondered how people would ever recover from this, and for a second he glimpsed an understanding of the scars on his own wife's soul.

'Thank you,' he told the attendant.

The orderly walked them down to the main entrance, and Docherty tried to give him a five-dollar bill, but the youth refused it. Glancing back over his shoulder as they went out through the main doors, Docherty could see the boy staring after them, a look of awe on his face, as if he'd just been privileged to meet visitors from another planet.

Outside on Saraci Street they inhaled the cold mountain air with unusual relish. As Docherty consulted their map there was a sudden loud explosion, followed almost immediately by another. Smoke billowed into the air a couple of streets away to the west.

'This way,' Docherty said, and the two men began to run. At first they thought the streets had magically emptied, but they soon realized their mistake. Every doorway held a group of people, sheltering from the man-made storm. The two SAS men found a niche for themselves, alongside two youngish women.

Minutes went by, and there were no more explosions. 'Just trying to keep us guessing,' Chris heard one of the women say. 'Bastards,' the other said quietly.

People started drifting away from their places of shelter, some shrugging their anxiety away, others casting nervous glances upwards, as if they thought the sight of an incoming shell would give them time to take evasive action. Docherty and Chris continued on past several badly damaged Islamic buildings and found Boscarsija Street.

The Princip Café was halfway down on the left, a European-style coffee house half full of students reading newspapers and smoking cigarettes. The walls were plastered with sepia photographs of days gone by, with pride of place given to a large portrait of Gavrilo Princip, the Bosnian Serb who had assassinated Archduke Franz Ferdinand in June 1914, and set in motion the events that led to World War One.

Docherty wondered where the assassination had actually taken place, and decided he would try to visit the location before they left. It seemed a thoroughly appropriate piece of tourism, he thought. He and Chris ordered two coffees, and found themselves sipping at a bitter, nutty-favoured brew which tasted strangely likeable. Inside the café men and women sat talking and laughing with each other, and at first the handguns laid casually down beside the coffee cups seemed ludicrously out of place. But gradually Docherty became more aware of the restless eyes, the twisting hands and fingers, the hasty drags on cigarettes. Then it was the laughter which seemed unreal, more like a nervous howl than a recognition of humour.

They had been waiting almost two hours when Dzeilana Begovic appeared, looking drawn with fatigue.

'What do you want to know?' she asked, after more coffees had been ordered.

'You know Nena's missing?' Chris asked in Serbo-Croat.

'Yes. But I don't know where she's gone.'

'Do you know any of her friends outside the hospital.'

'Only Hajrija.'

'Who is Hajrija? What is her other name?'

'Her best friend – haven't you spoken to her? Her last name? Let me think. It begins with M. Mejic? No, Mejra, that's it . . .'

Chris told Docherty what he'd learned.

'Ask her where this woman works,' Docherty said.

'She used to be a student at the journalism school,' was Dzeilana's reply. 'But she's in the Army now. One of the anti-sniper units. I saw her in Emergency a few weeks ago, with one of their men who'd been shot.'

'How could we find her?'

'I don't know.'

'You have no idea where she lives?'

Dzeilana searched her memory. 'No,' she said eventually.

'Does Nena have any other good friends at the hospital?' Chris asked.

'I don't think so . . .'

Chris questioned her for another five minutes, but she had no other real leads to give them.

'Hajrija Mejra,' Docherty murmured after she had left, having refused their offer of an escort with a look which clearly said: this is my town, and I know how to deal with it a damn sight better than you do. Still, she had smiled at them through the window as she walked past.

'How do we go about finding an anti-sniper unit?' Chris asked. 'Brindley or Thornton?'

Docherty grimaced. 'Thornton, I'm afraid.'

The MI6 man seemed pleased with himself when Docherty found him in the bar at seven that evening. 'Here's all the journalistic accreditations you'll need,' he said, passing a wad of papers across the table. 'UN, Bosnian Government, Croatian, local Serb. The last one doesn't travel well – it's only good for the immediate area. And I've done a deal with Muftic. Half a dozen MP5s for your team's safe passage through to open country. Delivery on completion. He just wants twenty-four hours' notice.'

'That's great,' Docherty said, his attention momentarily distracted by the fact that a man in tails had just sat down at the piano and begun playing a Chopin waltz. 'I need to get in contact with some people,' he told

Thornton. 'Do you know anything about Bosnian Army anti-sniper units?'

'Of course. The *crème de la crème*. The beautiful Strivela ...' He smiled at the thought. 'The name means "Arrow",' he explained. 'She's become a legend in her own time. Gorgeous textile-design student sees four-year-old child shot down, pleads to be allowed to join the anti-sniper unit, at first gets scorned by the men, then wins them over by her bravery, sharpshooting ability, etc., etc. It would make a great movie. Probably will when this is all over.'

'Is there only one unit?' Docherty asked patiently.

'Two or three, I think.'

'How can I reach them?'

Thornton took a sip of his whisky, trying to decide, Docherty thought, whether to ask the reason for the request. The fear of inviting more work overcame the curiosity.

'One of them's based in the Starigrad Hotel, about a quarter of a mile north of here, near the railway station. The other ones, I don't know, but they'll know at the Starigrad.'

'Thanks,' Docherty said, getting up.

'Dawn would be a good time to pay them a visit,' Thornton suggested.

Docherty walked across to the bar and inspected what was on offer. He chose a bottle of Glenfiddich, paid for it in dollars, and took it back upstairs. All three men were in his and Razor's room.

'You clowns may have forgotten it,' he said, reaching for the grimy glasses above the wash-basin, 'but this is New Year's Eve.' He poured two generous shots into the glasses, and then two more into the ones Chris fetched

105

from the other room. 'Here's to us,' Docherty said, 'and everyone we love back home.'

A thousand miles away, in their Glasgow home, Isabel was sitting on the couch, reliving in her mind's eye a scene from the morning on which he had left. She had come to their bedroom door and seen Marie seated at the dressing-table, her father kneeling on the floor behind her, lovingly running the comb through her dark hair. He had become such a gentle man, and though she knew the gentleness must always have been there inside him, she knew that she and the children had helped to bring it out. Now a part of her was afraid that in some impossible-to-know way it would make him more vulnerable. 'Please send him home to me,' she whispered, pulling her knees up under her chin and clasping herself tightly.

7

Docherty and Chris left the hotel at the first hint of light, leaving behind a mutinous Razor and the Dame. The PC could understand how frustrating it must be sitting in the hotel while he and Chris had all the 'fun', but he could see no justification for risking an extra two lives just to alleviate boredom. 'The moment something comes up which requires your talents, it's all yours,' Docherty told Razor.

'But who's going to charm the lovely Hajrija?' Razor wanted to know. 'You two?' he added disbelievingly.

Docherty grinned to himself as he followed Chris up the side of the wide boulevard. As on the previous morning the clouds were riding low in the valley, and despite the growing glimmer of dawn, visibility was still poor enough to deter any but the most determined sniper.

Halfway up the road a trio of burnt-out Japanese cars reminded him of what a dangerous walk this would be in sunlight. And then, as if to scoff at his presuming to know anything, a brightly lit bus sailed serenely past, crowded with people on their way to work.

'This place is like *Alice in Wonderland*,' Chris said.

'You can say that again.'

They crossed a meeting of five roads and found themselves in the more densely built-up area around the railway station. 'There it is, boss,' Chris said, pointing across the street to where an unlit sign bearing the legend Starigrad Hotel hung from a dingy three-storey building.

'Freeze,' a voice grated behind them. 'Hands on your heads.'

Chris rapidly translated the commands for Docherty. 'We're English,' he shouted. 'We're looking for someone.'

At least two pairs of footsteps came up behind them.

'Who?' another voice asked.

'Her name is Hajrija Mejra,' Chris said.

'Why do you want her?'

'We are looking for a friend of hers, and we think she might be able to help us.'

There was a silence lasting several moments.

'How did you know to look here?' the first voice asked.

'A journalist told us this was where one of the units was based,' Chris replied, deciding that something close to honesty was probably the best policy in this situation.

'Are you journalists?'

'No. We are with the UN.'

'You have papers?' the voice asked, its tone changing from hostility to mere caution.

'Yes.'

'Let me see them,' the man said, walking round to face them. He had long, brown hair surrounding a lean, bewhiskered face, and carried a machine pistol in his left hand. He looked, Docherty thought, like an extra in a spaghetti western.

He examined their papers with interest and then led them into the hotel. The drabness of the outside was mirrored within, where more pale, bearded men sat cleaning rifles on a black plastic sofa. They ignored the new arrivals.

The SAS men's interrogator had disappeared, hopefully to find Hajrija Mejra.

A minute passed, and another. He reappeared, leading a tall, slim young woman in camouflage fatigues. She walked gracefully, head held high, her face dominated by dark Latin eyes. Between twenty-five and thirty, Docherty guessed. A woman surrounded by men.

'I'm Hajrija Mejra,' she said without preamble, in English. 'Who are you?'

'My name is Jamie Docherty,' he said. 'This is Chris Martinson.'

'What do you want?' she asked simply.

'I was the best man at John and Nena's wedding,' Docherty said, as if that explained everything. 'I'm looking for Nena.'

Her face broke into a smile, which quickly became a frown. She looked around. 'There is nowhere to talk here,' she said. 'Come, follow me.'

She led them across the lobby, up a single flight of stairs, and into what had probably been a dining-room. Now it contained six mattresses and small piles of personal belongings. A man lay on one of the mattresses, listening to a Walkman. He grinned up at them. 'Beastie Boys,' he said.

A door on the far side led through to a smaller room, which showed signs of having once been an office. A small brown couch stood under the single, shuttered window, across from a desk, upright chair and wall of empty shelves.

'Please, sit down,' Hajrija said, offering them the couch and taking the chair.

Docherty sat down, but Chris decided to stand, rather than squeeze in next to him.

109

'Now,' Hajrija said. 'I will tell you. You know about the Russians?'

'What Russians?'

'The two journalists.'

'All we know is that she's missing,' Docherty explained. 'We don't know whether she's still in Sarajevo, or if not, where she's gone, or when . . .'

'She is not in Sarajevo. She leave here four days now. With the two Russians and my American journalist friend, Dwight Bailey . . .'

'Where were they going?'

'Nena and Dwight go to Zavik. She hear stories . . . you must know them, yes?'

Docherty nodded.

'She worries about her children. And John, but she never says that. Dwight hopes to get the big story about the Englishman fighting in our war.'

'And he never came back.'

'No, but the Russians, they come back. I go to see them at the Holiday Inn and ask them what happens. They say that they leave Nena and Dwight in Bugojno and not see them again, but they do not speak the truth.'

'How do you know that?'

'I know. They hide the truth. I know. I go to see the American journalist friends of Dwight and they agree. Something is smelly, they say. But they say there is nothing to do.'

Docherty considered what she had told them. Maybe she was wrong, and Nena was already in Zavik. If she was right, Nena could be anywhere, always assuming she was still alive.

'Why are you looking for Nena?' Hajrija asked.

'We are from the same regiment as John Reeve . . .'

'Ha! The famous SAS.'

Docherty smiled. 'Aye. Our political bosses are getting worried about what Reeve is doing in Zavik, for all sorts of reasons. We've been sent to find out what is happening there, and if it turns out that Reeve has lost his senses, I'm supposed to talk him back into them. Or something like that. It seemed a reasonable enough notion when it was first put to me.'

He shrugged. 'We came to Sarajevo partly to talk to people who know something about Zavik, and partly because we hoped Nena was here. I thought she'd be the best person to ask about Reeve's state of mind, and, if she was willing to come with us, the best person to make him see sense.'

Hajrija nodded. 'She understands him, I think. Though she is still very angry with him at the moment. Or she thinks she is angry – it is hard to know.' She smiled to herself. 'But I can tell you about Zavik – I am born there, and grow up there. Nena is my friend since I am a small girl. Our fathers are comrades in the partisans.'

'What we need is a good map of the town, and the area around it. Could you draw one?' Docherty asked.

'Of course. You go soon?'

'I don't know. Do you know where these Russians are staying?'

'At the Holiday Inn.'

'Probably down the corridor from us,' Chris said.

'Maybe we should pay them a visit,' Docherty decided. 'Do they speak English?' he asked Hajrija.

'Some, I think.'

'What are their names?'

'I only know Viktor and Dmitri. But I come with you, yes?' she said, her mouth setting in an obstinate line.

111

She had probably had a hard time getting accepted as a woman fighter, Docherty thought, but she needn't expect any opposition from him. He had married one. 'If you want,' he said simply.

'I go to speak with my commander,' she said. 'You wait here.'

She was only gone a few moments, and returned dressed for the outside world in a long, fur-lined anorak that had seen better days, though it looked warm enough.

The two SAS men were not looking forward to the walk back down the street, but they needn't have worried. Hajrija led them by a slightly longer, more circuitous route which only involved negotiating two open spaces. They sprinted across both without drawing fire.

At the Holiday Inn she tackled the receptionist with the insolent grin, and came away with the Russians' room number. 'He no see them this morning,' she said. 'They are sleeping still, I think. Russians all lazy,' she added conclusively.

'Let's pick up Razor and the Dame first,' Docherty said, as they headed for the stairs. 'With any luck sheer weight of numbers will scare the truth out of them.'

'This "Razor" and "Dame",' she asked, 'they are people?'

'As far as we know,' Chris said.

'They are nicknames,' Docherty said, 'names that friends use.'

'Silly names?'

'You could say that.'

Razor had, appropriately enough, just finished shaving. The Dame was, as usual, deeply engrossed in a trashy novel. Both men looked relieved to be offered a reason to leave their rooms.

'Just follow my lead,' Docherty said, as they climbed yet another flight of steps. The Russians were on the sixth floor, in a room at the back of the hotel.

Docherty knocked on their door and waited, ignoring the questioning voice inside the room. When the door inched open he shoved it backwards, pushing the man who had opened it back into the room. 'Viktor?' he asked.

The other Russian looked up from the edge of the bed, where he was sitting surrounded by what looked like bottles of pills, and said something sharply in his native language. 'Who are you?' he added, switching to English, as the other four crowded in, herding his colleague towards the bed. Razor closed the door and leant on it, feeling like someone out of *The Godfather*.

Then the darker of the Russians recognized Hajrija. 'You again,' he said. 'We have told you everything.'

'You lied to her,' Docherty said. 'We know that you lied,' he bluffed, 'and now we want the truth.' He casually reached under the hem of the Gore-tex jacket and pulled the Browning High Power handgun out from its cross-draw holster.

The eyes of the two Russians on the bed opened wider.

'Who are you?' the darker one asked again.

Docherty ignored the question. 'We want to know where you left the woman and the American,' he said. 'Tell us the truth and you won't get hurt. Keep lying and . . .' He shrugged.

'You cannot do this in the Holiday Inn,' the fairer Russian half-shouted, as if outraged by the damage such activities might do to the hotel chain's international reputation.

'This is Sarajevo,' Docherty said, 'and we can do just about anything we want.'

'We left them in Bugojno,' the dark one said, and they both stared defiantly back at him.

Hajrija had been right, Docherty thought: they were lying. He wondered how far he was prepared to go to force the truth out of them, and realized he didn't know. This war was already tugging at his notion of who he was.

He mentally shook his head, and tried another tack. If they were lying, why were they lying? To cover up misdeeds? He doubted it. To cover up shame? More likely.

'We are only interested in finding the woman,' he said. 'Anything you tell us will remain a secret between us. I promise you that. And I also promise you that if you do not tell us, one of you – you, I think,' he said, looking at the fair one, 'will be thrown out of that window there. And then your friend here will tell us to avoid the same thing happening to him.'

'You will not do this,' the dark one said.

'Lads,' Docherty said, gesturing Chris and the Dame forward, and catching the anxious look on Razor's face as he did so.

The two SAS men grabbed the Russian and pulled him to his feet.

Docherty watched with a stony face. Talk, he silently pleaded with the Russian, please talk. Don't call my bluff.

They started dragging him towards the window.

'OK, OK, I tell you,' the potential victim spluttered. 'They just say leave the woman behind . . .'

Chris and the Dame threw him back on the bed, turning away to conceal their sighs of relief.

'The whole story,' Docherty ordered.

The fair one shot a reproachful glance at his colleague and started recounting what had happened.

'Do you know where he means?' Docherty asked Hajrija when the Russian's account reached the roadblock.

'Yes,' she said, not taking her angry eyes off the two Russians, 'it is thirty kilometres in the west.'

Razor was watching her, and noticed the single tear that rolled down her cheek when she heard of the American's death, a tear that she didn't bother to wipe away, or even seem to notice. Her face remained unchanged, as if the part of her which grieved had no connection with the rest of who she was.

He was struck by how lovely she was, and wondered at how he could feel something like desire at such a moment. He remembered something his mother had said to him years before, that at heart he was a carer, and how bizarre it was that he'd opted for a life in the military, who only came into contact with needy people at the end of a gun.

The Russian finished his story, and then looked up with the unspoken question in his eyes: which of you would have preferred to die than run away?

Docherty had no answer for him. He put away the Browning and started for the door.

Hajrija had. 'You are cowards,' she said. 'Not for running away, but for lying to me about my friend.' Then she turned and strode from the room.

*　　*　　*

115

They reconvened in Docherty and Razor's room.

'Where is she likely to be now?' Docherty asked Hajrija.

The woman took a deep breath. 'There are three, how do you say, possibilities? One, she is dead. Two, the pigs keep her where she is taken. Three, they move her to one of the brothels in the area.' She ran a hand through her hair, anguish on her face.

'These brothels,' Docherty asked gently, 'are there many? Do you know where they are?'

'We know some. There is one in Visograd near border with Serbia, and one in Vogosca, which is only a few kilometres away on other side of mountain. And there are many others. The Serbs think they can make every Muslim woman pregnant with a Serb baby . . .' She shook her head, as if she was trying to shake out the thought of her friend in the beasts' hands.

'Is there any way we can find out if she has been taken to one of these?' Docherty asked, wondering how far he could take such a search. Finding Nena, which had been a means to an end, was becoming an end in itself. And so it should, he told himself, for a friend. But the other three men in the room had never even met her. Could he risk their lives for something that was only marginally relevant to their mission?

'I can try,' Hajrija said. 'There are always new people coming to the city, and someone can know something. But what good will it do? You cannot go and talk to her.'

'If she's only a few miles away we can try,' Razor said.

'We are the famous SAS,' Docherty told her with a wry smile.

*   *   *

An hour later Hajrija, Razor and the Dame were surveying the interior of what had once been the city's skating rink. Docherty had reluctantly accepted the need for the other two men to have their turn in the outside world. And if they needed a translator, they had Hajrija.

They didn't need one to describe this, Razor thought, as he studied the scene in front of him. Where there once would have been throngs of skaters gliding across the ice, and room for thousands more in the surrounding seats, there was now a refugee camp. Across the thawed rink, scattered across the seats and aisles, small groups of people were huddled listlessly together. The only heat came from a multitude of small butane stoves, and on most of these a saucepan containing water and a few desolate bits of greenery was quietly simmering. Most of the adults seemed to be staring into space, and only the younger children seemed unresigned to the passing hours.

'Most of them come from the city,' Hajrija explained. 'The big buildings, yes, and some have shells destroy their homes. We look for people from outside.'

They started working their way methodically through the hall, asking the groups where they came from. A few refused to say, but most seemed happy to tell them – what difference does it make now, their faces seemed to say. There was no one from Zavik, and none of those who had recently arrived from Serb-held territory recognized the photograph of Nena Reeve which Docherty had brought from home.

Until, that is, Hajrija stooped to ask two women who were sitting with their backs to the rink wall, heads bowed as if they were deep in thought. At the sound of Hajrija's voice both raised weary faces. Then, catching sight of Razor and the Dame behind her, they seemed to shrink back into the wall.

'We'll wait for you over there,' Razor said, nodding towards an area of empty seats. He and the Dame went and sat down, both feeling sombre.

'It's like something out of the Bible,' the Dame said.

'Yeah,' Razor agreed. He studied the back of Hajrija's head, which bobbed up and down as she talked to the two women.

The Dame was remembering his sister's wedding reception, and all the food they'd had to throw away. And all the petty problems everyone seemed so full of.

'What do you think of her?' Razor asked.

The Dame followed his gaze, and a slight smile crossed his face. 'Not my type,' he said.

'Not mine either,' Razor said. Or not usually, he thought.

Hajrija's shoulders suddenly slumped, as if she had just had bad news. Where Nena Reeve was concerned, Razor wasn't sure whether no news was good news. They would soon know.

But it was another ten minutes before Hajrija got to her feet, slowly walked across and sat down next to him. She had been crying, Razor instantly realized. 'Are you OK?' he asked, putting a hand on her shoulder.

'No,' she said and, half-falling forward, began sobbing into his chest.

A minute or so later, and almost as abruptly, she raised her head and ran a hand defiantly through her hair. 'I am sorry,' she said.

'Don't be,' Razor said.

She closed her eyes, took a deep breath. 'I have the

news,' she said, opening them again. 'Nena is at Vogosca. The women here, they come from there, and they are leaving when Nena comes.'

'When was that?' Razor asked.

'They think three days, but they are not certain.'

'Why did the Serbs let them go?'

Hajrija made a noise which was part sob, part laugh. 'Because they are pregnant six months. You understand? Too late for abortion.'

Back at the Holiday Inn, Docherty listened to what the women had told Hajrija. There were about forty women at Vogosca, most of them between fourteen and twenty-five, though there were a few older women, even a couple in their forties. They were kept at the Partisan Sports Hall, but each night different groups – which always included the youngest and prettiest – were taken to the Sonja Motel, about half a mile away, for the pleasure of the local Serb forces. The women Hajrija talked to had no idea how many guards there were around either the Sports Hall or the motel, but the town was full of Serb soldiers, uniformed and irregulars.

'How long would it take to walk there?' Docherty asked her. 'Avoiding contact with the enemy,' he added.

She thought about it. If they could get through the Serb lines without being seen – a big if, considering they had little knowledge of where the Serb positions were – she reckoned they could reach the town in between four and five hours. But, she went on, thinking out loud, unless they managed to extract Nena from her imprisonment without raising the alarm, the Serbs would be waiting for them on their way back.

'We wouldn't be coming back,' Docherty said. 'We'd be heading straight for Zavik.'

'But how can we leave all the other women behind?' Hajrija asked.

It was an impossible question. 'I don't know,' Docherty said. 'I don't know if we should be thinking about Vogosca at all.' He looked at the others, then turned back to Hajrija. 'You said "we" just now. Would you come with us as a guide?'

'Of course – she is my best friend. And I will ask others to come – good men. How many is the right number for this? Six? Ten? Twenty?'

'Hold on,' Docherty said, raising a hand. 'She's my friend too, but these three reprobates here have never set eyes on Nena Reeve. I want to know if they think I'm going over the top to suggest this little detour. The moment we start fighting alongside any of the local forces we're going way beyond our instructions. In fact, we'll be halfway to doing what we've been sent out here to persuade John Reeve to stop doing. Not to mention risking our necks in a country we hardly know at all.'

'Seems to me, boss,' Razor said, 'that we have to get to Zavik. Which means we have to get out of this city. No one told us which route we had to take. And I'd rather trust my luck with Hajrija's mob than go along with some deal that MI6 creep has done with someone we've never even met. And if we get to do good works on the way, then that seems like a bonus.'

'You old softie. Chris?'

'Seconded.'

'Dame?'

'Count me in.'

'OK.'

Docherty turned to Hajrija. 'I think around ten would be a good number, so if you can find four or five good men – men who can move quietly and won't start blazing away at rabbits – that would be ideal.'

She grinned at him. 'Would you like to give them audition?' she asked.

'No . . .'

'They may give you one,' she said, on her way to the door. 'I come back this evening,' she added over her shoulder.

8

They had waited, the ten of them, in the fourth-floor room of an abandoned building, taking turns at training the nightscope on the upper floors of the ten-storey high-rises half a mile away. There were six towers in the distant cluster, and from this vantage-point they looked like an array of giant skittles leaning forward, with the three at the rear looking out over the shoulders of the two in the middle, and this pair standing over the lone tower at the front.

There were occasional glimmers of light in the bottom two or three storeys of each building, but none above that. A mixture of stubborn long-term residents, refugees and people with nowhere else to go might risk life close to the ground, but throughout the city the top floors of such buildings were the exclusive preserve of snipers. Hopefully the man or woman they were looking for was still holed up in one of these six buildings, biding his or her time.

This sniper's latest victim had been a fourteen-year-old girl. She had been on her way home with the family bread when the dum-dum bullet had almost blown her in half, the fourth child victim in as many days in the same neighbourhood. Hajrija's unit was out to get him, and it had seemed like an ideal time to see what these Englishmen, the 'foreign super-soldiers', were made of.

The five male members of the unit had all seemed friendly enough, if somewhat sceptical of their guests' alleged prowess.

They were all in their twenties or thirties and, like most groups of Bosnians, looked remarkably heterogeneous. Two looked liked stereotypical Muslim guerrillas – Kaltak and the leader, Hadzic, were dark-haired, moustached and with stubbly chins – while Abdulahu was strikingly blond, and might have been taken for a Scandinavian. Began and Lujinovic were both brown-haired and blue-eyed. What all five had in common were an unkempt look, eyes red-rimmed from exhaustion, and the air of having been through the fire of combat and out the other side.

They had been passing round the nightscope for four hours now, and it seemed to Razor, whose shift it was, that the sniper was probably either asleep or gone. He started slowly scanning the top floor of the target building once more, searching for the movement he didn't really expect to find.

A small flare erupted in the corner of the nightscope, and vanished almost as quickly. Razor swung it back to where he thought it had been.

There was nothing. Had he imagined it?

No, there was another flare, fainter, much fainter than the last. The man's dragging on a cigarette, Razor realized. The first, brighter flare had been from a match or a lighter.

'Hajrija,' he said softly, liking the sound of the name. He passed her the nightscope, saying: 'Fourth building from the left, second floor down, second window from the left.'

She trained the scope. 'I cannot see . . . oh yes, there's the bastard.' She flashed Razor a smile in the dark, and got up to tell the others.

Two minutes later they were assembled and ready

to go. Hadzic led the way, followed by Docherty. The
SAS men were all carrying the silenced Heckler & Koch
MP5 sub-machine-guns, as well as Browning High Power
9mm semi-automatic handguns. Each Bosnian carried a
Kalashnikov and a Czech machine pistol, and Abdulahu
had a Dragunov sniper rifle strapped across his back. All
four SAS men were wearing American-designed passive
night goggles, or PNGs, while Hadzic sported a cruder
Soviet-made counterpart.

They marched down the stairs in single file, the sound
of their steps echoing in the empty building. As they
emerged into the night a series of tracer bullets arced red
across the sky in front of them, bright as flares through
the PNGs.

There was snow in the air now, falling desultorily for
the moment, but the flakes did not melt on impact. The
Bosnian commander led them off at a brisk pace, down
a long, sloping street towards the audible waters of the
River Miljacka. About fifty yards short of the bank they
turned right through an area of abandoned factories,
traversing several yards and clambering through old
holes in two high wire fences. This was a route the
unit had often used before, Docherty realized. Which
made him feel nervous.

They emerged on to a small road of houses, several
of which had been destroyed by shells. None looked
occupied. A scrawny cat suddenly darted across the
street, its eyes bright-green orbs in the PNGs, before
disappearing into the space between two high-rises. The
nearest of the towers was now not much more than three
hundred yards distant, looming above the expanse of
open ground which sloped upwards from the end of the
street. This looked to Docherty as if it had once been

used for allotments, but now only weeds and pieces of broken cane poked through the thin coating of snow.

'That is Serb territory,' Hadzic told Docherty, pointing forward. 'I used to live over there,' he added bitterly, 'with my fellow-Serbs.'

Docherty showed his surprise.

'Oh, I am a Serb,' the man said, 'though sometimes I am ashamed to be so.' He waved his hands outward, as if to dismiss the subject. 'And over there is a Serb cemetery,' he said, 'the only way in which is not guarded or mined. The dead make poor sentries,' he added, 'even in Sarajevo.'

They started across the open ground, the snow falling more heavily now. Soon there would be enough to leave noticeable footprints for any Serb patrol, which didn't bode well for their return journey. The cemetery was set on a shallower slope, and surrounded by a low wall. They clambered across it, and advanced in single file up a path between the rows of headstones. A sudden flurry of tracer fire turned everyone's head, and Docherty thought he caught a streak of red reflected in the distant river below.

They reached the far side of the cemetery, where a higher wall offered a good observation point. Beyond the wall there was a wide and empty road, and beyond that the nearest of the high-rises reared up from a concrete sea.

'We can use the front building as cover,' Hadzic said, 'but after that we're in the open.'

'Do they have nightscopes?' Docherty asked.

Hadzic shrugged in the gloom. 'Some of them do. But this bastard has only killed people in daylight.' He turned to make sure everyone was ready, and led them across the dark and empty road to the shelter of the first tower. There they waited another five minutes, scanning the neighbourhood for movement through the PNGs until they were satisfied that they had not been spotted.

Hugging the wall of the building, they moved round to its rear, where a line of rubbish containers offered convenient cover. The doorway of the target high-rise was now only an eighty-yard run away. Unfortunately, as Docherty discovered when he trained his nightscope on the doorway, two men were sitting just inside the glass doors, which looked as though they were chained. He passed the scope to Hadzic, who swore softly under his breath.

'Something's moving out there,' Razor whispered in Docherty's ear, pointing out to the left. Through the scope the mere impression of movement focused into two men pushing bicycles. Each had a rifle slung across his shoulder, and one was carrying what looked like a billy-can. Steam was escaping from around its lid into the freezing air, looking through the PNGs like a cloud of green gas rising up from a witch's cauldron.

The men were obviously expected. The two guards unchained the glass doors to let them in, and an indecipherable murmur of conversation drifted across the snowy ground before the new arrivals, complete with pot, disappeared into the building.

'Food for a sniper,' Hadzic said, his voice brimming with suppressed triumph. 'The bastard's up there all right.' He turned to Docherty, a knowing look on his face. 'But we must still find a way in without waking up the whole neighbourhood. I think maybe this is where you Englishmen show your skills.'

Docherty looked at Hadzic, just to make sure he was serious. He was. He then examined the two soldiers once more through the nightscope. They were little more than faint silhouettes: certainly there was no way Docherty could see their faces.

Which was fitting enough, he thought. If they wanted the Bosnians' help in rescuing Nena, then he had no choice but to order the killing of these two men, whom he knew nothing about, whom he had never seen before. They were enemies of his friends, that was for sure. And they were holding guns in a war zone, which he guessed made them fair game. It might not be the SAS's war, but tonight they seemed to be making a guest appearance.

'*Nema problema*,' he said softly. It was the only Serbo-Croat phrase he'd picked up so far.

The four SAS men squatted together to discuss how. 'There's only one safe approach,' Chris said, 'on our bellies until we're level with the front of the building, then we can move in from the side.'

'They haven't rechained the door,' Razor said, 'but there's no way of knowing how thick the glass is, and I don't reckon our chances of getting them both before they get a shot off. These guys' – he patted the silenced MP5 – 'just don't have the muzzle velocity.'

'We'll have to get them outside,' the Dame said thoughtfully.

'How?' Docherty asked.

'Curiosity,' Chris said, his eyes suddenly lighting up. 'And maybe hunger. Let the Dame and I handle it. OK, boss?'

Docherty hesitated, reluctant to let the two youngest men bear the burden of starting this undeclared war, but from the barely concealed eagerness on their faces it was clear that they had no such doubts. And their youth would come in handy when it came to crawling swiftly and unobserved through a hundred yards of snow. 'OK,' he agreed, and went back to brief Hadzic.

Ten minutes later, Chris and the Dame were standing against the wall of the target building, around the corner from the doorway, having successfully worked their bodies across the snow-covered concrete. Watching through the nightscope, Docherty saw Chris take something out of his pocket, but couldn't make out what it was. He put it to his lips and the noise of a duck quacking came wafting across on the night air.

The two guards inside the vestibule heard it too. They looked at each other, then out into the darkness. One came to the door and pushed it open.

'Quack, quack,' Chris went.

The man went back for his rifle, said something to his companion, and emerged into the night. He stood still, waiting for directions from his intended prey.

'Quack, quack.'

Chris was moving away from the building now, trying to convince the guard his potential supper was getting away.

It worked. As the Serb reached the corner of the block a hand reached out, and something flashed bright green in Docherty's PNGs. The man's hand flew up, then just as swiftly fell lifeless beside him, and he slumped forward into the snow, making only the slightest 'whumpf' as he did so.

'Quack, quack, quack, quaaaaack!'

The other man emerged from the doorway, and seemed to hesitate. Standing motionless by the wall, virtually invisible to the guard, the Dame tightened his finger on the MP5's trigger, prepared to risk only wounding the man with a silenced shot rather than let him re-enter the building.

'Radic?' the figure said, almost apologetically. 'Where the fuck are you?' he added, stepping forward into the darkness, holding his rifle at the ready.

Wanting to be sure, the Dame waited, the extended stock of the silenced MP5 pressing into his shoulder, until the man was within twenty feet of him. Then, his training instructor's voice sounding in his head, he aligned the sight on the centre of the Serb's head and squeezed the trigger, maintaining the squeeze while firing and for a moment more. The man's head flew back, his feet seemed to almost paw at the snow, and he collapsed awkwardly on to the ground.

The Dame walked swiftly forward, confirmed that the Serb was dead, and signalled to Docherty that the way was clear. Then he and Chris went in through the glass doors, and took up station at the bottom of the stairs. There were no signs of life in the stairwell, no indication that the men who had brought the food were on their way back down.

The rest of the group joined them a few minutes later. 'Who will go up?' one of the Bosnians asked Hadzic.

'All of us. We don't know how many there are up there. It is probably just the three of them, but it could be a unit of ten. But there is no need for our English friends to tire themselves out,' he added. 'They have done their bit.'

'We wouldn't miss the climax,' Docherty said.

All ten started climbing, as silently as they could manage. At each landing they stopped for a few seconds, ears straining in vain for the sound of footsteps coming down. On the eighth floor they waited for longer, while

Lujinovic scouted out the lay of the land. He returned five minutes later with the news that all the rooms seemed empty save the one in question. That one, number 96, had its door closed. There was music playing inside, and men talking as well, though he hadn't been able to tell what they were saying.

Hadzic's grin was visible even in the dark.

They climbed the last flight of stairs, and walked down the corridor towards the sound of the music. It was Prince, the Dame realized, singing 'Little Red Corvette'. One of his sisters had the CD back in Sunderland.

Hadzic and Began positioned themselves either side of the apartment door, like cops in an American TV series. 'Need to find a love that's gonna last,' Prince sang, as Kaltak launched his foot against the door, and the chorus was drowned in splintering wood as the three Bosnian soldiers burst into the room.

No gunfire greeted them. By the time Docherty and the other SAS men reached the front room three frightened-looking Serbs were being held at gunpoint. There was a heavy smell of marijuana in the air and several roaches in an ashtray that was overflowing on to the pink carpet. A large tarpaulin had been hung across the window, with a narrow opening for sighting and firing through.

The two men who had brought the food were still wearing their coats, while the sniper seemed to be wearing about five layers of sundry T-shirts and sweatshirts. The top one bore the logo 'Alice in Chains', and featured Lewis Carroll's Alice hanging from a noose. The fourfold Cyrillic C logo – 'Only solidarity will save the Serbs' – was tattooed on his right hand. The pupils in his pale-blue eyes were remarkably dilated.

One of the Bosnians was tearing down the tarpaulin,

revealing two broken windows. Then Began and Kaltak suddenly grasped the sniper's hands, pulling them back behind his head, causing some reaction at last in the lifeless eyes. His legs squirmed away from the hands that were trying to grasp them, but only for a moment.

'Shoot me,' he cried out desperately. 'I only shot people. Shoot me.'

The Bosnians ignored him. Grim-mouthed, they carried him to the window, where, since they neglected to impart any energy into the process, it was not so much a matter of throwing the sniper into the night as of simply tipping him out. His wail faded into a faint but sickening sound, like that made by a boot crushing a ripe fruit.

The other two captives both started talking at once. Hadzic stepped forward and shot one in the head, then the other.

Nena Reeve sat in the gymnasium of the Partisan Sports Hall in Vogosca, remembering good things about her estranged husband. Perhaps it was more than a little perverse to choose this place and time to remind herself of his better side, but she enjoyed the ludicrousness of it all. Soon after arriving at Vogosca, Nena had decided that only her sense of the absurd would get her through such an experience. Take it all straight, and she'd go mad.

Mad with outrage, mad with sadness, just mad.

Across the gym two women were softly crying, like violins intertwining a melody.

John, she told herself, think about John. Why had she left him, really? Because he was impossible. And why was that? Because he didn't listen – that was what it all came down to. He loved her, she knew that. He loved looking after her, but always on his own terms.

It was the same with the children. He'd be wonderful with them right up to the moment when they had wills and lives of their own, and then he wouldn't know how to deal with them at all.

The recurrent thought that the children might be dead crossed her mind. Though she'd always thought she'd know if anything happened to either of them. And John might be dead too. The thought brought a sinking feeling to her stomach. Whatever their differences, they were not finished as a couple. Not if they both managed to survive this.

One of the women had stopped crying, but the other carried on, making a low, moaning sound, as if she was mourning a death.

Perhaps she was. Almost all of these women and girls would have had men in their lives: husbands, fathers, lovers, brothers. Where were they now? Some were known to be dead. Some had been put to death in front of their wives and daughters, often after witnessing their violation. Some would be in labour camps, and a few might have escaped, across mountains, across borders to God knew where. Whatever had happened to them, wherever they might be, they were lost to these women.

Talking was not allowed in the gym, but the guards were not always inclined to enforce the rule, and the need for conversation, for contact, often outweighed the risk of one more bruise. Over the last few days Nena had spoken to most of her fellow prisoners, heard the stories of their abduction and humiliation. All of them were Muslims, and all but Nena herself were from villages that had been taken over by Serb irregulars since the summer. Separated from their families, they had been loaded on buses like the one which had brought Nena, and brought here to service the local fighters. The lucky ones were taken out at night to a nearby motel where they were raped by between one and a dozen men, and returned, crying, a few hours later. The younger ones had almost all been virgins, and thought that their chances of ever finding a husband were now over. They didn't believe that any man would believe that they had had no choice.

The unlucky ones were taken out and not returned.

Usually, according to the few women prepared to talk about it, the rapes were speechless affairs: the men were using the women to demonstrate their dominance and as substitutes for masturbation. Nena heard several accounts of men who couldn't get an erection seeking compensation by urinating on the woman.

She herself had not been molested since her arrival, and supposed she owed such tender mercy to her age. Hoping to encourage such neglect she had tied her blonde hair back in a tight bun. And every night when they came and took other women away she felt guilty for her own good fortune.

But not on this night. The man came with his torch, moving along the wall from face to face, picking out one girl who seemed to be always chosen, another who was selected almost as often, and finally, almost hesitantly, bathing Nena's face in the beam.

'A blend of youth and experience,' he muttered to himself, like a football coach.

Nena's first reaction was surprise, her second a sense of emptiness that came close to panic. In the back of the van she told herself she had survived the four men in the mountains, and she could survive as many more here as

133

she had to. This had nothing to do with her. It was like being shot by a total stranger: it might hurt like hell, but if the bullet didn't kill you, then the wound would heal. There was no need for her mind to get involved. Just turn off, she told herself, looking at the blank faces of the two younger women. Just turn off.

And it worked as well as anything could have worked, at least until the sixth and last man came into the motel room. He was no younger than the rest of them – in his early twenties – but he seemed to lack his comrades' macho shell of assurance. Seeing her laid out naked on the bed, fresh bruises growing on her breasts and bloody between the legs, he hesitated before reaching to undo his belt.

'Why are you doing this?' she asked, breaking her own rule of silence, and cursing herself for doing it.

'Your people are doing the same to our women,' he said, but not with any great conviction.

He might well believe it, she thought, but he didn't seem to find it a good enough reason to reply in kind. 'Does that make it right?' she asked him. 'What do you think your mother and sisters would say if they could see you now?'

'I don't have any sisters,' he said. The belt was undone, but he had made no move to drop his trousers.

'You have a mother,' she said.

'I have no choice,' he said, 'I don't *want* to . . .'

'Then don't.'

'We have to,' he whispered fiercely.

'No one will know,' Nena said. 'Think of your future. How will you ever know love if this picture is in the back of your mind?'

He closed his eyes. 'Shut up,' he said. 'Just shut up.'

134

9

The unit got back to the Hotel Starigrad shortly after dawn, tired but mostly satisfied with the night's work. Hadzic and Docherty agreed that their combined unit would leave for Vogosca an hour before midnight the following day. The next thirty-six hours would need to be spent gathering intelligence on the military situation between Sarajevo and their destination, working out the safest route and possible assault plans, and making sure that they had everything they needed, both for this op and the subsequent mission to Zavik.

Razor and Hajrija were charged with acquiring the necessary maps, and with interviewing refugees who knew anything of the current situation in Zavik or its surrounding region. Chris and the Dame were put to work securing supplies. Extra emergency rations would be needed for the Bosnians, and since the party would have to spend at least one night camping out in the snow, digging tools of some sort would also be necessary. Vogosca might be only four or five miles away as the crow flew, but there was a Serb-held mountain ridge in the way, and no chance of reaching the town, doing a proper recce, launching a rescue and getting back to Sarajevo, all in one night. The unit would have to spend a whole day hidden up in the hills above Vogosca, ready to launch their assault early the following night.

Docherty himself went to see Brindley at the HQ of the British UN contingent. The major's makeshift desk was overflowing with pending paperwork, and he seemed only too pleased for a chance to take a break. He led Docherty across a car park crammed with white UN vehicles and into the steamy Portakabin which did duty as the unit's mess. The coffee was even worse than Docherty expected, despite the generous nip of whisky from Brindley's hip-flask.

'So what have you lot been doing with yourselves?' the major asked.

'Oh, just getting acclimatized,' Docherty replied, wondering exactly how much he should be telling the other man.

'Have you found the woman?'

'We've found out where she is.'

'That's good.'

'Not really. She's in a Serb brothel in Vogosca.'

'Oh Jesus . . .'

'But not for long, we hope. We're going after her . . .'

Brindley's eyes widened. 'Is that . . .' he started to say.

'Is that what we're here for?' Docherty completed for him. 'Probably not. And that's why I'm here.' He paused, ordering his thoughts. 'You know how hard it is for the UN to be involved in a war and still not take sides . . .'

'You're not kidding.'

'Well, I don't think there's any chance of us keeping our hands as clean as you lot have to. If we're going to have any chance of doing what it was we were sent out here to do, then we can't afford to be choosy about accepting help. So our trip to Vogosca is a joint op involving men from a Bosnian Army anti-sniper unit . . .'

'Oh boy,' Brindley said with a smile.

136

Docherty smiled back. 'I wanted someone to know,' he said, 'and you've been selected. If we don't come back, at least they'll be some facts for the Regimental magazine.'

'And after Vogosca?'

'Then we head for Zavik. Just the four of us and Nena Reeve – assuming we've found her and she's willing to go.'

'And then?'

'Depends what we find when we get there. But I've no intention of making it my permanent address. If we say two days to Vogosca, another three to Zavik and a couple of days there, then add three or four to reach the coast . . . I'd like to be in Split again around two weeks from now.'

Brindley nodded. 'OK,' he said. 'I take it you haven't called Hereford since you got here. I could fix it,' he added. 'It might take a while, but there are ways . . .'

'We could call them ourselves,' Docherty said, 'but they know nothing about the situation here, and there's nothing they can do to help us. Anyway,' he added with a grin, 'they don't like to be bothered.'

Brindley wished them good luck as he and Docherty parted again in the vehicle park.

The PC made his way back to the Holiday Inn, wondering what Barney Davies would make of the decisions he was taking. There was no way he could officially agree to joint action with local forces, Docherty knew, so there was no point in telling him. The fact that HQ had made no attempt to reach them since their arrival in Sarajevo seemed to suggest that the CO had an equally firm grip on reality.

*   *   *

The combined unit's jump-off point was a house on the road to the mountain village of Nahorevo, just inside the city's northern boundary. The ten soldiers arrived in dribs and drabs throughout the day, so as not to tip off any watchers in the hills that an operation was imminent. They sat around drinking dandelion tea, smoking cigarettes, rechecking their equipment and reading one of several hundred copies of *Mad* magazine. The house's owner, a member of the anti-sniper unit who had been killed a few weeks earlier, had obviously been a subscriber.

They left the house at 2200 hours, following the Nahorevo road uphill for a few hundred yards before turning on to a path which ran diagonally up across the slope of the hillside. The ridge-line was still some five hundred yards above them. And up there were some of the Serbian guns that continued to pound what remained of Sarajevo.

There would also be some sort of encircling ring of troops, deployed to prevent goods and men from either entering or leaving the besieged city, but opinions in Sarajevo had differed as to how thick or thin this cordon would be. Hadzic was gloomy on the subject, and feared that they might not find a way through without alerting the enemy. His main hope lay in the silenced MP5s.

Docherty was of a different opinion. His experience told him that such cordons often existed mostly in the mind, and only needed minimal manning to reinforce a false impression of impregnability. Historically, in most sieges, both sides tended to become stuck in the roles of besieger and besieged, to the point where neither felt able to cross the line between them. The Serbs up above, Docherty thought, would not be expecting anyone to try what they were trying. Consequently, they would not be expending scarce manpower on blocking off such a possibility.

Or so he hoped. At least they were on the move, and in the right direction, away from Sarajevo. The evening before, in the bar of the Holiday Inn, he had got into a conversation with a fellow Scot, a journalist with one of the quality Sundays. The man, who looked around forty-five, had been pleasantly drunk, and most of the conversation had been small talk, ranging from Celtic's fall from grace to the fate of the SNP. But like a cloud-laden sky parting briefly for sunshine, their good-natured banter had parted to reveal a glimpse of something close to despair. 'Say what you like,' the journalist had said, 'but what has died in this city is the belief that humans have learnt anything from this century.'

Docherty had wanted to disagree, but could think of no reasons for doing so. Nor could he now, climbing the dark path behind Hadzic and Hajrija. And with that realization came another question: if the world was up shit creek without a paddle, then what the hell was he risking his life for?

A friend? He liked Reeve, but he had no sense of obligation to the man that would outweigh his responsibility to Isabel and the children.

Regimental duty? He'd done his share of duty. The SAS wasn't a religion, and Barney Davies wasn't the high priest. No, he'd accepted this job almost out of habit. And out of curiosity. And now he was beginning to wonder whether it had been the stupidest decision of his life.

A couple of Bosnians behind him, Chris was not

wondering about what might have been. He rarely did. In this life, he reckoned, you opened doors and then dealt with what was on the other side. And he loved opening them. Of course there was always the chance that he'd not beat the clock on this one, the way Eddie and Anderson had failed to beat it in Colombia, but that was the chance you had to take. Knowing that was the one thing he and Eddie had had in common, but it was so basic that it had made up for all the things they had disagreed on.

Eddie had loved moments like this, walking across a mountain in almost total darkness, senses attuned to every little noise, utterly alive in every respect. Christ did too. He loved the idea that every place they got to was somewhere he'd never been before. Even Sarajevo had been incredible. Downright tragic, certainly, but fascinating. It hadn't looked like he'd imagined it, but then places never did.

So far, his only regrets regarding this op concerned the paucity of birds he'd been able to see. There had been the usual Mediterranean coastal types around Split, but since their arrival in Sarajevo he'd hardly seen any at all. That said a lot for their intelligence, Chris thought. What birds in their right minds would want to winter in a city pounded by sustained artillery fire? Once they started out for Zavik, though, who knew what he might see. Maybe a booted eagle, or even a Bonelli's eagle.

Twenty yards ahead, Razor was thinking about a different kind of bird. Hajrija was walking in front of him, and, even bundled up like a bear, she was offering the Londoner more than enough food for his fantasies. No amount of clothing or equipment could quite disguise the grace of her walk, and the long wisps of hair escaping from the woollen balaclava seemed unbelievably feminine. Physically she reminded him a little of Maureen, which wasn't the best of omens.

Maureen had been a couple of years older than Hajrija, a divorced occupational therapist who lived in Hereford with her six-year-old son. She and Razor had met in a pub, and taken to each other immediately. They didn't have any interests in common, but the sex was great and he got on well with the kid. Within three months they had arranged to get married. He couldn't remember ever having been happier. Even his mother's announcement that she was remarrying, and going off to Australia for at least three years, had failed to really upset him.

Then the roof had fallen in. Maureen had called off the wedding a month before it was due to take place, and announced that, for the boy's sake, she was going back to his father. Razor had thought the man lived in London, but it turned out he had been back in Hereford for several months.

Six weeks later his mother, to whom he'd always been close, left for Australia. For the first time in his life Razor had felt uncertain of his own judgement, rootless, and mortal.

That had been two years ago, and things had not changed much in the intervening period. He had acquired a sense of time passing, and a tendency to reflect on the past, which he had never had before. His job in the Training Wing was interesting, even challenging, but seemed to be leading to nothing more than a distant retirement. And there was always the chance that the loss of his happy-go-lucky self had made him less of a soldier.

So far, though, he could detect no signs that it had.

And maybe it was the presence of Docherty, but he could feel all the old excitement at setting out on an operation. Hell, he thought, Docherty got the woman in Argentina – this time it's my turn. Hajrija, you're going to be mine, he silently told her back, and at that moment, right on cue, she turned her head to give him a quick smile. Razor thought how much he'd like to see her in sunshine, with considerably fewer articles of clothing on.

Towards the rear of the column, the Dame was enjoying the darkness. He had always preferred the city to the country, and the sort of vast terrain which made many people gasp with wonder tended to make him feel uneasy. It was all too much, somehow. It was so fucking eternal. He preferred not to have to look at it.

He thought about the other night, and the two men he'd killed beneath the high-rise. They'd never know who won this war, never know anything more. They wouldn't catch Bosnia's first appearance on the fucking Eurovision Song Contest. Life had just ended for them – just like that.

But where were they now? It was hard to imagine those men in heaven, but he doubted if they'd done anything bad enough to warrant endless torture by fire.

At the Holiday Inn he'd come across a guide to Yugoslavia, and one of the bits he'd read had been about a place called Medugorje, which was fifty miles or so to the south. In 1981 six of the village's teenagers had seen an apparition of the Virgin Mary, and the place had suddenly become a place of pilgrimage, not to mention a tourist attraction.

The Dame found it hard to believe that anyone had seen such an apparition, but then it wasn't much easier believing six kids from a dirt-poor village had conspired to make the whole story up. And apparently the apparitions had continued on a regular basis, usually on Mondays and Fridays.

He had laughed when he read that – it seemed such bullshit – but then it occurred to him that if there were no apparitions then why had none of the thousands of witnesses not blown the whistle on it all, and exposed the whole business as a fucking rip-off? Maybe it wasn't, or maybe they were all so desperate to see something that they had. Maybe that's what faith was, a sort of desperation. He could understand that. He knew death wasn't the end of everything – it couldn't be, or what was the point? There had to be a reckoning, a time to answer for what you had done. There had to be somewhere to wipe yourself clean.

The path led them slowly but remorselessly upwards, winding around the rims of indentations in the mountainside, passing through large stands of conifers that clung to the slopes. The snow was deeper the higher they went, and the trail they left became ever more marked. The good news was that no one else had used this path lately, or at least not since the last snowfall two days before.

About two hours into their journey Docherty and Hadzic agreed to call a halt. The column was now only some two hundred feet from the ridge top, and the two leaders thought it prudent to send scouts forward to check the situation. Chris and Kaltak were dispatched.

They returned less than fifteen minutes later with some welcome intelligence. Each Serb gun emplacement was obviously allowed a fire for cooking and warmth just behind the ridge top, out of sight of the city below. The two nearest fires were a couple of hundred yards to the west of their path, and rather more than that to the east. They should have no trouble slipping through.

The march resumed, with Chris out in front as lead scout. Five minutes later they crested the rise, and crossed what was obviously a much-used path along the top of the ridge. To left and right each of them could see the line of fires stretching into the distance. Ahead and below there was nothing but the ghostly light of the snow-covered slope falling away into darkness.

They worked their way down it, using what looked like a snowed-over stream bed to make their tracks less obvious, and eventually reached the trees. This side of the mountain, unlike the slopes looking down on Sarajevo, was mostly covered in forest, and their hopes were high that they could find a suitable observation point overlooking Vogosca without leaving the shelter of the trees.

It was almost two in the morning when they gave up any idea of finding such a spot. There just wasn't enough light. They were relying on the Bosnians' knowledge rather than eyesight to gauge where the small town was, and there was no way of judging what would be visible when daylight came. It was decided to make camp deep in the trees, and send a two-man team forward to set up an observation post just before dawn.

For the moment the SAS men concentrated on seeking out and enlarging spaces beneath the lower branches of conifers where snow had built up around them, leaving a pocket of air beneath. The Bosnians watched with initial astonishment as the SAS men dug into the snow beneath the spreading branches on the lee side of the trees, and unearthed these living quarters.

144

'Where do you learn this?' Hajrija asked Razor. 'There is no snow in England.'

'Norway,' he said. 'NATO exercises.'

An hour later two buttressed snow caves had been excavated, complete with removable doors. There were too many tracks for the hides to be completely secure, but they would only have to remain undetected for the nine or so hours of daylight.

There remained the matter of choosing the recce team. Hadzic picked Hajrija, and Docherty named Razor, repressing a smile as he did so. 'You know what we want,' he told his second in command. 'We'll see you at dusk. Be good,' he added in parting.

She seemed pleased it was him, Razor thought, as they made their way back down through the trees, aiming for the spot which their map had suggested would be the most promising. Walking down, he couldn't remember ever being in a darker place: the thick cloud cover, and lack of any moon, gave the snow nothing to reflect. The PNGs enabled them to avoid trees, but not much more, and he had to rely on all his dead-reckoning skills. Even then, once they had reached what he gauged was the correct location, there was nothing much to reinforce the supposition. Ahead of them the trees gave way to nothing but blackness; they could be staring out across the hollow which held Vogosca, or just gazing into an empty meadow. Only the dawn would tell.

It was still something between ten and twenty minutes away, so Razor suggested they use the time digging out the blocks of frozen snow they would need to cover the observation trench. Hajrija agreed and, following his example, used the spade to cut out blocks of snow half a yard square and roughly four inches thick. Once they had a dozen, Razor called a halt.

The faintest glimmer of light was now showing in the eastern sky, and they both squatted on their haunches watching the blackness in front of them slowly fade into browns, and the scene gradually swim into focus. It was the town, and their positioning was almost perfect. Razor selected a sight some ten yards to their left and just inside the line of trees, which gave them an overall view of not only the town but both major access roads, and started furiously digging their trench.

Hajrija carried the thick snow tiles across and then helped with the digging. Ten minutes later, with sweat running freely inside their winter clothing, they had a trench about eight feet long and about two and a half feet wide. Razor used the spade to cut a ledge along both sides just below the upper lip, and between them they balanced pairs of snow tiles against one another to make their roof. Once this was completed they used loose snow from the drifts beneath the trees to smooth out the angular outline of the structure and disguise its rectangular shape. Only twenty minutes had passed since first light when they took up residence, lying closely together side by side, their eyes looking out through the observation slit. The trench was designed to sleep one while the other observed, but both were too interested in what lay below for either to countenance sleep.

It was growing light enough now to pick out details. To their left the main road from Sarajevo swung down from the mountain, entering the town between two lines of dwellings and emerging on the far side before swiftly dropping from sight into an unseen valley. What looked like no more than a dirt track wound up into the hills to the east, beyond the river which ran down through the heart of the town.

This had no more than two hundred buildings, sprinkled apparently at random around the church in the centre. The only signs of socialist-style construction were two four-storey blocks on the western edge of town and a long, single-storey building on the road leading in down the mountain. That had to be the Sonja Motel, where the women were taken.

The Partisan Sports Hall was easy to spot: a large, almost windowless structure on the far side of the town, rising out of a complex between the river and the main road. So far, Razor thought, reality matched their map.

He started a more thorough search with the binoculars, and found his first signs of life, a soldier walking from the motel towards one of the last houses on the road out of town. There seemed to be a few upright chairs under a tree by the road. By day it had to be a checkpoint, he decided.

He trained the binoculars on the road beyond the town and found another, but the dirt track leading up to the right didn't warrant one. The Serbs here weren't expecting any trouble, he thought.

'More men,' Hajrija whispered by his side.

Razor followed the direction of her East German binoculars, down to where several men were gathering in the forecourt of the Sonja Motel. The faint sound of an engine starting drifted up from the town, and a dormobile emerged into view from under the overhang of the motel's roof. The men all climbed aboard, and the vehicle moved out on to the road, turning left, away from the centre of the town. At the checkpoint it slowed, and then accelerated away up the hill.

'The day-shift gunners,' Razor thought out loud. He turned to Hajrija, whose face was uncomfortably close. Her breath smelt faintly of the plum brandy they had all imbibed after completing the shelters back in the forest. Her eyes were dull with fatigue. 'Do you want to sleep first?' he asked.

'OK,' she said. 'But you wake me, yes?'

Razor looked at his watch. 'It will get dark around five,' he said. 'I'll wake you at twelve-thirty.'

'OK,' she said again, yawning.

He listened to her struggle her way into the sleeping bag in the confined space, and then her breathing in the silence. Just when he thought she was asleep, the words 'you make a nice house' emerged faintly from out of the darkness.

'Thank you,' he said, and smiled to himself.

The next four and a half hours he spent struggling to stay awake and alert, and noting down everything that happened in the town below, adding detail to their map. The amount of military traffic did not seem high, and seemed to consist mostly of men returning from or setting out for the Serb positions in the hills above Sarajevo. The exceptions were one lorryload of uniformed troops which arrived from somewhere down the valley and two cars carrying irregulars sporting broad-brimmed hats. Chetniks, Razor guessed, though one brief glimpse was not enough to ascertain whether they wore long beards. Like everyone else they disappeared into the Sonja Motel, which seemed to function as the local barracks.

As for the Partisan Sports Hall, there seemed to be no movement around it at all, and Razor began to wonder whether the women held there had been moved in the week since their informants' release. He could see no sign of guards, but with any luck they were positioned out of sight on the far side of the building. The thought of this mission coming up empty left a sinking feeling in his stomach.

At twelve-thirty he shook Hajrija by the ankle, eliciting what sounded suspiciously like a Serbo-Croat curse. She emerged by his side a few minutes later, bleary-eyed and beautiful.

He concentrated on the job in hand, listing what he'd seen, and sharing his anxiety about the Sports Hall. Her face fell as he did so, but the disappointment quickly turned to anger, and another indecipherable curse escaped her lips as she ran a hand angrily through her tangled hair.

'One day you must tell me what that means,' Razor said.

She shook her head, ran the other hand through her hair, and managed a faint smile. 'One day maybe,' she said, 'now you go sleep.'

'Gladly,' Razor said. He backed himself into the trench, found his way into the sleeping bag, and the next thing he knew she was tugging on his ankle and whispering that it was five o'clock. He lay there for a few seconds wondering where the light had gone and why he still felt dog-tired.

Hajrija's smile of welcome made him feel better for an instant, until he made out the change in the outside world. For the first time since their arrival in Sarajevo the sky was clearing, and the last vestiges of a visible sun were glowing orange above the mountains to the west. 'Shit,' he said succinctly.

149

'It works for us too,' she said.

'We have PNGs,' Razor said.

'The women have not. I think it will be more easy to get them away from there if there is some light.'

She had a point. 'Maybe you're right,' Razor agreed, 'but we don't even know if they are still here.'

'Some are,' she said. 'Take a look.'

He trained the binoculars on the area of the Sports Hall. A couple of streetlights burned in the growing gloom, and just to one side of them was . . . a bus.

'Ten women come in the bus,' Hajrija said. 'About one hour now. Two men come out and take them into the hall.'

'I suppose that's good news,' Razor said, aware of the irony.

'Yes,' she said, in the same tone.

'OK,' he said. 'What are we going to recommend here? What's the best way in and the best way out?'

'The river to go in,' she said. 'But out – we not know how many people or where we are going. If there are thirty women . . .'

'We shall need the bus,' Razor completed the thought. 'And I agree, the river is the best way in. How much longer do you think we should stay here?'

'Thirty minutes? It will be all dark then.'

'Yeah, and it'll give us a chance to see what the lighting's like down there,' said Razor.

They both watched in silence for the next few minutes.

'Are you married?' she asked out of the blue.

'No,' he said. 'Are you?'

'No.'

He asked a question that he'd been wanting to ask.

'That American journalist Bailey – was he . . . more than a friend?'

'You mean, do I sleep with him?' she asked, surprised.

'No. I mean, were you in love with him?'

'Oh no. But I like him. He is – was,' she corrected herself, 'a nice man. He has innocence, you know?'

So had she slept with him, Razor wondered. He decided to change the subject. 'How did you get involved?' he asked. 'In the Army, I mean?'

'Oh, that is an easy story,' she said. 'I am a student of journalism, and it seems more important to fight for what I believe than write it down.'

'Makes sense.'

'My boyfriend does not think so,' she said. 'He say it is crazy for a woman to do this. I tell him "fuck off".'

'Does he?' Razor asked.

She laughed. 'Who knows? I do not see for a long time. But why I am in the unit, I see children killed in the street and I know I want to fight the bastards who do this.'

'And the men accepted you?'

She grimaced. 'Not at the beginning. But slowly, yes, they realize I can run as good and walk as good and shoot better than any of them. They learn now, I think. I am just one of the boys,' she added sarcastically.

Razor found it hard to take that thought seriously. She might be a better soldier than any of them, but a boy she certainly wasn't.

Half a mile away Docherty was wondering why it seemed harder to sleep when you were older and needed it more. Or at least felt like you did. All these young men he was surrounded by hardly seemed in need of energy conservation, yet they slept like bairns.

He hoped it hadn't been a mistake sending Razor with the woman. The two of them obviously had something brewing between them, whether they knew it or not, and on the spur of the moment he had felt like indulging a romantic whim. Hardly appropriate in retrospect, and he hoped the two of them had risen above the temptation he had wilfully put their way.

Still, something inside him remained unrepentant. The business of being a soldier often involved putting the business of being a human on hold, but there was something about this war and this op, he felt, which made it more important than usual to keep the two men inside him tied closely together. If the human being slowed the soldier down then that was too bad.

As his favourite strategist Liddell Hart had been fond of pointing out, it didn't help to win the war if you lost the peace. And whether Liddell Hart had meant it or not, Docherty had always believed that any decent peace must include the soldier's peace of mind.

It was almost fully dark now, or at least as dark as it was going to get. Docherty pulled himself out through the narrow exit and on to the snow-covered forest floor. As he expected, the patch of sky visible between the treetops showed stars – the sky had cleared during the day. To his left the light seemed brighter, and he walked across to find a clearing no more than thirty yards from their hides. Here a few clouds could be seen scudding across the sky, and the stars seemed as bright as they ever did at this altitude. Deneb flickered like a roseate diamond to the north, and directly above the clearing the Milky

Way looked like a jewelled scarf that someone had tossed into the air.

Docherty stood there, revelling in the wonder of it all, thinking about Isabel. She'd be giving the kids their tea about now, and then maybe watching the news while they shared a bath. He could see the kids in his mind's eye, splashing water over each other.

He walked back down to the hides, grateful that they wouldn't be needing the wretched PNGs that night. If the clouds were anything to go by there'd be a stiff breeze blowing out there in the open, and that would make it that much easier to reach their target undetected. In Docherty's experience it was more often sound than sight which gave an attacker away.

He arrived back just in time to see two shadowy figures approaching through the trees, and froze in his tracks, just in case. Then the taller of the two extended an arm into the air – the prearranged signal. It was Razor and Hajrija.

Docherty gestured Razor into the British hide, and invited Hajrija to bring Hadzic over for a conference. Chris and the Dame were awake now and, once the two Bosnians had arrived, all six of them huddled together in the confined space, the much-amended map spread out on the small portion of hardened snow left between them. Three torches illuminated the map and faces surrounding it.

Razor and Hajrija took turns describing what they had discovered, and then he outlined their recommended method of approach.

'OK,' Docherty said. 'But let's start at the end and work backwards – it usually helps. Assuming we get the women out of the hall, where do we take them from there?' He looked at Hadzic. 'Where will they want to go?'

The Bosnian shrugged, or at least tried to. It was difficult when both shoulders were pinned by the person on either side. 'Somewhere safe,' he said drily. 'The way I see it,' he went on, 'there are two choices. The first is to take them back the way we have come, across the mountain to Sarajevo. But there are reasons not to do this. We don't know what condition the women will be in, and whether they can make such a journey. We do know that Sarajevo is not the best place to be in the world right now. So ... I think the second choice is better. We take the bus and we drive it west. We will have to go through the Serb lines somewhere between here and Ilijas, but it will be three, four in the morning, and if they are not expecting us our chances will be good ...'

'That's the main thing,' Docherty agreed. 'We have to get out of Vogosca without raising the alarm. Now, remember what the women told Razor and Hajrija about the lorry coming for them each evening around nine o'clock ...'

10

'Remember to bring the blonde again – the young one with the big tits,' his friend shouted.

'I'll bring what *I* fancy,' Dragan Kovacevic retorted, climbing unsteadily into the cab and almost knocking his hat from his head.

'Christ, I'd better come with you,' his friend said. 'The state you're in you'll probably come back with our grandmothers.'

He climbed into the driver's seat and belched loudly. 'That's fucking good beer,' he said. 'Hey, I need a piss,' he suddenly realized.

He climbed back down again and sent a long, steaming stream on to the slush-covered gravel, sighing loudly as he did so.

'Come on, get a move on,' Kovacevic said.

'What's your hurry?' his friend wanted to know, lifting himself back into the cab. 'The whores aren't going anywhere, are they?' He untucked his shirt and used it to dry his beard. 'It'll freeze solid,' he explained, as the other man eyed him with amusement.

'I'm going to cut mine off,' Kovacevic said, turning the key in the ignition and letting in the clutch. 'You see those boys from Goradze? They all had lice crawling in theirs. It was disgusting.' He pulled the lorry out of the motel forecourt and on to the road.

'What do you expect from that bunch? They've been living around fucking Muslims too long.'

The lorry rumbled down the road into the dark town,

its headlights picking out the twin tracks of clear tarmac in the snow-covered road.

'I wonder what they all do at night,' Kovacevic observed, his eyes roaming across the darkened houses. 'No electricity for TV, no light for doing anything.'

'They probably do what we do,' his friend said with a grunt. 'Except they don't get such a varied menu,' he added, laughing. 'You know, it's gonna be hard to get used to having only one woman after all this is over,' he went on.

'You . . .' Kovacevic started to say. A light was shining on the road ahead, waving to and fro. On the bridge, it looked like. He braked, wondering what sort of idiot could have ordered a checkpoint in the middle of the town.

There only seemed to be one man though, his face shadowed by the hood on his anorak. He didn't appear to be carrying a gun, which was strange for a checkpoint . . . 'What the fuck?' Kovacevic muttered, pulling the lorry to a halt some ten yards from the waving flashlight.

It was the last sound he ever made. The windows imploded as the silenced MP5s raked the cab with automatic fire, leaving an echo of breaking glass to compete with the swift-flowing river in disturbing the night's silence.

Docherty pulled open the cab door and yanked the bearded soldier out and down on to the icy road. Chris was doing the same on the other side. Razor and the Dame had taken up covering positions twenty yards back up the road. No lights had gone on in the nearby houses, but that was presumably because of a lack of electricity. No one had appeared out of the darkness, which suggested either bad hearing or a healthy instinct for survival.

The PC pointed the flashlight up-river, switched it on and off three times, and then set about heaving the Chetnik's body across to the stone parapet. Once there, he lifted the shoulders up across it, and then used the legs to lever the corpse out into space. The splash was barely audible above the sound of the rushing water.

The corpse from Chris's side followed it in, and Docherty had a momentary memory of a Saint book he had read as a youth, in which the hero had come across three men attacking one on a bridge like this in Innsbruck. Being the Saint, he had tipped all three into the icy river, only to belatedly discover that they were policemen trying to arrest a thief. *The Saint's Getaway*. He had loved those books.

The six Bosnians loomed out of the dark like wraiths and, without a word, clambered into the back of the lorry. They were good soldiers, Docherty thought. He checked that all the bergens had survived the journey and then, signalling Razor and the Dame to join the Bosnians, picked up the Chetnik's hat and climbed into the cab. Chris was already waiting at the wheel, broad-brimmed hat perched on his head, looking like anyone's idea of a drunken Australian.

There was a rap on the cab's back window. 'Let's go,' Docherty said. 'And keep it slow.'

Chris obliged, rumbling past the town's neat ortho-dox church, several official-looking buildings and an apparently empty supermarket with one large window boarded up. The road curved round to the left, and the Sports Hall came into view. 'Where the fuck do they park it?' Chris asked.

'Up against the side of the building,' Docherty suggested. There wasn't anywhere else he could see. 'But where's the fucking bus?' This lorry would do at a pinch, but it would be a real pinch, with thirty women to transport.

'It's round the back,' Chris said, braking to a halt. 'Razor's new girlfriend saw them move it there.'

'OK,' Docherty said. He took a deep breath. 'Ready?'

'Yeah.'

'Then let's do it.'

They got down from the cab, adjusted the hats as low across their faces as they could without looking ridiculous, and started walking towards the corner of the building. The entrance was reportedly on the other side, and they were just rounding the corner when they heard the sound of a door opening. Someone had heard the lorry arrive.

A man stepped out through the doorway, silhouetted against the dim light that came from within. Docherty didn't break step.

'*Zdravo*,' the man said.

'*Dobro vecer*,' Chris replied.

They were only a few yards apart.

'*Koja* . . .' the man began, suddenly suspicious.

Docherty flicked open his coat and fired the MP5 from the hip. The man was still falling as Docherty sped in through the doorway. Another two men, both well into middle age, were looking up from a makeshift table, cards spread around the yellow-glowing kerosene lamp. Docherty's finger tightened on the trigger, and then slowly unclenched itself.

'Tell them we're looking for a reason to kill them,' he said to Chris. 'And find out where the women are.'

He went back outside, dragged the body off into the shadows, and went to get the rest of the unit.

'The bus is round the corner,' he told the Dame, who sped off to check it out.

Lujinovic and Begen started off up the road back into town; their job was to provide early warning of any enemy approach. Docherty didn't know how long the Serbs at the motel would be prepared to wait for their victims, but, always assuming they weren't all too drunk to notice, he doubted if their patience would survive much more than half an hour.

Abdulahu and Kaltak had clambered into the lorry's cab, with Razor still seated in the back. They were waiting to move off in the opposite direction, towards the checkpoint a few hundred yards further down the road, once any problems in the Sports Hall had been dealt with.

Docherty led Hajrija and Hadzic round to the entrance. Chris was standing over the two Serbs, whom he'd ordered to lie flat on the wooden floor. 'In there,' he said, pointing towards double doors further down the corridor. 'This is the key,' he added, handing it to Docherty.

'Look after those two,' the PC said. He passed the key to Hadzic, and followed the Bosnian commander and Hajrija down the corridor. The Bosnian turned the key and opened the door on to the darkened gym. Almost immediately, it seemed, several invisible people started to cry.

Hadzic stepped in with his torch, and the wailing seemed to go up a notch in volume.

Sensing what was happening, Docherty went back outside to collect the kerosene lamp.

159

'We are here to rescue you,' Hadzic said in his native tongue, but there was no response, save perhaps a muting of the keening sound.

'Nena, are you there?' Hajrija asked, as Docherty came back in with the marginally brighter light.

A sound like a sob escaped from Nena Reeve's lips. 'Hajrija?' she said disbelievingly.

Hajrija shone the torch into her own face. 'It's me. We've come to take everyone away from here.'

Nena pushed herself up from the wall and walked across towards her friend, slowly, as if she feared speed would dissolve the mirage. 'I can't believe it,' she said, and at that moment she caught sight of Docherty.

'This is a dream,' she said.

'Hello, Nena,' Docherty said.

Outside in the parking area the Dame had found the bus. The destination board read Foca, but presumably hadn't been changed since the war began. The tyres were worn, but snow-chains had been fitted, which more than made up for them. There was no key in the ignition. He set about trying to hot-wire the vehicle, and a few minutes later was rewarded with the motor chugging noisily into life.

Rather too noisily. The Dame checked the petrol gauge, which seemed to be hovering between a quarter and half full, before switching off the engine and stepping back down to the ground. He had a momentary glimpse of a slim moon rising above the mountain before someone started shouting at him in a language he didn't understand.

A uniformed soldier was hurrying towards him, doing up his coat as he came. The Dame just stood there, his mind utterly calm, as the man strode up. He watched the soldier's face turn from anger to surprise, the body try and fail to apply the brakes, and then he stepped in like a ballet dancer, taking the man around the neck with one arm and pulling back, his knife slicing across the outstretched throat.

The warm blood gushed across his hand, and he let the body gently down to the ground, before doing a panoramic turn, eyes searching the shadows for other sources of trouble. Satisfied there was none, he pulled the body into the deeper shadow beneath the wall, and washed his hand in a small drift of snow. Looking down he had the momentary illusion that the stain was spreading towards him.

Once Chris had given him the green light, Kaltak had started the lorry down the road in the direction of the checkpoint. They quickly left the town behind, the road running between the river and a narrow meadow, aiming for the mouth of the valley. The lone house ahead was unlit, but beside it a yellow light seemed to be hanging in the air just above the road. As they approached, it revealed itself as a kerosene lamp perched on a wooden bench that was placed across the highway.

The lorry slowed, one of the Bosnians rapped his knuckles on the cab's window, and Razor leapt nimbly down to the road. He reached the bank of the river as the lorry came to a halt in front of the makeshift barricade. There was still no sign of life inside the house.

The Bosnians climbed down, and stood there waiting for a moment, wondering what to do. Razor asked himself whether they could trust the men inside the house – always assuming there were some – not to wake up at any time in the next hour. The answer, unfortunately, was no.

Kaltak and Abdulahu had obviously reached the same conclusion. The latter climbed on to the lorry's running board, reached in, and blew a short blast on the horn. It sounded almost deafening to Razor, but he doubted whether the noise had travelled across town to the motel.

For a moment it even seemed that the blast had failed to rouse anyone inside the house, but the door abruptly banged open, and a man stepped out, complaining loudly. He had no hat on, but the bottom half of his face was darkened by a beard. Razor waited until he was out in the open before knocking him down with a three-shot burst of the silenced MP5.

At the same moment another man came through the doorway, also apparently complaining, and ducked back instantly the moment he saw his comrade fall. Razor cursed and went after him, his mind registering the fleeting impression that the man had not been carrying a weapon. He leapt on to the low veranda and rushed in through the doorway, moving swiftly to his right to avoid being silhouetted against the lighter outside world.

He could hear the man running up the stairs, and restrained himself from instant pursuit. Five seconds, ten, and his eyes were more accustomed to the dark. As he made out the foot of the staircase there were raised voices upstairs, the thud of moving feet on the ceiling above.

Razor went for the stairs, climbing as swiftly and silently as he could manage. There was a faint light above, and three voices talking excitedly to each other, or maybe only two. The thought flashed through his mind that this was a modern house, probably someone's pride and joy before the present war. He wondered what had happened to the people who had lived there.

Thumping footsteps gave the Chetnik away before his silhouette appeared at the head of the stairs. The SAS man fired an automatic burst, and the man crashed backwards, his weapon bouncing past Razor down the stairs. By the time it reached the bottom another man had died. Driven into view by his own inertia, unable to find a target for his AK47, this Serb managed one shot before the MP5 took out his left eye and threw him back on to his partner's body.

The sound of the shot echoed round the house, dying into silence. Razor advanced carefully, ears straining for evidence that there was a third man present. He heard a whimpering noise, which was suddenly drowned out by the entrance of his two Bosnian allies downstairs.

Razor put an eye cautiously round the top of the stairs. The dim light was coming from the room across the landing. There were two other doors, both shut.

He edged his way on all fours towards the half-open door, and gently pushed it wide. The whimpering grew louder, but no shots came out.

'You OK, English?' one of the Bosnians whispered loudly from the bottom of the stairs.

'*Da*,' Razor whispered back, using half of his Serbo-Croat vocabulary and wishing the other half was the Serbo-Croat for 'wait'. The whimpering inside stopped suddenly, and for a few seconds the only sounds to break the silence were his own breathing. Then the shot resounded inside the room, followed in quick succession by the sharp thunk of something metallic hitting the floor and the duller thump of something bigger.

Razor put his eye to the crack between door and frame, and then wearily climbed to his feet. 'It's OK,' he shouted down the stairs. Inside the room he found the youth – he was about fifteen, he guessed – crumpled on the floor. The half of his head that was missing was still sliding down the wall. The AK47 which had put it there was lying in the middle of the room.

Why? Razor asked himself. He turned his head away, and found the answer. A young girl, younger even than the boy, was stretched out on the bed, naked but for the sock stuffed in her mouth and the scarf that had been tightly looped around her neck.

He yanked out the sock and undid the scarf, almost in a frenzy, wanting to cry out something, anything.

He reached for the carotid artery and felt life. The pulse was slight, but she was breathing, almost desperately now, and even in this light there was a blueness around the lips. There seemed no external injuries other than a redness around the vagina, and Razor turned her over, moving one arm and leg outwards to stop her lying flat. The breathing seemed to ease.

Abdulahu appeared in the doorway, took in the scene and said something in his own language, something that seemed to encompass surprise, resignation and sadness. He squatted down next to Razor by the bed. 'She OK?' he asked.

As if in answer the girl's eyes opened, slowly at first and then wide with fright.

Abdulahu said something and took her hand. She began shivering.

Razor looked round for her clothes, but could see none. He yanked the curtain violently down from the window and covered her with that, as her eyes seemed to search his face for understanding. He turned away and stood there for a minute, thinking furiously. 'You stay with her,' he told the Bosnian, miming to reinforce the other man's understanding.

Abdulahu nodded. 'She come with us,' he said.

Razor walked out of the room to where the two dead men lay twisted together and, on an impulse too strong to resist, lashed out a foot at the nearest body. Then, for the first time that he could remember in his adult life, he simply lost control, kicking and kicking the lifeless heads until Abdulahu gently pulled him away.

Back at the Sports Hall Docherty had heard the two shots in the distance, but only faintly. He very much doubted that they would have been heard across the town, and his only real worry was that Razor or one of the Bosnians had been on the receiving end.

In the gymnasium Hajrija and Nena were going from woman to woman, explaining what was happening and where they were being taken. It seemed to be taking a lot of time, but Docherty knew that he couldn't hurry the process. As Nena had explained it, slowly and carefully, as if she was talking to a child: 'These women were put into buses once, given no explanation, and they ended up here – there's no way we can just put them in another bus without telling them why and where they're going.'

The reactions of the women, as far as he could see, varied greatly. Some seemed in shock, blanked out, like mental patients. Others seemed simply tired, as if they'd been awake for days on end. Many were distraught, and found it hard to understand what they were being told. A few were simply brimming with anger.

Nena's state of mind was hard to gauge. Docherty

remembered her mostly as a woman with a ready laugh, a bundle of enthusiasms, and a defiant willingness to wear her emotions on her sleeve. He had always known she must have a more introverted side – he knew from Reeve how seriously she took being a doctor – but it had rarely surfaced in her social persona. The woman he could now see across the dimly lit gymnasium bore little obvious relation to the woman he had known.

What sort of people could do something like this? Docherty asked himself. He had always drawn a blank when trying to imagine the thought-processes of the men who had run the German concentration camps, and he found this no easier to understand. Anyone could turn off their humanity in the heat of the moment, or in longer periods of extreme stress, but this was something else. Evil was the word that came to mind, but it was only a word – it didn't explain anything.

'Boss,' Chris said at his shoulder, 'Kaltak just came back. The checkpoint's ours, but they found a girl there – in bad shape. She'll have to come with us.'

Docherty cupped his hands round his nose. 'Right,' he said, and took the hands away. 'How's the Dame doing?'

'He and Hadzic just got back with some petrol they stole from somewhere. They're putting it into the bus now. They've taken out the lights. How are we doing here?'

'Almost ready, I think.' He looked at his watch. 'The Serbs must be wondering where their women are.'

'It's a pity we don't have time to raze that motel to the ground,' Chris said.

'Yeah.'

'Who's going in what, boss?'

'I want Razor driving the bus – he's the maddest driver I've ever come across, and the best. And I think the Dame should ride shotgun. You and I'll go in the lorry with the Bosnian laddies. And I guess we'll have to take the two prisoners with us.' He rubbed his eyes. 'We'll all have to take the bus up to the checkpoint.'

Hajrija was walking towards them. 'We are ready,' she said, almost accusingly. 'Are you?'

'Yes,' Docherty said.

She turned and said something to the women, who all started getting to their feet. Hajrija said something more, and they started filing out, silently. The few eyes turned towards the men were full of anger.

Nena brought up the rear. She had shaken her golden mane loose, and looked more like the woman Docherty remembered.

'What are you doing here, Jamie?' she asked. 'Is this just a coincidence, you being here?'

'No,' he said. 'We were looking for you, and we heard you were in this place . . .'

'Why were you looking for me?'

'Because of Reeve.'

She looked at him. She had always liked Docherty, liked his Argentinian wife, and the way the two of them were together. She had even thought about them the other day when she was reflecting on her marriage to Reeve. Isabel and Jamie seemed to have got the crucial balance in any relationship, the one between independence and interdependence, about right. It was a hard thing to do. Certainly, she and Reeve had never managed it.

She looked around at the empty gymnasium. 'Aren't SAS wives allowed to leave their husbands any more?'

she murmured, her voice a blend of weariness, flippancy and bitterness.

The bus was ticking over in the Sports Hall car park. The women filed on board, filling up all but four of the forty-two seats. The two prisoners were ordered to sit in the aisle and did so, holding their hands over their heads as if expecting a rain of blows from the women they had guarded. Kaltak took the wheel, leaving the other seven members of the combined unit to squeeze into the seats and space at the front.

As they turned on to the main road Docherty cast a glance back up it, in the direction of the river and the motel. There was no sign of anyone coming to look for the lorry that hadn't returned. Maybe they were in luck: maybe the Serbs were all too drunk or full of pills to care.

They arrived at the checkpoint not much more than a minute later. Razor carried the heavily wrapped girl on board, and passed her on to Hajrija. Nena started to examine her.

'Are you all right?' Docherty asked him.

A bleak smile crossed Razor's face. 'I'm fine,' he said.

He didn't look it, Docherty thought. 'You're driving the bus,' he said.

'Right,' Razor said, his eyes taking in the sea of barely lit women's faces stretching to the back of the vehicle.

'Just follow the lorry,' Docherty said. 'If you think you need a rest, give the Dame a turn.' He gave Razor a few more instructions and then got down off the bus and walked across towards the lorry, noticing that someone had placed a bench and lighted lamp across the road

168

behind them. Presumably it had been that way when they arrived.

He climbed up into the cab where Hadzic and Began were already waiting, and nodded his assent to the question on the driver's face. The lorry moved away, and in the wing mirror Docherty could pick out the dark shape of the unlit bus following some thirty yards behind. No one seeing the lorry's headlights coming towards them would realize there was a second vehicle behind, not until it was halfway past them.

They were heading down a winding valley now, the road crossing and recrossing the rushing river in the confined space. Somewhere at the bottom of this road they would come across the dividing line between Serb-controlled and Muslim-controlled territories. There would be checkpoints of some sort, maybe physical barriers, maybe even an exchange of fire in progress. And the sooner they reached it the less chance there was that they'd be expected, Docherty thought. He was still surprised that no one had come looking for the lorry in Vogosca. Maybe by now they had, and found nothing but the empty Sports Hall.

He wondered whether they should stop and cut the telephone wires than ran along by the road, and decided it would be a waste of time – even if the telephones were operational, which he doubted, the Serbs would be using radio.

He also wondered whether he should have put the bus in front. If they had to force their way through an unexpected roadblock the rear vehicle would be the most vulnerable. But then again, if they ran into enemy forces . . .

Docherty told himself to stop worrying about decisions already taken.

Behind him Razor was guiding the bus by the lights of the lorry ahead. It was a favourite trick of Docherty's to disguise two vehicles as one, and they'd done something similar in Argentina, during their escape from the town where he and Ben had been taken prisoner. That had been a night to remember, all right. Like this one. Only this was different. Argentina had been hairy enough, but it had felt like an adventure. This one was getting to him. Had got to him.

He glanced across to where the Dame was sitting, MP5 cradled in his lap, face showing no emotion. Razor wondered what was going on beneath the surface. Maybe nothing. Maybe the Dame was like he himself had been for so many years, someone who just let it happen, and dealt with it when it did. He had rather liked being that way.

His mother had used to say to him: 'One day you'll get it.' 'Get what?' he had wanted to know. 'When you get it, you'll know,' she had said, affectionately enough. He knew he had driven her nuts, but she'd kind of liked him that way too.

He took a quick look in the rear-view mirror. Hajrija was sitting with the young girl on her lap, looking out of the window beside her.

He realized he knew no more about her than he had about any of the other women he'd really fancied, and that for once it seemed to matter.

The crescent moon was high in the sky now, shedding its thin light across a wider valley below. Lorry and bus passed under a bridge carrying the railway from Sarajevo, which turned in a long curve to run alongside the highway. On the left the river from Vogosca cascaded over stones to join with the broader Miljacka. On all sides a sharp line separated the darker mountains from the star-strewn sky.

A road sign appeared in the lorry's headlights.

'Which way?' Began asked his commander, slowing down.

'Both roads go to Visoko,' Hadzic told Docherty. 'The main highway will be easier to drive, but we'll probably meet less opposition on the smaller road.'

'Let's get off the highway,' Docherty suggested. He looked at his watch. It was a few minutes past three.

'OK,' Hadzic agreed. He said something in his own language to the driver, who took the right fork.

The road ran across a small stretch of bare meadow and tunnelled into a mostly coniferous forest. Curves and dips followed for several miles, and then the road suddenly emerged above a small town, before descending through a succession of hairpin bends to cross the railway tracks and pass the sign that told them they were entering Semizovac.

The town seemed dead at first, full of houses either burnt out or blown up, but as the lorry swung into the main square a line of military vehicles loomed into view, parked along one side. In the opposite corner a brazier was burning, with a soldier standing either side of it, their illuminated faces turned towards the unexpected arrivals.

Lorry and bus left them staring, burrowing down the town's main street.

'I think this is the last Serb-held town,' Hadzic said in English, than added something in Serbo-Croat to Began, who responded by pressing his foot down on the

171

accelerator. In the wing mirror Docherty could see the bus regaining its normal distance as Razor responded.

They seemed to be almost out of the town now, the road dipping suddenly to pass under the railway tracks. As they emerged from the underpass a tank loomed into view, its gun pointed down at the ground. Two armoured cars were parked beside it, also apparently devoid of occupants.

On the tracks to their right a line of covered wagons seemed to be serving as barracks. And a couple of hundred yards further down the road two burnt-out cars had been used to narrow the channel for traffic. There were no lights, but moving figures were visible in the gloom. The pinpoint of a torch suddenly appeared, like a star that had slipped out of the sky.

Docherty leant out of the window with his torch in hand and drew a circle in the air. In the bus behind Razor shouted 'Now!' at Hajrija, who passed on the news in Serbo-Croat. Most of the women responded, either burrowing down on to the floor in front of their seats or simply bending their heads down between their knees.

Razor by this time had brought the bus up level with the lorry, the two vehicles accelerating side by side towards the barrier. Seventy yards, sixty . . . and still no flashes erupted from the Serb guns. Fifty, forty . . . and the lorry slowed abruptly, letting the bus into the lead.

A single bullet passed through a window behind him, and he could hear a machine-gun open up, but they were ripping through the gap between the two hulks, metal screaming on metal down both flanks of the bus.

In the lorry behind, Docherty was firing the MP5 blind, his head jammed as far back behind the window

172

as he could get it. He had a flashing glimpse of trees and running men, a concrete building, another armoured car. Beside him Hadzic had his head down beneath the dashboard, but Began was sitting up behind the wheel, with only the look in his eyes to show that he wasn't going on a picnic. As the bus ahead blasted its way through the gap he let out a great whoop, which seemed made up in equal parts of triumph and terror.

His steering wasn't quite as good as Razor's, the lorry missing the car on the right by a foot or so and giving the one on the left an enormous side-swipe. It rocked on the road like a train on bad tracks, righted itself and sped on after the bus, the soldiers in the back still firing at the vanishing checkpoint.

Another half a mile down the road they found the Bosnian Army waiting to welcome them to what, by Bosnian standards, was safe territory.

One woman in the bus had been cut by flying glass, but everyone else was unharmed.

11

The bureaucratic niceties involved in relocating from one tribal patch to another took up the best part of an hour. The local Bosnian commander was not used to British soldiers emerging, guns blazing, from Serb-held territory, and he wanted more explanation than Docherty was prepared to give him. He spent several minutes reading the small print on their UN accreditation and then simply looked at Docherty, eyebrows raised, as if to say: 'Surely you don't take me for that big a fool?'

At this point Hadzic took over, speaking so fast in his own tongue that Chris had trouble understanding what he was saying. At the end of it all the local commander looked at them, sighed, and handed back their papers with slight distaste. 'OK, you can go,' he said.

'What the hell did Hadzic tell him?' Docherty asked Chris.

'I told him you were mercenaries,' the Bosnian said from behind them. 'And that we didn't have so much help from the outside world that we could afford to antagonise men who had just saved thirty of our women from a Serb brothel.'

Docherty laughed. 'I take it the man didn't approve.'

'He was regular army,' Hadzic said. 'Probably had a good career going for him before someone pulled the rug out from under his feet.'

They walked back out to the vehicles, which were empty.

'Where are they all?' Docherty asked Razor and the Dame.

'Having a bath,' was the reply. 'And then some food, I think. I could do with some breakfast myself,' the Londoner added.

They found the unit's mess by following their noses. A train of coaches stood on the nearby railway line, and on the ground in front of them several men were busy keeping up the fire under two large tureens of bean soup. These had presumably been ordered for the women, but there seemed plenty to go round, and the SAS men were soon offered bowls of the thick, steaming liquid. The unit's commander might not like mercenaries, but his cooks seemed more impressed by results than motivation.

There was bread too, stale perhaps, but delicious once softened by the soup. And each man was given a cup of a hot, bitter-sweet liquid that they later discovered was supposed to be coffee.

The women arrived in dribs and drabs, and were taken up into one of the coaches for their food. They all looked cleaner, and some looked readier to take on the world. Many, though, still seemed in shock. Nena was one of the stronger-looking. She glanced across to where Docherty was sipping coffee, perched on a pile of sacking, and a faint smile seemed to cross her lips, as if she was remembering another world.

Light was showing over the rim of the eastern hills as they resumed their journey. It was a bitterly cold morning, but the local commander had donated a recent shipment of blankets for the women on the unheated bus, and the clear sky promised a sunny day.

It was only about ten miles to Visoko as the crow flew,
but the actual driving distance was more than twice that,
and the drivers could rarely exceed twenty miles an hour
on the winding snow-covered road. The sun had cleared
the high horizon before they arrived, transforming the
countryside for the four SAS men, who had only seen
Bosnia under cloud.

Docherty was reminded of the area around Aviemore
in Scotland, until the road wound down into Visoko,
where a tall minaret broke the surface of the steep-roofed
houses.

The cobbled town square would have looked untouched
by the war, if the local military hadn't picked the old
town hall for its HQ. They drew up their vehicles in
front of it, and sat waiting while Hadzic went in to
report their arrival.

Their last hosts had radioed ahead, and they were
expected, though no mention seemed to have been made
of British soldiers, mercenary or otherwise. A group of
local women were waiting to take care of those rescued
from Vogosca and their rescuers had been allocated a
billet a hundred yards or so from the square.

It was an old stone house, probably dating back to
the days of the Austro-Hungarian Empire. 'Serbs lived
here,' Hadzic told Docherty as they pushed in through
the unlocked front door, but he either didn't know or
wouldn't say what had happened to them. Wherever the
Serbs were now, most of their possessions remained in
the house. There was a three-month-old newspaper lying
open on the table in the kitchen.

Hajrija having stayed with the women, the Bosnian
men divided up the two bedrooms between them, leaving
the SAS men to spread out their sleeping bags in the single

large downstairs room. All were exhausted, but sleep only came easily for Chris. Each of the others found it hard to turn off their minds, which seemed intent on running endless replays of the previous night's events.

As usual Docherty woke first, at around two o'clock in the afternoon, and went in search of a toilet. He found it occupied by a whistling Bosnian, and ducked out through the back door in search of an alternative. There he found Hadzic cheerfully pissing against a wall, eyes squinting against the smoke from the upturned cigarette between his lips.

It was a beautiful day, the sun high in a clear blue sky. Through a gap in the houses ahead, mountains rose across the valley, while above the roofs behind, a rock face rose almost sheer behind the town, before flattening out into pine-covered slopes. Some two hundred yards away the top of the minaret peeked up through the red-tiled roofs, looking strangely like a fairground rocket.

'You come with me now to see the General?' Hadzic asked.

Docherty reluctantly turned his eyes away from the illusion of a world at peace. 'Aye,' he said.

The two men walked down the narrow street to the square. There were not many people on the street, but there were some, and Docherty was thinking that at least some semblance of normal life had been preserved here. The distant sound of a hundred children shouting and screaming suggested a school that was actually functioning.

They found the 'General' in a small room at the back of the old town hall. He turned out to be a handsome young Bosnian named Ajanovic, with wavy, light-brown hair and green eyes. He was about twenty-eight, Docherty guessed, and had probably been a lieutenant in the old Yugoslav Army. He also, it turned out, spoke excellent English, thanks to a six-month stint in Australia, where half his family had long since emigrated. Docherty took to him instantly, without knowing why, and was pleased to see his judgement vindicated over the course of their discussion.

Hadzic went through the events of the last few days: the discovery that Nena Reeve was in Vogosca, the idea for a joint rescue mission, the rescue itself. Ajanovic listened with great interest, offered them both cigarettes, and said that all of that was very clear, but what were Docherty and Co. doing in Sarajevo in the first place? Who were they?

Hadzic looked at Docherty, who decided to take a chance. They were regular British soldiers, he said, and they'd been sent in to make contact with another British soldier, who was apparently leading a small army of irregulars in the vicinity of Zavik . . .

'That's in Serb-held territory,' Ajanovic said in his Australian-accented English.

'We know.'

Ajanovic looked at him and smiled boyishly. 'What a war,' he said.

The UN wanted Reeve out, Docherty went on, and the Croats, and the Serbs. 'And your Government,' he added diplomatically. 'Everyone is saying he makes it harder to get peace. And even if that only means he's everyone's excuse for continuing to fight, then it makes sense to get him out.'

'Are you supposed to kill him?' Ajanovic asked. 'Terminate him with extreme prejudice,' he enunciated

178

carefully. 'I saw that movie in Sydney. And this war is even crazier,' he added.

'He's a friend,' Docherty said simply.

'Ah, I'm sorry. And his name is Reeve, so the woman is his wife, yes?'

'Yes.'

Ajanovic leaned back in his chair. 'OK,' he said. 'So what do you want from me?'

'Three things, if possible. Some sort of authorization to get us as far as Serb territory, any intelligence you have of the military situation between here and Zavik, and a vehicle of some kind. The lorry we came in if nothing else. Something a bit smaller and more manoeuvrable would be better.'

'You know the British UN base is only forty kilometres up the road, in Vitez?'

'Aye. I was hoping to avoid involving them. You see . . .'

'Yes, yes, I can see why,' Ajanovic agreed. 'But you do understand – what you are doing may be for the good of us all, but it will not help my people in this war, and it is hard to justify giving away anything which we might find useful.'

'Aye, I understand that,' Docherty said. He would have felt the same in the other man's shoes.

'But,' Ajanovic continued, 'there is a – what do you call it? – a transit van? A van with seats . . .'

'Sounds ideal . . .'

'Ah, there is a catch. It needs repair, and we have lost our mechanic. If you have one . . .'

'We do.'

'OK, it is of no use to us. As for the other things, I could write you a hundred authorizations but it would do you

179

no good. I am the commander for this district, and that is all. I have no superiors giving me orders from outside, and no one outside will accept my orders. This is a war in compartments, yes? The next commander you meet may have you shot as spies.' He shrugged and laughed. 'I like the English,' he said, 'and I am grateful on my country's behalf that you risked your lives for our women. So any information we have is yours. But your own people in Vitez will know more.

'I will give you one more piece of advice. If you could travel as something other than what you are, it will be safer for you. Perhaps your people at Vitez can arrange for you to have journalists' papers.'

Docherty thanked him, but didn't see any reason to admit that they already had the various such accreditations Thornton had provided in Sarajevo. He asked where the van was, hoping it had the right number of wheels and an engine. Ajanovic left the room and came back a couple of minutes later with another uniformed soldier, this one barely out of his teens. 'Kemal will show your man the vehicle,' he said. 'And our intelligence man works in the office next to this. His name is Akim, and I have told him to give you any information he has that you need. Do you know when you will be leaving?'

'That depends on how good our mechanic is,' Docherty said.

'Then we may meet again.' Ajanovic offered his hand, and the two men shook. Docherty found himself hoping this man survived the war.

He and Hadzic walked back to the house, where the SAS men were in various stages of getting up. Razor was shaving, Chris rummaging through his bergen for a clean shirt, the Dame leaned up against the wall in his sleeping bag reading a Yugoslav tourist guide. 'Having a nice holiday, are we?' Docherty asked them.

'This is a good B&B, boss,' Razor observed, 'except for the lack of beds and breakfast.'

'Been out sightseeing, boss?' Chris asked.

Docherty told them whom he'd seen. 'There's a boy out here wants to show you a van,' he told the Dame. 'It needs some sort of fixing, but I don't know what. See what can you do.'

'What if it's unfixable?' Razor asked.

Docherty shrugged. 'I guess we fight Hadzic and his boys for the lorry.'

'I'm game,' Razor said.

'Yeah, we all know which of his boys you'd like to wrestle,' Chris murmured.

As if on cue, Hajrija appeared in the doorway. 'Nena is here,' she told Docherty. 'She likes to talk to you.'

'Where is she?'

'In the street.'

Docherty walked out to find her leaning up against a wall, apparently lost in thought. She was wearing the jeans they had found her in, and a large coat that she had since acquired from somewhere. She looked cold.

'Are you coming in?' Docherty asked her.

'No, I . . . I feel like being outside in the sunshine. You know? Can we walk?'

'Aye, of course. Just let me tell the lads.' He slipped back inside, told Chris and Razor to see Akim at the town hall and to start planning their route to Zavik, and re-emerged half a minute later to find her in the same position.

'This way?' he suggested, looking down the road towards the far-off mountains.

They started walking, in silence at first.

'I don't know what to say,' he eventually said. 'I can only try and imagine what you've been through . . . If you want to talk, I can listen.'

'No,' she said, 'I don't want to talk about it. Not to a man. Not even to a good man,' she added, looking straight ahead. 'Tell me what you are doing here. Hajrija told me some of it, but I'm not sure she understands it completely.'

Docherty went through it all again, from the moment he had picked up the phone and heard Barney Davies talking to him over the bar chatter at Glasgow Central.

She listened in silence, and when he had finished turned to him with a perplexed look in her eyes. 'Why did you say yes, Jamie?' she wanted to know. 'Why did Isabel let you?'

'I've been asking myself the same thing,' he said. 'And you know, there's a voice in my head saying "OK, you've been a soldier, you think you know what war is, well, you don't. You've just been through soldiers' games like Oman and the Falklands and Northern Ireland. You've been through wars where the rules get bent. But this is a war where there aren't any rules." I . . .' He stopped himself. 'I'm sorry,' he said, 'this is not what you need to hear right now.'

'I asked the question,' she said.

They walked on for another minute in silence. 'You'll take me to Zavik, then?' she asked eventually.

'Only if you're sure you want to go.'

'I've already tried to get there once.'

He wondered how long the bitterness would colour her voice, and thought about Isabel. It had left his wife's voice, but it had only been an outward manifestation of the breakages within. Her experience with the torturers would always be part of her.

They were almost at the edge of town. A hundred yards ahead their road joined the main highway, which bypassed Visoko to the north. Beyond that the wall of mountains bathed in the afternoon sunshine.

She shivered. 'When do we go?' she asked.

'I don't know yet,' he said. 'Maybe tomorrow.'

'That's an Everly Brothers song,' she said. 'You remember Reeve loves the Everly Brothers?'

'Aye.' The idiot had sung 'All I Have to Do Is Dream' at his own wedding reception. Badly.

'I can't believe he is doing what they say he is doing,' she said.

'No,' Docherty agreed, but a small doubt nestled in the back of his mind. He knew what this war had done to him in a week. God only knew what it had done to Reeve in nine months.

After Docherty's departure with Nena, Razor had found Hajrija standing in the garden, staring into space.

'Hajrija,' he said gently, but she jumped anyway.

'Don't do that,' she said angrily when she saw it was him.

'I'm sorry,' he said. 'I . . .' He shrugged helplessly.

'No, I am sorry,' she said. She pushed her hair back from her eyes in characteristic fashion. 'It is hard,' she said, looking at him almost pleadingly. 'To be with those girls after what happens to them. It breaks my heart. But I must be strong and make them happy, you understand.'

'Yeah,' he said, 'you need a hug.' He opened his arms. 'Come on,' he said, and she burrowed her head into his neck, her tears running down inside his shirt.

'Thank you,' she said after a couple of minutes, pulling herself gently away.

'You're welcome,' he said, thinking he'd never seen anyone he desired half as much. 'How's the girl?' he asked. 'The one from the house . . .'

Hajrija looked distraught again. 'Satka,' she said. 'Her name is Satka, and I forget to tell you – she wants to see you, "the man with the funny face" she calls you. She is . . . She is OK, I think. You know? Not sick.'

'I know,' he said. Not sick perhaps, but who knew what damage had been done?

'We can go now,' she said. 'It is not far. Two streets.'

'Why not.'

They went back into the house, where Chris was looking through his bird book as he waited for Razor.

'I've got a house call to make,' Razor told him. 'I'll meet you at the town hall in half an hour or so.'

Chris nodded and smiled knowingly at him.

'I'm the man with the funny face,' Razor shouted back over his shoulder as they left the house.

He didn't feel like cracking any jokes once they reached the place where the women had been temporarily housed. It was a large building next to the mosque, part of a religious school, as Hajrija explained. Satka, along with nine of the youngest women, was sharing one of five mattresses in an upstairs room. When Razor arrived all the other women seemed to shrink away from him, despite the presence of Hajrija.

Satka, though, was pleased to see him, and they talked for ten minutes, with Hajrija translating. She was twelve,

184

she said, and when the men had come to their village her mother had told her to hide. When she came out everyone was gone, and all the houses were burning. She'd stayed there for a couple of days but no one had come back, so she'd tried walking to the next village, and that was when the other men had found her and made her go with them in their car.

Up to this point she told the story almost as if entranced by her own narrative flow, but then abruptly she shifted into the third person, using 'she' instead of 'I' when describing how the men had hurt her and kept her tied up, right up to the moment when 'she' was rescued by the 'man with the funny face'.

Razor listened, smiling encouragingly, and thought that never before had he fully understood the meaning of the phrase 'a broken heart'. He wanted to promise this girl that he'd take her to England that very minute, but he knew that he couldn't, and even that he shouldn't.

At least she was alive, he thought, as they walked back down to the building's courtyard. It wasn't enough.

'I think you need hug now,' Hajrija told him, putting her arms round his neck.

After parting with Nena, Docherty let his feet carry him round the town. The temptation to stay another day was strong, and he could think of at least one good reason to reinforce the desire. They needed the rest, not so much from the physical stresses as from the emotional ones. None of them had ever been through anything like this before. So far the other three had performed in exemplary fashion, but the danger signs were there: a lack of jokes from Razor, almost total silence from the Dame, and his own tendency to let things slide, as evidenced by the fact that he was strolling round the town rather than doing what needed to be done.

Only Chris seemed to be taking it all in his stride. Maybe they should all take up bird-watching.

His stomach suddenly let loose an angry rumble, reminding him that he hadn't eaten for about twelve hours. And presumably neither had the others. 'The least you can do is keep your men fed, Docherty,' he told himself out loud.

Back at their lodging he found Began brewing tea in the kitchen. 'Where is Hadzic?' Docherty asked. Began grinned and shrugged.

Docherty came out of the kitchen door just as Hajrija came in through the front. 'Ah, I need you,' she said.

'I'm spoken for, love.'

She looked at him questioningly.

'What do you need me for?' he asked.

'I need to say I come to Zavik with you, yes?'

Docherty's first thought was that this would make Razor's day. His second was that it was impossibly irregular, his third that she'd be invaluable in several ways. His fourth, he expressed out loud: 'Will Hadzic let you go?'

'Of course,' she said. 'I join up, I leave. No problems.'

'It doesn't quite work like that in the British Army,' he said, 'but if it's OK with your boss, we'd love to have you along.'

She beamed at him. 'That is good.'

'You can ask Hadzic now,' Docherty said, catching sight of the Bosnian commander through the open door, crossing the street towards them.

Hadzic seemed rather less sanguine about letting

her go than Hajrija had led Docherty to believe, but after an animated five-minute exchange of opinions in Serbo-Croat he reluctantly acquiesced in the transfer of her loyalties.

'Is there any spare food in this town?' Docherty asked them both when they'd finished, 'or do we have to break open some emergency rations?'

'There is a place for soup,' Hadzic said. 'You want to go there now?'

'When the others get back.'

Began called out something from the kitchen.

'Who wants tea?' Hadzic translated.

'We do,' Razor said from the doorway. Chris was behind him.

'I come back later,' Hajrija told them all, on her way out.

The three SAS men took their mugs of tea and sat round a large-scale map of the region, discussing the information Razor and Chris had managed to glean at the town hall. Zavik was about ninety twisting miles away, all but twenty-five of them through allegedly safe territory. The first thirty miles to Vitez followed the main highway, and the road south from there to Gornji Vakuf was apparently being kept open by the British UN contingent of Cheshires as a supply route for themselves.

'With any luck we can hijack a Mars Bar shipment,' Chris said.

Razor grunted. 'The problems begin after that,' he said. 'The road to Bugojno is supposedly open, but the town's probably being bombarded by the Serbs. Beyond there, we have a very dicey road to Kupres, which the Serbs seem to hold, and then the last stretch to Zavik, right up in the mountains. I'm beginning to think even an HAHO drop would be preferable to driving this fucker.'

'We don't seem to have that option,' Chris said.

'That's why he's suggesting it,' Docherty said with a grin. 'By the way, Hajrija is coming along for the ride.'

Chris shook his head. 'The man's in danger of charisma overload,' he said.

Razor, though, didn't seem so pleased. 'Why, boss?' he asked seriously.

'She asked. I guess she wants to keep Nena company.'

'And why did you agree?'

'I think it will be good for Nena to have another woman along. And Hajrija knows Zavik. We already know she's a good soldier.'

'OK, boss.'

'If you think I've made a wrong decision, say so.'

Razor smiled. 'No, boss, I don't think you made a wrong decision. I guess I just don't like the thought . . . you know what I mean.'

'Aye.'

'If we're gonna be walking over snow-covered mountains she'll need some better gear than what she's been wearing,' Chris said.

'Aye, so will Nena. I have a horrible feeling we're going to have to visit the Cheshires after all.'

'Maybe they'll lend us a Warrior,' the Dame said from the doorway.

'No joy with the van?' Razor asked.

'It's outside,' the Dame said.

They filed out into the street, where a sorry-looking vehicle greeted their eyes. The VW Microbus had obviously seen some action, though whether in a war or a demolition derby was impossible to tell. The various wounds it had suffered had all been duly painted over, in a veritable kaleidoscope of different shades. The overall effect was of a mottled, rusty, hippie camper.

'Far out,' Razor said sarcastically.

'The motor's OK,' the Dame said. 'And it does about seventy.'

The interior had been customized, presumably to improve its troop-carrying capacity. Behind the solid front seat two wooden benches ran along either side of the vehicle. It was roomy enough, Docherty thought. Not as sturdy as the lorry perhaps, but easier on petrol and more manoeuvrable.

And a much more likely-looking transport for a group of journalists. From what Razor and Chris had discovered it was beginning to look as though the last stage of the trip was going to be difficult enough without Serb opposition, let alone with it.

'What do you think?' he asked the Dame. 'Does the engine seem reliable?'

The Dame looked at it. 'Yeah,' he said, 'I think so. And I wouldn't say the same for the lorry you lot came in.'

'That settles it,' Docherty said. 'We'll get off tomorrow morning at first light, and have lunch with our fellow Brits in Vitez.'

'I think we should call it Woodstock,' Razor said, staring at the Microbus.

Docherty had a sudden image of them all riding round Bosnia, flashing peace signs at burnt-out villages.

Two streets away, their positions of a fortnight before strangely reversed, Nena was trying to persuade Hajrija

189

not to make the journey. 'It's because of him, isn't it?' she asked. 'Rija, this is no time to go chasing after a man.'

'I am not chasing after a man,' Hajrija shouted back, thoroughly angry. 'I am coming with you because you are my friend, and the last time I let you go off alone . . .' She stopped herself. 'OK, I like him, but that's just a bonus. It is *not* why I am coming. Zavik is my home too, you know . . .'

'You have no family there any more.'

'I have friends. It's my home. I have a right to know what's going on there . . .'

'OK, enough,' Nena said. 'I just don't want you to put yourself in danger, for me or the Englishman . . .'

Hajrija burst out laughing. 'What do you think I was doing in Sarajevo,' she wanted to know, 'modelling swimsuits?'

They left Visoko at dawn the next day, with Razor in the driving seat, Docherty beside him, and the other four in the back with their gear. The previous day's clear skies had been filled with hurrying clouds, and except for those few occasions when the sun shone through, the road down the Bosna valley twisted and turned in perpetual twilight.

There was not much conversation to lighten the journey, with each of the travellers engrossed in thoughts of what had passed and what was to come. But neither were there any roadblocks to slow their passage. Traffic was virtually non-existent on the main highway – only two lorries went up the valley as they went down – and the signs of life were few: smoke from a farmstead on the other side of the river, a man trudging through snow high on the valley slope, a dog barking outside an abandoned roadside café.

After driving about twenty miles they left the Bosna valley and its highway, turning left up the Lasva valley. Nearly ten miles of steady climbing later they came into the small town of Vitez, where the British UN Protection Force was based. The depot was on the higher side of the town, an affair of temporary barracks and vehicle pound, surrounded by wire fencing still new enough to gleam.

Razor pulled up at the gate, where two Cheshires in UN berets waited, their SA80s held pointedly close to the firing position. Through the gates the new arrivals could see Warrior infantry carriers and Scimitar armoured reconnaissance vehicles, all painted UN white.

Docherty climbed slowly out of the van, approached the two sentries and introduced himself. They were impressed enough by the SAS credentials to let him through to see the duty officer, but insisted on the vehicle and its other five occupants remaining outside the gate. Serving under the UN flag did not seem to have filled these soldiers with a warm glow of security.

Five minutes and two go-betweens later Docherty reached the office of the unit commander, Lieutenant-Colonel William Stewart, a tall, fair-haired Yorkshireman. As luck would have it he was also an ex-SAS officer, whom Docherty had served with nearly twenty years earlier in Oman, when Stewart was a hyperactive young lieutenant who had only just been badged.

'Docherty!' he exclaimed. 'What the hell are you doing here? I heard they'd put you out to grass months ago.'

Even in his forties, Stewart found it impossible to sit or stand still. As Docherty explained that his SAS patrol was on an undercover mission, and that they would appreciate some unofficial help, Stewart paced up and down his cramped little office like a caged tiger. 'We need Arctic gear for two, and the latest intelligence on the roads between Vitez and Bugojno,' Docherty said. 'And some breakfast wouldn't go amiss,' he added.

'I dare say we can manage all that without breaking the UN Charter,' Stewart said. 'I don't suppose you're going to tell me what you're up to in this neck of the woods?'

The answer should have been no, but Docherty told him anyway.

Stewart was envious. 'We spend most of our time here

wishing we could do more than just watch it all happen. It's like holding the coats of two men who've decided to beat each other to death.' He reached for the door. 'Let's go and fill your order.'

An hour later they were on their way again, having been supplied with Arctic clothing for the two women – both of whom, fortunately, were tall – an optimistic assessment of their road as far as Gornji Vakuf, and a fry-up in the Cheshires' mess. Cholesterol-rich it definitely was, but the men hadn't had a better meal since Split, and the two women hadn't eaten as well for months. A couple of Cheshires at the next table couldn't keep from commenting on the two women's appetite, and were met with looks from the SAS men which would have silenced Cilla Black.

Razor's benign mood had been further lifted by the news that Tottenham had won on the previous Saturday. Sunderland and Celtic, however, had both lost.

'I don't suppose you remember Tottenham's games against Rangers in '62?' Docherty asked Razor, as the latter steered the Microbus up the long incline leading out of town.

'I was only four, boss.'

'I was eleven. I can't remember which European competition it was, but they were really big games. English and Scottish club teams had hardly ever played each other before then, and then those two were drawn against each other and there was this enormous expectation, enormous curiosity, because no one really knew whether English teams were much better than Scottish teams, or much the same, or vice versa.'

'I take it we won.'

'Oh aye, you won all right. Five-two, I think, down in

London. But Rangers played well enough to make people think they could turn it round at Ibrox. They had some great players then – Willie Henderson, Jim Baxter. And then the second leg was only about five minutes old when Jimmy Greaves ran half the length of the field and scored. People who were there said the silence was so deep you could hear sheep farting in the Outer Hebrides. Spurs won that one three-two.' Docherty smiled to himself. 'I always remembered those games because I felt so torn. Being a Scot I wanted Rangers to win, and being a Celtic supporter I wanted to see them thrashed. I guess it was the first time I understood how loyalties could cut across each other.' He looked out of the window. 'But it was a long time before I realized what a good thing it was that they did. Because people with only one loyalty have nothing to restrain them.'

'Like here in sunny Bosnia?'

'Aye.'

A few miles further on they turned left, on to a small road which climbed across the mountains towards Bugojno. In normal times this would have been closed to traffic, but the UN Protection Force needed it open for resupply purposes, and the necessary vehicles and equipment had been brought up by road from Split two months earlier. Piled snow on either side of the twisting road offered evidence of the use to which they had been put.

In the back of the Microbus the euphoria provided by breakfast soon dissipated. As they got nearer to their destination Nena was finding her anxiety for her children beginning to grow, and Hajrija was finding no reason to worry less about Nena. Her friend still seemed locked inside that mental shell she had grown to protect herself during captivity, and Hajrija didn't know how to react. Should she try breaking it open from the outside or wait for Nena to free herself?

And there was also the Englishman to think about. Feeling desire for a man didn't seem very appropriate after what her best friend had just been through.

Sitting opposite each other by the back door, Chris and the Dame were also in very different states of mind. Since the bus ride from Vogosca the Dame had been unable to shake the picture of all those traumatized women and girls out of his head. Memories of his sister's wedding reception kept coming back to haunt him with their pettiness. If people only knew how bad it could get, then they wouldn't waste love in the stupid way they did. They would cherish it, look after each other, thank God that their sisters and wives were not on a bus to somewhere like Vogosca.

Facing him, Chris was watching the sky above the snow-covered moorland, and occasionally catching sight of a hovering bird of prey too far off to identify. He wanted to stop the van, get out and climb into these unknown hills, and feel as free as the birds that circled above them.

They reached Gornji Vakuf around eleven and turned off the main road to Split, following another, wider road north-west towards Bugojno. The most recent hard intelligence available at Vitez had placed the Serbs within a few miles of Bugojno, and there was an unconfirmed report that long-range shelling of the town had begun in the last few hours. The small UN unit stationed there had been incommunicado for almost twenty-four.

The SAS men found out why a few miles short of the

town, when they came upon the UN unit's two vehicles and five men eating an early lunch in a convenient picnic spot beside the highway. The town, the men from the Cheshires told them, was now under almost continuous bombardment by Serb artillery, and they had been ordered out by the overall UN command. The five Cheshires seemed pleased enough to be out of immediate harm's way, but, as one of the younger men put it succinctly: 'What's the fuckin' point of it all?'

The major in charge had more recent information on Serb movements in the area, but warned them not to take anything for granted. 'The bastards could be in the town square by now,' he said cheerfully. When Docherty asked him about Zavik the major raised a knowing eyebrow, and said that there had been no news of the town for weeks. 'Which could mean that they're all still hung over from Christmas, or it could mean that the Serbs have burned the place to the ground. Who knows? I just want to get back to the Falls Road,' he concluded, with only the faintest trace of irony.

Another few miles down the valley they could hear the big guns firing up ahead. Razor stopped the Microbus on a convenient rise and all six of them got out on to the road for a panoramic view of the distant town. Smoke was already rising from half a dozen buildings, and every few minutes another flash of white light would be followed by the sound of a shell exploding.

'I don't suppose there's a way round,' Razor muttered.

'Not on this map,' Docherty replied.

'The shells are landing about every three minutes,' Chris said, looking up from his watch as another white flash erupted, 'and they just seem to be lobbing them

196

in at random. Our chances of being hit by one are not much worse than our chances of being knocked down by a London bus.'

'Oh well, that's all right then,' Razor said sarcastically. He looked round at the Microbus. 'Boss,' he said more seriously, 'I think everyone should get in the back with the bergens up against the windows. And keep your heads down, no matter how good the architecture down there used to be. If I see a one-winged, purple-crested parrot flying out of the smoke I'll give you a shout,' he told Chris. 'OK?'

They did as he suggested, and huddled together between the rows of seats in the back. Razor started off down the hill, trying to gauge times and distances. The town didn't look so big, and it shouldn't take much more than five minutes to reach its centre, find the road which they wanted, and drive back out again. If he entered the town just after a shell landed, then with any luck there would only be one to avoid before they made their exit.

'You're a genius, Razor,' he murmured to himself, easing his foot down on the brake as the Microbus drove past the first houses. At that moment there was a loud explosion, a far louder one than he'd expected, and half a house not fifty yards away seemed to rear and crash down into the street ahead. Razor moved slowly forward, poised on the accelerator, and when the dust had cleared sufficiently for him to see a path through the rubble, rammed his foot down. And then he was racing along the empty street towards the town centre, where a mosque's minaret contested the sky with a Christian spire.

The road signs were still up, and he was swinging

across the small square towards the Kupres road, thinking the worst was over when several bees seemed to whizz past his head. Pretty solidly built bees, to judge by the holes they had left in the windscreen.

Razor pulled down the steering wheel, first one way and then the other, careering in violent curves down the road away from the square. He thought he heard other shots, but no more bees came through the cab, and a minute later the Microbus was back in open country, beginning a slow climb towards a distant cleft in the valley's side.

He could feel the adrenalin pumping through his veins. 'Is everyone OK back there?' he called out anxiously, risking a glance in the rear-view mirror in search of Hajrija. She was there. And everyone else.

'What did you see?' Docherty wanted to know.

'Nothing. Not a soul,' said Razor. 'Maybe they were all in their basements, or maybe the Serbs are just firing at an empty town.'

'Who fired at us?'

'No idea. Didn't see them either.'

'We'd better stop and make sure there's no real damage.'

Razor brought the van to a halt just above a hairpin bend, and they got down to make an examination. Three bullets had passed through the vehicle, all of them in through one of the door windows at the back and out through the windscreen to Razor's right. If Docherty had still been sitting in the passenger seat there wouldn't have been much left of his head. As it was, the only lasting consequences of the attack were an increased draught of cold air and an obscuring of the view through the affected windows.

They got back on board, Docherty resuming his front seat. For the next six miles the road clambered out of the valley in ever-tightening spirals, the Microbus's wheels slipping and sliding far more than Razor liked. The way down was even more treacherous, and their progress often slowed to no more than a crawl. It was only when they reached their intended turn-off that the way became easier, and not for a very comforting reason. Tracked vehicles had used this road not long previously; the Microbus had obviously entered Serb-controlled – or at best Serb-contested – territory.

According to the Cheshires they had met outside Bugojno there was a checkpoint in the village of Dragnic, another six miles up this road. They were planning to abandon the Microbus half a mile short of the village and take to the hills, literally. It would be a twenty-mile hike to Zavik, across a 6000-foot range of snow-covered mountains, but Docherty had no doubt that Hajrija and the four men could cover the distance in reasonable time. Nena, though, was a different matter. She had told him she could do it, but . . .

He was still worrying this over in his mind when the tell-tale drift of smoke came into view, curling up above the next rise.

'I see it,' Razor said, as Docherty pointed forward.

'Stop short of the next crest,' the PC said. 'And we'll go take a look.'

They did, inching their heads above the skyline to see the roadblock a quarter of a mile ahead: a car and a transit van nose to nose in the middle of a river bridge, and on the bank beyond a blazing fire surrounded by several men in the familiar broad-brimmed hats.

'I love barbecues,' Razor said.

'Shit,' Docherty muttered. This had added another five or six miles to their walk.

They had no other choices. They couldn't ram a path through this roadblock, and there was no way they could get within killing distance of the enemy without being seen. At least not before nightfall, and that was five hours away. Who knew what might appear on the road behind them in the meantime?

Docherty glanced to the right, where the ground fell brokenly towards the same river, and then rose up beyond it in pine-covered slopes. That was the way they had to go.

He and Razor inched their way back from the crest, then hurried back down to the van. 'Bad news, folks,' Docherty said. 'We're on foot from here on.'

They unloaded their gear.

'What about Woodstock?' Razor asked.

Docherty thought for a moment, wondering whether to bury the Microbus in a snowdrift, or drive it back to the top of the last rise and give it a push. 'We'll leave it here,' he decided. 'They're not going to follow us across country.'

'Ready?' he asked, looking round at them all. Chris was smiling with anticipation, the Dame poker-faced as ever, the two women tensely determined. 'Dame, you take lead scout,' Docherty said. 'Chris, you're Tail-end Charlie. Nena, I want you and Hajrija between me and Razor, OK?'

They hoisted the bergens on to their backs and started off in order of march across the sloping meadow, all but Nena holding an SMG cradled in their arms. The snow was about a foot deep, and the going was slow. At this rate, Docherty thought, it would take about a week to reach Zavik. He hoped the forest would be easier walking.

They found a dry way across the river without much difficulty, and were soon under the cover of the trees, where the going was not appreciably easier. After half an hour they seemed to have covered only about a quarter of a mile.

Docherty called a halt. 'Any ideas?' he asked.

'The plan was to get off the road about six miles further up, right?' Chris said. 'And then take this track Hajrija knows across the mountains and in through Zavik's back door?'

'Right.'

'So why not work our way round the roadblock we know is there, wait for dark, and then walk up the road?'

It was so obvious Docherty wondered why he hadn't thought of it. He consoled himself with the thought that the Incas hadn't managed to come up with the wheel. 'Can anyone see a flaw in that that I can't?' he asked.

'Sounds good to me,' Razor said.

'There is one problem,' the Dame said slowly. 'If we have to hang around somewhere until it gets dark then anyone following our tracks will have time to catch us up.'

'Good point,' Docherty agreed. 'We'll have to keep our eyes open.'

As it happened, it took them most of the remaining daylight hours to work their way around the Serb roadblock, and anyone following their tracks would presumably be making no better progress. They eventually reached a position on the edge of the trees just above the road, which was now hugging the eastern side of the valley. Chris was sent back fifty yards along their tracks to provide any advance warning of pursuit, while the other five retreated further into the trees for rest and refreshment. Since it was still light Docherty risked using the hexamine stoves to boil water for soup and tea.

They needed all the warmth they could get. The sky was clearing once more, and the temperature seemed to be dropping like a stone. After their struggle through the snow their limbs needed rest, but there was no doubting that it was warmer on the move, and once darkness had fallen they lost no time in getting started once more.

About twenty minutes later the sound of a vehicle on the road behind caused them to scurry up the bank and into the trees. A few moments later a lorry rumbled by, with two men sitting in the cab and another half dozen or so barely visible in the rear, their cigarettes glowing like fireflies.

'Our chums from the roadblock,' Razor observed.

'Pigs,' Hajrija said contemptuously.

They continued their march up the long road, the stars shining in the sky above the valley, the river singing its way across the stones. In any other circumstances, Docherty thought, this would be almost magical. He could be walking down a glen on New Year's Eve, on his way to visit a warm and welcoming pub by the side of the loch.

Some hope. He turned to check on Nena, walking some five yards behind him. She seemed steady enough on her feet, and even managed a faint smile in his direction. She was strong, Docherty knew, and as far as he could tell her experience didn't seem to have taken any great toll on her body. The mind was a different matter. He wondered how Reeve was going to react to the news that his wife had been repeatedly subjected to multiple rape, and realized that he didn't have much of a clue. Reeve had often surprised him in the past, behaving badly when expected to behave well, rising above his usual self when Docherty had expected the worst. He hoped this would be one of the latter cases. The woman had been through more than enough already.

Four hours and twelve miles later they had skirted round two small villages – though no lights shone to suggest there might be anyone to watch or listen – and carefully approached the location of the roadblock they had been told about, only to find an empty stretch of road. Soon after they reached the spot where Hajrija's track took off to the east, and started following it up a wider valley towards the first village, which she said was only a couple of kilometres away. She knew some of the people who lived there, and hoped for news of what was happening in Zavik.

They reached a slight rise overlooking the village about half an hour later. The moon was up now, reflecting in the tiles of the roofs and the bend of the river which enclosed most of the dwellings. There were no lights shining, but none could be expected at such an hour.

They walked carefully down towards the first house, keeping to the shadows beside the road. A burnt-out Lada by the side of the house offered proof that the war had come to call. The whole place felt dead, Docherty thought. He remembered villages in Dhofar which had felt as empty as this.

The door of the first house was open. Razor entered cautiously, and walked through the house, sweeping it with his torch. There was no one there – alive or dead.

They went through the next two houses with the same result.

'They've gone,' Hajrija said.

'There's no point in going through every house,' Docherty decided. 'We'll just borrow one for a few hours, get some sleep, and move on at first light. We should be in Zavik by noon.'

Chris had the penultimate watch, and, when Docherty came to relieve him half an hour or so before dawn, he decided to walk up through the forest rather than try for a few minutes' more sleep. Some chaffinches were soon chirping in the trees around him, but the dawn chorus as a whole was disappointing. Chris emerged from the forest above the other side of the village, and stopped for a moment in the shelter of the trees to check that there were no signs of life below. There were not, but several huge birds were lazily circling in the dawn sky. He fixed the binoculars on one of them, and saw a pale-grey head which hardly protruded at all from the yellow-brown body. A large, hooked beak adorned the head, while the tail was short, dark and square. It was a griffon vulture.

He watched it through the binoculars for a few moments, marvelling at the sheer size of the bird. Then the realization dawned – these creatures only came together for carrion. Chris started walking down through the houses, towards the centre of the village, above which the predators were circling.

He found a space where a building had been, and the charred wooden moon and star lying half-buried in the snow told him what it had been. He walked forward, expecting the worst, and found it. The snow lay across

204

a pile of charred and half-consumed corpses. A large metal padlock, still locked around the two halves of an iron hasp, lay where the entrance had been.

Time and winter had taken the smell away from the vultures' refrigerator. He walked round the site, conscious of the huge birds hissing in the sky above. At least fifty bodies, he reckoned. The whole village, perhaps.

Chris walked back down the road to the house they had borrowed for the night, and told Docherty what he had found. The PC closed his eyes for a second, then looked at the ground. 'How long ago?' he asked.

'Hard to say. Weeks, at least. Maybe months.'

Twenty minutes later the whole party was staring dull-eyed at the scene of the massacre. There was no time to sift through the wreckage, or to disentangle what remained for burial. If the time for grieving ever passed, Docherty thought, then it had passed for those who had perished here.

They walked up the dirt track that led out of the village, into the innocence of the forest. The morning sunshine slanted down through the tall pines and lit the virgin snow that covered the more open parts of the forest floor, giving the Dame, again leading the way, the impression that he was walking through a huge cathedral. Images of the burnt mosque back in the village, the women on the bus, the sniper flung from the window . . . all passed through his mind and were somehow consumed by the beauty of the forest, like the heavenly sound of interweaving requiems.

Ten yards behind him, Docherty felt numb. This is Europe, he told himself. The house they had stayed in had been a European house, connected to an electricity grid, plugged in by radio and TV and cars to the rest of the continent. There had been a record player, and records ranging from Rachmaninov to Elton John. And the family who had listened to 'Crocodile Rock' had probably been among those herded into the time warp, taken back to an age in which they could be herded into a mosque and burnt alive.

Why? he asked himself. What had happened in this country? Were these people so different from all the other peoples of the world who could take the body's needs for granted? Or was this just the place where the surface had cracked to reveal the rotten ooze welling up below?

For the first time in his life Docherty felt a stirring of fellow-feeling with his late father. The old union man hadn't liked the way the world was going; he always said that people were getting more and more of what they wanted, and less and less of what they really needed. And because they were getting what they wanted they couldn't understand why they were so unhappy. And that made them angry.

Docherty wished he could feel angry, but felt something closer to despair.

They walked on through the forest for several miles, to where the track finally emerged in a high valley. They prudently waited for several minutes, scanning the surrounding countryside for signs of an enemy, but in this empty place there were none. They walked on, following an infant stream which trickled down between wide, snow-covered moorland slopes.

For half a mile or so the going was hard, but then they passed across a small crest and down into another, more sheltered valley, where bare trees gathered in the bends of a wider stream. They were now only about a mile from the next and last village on their route, and no one in the party was feeling particularly sanguine about what they would find when they got there.

Of the two women, Hajrija had been more affected by what they had found in the previous village, despite seeing more than her share of death and cruelty in Sarajevo. 'It's different,' she told Nena. 'In the city we are fighters against fighters, and the shelling, well, somehow it's not personal. But to take people like that . . . to see their faces and hear them . . .' She shook her head, refusing to let the tears flow.

Nena put an arm around Hajrija's shoulder but said nothing. In her mind's eye she could see her children being marched into the mosque in Zavik.

Behind them, Razor was wondering about himself and Hajrija, and about whether they would ever get the chance to be together. If they got out of this trip alive, then he would be going home to England and she . . . she might be going back to Sarajevo, or she might even want to stay in Zavik, if the town was still there. He could hardly send her love-letters at either address. And she could hardly come and visit him when the anti-sniper unit had their summer holidays.

What a fucking mess, he thought. And in any case, what did it say about him that he was worrying about his love-life after what they had just left behind? That he was an insensitive git? Or that he was more interested in life than death? Who the fuck knew?

A hundred yards ahead, the Dame gave Docherty the hand signal for halt before dropping to his knees and carefully advancing to the latest crest in the path.

Reaching it, he lay flat in the snow and slowly scanned the valley below with his binoculars.

Docherty watched him, waiting for the thumbs-up to tell him that no enemy was in sight or suspected. Instead he saw the Dame's shoulders slump momentarily, and then the Wearsider seemed to lie motionless for a minute or more, before placing his hand on his head to indicate he wanted Docherty to join him.

The PC wriggled forward, and found himself with a panoramic view of hills stretching away into the distance. A quarter of a mile away, the next village nestled in the valley below. He could see no sign of movement.

Docherty turned to the Dame, and saw tears running down his cheeks. With a sinking feeling he picked up his own binoculars and started scanning the village below. The first few houses seemed untouched, but then several came into view that had been burnt to the ground, and in the centre of the village, once more, there was the remains of what had probably been the mosque. He must have sealed his heart against this, Docherty thought, because he felt immune to grief.

And then he saw them, as the Dame had seen them, the crucified bodies on the side of the barn, and he felt the tears welling up in his own eyes.

They took down the corpses and, lacking the time to dig graves in the frozen earth, simply buried them beneath mounds of snow. Why, in any case, did these deserve graves when those bodies in the burnt-out mosque did not? They could not bury all the dead of this village, any more than all the dead of the last.

As before, a group of vultures hissed overhead, waiting for them to leave.

The road which ended here ran south down the valley, but they took the path to the east, which would lead them up over the last range of hills and down into Zavik's valley. It was almost noon now, and the sky was clouding over again, the wind whipping up fine sprays of snow and flinging them at the walkers.

The women were feeling the strain now. Unlike the four SAS men, neither had been forced to endure walks of nearly thirty miles across the Brecon Beacons, and both had developed blisters from wearing boots that were slightly too large for them. But they didn't complain, and they kept up with the pace.

The weather conditions continued to deteriorate. As Docherty halted to check the map against a world of snow and mist and pale, shadowy pines, one which seemed devoid of any reference points, Hajrija arrived at his shoulder to tell him where they were: only a hundred yards or so from the crest of the last ridge.

The view when they reached it was disappointing, merely one more white meadow below, and a hint of tree-covered slopes through the mist ahead.

'You can't see the town from here,' Hajrija said, 'but it's down there. This is where a lot of the townspeople come to ski on winter Saturdays,' she added. 'Or used to. There's a lodge down there, just above the trees. It was the only shelter up here.'

They moved slowly down the slope, waiting for the lodge to swim out of the murk. When it did so the binoculars revealed no sign of life. They advanced on it carefully nevertheless, watching for tell-tale tracks in the snow.

There was a musty smell inside, but no bodies. Cigarette ends and beer bottles littered the floor of the main room, and there were several cartridge cases arranged in a neat line along one of the window-ledges. Fighting men of some description had been here, but not for a while.

If the only shelter on the hills behind the town was unoccupied in this sort of weather, Docherty reasoned, then it seemed unlikely that there were any enemy units between them and the valley below. It was a comforting thought.

He put it to Hajrija, who agreed.

'In which case,' Docherty said, 'our first contact will probably be with Zavik's defensive perimeter. Assuming it has one. So where would it be.'

Hajrija shrugged. 'There is only one easy way down. It is a very – how you say?' – she drew hairpins in the air with her finger . . .

'Winding,' Docherty supplied.

'Yes, the Beatles. The long and winding road. But this is short and steep and winding.'

'There is no other way?'

'There's the Stair,' Nena said.

'Not in the winter,' Hajrija objected.

Nena shrugged. 'Maybe not. There is a long climb down past the waterfall,' she said to Docherty. 'We used to go up and down it when we were children, mostly because our parents said we should not. In winter it will be slippery and maybe impossible.'

'Which do you think will be safer?' Docherty asked the two women.

'The road,' Hajrija said flatly.

'Yes, I think so,' Nena agreed reluctantly. 'Though anyone below will be able to see us coming down the road long before we can explain who we are.'

They set off down the mountain, following the narrow road through a wide swathe of pines and out alongside another meadow. Then there were more trees and the road suddenly fell away. About two hundred yards below, the roofs of a town were dimly visible above the intervening trees, tucked inside a sharp bend of the pale-grey river. Docherty turned the binoculars on the road down, and found what looked like an ominous gap. He passed the binoculars to Hajrija.

'There is a bridge there before,' she said.

'Will there be a way across?'

'Not an easy one,' Nena said. 'The road crosses a stream there, almost like a waterfall. It is a long way down.'

'The Stair, then.'

'There is no other way.'

They left the road and hiked across the bottom of the meadow, and worked their way up across a tree-covered ridge and down into another cleft in the mountain face. This one was even steeper, and the depth of the snow varied wildly, making progress extremely slow. Docherty alternated between imagining how beautiful this would be in the summer and cursing the difficulty of their passage.

After an hour which seemed like three they arrived at the head of the Stair. The waterfall, no doubt deafening in spring, was barely audible above the wind, and with good reason. Only a trickle of water was actually falling – the rest was frozen in mid-flight, waiting for spring to set it free.

The Stair itself was easier than the SAS men had been led to expect. Flat rocks had been inset into the steeply sloping ground beside the waterfall, and though some were definitely slippery, and almost any slip potentially fatal, there was always a handhold to spare. Every twenty yards or so, there was a larger ledge to rest on.

Descending such a path with a fully laden bergen wasn't anyone's idea of fun, but after what they'd seen that day just being alive seemed like something to be thankful for. Hajrija was less than twenty feet from the bottom when they all heard the voice from below.

'Keep coming, and keep your hands away from your guns,' it said in Serbo-Croat.

Chris quickly translated the order, but in any case no one was going to risk opening fire on probable friends whom they couldn't even see.

'If it wasn't for the women you would be dead by now,' the voice said cheerfully.

It wasn't until they were all off the Stair that the three men stepped out from behind the overhanging rock. Each was carrying a Kalashnikov in firing position.

'Jusuf!' Hajrija said, recognizing the face of the oldest man. 'You can put down the guns.'

The man stared at her in bewilderment for a moment, and then recognition dawned. 'Hajrija Mejra? I did not see the girl inside the uniform. Where in God's name have you come from?'

'Sarajevo. And you know Nena.'

Jusuf's eyes grew even wider. 'Yes, yes, of course. Does the Commander know you are here?'

'My children,' Nena asked, heart in mouth, 'are they . . . are they well?'

'Yes, yes, I think so. My boy has the chickenpox, but . . .'

The sense of relief took Nena's breath away.

'Where is Reeve?' Hajrija asked.

'At the HQ' I think.'

'And where is that?' Hajrija asked patiently.

'First you must tell me who these men are,' he said obstinately.

'They are English. They are friends of Reeve.'

Jusuf's face lit up. 'That is wonderful news,' he said. 'Did he know you were all coming?'

'No, but if you take us to him . . .'

13

Nena Reeve strode purposefully across the town she had grown up in, towards the house on the hill where she had been born. The mist seemed to be thickening again as darkness began to fall, but from what she could tell the town seemed much the same as it had always been. There were no scars of war, and there were people on the streets, even a couple she recognized. She hurried past them, head down – the last thing she wanted to do now was stop and explain herself to mere acquaintances.

There were no lights showing in her parents' home, but the house itself looked the same as it always had. She pushed open the front door, and felt the warm air of life on her face. Voices sounded from the kitchen at the back, children's voices.

She stood a second by the parlour door, feeling almost limp, and then turned the old handle and walked across the threshold. By the light of the single kerosene lamp she could see the four faces turned towards the door – those of her father, mother, son and daughter. There was a moment of stunned silence, and then both children cried out in unison: 'Mama!'

On the other side of town John Reeve and two of his fellow-officers in the Zavik Militia were poring over a map in the back room of the Youth Hostel which served as their HQ.

'Hello, Reeve,' a familiar Scottish voice said from the doorway.

Reeve looked round, utter astonishment on

his face. 'Jesus Christ,' he said, 'the fucking cavalry's arrived.'

Docherty grinned at him. Reeve wasn't wearing any sort of uniform, but he appeared fit and well. There were no weapons visible, but the looks of the other young men, the maps on the table and wall . . . the scene had all the makings of a military unit which knew what it was doing. And it was about as far removed from Brando's camp in *Apocalypse Now* as Docherty could imagine. He wasn't surprised, but he had been prepared to find the worst, and this wasn't it.

The two men shook hands, and Docherty introduced Razor, Chris and the Dame. Reeve in turn introduced the two Bosnians. The taller of the two, a serious-looking man with short, black hair and a pronounced Slavic face, was named Latinka Tijanic. The other man, also dark-haired, but with a rounder face and moustache, was Esad Cehajic.

'So what the fuck are you doing here?' Reeve asked.

'We've come to see you, but . . .'

At this moment Hajrija, who had been talking to their escort outside, appeared in the doorway.

'Hajrija?' Reeve said, staring at her with renewed astonishment. The last time he's seen her she'd been a student in jeans and T-shirt.

'*Zdravo*, Reeve.'

'How are you? How is Nena?'

'I was just about to tell you,' Docherty said. 'She came with us. She went straight on up to her folks' place. Are they OK? And the children?'

'They're fine. All of them.' Reeve seemed momentarily stunned. 'Jesus, Jamie, what's she doing here? How did you all get here?'

'It's a long story. Maybe . . .'

'I'd better get over there,' Reeve said suddenly. He grabbed his coat and looked around. 'Lads, make yourselves at home. Esad, look after them, will you? I'll be back.'

'How are you, Nena?' her father asked, when the children finally allowed him the opportunity. He looked older, Nena thought, whereas her mother looked much the same. He had been a schoolteacher by profession, but his life's vocation – from the years as a partisan in World War Two to his years as Mayor of Zavik – had been the Party and the idea of Yugoslavia. The collapse of everything he had fought and worked for must have been terrible for him, Nena realized. The erasure of a life.

'I'm fine,' she said. Two years before she might eventually have told her parents what had happened to her, but not now. There would be no point. 'But what has happened here, Papa?' she asked, partly to move the conversation away from herself.

'We have fought them, that is what has happened,' her father said. 'Your Reeve has been wonderful, Nena. Without him I dread to think how things would have gone.'

There must have been a trace of irony in her expression, because her father gave her an aggrieved look. 'This is a good man,' he insisted.

'I know,' she said.

'So why . . .'

She was saved by the good man's arrival. There was a rare look of uncertainty in his eyes, Nena thought, as she got up, fighting her own reluctance, to embrace him.

'How are you?' he asked.

'Fine. Tired. Happy to see these two,' she said, putting an arm around each child. They were looking wary, perhaps remembering the arguments which had been so frequent the last time their mother and father had been together.

'Are you sure you're OK?' he asked.

'I'm just exhausted. It was a hard journey.' Now that she knew everyone was safe all she wanted to do was sleep. In a proper bed, for a long time.

At the Youth Hostel Esad had made the visitors the best coffee they'd had since leaving England. They sipped at it gratefully, sitting in silence and resting their aching legs. Hajrija, meanwhile, was conducting an animated conversation in her native tongue with the serious-looking Tijanic, and Razor was torn between pleasure at her obvious happiness to be home and more than a slight stirring of jealousy. The darkness seemed to have gone from her eyes, he thought. She seemed so natural here, but it made him wonder whether the months in the anti-sniper unit had wrought changes inside her, hardened her in some way, or whether she had somehow managed to keep her real self at a distance from it all.

And that made him think about what the years in the Army had done to him. He knew men in the SAS who had been unable to cope with what they were required to do – some who had simply decided it wasn't for them and left, others who had turned themselves into machines – but he had never felt pushed in either of those directions. His defence had been not to take it too seriously; to stay loose and not get wound too tight by it all, the way the

Dame seemed in danger of doing. When the feeling was there, you had to let yourself feel it, and then get on with the job in hand.

He was a survivor, he thought. And he had the feeling she was too. If only . . .

'There is a café,' she said suddenly in English. 'It is open, with food and drink. Not far. Not steaks and wine, you understand, but maybe music.'

'I could eat a horse,' Razor said.

'There'll probably be one on the menu,' Chris said.

They turned to Docherty. 'Go and eat,' the PC said. 'I'll wait here for Reeve to come back.'

Outside darkness had fallen, and the mist still clung to the valley floor, making it hard to see each other, let alone the direction they were supposed to be taking. Hajrija grabbed hold of Razor's hand. 'Make chain,' she said, and they did so, unable to think of a less embarrassing alternative. Chris found himself remembering a game they played at school, the chain of tagged kids reaching and twisting for one of the untagged to release them with a touch.

Hajrija led them unerringly down one street and then another, buildings occasionally looming through the patchy mist, until a hazy light announced their destination. The words René's Café on the glass door stood out against the yellow light within.

'What?!?' Razor exclaimed.

Inside, a large poster of the cast of *Allo, Allo* took pride of place behind the serving counter. The three Englishmen gazed at it open-mouthed.

'It is big hit on Yugoslav TV,' Hajrija explained. 'Like the Fools and Horses. Del-boys and lovely-jubbly,' she added gratuitously.

The café was empty when they arrived, but the menu surpassed expectations by containing both cheese and beer, and their own arrival seemed to trigger an avalanche of customers. The beer was strictly rationed to two bottles a customer, but this didn't seem to get in the way of the good feeling which encompassed everyone there. Men and women, old and young, talked in groups and pairs, sometimes reaching out to join in other conversations which caught their ear. Razor had grown up the only child of a single parent, but this was what he had always imagined a huge family gathering would be like. A sort of chaotic warmth.

'This is how it used to be,' Hajrija said, her breath brushing his cheek.

René stared down at him from the poster. 'I will only say this once,' Razor murmured to himself.

Reeve arrived back at the hostel looking more subdued than when he'd left. He didn't seem surprised to find only Docherty. 'Well, Jamie, this is a surprise,' he said, lighting a cigarette and blowing smoke at the ceiling.

'Aye, I expect it is,' Docherty agreed, thinking that Reeve seemed much the same as he'd ever been.

'I don't suppose it's a coincidence that you and Nena have turned up here together. You didn't just run into each other on Sarajevo Station, I suppose?'

Docherty smiled without much humour. 'She's had a bad time, Reeve. A really bad time.'

Reeve took a drag on the cigarette. 'Sarajevo used to be a lovely town,' he said mildly. 'She didn't tell me anything,' he added. 'So why are you all here?'

'To check you out,' Docherty said bluntly. 'Our

219

beloved Government has been getting stick from all sides about this lunatic Brit in the Bosnian hills . . .'

'You're kidding. What's it matter to John Major, for Christ's sake? It's not as if any of those bastards *care* what's happening here.'

Docherty looked at him. 'You are still a serving soldier in their Army. They may not give a flying fuck about Bosnia but they have to care about that.'

Reeve grinned. 'Tell 'em I resign. Tell them I've taken out Bosnian citizenship and I'm as entitled to my piece of the war as any other Bosnian.'

'Have you?'

'You're joking. How the hell do you think I'd do that – by post? On the phone?'

'Aye, OK.'

'I mean, this is hard to believe,' Reeve went on. 'They actually sent you and three other guys into all this just to tell me to keep a low fucking profile? It's like infiltrating a patrol into Saddam Hussein's palace to steal his bog paper.'

'We weren't sent to tell you to keep a low profile,' Docherty said calmly. 'We were sent to find out what's been going on.'

Reeve stubbed out his cigarette, walked across to a cupboard and pulled out two glasses and a bottle. 'OK,' he said, unscrewing the top and pouring two respectable shots of plum brandy, 'I'll tell you.'

Docherty leaned back in his chair and sipped at the brandy. It was good.

'You know why I came back here?'

'To see the kids.'

'And you know about Nena and me splitting up?'

'Aye.'

'Well, when I came to see them she took the chance to go to Sarajevo, and then because of the war she couldn't get back here. Didn't want to either, from what I could tell. Doctoring's always been important to her, and she knew her parents were here to look after the kids if I left.'

'Why didn't you?'

'The Serbs came to call, like they did everywhere else around here. Only we stood up to the bastards – all the town, most of the local Serbs included – and kicked them back out again. We knew they'd try again, so we had to get ourselves organized properly, do some thinking about how to defend the place, and how to survive in a siege. And I was the only one with any real experience of anything like that. I couldn't leave.'

'You became "the Commander".'

'It's not like it sounds. No one else here could have handled it. Plus, I was English, so there didn't have to be any arguments about whether a Serb or a Croat or a Muslim should be top dog.' He smiled. 'I became sort of a mini-Tito,' he said. 'And I've done a good job.'

'I bet you have. Did you blow the bridge on the road behind the town?'

'Yeah, but only as a precaution. The Serbs can't get people in numbers up on this side of the valley. We blew the bridges over the river further down, and they can't get anything across. They could try from the back – I suppose that's the way you came in – but there are no roads and nowhere to shelter, and nothing much to build a shelter with. They couldn't get any heavy guns up there.'

'So what have they tried?'

'After the first visit they left us alone for a week, then tried surprising us in the middle of the night. We killed about twenty of them, and they left us alone for a couple of months after that. Except of course they blocked up the valley at both ends so nothing could come in or out. That was around August, and there was plenty of food in the town, but we had to start thinking about how we were going to survive the winter. We could cut down trees behind the town for fires, but the only generators we had needed oil, and there was hardly any left. So' – he opened his palms – 'we had to steal some.

'By this time I'd got a pretty good training programme going. I based it on what we taught the Dhofaris in Oman, remember? Once they were ready I took some of the lads on a recce, and we found the Serbs' local fuel depot in Sipovo. Nicking two tankers was easy enough – the depot wasn't even guarded – and we managed to bluff our way back through their roadblock. You can get a long way around here singing the right songs and sporting the right tattoos.' Reeve grinned reminiscently. 'Plus, of course, about a third of our men don't have to pretend – they really are Serbs.'

Docherty grinned back, relief spreading through him. Reeve hadn't been driven off the rails by the madness around him. In fact, as far as Docherty could tell, he seemed more insulated from it all than anyone they had met since leaving Split.

Reeve poured another two measures of plum brandy and lit another cigarette. 'The weaponry situation wasn't too good either,' he said. 'We had plenty of Kalashnikovs, and a couple of mortars we stole from the Serbs, but only a few SMGs and hardly any explosives. Luckily, we had an ex-Yugoslav Army officer in town – a Croat – who could lead us straight to an armoury outside Livno. The Croat Army was pissed off when we stole half their ordnance, but what the fuck?' He laughed. 'The main problem was carrying the goddam stuff back over the hills. We didn't think the Serbs would fall for the bluff twice, though God knows there's enough of them popping acid that they probably wouldn't have noticed. Probably just see pretty patterns as we went past.'

'How did you manage to piss off the Bosnian Government?' Docherty asked. 'And the UN?'

'Ah, that was a bit naughty,' Reeve admitted. 'We stole one of their supply shipments – mostly food.'

'You what!?'

'They had plenty to spare, Jamie. It was when they were still using the Kupres road to supply Vitez. The idiots left the key in the ignition when they stopped for a picnic lunch. They ran along behind us for about a quarter of a mile, shouting at us to bring it back.'

Docherty laughed. 'I talked to the commander at Vitez, and he didn't mention it,' he said.

'I'm not surprised,' Reeve said. 'It hardly adds lustre to the Cheshires' image, does it?'

'And the Bosnian Government?'

'We borrowed one of their armoured cars from Bugojno. It's not exactly state-of-the-art, I'm afraid – it was probably abandoned by the Red Army in 1945. But it works. We just drove it home through the Serb roadblock – and I mean through it – all hatches down. They didn't know what to make of it either, watching this armoured car blithely totalling one of their beloved Toyotas.' He took a gulp of the brandy. 'I've got to like this stuff. Where were we?'

'Stealing an armoured car.'

'Yeah, well. I don't see how the Bosnian Government can object to us doing their job for them. They should be holding us up as a shining example. Izetbegovic is fond of saying that Bosnia was overflowing with brotherly love and tolerance before the Serb shit hit the fan. I don't know how much of that is wishful thinking on his part, but Zavik is definitely Bosnia as it ought to be. We've got Serbs, Muslims, Croats, Jews, even a few Albanians, and yours truly, all getting along with each other. You take a walk through the town tomorrow morning – you'll find a mosque, an Orthodox church and a Catholic church, all in the same square, all open for business.'

'What about the Serbs outside the town?' Docherty wanted to know. 'Are they still keeping their distance?'

'No, they're hatching something. And they're more or less all around us now. Sooner or later they're going to drag some guns on to the hills opposite and start throwing shells at us. If they can be bothered. I hope they can't.' He took a last drag on the cigarette. 'And of course there's always a chance that peace will break out.'

'I wouldn't hold your breath,' Docherty said mildly. 'And I wouldn't be too optimistic about reconciliation,' he added. 'We've been in this country about a week, and I've seen things to trouble my sleep until I die.'

'Like what?'

Docherty told him about the villages in the hills, the hospital at Sarajevo, the women at Vogosca.

'What were you doing there?' Reeve asked.

Docherty cursed himself for the slip, but decided there was no going back. 'Rescuing Nena,' he said.

Reeve looked at him, sudden bleakness in his eyes. 'Oh Christ,' he said.

'She wasn't there long,' Docherty said, realizing as he did so how ludicrous it sounded.

224

Reeve was getting slowly to his feet. 'I should be with her,' he said. 'I . . .'

'Maybe you should let her come to you,' Docherty said gently, wondering if she would.

A quarter of a mile away, Nena lay in her old childhood bed in the house on the hill, curled up like a foetus, unable to sleep. Her mind was whirling around, and she seemed to lack the will to stop it. It was like a waking dream, a sort of seamless merging of scenes and people.

There was Docherty at their wedding, still treating Isabel as if she was an invalid, and there was Reeve on the day their son was born, looking like a boy himself, so young and proud, and there were the crucified bodies on the wall, the man and the woman and the two children, and there she was in the gymnasium at Vogosca with the waves of crying ebbing and flowing like a sea of sadness.

'Will you ever be the same again?' a voice asked, and she answered, angrily: 'No, of course not!' and then there was silence for a moment, a silence of snow and blue sky. Then the voice asked: 'Will you ever be happy again?' and she said: 'Yes, yes, I promise!' and she wondered if it was a promise she could keep.

They had been told to take their pick of the empty rooms at the youth hostel, and Hajrija picked out one on the first floor. 'Razor, can I talk with you,' she asked, beckoning him in.

'Sure,' he said, surprised but daring to hope.

She pushed the door shut behind him and stood there, not saying anything, just looking at him, waiting.

In the dark she looked so serious, he thought. So sad.

He leaned forward and kissed her on the lips, and felt her arms reach around his neck, and her body press into his.

They kissed for what seemed like minutes, and then finally managed to shed their jackets and hats and belts before kissing for several more. They shed their boots and half tripped on to the narrow bed, slowly disentangling themselves from the top half of the Arctic gear, and lying there half-naked, oblivious to the cold. He kissed her breasts and raised his face to hers. In the darkness of the room all he could see was a faint glow on either cheek and two excited eyes that shone deep and dark.

They made love as if they never would again, and then sank into an exhausted sleep.

Soon after dawn, as they were disentangling themselves for the third time, the window blew in, swiftly followed by the sound of an enormous explosion.

The first Serb shell had landed on Zavik.

They gingerly slid out from under the glass-strewn blanket. 'Are you OK?' Razor asked, holding her naked body against his own.

'Yes,' she answered. She was shivering, and not all from the cold.

'Some couples feel the earth move,' Razor murmured. 'We seem to hear the sound of breaking glass.'

The bombardment continued throughout the day. At first a shell would land every few minutes, but from mid-morning onwards the gaps became longer, as if the Serbs were either growing bored or intent on conserving ammunition. The previous day's mist had lifted, revealing a layer of clouds which grew more broken as the morning progressed. Whether this improvement in visibility was a good thing, Docherty was unable to decide. It presumably gave the Serbs more chance of hitting what they were aiming at, but since they were apparently content with landing their shells anywhere in the town, that didn't seem such an important consideration. For the townspeople, he suspected, a first taste of artillery bombardment in yesterday's mist would have been even more unnerving than what they were having to endure.

Most of the town's population – reckoned by Reeve at just over two thousand – were now sheltering in their own or a neighbour's basement or cellar, listening to each crack of man-made thunder and wondering where on their mental map of friends and acquaintances each particular blow had fallen.

One of the first shells had landed on the school. Two children had been crushed by a falling roof, and another dozen injured, some of them seriously. About the same number of adults had been injured during the confusion of the first hour, and three men and two women had been killed, all in their beds, when their houses exploded around them.

Once the initial shock had subsided the more or less regular gaps between shells gave people a chance to move around in relative safety. It was Sarajevo without the snipers, Nena Reeve thought bitterly, as she hurried down the street towards the youth hostel. Optimistically, as it turned out. She arrived in the hostel's basement at the same time as one of Reeve's young soldiers, who had come with the news that a man had just been shot dead in the main square. Almost certainly by a sniper.

'What are you doing here?' Reeve asked, seeing her standing in the doorway.

'I assume you need doctors,' she said.

'Christ, yes. Hold on a minute.' He barked rapid-fire orders at two men, both of whom Nena suddenly recognized as the sons of an old friend. The last time she'd seen them they were about sixteen, and on their way to university in Belgrade.

Reeve stood up. 'We'll wait for the next shell and then I'll take you over to the hospital,' he said.

'Hospital?'

'We've cleared out one of the underground crypts in the old castle ...' He raised a hand. 'I know it's not the ideal place, but it's safe from shelling. And it's the best I could think of at a moment's notice.'

She looked at him. 'You really are running this town, aren't you?' she said.

'Just about.'

'What about your career? The SAS?'

He shrugged. 'I couldn't leave the children at the beginning, and then I became kind of indispensable all round. I haven't had many choices, Nena ...' He grinned suddenly. 'But in any case ...'

228

There was the thud of an explosion, some distance away.

'Come on,' he said.

They went up the stairs, out into the street and turned uphill towards where the old ruined castle looked out over the town from its perch just beneath the clifftop. Away to the right the frozen waterfall was glistening in the sunlight.

'And some things are more important than the SAS,' he added, as if to himself. This was not the time to ask her about herself, he thought.

'You never used to think so,' she said. 'No, I'm sorry, that's not fair.'

'Maybe it is,' he said, as they reached the castle entrance. The booth where tourists had bought their entrance tickets was lying on its side in the snow like a badly made toboggan.

'How many other doctors are there in the town?' she asked.

'Two,' he said. 'Dr Muhmedalisa, remember him? He should be here. And then there's old Bosnic. He should have retired ages ago, but ... His eyesight's more or less gone altogether, I'm afraid ...'

They walked down steep stone steps and found themselves in a large, medieval-style chamber. Two oil stoves had been brought in to provide heat, and a man was busy trying to shut off the draughts. Mattresses had been arranged in two rows along either wall, and most were already occupied. The only doctor visible was patiently trying to undo a new bandage, holding it up to within an inch of his eyes. At the other end of the room a young girl was screaming in pain.

Nena went to look at her.

'Where's Muhmedalisa?' Reeve asked Bosnic.

'He was killed about two hours ago,' Bosnic said curtly.

'Oh shit.'

'That child needs morphine,' Nena said, hurrying up. 'Where are the drugs?'

'What we have are there,' Bosnic said, peering at her myopically. 'You're Nena Abdic, I remember your voice. You're a nurse.'

'A doctor now.' She was looking through the box. 'There's hardly anything here,' she said.

'It's all there is,' Reeve said.

'Won't Jamie and the others be carrying medical kits? And at least one of them should have medical training. That's the way it works, isn't it?'

'I'll go and find out,' Reeve said. 'Welcome home,' he added, as the girl started screaming again.

An hour later Chris and Razor were both helping out at the improvised hospital, and the SAS medical kits had been added to the town's supply. Docherty and the Dame were halfway up the mountain by this time, accompanying Reeve and Tijanic on a mission with two objectives. First they wanted to pinpoint the location of the Serbs' artillery piece, and second that of the sniper. In case they discovered the latter, the Dame had brought along the Accuracy International.

They hadn't needed to take the Stair; a couple of extended planks were available on the town side of the blown bridge. After they had walked across, another of Reeve's men had retracted the makeshift crossing and settled down to await their return.

It took them half an hour to reach the top of the

toboggan meadow, and another to find a suitable place to sweep the far side of the valley with their binoculars. The gun wasn't immediately visible, but they had doubted whether it would be, even from the crest above them. The Serbs would have taken care to camouflage it at the very least, and probably to remove it completely from any possible enemy line of sight.

It was the Dame who found it, behind the crest of a hill away to the right of the town. He had the rifle's telescopic sight trained in just the right direction to catch a shimmering in the cold air as the Serb gun fired. As he patiently waited to confirm his suspicion, a head momentarily popped up above the horizon. A minute later the same shimmering accompanied the sound of the gun firing.

They marked a line in on Reeve's map and then moved a few hundred yards through the trees to the east. From there they were able to draw an intersecting line and plot the exact location of the gun.

Then they started scouring the whole far side of the valley, looking for the sniper. Two hours of lying in the snow later, they were beginning to despair of finding him when Reeve let out a quiet whoop of triumph. 'Start at the top of the minaret,' he said, 'and go straight up until you hit the track on the hill. Just to the right there's a group of trees. The one on the right-hand end just moved, and none of the others did.'

The Dame cradled the Accuracy International to his shoulder and stared through the sight. He thought he could detect a darker shadow inside the tree but he wasn't sure. 'Too far away,' he said. 'And in any case I can't get a clean shot from here. If I miss he'll just disappear into the trees.'

'How about from down in the town?' Docherty asked.

'No reason why not.'

Back in Zavik, Docherty and Reeve visited the hospital, where the situation, though far from good, had at least improved since the morning. 'There have only been a couple more wounded this afternoon,' Razor told them.

'Are any of these in danger?' Reeve asked, looking round.

'Quite a few.'

'We can't treat them here,' Nena said, coming over to join them. 'We don't have enough medicine, and I don't have the right kinds of skills.' She looked exhausted, Docherty thought, but something else as well. There was more than a trace of her old self present – having others to take care of had at least been good for her.

'There's nowhere else to take them,' Reeve was saying. 'You can give me a shopping list of medicines and I'll try and fill it, but we're talking about a minimum of several days. I can't risk the few men I've got on half-thought-out operations.'

'If you don't, then some of these children will be at risk.'

'OK, OK. But first we have to deal with the gun up there, or there'll be more and more wounded to deal with. Are you and your boys in on this, Jamie?'

Docherty gave him a wry smile. It was a question he'd been expecting since their location of the Serb gun. 'Probably,' he said. He looked at Reeve. 'But we're here in the first place because our bosses were pissed off at one Brit taking sides in this war. I think I'd better talk to the others before we add four more to the charge sheet.'

'Fair enough,' Reeve said equably.

'Are you two needed here?' Docherty asked Razor and Chris.

'Not at the moment,' Nena answered for them.

The three SAS men waited several minutes for the sound of a shell landing, then hurried back down to the hostel, taking care to make use of all the available cover.

'Where's the Dame?' Chris asked Docherty.

'Out hunting,' the PC said.

It had taken the Dame fifteen minutes to find what seemed a suitable location, in the upstairs room of an empty house on the western edge of the town. The tree in question was now only three hundred yards away, just within the limits of the Covert PM variant of the Accuracy International. He erected the built-in bipod support, put his eye to the Schmidt & Bender telescopic sight, and there was the Serbian sniper, or at least the edges of his body. The man was perched about ten feet up in the cedar tree, but mostly hidden behind the trunk, his rifle resting against a convenient branch. When he next went to use it, the Dame would have him.

The minutes went by. The Dame thought he could see cigarette smoke drifting out from behind the trunk, and had a mental picture of his dead father lighting one of the forty Players No. 6 he had smoked each day. Every time he had lit one up at home his mother had coughed, just the once, to register her disapproval. What with the all the new stuff about passive smoking, he supposed she'd been right.

There was movement in the tree, and the man's face came into view, a hand putting the cigarette to his mouth.

The light was beginning to fade and there was a slight glow as he dragged on it. The man was an amateur, the Dame thought.

He watched as the Serb picked up his rifle – which looked suspiciously like a British Lee-Enfield – and slowly scanned the town across the river, looking for a target. An almost imperceptible tightening of the shoulders told the Dame he had found one.

The SAS man wriggled his shoulder to make sure the rifle's butt was comfortable, worked the bolt action, aligned the cross-hairs above the bridge of the Serb's nose, and squeezed the trigger. A black hole appeared where it was supposed to, and then the man was gone. The Dame shifted the telescopic sight downwards, through the cloud of snow that was still falling from the disturbed branches, and found the dark shape lying motionless beneath the tree.

One more, he thought. One more.

He packed up the rifle and went back down through the empty house. At the doorway something strange made him pause. Then he realized: no shell had landed on the town for quite a while. Maybe the bastards had run out of them. Maybe they were having their tea break.

Back at the hostel he found the other three having one.

'Did you get him?' Docherty asked.

'Yep,' he said, looking round. 'Where's my cup of tea?'

Razor did the honours.

'OK,' Docherty said, when the requisite cup had been poured and sugared, 'we have some decisions to take.' He grunted. 'Like decide what the fuck we're doing here.'

'What are the choices, boss?' Chris asked seriously.

'This is not our war. I mean, I don't know who's in the right. Does anyone?'

'Ah, c'mon,' Razor said. 'You've just spent the day trying to patch up kids who've been hit by indiscriminate shell fire. You know that's not right.'

'Sure,' Chris said. 'And what happened to those women, I know. But what I don't know is whether we've just seen one side of all this. You were there when they threw the sniper out of the window. That wasn't right either.'

'He'd shot half a dozen kids!'

'I know. But my point is, I think the whole country's gone mad.'

'But . . .'

'Aye,' Docherty interjected, 'the whole country has gone mad, and it's not up to us to sort it out. Like Chris says, it's not our war. But . . . we're here, and I don't think we can just walk away from what we see with our own eyes. It may be only one side, but right here, right now, there's a town being destroyed for no other reason than that it wants to live in peace.'

'What are you saying we ought to do, boss?' Razor asked.

'I'm not. I don't know. And it's different for me – I don't have a future with the Regiment to worry about . . .'

'Fuck that for a game of soldiers,' Razor said.

'Yeah,' Chris agreed, 'that's not a problem.'

'Anyway, us three can say we were just following orders,' Razor said with a grin.

'Be my guest,' Docherty agreed. 'Problem is, I still haven't got any orders for you to follow.'

'OK,' Razor said. 'Try this. We're not hanging around

to win the war for anyone, but we're not just making a run for good ol' Blighty. So we're going to do what we can and *then* head home. So what can we do?'

'Take out the Serb gun,' the Dame said.

'Aye. And maybe do something about those children. I have a feeling it's time I reported in. And I'm going to ask if someone can arrange choppers to take out the badly wounded and any other children whose parents want them to leave.'

'You think there's any chance they'll agree to that?' Chris asked doubtfully.

'Split's less than an hour away, and I can't see how anyone could see it as anything other than a humanitarian mission . . .' He shrugged. 'But I expect they'll say no. I can only find out by asking.'

'What are you going to say about Reeve?' Razor asked.

Docherty shrugged. 'I'll just tell them what's happened here. If they ask me, I shall say that in my opinion Sergeant Reeve has acted in the best interests of the people here and in the best traditions of the Regiment.'

'You're not going to mention the Cheshires' lorryload of frozen oven chips then, boss?' Razor asked.

The PC grunted. 'I don't think so,' he said, laughing. 'But I'd better talk to Reeve first, in any case. And I'll tell him we're on for tonight.' He paused. 'If any of you don't want to be involved in this, that's fine,' he said. 'If I wasn't a friend of Reeve's I'm not at all sure whether I'd be going.'

'We are, boss,' Razor said.

'I don't like people who can't even be bothered to aim their artillery,' Chris remarked.

* * *

Docherty found Reeve standing alone, smoking a cigarette, outside the entrance to the makeshift hospital.

'You're not running short on them, then?' he asked.

'These? No, we were lucky. There was a delivery lorry here a few days before the blockade was tightened. The driver was a Serb and wanted to risk it, but we dissuaded him.' Reeve smiled. 'He married one of the local girls a few weeks ago – a Croat. It's been an education, Jamie, this war. I wouldn't have missed it for the world.'

'I'm going to report in,' Docherty told him, 'tell them what the situation is here, and ask if they can arrange to fly out however many of those kids Nena thinks need to go.'

'OK,' Reeve said, after a moment's hesitation. 'And what's my report card going to say?'

'I'll just tell them what's happening. Tell them you've been looking after your kids, maybe offering some advice every now and then to the locals.'

'Thanks, Jamie.'

'Don't mention it. And you have four volunteers for tonight,' Docherty told him. 'And then I think we'll be on our way.'

'Missing Isabel?'

'You bet.'

'I've been missing Nena. More than I thought I would.' He grimaced. 'Have you talked to her? I haven't had a chance, yet. How is she, really?'

'I don't know, Reeve. But I don't think people bounce back from what she's been through. It'll take a lot of time.'

At the hostel, Docherty's departure left silence in its wake, as each of the other three men tried to make some sense of what he felt about the situation. For Razor there was the additional problem of what was going to happen between him and Hajrija. He hadn't seen her since their rude awakening that morning, and had no idea where she was. He hoped she wasn't regretting what had taken place the previous night.

He looked at the other two – the Dame sitting back with his eyes closed, Chris studying the map on the table – and wondered why there'd been no ribbing that morning. Maybe because they didn't think they knew him well enough, but he doubted it. Maybe because they knew he was serious about her.

Would she stay on in Zavik? It was her home town, after all. The thought of staying here with her crossed Razor's mind. He could certainly help out on the military and medical fronts – he wouldn't just be in the way. It would mean throwing career and pension out of the window, but that thought didn't deter him. If he'd been the type to care about things like that he wouldn't be in the fucking SAS, would he?

But he'd have to go with the others, at least as far as Split. They'd come in together and they'd go out the same way. He owed them that much.

'Assuming there's no reply from International Rescue,' he asked Chris and the Dame, 'how do you think we're going to get home?'

'The way we arrived, probably,' Chris said. 'A long walk out of here, and then . . .' He shrugged. 'We could walk to the coast in a few days. We've still got enough emergency rations.'

'We could,' Razor agreed, 'but I can't say as I fancy it. Unless you two are willing to carry me in a sedan chair.'

The Dame opened one disdainful eye, and closed it again.

'It was just a thought,' Razor said. He heard someone come in through the door upstairs and hoped it was Hajrija.

The boots which appeared on the stairs belonged to Docherty. 'You three could have a look at that map and come up with some suggestions for tonight,' he said, working the case containing the PRC 319 out of his bergen.

'I am, boss,' Chris said in an aggrieved tone.

Docherty grinned. 'Sorry.' He went back up the stairs with the radio, and out into the rapidly darkening street. Not far away he found a large enough expanse of open ground and set up the system, pointing the two tuning antennae up into the western sky and searching out the correct frequency. The PRC 319 was capable of carrying voice transmissions, but Docherty decided, mostly on instinct, to use the burst facility instead. He typed out 'Tito calling Churchill' and sent it. Almost instantaneously the words 'Churchill receiving' appeared on the tiny screen.

Docherty started typing with one finger. 'Tito group now in Zavik. Stop. No casualties. Stop. Our friend is here. Stop. Rumours unjustified. Stop. Town under artillery attack as of yesterday. Stop. Request helicopter extraction for seriously wounded children, numbering nine as of today. Stop. Will expect reply tomorrow 0700 GMT. Out.'

He packed up the set and squatted in the dark for an instant, looking up at the dark line of hills across the valley. Just one gun, he thought.

Better one less than one more.

15

They left the town shortly after nine o'clock, eleven men and one woman, walking in single file down the road which led up the valley to the west. Hajrija's presence was not appreciated by all – the acceptance she had won from her comrades in Sarajevo was only hearsay as far as Reeve and his men were concerned – and Docherty had felt more than a little reluctant when called as a witness to her competence. He suspected she was every bit as good a fighter as any in Reeve's unprofessional army, but the look on Razor's face was not a pretty sight.

The latter had already tried to dissuade her, and failed utterly. 'If you think I lie in bed all night waiting for you, you crazy,' Hajrija had told him. Now, walking along behind her, Razor was consoling himself with the thought that at least she was thinking about being in bed with him.

The twelve of them had a long way to go that night. The fact that Reeve and Chris had drawn up virtually identical plans of action might have reflected their common SAS training, but it also pointed to the paucity of options open to them. There were two ways up the three hundred-yard slopes opposite the town, one obvious, one not so obvious. But any attacking force had first to cross the river, and here the options were more limited. With the road bridges already blown there was only one spot close to the town where a force could ford the icy waters with any ease, and if the Serbs had any sense at all they would surely have night glasses

240

trained in that direction, particularly on the first night after beginning their bombardment.

So both the local ways up the slope were out. Instead, the two planners had recommended a four-mile walk up the valley to another crossing spot. From there they could climb up out of the valley, and then undertake a wide, flanking march around to the Serbs' rear. Such an approach might be exhausting, but, Reeve and Chris had both decided, offered the only reasonable chance of surprise.

And with any luck they would also come across the road the Serbs must have constructed to get the gun up to the top of the hill. It wouldn't do much good to take out one artillery piece if the enemy could just bring up another.

The walk was long but for the most part uneventful. The sky was full of broken cloud, and the quarter moon, when it rose, was bright enough to facilitate track-finding on their way out of the valley. Up on the rolling plateau it was almost too bright, combining with the snow to create a light that felt almost artificial. To Razor, walking at the rear, the column of black silhouettes against the moonlit white hills seemed like a scene caught by a camera's flash and then for ever frozen, locked in a denial of darkness.

It was almost three by the time they reached the Serbs' approach road. It had been a mere footpath on Reeve's local map, but the Serbs had widened and smoothed it, cutting down trees and inserting makeshift vehicle-width wooden bridges where dips or water made them necessary. Judging by the overlapping tracks in the snow they were making considerable use of it.

When the party reached the first bridge Reeve sent two

of his men forward as advance scouts. The rest waited while a third man rigged the bridge with Czech-made Semtex – part of Reeve's Livno Armoury haul – and set up a time fuse. He did the same at the next, and the next, a formidable piece of construction that spanned a narrow ravine. Considering that Zavik had no apparent military value, Docherty thought, the Serbs were taking a lot of trouble over it. Someone had to be very angry – maybe Reeve had overdone it a little. But it was obviously too late to kiss and make up.

One of the two advance scouts returned with news of a sentry point a couple of hundred yards further up the mountain. The location had been chosen well, he said: the two men were on the far side of the next bridge, which crossed another long ravine. There was doubtless a way round it, but it would take time to find.

'Are they just standing there?' Reeve asked.

'No, they're sitting by one of those braziers warming their hands and chattering on about what a bastard their commander is.'

'Can we get a clean shot at them? Are they holding their guns?'

'Yes and yes,' the scout said.

Reeve turned to Docherty, who had been receiving a translation of all this from Chris. 'We need your silenced MP5s,' he said.

'What's the range?' Docherty asked the scout, Chris translating the question.

'From cover? About sixty yards.'

'Too far,' Docherty said, cursing the fact that they'd only brought one scope for the MP5s. 'Dame,' he said, 'do you think you could take out two before the second man raises the alarm?'

'No reason why not,' the Wearsider said. Two more, he thought.

The scout led him up the widened path, which now ran diagonally across a forest-covered slope. A few minutes later they were joining the first scout, squatting down and staring out across a wide expanse of snow at the bridge and the two men by their brazier. It looked ridiculous, the Dame thought, just these two men on the side of a mountain sitting by a fire in the middle of the night.

He stood up, taking care to keep his body behind the trunk, and then inched himself slowly outwards, the MP5's retractable stock cradled against his shoulder, the telescopic sight to his right eye. It didn't feel as comfortable as the Accuracy International, but in this situation silence was everything. He examined the face of the Serb on the right, lit by the orange fire and big enough to fill the sight at this range.

He shifted the aim to the left and found the other face, which was laughing at something. He moved back swiftly to the first face, trying to accustom himself to the quick shift he would need. He was too close really: a hundred yards further back would have been better. Still, at that distance the gun would be reaching the limits of its effective range. And in any case he didn't fancy crawling back through the snow.

He felt easier moving from the right target to the left than vice versa. He aligned the cross-hairs on the side of the right-hand man's head, just above the ear. Aim by not aiming, he told himself, and let his grip slacken for a second.

Now. He squeezed the trigger once, smoothly slid his aim to the left, found the other target, squeezed again. He lowered the gun, and confirmed with his naked eye what his brain already knew. Both men were dead.

One of the two scouts was already scurrying back through the snow to collect the rest. The other was hurrying forward to check out his marksmanship. The Dame walked forward to join him, and they were both warming their hands on the brazier when the main party caught up with them.

Once the bridge had been rigged they resumed their climb, again through an expanse of forest. They were nearing the top now, but the scouts ranging fifty yards or so ahead found no more sentries. Instead they found a large clearing just below the ridge top. The gun which had done such damage sat to one side on its reinforced base, and the breakdown lorry which had presumably towed it up the mountain stood close by. On the other side of the clearing three transit vans were parked in a line, two of them in darkness, one showing a faint aura of light. Barely audible music seemed to be coming from the latter.

The snow had been mostly swept away from the clearing and the embers of a small fire were still glowing. Cooking utensils sat in a pile, and a pot had been filled with snow for whatever it was that Serb gunners drank for their breakfast.

'What now?' Docherty asked, as he and Reeve surveyed the scene from just inside the trees.

'We can't take prisoners,' Reeve said, looking at Docherty as if he was expecting an argument.

Docherty had none. These men were responsible for the children screaming in Zavik's makeshift hospital. And who knew what else, either in the past or the future. 'Let's do it quietly though,' he said. 'There may be more men on our route home, and I'd rather we surprised them than the other way round.'

'Semtex under each van, then,' Reeve said, as if he was decorating a stage. 'And one for the gun.'

'A fifteen-minute fuse for the vans, a couple more for the gun,' Docherty suggested.

Since both were demolition specialists, Reeve and the Dame supervised the laying of the charges. The latter approached the dimly lit van with appropriate caution, but the two men inside seemed fast asleep, oblivious to the Thin Lizzy tape playing on the van's stereo. Even outside the tightly shuttered van the smell of marijuana filled the cold air.

In ten minutes they were finished and the twelve-person patrol was on its way again, crossing the ridge top and starting down the slope on the quick route home. Once again two men were sent ahead to scout for the enemy.

The path wound steeply down through trees, and the going was easy enough to suggest it had been used with some regularity in recent days. After fourteen and a half minutes had passed on his watch Reeve halted the column, and they all waited in silence, hoping that nothing had gone wrong.

The first explosion was out by only two seconds, sending a yellow-white flash into the sky behind them. An image of the transit vans exploding in three simultaneous shafts of light came to Docherty's mind, and in his imagination he looked across the clearing to where the gun was still standing.

The second explosion was louder than the first, but not as spectacular. With grim smiles on their faces, and renewed caution, the twelve resumed their journey down the slope. About ten minutes later they emerged from a stand of trees to find the town spread out below them in the moonlight. Perhaps it was this which took the edge off their alertness, or maybe it was just that everything had gone too smoothly. Either way, they were halfway past the Serb observation platform before they knew it was there.

It had been dug into the mountainside to give the Serbs a panoramic view of the town and valley below, and the radio link with the camp on the hilltop gave the gunners at least the option of directed fire. The explosions above had woken the two men who manned the platform, and the failure of their efforts to raise their superiors had made them jumpy. It might just be a lot of stoned fun going on up on the hill – maybe someone had fired a Croat from the gun or something – but it might be something dreamed up by the English lunatic in the town below.

They had been watching and waiting for several minutes, when the first shadows walked into their line of sight. Despite this, one Serb was surprised enough to shout rather than shoot. The other was either quicker of thought or more prone to violence, because he opened up immediately, killing one of Reeve's men, wounding another in the shoulder and giving Razor a second parting in his dark hair. The shock made the Londoner slip on the snow, and he went down flat on his back.

It seemed as if the whole party opened fire at the same moment, and in retrospect Docherty reckoned it a minor miracle that no one had been killed or wounded by friendly fire. The observation post, though, was riddled with enough bullets to kill ten, let alone two. And any chance of surprising any

Serbs lower down the path had been shot just as comprehensively.

Razor's scalp hurt like hell, but there wasn't much blood, and he received some compensation from Hajrija's instant appearance at his side as he lay in the snow. Chris made quick examinations of both him and the man with the shoulder wound, and found nothing which would prevent them from walking. The party resumed its downward progress, with two men carrying the body of their dead friend. Reeve and Docherty spent the journey waiting for the scouts to report Serbs on the path ahead, but if any had been deployed there, they had apparently gone. An hour before dawn the troop forded the river below the broken bridge and re-entered the town.

The injured men were accompanied to the castle crypt, where Nena was found dozing fitfully on one of the few empty mattresses. After she and Chris had applied the necessary dressings, Docherty took her to one side, and told her he'd asked for nine of the children to be air-lifted out.

'Why nine?' she wanted to know.

'It seemed like a convincing number. I don't think they'll come anyway, but if they do, then we can ask them to take as many as you think should go.'

'Nine was a pretty good guess,' she said looking round.

Her eyes were bloodshot with exhaustion, Docherty noticed. He expected his own were too.

'If they don't come, most of those nine are going to die,' she said quietly.

It was getting lighter outside as Docherty walked back down to the hostel. Most of the townspeople were probably in their basements by now, waiting for the bombardment to resume. Well, they would be spared that, at least for the time it took the Serbs to repair their road, replace their personnel and find another gun. Weeks, he guessed. And then Reeve would go back up the mountain and destroy that one too.

The really different thing about this war, Docherty thought, was the lack of air power involved. It had to be the first war in Europe since World War One in which the aeroplane hadn't played a decisive role. Maybe that explained the medieval feel of the whole business.

It didn't explain crucifixions, though.

At the hostel he found all the others had disappeared to their beds, keen to grab back at least some of the sleeping hours they had lost. Docherty made himself some tea and sat in the basement room, thinking about his children, and wondering what they would think of their father's life when they were old enough to understand it. If they ever were, he thought wryly. When it came to the bigger picture he seemed to grow more confused as he got older, not less. A sign of growing wisdom, as Liam McCall would say. But not an excuse to stop looking.

At five to eight he collected the PRC 319 and went back up the hill to set it up for reception. At precisely 0800 Central European Time the words 'Churchill calling Tito' appeared on the tiny screen. 'Tito receiving' Docherty typed out, and waited, hoping against hope.

'Tito group return base soonest. Stop. Require Friend to accompany. Stop. No air assistance possible. Out.'

'Bastards,' Docherty murmured.

He packed up the radio and took it back to the hostel, then went up to the castle to tell Nena the bad news. She took it more stoically than he expected, but then he guessed she was used to such news after her months

248

working in the Sarajevo hospital. Back at the hostel he set his alarm for noon, and sank into an exhausted sleep.

Almost instantly, it seemed, he was woken by the clock. The sun was shining full on his face, and outside he could hear people talking. From the window he could see two women walking away down the street, as if the previous day's bombardment had been just a bad dream.

He went to wake the others, but found their rooms empty. Chris and Razor were in the basement, drinking tea and waiting for him. Both looked pointedly at their watches as he came in.

Docherty poured himself a cup and sat down. 'I've got bad news,' he began.

'We know, boss,' Razor said. 'Nena told us. But Reeve has had an idea.'

'That sounds ominous,' Docherty murmured, just as Reeve himself appeared on the stairs, the Dame behind him.

'It seems to be OK,' the Wearsider said. 'Both cab windows are broken, so it's going to be a bit on the cold side . . .'

'What's OK?' Docherty asked.

'The cigarette lorry,' Reeve explained. 'The one you're taking the kids to Split in.'

Docherty looked at Razor, whose bandaged head gave him the look of a punk pirate.

'It's the only way, boss. If we can't fly the kids out, we have to drive them out, it's as simple as that.'

Docherty supposed it was.

'And we've got something else to show you,' Reeve said.

They all trooped up the stairs and out into the street.

249

In front of the lorry stood an extremely basic-looking armoured car – one which looked old enough to have done service with Rommel in the desert. Its gun was obviously long gone, but it looked robust enough to shoot Niagara Falls. More surprisingly, given its age, the white vehicle bore the letters UN on its side.

'I told Reeve we had UN berets,' Razor explained.

'We'd already painted it white for winter camouflage,' Reeve added, 'but the logo is still wet.'

Docherty looked round at them. 'Let me get this straight. We're going to use this antique to escort a lorryload of children to Split, passing through at least one Serb blockade, and possibly several others, *en route*?'

'That's about it,' Reeve agreed.

Docherty shook his head and smiled. 'I like it.'

'We thought you would,' Razor said.

'I assume there's no problem with fuel?'

'Nope.'

'So who's coming on this jaunt?'

It was Reeve who answered. 'Eight children and two adults – they're a husband and wife, and they're in their seventies. Their basement ceiling collapsed on them yesterday. And Hajrija wants to come with you. She thinks it'll be easier to get back to Sarajevo from Split.'

'What about Nena?'

'She's staying here. She says there's nothing more she can do for the ones you're taking, and you have Chris and Razor. Zavik needs her more.'

And so do you and the kids, Docherty thought. He was glad they would at least have the chance to try again.

'When do we leave?' he asked.

'You're the boss,' Razor said.

Night or day, Docherty wondered. He was fed up with darkness. 'Dawn tomorrow,' he decided.

Later that evening Docherty visited Nena at her parents' home. She had managed to catch a few hours' sleep, and looked more like the woman he had known in years gone by, one with life in her eyes and a tendency to laugh. Not surprisingly, the children were still intent on monopolizing their mother, and there was not much opportunity for the two adults to share a serious conversation.

But there was one thing Docherty felt he had to say. 'If you ever decide to send the children out of here,' he said, 'but can't or don't want to leave yourself, then we'll be happy to look after them for you.'

'I can't imagine letting them go again,' she said, 'but thank you.'

'And as for Reeve,' Docherty said, 'you know him better than I do . . .'

'I think we know different sides.'

'Aye, maybe. But I know he's missed you, because he told me so. What that means . . .' He shrugged. 'Just thought I'd pass it on.'

She smiled ruefully at him. 'We'll see,' she said, just as her son imposed his head between theirs and began talking nineteen to the dozen.

An hour later Docherty and Reeve were drinking each other's health in René's Café. 'Didn't London even bother to mention me?' Reeve wanted to know.

'Oh aye, they bothered. "Require Friend to accompany." The friend is you.'

'What do they expect you to do – tie me up and throw me over your shoulder?'

'Christ knows. Who bloody cares?'

'What are you going to tell them?'

Docherty grunted. 'That you're more valuable here than they'll ever be anywhere. And that they can go fuck themselves.'

Reeve grinned. 'You know, I didn't think it was possible that you could grow more insubordinate with age, but you've managed it.' He raised his glass. 'Here's to the journey.'

16

The sun was still hidden behind the mountains, the town still far from awake, as the convoy began threading its way out through Zavik's narrow streets towards the road that ran west up the valley. A Renault Five containing Reeve and three of his men led the way, followed by Docherty and the Dame in the armoured car, with the lorry bringing up the rear. Razor was driving the lorry, while Chris and Hajrija served in the back as combination nurses and tail-gunners.

The number of passengers had dropped over the past twenty-four hours. The old woman had passed away in the night, and her husband's determination to live seemed to have died with her. It had taken all of Nena's persuasive powers to get him aboard the lorry.

One of the nine children had also died, and another two were withdrawn by parents unable to bear the thought of dispatching their only child into the void beyond the valley. Of the six that remained, four had been orphans since the first hour of the Serb bombardment forty-eight hours before, and the other two came from large families.

Half a mile outside the town the convoy passed through the inner ring of Zavik's defences, an apparently unmanned checkpoint where the road was hemmed in between a steep cliff and the river. The guards, Reeve had told them, were stationed out of sight above the road. With a flick of a detonator switch they could send half the cliff down on top of any hostile intruder.

They continued on up the winding valley, with all concerned keeping their eyes skinned for signs of an enemy presence. Reeve had sent scouts back up the mountain the day before, and they had found vultures hovering over the three burnt-out transit vans, but no sign that the Serbs below had discovered what had happened to their mountaintop unit.

It was this chronic lack of coordination between the various bands of irregulars which gave Docherty hope for the break-out attempt. As long as they could deal with the enemy piecemeal, they had a fighting chance of making the coast. But if one band managed to get word back to another, and give the other time to prepare a hot reception, then getting through might well prove impossible. There were simply too few of them, particularly since they also had six children to protect.

The convoy reached the checkpoint which marked the outer ring of Zavik's defences. Here the road was constrained between trees and the river, and two of the former had been cut down to block the road. The ropes and pulleys used to lift them aside were operated by men hidden deep in the trees – a technique which Docherty remembered Reeve using in a jungle exercise in Brunei twenty years before.

Sunlight was now slipping down the slopes across the river, and the only definite Serb checkpoint was not much more than a mile away. According to Reeve, it was usually manned by only three or four men, and then only out of habit. Why, after all, would anyone want to break out of Zavik into Serb territory?

The convoy came to a halt a quarter of a mile from the checkpoint, and the occupants of the Renault transferred to the armoured car. The vehicle was quite spacious inside, its Soviet makers having dispensed with luxuries like seats and equipment, but with six men aboard it was still something of a tight squeeze. Docherty was reminded of the stateroom scene from the Marx Brothers' *A Night at the Opera*, and hoped that they would burst out with as much alacrity, and rather more control, when the time came.

The armoured car rumbled down the road with its hatch down, the Dame peering forward through the open slit as he drove. Some way behind, Razor was edging the lorry slowly forward, letting the distance between the two vehicles lengthen.

As the leading one rounded a bend in the valley, the Dame saw the checkpoint up ahead. No attempt had been made to block the way, but two cars were parked between the road and a house set back from it. There were no people in sight.

The Dame picked up speed slightly, causing the armoured car to shudder violently for a second. The sound of its passage would be enough to wake the dead, he thought.

It woke the Serbs. One man half-clambered, half-fell out of one of the car doors, a rifle in his hand. He stood there for a moment, peering at the strange white object rumbling towards him, and then opened his mouth wide, presumably to shout. It was impossible to hear anything above the din of the armoured car.

As if by magic, three other figures emerged from the two cars at the exact same moment. Two were carrying Kalashnikovs, one an SMG. The Dame relayed this information to the men crowded in behind him. It was a pity the armoured car had no gun, the Dame thought, as he slowed the vehicle down.

The four Serbs had fanned out like Western gun-fighters, but the expressions on their faces were more amused than hostile. The Dame could almost hear the thought running through their minds: the fucking UN busybodies had gone and got themselves lost in the mountains.

The armoured car came to a full stop. 'They're ten yards away,' the Dame said, 'at ten o'clock, eleven o'clock, noon and two o'clock. The man at eleven o'clock has the SMG.'

'Ready?' Docherty asked. 'Steady. Go!'

In the same instant both side doors and the hatch swung open. Docherty was up through the latter like a jack-in-the-box, swinging the Browning toward the eleven o'clock position, fine-tuning his aim and firing before the man with the sub-machine-gun had time to raise it. He fell back, hitting the ground with the SMG still gripped in his lifeless hand.

Less than a second later the other three had joined him in death. Reeve and his three men had thrown themselves out through the side doors, and before the surprise had time to die on the faces of the Serbs, the attackers had rolled to a halt in the snow, guns already blazing.

The sound of the river re-emerged as the echoes of gunfire faded down the valley. Reeve and his men went to check out the house but, as expected, found no one there. Razor, meanwhile, was bringing the lorry forward on Docherty's signal.

'You know where you're going, then?' Reeve said. 'When you get to the crossroads go left, follow that road for about twelve miles and you'll reach the main road to the coast. Once you're on that I reckon your chances of getting hassled are less, especially with such a finely drawn UN logo. You could be in Split for lunch.'

Docherty offered Reeve his hand, wondering if they'd ever see each other again. 'Good luck, Reeve,' he said.

'Seconded,' Razor said from the lorry cab.

'You too. Now get going.'

Docherty climbed back aboard the armoured car and gave the Dame the nod. With a great whoosh of black smoke the vehicle started off, the lorry behind it. In the latter's side mirror Razor had a last glance of Reeve and his men walking back down the valley to where they had left the Renault. Behind them the bodies of the four Serbs lay sprawled and already forgotten in the snow.

The road continued up the ever-narrowing valley, until slopes seemed to rise up ahead of them as well as to either side. The crossroads finally appeared. The straight-ahead road was no more than a dirt track, the one across the river rendered unusable by the destruction of the bridge which had carried it. Their road climbed up through the trees in a succession of hairpin bends, emerging on to a snowswept plateau.

The armoured car, which had struggled up the steep incline, now found a new lease of life, and Docherty's worries about its staying power receded somewhat. He was riding with his balaclava-clad head out of the hatch, prepared to endure the stinging-cold wind if it meant having advance warning of any trouble on the road up ahead.

For the first few miles he might have been travelling in Antarctica. There were no signs of human habitation;

the road itself offered the only proof that humans had ever passed that way. A polar bear sunning itself in a meadow wouldn't have seemed out of place.

They soon left the barren heights, winding their way down into another forested valley. The armoured car enjoyed descending even more than riding on the flat, and for the next few miles they made excellent speed. Docherty was just beginning to take Reeve's idea of lunch in Split seriously when disaster struck.

The two vehicles were nearing the bottom of a long, curving slope when the armoured car suffered a tremendous jolt, strong enough to almost launch Docherty out through the hatch. The PC was still thanking his lucky stars that no permanent damage had been done to the vehicle when the horn sounded behind them. The lorry was limping to a halt by the side of the road.

Docherty walked back to where Razor was examining the underside of the vehicle. The Londoner got back to his feet with a grim look on his face. 'The front axle's fucked,' he said. 'I'm sorry, boss, I didn't see the trench until it was too late.'

'Neither did the Dame,' Docherty said, looking around. The road ran uphill in both directions, and everything else was forested slope. The wind had got up, and it seemed to have grown appreciably colder since their departure from Zavik. He wondered what the fuck were they going to do now.

Chris emerged from the back of the lorry looking sombre. 'One of the kids got a knock on the head where he was already wounded,' he reported. 'Doesn't look good.'

Razor went to take a look, leaving the other three SAS men standing in the road.

'Any suggestions?' Docherty asked.

'Could we all get into the armoured car?' Chris asked.

'Not unless you're into breaking the number of people in an armoured car record. You might be able to get all the patients in, but not in the sort of comfort they'd need to survive a sixty-mile journey. And we'd be sitting ducks on top.'

'We could take the armoured car and go looking for another lorry,' the Dame suggested.

'How far are we from the main road?' Chris asked.

'About nine miles last time I looked,' Docherty said, taking the map out of his pocket and unfolding it. 'Yeah, I reckon we're about here,' he said, pointing with a finger. Between seven and nine miles.'

'Boss, I think someone's going to have to walk,' Chris said. 'The temperature's going down like a stone. I was already getting worried about how cold it was in the back of that lorry, and with this wind . . . I think the kids should be moved into the armoured car, where there's a heater.'

Docherty blew into the hands he was holding over his nose. 'OK,' he said eventually. 'I can't think of a better plan. Can either of you?' he asked Razor and Hajrija, who had just appeared beside them.

They couldn't, and for the next fifteen minutes Hajrija and the four SAS men ferried the wounded from one vehicle to the other, with Chris dividing up the small space between them, and keeping up a constant conversation with each child as he did so. The old man, once he realized how small the space was, adamantly refused to take up any of it. It took an almost superhuman effort on Hajrija's part to make him sit in the cab of the lorry, whose heater was fighting a losing battle with the broken windows.

'Say, three hours to get there, and, at best, twenty minutes to get back,' Docherty told those who were staying.

He and the Dame set off up the road, one ten yards behind the other, their MP5s cradled in their arms.

Once they were gone Razor and Hajrija took up stations about a hundred yards either side of the stranded vehicles. They had no idea what the chances of traffic were, but there had to be some, and anything which passed would inevitably see both lorry and armoured car. It might have been possible to get the latter off the road, but only at the expense of either lengthening the ferrying of the children or jolting them around inside.

Chris was left to look after them, which presented some difficulty. There was no room for him to get in with them, and he didn't think it would be wise to shut them up in the dark, no matter how warm they might then be. He compromised by keeping the hatch open, and talking to them through it.

It was mostly a one-sided conversation. Nearly all the children were in considerable pain, and their powers of concentration greatly diminished. What amazed Chris was their fortitude – though none was older than ten he heard no whining and saw very few tears. While telling a funny story he even had the feeling that some of the children were forcing themselves to smile out of sheer generosity.

As he looked down at their upturned faces, eyes bright in the gloom of the armoured car's belly, he had the feeling that here was a sight every soldier should see.

And it tore at his heart.

*   *   *

As the morning passed Docherty and the Dame ate up the miles. The road ran roughly south down the widening valley, keeping close to the river, and such houses as they saw in the distance were perched on the lower slopes. Several times the PC thought he saw far-off moving figures, but none appeared before them on the road, and no vehicles passed in either direction.

After an hour and a half's walking they found themselves looking down on a village which straddled the road, and which Docherty thought it prudent to bypass. The resulting trudge across forested slopes added an extra hour, and it was almost eleven o'clock before they came in sight of their destination. From a convenient hilltop they surveyed the cluster of buildings which marked the spot where their road met the main highway to Split.

One had been a garage, and one of the others probably a roadside restaurant. Maybe it still was, because two lorries were standing outside it. Through the binoculars Docherty could see that there was no one in either cab. Nor could he see any light or sign of life through the building's windows. That was the good news. The bad news was that any approach would involve a ten-minute walk across open country. The two men lay there in the snow, considering the situation. Another lorry came into view on the main road, a large articulated vehicle, and drove through the junction in the direction of the coast. A man appeared in the doorway of the supposed restaurant, looked out, and then disappeared back inside.

'We could wait for dark, boss,' the Dame said doubtfully, 'but the lorries might be gone by then.'

'And we can't leave the others stuck on an open road for the whole day,' Docherty said. 'I'm afraid we don't have many options where this one's concerned.'

The Dame smiled to himself, 'Then let's go, boss.'

'Aye, but by the road, I think. Let's just be two lonely soldiers trudging homewards in the snow.'

'Pity we don't know any of those Serb songs your mate Reeve was talking about.'

'I want us to look natural, not wake up the town.'

They worked their way back to the road and started off down the slight slope towards the junction. There were fields on either side, with a few bare trees by the banks of a meandering stream. A large, black bird suddenly detached itself from a branch, and whirled up into the sky, cawing loudly.

The sound of an approaching vehicle grew louder, and then came into view to the right. It was another large lorry, and like its predecessor, sped on through the junction. If there was no checkpoint here, Docherty thought, then there was no reason for there to be any soldiers.

They crossed the stream by a stone bridge and left the road, working their way along behind the buildings that faced the main highway. These were fairly new affairs, long and windowless. Agricultural storage sheds of some sort, Docherty guessed. He halted at the end of the second, dropped to his haunches, and inched an eye round the corner. As he expected, the restaurant was visible across the highway. No name or sign was visible, but a Coca-Cola sign hung drunkenly from a single fixing beside twin entrance doors. The two lorries were parked side by side and roughly parallel to the highway, their rear ends no more than five yards from the doorway.

262

He gave the Dame the hand signal for follow, and slipped across the gap. The next building looked like someone's house, but as was the case with so many of the Bosnian houses they had seen, no one seemed to be at home. They trudged their way through the untouched accumulation of winter snow, pushed aside an already rickety fence, and reached the next gap. Again Docherty edged his eye round the corner. This time part of a disused garage was in view – two old-fashioned petrol pumps wearing what looked like hats of snow.

They moved cautiously down the gap between the two houses, to where they could get a view up and down the highway. As Docherty had hoped, the doors and windows in the front of the restaurant were hidden from view by the two lorries.

The two SAS men jogged across the highway, Docherty keeping an open eye to the left, the Dame doing the same to the right. No one was in sight. Another ghost town, Docherty thought. Or at least he hoped it was.

They reached the space between the cabs of the two lorries. While the Dame kept guard Docherty hoisted himself up to see if there was a key in the ignition of the first lorry. There wasn't, but there was in the second. He took off his gloves and felt the bonnet. It seemed faintly warm.

'Check it out,' he whispered to the Dame, and moved down between the two vehicles towards their rears. He sank to his haunches so that he could see the bottom half of the restaurant's front door.

Behind him, the Dame climbed up into the cab and released the bonnet lock. It sprang loose with a sharp clunk. He sat there for a few seconds, ears straining for a sign that someone had heard, and then climbed back down. He leaned the MP5 up against a wheel and pushed up the bonnet. The engine was hot to the touch. He pushed the bonnet gently back down, just as the men emerged from the side door of the restaurant.

It all happened very quickly.

As one man shouted something in an indignant voice, the Dame considered and rejected the option of diving for the MP5. Maybe one of the Serbs was telepathic, because at that moment he saw the SMG, and pulled his AK47 into the firing position, screaming something as he did so. By this time the Dame's Browning was clearing the holster on his right thigh.

The two guns fired simultaneously, the Dame's 'double tap' piercing the man's upper trunk as his automatic burst stitched fire across the Dame's chest.

The Wearsider was already going down as the other Serbs opened up.

About five seconds had elapsed since the first shout, and Docherty had only moved a few yards down the corridor between the lorries. He saw the Dame fall, and sank to the ground himself. Six legs were visible beneath the lorry, and he opened up on them with the MP5.

Cries of pain told him he had hit at least some of them, but he was already rolling forward, under the lorry closest to the restaurant and out into the gap between the two. The Serbs leapt into view, two of them already down, one still on his feet. As the six eyes flashed towards him he opened up again with the silenced MP5, knocking the third man back across the other two.

He rolled again, into a small snowdrift at the foot of the restaurant wall, but no bullets came his way. As he got to his feet, he heard sounds through the wall behind him. He swung the MP5 round towards the front door just as it swung open, and a child stepped out. Somehow he didn't squeeze the trigger.

A voice shouted a question in a foreign language. A woman's voice.

Docherty strode across to the door, the small boy retreating before him, and edged his eye around the frame. A blonde woman was standing by a pile of chairs and table, frozen to the spot. She suddenly started screaming at him, though whether in anger or fear Docherty couldn't tell. He marched past her, and found the side door they had neglected to notice. Outside the dead Serbs lay twisted together. Like the stupid tattoo they were all wearing, Docherty thought. Solidarity hadn't saved these Serbs.

He glanced up and down the highway and saw nothing. The Dame was still breathing, but with difficulty and not, Docherty guessed, for long. Even if the heart had been spared the lungs seemed to have been shredded.

He lifted the Wearsider's body up into the cab, and propped him up in the driving seat with the aid of the safety belt. Then he took the MP5 and burst the other lorry's rear tyres.

As Docherty clambered back up into the cab the Dame's eyes seemed to flicker open briefly, and what could even have been a smile twitched at his lips. Then the eyes closed again. Docherty felt the carotid artery. The Dame was dead.

As he let in the clutch the door of the restaurant burst back open, and the child stumbled out. He had come to wave goodbye.

His mouth set in a grim line, Docherty hurled the lorry as fast as he could down the treacherous road. He knew there was nothing to be gained from blaming himself for the Dame's death, but he couldn't help doing so. How could he have missed the side door? How could either of them?

Just concentrate on the job, he told himself. He could wallow in guilt later.

There was no choice but to drive through the village they had avoided on the way down. He roared through faster than the road warranted, but no one stepped out with an upraised hand, and no bullets pursued him. The village was alive, though, and he saw several people watch the lorry go by, their bodies still and their expressions vacant, as if they feared doing something which would cause him to stop.

Less than twenty minutes had passed when he found himself driving down through the forest towards the armoured car and lorry. He flashed the headlights twice as he approached, and Razor materialized from behind a tree, a smile on his face.

'Hiya, boss,' he said, and then he saw the Dame. 'Oh shit,' he murmured, closing his eyes for a moment.

'Aye,' Docherty agreed. 'Come on, let's get out of this fucking country.'

With Razor on the running board, the lorry rolled on down the last hundred yards.

Chris leapt down from the armoured car and came across to meet it. 'The clock beat the Dame,' Razor said quietly, stepping to the ground.

Chris stopped in his tracks, opened his mouth to say something, and then saw his friend propped up in the seat. He walked round to the other side and looked at him. Docherty had closed the Dame's eyes and the Wearsider seemed strangely at peace, as if he'd finally come to terms with something.

'We'll mourn him later,' Docherty's voice said in his ear.

Chris nodded. 'Goodbye, mate,' he said to the dead man, and turned away.

'Razor, go and get Hajrija,' Docherty ordered. 'How are the children?' he asked Chris.

'As well as can be expected. Better, in fact.'

'Well, let's start shifting them.' As he walked round to the back of the lorry it occurred to him that he had no idea what was inside it. He swung one of the doors open to reveal wall-to-wall pinball machines.

'Christ almighty,' Docherty muttered. Of all the things he'd seen since landing in Split this took the biscuit. In the middle of a medieval war someone had been scouring the country – and presumably restaurants like the one he'd just returned from – and either buying up or stealing pinball machines.

A sudden rage filled him, and he leapt up into the lorry and began tearing the restraining ropes from the mute machines. The first one crashed down into the road, and the second followed. Soon there was a pile rising up beneath the tailgate, and he had to move the lorry forward to free it from their grasp.

He sat in the cab for a few seconds, letting the rage subside.

'You OK, boss?' Razor asked him through the open window.

'Aye,' Docherty said. He wanted to see Isabel, he thought. He wanted to see her that very moment.

It wasn't possible, so he got down from the cab and

helped ferry the children from the armoured car to their new temporary home.

'What about the Dame?' Chris asked when they were finished.

'Wrap him in his sleeping bag, and put him in with the kids,' Docherty decided. He was wondering whether it was worth taking the armoured car any further. It really needed a crew of two – a navigator and a driver – and he wanted both Chris and Razor in the same vehicle as the children. Hajrija, when asked, said she was willing to try driving, but no, she had never actually driven anything, even a car . . .

There was also the chance of the ludicrous UN camouflage doing more harm than good. Anyone with half a brain wouldn't be fooled for more than a few seconds, and anyone in a real UN vehicle might decide the deception had hostile intent. Besides, driving along in the damn thing felt a bit like robbing orphans in a Mother Teresa mask.

He decided to abandon it, along with the mound of pinball machines. The old man too was left behind, in the cab of the broken lorry where he had fallen asleep and died.

With Razor at the wheel, Hajrija and Docherty beside him in the front seat, and Chris in the back, they set out once more. It was now the middle of the afternoon, and the wind had dropped again, leaving a slowly moving cloud mass to block out the sun.

They reached the junction within an hour of Docherty's last visit. Everyone had their guns at the ready as Razor turned on to the highway, but nothing moved in the cluster of buildings. The four dead men still lay in their tangled pile, and Docherty could see no sign of the woman or child.

The road soon started climbing up across a vast plateau, a thin strip between a sea of snow and the leaden sky. Two other lorries appeared, growing from dots in the distance to juggernauts thundering by, their drivers staring straight ahead, not risking eye contact.

After not much more than an hour the road was winding down towards Livno, and there they met their first checkpoint, manned by Croatian regular army forces. The officer in charge inspected their UN accreditations, no doubt took note of the pale-blue berets, and declined to make an issue of the fact that Hajrija was obviously only along for the ride. When he saw the children in the back, his face even softened, and they were waved on through.

'So far so good,' Razor said. 'And we're in Croat territory from now on, right?'

'Looks like it,' Docherty agreed. If it hadn't been for that one mistake, they would all have survived.

There was now only one more mountain range to cross, and the road ran steadily uphill, a huge lake below and to their left. The character of the country was changing too – even under the snow this land seemed more barren, with only a few twisted trees and sharp outcrops of dark rock jutting up out of the white overlay.

'This is Hercegovina,' Hajrija told them. 'There is nothing here,' she added. 'Even the water is in rocks, you understand?'

It was limestone country, Docherty realized. Where the rivers ran underground and people went potholing, for reasons that only they knew.

In the far distance he could see a large bird hovering in the air, and wondered idly what it was. Chris would know, he thought, and for a passing moment even wondered whether to stop the lorry and let the twitcher out of the back to identify it for him. You're getting senile, he told himself. And that was yet another reason for this being the last mission of his soldiering career.

'Boss,' Razor said, interrupting the PC's reverie.

Docherty focused his attention on the two cars blocking their passage a couple of hundred yards ahead. The road was clinging to the side of a bare valley, and all around them precipitous slopes either rose to the sky or dropped to the depths. A wooden cabin had been erected in a rare piece of flat land adjoining the road, maybe as a hunting cabin, maybe a roadside café. From its roof fluttered the red-and-white checked flag of the Croats. Standing outside its doors was a transit van which had been plastered with metal sheets, apparently by a gang of deranged welders.

What the fuck was anyone doing up here? Docherty asked himself. Nothing good, was the likely answer.

He turned and rapped three times on the partition, giving Chris the signal for possible danger.

Razor sized up the two cars blocking the road as he slowed the lorry. They looked ripe for pushing aside, but to do so at speed might well kill one or more of the children.

'Stop twenty yards short,' Docherty told him, as the first figure emerged from the cabin. Like the men they'd seen in the Split restaurant he was dressed all in black, from the polished boots to the peaked leather cap. He was carrying an Uzi, as were the three identically dressed men who followed him out through the door.

Four again, Docherty thought. In this country the bastards did everything in fours. He loosened his anorak, checked the butt of the Browning in the cross-draw holster, and stepped down to the road.

'United Nations,' the leading Croat said, mouthing the two words as if he had just learnt them. He had short, dark hair and a handsome, clean-shaven face. Only the yellow teeth would have hindered a career in Nazi propaganda films.

Docherty passed over the UN and Croat accreditations and examined the three men behind the leader. Between them they had enough intelligence for a cabbage, he decided. One was still listening to the Walkman clipped to his belt.

'I speak English,' the leader said, looking at Docherty.

'Good,' the PC replied. What do you want, he thought – a diploma?

'What is in truck?' he asked.

'Sick children.'

'I see,' the leader said, and strode off up the road, only missing half a step when he saw Hajrija in the cab. Razor smiled down at him.

At the rear of the lorry Docherty called out a warning to Chris, and slid the back door up. The Croat surveyed the improvised ambulance.

'Where are children from?' he asked.

'Many places,' Docherty said. He signalled with his eyes for Chris to join them in the road.

The Croat walked back down the other side of the lorry and stared in at Hajrija. The other three men in black had moved closer, but the Uzis were still loose in their hands. 'The woman is not United Nations,' he said.

271

'She is . . .'

'The children are Muslims,' the Croat said. 'But you can go. Only leave the woman.' He smiled up at Razor, who smiled back at him.

There were a few pregnant seconds of silence.

'I said, leave the woman behind, motherfucker!'

Razor took Docherty's signal, pulled the Browning up from under the window and shot the man through the forehead.

Docherty and Chris were both drawing their Brownings at the same moment, the lessons of the Regiment's 'Killing House' training ground flashing through their minds, as they took out the three fumbling targets in front of them. Only one Uzi was fired, a short burst at the sky, as its holder fell backwards.

The man with the Walkman had got entangled in his earphone wires, and yanked the cassette player off his belt with the Uzi. The last sound to echo in the silence was of a spilt cassette tape landing in the middle of the road.

Docherty looked around. In the cab Razor had his arm around Hajrija. Chris had disappeared, probably to reassure the children. Another four men lay dead in front of him.

He walked across and began pulling the corpses out of the road. The tape caught his eye, and he picked it up. The writing was in English. The album was called *Cowboys from Hell*, by a group he'd never heard of called Pantera. One song was called 'Psycho Holiday', another 'Message in Blood'.

He looked at the four black-clad Croats, who had taken so much more trouble with their clothes than they had with their hearts or minds. If he looked inside the cabin, he'd probably find some sort of dope, some German beer or American Pepsi, a few hard-core porn magazines. All these men had needed for their perfect life was a woman toy, and they had just died trying to steal one.

Docherty looked up at the twisted rocks, the alien landscape. He had wanted to believe that this was a foreign war, a throwback, but somewhere deep inside himself he had always known otherwise. This was a war that came from the heart of what the world had become.

He climbed wearily back aboard the lorry, and nodded for Razor to resume their journey down to the sea.

Epilogue

They arrived in Split early in the evening, with the sun hanging low over the sea like a tourist postcard. The children were passed over to the care of the town's hospital, and hopes were high that all would recover. Where they would end up seemed to be anybody's guess. Once fit, Docherty guessed, they would just become one more group begging a home from a reluctant rest of Europe.

The SAS men were made to wait almost thirty-six hours, without explanation, for a flight home to the UK. After enduring an irritatingly lengthy stopover in Germany, they arrived at RAF Brize Norton shortly after nine in the morning. Rain was falling from a dull sky as they walked across the tarmac.

Barney Davies was there to meet them, along with an MoD man in civilian dress named Lavington. Before the tired returnees knew what was happening they found themselves being corralled into a small office. A tray had been set out with cups and a percolator full of coffee.

Docherty dropped his bergen on the floor. 'I'm going to ring my wife,' he said, and started back for the door.

'Can you do that afterwards, please?' the MoD man asked coldly.

Docherty stopped, turned and stared at him.

'She has already been informed that you're all right,' Lavington said.

'I want to hear her voice,' Docherty said quietly, and walked out of the office.

Lavington watched him go, a thoughtful look on his face, then turned his attention to Hajrija. Having apparently satisfied himself that she wasn't a member of the SAS, he asked the others who she was and what she was doing there.

'She wanted to see if England really was full of pricks like you,' Razor told him, at which point Barney Davies suggested they all have some coffee.

Out in the building's foyer Docherty was listening to the phone ring in Liam McCall's Glasgow house. 'Hello?' a voice answered in the familiar husky accent.

'Isabel,' he said.

'Jamie,' she said back, remembering how she'd felt when Barney Davies rang her two evenings before. Then she'd just uttered the two words '*dios gracias*' and almost collapsed with relief. 'Where are you?' she said now, her voice so happy it made him want to sing.

'Brize Norton. I'll be home tonight. Somehow or other.'

'I can't wait,' she said.

A few minutes later he was walking back to the office, wondering if it was worth even being polite. Probably, he thought. The others had careers to think about.

He found everyone drinking coffee in strained silence. After pouring himself a cup he sat down opposite Lavington. 'Let's get on with it, then,' he said.

'Very well,' the MoD man said stiffly. 'This is only a preliminary debriefing, of course. First, where is John Reeve? Your orders were clear — to bring him home.'

'He didn't want to come,' Docherty said. 'And there was no way we could have brought him against his will, even if I had thought that doing so was in anyone's best interests. Which I did not.'

Lavington pointed out that they were paid to obey the Crown, not formulate policy on their own. Docherty told him that in the SAS they tended to believe that the man on the spot was usually the man best placed to take decisions. 'John Reeve is looking after his children,' he added, 'as any father would.'

'If you could get out with a lorryload of children,' Lavington insisted, 'then so could he.'

'He also has a wife and her parents to worry about . . .'

'And a private army to lead.'

'He has no such thing,' Docherty lied. 'He may have given them some advice in the early days, but that's all. And I might add that we didn't all get out with the children. One of my men is still on the plane, in a coffin.'

Lavington looked at him. He could see they were all tired, he said. The debriefing would have to be postponed. After telling Barney Davies that he would call the next day the MoD man made his exit.

'Is that who sent us?' Razor asked disgustedly.

'No, I sent you,' Davies said. 'His masters sent the message you received in Zavik. I'm sorry about that, but the MoD and the politicians were adamant, and there was nothing I could do.' He gave them a wintry smile. 'I assumed you would ignore the part about Reeve, unless he really did need putting in a strait-jacket.'

'He's one of the sanest men in Bosnia,' Docherty said, 'though that's not saying very much.'

'And is he running an efficient private army?' Davies asked.

Docherty grinned at him. 'What do you think?'

*   *   *

Three days later Docherty was back in Hereford for Corporal Damien Robson's memorial service. Many of the men who had served with him were in attendance, including Chris and Razor. Joss Wynwood, who had led the patrol out of Colombia four years earlier, flew back from Hong Kong to be there.

An appreciable number of family members had also driven down from Sunderland, and after the service they were given a guided tour of the Stirling Lines barracks by Docherty and Barney Davies. Most walked around with a sort of wide-eyed wonder, as if they couldn't believe that their relation really had lived and worked there for the past seven years. From the conversations he had with several of them, Docherty got the impression that the Dame, though undoubtedly much loved, had been even more of a mystery to his family than he had been to his comrades in the SAS.

The day after the service Chris Martinson drove down through Hay-on-Wye and up into the Black Mountains. He had binoculars and book with him, but on this day his heart wasn't in it. Even the sudden appearance of a merlin only produced a brief burst of enthusiasm.

Over the last week he had been turning several important things over in his mind, trying to arrange them in some sort of pattern which made sense of his life, both now and in the future. The Dame's death had not shocked him – how could a soldier's death ever be surprising? – but some of the things they had seen in Bosnia continued to haunt him. The Sarajevo hospital for one, and the faces of the children they had brought out of Zavik and left to an uncertain future in Split.

He was over thirty now, and more than half convinced

that it was time to consider a change of career. He already possessed sufficient medical skills to be useful in much of the Third World, and he had written off for more information about how to turn these skills into whatever qualifications he might need.

Chris didn't know how or why, but the time in Bosnia had tipped some balance in his mind. When it came down to it, he felt more comfortable helping children than he did killing evil men. He was not running away from the world as it was. He didn't just want out. If anything, he wanted in.

He looked up at the grey clouds scudding across the Welsh sky and wondered about the bird life in India. Or Africa. Or anywhere he could feel needed.

Razor was also aware that his life had reached a crossroads, and a happy one at that. He could still hardly believe that Hajrija had come to England with him, or how much they had enjoyed each other in the days that had followed.

He guessed he had the long wait at Split to thank. If she hadn't read all those English papers, and got so incensed at their reporting of the war in her native country, then she might not have come. 'Why don't you go back to journalism, then?' Docherty had suggested. 'Come back to England with us and start pestering them with the truth.'

Maybe she had just been waiting for the excuse, but she had come in any case, and they had enjoyed what felt like a four-day honeymoon in a Hereford hotel, emerging to eat and drink and ride round the wintry countryside, going back in to make love and talk and make love again.

Razor couldn't remember ever feeling happier, and the only shadow on this happiness was a slight but persistent sense of guilt. How could something so good, he asked himself, have come out of something so bad?

A week or so later David Owen and Cyrus Vance came up with their peace plan for Bosnia, which involved breaking the country into ten semi-autonomous and ethnically based cantons. The central government, although remaining in existence, would have little in the way of real power.

John and Nena Reeve heard the news as they sat round the kitchen table listening to the World Service. 'Maybe it means peace,' Reeve said.

Nena disagreed, but she didn't say so. Reeve had always had a child's naïvety when it came to politics.

They were both living in her parents' house, but despite parental disapproval were not sharing his bed. She had eventually told him the full story of what had happened to her, almost as much to hear herself tell it as for him to hear.

He had not disbelieved her, or accused her of not resisting; he had not behaved the way most of the Muslim women expected their men to behave. For that she supposed she was grateful, but she had expected nothing less, and rather hoped for more.

When it came down to it he didn't know how to react. He wanted to help, but he didn't know how to give himself, and that was all she wanted. He was still a child in more than politics, she reluctantly admitted to herself.

She looked across the table at him, and he grinned at her. This is the child who saved a town, she thought.

*   *   *

The trouble with being a soldier, Docherty thought to himself, was that you tended to see your comrades at their best and other people at their worst. Which, all in all, engendered a somewhat warped view of humanity.

He stared out at the islands and highlands silhouetted by the rising sun, and wondered whether humankind could claim any credit for its collective sense of what was beautiful.

The family was on its way back from a long weekend in Harris, where they had stayed with Docherty's friend, the retired priest Liam McCall. They had been lucky to hit one of those rare calms in the Hebrides' winter storm: the children had been able to run wild on the beach without being blown away to the mainland, and at night, while they slept the sort of sleep only fresh air exercise could induce, the three adults had been able to talk and work their way through a couple of bottles of malt whisky.

Docherty had so far been reluctant, without really knowing why, to tell his wife much of what had happened in Bosnia, but in Liam McCall's cottage, with the two people he cared for most in the world ready to listen, he found himself going through the whole story.

'The centre cannot hold . . . mere anarchy is loosed upon the world,' Liam had murmured, quoting his beloved Yeats.

'Aye,' Docherty had agreed. 'In Bosnia there was no sign of any centre that I could see.' He had stared into the whisky glass and said, surprising himself: 'And I think I've lost my own, at least for a while.'

'I lost mine a long time ago,' Isabel had said softly. 'But you can live without one. You can even love without one.'

For a second he had felt almost terrified, catching a dreadful glimpse of a world in which there was nothing to hang on to. And then his eyes had met Isabel's in a sharing that seemed infinitely sad.

Here now, on the deck of the ferry, with the sunlight dancing across the waves, the love of his life by his side, and their children running riot somewhere else on the ship, that world seemed far away.

But then the light was always brighter, coming out of the dark.

SOLDIER P: SAS

NIGHT FIGHTERS
IN FRANCE

SOLDIER P: SAS

NIGHT FIGHTERS
IN FRANCE

Shaun Clarke

Prelude

Operation Overlord, the Allied invasion of Europe, commenced on the night of 5 June 1944 with the concentrated bombing of German positions on the north coast of France by 750 heavy bombers, an onslaught against the Normandy defence batteries by hundreds of medium bombers, the clearing of broad sea highways thirty miles long by 309 British, 22 American and 16 Canadian minesweepers, and landings by parachute and glider in the vicinity of the east bank of the Caen canal and astride the Cherbourg peninsula. Fires were already burning all along the coast of Normandy, acting as beacons to the invasion fleet, when, just as dawn broke on D-Day, 6 June, Fortresses and Liberators of the US 8th and 9th Air Forces, covered by an umbrella of fighters, dropped 2400 tons of bombs on the British beaches and nearly 2000 tons on the American beaches.

Shortly after dawn, the warships heading for Normandy opened fire with their big guns, covering the coastline with spectacular flashes and clouds of brownish cordite while the British 'Hunt'-class destroyers raced in to engage the enemy's shore batteries. To the west, American destroyers were doing the same, with the heavier guns of their battleships hurling fourteen, fifteen and sixteen-inch

1

shells on to the beaches and the German fortifications beyond them. The final 'softening up' was achieved by rocket-firing boats which disappeared momentarily behind sheets of flame as their deadly payload rained down on the beaches, adding to the general bedlam by causing more mighty explosions, which threw up mushrooms of flying soil and swirling smoke.

At 0630 hours American forces swarmed on to the western shores, where a broad bay sweeps round to Cherbourg. They were followed fifty minutes later by British and Canadian troops, put ashore by more than 5000 landing-craft and 'Rhino' ferries on the eastern beaches. Many of the assault craft were caught by sunken angle-irons and, with their bottoms ripped open, foundered before they made the shore; others were blown up by mines.

Nevertheless the men, each heavily burdened with steel helmet, pack and roll, two barracks bags, rations, two cans of water, gas mask, rifle and bayonet, bandoliers of ammunition, hand-grenades and, in many cases, parts of heavy weapons such as machine-guns and mortars – a total weight never less than 132lb – continued to pour ashore on both the eastern and western fronts, advancing into the murderous rifle and machine-gun fire of the Germans still holed up in their concrete bunkers overlooking the beaches. Likewise savaged by a hail of enemy gunfire were the Royal Engineers and American sappers, who continued bravely to explode buried German mines to create 'safe' paths for the advancing Allied troops.

Within minutes, the beaches, obscured in a pall of smoke, were littered with dead bodies and black shell holes. The sounds of machine-guns and mortars increased the already appalling din. Out at sea, the guns of Allied cruisers, battleships and destroyers continued a bombardment that would account for 56,769 shells of various calibres. Simultaneously, the Air Force continued to pound the enemy positions: more than 1300 Liberators and Fortresses, escorted by fighters, bombed the German positions for another two and a half hours.

By evening the Germans overlooking the beach had been pushed well back and Allied forces were as far as six to eight miles inland. While British Commandos and American Rangers were having spectacular successes on their separate fronts, a Royal Marine Commando, even after the loss of five of its fourteen landing-craft, fought through Les Roquettes and La Rosière, quelled several German machine-gun and mortar nests, and finally captured Port-en-Bessin. There, making contact with the Americans, it linked up the whole Allied front in Normandy and paved the way for the major push through France.

Strategically vital bridges, locks and canals soon fell to the Allies and in many small towns and villages French men and women emerged from rubble and clouds of dust to wave the tricolour and rapturously greet their liberators.

Even though German resistance was heavy, by the evening of the first day a bridgehead twenty-five miles wide had been established, forming a continuous front, with American forces in the Cotentin peninsula and just east of the River Vire, and Canadian and British troops on the left flank. To the east, British troops advanced to within three miles of Caen, while to the west US forces penetrated to a depth of five miles south of Colleville and crossed the River Aure to the east of Trévières. Two days later, Isigny, six miles from Carentan, was captured. Carentan itself fell to US troops on the 12th.

Violent fighting broke out around Caen, with both sides changing positions constantly, but the Americans entered St-Sauveur-le-Vicomte on the 16th, reached the main defences of Cherbourg on the 21st and, after fierce fighting, but with the aid of an intensive aerial bombardment and artillery fire, captured the town on the 27th, taking 20,000 German prisoners of war.

By this time, British troops had cut the road and railway between Caen and Villers-Bocage to reach the River Odon at a point some two miles north of Evrecy. A strong bridgehead was established which resisted the counter-attacks of eight Panzer and SS Panzer divisions. When the Germans retreated, the bridgehead was secured and enlarged.

On 3 July, having cleared the north-west tip of the Cotentin peninsula, the US 1st Army advanced in a blinding rainstorm on a wide front south of St-Sauveur-le-Vicomte. By the following day they had captured the high ground to the north of

La Haye-du-Puits and, after eight days of fierce fighting, finally captured the town. Simultaneously, other US troops were battling their way up the steep, wooded slopes of the Forêt de Mont Castre and advancing down the Carentan–Périers road to force a passage across the Vire in the direction of St-Jean-de-Daye, which fell on the 8th. By the 11th they were advancing through waterlogged country to take up positions within three miles of the vital German communications centre of St Lô.

British and Canadian forces, meanwhile, had attacked eastwards towards Caen, and early on the 8th, after a concentrated bombardment from heavy and medium bombers, launched an attack that carried them to the outskirts of the town. Supported by sustained fire from massed artillery and British ships, they took the northern part of the town by nightfall.

St Lô fell to the US 1st Army on 18 July after eight days of bloody fighting. Following the capture of the northern part of Caen, the British 2nd Army, under Montgomery, launched an attack southeast of the town. Over 2000 British and American heavy and medium bombers dropped nearly 8000 tons of bombs in an area of little more than seventy square miles, blasting a 7000-yard-wide passage that enabled armoured formations to cross the River Orne by specially constructed bridges and drive strong wedges in the direction of Cagny and Bourguébus.

While this armoured advance was temporarily halted by a combination of determined enemy resistance and violent rainstorms, Canadian troops were successfully clearing the southern suburbs of Caen and British infantry were thrusting out eastwards towards Troarn to clear several villages in the area. A further Canadian attack across the Orne, west of Caen, resulted in the capture of Fleury and the clearing of the east bank of the river for three miles due south of the latter town.

A week after the British 2nd Army's offensive began, the US 1st Army attacked west of St Lô, captured Marigny and St-Gilles, then fanned out in three columns, west, south and south-west, to capture Canisy, Lessay, Périers and Coutances, and join up with US forces advancing from the east. By nightfall of the 30th, American armour had swept through Bréhal and, the following day, captured Avranches and Graville. Further east, Bérigny was captured.

Aiding the American success were two attacks in the British sector: one by the Canadians down the Caen–Falaise road, the other in the area of Gaumont, where, after a heavy air bombardment, a British armoured and infantry force secured Cahagnes and Le Bény-Bocage. Five more villages, including the strategically important Evrecy and Esquay, south-west of Caen, were captured on 4 August and Villers-Bocage, which was by now in ruins, the next day.

American armoured columns reached Dinan that same week, turned south and, heading for Brest, liberated several Breton towns *en route*. Rennes, the capital of Brittany, was captured on the 4th and the River Vilaine was reached two days later, sealing off the Brittany peninsula. The fall of Vannes, Lorient, St-Malo, Nantes and Angers soon followed, and US patrols had crossed the Loire by 11 August.

With British and Canadians, plus the 1st Polish Armoured Division, advancing from the north, and the Americans, along with the French 2nd Armoured Division, closing in from the west and south, a large part of the German 7th Army was almost surrounded. Their only escape route – the narrow Falaise–Argentan Gap – was sealed by the Americans advancing from Le Mans, which they had liberated on 9 August.

By 19 August, the Falaise Gap was closed and, after a terrible slaughter of German troops, whose dead choked the village streets and surrounding fields, the sad remnants of von Kluge's 7th Army were taken prisoner.

Four days earlier, on 15 August, General Eisenhower had taken command of the Allied Expeditionary Force, leaving Montgomery at the head of the 21st Army Group, which consisted of General Dempsey's British 2nd Army and General Crerar's 1st Canadian Army. Lieutenant-General Omar Bradley was at the head of the 12th Army Group, comprising General Hodge's US 1st Army and General Patton's 3rd Army.

The latter was driving towards Dijon as other Allied forces advanced from the south.

To aid the advance of Patton's 3rd Army, the Allies planned airborne landings in the Orléans Gap, and to soften the enemy before the landings, they decided to drop a squadron of men and jeeps by parachute in the area of Auxerre, central France. The squadron's task would be to engage in a series of daring hit-and-run night raids against German positions to distract the enemy from the landings taking place elsewhere.

While the Allied advance was under way, the French Forces of the Interior (FFI) were seizing high ground in advance of the American armour and engaging in guerrilla warfare, to harass the Germans and protect Allied lines of communication. In central France, the Maquis – Frenchmen who had fled from the Germans and were living in makeshift camps in the forest – were conducting sabotage missions behind enemy lines. Among their tasks were blowing up bridges, putting locomotives out of action, derailing trains, and cutting long-distance underground communications cables between Paris and Berlin. Montgomery, knowing of these activities, decided that the men chosen for the parachute drop should establish a base and make contact with the Maquis.

The men deemed most suitable for this mission, known as Operation Kipling, were those of C Squadron, 1 SAS, based in Fairford, Gloucestershire. Formed in North Africa in 1941, 1 SAS had already

8

gained a reputation for uncommon daring. That reputation would be put to the test over the weeks to come.

1

The men crowding into the briefing room in their heavily guarded camp near Fairford, Gloucestershire on 10 August 1944 were not ordinary soldiers. They were men of uncommon ability, members of the Special Air Service (1 SAS), which had been formed in North Africa in 1941 as a self-contained group tasked with clandestine insertion, long-range reconnaissance patrols behind enemy lines, and sabotage and intelligence-gathering missions, often with the Long Range Desert Group (LRDG).

Originally, 1 SAS had been conceived and formed by Lieutenant David Stirling, a former Scots Guard who, having joined No. 8 Commando, was promptly dispatched to the Middle East on attachment to Colonel Robert Laycock's Layforce. After taking part in many relatively unsuccessful, large-scale raids against German positions along the North African coast, Stirling became convinced that raids with small, specially trained units would be more effective. In the spring of 1941, hospitalized in Alexandria after a parachute accident, he passed the time by formulating his plans for just such a unit, based on the belief that 200 men operating as five-man teams could achieve the surprise necessary to destroy several targets on the same night. Subsequently, with the support of Deputy

Chief of Staff General Neil Ritchie, L Detachment, Special Air Service Brigade, was born.

The new SAS Brigade's first raids behind enemy lines in November 1941, which involved parachute drops, were a complete failure. However, later raids against Axis airfields at Sirte, Tamit, Mersa Brega and Agedabia, during which the men were driven to their targets and returned to base by the highly experienced LRDG, were remarkably successful, gaining L Detachment a legendary reputation. By October 1942, when L Detachment was given full regimental status as 1 SAS, it had grown to include the 390 troops of the existing 1 SAS, the French Squadron of 94 men, the Greek Sacred Squadron of 114 men, the Special Boat Section of 55 men and the Special Interrogation Group.

Lieutenant Stirling was captured in January 1943, incarcerated in Gavi, Italy, from where he escaped no less than four times, then transferred to the German high-security prison at Colditz. In April 1943, while Stirling was embarking on a series of daring escapes from Gavi, the French and Greek Squadrons were returned to their respective national armies, the Special Boat Section became a separate unit, the Special Boat Squadron (SBS), under the command of Major Jellicoe, and 1 SAS became the Special Raiding Squadron. In May 1943 2 SAS came into existence and, later that year, the Special Raiding Squadron reverted to the title of 1 SAS. Finally, in January 1944, the SAS Brigade was formed under the umbrella of

1st Airborne Corps. It consisted of 1 and 2 SAS, 3 SAS (3 French Parachute Battalion), 4 SAS (4 French Parachute Battalion), 5 SAS (Belgian Independent Parachute Company), HQ French Demi-Brigade, F Squadron, GHQ Liaison Regiment and 20 Liaison HQ, which was the SAS link with the Free French.

The men crowding into the briefing room at Fairford, however, were the British founder members of the SAS Brigade, having joined it in North Africa in 1941 and taken part in its first daring raids. The 'Head Shed' in charge of the briefing and now taking up his position in front of the covered blackboard on a raised platform was the squadron commander, Captain Patrick 'Paddy' Callaghan, No. 3 Commando, an accomplished boxer and Irish rugby international who had, at the time of the formation of L Detachment, been languishing in a military-police cell in Cairo, waiting to be court-martialled. Though normally an amiable, courteous man, Callaghan had a fiery temper and had often landed in trouble because of it. Nevertheless, he was one of the most able officers in the SAS, often mentioned in dispatches for his bravery in action. Thus, though he had not been promoted since 1941, his abilities had been officially recognized when his superiors put him in charge of C Squadron.

Standing beside the heavily built Captain Callaghan was his slim, handsome second in command, former Lieutenant, now Captain, Derek 'Dirk' Greaves. Like Stirling, Greaves had been a member of No. 9 Commando, posted to General Wavell's Middle Eastern

Army on attachment to Layforce. With Layforce he had taken part in raids against the Axis forces in Rhodes, Crete, Syria, around Tobruk and all along the seaward side of Libya's Cyrenaica Desert, before being wounded, meeting Lieutenant Stirling in the Scottish Military Hospital in Alexandria and becoming his right-hand man in the formation of L Detachment. Single when with Layforce, he had since married his Scottish fiancée, Mary Radnor, and now missed her dreadfully, though he took comfort from the knowledge that she was living safely in the family home in Edinburgh, and now eight months pregnant with their first child.

'All right, men, quieten down!' Captain Greaves shouted. 'We haven't got all day!'

When the spirited babble continued even as Captain Callaghan was taking up his position in the middle of the dais, Sergeant Ralph Lorrimer bawled: 'Shut your mouths and let the boss speak! Are you men deaf, or what?'

Formerly of the Dorset Regiment, then with the LRDG, an expert in desert tracking and warfare, but also unbeatable with the Browning 12-gauge autoloader, Lorrimer had been approached by Stirling and Greaves to join L Detachment when he was spending his leave in Tiger Lil's brothel in Cairo's notorious Sharia el Berka quarter. He was therefore respected by the men for more reasons than one and, when he shouted for them to be silent, they promptly obeyed and settled down to listen to the Head Shed.

'Can I just open,' Captain Callaghan asked rhetorically, 'by saying that I know how frustrated you men have been, stuck here in Gloucestershire, when the battle for Europe is under way in France.'

'Damned right, boss!' Lance-Corporal Jack 'Jacko' Dempster cried out. 'The best bloody brigade in the British Army and they leave us sitting here on our arses while lesser men do all the fighting. A right bunch of prats, that's how we feel.'

As the rest of the men burst into laughter or murmurs of agreement, Sergeant Lorrimer snapped: 'We don't need your bloody nonsense at this time in the morning, Jacko. Just shut up and let the boss speak or I'll have you out in a guard box.'

'Yes, Sarge!' the lance-corporal replied with a smirk.

Nevertheless, Lorrimer was grinning too, for he had a great deal of respect for Dempster and the rest of the 'other ranks'. Jacko, as everyone knew him, was just one of the many men in the room who had been founder members of L Detachment when it came into existence in 1941. Known as the 'Originals', they included Sergeants Bob Tappman, Pat Riley and Ernie Bond; Corporals Jim Almonds, 'Benny' Bennett, Richard 'Rich' Burgess and Reg Seekings; and former Privates, now Lance-Corporals, Neil Moffatt, Harry 'Harry-boy' Turnball and, of course, Jacko Dempster.

Each one of these men had gone into the North African desert with minimal knowledge of desert warfare, learnt all there was to know from the Long Range Desert Group, and then taken part in daring, mostly successful, raids against Axis airfields located well behind enemy lines. Remarkably, only one of them – the revered Lieutenant John 'Jock' Steel Lewes – had died during those raids. As a brutal climax to the final raid of that period – a simultaneous attack by three different groups against Sirte, Tamit and Nofilia – the survivors, all now present in the briefing room, had made it back to the forward operating base after an epic trek across the desert, most of them practically crawling into their camp at Jalo Oasis. Though they never openly said so, they were proud of what they had accomplished and stuck together because of it, keeping themselves slightly apart from the other, more recent arrivals in the SAS Brigade.

Furthermore, as Sergeant Lorrimer knew only too well, the Originals had developed a low boredom threshold, and this had caused immense frustration when, at the end of 1943, 1 SAS were returned to Scotland for training and operations in northern Europe. Initially they were kept busy establishing a base near the remote village of Darvel, east of Kilmarnock; but in May the following year the SAS Brigade had been moved to Fairford, where the men had been able to do little more than constant retraining in preparation for Operation Overlord. Small wonder they had become even more frustrated when D-Day passed without them. Now Lorrimer was hoping that what the CO was about to tell them would make amends for that.

'Well, gentlemen,' Captain Callaghan continued, 'to end the suspense, we've been assigned a specific task in France and it commences forthwith.'

When the cheering, clapping and whistling had died down, the captain continued: 'At this moment, General Patton's 3rd Army is driving south towards Dijon.'

'Mad Dog Patton!' shouted Corporal Richard 'Rich' Burgess.

'I wouldn't let him hear you say that, Corporal,' Callaghan admonished him, 'because although he may seem mad to you, he's a damned good soldier and proud of it.'

'Sorry, boss.'

'Anyway, to aid Patton's advance, Montgomery has asked for airborne landings in the Orléans Gap.'

'That's us?' Lance-Corporal Harry 'Harry-boy' Turnball asked hopefully.

'No,' Callaghan replied. '*Our* task is to soften up the enemy before the landings – and to distract them from the landings – by engaging in a series of hit-and-run raids against their positions. For this mission, Operation Kipling, you and your jeeps will be inserted by parachute in central France. Once you've all been landed, you'll establish a base, lie low and make contact with the Maquis.'

'Frogs?' Lance-Corporal Neil Moffatt asked dubiously.

'French partisans,' Captain Callaghan corrected him. '"*Maquis*" is a Corsican word meaning "scrub"

16

or "bush". The Maquis are so called because when the Krauts introduced compulsory labour in the occupied countries, many men fled their homes to live in rudimentary camps in the scrubland and forests. Since then, with the aid of our Special Operations Executive and America's Office of Strategic Studies, they've been engaged in highly successful sabotage activities behind German lines. They may be Frogs to you, but they're a bunch of tough, courageous Frogs, so don't knock them.'

'Sorry, boss,' Neil mumbled.

'Good or not, why do we need 'em?' Rich Burgess asked.

'Because we believe their local knowledge will make them invaluable for planning raids, particularly those behind enemy lines.'

'Are they troublesome?' Sergeant Bob Tappman asked.

Callaghan nodded. 'Unfortunately, yes, and for a couple of reasons.'

'Which are?'

'The Maquis are split between those who support General de Gaulle's Free French and those who sympathize with the communists. Unfortunately, the latter believe, as do the communists, that de Gaulle is no more than Britain and America's stooge, to be used and then discarded.'

'Bloody marvellous!' Corporal Reg Seekings murmured, then asked: 'Anything else?'

'Yes,' Callaghan said. 'A lot of the Maquis have

shown more interest in storing weapons for after the war, to use against de Gaulle's supporters, than they've shown in actually killing Germans.'

'Beautiful!' Jacko said, laughing. 'I can't wait to work with them.'

'Also,' Callaghan pressed on, 'the SOE views the Maquis as its own concern, has its own teams to arm and organize them, and therefore won't take kindly to us becoming involved. In fact, they've already unofficially voiced their complaints about the plan to insert us in what they view as their own territory.'

'Well, stuff the SOE!' Rich exploded.

'I agree,' said Bob Tappman. 'Those sods don't know anything about the real world. We can deal with the Maquis better than they can, so let's go in and get on with it.'

'Nevertheless,' Callaghan continued, 'even given these negative points, we *do* believe that with the advent of D-Day and the continuing advance into Europe, the Maquis will be more co-operative than they've been in the past. They'll want the war to end as soon as possible . . .'

'So that they can get stuck into each other,' Jacko interrupted, copping a laugh from the other men.

'. . . to enable them to sort out their differences,' Callaghan continued, ignoring the interjection. 'We're banking on that.'

'And what if it doesn't work out that way?' Bob Tappman asked bluntly.

Callaghan nodded to Greaves, then stepped aside to

let his fellow captain take centre stage. 'Where we're going,' Greaves explained, 'the situation is changing constantly, so our own position there will be highly unpredictable. Therefore we have to be ready to change our plans at a moment's notice. What I'm about to outline to you is a preliminary course of action that'll be subject to changing circumstances on the ground.'

'I love surprises,' said Jacko.

'I should point out, first thing,' Greaves continued, 'that we won't be alone. The Special Air Service Brigade, consisting of British, French and Belgian components, was flown into France shortly after D-Day and has since set up a wide network of bases in Brittany, the Châtillon Forest, east of Auxerre, the area around Poitiers and the Vosges. Some of these groups are working hand in glove with the Maquis; others are out there on their own. Either way, they were inserted in order to recce the areas, receive stores, and engage in active operations only after our arrival.'

'So when and where do we arrive?' Bob Tappman asked.

In response, Greaves picked up a pointer and tugged the canvas covering off the blackboard, to reveal a map drawn in white chalk and showing the area of central France bounded by Orléans to the west, Vesoul to the east, Paris to the north and Dijon to the south. 'We'll parachute in here,' he said, tapping a marked area between Rennes

19

and Orléans, 'and then make our way by jeep through the forest paths north of Orléans. The vehicles will be dropped by parachute once you men have landed. They're modified American Willys jeeps equipped, as they were in North Africa, with twin Vickers K guns front and rear, supplemented with 0.5-inch Browning heavy machine-guns. The modified versions have a top speed of approximately 60mph and a range of 280 miles, though this can be extended by adding extra fuel tanks, so you should get anywhere you want to go with a minimum of problems.'

'And where do we want to go?' Jacko asked.

'With the recent American breakthrough at Avranches, we've been presented with a fluid front through which small vehicles can pass. The American Advance Party already has one troop spread across a direct line from Normandy to Belfort, roughly across the centre of France. With those men already in place, and with ensured air supply for our columns, we're in a good position to cause chaos behind the Germans who're withdrawing in front of the US 3rd Army led by General Patton. Therefore, in order to lend support to Patton's advance and help his 3rd Army reach Dijon, you men will head initially for the Châtillon Forest and, once there, make contact with the Maquis. You will then learn everything you can about the area from the Maquis and, using that knowledge, embark on a series of hit-and-run raids, preferably by night, against enemy positions.'

'How far do we take the raids, boss?' Bob Tappman asked in his customary thoughtful manner.

'Nothing too daring, Sergeant,' Greaves replied. 'Nothing too risky. The point is to harass them – not engage in unnecessary or lengthy fire-fights – and to sabotage their channels of communication and, where possible, destroy their transport. The task is harassment and distraction, rather than elimination – so just get in and out as quickly as possible. And no heroics, please.'

'You won't get any heroics from us, boss,' Jacko said, lying for all of them. 'No one here wants a bullet up his arse if he can possibly avoid it. We all want to live to a ripe old age.'

In fact, Jacko was not alone in thinking that the last good time he had had was a month ago, when on a weekend pass to London. After the peace and quiet of Gloucestershire, he and the other Originals had been thrilled to find the West End so lively, with staff cars and troop carriers rumbling up and down the streets, Allied bombers constantly roaring overhead, protected by Spitfires and other fighter planes, flying to and from France; the pavements thronged with men and women in the uniforms of many nations; the parks, though surrounded by anti-aircraft guns, packed with picnicking servicemen and civilians; ARP wardens inspecting the ruins of bombed buildings while firemen put out the latest fires; and pubs, cafés, cinemas and theatres, albeit with black-out curtains across the windows and their doorways protected behind sandbags, packed with people bent on enjoying themselves.

Even during the night, when diminishing numbers of German bombers flew over to pound London and V-1 and V-2 flying bombs caused further devastation, the city was packed with soldiers, pilots, sailors and their women, all having a good time despite the wailing air-raid sirens, exploding bombs, whining doodlebugs, blazing buildings and racing ambulances. Compared with tranquil Gloucestershire, the capital was a hive of romance and excitement, for all the horrors of war. In truth, it was where most of the Originals wanted to be – either on leave in London or taking part in the liberation of Europe. The latter was, at least, now happening and they would soon be part of it. That made Jacko, and most of the others, feel much better. They were back in business at last.

'What's the transport situation?' Sergeant Pat Riley asked.

'Handley-Page Halifax heavy bombers specially modified to carry men and supplies and drop jeeps and trailers from its bomb bay,' said Greaves.

'Bloody sitting ducks,' Neil Moffatt whispered to his mate, Harry 'Harry-boy' Turnball.

'Not any more,' the captain said to Neil, having overheard his whispered remark. 'In fact, the Halifaxes are now armed with two .303-inch Browning machine-guns in the nose turret, four in the tail turret, and two in manual beam positions, so we should have adequate protection should we be attacked by enemy fighters during the flight.'

'Thanks, boss, for that reassurance,' Neil said wryly.

'Is it true, as some of us have heard, that we're having problems in getting enough aircraft?' Rich Burgess asked.

'Unfortunately, yes. Because we don't yet have our own planes, all arrangements for aerial transport have to be co-ordinated by 1st Airborne Corps and 38 Group RAF at Netheravon and Special Forces HQ. This means that we practically have to bid for aircraft and we don't always get enough for our requirements. For this reason, you should expect to be inserted in batches over two or three successive nights; likewise for the jeeps.'

'Which means that those who go earliest have the longest, most dangerous wait on the ground,' Rich said. 'More sitting ducks, in fact.'

'Correct,' Greaves replied with a grin. 'Which means in turn that the most experienced men – including you, Corporal – will be in the first aircraft off the ground.'

'Gee, thanks, boss,' Jacko said, imitating an American accent with no great deal of skill.

'Do we take off from Netheravon?' Bob Tappman asked.

'No. From RAF Station 1090, Down Ampney, not far from here. Station 1090 will also be giving us support throughout our period in France.'

'So when do we get out of here,' Rich asked, 'and get to where it's all happening?'

Greaves simply glanced enquiringly at the CO, Captain Callaghan, who stepped forward to say: 'Tomorrow night. You'll be kitted out in the morning, collect and manually test your weapons throughout the afternoon, and embark at 2250 hours, to insert in central France just before midnight. Any final questions?'

As the response was no more than a lot of shaking heads, Callaghan wrapped up the briefing and sent the men back to their barracks with instructions to pack as much as they could before lights out. They needed no encouragement.

2

Next morning the men rolled off their steel-framed beds at first light, raced to the toilets, then had a speedy cold shower and shaved. Cleaned and jolted awake by the icy water, they dressed in Denison smock, dispatch rider's breeches and tough motor-cycle boots. The smock's 1937-pattern webbing pouches held a compass and ammunition for the .455-inch Webley pistol, which was holstered at the hip. Though most of the newer men wore the paratrooper's maroon beret with the SAS's winged-dagger badge, as ordered by a directive of the airborne forces, of which they were presently considered part, the Originals viewed the directive as an insult and were still defiantly wearing their old beige berets.

Once dressed, they 'blacked up' their faces and hands with burnt cork, which they would keep on all day and at least throughout the first night in France. They then left the barracks and crossed the parade ground to the mess hall at the far side, most glancing up just before entering the building to see the many Fortresses, Liberators and escorting Spitfires flying overhead on their way to France for the first of the day's bombing runs. In the mess, which was filled with long, crowded tables, steam, cigarette smoke and a lot of noisy conversation, they had a substantial breakfast of cereal, bacon, fried eggs and baked beans, with buttered toast or fried bread, and hot tea.

'The last day we're going to get decent grub for a long time,' Jacko said to the men at his table, 'so enjoy it, lads. Only two more to go.'

They tucked in as best they could in the time allocated to them, which wasn't much; then, with full bellies, they left the mess hall and walked briskly to the armoury, where they collected their personal and other weapons. These were, apart from the Webley pistol, which they already had, of a wide variety, most chosen by the individual for purely personal reasons and including 9mm Sten sub-machine-guns, Thompson M1 sub-machine-guns, more widely known as 'tommy-guns', and Bren light machine-guns. Their criss-crossed webbing was festooned with thirty and thirty-two-round box magazines, hand-grenades, a Sykes Fairburn commando knife, a bayonet, binoculars and some Lewes bombs – the latter invented by the late Lieutenant John 'Jock' Steel Lewes and first used in the North African desert in 1941.

Burdened down with their weapons, they scrambled into Bedford QL four-wheel-drive trucks and were driven to a firing range at the southern end of the camp. There, as the sun climbed in the sky and the summer heat grew ever stronger, they lay in the dirt and took turns at firing their various weapons, simultaneously practising their aim and checking that the weapons worked perfectly and did not jam. After a couple of hours, they stripped and cleaned the weapons, slung them over their shoulders, then clambered back into the trucks and were driven back to their barracks. There they deposited their weapons in the lockers by their beds before returning to the mess hall for lunch.

'The second-to-last decent meal for a long time,' Jacko reminded his mates, 'so tuck in, lads.'

After lunch they were marched to the quartermaster's store, where they picked up their bergen rucksacks, groundsheets, survival kit, including water bottles, first-aid box, tin mug and plates with eating utensils, and finally their Irvin X-Type parachute. Another hour and a half was spent packing the kit into the rucksacks and checking thoroughly that the chute was in working order, then they strapped the rucksacks, rolled groundsheets and parachute packs neatly to their backs, picked up their weapons and left the barracks like beasts of burden.

'All right, you ugly mugs,' Sergeant Lorrimer growled at the men, standing before them with his clenched fists on his broad hips, as bombers rumbled overhead on their way to France, 'get in a proper line.'

After being lined up and inspected by their respected sergeant, who had an eagle eye and a sharp tongue when it came to error and inefficiency, they were marched to the waiting Bedford trucks, clambered up into them, and were driven out of the base and along country roads to Down Ampney and RAF Station

1090. On the way they passed columns of troop trucks heading away from many other staging areas and bound for various disembarkation points along the coast, where the boats would take them to France to join the Allied forces already there. Above, the cloudy sky was filled with Allied bombers and fighter escorts likewise bound for France. Such sights gave most of the men a surge of excitement that had been missing too long, and eased the bitter disappointment they had been feeling at missing D-Day.

'Nice to know we're joining them at last,' Rich said to his mate Jacko. 'We've been stuck here too long.'

'Bloody right,' Jacko replied, waving at the troops heading in the opposite direction in Bedfords. 'And we'll be there in no time.'

After passing through the heavily guarded main gates of the RAF station, they were driven straight to the airfield, which was lined with both British and American bombers, as well as the fighters that usually escorted them to Germany. Disembarking from the trucks at the edge of the airfield, near a modified Halifax bomber being prepared for flight and the Willys jeeps waiting to be loaded on to it, they were greeted by Captains Callaghan and Greaves.

'How goes it, boss?' Sergeant Lorrimer asked Callaghan.

'Not too well,' Greaves replied bluntly. 'Captain Callaghan and I have wasted most of the day desperately phoning between 1st Airborne Corps and 38

Group RAF at Netheravon and Special Forces Unit, begging for more aircraft for the drop.'

'Bloody waste of time,' Callaghan said curtly to Sergeant Lorrimer and the other ranks grouped around him. 'By the time we'd finished we still had only one Halifax to go with – this one here.'

'Which means,' Greaves cut in, 'that we will, as feared, have to insert the men and jeeps over two or three nights.'

'Wonderful!' Lorrimer murmured sardonically. 'What a bloody waste of time!'

Callaghan nodded wearily, then continued: 'Since then, we've been rushing around trying to finalize routes, supplies and men, and liaise with the units across the water. Everything's now set for the drop, but the insertion will necessarily be tedious. The most experienced men will therefore go first.'

'That's us,' Jacko said.

'Lucky us,' Rich added. 'We'll be on the ground with Krauts all around us and we won't be able to do a sodding thing until the others are dropped. Two or three days of high risk coupled with boredom – a fitting reward for experience.'

'Stop whining,' Lorrimer told him. 'When it's over you'll be boasting about it in every pub in the land. You should *thank* us for this.'

'Gee, thanks, Sarge!' Rich replied.

'All joking aside,' Callaghan said, 'this business of not having our own aircraft means we're practically having to beg for planes that are constantly being allocated elsewhere at the last moment, leaving us strapped. I don't like being at the mercy of 1st Airborne Corps or 38 Group RAF. Sooner or later, we'll have to get our own air support – always there when we want it.'

'I agree,' Greaves said. 'But in the meantime we'll have to live with our single Halifax.'

'All right, let's get to it.'

Already well trained for this specific task, the Originals of C Squadron, who would go on the first flight, removed the twin Vickers K guns normally mounted to the front and rear of the modified American Willys jeeps, along with the 0.5-inch Browning heavy machine-guns, and placed them in separate wooden crates. Then, with the aid of short crates and nets operated by REME, the jeeps were placed in their own crates, which had air bags underneath to cushion the impact on landing. When the lids had been nailed down, four parachute packs were attached to each crate. To facilitate the drop, the aircraft's rear-bay doors had already been removed and a long beam fastened inside, so the men rigged each crated jeep with a complicated arrangement of crash pans and struts, then attached it to the beam to spread the load.

'Those should slow your darling down a bit,' Jacko said to the RAF pilot standing beside him, referring to the crated jeeps and weapons.

The pilot, who was chewing gum, nodded. 'They'll certainly have an adverse effect on the aircraft's performance, but apart from making it sluggish to fly, there should be no great problems.'

'Unless we're attacked by Kraut fighters.'

'Hopefully they'll take care of that,' the pilot said, pointing at the other RAF men who had already entered the Halifax and were taking their positions behind the two .303-inch Brownings in the nose turret and the four in the tail turret. The remaining two guns in the manual beam positions would be handled in an emergency by one of the other seven crew members. 'They'll make up for our sluggishness,' the pilot added.

'Let's hope so,' said Jacko.

By the time the last of the crates had been fixed to the beam in the rear bay, darkness was falling. Once the rest of the RAF crew had taken up their positions in the aircraft and were checking their instruments, the men of C Squadron were ordered to pick up their kit and board the Halifax through the door in the side. After forming a long line, they filed in one by one and sat side by side in the cramped, gloomy space between the fuselage and the supply crates stowed along the middle of the dimly lit hold. Shortly after, the RAF loadmaster slammed the door shut and the four Rolls-Royce Merlin 1390-hp, liquid-cooled engines roared into life, quickly gained power, and gradually propelled the Halifax along the runway and into the air.

Flying at a speed of just over 685mph, the aircraft was soon over the English Channel, though the SAS men in the windowless hold could not see it. All they could see directly in front of them were the wooden supply crates which, though firmly strapped down, shook visibly each time the aircraft rose or fell. Glancing left or right, all that each trooper could see were the profiles of the other men seated along the hold, faces pale and slightly unreal in the weak yellow glow of the overhead lights.

The hold was long, too crowded, horribly noisy and claustrophobic, making many of the men feel uncomfortable, even helpless. This feeling was in no way eased when, over France, the Halifax was attacked by German fighters and the Brownings front and rear roared into action, turning the din in the hold into absolute bedlam. To make matters worse, the Halifax began to buck and dip, obviously attempting to evade the German Stukas, and the piled crates began banging noisily into one another while making disturbing creaking sounds.

'Christ!' Neil shouted, to make himself heard above the noise. 'Those bloody crates are going to break away from their moorings!'

'If they do, they'll fall right on top of us,' his friend Harry-boy Turnball replied, 'and crush more than our balls. They'll bloody flatten us, mate!'

'Or crash right through the fuselage,' Jacko put in, 'and leave a great big fucking hole that would see us sucked out and swept away. Put paid to the lot of us, that would.'

Even above the clamour of the Halifax's engine and

the banging, groaning supply crates, they could hear the whine of the attacking Stukas and the deafening roar of the Brownings.

Suddenly, there was a mighty explosion outside the Halifax, which shuddered from the impact, followed by cheering from the front of the plane. The RAF sergeant acting as dispatcher, standing near the crated jeeps in the bomb bay, gave the thumbs up.

'They must have knocked out one of those Kraut fighters,' Rich said. 'I just wish I could see it.'

'Right,' Jacko replied. 'Bloody frustrating being stuck in here while all that's going on outside. Makes a man feel helpless. I'd rather be down there on the ground, seeing what's going on.'

'Too right,' Rich agreed.

In fact, they didn't have long to wait. The buzz of the Stukas faded away, the Brownings ceased firing, and the Halifax, which had been dipping and shaking, settled back into normal, steady flight. Ten minutes later, it banked towards the drop zone (DZ) and the dispatcher opened the door near the bomb bay, letting the angry wind rush in.

'Five minutes to zero hour,' he informed the men, shouting above the combined roar of the aircraft's engines and the incoming wind, which beat brutally at the seated men. 'On your feet, lads.'

Standing up, the SAS paratroopers fixed their static lines to the designated strong points in the fuselage and then waited until the dispatcher had checked the connections. This check was particularly important as

the static lines were designed to jerk open the chutes
as each man fell clear of the aircraft. If the static line
was not fixed properly to the fuselage, it would slip
free, the canopy would not open and the unlucky
paratrooper would plunge to his death. A man's life
could therefore depend on whether or not his static
line was secure.

Satisfied that the clips would hold firm, the dispatcher went to the open door, leaned into the roaring
wind, looked down at the nocturnal fields of France,
hardly visible in the darkness, then indicated that the
paratroopers should line up, ready to jump. As they
were already in line, having been seated along the
length of the fuselage, they merely turned towards
the open door, where the wind was blasting in, and
stood there patiently, each man's eyes focused on the
back of the head of the soldier in front of him.

Because he could not be heard above the roar of
wind and engines, the dispatcher mouthed the words
'Get ready!' and pointed to the light-bulb above his
head. Looking up at the light, which would signal
the start of the drop, the men automatically tried
to become more comfortable with their harnesses,
moving the straps this way and that, checking and
rechecking their weapons, then doing the same with
their equipment.

'Close your eyes and think of England,' Rich
murmured, though most of the others merely took
very deep breaths and let it out slowly, each coping
with the rush of adrenalin in his own way.

The light turned to red. Two minutes to go.

As CO, Captain Callaghan was back at base, waiting to come out with the third and last group, and Captain Greaves was heading Group One. Greaves therefore took up a position beside the open door, from where he could check that each man had gone out properly before he became the last man out. The first man to jump was Sergeant Lorrimer, not only because he was the senior NCO, but because he was going to act as 'drifter', indicating the strength and direction of the wind.

Taking his place by the open doorway in the fuselage, Lorrimer braced himself, leaned into the beating wind, took a deep breath and looked down at what appeared to be a bottomless pit of roaring darkness. Eventually the dispatcher slapped him on the shoulder and bawled: 'Go!'

Lorrimer threw himself out.

First swept sideways in the slipstream, he then dropped vertically for a brief, deafening moment. But suddenly he was jerked back up when the shoot was 'popped' by the fully extended static line secured inside the aircraft. Tugged hard under the armpits, as if by the hands of an unseen giant, he then found himself dropping again, this time more gently, as the parachute billowed open above him like a huge white umbrella.

In just under a minute the seemingly infinite darkness beneath him gained shape and definition, revealing the moon-streaked canopy of the dense forest north of Orléans. No sooner had Lorrimer glimpsed this than the trees were rushing up at him with ever-increasing speed. Tugging the straps of the parachute this way and that, he steered for the broad, open field that was now clearly visible and watched the trees slip away out of view as he headed for the DZ. The flat field seemed to race up to meet him and he braced himself for contact. The instant his feet touched the ground, he let his legs bend and his body relax, collapsing to the ground and rolling over once to minimize the impact. The whipping parachute dragged him along a few feet, then collapsed, and he was able to snap the straps free and climb to his feet, breathless but exhilarated.

Glancing about him, he saw no movement either in the dark expanse of field or in the forest surrounding it. Relieved that he had not been spotted by the Germans, who were doubtless in the vicinity, he looked up at the sky and saw the blossoming white parachutes of the rest of the men, most of whom were now out of the Halifax.

Having carefully observed Lorrimer's fall and gauged from it the wind's strength and direction, the pilot had banked the Halifax to come in over an area that would enable the paratroopers to drop more easily into the field, rather than into the forest. Now, they were doing so: first gliding down gently, then seeming to pick up speed as they approached the ground, hitting it and rolling over as Lorrimer had done, then snapping the straps to set themselves free from the wildly flapping parachute.

Having disengaged himself, each man used the small spade on his webbing to quickly dig a small hole in the earth. Then he rolled up his chute and buried it. This done, he unslung his assault rifle and knelt in the firing position, all the while keeping his eyes on the trees. By the time the last man had fallen, the paratroopers were spread out across the field in a large, defensive circle, waiting for the Halifax to turn around and drop the crates containing the jeeps and supplies.

This did not take long. The aircraft merely turned in a wide circle above the forest, then flew back to the field. When it was directly above the DZ, the crates were pushed out of the open rear bay and floated down, each supported by four parachutes. The men in the field had to be careful not to be standing under a crate when it fell, even though its landing was cushioned by the air bags beneath it.

Soon those not on guard, keeping their eyes on the surrounding forest, were using their special tools to split the crates open and get at the jeeps. Once out of the smaller crates, the twin Vickers K guns and the 0.5-inch Browning heavy machine-guns were remounted on the Willys jeeps and the vehicles were then driven into the forest and camouflaged. When the field had been cleared, the wood from the packing crates was buried near the edge of the trees and the upturned soil covered with loose leaves.

'Now let's get into hiding,' Greaves told his men,

'and wait for the others to be dropped tomorrow night.'

'*And* the next night,' Lorrimer said in disgust.

The men melted silently into the edge of the forest flanking the DZ, taking up hidden positions near the field's four sides. There, they proceeded to make individual lying-up positions, or LUPs, by scraping small hollows out of the earth, covering them with wire, and laying local vegetation on top. Having eaten a supper of cold rations washed down with water, the men bedded down for the night, most of them in their LUPs, others taking turns at guard duty. Placed in the four directions of the compass on each side of the field, the lookouts scanned the forest for any sign of the enemy.

There were no land movements apparent that night, though many aircraft, both Allied and German, flew overhead to engage in bombing runs or aerial fights far away. While the surrounding forest was quiet, the sounds of distant explosions were heard all night as battle was engaged on several fronts and the Allied advance across France continued. When dawn broke, the mist of the horizon was smudged with clouds of ugly black smoke.

'Poor bastards,' Jacko murmured, thinking of the unfortunate men who had endured the relentless bombing all night near that murky horizon.

'Poor *Kraut* bastards,' Rich said ironically.

'A lot of them are Allied troops,' Jacko reminded him, 'being bombed by the Germans. But whatever side they're on, they're poor bastards, all of them. I don't like bombardments.'

'I grant you that, mate. We had enough of them in North Africa and Sicily to last us a lifetime. I'm amazed we've still got our hearing as well as our balls.'

'Some would dispute the latter assertion,' Sergeant Lorrimer whispered as loudly as he dared, raising his head from the LUP beside them. 'Now shut up, fill your mouths with some cold food, then go and replace those poor frozen sods out on point.'

'Yes, Sarge!' Jacko and Rich whispered simultaneously.

For most of the men, the rest of the day was long and boring, with nothing for them to do but either lie in their LUPs or crawl out to replace one of the guards. Aircraft, mostly Allied, flew overhead constantly, Fortresses and Liberators and accompanying Spitfire fighters, intent on keeping up the relentless bombing of German positions further inland.

Also, throughout the day, German convoys or individual jeeps and trucks could be seen passing by on the nearby road, half obscured by the hedgerows that bounded the fields, heading towards or away from the front indicated by the distant sounds of battle. Luckily, none of them turned off the road to cross the field to the forest and the SAS men remained undetected.

When darkness fell, the sounds of distant battle were accompanied by spectacular flashes that lit up the horizon and lent a magical glow to the dense clouds. Shortly before midnight, the Halifax reappeared overhead and the white parachutes of the second batch of SAS men billowed in the darkness as they drifted gently to earth. They were followed by another consignment of wooden crates, each one descending beneath four parachutes and landing on their air bags.

When the aircraft had disappeared again, the new men did exactly as the first batch had done: drove their jeeps into the forest, buried the wooden planking from the crates and covered the disturbed earth with leaves, then scraped out LUPs in areas selected for them by the Originals, who had landed the previous night.

Another night passed uneventfully, except for distant explosions from the front and eerie flashes which lit up the horizon, revealing swirling clouds of smoke. The smoky dawn heralded a second tedious day, with Allied aircraft rumbling almost constantly overhead and helmeted German troops heading to and from the front on the road beyond the field, at the other side of the hedgerows. Hidden in their LUPs, the men were not seen by the German troops, though some were already so bored that they wished they had been.

That night the third and last of the SAS groups, headed by Captain Callaghan, was brought in to the DZ by the Halifax. This time, however, one of the jeeps dropped from the aircraft broke free from two of its four parachutes and crashed to the ground, causing the crate to shatter and the waiting soldiers to run for cover. The jeep had embedded itself so deeply in the ground that it had created a large crater. Because the vehicle was badly damaged, it was left buried there, along with all the other debris, and then the hole was filled in with soil and camouflaged with loose foliage.

This time, instead of melting back into the trees, the new arrivals helped the first two batches of men to fill in their LUPs and hide all trace of their presence in the area. Then the men of C Squadron, now safely on the ground, dispersed to their individual jeeps and the column, totalling twenty vehicles, moved off along a forest track, heading for the open country behind enemy lines.

3

Aided by bright moonlight, which illuminated the narrow road through the forest, the column of jeeps had a relatively easy first morning, heading without lights for open country dotted with small farming communities. Some of the villages, as the men knew, were still occupied by the Germans and so had to be approached carefully; others had been freed but were surrounded by the advancing and retreating armies, which meant that the Germans could return unexpectedly; and an increasing number were well out of the danger zone and preparing to give a heart-felt welcome to their Allied liberators.

Progress was frustratingly slow because one jeep was out ahead on point, its crew having been given the dangerous job of acting as advance scouts, prepared to either engage the enemy or, if possible, return unseen to the main column and report the enemy's presence to Captains Callaghan and Greaves, who would then jointly decide if they should attack or simply make a detour. The brief, as outlined by Callaghan, was to avoid engaging the enemy whenever possible and instead reconnoitre the area for a suitable base camp from where they could move out to find the Maquis.

In fact, more than once the men on point in the

jeep – Sergeant Lorrimer as driver, Jacko on the twin Vickers K guns and Rich on the Browning heavy machine-gun – noticed the glow of camp-fires and oil lamps in the forest and assumed them to be from German camps. Invariably, closer inspection, usually on foot, revealed this to be true and the men therefore always had to backtrack to meet up with the column behind and inform Callaghan and Greaves of the enemy presence. The column, now split into two, with Callaghan in charge of Group One and Greaves leading Group Two, would then take the nearest side road and make a wide detour around the enemy, to travel on unmolested.

This was the situation for most of the first six hours, as they travelled through the night and early morning in the depths of the forest. By dawn, however, the trees were thinning out and they were emerging into open countryside with wide, rolling fields dotted with hamlets and crossed by a web of major and minor roads, including German military supply routes (MSRs).

'It looks so peaceful out there,' Callaghan said.

'Except for that smoke on the horizon,' Greaves replied. 'It's all happening there.'

Now out in the open, they had to travel much more carefully. To get from one side of an MSR to the other, they usually drove alongside it, out of sight behind hedgerows or trees, until they came to where the road was crossed by a track. There they would wait until the track was inspected by the jeep on point; when it was reported clear, the column of jeeps, using the track, would cross at top speed. Once or twice the last of their jeeps crossed just as retreating German columns appeared along the MSR and headed towards them; but that first day, at least, they managed to push on unseen.

The first village they came to was on the banks of the Loire. Arriving there just before noon, they were greeted by villagers, mostly women, children and elderly men who cheered, applauded and placed garlands of flowers around the soldiers' necks. The soldiers then learned that they were the first Allied troops to arrive; that the Germans had only recently fled from this village; that three of the villages around it were still occupied by sizeable German columns; and that the Germans were reported to have recently fled from the next village along the SAS men's route.

As most of the soldiers settled down in the sunny village square to flirt with the bolder local girls while enjoying a lunch of fresh bread, cheese and calvados, all supplied by the grateful villagers, Callaghan and Greaves received a visit from the mayor and the sole remaining member of the Maquis. The mayor was a portly, good-humoured individual who gave them invaluable information about the German forces who had occupied the village. The Maquisard was a young man, Pierre, who wore shabby grey trousers, a torn tweed jacket, shoes with holes in the soles and a rakishly positioned black beret. With a stolen German semi-automatic rifle slung over his shoulder, he grinned cockily as he told them, in French, that the rest of his Maquis friends had left the village in pursuit of the fleeing Germans and that he had been left behind to act as guide to the first Allied troops to arrive.

'That means us,' Callaghan said.

'*Oui, mon capitaine*. I will be proud to serve.'

'Ah, you speak English!'

Pierre grinned and placed his index finger just above his thumb, leaving a tiny gap between them. 'Only a little.' Then, reverting to his own language, he said: 'But your French, I notice, is excellent.'

'It's good enough,' Callaghan said, though he spoke the language well. 'I'm sure we'll get by with it. What was it like with the Germans here?'

Pierre shrugged and stopped grinning. 'Not good, *monsieur*, but other villages had it worse. Here, though the Boche commandeered the best houses and took most of the food we grew, they were a disciplined bunch who neither harmed the older folk nor abused the women. They *did* take the few remaining young men away for forced labour in Germany, but as most of us knew they would do that when they came, we fled into the forest and made our own camps there.'

'And were very successful at harassing the Germans,' Greaves said diplomatically.

'In a limited way only – at least until the invasion was launched. Before that, we had to be careful about coming out of the forest to attack the Germans, because if we did they would exact some terrible form of vengeance. Sometimes they shot three or four Frenchmen for every German shot by us, or even worse, in one case they herded every member of a village into the church and then set fire to it. So some of them have done terrible things, but here we were lucky.'

'And your fellow Maquisards are now pursuing those same Germans?'

'Sniping on them as they retreat. The main German supply route, along which they are retreating, runs through hilly, densely forested countryside. The Maquis are well protected by the trees and pick them off from the hills. This not only reduces the Germans in number, but also makes them constantly nervous. I wish I was there!'

'You can be,' Callaghan told him. 'It's imperative that we link up with the Maquis and learn all we can about the Germans' movements and habits. If you act as our guide, you'll be able to rejoin your companions.'

'Then I'm your man, *mon capitaine*.'

'Thank you, *monsieur*.'

Callaghan glanced across the village square and saw that the SAS troopers not on guard at the edge of the forest encircling the village were sprawled around the fountain in the middle of the square, in the shade of the leafy trees, finishing off their bread and cheese, swigging calvados, and shamelessly flirting with the younger, bolder girls. The girls' parents were looking on, not offended, simply thrilled to see the British soldiers here, scarcely believing that they were human like other men, and might seduce their daughters. The fountain itself, Callaghan noticed, had been hit by a bomb and was now half demolished and covered with its own rubble and pulverized cement. There was no sign of water.

'When do we move out?' the young Maquisard asked, removing his semi-automatic weapon from his shoulder and laying it across his thighs, where he lovingly stroked it.

'When we've checked that the next village has been cleared, I want you to go with a forward patrol, lead them to the village, see what's happening, then return here. If we know that the village is cleared, we can move on to link up with the Maquis.'

'Very good,' Pierre said.

Nodding at Sergeant Lorrimer, who was kneeling beside the young Frenchman, Callaghan asked: 'Do you mind doing this?'

'My pleasure,' Lorrimer replied. 'That calvados perked me up no end and now I'm raring to go.'

'Then take Pierre with you and try to get back here as soon as possible. Be careful, Sergeant.'

'I will, boss,' Lorrimer said. 'OK, Pierre, come with me.' When Pierre stared uncomprehendingly at him, Lorrimer stood up and jerked his thumb, indicating that the Frenchman should follow him. With Pierre beside him, he walked around the smashed fountain to where Jacko and Rich were sitting on the steps of a house, enjoying themselves by trying to communicate with two giggling girls who spoke almost no English.

'No, you don't understand,' Jacko was saying, indicating himself and the dark-haired girl nearest to him by jabbing at her and himself with his index finger. 'Me . . . love . . . you. Me want to get in your knickers.'

The girl, not understanding what he was saying, started giggling again, though Rich silenced her by saying: 'That's bloody rude, Jacko! They're decent girls.'

'And we're their conquering heroes, so we might as well . . .'

'Shut your filthy mouth, Jacko,' Lorrimer growled as he approached the men, 'and get to your feet. Before you cause offence here by saying the wrong thing in front of a Frog who knows English, I'm taking you on a little patrol.'

'Aw, come on, Sarge!' Jacko protested, wiping his wet lips with the back of his hand and waving his bottle of apple brandy. 'I haven't finished my lunch!'

'You've had enough for now. And if you have any more of that stuff you'll be even more stupid and loose-tongued than you are normally. So put that bottle down, pick up your rifle, and get on your feet. You, too, Burgess.'

'Very good, Sarge,' Rich said, slinging his rifle over his shoulder and winking at the moon-eyed French girl beside him. 'Unlike some we could mention, I never complain about being asked to perform my duty. Backbone of the squadron, me, Sarge.'

'And humble with it, I note,' Lorrimer responded. 'Now say goodbye to your two little girlfriends and let's get to the jeep.'

Rich shyly mumbled his farewell to the girl sitting beside him, but Jacko, climbing to his feet, was considerably more theatrical, bowing, sweeping his beret across his chest and saying with a dreadful accent: '*Au revoir, mademoiselle. Je t'adore.*' When the girl burst into giggles again, Jacko grinned from ear to ear, then followed Lorrimer, Rich and the young Maquisard across the square to their jeep.

'I didn't know you spoke French,' Rich said.

'I don't,' Jacko replied. 'Those are the only Frog words I know. Picked them up from the films.'

'What a fucking prat!' Sergeant Lorrimer muttered to himself, shaking his head in exaggerated disgust. Then, indicating the young Frenchman with the German rifle, he said: 'This is Pierre, of the Maquis. If you understand what I'm saying, Pierre, this is Corporal Burgess, known as Rich, and Lance-Corporal Dempster, known as Jacko. As neither speaks French, you won't have to put up with their bloody awful conversation.'

'Well, thanks a lot!' Jacko exclaimed.

'I understand,' Pierre said proudly, smiling at everyone. 'Rich and Jacko! Nicked names!'

'Nicked names,' Lorrimer said. 'You've got it.' He

sighed in exasperation and turned to the other two. 'Pierre's going to act as our guide and hopefully lead us to his fellow Maquis. But first he'll take us to the next village on our route. If it's been cleared, which we think it has, we'll come back and tell the others about it. Then we head out.'

'You picked the right men for the job,' Jacko informed him.

'I'm sure,' Lorrimer said, then he clambered up into the driver's seat of the Willys jeep, indicated that Pierre should sit beside him, and waited patiently until Jacko and Rich had climbed into the back, the former behind the twin Vickers guns mounted in the middle of the vehicle, between the front and rear seats, the latter behind the Browning heavy machine-gun mounted on the rear. 'All set?' Lorrimer asked.

'Of course,' Jacko replied.

'Fire away,' Rich added.

'Hold on,' Lorrimer said. Just to take the wind out of the sails of his two cocky passengers, he released the handbrake and accelerated quickly, making the tyres screech in the soil as the jeep shot forward, practically taking wing. Jacko and Rich were nearly thrown out and had to hold on to their mounted machine-guns to stay upright; they were still frantically trying to keep their balance when their SAS mates in the square, still eating and drinking, clapped their hands and cheered, before being obscured in the cloud of dust churned up by the departing jeep.

'Mad bastards!' Callaghan muttered as he watched

the jeep disappear around the first bend in the track, heading into the forest.

'Lorrimer's just having some sport,' Greaves replied, grinning. 'They'll be all right.'

In the jeep, as Lorrimer slowed it down to a less suicidal speed, Jacko spread his legs and continued to steady himself by holding on to the grips of the twin Vickers. 'Very good, Sarge!' he bawled above the roaring of the vehicle. 'A real smooth getaway!'

'Designed to wake you up,' Lorrimer replied. 'And clearly it did.'

'Bloody right,' Rich confirmed, likewise holding on tight to his machine-gun.

'Very quick! Most admirable!' Pierre added, trying out his English. 'We will be there in no time. Take this track, s'il vous plaît.'

Following the direction indicated by the Frenchman, Lorrimer turned off the main road and took the narrower track heading east, winding through dense, gloomy forest. The narrowness of the track and its many bends, and the overhanging branches of trees, slowed him down considerably, but he would have gone slower anyway to enable Jacko and Rich to thoroughly scan the forest for any sign of German snipers. In this task Pierre was even more of a help, knowing the forest intimately, but no movement was evident among the dense trees.

Ten minutes later they were, Pierre loudly informed them, approaching the next village.

'Slow down when I signal,' he managed to say in a

mixture of French, English and sign language. 'Stop, please, when I tell you.'

Lorrimer slowed down and stopped entirely when Pierre, at a bend in the narrow track around which they could not see, dropped his right hand with the palm face down. When Pierre indicated that they were going to walk the rest of the way to the village, Lorrimer executed a difficult turn on the narrow track, so that the jeep was facing back the way it had come. Having cut the engine and applied the handbrake, he picked up his 9mm Sten sub-machine-gun and jumped to the ground.

'You, too,' he said to Pierre, then turned to Jacko and Rich to say, as Pierre jumped down beside him: 'You two keep manning those guns. If you hear us running back – or hear or see anything else indicating that we're being pursued by Jerry – get ready to open fire. Understood?'

'Yes, Sarge,' both men replied, simultaneously swinging their machine-guns around on their swivel mounts until the barrels were facing the track at the rear of the jeep.

'Good. Let's go, Pierre.'

Lorrimer and the Maquisard walked away from the jeeps and turned the bend in the track, both with their weapons unslung and at the ready. At the other side of the bend, the track ran straight to the tiny village, and gave a partial view of the sides of several stone cottages with red-slate roofs. The village, Lorrimer noted, was only about five hundred yards away and smoke was coming out of the chimneys.

Using sign language, he indicated that he and Pierre should leave the track and advance the rest of the way through the trees. This they did, encountering no one and soon emerging near the backs of the cottages.

From the open window of one of the cottages, they could hear a crackling radio on which someone was speaking in French. Though not familiar with the language, Lorrimer understood enough to realize that he was hearing news of the Allied liberation of the country. The advance seemed to be going well.

Stepping up to the house and glancing through the open window, Lorrimer saw that the kitchen was filled with people, all seated around a huge pine table, drinking wine or calvados, smoking cigarettes and listening with obvious pleasure to the news on the radio. That they were doing so was a clear indication that the Germans had already left.

Sighing with relief, but still not taking any chances, Lorrimer checked the rear of the other cottages in the row, and found similar scenes inside, so he let Pierre lead him out into the village's only street.

The street was no more than a flattened earth track running between two straight rows of stone cottages and a grocer's, animal feed store and saddlery, bakery, dairy, blacksmith's, barber's shop, one bar and, at the far end, a church, graveyard and school. Many of the locals – mainly farmers and their wives, most surprisingly plump and red-cheeked given the spartan existence they must have led during the German occupation – were sitting either on their doorsteps or on rush chairs outside the houses, taking in the sun, eating and, like those Lorrimer had seen in the kitchens, celebrating with wine or calvados.

When those nearest to Lorrimer and Pierre saw them, they came rushing up excitedly to embrace them, kiss them on both cheeks or shake their hands, and then plied them with bread, cheese, alcohol, all the while asking about the Allies' progress. After refusing the wine and telling them as much as he knew, Lorrimer asked if all the Germans had left the village.

'They left two behind as snipers,' he was informed in English by a solemn-faced, gaunt man wearing an FFI armband. 'But they didn't last long.' Straightening his shoulders and grinning, he turned away to point along the street. Looking in that direction, Lorrimer saw two German troopers sprawled on their backs in the dirt, their helmets missing – probably taken as souvenirs – and their heads a mess of blood and exposed bone where they had been shot. The FFI man patted the pistol strapped to his waist and smiled again at Lorrimer. 'Me,' he said proudly. 'I killed both of them. There are no more Boche here.'

'Good,' Lorrimer said. 'We intend bringing our men through here, so please send someone back to warn us if any Germans return.'

'Naturally,' the man said, clearly relishing his role as protector of the hamlet.

Lorrimer thanked the man and walked back along the village street, with Pierre beside him. 'A good man,' Pierre said. 'He hates the Germans. And those who fraternize.' They were passing a crowd that had gathered around the barber's shop and walked over to see what was happening. An attractive young woman of no more than twenty was having her head shaved by the village barber while the excited crowd, mostly women and children, looked on, laughing and occasionally spitting at the weeping woman. 'She slept with a German soldier,' Pierre explained, smiling brightly at Lorrimer. 'A collaborator bitch.'

'Probably just in love,' Lorrimer said, turning away in disgust.

Pierre shrugged. 'In love . . . a whore . . . whatever – she still collaborated. That's all we care about here.'

'Let's get back,' Lorrimer said.

They returned via the narrow, winding forest track to the jeep, where Jacko and Rich were keeping the bend covered in silence.

'The village has been cleared,' Lorrimer told them, 'so let's get back to the squadron.'

'They must have heard you coming,' Jacko said.

'And got scared shitless,' Rich added.

'Any more fancy remarks and you'll be *walking* back,' Lorrimer said as he climbed into the driver's seat and turned on the ignition.

'These lips are sealed,' Jacko said.

'Same here, Sarge,' Rich added.

'Glad to hear it, lads,' said the sergeant, waiting

until Pierre was sitting in the seat beside him before releasing the handbrake and heading back to the first village.

Twenty minutes later they emerged from the gloomy forest and drove into the centre of the sunlit village, where Lorrimer told Jacko and Rich to remain in the jeep until he had reported to Callaghan and Greaves. The two captains were sitting in the shade of a tree near the remains of the fountain, studying a map.

Though disgruntled at being prevented from again fraternizing with the pretty village girls, Jacko and Rich received some consolation when they hurried up to the jeep, gave them more bread, cheese and wine and began flirting with them. Shaking his head in mock exasperation, but unable to conceal a grin, Lorrimer ignored them while he crossed to the square, accompanied by Pierre, and knelt in the dirt beside Callaghan and Greaves.

'The next village has been cleared,' he informed the offices. 'The only Germans still there are the two dead ones lying in the street.'

'The FFI took care of them?' Callaghan asked shrewdly.

'Yes, boss.'

'Where would we be without our French patriots? Right, Sergeant, let's get doing.'

The column of jeeps moved out shortly after, churning up great clouds of dust that descended on the men, women and children in the square, most of whom waved goodbye and threw flowers over the departing vehicles. Once back on the forest track, amid the now familiar gloom and silence, the men manning the guns in the jeeps carefully scanned the trees on both sides, on the lookout for snipers. In the event, nothing happened and soon they were rounding the last bend in the track and emerging on to the sunlit road that ran straight through the village.

The SAS men responded with understandable pleasure to the women and children who ran alongside their vehicles, throwing flowers and handing up more bottles of calvados. Their spirits, however, were momentarily dampened when they passed the woman who had had her head shaved and now, completely bald and streaked with blood, was kneeling in the dirt, covering her face with her hands and trembling as she sobbed. Thankfully, they were soon past her and circling around the two dead German troopers spread-eagled in the middle of the road; then they were leaving the village behind and heading out into open country again.

In the dimming light of the late afternoon, they could still see the smoke on the horizon, where battles were raging along the constantly shifting front. Throughout the journey they saw no German troops, though Luftwaffe planes occasionally passed overhead, mainly bombers escorted by Me-109 fighters, heading for England and some desperate, last-minute air raids. How these aircraft managed to get as far as Britain was a mystery to most of the SAS men, since the sky above them seemed to be filled constantly with Allied aircraft flying in from Britain and recently recaptured Normandy airfields to bomb German positions in front of the advancing Allied troops.

'They must just ignore one another,' Rich suggested, 'because the missions they're on are more important. Just fly right past each other.'

'I s'pose so,' Jacko replied. 'No sense in it otherwise.'

Later in the evening, as the sun dimmed and huge shadows crossed the rolling green and brown hills, the smoke on the horizon was illuminated by the silvery flashes of countless explosions. It was not a welcoming sight.

'We'd better find somewhere to stay for the night,' Callaghan said. 'I think we've travelled far enough from the DZ and the men could do with a break.'

'I agree,' said Greaves.

They picked the next isolated farmhouse they came to. Not wishing to act like the Germans and commandeer the farmhouse itself, they decided to make simple LUPs on the unused field directly behind it. Nevertheless, when Callaghan and Greaves climbed down from their respective jeeps and knocked on the door of the farmhouse, the farmer refused to come out. Frustrated, the short-tempered Callaghan forgot his manners and blew the lock off the door with his Webley. He then kicked the door open and strode in, followed closely by Greaves.

Inside, in a living-room smelling of dry rot and

filled with crying cats, saucers brimming with milk and cat food, strung-up dead rabbits, and ancient rustic furniture, they found the French farmer and his wife cringing behind a moth-eaten sofa and tentatively raising their hands above their heads.

Exasperated, Callaghan spoke to them in French, explaining that he and his men were English and merely wished to camp for one night at the back of the farm and have access to water and the outdoor toilet. All cooking, he explained, would be done by his men on their own portable stoves. Even so, because the farmer had been under the yoke of the Germans for years, the proposal terrified him.

'But what if the Germans return and learn that I've helped you?' he asked, his voice shaking. 'They would shoot me!'

'Then let them bloody well shoot you!' the increasingly irate Callaghan exploded in English, unable to reconcile the difference between this trembling wretch and the warmly welcoming French people in the last two villages they had past through. 'If they don't shoot you, I will!' he added in French. 'We're staying! You understand?'

'*Oui, monsieur!*' the shocked Frenchman snapped.

'Damn it, we're here to help you!'

'*Oui, monsieur!*' the farmer's wife said quickly.

'You have a pump round the back?'

'*Oui, bien sûr.*'

'Good. We'll use it for our water. We'll use your outdoor toilet and ensure that it doesn't get blocked.

We'll do our cooking on our own stoves and ensure that the leftovers and rubbish are burried in the field. We'll leave no mess. Your house will not be entered. When we leave tomorrow, you'll hardly know we've been here. Is that acceptable to you?'

'Of course, *monsieur*!' the farmer said. 'Naturally, Captain!'

'Good,' Callaghan repeated. 'We'll do all this on the grounds that you don't leave your farm and tell no one, French or German, that we're here. Should you do so – or should you, in any other way, give us trouble – I personally will put a bullet through your thick head. Is that understood?'

'Yes, *monsieur*!' the farmer replied, practically babbling.

'Then good night to you, sir.'

Flushed with anger, Callaghan turned away from the cringing farmer and his wife, and, followed by Captain Greaves, went to the back of the house to organize his sixty men, most of whom were now sitting or stretched out on the field by their parked jeeps.

As they were only staying for one night, and as tents could more easily be seen by a passing enemy, Callaghan told the men to make LUPs similar to those they had used at the DZ when first inserted on French soil. As they had done before, the men merely scraped small hollows out of the earth, covered them with wire and spread foliage on top. Since they had not had a hot meal since their arrival in France – though they were certainly grateful for the bread, cheese, wine and calvados generously proffered by the grateful locals – they were given permission to use their hexamine stoves for simple fry-ups and making tea.

A couple of hours later, when the food had been consumed, each trooper doused the flames of his still-burning hexamine blocks, cleaned his stove and put it back in his bergen rucksack. He then queued up for as long as forty minutes to use the outdoor toilet, before gratefully lying down in his LUP for a fitful sleep punctuated by the sound of explosions from the distant front, accompanied by spectacular, silvery flashes illuminating the dark horizon where soldiers, British and German alike, were dying all through the night.

Nevertheless, they managed to rise at first light from their LUPs, if not exactly full of the joys of spring, at least sufficiently rested to face the new day.

4

Passing through more scattered villages from which the Germans had fled, the SAS column naturally attracted the attention of the locals, who plied the men with food, alcohol and information about enemy troop movements. Unfortunately, in many cases they were more enthusiastic than accurate and while much of the information was valuable, a lot of it had to be discarded after causing great confusion, such as sending the SAS men off in the wrong direction, sometimes practically right into enemy hands, sometimes into areas being bombed or shelled by the Allies. Nevertheless, while this led to some hair-raising experiences, by nightfall the column had travelled another fifty miles, or a third of its planned journey, and Captain Callaghan was well satisfied.

By now Callaghan had learnt that because of the constant Allied bombing, the Germans were mostly moving under cover of darkness. Therefore he decided that his own men would move during the day and rest in LUPs during the night. He also decided that it would be safer to divide into three smaller columns, spaced approximately thirty minutes apart, to ensure that the whole squadron could not be attacked at once. He placed himself in charge of the first column of seven jeeps, Captain Greaves in charge of the second, also seven jeeps, and Sergeant Lorrimer in charge of the third, consisting of the remaining six jeeps. It was the latter who had the first encounter with the enemy.

The three columns had been advancing all morning and into the early afternoon, ever deeper behind enemy lines, guided by the excitable Maquisard Pierre, now in Callaghan's jeep, and always keeping well away from the smoke-wreathed horizon where the main battles were raging along a broad front. The squadron had divided earlier that morning, with the second two columns moving out at thirty-minute intervals after the first and fanning out in opposite directions. Every two hours, however, they circled back to meet at prearranged RVs, where they would rest, eat cold rations and trade information about what they had seen and heard, before parting again.

Soon after emerging from the darkness of the Forêt de Dracy and *en route* to the next RV, which was near Avallon, Lorrimer, following Callaghan's Group One and well in front of Greaves's Group Two, found his way blocked by a broad river.

'Shit!' he hissed, then checked his map and looked up at Jacko and Rich. 'The River Yonne,' he informed them. 'It runs south, right past Avallon, which is on the east bank. We've got to get to the other side, so let's follow it downstream until we find a bridge.'

'You're the driver, Sarge,' Jacko said chirpily from behind the twin Vickers guns. 'Ours is to obey.'

'I should bloody well hope so,' Lorrimer said, rising once again to the bait. He stood behind the steering wheel and used a hand signal to indicate that the five other jeeps should follow him, and then sat down again, engaged the gears and led the column south, following the muddy track alongside and above the river.

The jeeps bounced roughly along the track for a distance that should have taken them half an hour but actually took almost three because they got bogged down again and again, with the jeeps' noses tipped forward and the front axles buried deep in the mud. When this happened, the men, groaning with frustration, rescued the vehicles with a variation on a system first devised in the deserts of North Africa. First they unloaded the heavy kit and weapons to lighten the jeep; then, after scraping or digging away the mud from the trapped wheels, they placed modified five-foot-long steel sand channels under them. When these were firmly in place, the jeep, with its engine running in low gear, could be pushed forward on to a succession of further channels until it was back on firm ground.

It was sweaty, exhausting, filthy work that left the men caked in hardening mud, but it had to be done.

'Bloody awful,' Lance-Corporal Neil Moffatt complained, kneeling on the river bank and trying to rub the mud from his face and hands with a wet cloth, which only seemed to spread it even more. 'I hate this filthy business. It was bad in the heat of the fucking desert, but at least it was sand, not this stinking mud. I could scream doing this.'

'Right,' said his mate, Harry 'Harry-boy' Turnball, who was kneeling beside him and also trying to clean himself. 'And Christ knows what slimy bastards are crawling about in this mud, itching to give us some filthy disease. I *hate* this bloody stuff!'

'The only disease you're going to get,' Corporal Reg Seekings told him, 'is the clap from some poxy French tart.'

'He should be so lucky,' Jacko told them, standing behind them and looking on, amused, smoking. 'The way they responded to him in the villages we've already passed through, I'd say he'd be lucky even getting himself a hag. A dead dog's about all he'd get near – and even that might be shocked back to life and run away at the sight of him.'

'Very funny,' Harry-boy said. 'I'm splitting my sides here.'

'All right, you men, you're filthier than you were before,' Lorrimer bawled at them. 'Let's waste no more time. Get back in the jeeps.'

The journey along the river bank continued, with the jeeps continuing to get stuck in mud every few minutes. Eventually, however, they came to a bridge linking two MSRs. About a hundred yards wide, it was constructed from wooden planks lashed together, but was strong enough to support heavy vehicles.

Stopping at the bridge, Lorrimer carefully scanned the far bank for signs of enemy troops, but saw no sign of movement in the murk of the dense forest.

'What do you think?' he asked Jacko and Rich.

'Impossible to say,' Jacko replied. 'The only way we'll find out if Jerry's covering that bridge is to drive across it.'

'As fast as we can,' Rich added thoughtfully.

'All right, let's do it,' Lorrimer said. 'Hang on to your berets, lads.'

After letting the jeep bounce down on to the planks, Lorrimer accelerated and started to race across. The bridge shook dramatically as the other jeeps thumped down on to it one after the other; the tyres made the planks rumble like jungle drums and the wind, whipping at the exposed men, followed the course of the river with a loud, rushing sound.

Lorrimer was about halfway across when a machine-gun roared on the far bank. Instantly, a hail of bullets ricocheted noisily off the struts of the bridge just above the jeep.

Jacko and Rich returned fire with their machine-guns, sweeping left to right in a broad arc that tore branches and leaves off the trees along the opposite bank. Unable to see where the enemy fire was coming from, they just hammered away in a sweeping motion as bullets ricocheted around them and the jeep raced towards the relative safety of the bank. They stopped firing when the jeep practically flew off the bridge at the far side, smashing through the overhanging foliage and racing along the track into the forest.

As Lorrimer put his foot on the brake, Jacko and Rich clung once again to their machine-guns, using them for balance. Glancing back, they saw the next two jeeps following each other off the bridge, bouncing dangerously as they did so. However, the tyres of the third exploded when it was peppered with German bullets and it slewed left as it bounced off the track and crashed into a tree trunk.

Accurately judging where the gunfire was coming from, Jacko opened fire with his .303-inch twin Vickers, squinting grimly along the sight, which was located between the two round-shaped 250-round belt feeds, firing in long, savage bursts, and turning the forest to his left into a storm of flying leaves and branches. Rich followed suit, raking broadly from left to right, the combined guns making that part of the forest look like it was being torn apart by a tornado.

A man's scream rang out above the harsh rattling of the machine-guns and the German fire stopped abruptly. This enabled the men in the damaged jeep – Sergeant Tappman and Lance-Corporals Moffatt and Turnball – to jump out and run for the shelter of the nearest trees. As they were doing so, the second two jeeps screeched to a halt close to Lorrimer's and the last two bounced off the bridge and managed to get into the shelter of the trees before the German Spandau machine-gun started up again.

'I don't bloody believe this!' Jacko yelled, then raked the same area, tearing the trees to shreds and this time making the Germans stop firing.

'Get in there!' Lorrimer bawled to the men who

had escaped from the damaged jeep and were frantically unslinging their assault rifles. 'Finish off those bastards!'

Tappman and the two lance-corporals instantly raced towards the area devastated by the machine-guns of Jacko and Rich. Spreading out, crouched low, their weapons at the ready, they disappeared into the undergrowth. Seconds later, their combined 9mm Sten sub-machine-guns and Thompson M1 sub-machine-guns roared in short, savage bursts. Then there was silence.

When the three men reappeared, Tappman stuck his thumb in the air, indicating that the remaining Germans had been dealt with.

'A single machine-gun crew?' Lorrimer asked when the men had returned to his jeep.

'Yes, Sarge, just one. Four men, one machine-gun.'

'What about your jeep?'

'All the tyres have been blown out and the petrol tank's shot to buggery. We can kiss it goodbye.'

'Any of you men hurt?'

'Not a scratch.'

'Lucky you,' Lorrimer said dispassionately. 'So, since you're still alive, strip everything out of that fucked jeep and spread it around the other vehicles. Then each of you can take the spare seat in one of the others.'

When the spare kit and weapons had been removed from the abandoned jeep and distributed around the squadron, the three men took spare seats and the column moved off again, winding through the dark forest until they emerged on the edge of another village deserted by the Germans. As they drove along the single street, the villagers swarmed excitedly around them, cheering, shouting greetings in French and offering the customary bread, cheese and wine.

One of them, who had an idiot's grin, clambered on to the bonnet of Lorrimer's jeep to rant in a mixture of French and pidgin English about how he would help the SAS kill more of the Boche. When he refused to get down, Lorrimer removed his Webley from its holster and tapped the barrel against the man's forehead.

'Off the jeep,' he said firmly.

The man's eyes widened and turned, almost crossing, to focus on the barrel of the pistol, then he grinned, slipped to the ground and disappeared back into the crowd.

As the others closed in on the jeep, offering greetings and gifts, an attractive, dark-haired woman in her mid twenties, wearing muddy dungarees and flushed with excitement, said in English: 'God, I can't believe it! You're actually here at last!'

Stunned to recognize a West Country accent, Sergeant Lorrimer asked: 'Are you English?'

'Yes,' the young woman replied. 'Anne Gardner.'

'What on earth are you doing here?'

Smiling as if slightly embarrassed, the woman glanced at the villagers packed tightly around her and now listening in as best they could without knowing the language. 'Oh, I married a Frenchman

I met in St Austell, where I lived with my family before the war. I was only eighteen then. He was a farmer and he brought me back here. I've lived here ever since.'

'You were here when the Germans occupied the village?'

'Yes.'

'How did they treat you?'

'No different from the others, thank the Lord. I always spoke French and they never asked to see my papers – only my husband's. Then they took him away.' When tears started from her eyes, she quickly wiped them away. 'Forced labour in Germany.'

'He's there still?'

'I presume so.'

'I'm sorry.'

The sound of laughter and shouting made Lorrimer glance over his shoulder. Directly behind him, in the jeep, Jacko and Rich were still at their machine-guns, though Jacko was leaning down to take a bottle of calvados from one of the women. 'No more drinking!' Lorrimer bawled. 'Give them back the bottles. And pass the word along the column.'

'Aw, come on, Sarge, just . . .'

'*Give it back!*' roared Lorrimer.

Hearing the tone of the sergeant's voice, Jacko shrugged and rolled his eyes at the woman with the bottle, indicating that he could not accept it.

'Sooner or later we'll be confronted by more Germans,' Lorrimer explained, 'and I don't want you men pissed when that happens. So pass the word down the line: no more drinking today.'

'Right, Sarge, will do.'

Still holding the grips of his twin Vickers, Jacko turned away to shout Lorrimer's order along the column. As the expected moans and groans arose from the other jeeps, Lorrimer, ignoring them, turned back to the Englishwoman.

'We were ambushed by a lone bunch of Germans when we crossed the river back there,' he told her. 'Are there any more that you know of still around?'

The woman nodded and pointed her finger. 'Back there,' she said, 'is a whole regiment – about a hundred men in all.'

Seeing that she was pointing south, where the other two SAS columns were exploring, though thirty minutes apart, Lorrimer decided that he had better check the area and, if necessary, mount a rescue operation if one or other of the columns, led by Callaghan and Greaves, had got into trouble.

'Would you show me where the Germans are?' he asked.

'Of course,' the Englishwoman said. 'I'll take you most of the way. Then you can drop me off and I'll walk back. I can't fire a gun.'

'I'm very glad to hear *that*,' Lorrimer said, grinning, charmed by the young woman's manner. 'Take the seat beside me.'

When the woman had climbed up beside him, Lorrimer drove off, following her directions. Within five minutes they had passed through more thick forest and eventually emerged to where the road suddenly snaked around the top of a steep cliff and back down again. At the bend, the woman told Lorrimer to stop the jeep.

'They were just around that bend,' she said. 'At the base of the cliff. You should see them if you get out and walk along, using the ditch at the side of the road for cover.'

'You'd make a good soldier,' Lorrimer told her, jumping down from the jeep as the woman did the same the other side. 'Thank you and goodbye.'

'Good luck,' the woman replied, then, after waving to Jacko and Rich, she hurried back along the road and disappeared around the first bend. Unslinging his 9mm Sten gun, Lorrimer said to the two men: 'I'm going around that bend alone, but keep your eyes peeled and your ears unblocked.'

'We're right behind you,' Jacko said.

'That's what I'm afraid of,' Lorrimer replied. 'I don't want my arse shot off.'

He walked to the side of the road and slithered down into the ditch that ran alongside it. The ditch was narrow and, being filled with stones, was awkward to walk along, but he made his way carefully around the corner with only his head visible above the rim.

That was enough. The instant he rounded the bend, the roar of a Spandau machine-gun split the silence and bullets ricocheted noisily off the lip of the ditch,

72

sending pieces of stone and earth raining down, cutting his face and temporarily blinding him.

Ducking low, but then carefully raising his head again, Lorrimer caught a glimpsed of the Germans. Their jeeps, armoured cars, tanks and horse-drawn gun carriages were resting under the trees by the road below, obviously hoping to ambush passing Allied troops. Having kept in contact with Groups One and Two by means of the No. 11 wireless set in the radio jeep, he knew that if they had not already done so, both groups would be returning along that same road just before sunset, heading back to the RV. If either group did so, it would be ambushed.

'Damn!' Lorrimer murmured.

Judging by the number of vehicles visible through the trees, there were certainly a lot of Germans – probably a hundred or so, as the girl had suggested – and they were clearly well armed.

The team firing the Spandau had spotted Lorrimer's head from the back of their horse-drawn gun carriage. Even now, their spotter, just about visible through the overhanging branches, was scanning the upper road with binoculars, only lowering them when he wanted to indicate a new line of fire by jabbing his finger in Lorrimer's direction. The bullets continued to tear up the lip of the ditch, coming closer to him each second.

Satisfied with what he had seen, Lorrimer began making his way back, but before he reached the bend again the other jeeps raced towards him, with Rich driving the lead vehicle and Jacko already firing bursts from his twin Vickers. The guns of the other jeeps roared into action as the vehicles rounded the bend, strafing the German positions below and temporarily silencing the machine-gun that had been trying in vain to find Lorrimer.

Glancing back over his shoulder, Lorrimer saw that the forest all around the German vehicles was being torn to shreds by the hail of bullets from the machine-guns mounted on the SAS jeeps. Even so, the German troops were well protected in their armoured cars and behind their truck, and clearly something more forceful was required.

Even as Lorrimer was deciding that a few mortar shells might do the tricks, the German machine-gunner started firing again and the ground along the rim of the ditch spat soil and stones, encouraging Lorrimer to hurry back along the ditch until he came abreast of his jeep, still in the lead. The column was placed near the far side of the track, which gave it a certain degree of cover behind the lip of the ditch, but the top half of the vehicles, from where the men were firing, was exposed to enemy gunfire.

'I want a couple of mortars in that ditch,' Lorrimer bawled at Jacko, 'to put out that Spandau and damage some of their armoured vehicles. Pass the word down the column.'

Jacko shouted Lorrimer's instructions to the jeep directly behind him and Corporal Jim Almonds, heading that vehicle, shouted the instructions on to the men in charge of the group's two 3-inch mortars.

As the fire from the Spandau was joined by that of other machine-guns, showering the SAS troops in earth and vegetation from the overhanging trees, the two mortar teams clambered out of their jeeps and hurried as fast as they could across the road to the ditch, burdened as they were by their heavy equipment, including the mortars and steel base plates. Once in the relative shelter of the ditch – where they were nevertheless constantly showered by soil and stones – they expertly bedded the base plates by packing them in with some of their smoke bombs.

In one team, Corporal 'Benny' Bennett, one of the Originals from the war in the North African desert in 1941, was directing the firing, which was done by Neil Moffatt. In the second team, Harry-boy Turnball was directing and Reg Seekings firing.

The first shells used were smoke bombs – selected not only to cause discomfort to the Germans, but also to provide a visual aid for the two men directing the fire. The mortars roared and their shells exploded in the forest about 200 yards beyond the German positions.

Using the rising columns of smoke as markers, Bennett and Turnball gave new instructions to the two gunners, who fired two more smoke bombs at a much sharper angle. This time, the smoke billowed up darkly from close behind the last German armoured car visible through the trees. Knowing that a slightly sharper angle of fire would land the shells directly on target, Benny and Harry-boy gave revised instructions and were gratified to see the resultant columns of smoke billowing up from between the enemy's armoured vehicles.

Satisfied, they instructed the gunners to replace the smoke bombs with 4.54kg high-explosive shells, which erupted with a mighty roar, tearing the trees to shreds and setting fire to some of the branches. When the first two HE shells were followed by another two, the combination of smoke, fire and flying debris forced the Germans to flee in all directions, some of them running out into the road. There, they were cut down by a savage fusillade from the SAS machine-guns, semi-automatic weapons and assault rifles.

Deciding to risk the mortar explosions rather than the withering hail of SAS fire, the surviving German troops rushed back into the blazing, smoking forest, leaving their many dead and wounded on the road behind them. Within minutes Lorrimer and his men had the satisfaction of seeing the undamaged German vehicles pulling out of the trees and tearing off along the road, weaving to avoid the exploding mortar shells and continuing gunfire. When they were out of sight, with only the dead and wounded still on the road or in the forest, Lorrimer hand-signalled 'Cease fire' and a startling silence descended.

'Tell the signaller to get on the radio,' the sergeant

said, 'and inform Captain Callaghan that the route to the RV has been cleared.'

'Will do, Sarge,' Jacko replied, releasing the grips of his Vickers and vaulting over the side of the jeep.

'And get confirmation that we can all proceed to the RV straight away,' added Lorrimer.

'Got you, Sarge.'

'And while you're at it, check if we have any casualties.'

'Anything else, Sarge, before I leave?'

'That'll do for now, Jacko.'

'I am on my way, Sarge.'

Lighting up a Senior Service and puffing a cloud of smoke, Jacko hurried back along the column to have words with the signaller in the radio jeep. While Jacko was away, Lorrimer and Rich both lit up Players and puffed away with great pleasure while gazing down at the dead and wounded Germans on the road. As there was little sign of movement down there, the wounded had to be few in number.

'We'll have to pick them up,' Lorrimer said thoughtfully.

'Why?' Rich asked in his quiet, oddly dispassionate manner.

'Can't just leave 'em there to die,' Lorrimer replied. 'Too slow. Too painful. They could freeze to death tonight or even get eaten by wolves.'

'So be it,' Rich said. 'What would we do with them, Sarge? They'd just be a bloody nuisance.'

'Certainly bloody,' Lorrimer replied, surveying the

dead and wounded. 'But we can't leave them there. If we meet up with the others at the RV, where we'll also join up with the Maquis, we can load those poor bastards on trucks and drive back to the nearest field hospital.'

'Those poor bastards were trying to kill us,' Rich said, exhaling a cloud of cigarette smoke.

'We were trying to kill them,' Lorrimer answered, 'so I reckon we're even now.'

Jacko sauntered back with the cigarette still smouldering between his lips. Clambering up into the jeep, he said: 'No, we have no casualties. Yes, we can proceed directly to the RV.' He took up his position behind his Vickers, then continued: 'Group One is at the RV already, having managed to get past that stretch of road down there before Jerry arrived. We're to take off now and Group Two, which is about thirty minutes south of here, will follow in about thirty minutes. Captain Callaghan said to thank us for clearing the road for him. He would have copped it otherwise.'

'That he would,' Lorrimer said. 'A right little massacre.' He raised his right hand, then brought it down in a cutting motion, indicating that the column should move out after his jeep. Taking his seat behind the steering wheel, he turned on the ignition and set off, following the road as it curved sharply left and dropped steeply, until the column reached the dead and wounded Germans far below the cliff top. There, Lorrimer demanded that two men get out of each jeep to drag the German dead to the side of the road and hump the wounded into the SAS jeeps. This they did with a great deal of grumbling, many of them agreeing with Rich that the enemy wounded could become a nuisance, others wanting to put a bullet through their heads and be done with it. Eventually, however, the route was cleared, the German dead heaped up around the trees by the side of the road and their four wounded stretched out on the rear seats of the jeeps, one man to each vehicle.

'Right,' Lorrimer said, squinting into the setting sun, 'let's get to the RV.'

As the sun sank and the shadows lengthened, they found themselves driving into hilly, densely forested country around the Forêt de St Jean, where, they knew, the Maquis were in hiding. Darkness had just about fallen when, following the grid references on their maps, they approached the RV. Guided in by Morse code flashed on lamps held by fellow SAS troops on the hills, eventually they found themselves driving into a huge, uncompleted laager formed by Groups One and Two in a clearing surrounded by protective hills and forest.

Only when their own column was parked, completing the laager, and when the four wounded Germans had been placed temporarily on camp-beds in the hospital tent, were the men of Group Three allowed to climb down and join the other men sitting in clusters near their camouflaged bell tents, cooking hot food and boiling tea over open fires or on hexamine stoves.

As the Maquisard Pierre told Lorrimer when the sergeant reported to Captain Callaghan, the bell tents actually belonged to the men of the Maquis, most of whom were presently patrolling the hills and would not be back until first light. The SAS men had been allowed to light fires and use their portable stoves because only Allied aircraft were flying over this area and the laager itself was well guarded by troopers taking four-hour stints on watch.

Exhausted by their long, eventful journey, the men of Group Three enjoyed a hot meal, then unrolled their sleeping bags and stretched out around the bell tents, under the stars, to catch up on some badly needed sleep.

5

As the gentle shafts of first light fell on the bell tents of the Maquis and the laager of SAS vehicles, some of the men woke to see figures emerging spectrally from the mist that still wreathed the trees of the thickly wooded hills. Unshaven, dressed in baggy grey or black trousers, black boots or heavy shoes, and drab, faded jackets, and with peaked caps on their heads, they might have been taken for farmworkers were it not for the bandoliers of ammunition criss-crossing their bodies, the hand-grenades hanging from their belts and the mixture of British, American and German weapons they were holding at the ready.

If this surprised the watching SAS men, many of whom were still sitting up in their LUPs and rubbing the sleep from their eyes, they were even more surprised to see that some of the shabbily dressed men were in fact women.

'I think I must be dreaming,' Callaghan said to Greaves as the two slipped out of the sleeping bags laid down in the shallow LUPs they had diplomatically decided to dig near those of their NCOs and troopers.

'Some of them are pretty as well,' Greaves replied, 'as you can see when you get a good look at their faces.'

'Not so easy under all that dirt – and not so easy to see their bodies beneath those baggy clothes. But, yes, some of those girls *are* attractive!'

Indeed, one of the consolations of this war, Callaghan was thinking as he stood up and adjusted his uniform, having slept in it, was that the squadron was moving through a land populated with ordinary people – not just fellow troopers, enemy soldiers, or male Arabs and camels, as it had been in the North African desert back in '41. Here, particularly in the liberated villages, they had seen many women, young and old. Clearly, some of them had decided to do their bit with the Maquis and were, as he noted when they drew closer, mostly young and pretty, albeit smeared with the dirt used as camouflage.

He and Greaves were distracted from their instinctive study of the womenfolk when a lean, handsome, unusually intense man, about thirty years old, stepped out from the group and stopped right in front of them.

'Ah!' he exclaimed softly but sardonically. 'The English have arrived at last!'

'Yes,' Callaghan replied.

'British Army?'

'Yes. The Special Air Service, 1st Airborne Division.'

'Ah, yes, the SAS! I have heard much about you.' The man adjusted his M1 carbine on his left shoulder and held out his right hand. 'André Flaubert, leader of the local Maquis.'

Callaghan shook his hand. 'Captain Patrick Callaghan, Commanding Officer of C Squadron. And this is Captain Derek Greaves, my second in command.'

'Pleased to meet you,' Greaves said formally, shaking the Frenchman's hand.

André Flaubert nodded toward the sleeping bags. 'You slept there?'

'Yes.'

'As Commanding Officer and second in command you should have better than that.'

'As the men were sleeping like that last night, I thought we should do the same. We'll fix up better accommodation when the tents arrive with the resup planned for tonight.'

'Resup?'

'Further supplies. Dropped by parachute.'

'Ah, yes, I see.' Nodding, not smiling, the Maquis leader glanced back over his shoulder to see the rest of his group, men and women, dispersing to their individual tents. Then he looked back at Callaghan and Greaves. 'Come,' he said. 'We can talk in my tent. Have you had breakfast yet?'

'No.'

'Then we can talk while we eat.'

The SAS men, apart from those on guard duty, were already splashing cold water on their faces or lighting their hexamine stoves, to make breakfast, as the officers accompanied André to his tent. It was only slightly bigger than the others, though big

83

enough to contain not only the usual camp-bed, but also a trestle-table, a blackboard with maps of the local area draped over it, and at least three wooden chairs for guests. A portable wood-burning stove had been set up on a table just outside the tent and one of the dirt-smeared Resistance women was heating coffee on it while filling bread rolls with cheese and tomato.

'Please,' André said with a distracted wave of his hand, taking the chair at the far side of the trestle-table, just in front of the blackboard. 'Take a seat.'

Callaghan and Greaves each took one of the wooden chairs at the other side of the table, feeling as if they were being interviewed in someone's office. The woman outside, hardly more than twenty and already an experienced fighter by the look of her, had prepared the food and was pouring the coffee into four tin mugs.

'How long have you led this group of Maquisards?' Callaghan asked, to get the conversation rolling.

'Four years,' André replied, still not smiling. 'Since the Germans first came to the village. We knew they were on the way and also knew, from the experience of those in other villages, that they would take most of the young men away for forced labour in Germany, so we fled into the woods just before they arrived. Since then, we've been making a nuisance of ourselves, though never with the Germans in local villages. We only attack passing convoys,

84

blow up bridges and railways, and send as much information as we can gather to the Allied forces. We limited ourselves in this way in order to prevent retaliation against the villages. So far it seems to have worked.'

'Your resistance work is much admired in London,' Callaghan said with genuine admiration.

André nodded. '*Merci, monsieur.*' He glanced up when the young woman came in, carrying two of the steaming cups of coffee, and gave one each to Callaghan and Greaves, merely nodding and smiling silently when they offered their thanks. She then went back outside and returned almost immediately with the other two cups, placing one in front of André, the other at the left-hand side of the table. When she came back a third time, she was carrying a tray containing four plates and the rolls. In silence, she placed the tray in the middle of the table, handed each man a plate, transferred one of the rolls from the tray to her own plate, then pulled up the remaining chair and sat down. Nodding to Callaghan and Greaves, she said in English: 'Eat, please.'

'*Merci, mademoiselle,*' Callaghan and Greaves said simultaneously.

'This is Maxine,' André told them. 'She left the village with me four years ago. She was then only eighteen years old and already my mistress. She has fought by my side ever since and I don't know what I would do without her. She'll slit a German throat or

85

blow out German brains without thinking twice. If you need a guide, she's at your disposal. Now, please, gentlemen, eat.'

As Maxine was already biting into her roll, the three men helped themselves and ate in silence, meanwhile glancing uneasily, first at one another, then at Maxine, who, though only twenty-two years old, seemed much older.

Eventually, putting his empty plate down, André asked: 'So what is your purpose here?'

'Our original brief,' Callaghan replied, 'was to establish a base, lie low and make contact with the Maquis, then work with you to aid the airborne landings scheduled to take place this week in the Orléans Gap. The main task would have been reconnaissance and sabotage, avoiding direct confrontation wherever possible. However, this morning, just before you returned, we received a coded radio message informing us that the airborne operation has been cancelled. Because of this, because General Patton's advance on Dijon is continuing, and because we're already here and can't go back, we've been ordered to include aggressive patrolling in our future activities in this area.'

'Did your brief include how to deal with us?'

'With your group in particular or the Maquis in general?'

'The Maquis in general.'

'Yes. We were told to try to unite the various local groups and use their pooled intelligence about

German locations, activities and troop movements. In return for this, we were to supply you with all the weapons and equipment you need, as well as the benefit of our military experience.'

André nodded and smiled for the first time, though the smile was world-weary and slightly mocking. 'It's nice to know that we'll receive the benefit of your superior military expertise.'

'I'm sorry, André,' Callaghan said. 'I didn't mean to insult the invaluable work being carried out by your group – and, of course, the others. But as you yourself have admitted, your activities have been restricted to relatively minor raids, ambushes and acts of sabotage. What we need now are more ambitious plans and greatly increased manpower and supplies. That's why we're here.'

'But the Maquis already aid the British and receive supplies, weapons and other kinds of aid from them, courtesy of the SOE.'

'Not enough,' Greaves said firmly, since he was the man who had to deal with the Special Operations Executive, a duty that he found frustrating and even counter-productive.

'You mean, not enough in view of the fact that the liberation of Europe has commenced,' André said sarcastically.

'I mean that precisely,' Greaves said. 'The more united we are, the more powerful we are – and the quicker this war comes to an end. It's in your own interests.'

André nodded solemnly, his face serious now. Maxine, sitting to his left, was still nibbling her roll, sipping her hot coffee and listening intently. A petite brunette with delicate features, she did not, to Callaghan's experienced eye, look like the type who could slit throats, German or otherwise.

'So do you have SOE backing for this?' André asked.

'No,' Callaghan replied honestly. 'We have the official backing of 1st Airborne Division and 21st Army Group. We have the discreet, though reluctant, backing of SOE.'

'Why reluctant?'

'Because the SOE sees the Maquis as its own concern. Because it has its own teams to carry out such tasks, it doesn't approve of the SAS arming and organizing Resistance groups.'

'But you insist that you can do it better,' André said.

'Yes. The SAS is widely experienced at insertion, supply and aggressive action behind enemy lines. Therefore, if we linked up with the Maquis, we could accomplish an awful lot together.'

André nodded again, though his smile remained sardonic. When the rumble of Allied aircraft flying to the front became too loud to speak, everyone glanced up automatically. Only when the sound of the aircraft had faded away did they return their attention to the matter in hand.

'So your aim,' André said, 'is to unite the numerous

local Maquis groups and place them under a single command, preferably your own.'

'Correct. For the good of all, André.'

The Maquis leader sighed. 'That may not be so easy, Captain. Unfortunately – and I am loath to admit this – the Maquis are split between the supporters of General de Gaulle's Free French and the communists. It sickens me to say so, but the latter regard de Gaulle as no more than the puppet of the British and Americans. They'll use him now – but they've made it perfectly clear that they'll discard him the instant they feel they can do so safely.'

'Yes,' Callaghan said. 'We've heard of the problems caused by that division, but we feel we can live with it and still benefit. How serious do you think it is?'

'Serious enough. Sadly, many Maquisards are more interested in storing weapons for after the war, when they intend to settle scores with de Gaulle's supporters. Frankly, they're more interested in that than they are in killing the Germans.'

'That explains why there are traitors in your midst.'

'Yes, I fear it does. With that fact you will have to learn to live – as indeed we do.'

'I'm willing to try it.'

Now looking more friendly, André, after glancing at Maxine, said: 'I can only assure you, Captain, that apart from the problems mentioned, you will find my men – I can only speak for my own, of course – well organized and highly motivated. If you're willing to try this, you'll have their full co-operation. I personally guarantee it.'

'Thank you, André.'

Both men shook hands across the table, then the Maquis leader pulled a packet of cigarettes from his jacket pocket and passed them round. Everyone lit up and puffed contentedly, including Maxine, who, sounding surprisingly sure of herself, despite her imperfect English, asked: 'So what happens now that you are here?'

Noticing that she was smiling and appeared charming, after all – suddenly realizing, in effect, just how young she really was – the Englishmen both relaxed.

'The first thing,' Callaghan said, 'is to bring in the rest of the equipment required for both groups – by which I mean the SAS and the Maquis. This will include tents for my men, decent food, more weapons and ammunition, and anything that your people may require. I'll brief my men in the morning, once they've had a proper rest, and arrange for the first drop tomorrow night at a DZ chosen by you. Once the supplies have arrived, we'll convert this tent city into a proper forward operating base, although still in tents, with ringed fortifications and good communications. Should all go well, we'll then be in a position to immeasurably aid the Allied advance through France. What do you say?'

André stared gravely at Callaghan and Greaves, glanced at his smiling girlfriend, then reached into another pocket and withdrew a hip-flask. Uncorking it, he poured its contents into each of the empty coffee cups. He then raised his cup in a toast and the others did the same.

'Calvados,' he explained, then at last smiled and said: 'Welcome, gentlemen! To friendship.'

6

Taking advantage of what Callaghan viewed as a day of rest, the men of C Squadron spent the morning cleaning and checking the firing mechanisms of their weapons, the afternoon studying maps of the area with the help of the Maquis, and then were called to an open-air briefing around five o'clock. Already exhausted, they squatted on the spare ground between their LUPs and the Maquisards' tents while the seemingly inexhaustible Captain Callaghan, with Captain Greaves by his side, told them about the recent change in plans.

'So,' Callaghan summarized, after telling them what he had already told André Flaubert, 'with the airborne landings cancelled, we can forget lying low and instead embark on a series of aggressive patrols.'

The men spontaneously began to clap, cheer and whistle, bringing a smile to the faces of both officers, who knew that the very idea of 'passive action' had been frustrating them. When the noise had subsided, which it did only after Sergeant Lorrimer bawled for silence, Callaghan continued.

'Our main tasks are to cut railway lines used as German supply routes or for troop movements, cause general disruption to enemy MSRs, respond to requests from 21st Army Group, 1st Airborne

Group, SOE and our own HQ back at Moor Park for information that will help them select targets for Allied bombing raids, and, when not specifically engaged in a task for the aforementioned, simply go out and attack German convoys or FOBs.'

This last remark caused another outburst of jubilation, which was instantly silenced by Lorrimer. When the noise had subsided, the ever-thoughtful Sergeant Bob Tappman asked: 'Do we operate under instructions from 21st Army Group, 1st Airborne Group or the SOE?'

'We operate under instructions from all three, but only when they have a specific task for us. Otherwise, we're on our own and can choose our own targets.'

Another bout of cheering was silenced when Bob Tappman asked: 'Do we make direct attacks on our own initiative?'

'Yes. Aggressive patrolling is now the order of the day. When not set a specific task by SOE, 21st Army Group or our own HQ, we're to attack the enemy where seen and, if possible, destroy their armoured vehicles with our Bofors anti-tank guns.'

'That's my kind of music!' Jacko said, laughing.

'What about communications?' It was Bob Tappman again, thoroughgoing as ever.

'Arrangements have been made for instructions or information to be received from, or sent to, Great Britain in a number of ways. One is the time-honoured use of homing pigeons carrying maps or coded information that will either help our bombers locate their targets or guide us to new targets for our hit-and-run raids.'

'Pigeons!' Harry-boy Turnball breathed melodramatically. 'We're back in the Dark Ages!'

'That's only one system,' Callaghan responded, unperturbed, 'and it's certainly more effective than you can imagine. Pigeons don't get shot out of the sky like aircraft and they don't argue like agents on the ground. In short, they're reliable.'

'The man's faith in human nature is amazing!' Jacko whispered to Rich.

'It's positively inspiring,' Rich whispered back. 'It gives me hope to go on.'

'Naturally,' Callaghan said, 'we'll continue to rely on the field radio, utilizing Morse code. But coded messages will also be put out by the BBC and received by our signallers working in the field with the resistance forces on various types of miniature receiver, such as the MCR1, known and loved by you all as the "biscuit receiver".' Callaghan was referring to the fact that the MCR1 was small enough to be slotted into a Huntley & Palmer's biscuit tin that also contained an additional three batteries and five miniature valves. 'However,' he continued, 'having learnt to our cost that German D/F – direction finding to the uninitiated – has become frighteningly efficient, it's recommended that those of you using the receivers change location and frequency as often as possible, to avoid being tracked down. You should also keep your transmissions as brief as possible. To help in this, a series of 600 four-letter codes has been devised and printed out on large silk scarves. Each of you – not just the signallers – will be supplied with one of these scarves and you're expected to carry it on your person at all times.'

'I always wanted a silk scarf,' Jacko said loudly. 'Now I can walk with a wiggle!'

'You'll get my boot up your arse if you do,' Lorrimer growled at him. 'Now shut up and let the boss get on with it.'

'What about air support?' Bob Tappman asked.

'No problem. As part of 1st Airborne Division, we've been promised strong support from the RAF, including the use of the Lancasters, Halifaxes, Stirlings and Dakotas of 38 Group, as well as others from 46 Group and the Special Duty Squadron based at Tempsford in Bedfordshire. If necessary, these will be supplemented by gliders. Supplies will include not only general kit, food and light weapons, but heavy-duty vehicles such as Bedford QL trucks, the latest, modified four-wheel-drive Willys jeeps, and the Bofors six-pounder anti-tank guns required for the task just mentioned.'

'Excuse me, boss,' Rich asked, 'but we all think the Willys jeeps are fine as they are, so how have they been modified?'

'Nothing that should bother you,' Callaghan replied, 'and a lot that should please you. The latest model is fitted with special armoured plating across the front bumper. That modified bumper has a wire-cutting device fixed to it. Another innovation is bulletproof Perspex screens in front of the driver and front gunner. The old condensers have been removed to enable reserve fuel tanks to be fitted under the driver's seat and over the lockers at the back, giving the jeep a range of over 600 miles. The new jeeps, like the previous models, are fitted with twin Vickers .303-inch K guns front and rear, but these now have heavier tubular-steel mountings. In addition, a fifth K gun has been mounted beside the driver, enabling him to fire while still driving with one hand.'

'I love it!' Jacko exclaimed.

'As the K guns can empty their 100-round magazines in half a second,' Callaghan continued, grinning at Jacko's enthusiasm, 'shooting tracer, armour-piercing and incendiary bullets, and rounds of ball ammunition, this additional gun for the driver has turned the jeep into a formidable mobile fighting unit. I think you will indeed love it.'

'Just let me at it!' the cocky Neil Moffatt called out.

'Also included with the weaponry for each jeep,' Callaghan continued briskly, knowing he had won the men's hearts, 'are a Bren gun for firing outside the jeep, grenades for dropping over the rear to deter pursuers and, of course, either a 9mm Sten sub-machine-gun or a tommy-gun as a personal weapon – you can make your own choice. Finally, for the purposes of communication, each jeep comes with a No. 11 radio, already mounted, and a set of S-phones and Eureka beacons which, being compact and lightweight, can be carried easily when you're out of the vehicle.'

'Do we use the radio for communication with our air support?' Bob Tappman asked.

'No,' Callaghan replied. 'Its transmissions take too long and could be picked up by the German D/F, so we'll only use it for on-the-ground communications. For anything else, particularly air support, we'll be using the S-phones and Eureka beacons. The former can be detected at a distance of up to six miles by an aircraft flying at 10,000 feet, while the latter can be picked up from up to forty miles away by any aircraft equipped with Rebecca radar. Even better, by using a narrow emission beam and ultrashort waves, both systems are virtually invisible to enemy D/F.'

'Can I take it we'll be working with the Maquis, boss?' Bob Tappman asked.

'Yes.'

'That could be tricky.'

'Yes. For one thing, they don't know too much about keeping under cover – they still tend to gather in large, noisy groups. More importantly, they're split between the supporters of de Gaulle and the communists, which means their network is riddled with traitors. We therefore have to be extremely careful when engaged in joint operations with them. If, for instance, they pick a DZ for us, we'll use it because of their knowledge of the local area – which means it will basically be a safe DZ – but we'll do so in the full awareness that it might have been compromised by a traitor passing on information about the drop to the Germans. What I'm saying is that I'm expecting a high level of co-operation between us and the Maquis, and that I believe them to be well organized and highly motivated in general, with invaluable local knowledge, but that the divisions between them, including their communist and Nazi sympathizers, could lead to dangerous complications. In short, respect them but treat them with caution. Finally, I should warn you that although you'll be wearing uniforms, the fact that you're working with the Maquis will get you branded as agents by the Germans.'

'What's the difference?' Jacko asked, being serious for once.

'The difference,' Callaghan told him bluntly, 'is that if the Krauts catch you, they'll ignore the rules of war, probably torture you for information, and almost certainly have you executed as enemy agents rather than soldiers.'

'So we don't let them catch us,' Jacko said.

'Precisely, Lance-Corporal.' Callaghan shifted his uncommonly direct gaze from Jacko to the other men. 'Any specific questions, gentlemen?'

'Yes, boss,' Harry-boy said, putting up his hand to be noticed, as if back in the schoolroom. 'When do we start?'

'Immediately. In fact, the first supplies are being dropped in about half an hour – ten minutes after last light – and I want you out there to collect the containers. I'm taking you there myself to show you how it's done. So get off your backsides and let's go. I want you in full battle kit in the Maquis transport five minutes from now.'

'Hop it!' Lorrimer bawled.

The open-air meeting broke up and the men hurried back to their LUPs to collect their webbing and weapons. Once kitted out, they hurried to the black Citroën vans and nondescript trucks used by the Maquis instead of jeeps because they reduced the chances of being stopped by German patrols. When everyone was in a vehicle, the column moved out of the camp, following a Citroën van which contained Captains Callaghan and Greaves and, right behind it, a similar vehicle carrying André Flaubert, Maxine, and other Maquisards, including a few women, to a drop zone some two miles from the camp.

They reached the DZ ten minutes later. There, in a huge field about 1000 yards long, watched carefully by the SAS troops, the Maquisards piled brushwood up in three piles approximately 100 yards apart to form an L shape, then poured the contents of cans of petrol over them. As they were doing so, some of the SAS men were dispatched to point positions north, south, east and west, first to check that no Germans were waiting in ambush and then to keep their eyes peeled for the enemy in general. Meanwhile, Callaghan, with his signalling torch in his hand, walked off to take up a position thirty yards to the west of the three brushwood beacons.

His signaller, Corporal Jim Almonds, had removed his S-phone from its aluminium box and was clipping it to the webbing on his chest, preparing to use it both as a homing beacon for the incoming Dakota and as a radio-telephone link with the plane's radio operator.

'When the incoming aircraft crosses the right angle formed by the brushwood piles and the recognition signal flashed by Captain Callaghan,' Captain Greaves explained to his men, 'the pilot will know he's at the DZ, flying into the wind, and can order his loadmaster to drop the supplies. Naturally, this is a system devised by the Maquis in the absence of proper equipment. When the Dakota drops its supplies, we'll be able to use the same set-up for other DZs, but with three red lights instead of the bonfires and a proper white light for flashing Morse instead of this torch. Got that?'

'Got it, boss,' Rich said.

'Good. Now I want you men to stand at regular intervals along both sides of the DZ – west and east of it – ready to run in and collect the containers being dropped by parachute. Clear the field before the aircraft makes its second pass to drop some more of our men. OK, get going.'

Running with their backs to the wind, which was blowing strongly, but facing the anticipated direction of the incoming plane, the SAS troopers took up their positions at regular intervals in two long lines either side of the DZ. Once in position, they divided their attention between watching for the Dakota, keeping their eyes peeled for Germans beyond the guarded perimeter of the field, and waiting for the Maquisards to set fire to the piles of brushwood. Though the resistance fighters waiting by the beacons included some young, attractive women, the SAS men kept their thoughts to themselves and did not make the usual chauvinistic remarks. Indeed, they were all as quiet as mice and the only sound to be heard until the plane came in was the wind's soft moaning.

Eventually, after what was only five minutes though it seemed much longer, Callaghan heard the distant drone of an approaching plane and instantly alerted Corporal Almonds, who plugged in the short-directional aerial of his S-phone. This would send out a beam that would vibrate the needle of the direction indicator on the controls of the incoming Dakota, enabling the pilot to fly directly towards the source of the signal. At the same time, the Maquisards lit blazing torches and threw them on to the three petrol-soaked piles of brushwood, which burst into flames and were soon burning fiercely.

This was the most dangerous part of the operation because the beacons could be seen a long way off and reveal the men's presence to passing German patrols. As a result, they grew increasingly nervous and wary as they waited for the aircraft.

Eventually it appeared in the southern sky, homing in on Almonds's S-phone and heading directly for the beacons. As it did so, Callaghan flashed a Morse confirmation that the DZ was clear. A back-up confirmation conveyed by the signaller's S-phone brought the aircraft right in over the DZ and the first of the canisters floated down beneath billowing white parachutes.

When the canisters had all landed, with their collapsed parachutes being whipped dramatically by the wind and the Dakota circling around to come back for the second drop, the SAS men on both sides of the DZ rushed in to collect them. The sheet-metal cylinders were all some six feet long, though there were two different kinds: C-type and H-type. The former contained weapons and clothing, packed carefully to fill the whole of their length, while the latter each held five smaller cylinders, locked together with restraining rods and carrying ammunition, rations and other supplies.

After sliding a thick wooden pole through each pair of carrying handles on the cylinders, some of the SAS men, in teams of four, carried the C-type containers away from the DZ and loaded them into the back of the Maquis trucks. To remove the H-type canisters from the field, they released the restraining rods, separated the five smaller cylinders, and carried them by straps slipped through their carrying rings.

A few minutes later the Dakota returned for its second drop, but this time it disgorged hampers, panniers, and even wicker baskets containing radio spares. Finally, when the aircraft made its third run, twelve more SAS paratroopers drifted down. As soon as they hit the ground, they were met by their comrades and escorted to the waiting trucks, which drove them away even as the Dakota was disappearing in the dark sky on its way back to England.

The men still in the field climbed back into the Maquis vehicles to be driven the two miles back to the camp. Once there, they emptied the containers, then buried them in ditches dug for the purpose and covered the upturned earth with foliage.

Fully equipped, they were now all set to attack.

7

The modified Willys jeeps were dropped by a Halifax the following night and quickly assembled by the SAS troopers. The original jeeps were passed on to the Maquis and at first light the next morning the SAS, guided by André, Maxine and a handful of other Maquisards, were on the road, looking for targets.

As before, they broke up into three columns and headed off in different directions, having agreed to meet up every two hours at a forest RV near the town of Châtillon. Group One was led by the jeep containing André, Maxine and two other male members of the Maquis. Directly behind the lead jeep was the one containing Sergeant Lorrimer, Jacko and Rich, with five more jeeps behind them, the last two filled with Maquisards.

Having left the camp just as the sun was rising over the green hills, they were soon racing along a road that wound pleasantly around hilly fields, between dense stands of birch trees and tall hedgerows. The roads and fields seemed empty, but the men knew that this appearance could be deceptive as skirmishes were taking place to the north, south and east, beyond the horizon, and in any case the movement of German troops was unpredictable. They were reminded of the larger war by the frequent passage of Allied bombers and, depending on the direction in which the constantly winding road took them, by the smoke darkening the sky to the east where General Patton's 3rd Army was advancing despite strong resistance.

As he passed a farmer in a horse-drawn cart – the first soul they had seen since setting out forty minutes earlier – André slowed down, ran alongside him and asked if the next village was clear of Germans. The farmer nodded. Hoping to pick up information about enemy movements from the villagers, André drove on with the rest of the column strung out behind him.

A sharp bend in the road led abruptly into the single street of a picturesque village, where a bunch of Afrika Korps troops were spilling out of a truck, probably intending to stretch their legs. Slamming his foot on the brake, André went into a brief, noisy skid and screeched to a halt, the jeeps behind doing the same.

Instantly, the Germans scattered to both sides of the road and behind their truck, unslinging their rifles on the move. The first shots were fired before the SAS and the Maquisards could get out of their vehicles – a fusillade that peppered André's jeep and blew out the front tyres. Even as bullets were ricocheting off the vehicle, the two men in the back were jumping out. André and Maxine scrambled over the rear seats to do the same.

Jacko's twin Vickers roared into action as he gave the men in the first jeep covering fire with a savage, sustained burst, swinging the weapon from left to right, cutting down the enemy soldiers still racing across the road. They screamed, dropped their weapons, flung their hands up, spun away and collapsed in clouds of dust. The survivors frantically pressed themselves flat against the front doors of the stone houses lining the street and returned Jacko's fire.

Behind Jacko, Rich let rip with his own machine-gun, aiming at the Germans on the left side of the road, spraying the walls around them with bullets, showering them with dust and flying fragments of stone. Meanwhile Lorrimer was kneeling behind the jeep, swinging in and out constantly to pick off individual Germans with short, deadly bursts from his 9mm Sten gun.

As André and Maxine dropped to the ground behind their vehicle, between the other two Maquisards, both of whom were leaning out to fire their rifles at the Germans shooting at them from behind their truck, the few civilians still in the street either threw themselves to the ground or bolted for cover into the nearest house or shop.

The SAS men not manning the mounted machine-guns were either firing their weapons from behind the jeeps or boldly darting across the road, dodging the whipping lines of dust created by German bullets, to take up positions in vacant doorways, from where they had an oblique view of the Germans hiding behind the truck. Having taken careful aim with their Sten guns and tommy-guns, they unleashed a hail of fire that cut down many of the Germans and forced the rest to flee from behind the truck and try to reach either side of the road, and the shelter of the doorways.

Few made it. Caught in a fusillade that turned the road into a storm of spitting dust and flying stones, most of them were cut down within seconds, screaming, shuddering, spinning and falling to the ground. The few who managed to reach cover failed to find the protection they had sought. Jacko and Rich had taken opposite sides of the road and were pouring a murderous hail of fire from their machine-guns into the doorways, so that the Germans trying to fire from there were blinded and choked by the dust and debris thrown up by the stream of bullets. As they leant forward gingerly to see and breathe properly, they were savagely cut down.

At that moment, Lorrimer unclipped the pin of a 36 hand-grenade and hurled it at the rear of the troop truck. The grenade looped upward in a languid arc, then fell into the back of the vehicle. Less than a second later, it exploded, blowing the canvas covering to shreds, setting the flying tatters on fire and buckling the exposed metal supports. Simultaneously, the petrol tank exploded with a deafening roar, creating an inferno of yellow flames and boiling black smoke, from which emerged two screaming Germans, both on fire and quivering epileptically as they slumped to the ground.

'Go after them!' Lorrimer yelled, jabbing his finger to indicate both sides of the street, where the few remaining German soldiers were scurrying into the houses.

As the SAS troops inched along both sides of the street, darting from door to door, the eight Maquisards from the last two jeeps split into two groups and hurried behind the houses, intent on stopping the Germans making their escape by the back doors.

'The top floors!' Lorrimer bawled as he dropped back on his haunches and aimed his Sten gun up at the top window of one of the houses. His short, controlled burst blew out the window, where a shadowy figure had appeared, and the figure dropped back out of sight. Lorrimer then jumped up and ran towards the houses on his right, following André and Maxine and screaming over his shoulder to Jacko and Rich: 'Keep manning those guns!' Frustrated, Jacko and Rich had to remain in the jeep while Lorrimer and other troopers rushed into the houses, kicking in doors where necessary, and began to flush out the remaining Germans as the occupants huddled in panic behind the furniture.

As the SAS men were entering the houses, following the example set by André and Maxine, most of the remaining German soldiers were fleeing through the back doors – where they were cut down by the Maquisards waiting for them. Lorrimer heard the harsh chatter of their lethal gunfire as he raced through the small living-room of the house he had entered, then saw the frantically jabbing finger of the white-faced housewife, indicating that a German soldier was upstairs.

Aware that the villagers could ill afford the damage being inflicted on their houses, but knowing too that it was unavoidable, Lorrimer went carefully to the stairs, looked up, saw nothing, then started to ascend as quietly as possible. He was halfway up when, to his relief, he heard the loud chatter of a Schmeisser being fired from inside the front bedroom. The noise drowned his footfall on the creaking stairs as he covered the last treads and turned into the short, gloomy hallway.

An Afrika Korps trooper was at the window of the bedroom to Lorrimer's left, firing down on the men in the street. Temporarily deafened by the roar of his machine-gun, he did not hear the SAS man until it was too late. At that point he jerked his head around, saw Lorrimer aiming at him, and tried to turn his whole body so as to fire his weapon. Lorrimer's burst took him in the chest, punching him back against the window frame, which rattled violently, and turning his tunic into a bloody rag. Bouncing off the wall, he flopped face down on the floor as his Schmeisser clattered noisily across the bare boards.

Lorrimer checked that he was dead, then went downstairs and said in his halting French to the frightened woman: 'I'm sorry. Don't go up there. Wait until we come back for the body. We'll be as quick as possible.'

The woman was speechless with fright and merely

nodded at Lorrimer as he went back into the street. Short bursts of gunfire could still be heard from behind the houses on both sides, but most of the SAS and resistance fighters were now coming out of the houses, having killed off any snipers found inside.

Lorrimer was learning from Rich that there were no SAS or Maquis casualties when two Afrika Korps troopers emerged from a house with their hands up, being covered by André and the delicate-featured Maxine. The Maquis leader was carrying the Germans' Schmeissers in his free hand. When they were back on the road, near the smouldering ruins of the troop truck blown up by Lorrimer's grenade, Maxine kept them covered with her American M1 carbine as André questioned them about the strength and movements of other German units in the area. When both men refused to answer, Maxine placed the barrel of her weapon against the back of the head of one of them.

'Talk or I shoot,' she said in German.

Both men shook their heads.

Maxine pressed the trigger and the German's head exploded into a torrent of blood and flying bone as his body convulsed and collapsed.

'What the hell . . .!' Outraged and red-faced, Sergeant Lorrimer marched up to André and Maxine and glared at each of them in turn. 'That man was our prisoner!' he bawled.

'He refused to talk,' Maxine said quietly. 'You can rest assured that this one will.' Then, unconcerned by

Lorrimer's rage, she placed the barrel of her carbine against the second soldier's head.

'Talk or I shoot,' she said.

The German started babbling to André, who listened attentively while Lorrimer, disgusted, hurried off to give his men further instructions.

'Jesus Christ, did you see that?' Jacko asked Rich, both of them still standing at their mounted machine-guns.

'Christ, yes! She didn't hesitate for a second – just blew his brains out.'

'Bloody barbaric,' Jacko said, spitting over the side of the jeep.

'She's such a sweet-looking young thing,' Rich said, studying Maxine with disbelieving eyes. 'You'd think butter wouldn't melt in her mouth . . . And then she does that.'

'Fucking hard life in the Maquis. If they're caught, the Germans routinely torture them before executing them. That knowledge toughens them up.'

'I'll say it does!'

'All right, stop your jabbering,' Lorrimer told them when he reached the jeep. 'We're not finished yet. Listen to me, everyone!' he bawled down the column. 'I want one man to remain in the jeep, manning a machine-gun. The others are to form two-man teams and go back into the houses to drag out any dead Germans you find there.' He waited for the inevitable groans to die away, then continued: 'When you bring the dead out, line them

111

up along the street near the blacksmith's . . . *Corporal Almonds!*'

'Yes, Sarge!' the signaller called back from the radio jeep.

'We can't have these Krauts stinking up the village and maybe causing disease, so get on the radio and tell base camp to send out a burial detail.'

'Will do, Sarge!'

'All right, men, get to it.'

Most of the SAS men tossed coins to determine who would stay in the jeep and who would get the less pleasant job of gathering up the dead. As the losers were dispersing, muttering under their breath, the Maquisards who had gone round the back of the same houses, to cut down the Germans trying to escape that way, appeared around the corners at both ends of the short street, walking backwards with their weapons slung over their shoulders, dragging the German dead by their feet. Lorrimer told them to use the area in front of the blacksmith's. Eventually, the SAS men had dragged out the others and the many blood-soaked dead were lying on their backs in the street, being studied by the curious, often delighted, villagers.

'So,' Lorrimer said to André, still furious with them both. 'Did you get anything valuable out of the prisoner you didn't execute?'

'A little, but not much,' said André. 'I think he genuinely didn't know much about anything other than the plans for his own squadron.'

'So the other one died in vain.'

'We all do, Sergeant.'

'And what have you done with the survivor?'

André pointed to inside the blacksmith's shop, where the prisoner was resting on the ground, his hands and legs tied, one of the Maquisards keeping him covered with an M1 carbine. 'My man will protect him from the wrath of the villagers, then hand him over to the SAS burial party when they arrive.'

'Good,' Lorrimer replied, only slightly mollified. 'Let's move on.'

The column moved out of the village, leaving behind the German dead and the grateful, cheering residents. Almost immediately the jeeps were back in the narrow lane that wound in a leisurely manner between smooth, green hills and tall hedgerows. The sun was now high in the sky and the birds were singing lustily. Only the smoke staining the blue sky in the distance reminded them that the war was still being fought at that very moment.

'A nice little drive,' Jacko said, sitting beside his Vickers, which was now in the locked position, its barrel pointing skyward. 'A pleasant day in the country.'

'Apart from nearly getting our balls shot off, it's been *very* pleasant,' said Rich, who was now likewise sitting relaxed, though his dark eyes remained watchful.

'At least it's better than North Africa,' Jacko said. 'Lots more to see. Not least some pretty French fillies. Does the heart good, that does.'

'They're supposed to be pretty liberal, aren't they?' Rich asked doubtfully.

'So they say. At least, they think the English are a bunch of puritans by comparison, so they must be pretty quick off the mark when it comes to pulling their knickers down. I wouldn't mind a taste of it.'

'Maybe when we get leave.'

'In Paris,' Jacko said.

'I always wanted to see Paris,' Rich revealed, 'and I can't wait to get there.'

'I wouldn't argue with that. Cheap cognac, naughty nightclubs and fast fillies. That'll do me, mate.'

The roar of a 75mm gun cut short their conversation as the jeep turned a corner. Both men ducked instinctively when the shell whistled over their heads and exploded between them and the jeep behind, showering them with soil, stones and grass as the blast slammed their jeep forward into the ditch by the side of the road.

As the other jeeps screeched to a halt at both sides of the road, spilling out their men, Lorrimer, Jacko and Rich crawled from their wrecked vehicle and wriggled down into the ditch, between darting, spitting lines of dust kicked up by a torrent of machine-gun bullets. Looking up, they saw a good number of German troops advancing boldly from a sandbagged gun emplacement at the side of the road, most firing Schmeissers from the hip.

More bullets ricocheted around them, shredding the foliage and making the dirt spit in jagged lines as

Jacko and Rich unslung their tommy-guns. Hearing a scream, Lorrimer glanced behind him and saw that one of the Maquisards had been hit and was rolling on to his back, grabbing frantically at his smashed and bloody kneecap. The SAS troops beyond him were either resting on one knee or were down on their bellies, firing at the advancing Germans.

'*Bring up some Bren guns!*' Lorrimer bawled as a medic crawled towards the wounded man.

The sergeant turned back to the front as a big, blond German ran straight towards him, firing from the hip. As Jacko and Rich were still disentangling the personal weapons slung across their shoulders, Lorrimer raised his Sten gun and fired a burst into the advancing soldier. The giant screamed, convulsed, dropped his weapon and clutched his stomach, then pitched forward into the dirt.

Nevertheless, more German troops were advancing along the edge of the field on the other side of the hedgerow, which their relentless fire was tearing to shreds. The bullets tore up soil and dust around Lorrimer and his men, and leaves and smashed branches showered down on them. The noise was atrocious.

Spitting dirt and rubbing it from their eyes, Neil and Harry-boy crawled past the wounded, screaming Maquisard as Jacko and Rich opened fire with their tommy-guns.

Squinting through a gap in the hedgerow, Lorrimer saw that the road bent back almost at a right angle and that the last two of his jeeps were parked there, with the men clambering out and clearly about to crawl around to the front. Wanting to use those same men to attack the German flank instead, he shouted to Neil and Harry-boy: 'Keep those bastards back!' Then he crawled away.

The roar of the two Bren guns joined the noisy chatter of Jacko and Rich's weapons as Lorrimer crawled past the wounded Frenchman, who was quieter now that he was being attended to by the medic.

Another 75mm shell whistled overhead and exploded with a mighty roar between two of the jeeps. No one was hurt, though Lorrimer found himself crawling through swirling dust and soil with a loud, ringing noise in his head.

As the murk cleared, André came into view, jumping up from behind a jeep and swinging his free hand to release a 'potato-masher' – a captured German hand-grenade which had a wooden handle with a screw-on exploding canister at one end. Even as the long, thin device was curving through the air, André was dropping back behind the jeep, beside the petite but murderous Maxine, and firing another burst from his M1 carbine, as his girlfriend was doing.

The potato-masher exploded in the midst of the Germans advancing along the side of the ditch, slamming them in opposite directions, some into the hedgerow, others on to the road, and covering the areas in a choking black smoke.

Lorrimer crawled on, passing André and Maxine,

until he came to the bend in the road. There, he jumped up and ran at the crouch around the curve to meet the SAS men coming the other way, also crouching and with weapons ready.

'Get back,' he shouted. 'I don't want you at the front. There are more Krauts advancing along the other side of the hedgerow, just down from the gun position. I think we can attack their flank from further along this lane, where it curves sharply back on itself. So turn around and go back the way you came, past your jeeps, until we find a direct line of fire to that gun position. *Now move it!*'

The men, led by Sergeant Bob Tappman and Corporal Benny Bennett, did as they were told and hurried back with Lorrimer around the bend to their jeeps as a German mortar shell exploded nearby, showering them with soil and slapping them with its shock waves. As they passed the jeeps, Lorrimer made the men stop and told Benny to pick up the 2.36-inch bazooka and some 60mm shells. This done, Benny and the others kept going until they came to where the road curved dramatically and gave a direct view across the field to the back of the gun emplacement. It also gave a clear line of fire into the flank of the Germans who were inching their way along the edge of the field and firing through the hedgerow at the SAS and the Maquisards.

'Perfect,' Lorrimer whispered, then turned with a triumphant grin to Sergeant Tappman. 'Bob, set that Bren gun up on its bipod and fire the instant the first shell from the bazooka explodes. Corporal Bennett will fire the bazooka at my command. The rest of you will join the Bren gun in putting a stop to those bastards inching along the field. Let's give them what for, lads.'

While Bob Tappman was setting up his Bren gun, Benny Bennett stretched out on his belly on the ground, rested the relatively light bazooka anti-tank weapon on his right shoulder, loaded it with a 60mm shell, then took hold of the grips and aimed at the centre of the enemy position. Lorrimer waited until both men were ready, then tapped Benny on the shoulder and said: 'Fire!'

The bazooka appeared to explode on Benny's shoulder, spitting a fierce flame, jerking backwards to rock the corporal's whole body, and propelling the shell out of the barrel on a tracery of smoke that showed exactly where the shell was going. It shot in a virtually straight line into the rear of the sandbagged gun emplacement, then exploded with a deafening roar and a force that made the ground shake.

Even as the position was blown apart, with human limbs, twisted metal and sand from the shredded sandbags spinning out and upwards amid clouds of boiling smoke, Bob Tappman was opening fire with his Bren gun, sweeping it left and right to pour his bullets in a long arc into the flank of the Germans advancing along the edge of the field. As he did so, the other SAS men added a murderous hail of fire from their 9mm Sten sub-machine-guns and tommy-guns.

The hedgerow framing the Germans was torn to shreds, leaves raining down and broken branches flying everywhere as they jerked, twisted, shook spasmodically and finally collapsed. Those at the beginning and end of the column managed to run in opposite directions out of the line of fire, but Bob Tappman and his troopers adjusted their aim and had cut them down too within seconds.

When the smoke from the devastated emplacement had cleared, there were only dead Germans in the field to the side of it. The position itself was a mess of burning canvas, smouldering sandbags and charred, lifeless bodies. This side of the field had been brutally, efficiently cleared.

'Now we can cross the field and catch the other Germans on the road between us and the rest of our column,' Lorrimer said. 'Come on, men, let's go.'

While Bob Tappman folded up the bipod of his Bren gun in order to tuck the weapon into his side like an assault rifle, Benny Bennett broke the bazooka in half to make it easier to carry. They and the rest of the men then spread out in a long line, so as to reduce the risk of being hit by enemy fire, and advanced toward the dead Germans sprawled by the hedgerow near the destroyed gun emplacement.

As they advanced across the empty field, they could hear the continuing gunfire from the road on the other side of the hedgerow, where the Germans were still moving slowly along the rim of the ditch. Approaching the hedgerow carefully, the

SAS men spread out even more to give themselves individually selected targets. Through gaps in the hedgerow they could see the German soldiers making their painfully slow progress and, further along, the SAS and Maquisards firing at them from behind the parked jeeps.

At a hand signal from Lorrimer, the men fired through the hedgerow, their combined fire-power tearing much of it to shreds and cutting down the Germans on the other side. Taken completely by surprise and shocked by the massacre, the remaining Germans panicked and either jumped down into the ditch or leapt over it on to the road. Either way, they made themselves prime targets.

A minute or so later, the last of the Germans had fallen and silence descended over the road. Lorrimer then led his group around the opening in the hedge, near the wrecked enemy gun position, and back up the road to join the others. Even as he was approaching them, he saw André, Maxine and the other Maquisards giving the *coup de grâce* to the German wounded. Knowing that he could do nothing to stop them, Lorrimer just looked the other way.

'Let's head for the RV,' he said to Jacko and Rich. 'We've got to get there before dark.'

'We should be sleeping during the day,' Jacko said, 'and fighting at night. Driving about here in broad daylight is crazy. What do you think, Sarge?'

'I think you're right, Jacko.'

When the single Allied casualty, the wounded Maquisard, had been placed in the jeep and the other men were all seated, the column moved off.

8

Arriving at the RV just before sunset, Sergeant Lorrimer's group met up with the other two, headed by Captains Callaghan and Greaves. As they would do for the rest of their sojourn in France, even before making up their bashas the men carried out their customary inspection of the jeeps, checking the oil, water, petrol, carburettors and tyres before the sun set. While they were doing so, Corporal Jim Almonds was using two improvised systems to simultaneously recharge exhausted radio batteries. For some he was using a small windmill mounted on a collapsible ten-foot pole. For others he was using a steam recharger consisting of a boiler hung over a brazier and attached to a portable two-cylinder engine coupled to a generator. The pressure resulting from the steam in the boiler was then used to recharge the six-volt batteries. The signaller was also checking the five miniature tubes, three thirty-hour batteries and MCR1 receivers housed in biscuit tins and generally carried by the men when on foot for clandestine operations.

'Albert bloody Einstein,' Harry-boy Turnball said mockingly as he passed by to have a piss in the bushes.

'Who's he?' said Almonds.

'A Kraut scientist,' Harry-boy informed him, so in love with the idea of being superior that he temporarily forgot his bursting bladder.

'The enemy,' the signaller replied.

'A genius,' Harry-boy corrected him.

'Then how come he's a fucking Kraut,' Almonds asked. 'They're all blockheads, they are.'

'Conquered most of Europe, mate.'

'Soft twats, the Europeans, that's why. Frogs and Eyeties and what have you. Not worth pissing on.'

'Which reminds me,' Harry-boy said. 'I'm going to piss in a hole in the ground, but I should be pissing on you instead.'

'What have *I* done?' Almonds asked.

'It's not you; it's your mother.'

'What's me mum got to do with this?'

'She gave birth to you, you daft arsehole.' Harry-boy said, then strode off to empty his bladder.

Ignoring the banter, Sergeant Lorrimer reported to Captain Callaghan, who was sitting with Captain Greaves in the shade of a tree, comparing notes and checking maps. When Lorrimer had reported his group's activities of the day, Callaghan said: 'Not much different to ours. We ran into Jerry wherever we turned and went up against mortars and machine-guns. I was told they only travelled by night, but clearly that's rubbish.'

'Right, boss,' Lorrimer replied. 'Even Jacko – Lance-Corporal Dempster – said we should start going out on patrol only at night, and I think he's right.'

'What do you think, Dirk?' Callaghan asked Greaves.

'I agree. The very idea that Jerry would only travel by night is patently ridiculous. Allied aircraft are pounding their main positions night and day, so they're moving whenever they can and doing it in every damn direction. About the only constant in this fluctuating picture is the knowledge that they're all hoping to get to Germany in the end. Apart from that, they're certainly on the move twenty-four hours a day, which means that we can use the benefit of darkness.'

'Fine,' Callaghan said. 'We're all agreed on that. We'll take tonight and tomorrow off, then move out again tomorrow night. Otherwise we'll use the same tactics, mainly hit-and-run.'

'I'm not sure about having three different groups, though,' Greaves said. 'I had four separate encounters with Jerry today and lost three jeeps in the process. You lost two jeeps, boss. What about you, Sergeant Lorrimer?'

'One.'

'Lucky man!'

'But you're right, Dirk,' Callaghan said. 'That's six jeeps down in the first day – and that's too many for my liking. So I agree that we should divide into two instead of three groups. Do you agree, Sergeant?'

Though Lorrimer was far from being the only

sergeant in the squadron, he was treated as virtually a second in command because he was one of the Originals. 'Yes,' he said, 'I do.'

'That means I command one group,' Callaghan pointed out, 'and Captain Greaves the other.'

'Agreed,' Lorrimer told him.

Relieved, both officers glanced out of their natural shelter to where the rest of the men, in gathering darkness, having checked their vehicles, weapons and other kit, including radios, were starting to put up their personal choice of basha. The simpler option was a hollow scraped out of the earth and covered with a roof of thatch and wire. The other type of basha was a simple lean-to, to construct which two Y-shaped sticks were hammered into the earth and a crossbar, usually the branch of a tree, was placed horizontally between them and hooked into the upright Y shapes. A waterproof poncho was then draped over the branch, with the long end facing the wind and the short end tied to the ground with the cords attached to its edges. Inside both kinds of basha, a sleeping bag was unrolled on the ground. Foliage was then spread over the top of the basha so that it blended in with the surroundings, especially when viewed from the air.

As soon as they had finished their bashas, the men began to open their cold rations. Hot food was permitted only during the day, when the flames from the hexamine stoves could not be seen by the enemy.

'What about the Maquis?' Lorrimer asked.

Without thinking, Callaghan and Greaves glanced at each other, then both looked at the sergeant.

'Why do you ask?' said Callaghan.

'Frankly, boss, I think our views are so different that we won't be able to work comfortably together. The Maquis have had, shall we say, a more . . . *intimate* contact with Jerry than we have. I mean, they've had relations and friends captured, tortured and killed, so they tend to ignore the rules of war. This morning, during our first engagement, one of them, a woman, cold-bloodedly shot a prisoner in the back of the head just to scare another into talking. The second German talked all right, but I don't think it's the kind of thing we should be encouraging, let alone allow the men to see.'

'Did you try talking to them about it?' Callaghan asked.

'I did, but it made no impression on them. Obviously they thought I was soft. Anyway I have my doubts that we can exercise any kind of control over the Maquis – and that could make them dangerous to us. So I say let's consider not sharing any further missions with them.'

'I'm inclined to agree with that,' Greaves said. 'Not only for those reasons, but for others.'

'Such as?' Callaghan asked him.

'Already there have been fights between the Maquis in our group because some of the weapons distributed during the resups have disappeared and the de Gaulle supporters believe that the communists have stashed them away for use after the war – against the Gaullists, that is. The communists have denied this, but what can't be denied is that the weapons are missing and both sides now resent each other – which doesn't help when we're trying to plan a raid. The two branches of the Maquis are at each other's throats and that could lead to trouble for us. So, yes, I agree with Sergeant Lorrimer.'

The rumble of aircraft overhead made them all look up. The sky was now nearly dark, with few stars and gathering clouds, but they could see the dimmed lights of what appeared to be a huge armada of heavy bombers, all heading for the front further south. The dark southern horizon was frequently illuminated with silvery flashes, indicating that bombing raids were already under way. Over there it would certainly be hell on earth, but from where they were it looked pretty and dreamlike.

Callaghan sighed. 'Well, I must say I *did* find my particular bunch of Maquisards pretty undisciplined, with a tendency to gather in large groups and make a lot of noise at the wrong moment. Also, when engaging Jerry, they tended to act like a bunch of cowboys, following their own bent instead of sticking to what had been planned between us. I suspect they may have been doing this more than they normally would because their leader, André, wasn't present, being in your group, Sergeant, but it was certainly enough to make me think twice about depending on them too heavily in the future.'

'So what do you propose?' Callaghan asked.

'A loose affiliation. In future, if we must go on raids together, let the Maquis act independently of us, doing their own thing. They will, in effect, become the third group we'd decided not to have because our jeeps are down in numbers already. In other words, Group One headed by me, Group Two by Captain Callaghan, and Group Three, the Maquis under André. In this way we can utilize their local knowledge and considerable talents for clandestine operations without actually trying to operate alongside them.'

'Sounds sensible,' Greaves said.

'I agree,' Lorrimer added.

Glancing at the lights flashing spasmodically on the otherwise dark horizon, Captain Greaves, while thinking the sight was strangely beautiful, knew just how hellish it must be for those on the ground. His own early involvement with the SAS, in its original form as L Detachment, had sprung indirectly from his being wounded in the great battle for Mersa Brega and Tobruk in the Cyrenaica Desert in March 1941. Then acting as an observation officer for the Middle East Headquarters (MEHQ) in Cairo, he had been in the sprawling Allied camp outside Mersa Brega when it was attacked by the combined might of Rommel's Afrika Korps Panzer divisions, with their deadly Mark III and Mark IV tanks, a horde of Ju-87 Stuka dive-bombers, six-wheeled armoured cars and motorized infantry.

When the appalling din of the British ack-ack guns,

Bren guns and 0.5-inch Browning machine-guns was added to that of the German big guns and Panzer 55mm and 75mm fire, the noise became an almost palpable pressure around the head and the air filled up with choking, blinding dust, weirdly illuminated by darting flames and exploding flares.

Even now, Greaves could clearly recall the sensation of the ground shaking beneath him from the explosions, the screaming of wounded and dying men, the roaring, banging and rattling of tanks and other armoured vehicles and, to top it all, the demented scream of the Stukas. It had, indeed, been hell on earth – so much so that Greaves had almost been relieved to have his leg shattered by a round of bullets just outside the harbour town of Tobruk, from where he was casualty-evacuated to the hospital in Alexandria, where he first met the former Scots Guard officer and No. 8 Commando lieutenant, David Stirling, the creator and former head of the SAS.

Once L Detachment had gone into action in North Africa, Greaves saw lots more action, much of it extremely dangerous, but none of it could compare for sheer horror to that mighty battle in Cyrenaica. The combination of smoke, dust and infernal noise had been almost unbearable. So, while the distant lights of the present front were bewitching from where he stood, he didn't envy the men suffering under that bombardment.

* * *

'So we become night raiders,' Lorrimer said. 'What are your plans, boss? Anything definite?'

'Not really,' Callaghan replied, 'other than to avoid any more accidental encounters with Jerry and only attack him when we can take him by surprise.'

'Which means?' Greaves asked.

'For a start, it means a great deal of avoidance. According to what a French farmer told me this afternoon, there are Panzer troops strung over this whole area, albeit without their armoured vehicles in most cases. I therefore suggest that we leave tomorrow night, at 2200 hours, drive to Semur, find a suitable location for the next RV, then break up to cover as wide an area as possible, returning to the RV before dawn. Once there, we'll decide on the following night's general target area – and so on each day.'

'Each night, to be precise,' Lorrimer said.

'Sounds rather enjoyable, actually,' Greaves put in. 'I have to admit to finding this kind of war pleasurable compared with what we've been through before. A bit like cowboys and Indians.'

'That's a glib way of putting it,' Callaghan told him, 'but I'll admit it's a bit like that. Not your average kind of war.'

There were, as Callaghan well knew, many different kinds of war and this was the kind that he liked most – it was certainly preferable to being one of those foot soldiers beyond the horizon. The uncomfortable truth, he realized, was that while there were certain horrors of war which he could well do without and, in some instances, indeed dreaded, generally speaking he enjoyed being at war and couldn't really imagine living without it. Though happily married, with one son, Callaghan was forced to accept that no matter how much he loved his family, he could never stay at home for long. This was common to many soldiers, he knew, particularly SAS men, but it was something that few of them would admit.

Take Greaves, he thought. Though soon to be a father and clearly in love with his young wife, Mary, it was highly unlikely that he would even have considered giving up the SAS for her. Like Callaghan – and like most of the other men in the regiment – Greaves was a decent man who simply could not lead a normal life, being constantly hungry for adventure. Indeed, as Callaghan now recalled with a wry smile, being in love with his wife had not stopped Greaves, back in 1941, when still engaged to his sweetheart, from having a brief fling with Frances Beamish, the attractive Royal Army Medical Corps nurse who had ministered to his needs when his broken leg was healing in the Scottish Military Hospital in Alexandria. That brief affair, Callaghan knew, had sprung out of Greaves's insatiable desire for romance and adventure. In fact, for him, love was rather like war: a form of distraction.

Sergeant Lorrimer was no different. Though reportedly happily married with three children, he had confessed to Callaghan that he was always restless at home and couldn't wait to get back to the regiment, particularly if there was a war to be fought. Nor was it an accident that when first approached to join L Detachment, he had been found in Tiger Lil's brothel in Cairo, where he had actually rented a room for the whole of his leave. When asked why he had done so, he had answered with a single word: 'boredom'.

Lorrimer was a man who liked a man's world and had been toughened by it. Though decent, he had his steely side and made it work for him. War may have been hell to some, but Lorrimer loved it. That's what few can admit, Callaghan thought. The love of war, which many insist is uncivilized, is, rightly or wrongly, an ineradicable part of man's nature. Some truths a lot of people would rather reject. Some are too hard to bear.

'So what are our targets for the night raids?' Lorrimer asked.

'Railway lines, trains, airfields, grounded aircraft, radar stations, communications cables, bridges of strategic value, troop convoys, German FOBs, individual vehicles or foot patrols – anything we can attack before Jerry knows what's happening to him. No more direct encounters like those we had today. No flamboyant gestures.'

'Tell that to the Maquis,' Greaves said sardonically. 'They'll be all ears, I'm sure.'

'I'll go and see André right away,' Callaghan said.

'You won't have to,' Lorrimer told him. 'Here he comes with his sweet, murdering girlfriend.'

The Frenchman was emerging from the darkness of the trees, with Maxine by his side, both of them criss-crossed with webbing and spare ammunition, both with M1 carbines in their hands and Lugers holstered at the hip. When they reached the SAS men, they nodded sombrely.

'A very good first day,' André said with more enthusiasm than they had seen in him before. 'So what plans for tomorrow?'

'You thought that was a good day?' Callaghan asked with an ambiguous smile.

'Of course!' the Maquis leader exclaimed, looking almost happy. 'We killed many Germans!'

'And lost six jeeps,' Callaghan reminded him.

'Six jeeps for twenty Germans,' Maxine said, her brown eyes direct and challenging. 'That's a good trade, Captain.'

'It might have been if we'd planned it that way,' Callaghan countered. 'But we didn't, which means it was no gain. It was simply an accident.'

Maxine frowned and glanced at André, who merely shrugged and then returned his gaze to Callaghan. 'There are many beneficial accidents in war, Captain. They should not be disowned.'

'Accidents of any kind should be avoided at all costs, André. Certainly, an accident that just happens to turn out right for us should not be treated as something worth celebrating.'

133

'I'm confused, Captain. We killed a great many German soldiers, yet you . . .'

'We were lucky, that's all. We didn't plan to kill them. We didn't even plan to attack them. All three groups fought the Germans in self-defence and desperation. We didn't take them by surprise, as a result of planning. We just ran straight into them. That we only lost six jeeps, instead of a lot of men, was extremely fortunate. As for the jeeps, six were anyway too many to lose in the first day. We made a mess of it, André.'

The Frenchman stared at Callaghan as if he couldn't believe his ears, then glanced at Maxine. The young woman's gaze, though remaining steady, was more intense than before. It was a look of pure anger.

'Shit!' she exploded. 'That's what you're trying to give us! You turn our triumph into a turd because you want to control us. Well, Captain, it won't work. We know too much for that. You come here as our liberators, filled with the confidence of the free, but you don't know a damn thing. *We* know! We have borne witness for years. We know how the Germans think, what they will do, and we react accordingly. You do not like to see Germans executed? Unplanned fire-fights disturb you? Then get out of our way, Captain Callaghan, and let us win the war our way.'

'I don't think I can do that,' Callaghan replied calmly. 'Before the invasion, the war was between only you and the Germans – they were in control and you were underground – but now the war's out in the open and your many allies are also involved – British, American, Canadian, Australian, freed Europeans, your fellow Frenchmen – so you can't fight the way you did before, as if you're the only ones. Instead, you must think of what's happening elsewhere and plan according to that.'

'Which means?'

'No more accidental encounters, André. No summary executions. No driving about in the daylight just to find a fire-fight. We have to move under cover of darkness and make our plans carefully. We have to be more precise.'

'He's insulting you!' Maxine hissed.

André looked steadily at her, admiring her fierce courage and conviction. Then he smiled slightly and said: 'No, I think not.' Turning back to Callaghan, he asked: 'You want to take control of my men, Captain?'

'No, I don't think that would help.'

'Why not?'

'I don't think they would take orders from me.'

A sly form of flattery, this made André smile.

'Correct, Captain. They would not take orders from you. If you angered them, they would shoot you in the back and throw your body into a ditch. They have no time for doubts.'

'That I appreciate,' Callaghan informed him. 'You've lived close to the edge.'

'On the edge of a razor,' Maxine told him, 'so we do things our own way.'

Callaghan smiled. 'All right, I'll grant you that. Nevertheless, we have to somehow work together and take the best from each other.'

'Agreed,' André said. 'We have fought too long without support and now we need yours.' Maxine glared at him, but he ignored her. 'What do you propose?'

'We retain the concept of three groups, but instead of the Maquis being divided between the three, they will now form the whole of the third group, operating under your leadership. We will travel by night instead of by day, to avoid accidental confrontations with the enemy; and only hit hard targets that can be taken by surprise.'

'What does that mean?' Maxine asked, her delicate features showing a tightly controlled rage mixed with a grudging interest.

'Railway lines and trains; aircraft and airfields; radar installations and other communications centres; convoys on the move with the troops still in the trucks; FOBs . . .'

'Pardon?' André interjected.

'Forward operating bases or, for the purpose of your attacks, any German bases or camps which, at night, are in a state of relative inactivity and can be attacked with the benefit of surprise.'

'The British have turned cowardice into an art form,' Maxine spat.

136

Callaghan shrugged and spread his hands in the air as if asking to be pardoned for his sins. 'What can I say? War is war and the loser loses all – and we can't afford that. We have hundreds of thousands of Allied troops advancing through France towards Germany and we can't risk their lives for misplaced feelings of honour. In other words, we do not invite the Germans to shoot us before we fire our own weapons. We do not travel in broad daylight only to run unexpectedly into well-armed German columns. We do not announce our arrival to the enemy and trust they will let us win. This isn't cowardice, *mademoiselle*; it's simple common sense. I trust you will see that.'

There was silence for a moment, then, after glancing at André, Maxine nodded her agreement.

'Good,' Callaghan said. 'Now why don't we pool our information about German strength and movements, about the locations of their most strategically important camps, airstrips or communications centres, and work out a precise plan of attack based on three different groups all attacking in different areas at once?'

'I have everything marked up on these maps,' André said, tugging a handful of maps from the rucksack on his back. 'Let's work out who does what.'

'Excellent,' Callaghan replied, smiling at Greaves and Lorrimer.

By the time the meeting ended, an hour later, each group leader knew what the other group was doing and was prepared to do it.

Even Maxine was pleased.

9

The men had a good rest that night, sleeping in their lean-tos or LUPs hidden by the trees, but they were up at first light the following morning to wash in the nearby stream, have a quick breakfast of cold rations with water, and then organize the temporary camp as a proper FOB. While some of them remained in the camp itself to clean and oil weapons, study maps of the areas, practise their French and check the supplies and vehicles, others were sent out in four different directions to construct observation posts and keep a record of the direction, frequency and size of passing enemy columns and aircraft.

'Every last damn vehicle,' Captain Callaghan warned them. 'Every tank, armoured car, truck, jeep, motor-bike or bicycle. As for the aircraft, I want to know the type – heavy bomber, light bomber, fighter plane, escort – the direction of flight, and the time it was spotted. I want nothing missed nor forgotten. Now get to it, men.'

As they were planning to be there for some time, the men constructed rectangular observation posts, which were deeper and larger than the short-term, diamond-shaped OPs. Facing outwards, away from the camp, the rectangular OP contained four shallow scrapes: one for the observer, one for the sentry, one for the man assigned to keep records and a fourth as a rest bay. A small well was dug in the centre, to drain off excess water such as rain, and the roof was made of chicken wire, camouflage netting and foliage that helped it blend in with its surroundings. The OP had a camouflaged entry cum exit hole and there was a long, thin viewing slit between the upturned earth and the artificial roof in the side that faced away from the camp.

Once constructed, the OP was filled with everything the men would need for long-term observation of both sky and land, including black-painted binoculars and a tripod-mounted telescope, maps, log book, cipher book, camera, S-phone and MCR1 receiver for contact with SAS foot patrols or the FOB, water and rations, sleeping bags for the shallow scrapes, spare batteries and clothing, and personal and close-support weapons, including a Webley pistol, 9mm Sten gun, Thompson M1 sub-machine-gun and two .303-inch Lee-Enfield bolt-action rifles. Thus equipped, the men settled down and began their observation.

At the same time, Captain Callaghan was huddling with Corporal Jim Almonds, giving the squadron's signaller a list of requirements for a resup drop to take place that night. Almonds relayed the request by Morse code over the No. 11 radio set to London, from where it would be passed on to their air-support group at RAF Station 1090, Down Ampney,

Gloucestershire. The supplies, which included replacement Willys jeeps for the six lost, would be flown out from there.

While the men were setting up their OPs and Callaghan was contacting London, Greaves was decoding messages received in code from the BBC regarding the progress of the battle for Europe. When the messages were decoded, he was able to tell those gathered around him – Jacko and Rich, Harry-boy and Neil – that since they had parachuted into France a massive Allied invasion force of British, American, Canadian and French troops had started advancing along a 100-mile front from Nice to Marseilles; Paris had been liberated by General Leclerc's French 2nd Armoured Division; American forces were continuing to advance on Reims and Verdun; the British 2nd Army was sweeping across the bridgeheads of the Seine, heading for Amiens; and French troops and General Patton's 3rd Army were racing in from opposite directions to capture Dijon.

'I'll take Paris,' Jacko told his mates when Captain Greaves had departed. 'The rest of those Frog towns you can keep, but Paris should be worth seeing.'

'The way the war's going it should all be over in no time,' Rich informed them, 'so we might get there sooner than you think.'

The four men were sitting in a small circle on the grass, cleaning and oiling their personal weapons.

'We'll probably liberate France pretty soon,' Neil

said, 'but we've still got the whole of Germany to cover.'

'The Russians are practically there already,' Jacko told him, 'so that won't take long either. Before you know it, this war's gonna be over and we'll all get leave in France.'

'I don't think *everyone* in the Allied armies can be given leave in France,' Harry-boy put in. 'Too many of us, mate. So I reckon that as soon as the war ends, we'll all be shipped home. No Paris. No French tarts. *Nothing.*'

'Or get shipped to Italy,' Rich said solemnly. 'The war's still being fought there.'

'Right,' Neil said. 'But Florence has already fallen to the Allies and the rest of Italy's set to fall.'

'That's 'cause the Eyeties don't like fighting,' Harry-boy said. 'They just like wine, women and song. They don't even care who runs Italy, so long as they can still have a good time. Carefree, that's what they are.'

'Bloody useless Eyeties,' Jacko opined. 'About all they're good for is making pasta and yodelling.'

'They don't yodel,' Rich corrected him. 'They sing opera.'

'Can't understand a word of it, mate, so it sounds like yodelling to me.'

'They aren't as bad as soldiers as people say,' Harry-boy insisted. 'They certainly fought well in Sicily.'

'Fought well?' Jacko repeated in disbelief. 'The only English word they learnt is "surrender" and they used it a lot, mate!'

'Not in Sicily,' Rich said. 'I agree with Harry-boy on that. The Eyeties, they may not be great soldiers, but they did their best down there.'

'They just don't want to die, see?' Harry-boy put in. 'They're philosophical, like, when it comes to being alive, and they think more of the good things of life than they do of fighting wars.'

'They don't believe in dying for their country,' Neil said. 'That's what Harry-boy means when he says they're carefree. You say there's a war on and it's very important and your average Eyetie will reply: "What's important?" They don't know what that means, like.'

'Jesus!' Jacko exclaimed. 'I don't believe my own ears! You bastards are defending the soldiers who're so busy keeping their hands above their heads they can't even wank.'

'Jacko's famous filthy tongue!' Rich said in disgust.

'I'd recommend him to wash it out with iodine,' Neil said, 'but as we know, the bastard could drink anything and get the best out of it.'

'Anyway, we weren't talking about the bloody Eyeties,' Harry-boy said. 'We were talking about the end of the war in Europe and us getting to Paris.'

'Gay Paree!' Neil said, laughing. 'The old in-and-out in Montmartre! What more could a man want?'

They all stared at him, stunned. They hadn't realized he was educated.

'What the fuck's Montmartre?' Jacko asked. 'A Frog *museum* or something?'

'The cancan!' Neil informed him, warming to his theme. 'Women dancing and throwing their skirts above their heads. Music! Nightclubs! Striptease! For Christ's sake, Jacko, don't you know *anything*?'

'You mean you've already *been* there?' Jacko asked, taken aback.

''Course not,' Neil replied, coming back down to earth. 'But I've seen it at the pictures, see – and read all about it. Bloody fantastic place! I mean, Montmartre *is* Paris, for God's sake!'

Caught between monumental relief – the very thought that Moffatt had *already* been to Paris – and bitter disappointment, Jacko rolled his eyes and said with a sneer: 'Well, isn't that a bleedin' revelation? The halfwit thinks Paris is great because he's never been there. I bet it's just another French piss-hole.'

'I thought you wanted to go to Paris,' Rich said. 'In fact, you're the one who started this bloody conversation by saying you wanted to spend your leave in Paris, so why . . .?'

'Fuck all this rubbish about Paris,' Jacko replied rather too quickly. 'What *I* want to know is why we're sitting here on our arses when we could be out doing damage to Jerry.'

'We're waiting to go on a resup collection,' Rich solemnly reminded him.

'Ah, yes!' Jacko said, pretending that he had needed the reminder. 'A soldier's work is never done.'

They were still talking at last light when, just as boredom was setting in, they were called by Sergeant Lorrimer to help out at the night's resup DZ.

Again, Callaghan had picked a drop zone approximately two miles from the camp in case the Germans saw the landing lights. Again, he picked a field nearly 1000 yards long and encircled it with SAS and Maquis armed guards, all facing away from the field, towards where an advancing enemy could be seen. This time, however, instead of brushwood beacons, the DZ was marked with four proper lights, three red and one white, though as usual spread 100 yards apart in an L shape, with the white light at the end of the short leg.

When the distant growling of four powerful Rolls-Royce Merlin engines announced that the Halifax was approaching, Callaghan, using Morse code, flashed clearance to land, but this time using a large signalling lamp instead of a hand torch. Once the Halifax had banked towards the illuminated DZ, Corporal Almonds plugged in the short-directional aerial of his S-phone and used it both as a homing beacon and as a radio-telephone link with the aircraft's pilot for final instructions. At the same time, another group of SAS troopers, including Jacko, Rich, Neil and Harry-boy, ran with their backs to the wind, facing the incoming plane, to take up positions on both sides of the long leg of the DZ, ready to race in and collect the dropped canisters.

When the Halifax was overhead and the mass of

crates and canisters floated down on the end of their multiple parachutes, the men carefully avoided being hit by them but rushed to collect them once they had landed in the field. Within minutes the canisters had been opened, emptied and buried, and the men transferred their contents to the waiting trucks.

Even as the trucks were moving away from the DZ, more brilliant-white parachutes billowed up above as the crates containing the replacement jeeps floated down. When the crates were on the ground, the men broke them open, buried the separate pieces of wood, covered the disturbed soil with loose leaves and other foliage, then hurriedly loaded the smaller crates containing the weapons into the jeeps and drove away.

The Halifax turned back the way it had come and disappeared in the dark sky.

'Perfect,' Callaghan whispered. 'Not a German in sight. Let's get out while we can, men.'

The drive back through the dark, wind-blown countryside was uneventful, except for the jagged flashes illuminating the horizon and reminding them that the war was continuing. Once at the FOB, the men gave the new jeeps a thorough mechanical check. When this proved satisfactory, they carefully mounted the twin Vickers .303-inch K guns front and rear and fixed a fifth to the driver's side. Next, they attached the wire-cutter to the armour plating across the front bumper; slotted the bulletproof Perspex screens into place; hooked the reserve fuel tanks under the driver's seat and over the lockers at the back; then packed in as many boxes of spare ammunition as they could – armour-piercing and incendiary bullets, tracer, and rounds of ball ammo – plus water cans, food supplies, flares and an S-phone and Eureka beacon. Modified and fully loaded, the jeeps looked formidable indeed.

Finally, with everything unpacked and prepared for the next day's patrol, the men were allowed to relax and open the most precious boxes of all: the ones containing cigarettes and letters from home. Seated on the ground, either in or near their own bashas, they smoked and read their letters by the light of hand torches pointed downwards, some in silence, others shouting comments back and forth.

'Look at that!' Neil exclaimed. 'Jacko's got two letters from home and he can't even read!'

'I may come from Shoreditch, mate, but I can read and count.'

'Learnt it working on your old man's fruit cart, did you? That only means you can count – probably up to twelve.'

Neil was referring to the fact that Jacko was a true East Ender, who had left school at fourteen and worked for years in Petticoat Lane, selling fruit and vegetables from his father's cart. All of that, of course, was before he enlisted in the Army.

'If I've got two letters,' Jacko said, 'it shows that at least I know people who can write, which is more than we can say for you, Moffatt.'

'Below the belt, Jacko!' Harry-boy exclaimed. 'Just because my mate Neil's from up north doesn't mean he's illiterate. They have schools in Blackburn, you know, and the teachers teach English.'

'Lancashire English!' Jacko replied, speaking and scanning his letters at the same time. 'I don't think that counts, mate. Might as well be a bloody Welshman, coming out with all that garbled Celtic shit.'

'I speak perfect English,' Rich cut in, putting down the letter from his mother, who still lived in their tiny family home in the Welsh coalmining town of Aberfan, where Rich had worked before being called up. 'I just happen to have a very distinctive accent, of which I am proud.'

'The Welsh accent is an abortion,' Harry-boy told him. 'My ears ache when exposed to it.'

'Must be wonderful to come from Islington and learn perfect English from your Paddy neighbours and other working-class foreigners. I stand in awe of your background.'

'Listen, mate, they're bloody good people in Islington, I tell you. At least they speak to each other in English, which is more than the Welsh do.'

'We have our own mother tongue and are proud to speak it. The Welsh are a proud race.'

'I must remember to tell my kids that,' Jacko said, glancing again at one of his letters to learn from his wife's scrawl that his son, Tommy, had just turned six and had a nice party with the in-laws, Tommy's sister, Maggie, who was a year younger, and some neighbours' kids. The party had taken place in the house in Shoreditch, an area full of factories, in the middle of a German air-raid, but that had spoiled no one's fun.

After recounting this little incident to his mates, Jacko said: 'We're a right tough breed down Shoreditch way. It takes a lot to put us off our stride.'

'Not as tough as they are in Aberfan,' Rich told him. 'The coalmines get flooded, escaping gas causes explosions, the tunnels cave in, the dust fills your lungs – but still the men go down there to earn their crust. On top of that, we get bombed night and day by Jerry – so you're not *so* tough in London.'

'I agree,' Neil said. 'I mean, even the women in the cotton mills where I come from . . .'

'Heavenly Blackburn!' Harry-boy interjected.

'. . . are tougher than this lot from the south. About the only thing they're good for in London is shooting their mouths off.'

'That's because we Londoners are literate,' Harry-boy informed him, 'and know how to form complete sentences which, when strung together, actually mean something. Try that with a Welshman or your average halfwit from Lancashire and you'll be wasting your breath.'

'I don't have to listen to this,' Rich said, lighting a cigarette and exhaling a cloud of smoke as he sat back against the tree under which he had made his lean-to. 'I've heard more intelligent conversation between two-year-olds. I'm putting plugs in my ears.'

'Me, too,' Neil said. 'I've been insulted enough for one day. What's worse, I've now got to watch the twat who's insulting me run his fingers along the letters and silently mouth the words he's trying to read. A sight for sore eyes, that is.'

'I've had enough of it myself,' Jacko said, folding up his second letter, then stuffing both letters into the rear pocket of his dispatch rider's breeches. 'I'm going for a piss.'

Adjusting the maroon beret on his head, he moved off at the crouch to find the area designated a common latrine – in the bushes about 200 yards away and about 100 yards behind the men keeping watch out on point. As Jacko disappeared around the far end of the segregated Maquis bell tents – only the SAS slept in LUPs and lean-tos – a distant thunder was heard and the dark horizon was illuminated by a series of silvery-white flashes that appeared to be a hundred miles long.

'Twenty-five pounders,' Harry-boy said.

'Yeah,' Rich agreed. 'But firing across a very broad front, covering half the bloody country.'

'That must mean another push by the Allies advancing on Sombernon, to the west of Dijon. Glad I'm not there, lads.'

'Bloody right,' Neil said. 'A barrage like that can drive you nuts if it doesn't actually kill you. At least we don't have to deal with that.'

'I wouldn't like to be back in Blighty either,' Harry-boy said, squinting as he studied his letter from home by the light of his torch. 'According to what my mum says, Jerry's started dropping his new V-2 rocket bombs. Not nice, she says. Blowing London to hell.'

'They sometimes get it worse than we do, true enough,' Neil told him. 'The Home Front suffers as well.'

'I don't bloody well believe it,' Jacko said, returning at the crouch as the relentless Allied bombardment filled the air with muffled thunder and illuminated the dark horizon with jagged sheets of silvery light.

'Don't believe what?' Harry-boy asked him.

'That fucking Maquis leader, André,' Jacko said, slipping into his shallow LUP, 'and that sweet-faced, murderous little minx.'

'What about 'em?' Neil asked.

'Going at it like dogs in the street,' Jacko explained, outraged. 'They were doing it in André's bell tent and making no bones about it. All yelps and groans. The tent's actually shaking!'

'You're kidding!' Rich exclaimed.

'No, I'm not, mate. They're going at it like two pigs in a trough and making twice as much noise.'

The other three soldiers stared automatically at the bell tents, but they were too far away for any sounds to reach them.

'They're really doing it?' Rich asked, hardly able to credit it, and beginning to colour up.

'Bouncing away like they're on a trampoline,' Jacko

151

confirmed, enjoying Rich's embarrassment, 'and not being remotely quiet about it.'

'Well, I never!' Rich muttered.

'That's the French for you,' Neil told them. 'That's why I want to get to Paris – those Parisian girls are easy.'

'Not that again!' Jacko protested. 'Not more talk about bleedin' Paris. If I hear one more word about Paris I'm gonna throw up.'

'You haven't time,' Harry-boy informed him. 'It's our shift on guard.'

'Already?' Rich asked, checking his illuminated wristwatch. 'Christ, yes, you're right! Let's get up and go.'

Wearily, the men all emerged from their respective LUPs or lean-tos, carrying their personal weapons – a 9mm Sten gun for Jacko, a tommy-gun for Rich and .303-inch Lee-Enfield bolt-action assault rifles for Neil and Harry-boy – and made their way to their separate points to replace the men already there. Lying in carefully concealed scrapes, they spent the next four hours staring at the dark fields and forest straight ahead and at the flashes on the distant horizon. Not able to see each other, peering into the darkness, they spent a tense, lonely vigil, during which they could not relax for a minute. They did, however, ease their loneliness and tension by thinking of various things even as they kept their eyes peeled and their other senses alert.

Jacko thought of his wife and kids in Shoreditch,

surprised at how little he missed them. He then dwelt on the more exciting times he had had with the Long Range Desert Group in North Africa just over three years ago. He also thought of the many different women he had had – both before and since his marriage – and started imagining the kind he would meet if he ever got to Paris – women like that bitch Maxine, the very sight of whom gave him an erection. Normally, however, Jacko liked unsophisticated women with big tits and a subservient nature. He figured he might find that kind in Paris and the possibility was exciting. The thought that he was betraying his wife never entered his head.

Harry-boy distracted himself with more mundane recollections of his home off Islington's Caledonian Road, where, when not with the Army, he still lived with his parents. His father was a driver for a local furniture store and even now Harry-boy could only look back with unalloyed pleasure on the many days he had bunked off school and helped his dad deliver anything from a footstool to a three-piece suite on his rounds all over north London. He also thought of his girlfriend, Linda, from just up the road in Holloway. She had once wanted to marry him, but had since sent him a letter saying that since she hadn't seen him since 1941, when he had put off marrying her, she was now getting engaged to someone else. Despite the fact that what she had said was correct, Harry-boy burned up with humiliation and anger each time he thought of that letter. Nevertheless, it was the humiliation and rage that kept him alert throughout his long vigil.

Rich thought a lot about his early days in Aberfan, where he had been a miner. Though life was hard, the people were good and the community spirit a great comfort. For that very reason Rich had not wanted to join the Army and had resented being conscripted, but since being accepted by L Detachment in 1941, he had come to love being a soldier and now knew he would never go down the mines again. Nevertheless, when he felt lonely, he took comfort from thoughts of Aberfan and its close-knit community. You didn't have that kind of life in London, no matter what Jacko said; it was more impersonal there. So Rich took a lot of comfort during his lonely vigil by thinking of home. He hadn't been back there for five years, but it still lived inside him.

Neil, on the other hand, had few fond memories of his childhood and youth in Blackburn. Contrary to what he had told Jacko, he'd had a miserable upbringing both at school and, later, when he had become an apprentice textile machinist in one of Blackburn's largest cotton mills. Neil's father and mother between them had run a small electrical goods business in the centre of town and made Neil work there at weekends, even when he was still at school. For that reason, he had not had much spare time to spend with his school chums and, by the time he left school, at fourteen, and went into the cotton mill, he had very few friends left. Perhaps it was his feelings of loneliness that made him sign up with the Territorial Army in his local drill hall in 1939; certainly, once in the TA, he had found the kind of camaraderie he had lacked throughout his childhood and it had brought him out of himself a little. Within months of joining the TA, which he attended at weekends, he had become involved with a girl, Florence, from the cotton mill, with whom he had had many sweaty evenings that had not led to sex. Indeed, he still hadn't been to bed with Florence eighteen months later, when he transferred from the TA to the regular Army and was shipped to North Africa. Now, proud to be one of the Originals of L Detachment, and now a member of 1 SAS Brigade, he wasn't sure if he actually loved his plump Florence, though he certainly thought a lot about her and burned up at the thought of touching her large, bare breasts, which is all she had ever let him do. Those thoughts, though sometimes giving him an erection, also managed to keep him alert throughout his lonely vigil.

Jacko, Harry-boy, Rich and Neil were relatively lucky. Their shift on point was from midnight to four in the morning, which meant that they could catch three hours' sleep before, at first light, they had to rise again, have a quick breakfast, and then spend the rest of the day on foot patrol, reconnoitring the area, checking the local farms for German troops and marking points of strategic interest on their route maps.

They were, however, only relatively lucky, for that

long, hot, exhausting day was not followed by another period of rest. Instead, at 2200 hours, as planned, all the men were ordered into the jeeps and moved out in three separate columns for the first of their night raids.

10

The three separate groups moved out at thirty-minute intervals, with Group One, led by Captain Callaghan, following the road south, Group Two, led by Captain Greaves, forking off to the east, and Group Three, the Maquis group headed by André, branching off to the west.

The two SAS groups were strung out as they would have been in single file on foot patrol: the jeep containing Sergeant Lorrimer, Jacko and Rich was up at the front on point, constantly checking what lay ahead. The jeep containing Captain Greaves, Harry-boy Turnball and Neil Moffatt was second in line, followed by the radio jeep, manned by Sergeant Pat Riley, Corporal Jim Almonds and Corporal Benny Bennett, then three other jeeps. Finally, the seventh jeep, manned by Sergeants Bob Tappman and Ernie Bond, with Corporal Reg Seekings driving, was acting as 'Tail-end Charlie'.

Being out on point, the job of the gunners in the first jeep was to cover an arc-shaped area of fire in front of the column. The jeeps in the middle not only protected the radio jeep, but covered arcs to left and right. Those in the last jeep had to constantly swing around to face the direction from which they had come, not only covering the column's rear but also ensuring that the patrol had no blind spots. Given that in some way or another every man in the column had to constantly look for signs of enemy movement, either on the road ahead, on the road behind or in the fields on either side, as well as check repeatedly that the jeeps front and rear were still in place, the watch routines were emotionally and physically demanding, often leading to a great deal of tension and eventual exhaustion. Nevertheless they could not be ignored.

The column travelled into the darkness along a lane that wound like a snake and often appeared to curve back on itself, though in fact it passed through hamlets of white-roofed cottages, small fields of crops, hedges and gently undulating hills. In daylight, they would have had to drive very slowly to avoid throwing up a tell-tale dust cloud, but in the early morning darkness there was no such risk and they could travel as fast as they pleased, which was as fast as the narrow roads and sharp bends permitted.

Eventually, after a couple of hours, during which nothing was seen, the lane came to a dead end at a gate leading into a farm. Immensely frustrated, and to moans and groans from the men in the other jeeps, the column had to reverse back along the lane until the last jeep came parallel to a track that cut across the dark fields. The whole column reversed past the track until the first jeep could turn into it; the others then followed, which kept them in the same order as before. They then travelled across the fields, along what was no more than a narrow dried-mud track filled with potholes and mounds, making the jeeps bounce up and down constantly as they passed herds of cows and sheep.

After about an hour of this, during which they seemed to have travelled hardly any distance at all, they were further frustrated when they came to a fast-running stream about six feet wide. Luckily, when Sergeant Lorrimer got out to check the depth of the water and the consistency of the bed with a stick, the water was only ten inches deep at its deepest and the bottom was mostly gravel on compacted earth. The jeeps were therefore able to cross by inching slowly down the bank and into the water, then moving through the stream even more slowly and revving dramatically to get up the other bank and back on to the track.

When the radio jeep, the heaviest vehicle, sank into a patch of mud in the middle of the stream, Corporals Almonds and Benny Bennett lightened the load by clambering out and taking a lot of the gear with them; then, with Sergeant Pat Riley at the steering wheel, the mud was scraped away from under the wheels, steel sand channels were shoved under them, separating them from the bed, and the jeep, with its engine running in low gear, was pushed out by the soaked, cursing Almonds and Bennett. Once the wheels were free of the mud, Riley gunned the engine and the jeep screeched up the far bank, following the others.

From there, they took an even more unpredictable

and narrow track across country, using the wire-cutters fixed on the front armour plating of the jeep to break through the many wire or barbed-wire fences, as well as to hack through the many hedges they encountered. In this way they came eventually to what was, according to their maps, the village of Jeux, and drove as quietly as possible into its darkened, deserted main street.

Not quite deserted. They were, in fact, all taken by surprise when the door of the village bistro opened a little, shedding light briefly into the darkness, and an obviously drunken French farmer emerged. Seeing him, Sergeant Lorrimer stopped his jeep, then used a hand signal to stop the column behind him. Then, while the Frenchman, though drunk, stopped and stared in growing surprise at the column of 'liberators', Lorrimer glanced quizzically over his shoulder at Captain Greaves, whose jeep had braked to a rapid halt, almost hitting his own. Greaves nodded his agreement, then spoke in French to the farmer.

'Good morning, *monsieur*.'

The farmer hiccuped, then managed: 'Good morning. English, yes?'

'Yes.'

'We have already been liberated, which is why . . .' The farmer hiccuped again, then smiled benignly and spread his hands in the air as if praying to God for forgiveness. 'Which is why I am drunk, *monsieur*. The whole village has had an evening of wine and calvados. That place behind me . . .' – he indicated

160

the closed door of the bistro – '. . . is still packed with villagers.'

Greaves and the others could now hear laughter and singing from within. The captain grinned at the Frenchman. 'Yes, I understand, *monsieur*. These are good days for all of us.'

The Frenchman hiccuped. 'Good days. We've waited a long time for this. It is good to see you and those who came before you. But tell me, what are you doing here at this time of night – or rather morning?'

'We're looking for Germans.'

'Ah! Yes! Very good!' The Frenchman placed his index finger to his nose, then used the same finger to point beyond the town. 'A whole Panzer division without its tanks – I mean, a division of Panzer troops – is. strung out right across this area, though mainly between Semur and Montard. What are such troops without tanks? Go after them, Captain!'

'We will.'

The Frenchman hiccuped again and winked. 'Annihilate them, Captain. Get rid of them. Exterminate them like the vile scum they are.'

'We will,' Captain Greaves promised.

In fact, he had no such intention. An open conflict with such a sizeable company could only have led to disaster and Greaves had other fish to fry. Nevertheless, it was diplomatic to let the Frenchman think otherwise – his story of this encounter would doubtless resound throughout the village tomorrow.

In the meantime, Greaves felt it expedient to go on to more realistic matters.

With Sergeant Lorrimer's jeep out on point, the SAS column drove on into the night, making a wide detour around the estimated location of the German Panzer division to avoid a damaging conflict with them. Before long, however, the lane they were driving along turned into a bewildering maze of cart tracks that soon had them driving in circles, only knowing that they were east of the main road. Attempting to get back to it, they found themselves bouncing roughly over a ploughed field that led them to the summit of a hill overlooking the very road they were trying to find. As all of the jeeps, one after the other, came abreast on the summit, the whole squadron found themselves looking down at the moving headlights of a German convoy of trucks passing right by them.

Immediately, they switched off their engines and sat in complete silence, waiting until the last truck had passed. Then they drove down the winding track to the same road and headed off in the opposite direction, taking the first side road that led in the direction marked on their route maps. Eventually, about three in the morning, they arrived at a closed level crossing at the foot of a sharp incline. Before there was time to withdraw the jeeps, they heard the sound of a train coming round the shoulder of the hill. The chugging gradually became louder until they were able to see that it was a goods train of about twenty wagons, boldly flying a large swastika, and still about half a mile down the track.

Lorrimer instantly switched on his S-phone and contacted Greaves, telling him the situation and adding: 'It's too good to resist, boss.'

'I agree,' Greaves said. 'I want the jeeps to spread out into the fields on both sides of the road, covering both sides of that level crossing. At my signal – which will be when the train is exactly halfway across the crossing – we'll open fire on it with everything we've got, including the mortar. Convey that order to the men, Sergeant.'

'Yes, boss,' Lorrimer said. Still using his S-phone, Lorrimer passed the order down the line. The jeeps, in single file, pulled around each other and, in most cases, bounced off the road until they were forming a long line parallel to the railway track, on both sides of the level crossing. Once in position, the gunners, not including the drivers, cocked their Vickers K guns and prepared to fire. As they were doing so, the mortar team jumped out of their jeep, quickly dug a shallow hole for the steel base plate, buried it, packed it tight with shells, and then fixed the mortar to the base plate and looked towards Greaves.

When the train reached the gates of the level crossing, Greaves raised his right hand.

When the train had passed the gates and the line of transport carriages was halfway across – when, in fact, the German machine-gun crews on the open platforms were clearly visible in moonlight – Greaves dropped his hand abruptly.

Instantly, the mortar sent its shell in a great arc towards the track just in front of the engine. Even as the shell exploded with a startling roar, hurling up twisted metal, lumps of wood, soil and gravel in a billowing cloud of smoke, causing the driver to apply the brakes and the locked wheels to screech, the massed Vickers opened up, pouring streams of mixed incendiary, tracer and armour-piercing bullets into the whole length of the train, including the open platforms bearing the German machine-gun crews.

It was a spectacular sight. Before the German troops knew what had hit them, the train became a bizarre carnival of criss-crossing lines of green tracer, spitting flames, billowing smoke and exploding splinters of wood. The German machine-gun crews on the open platforms were torn apart with shocking speed and ferocity, with men screaming, throwing their hands up, then either jerking violently and collapsing around their weapons or falling off the edge of the still-moving train, to bounce brutally down the sides of the track, through loose gravel and clouds of sand.

The engine was unharmed by the first mortar shell, but the second explosion tore the tracks up right in front of it, derailing it and causing it to plunge down into the field, dragging the carriages with it. Then, like a giant accordion played by a mad musician, the carriages smashed into one another, rising up like a pyramid, then crashing back down in a dreadful tangle of steel, wood and exploding glass. Finally, even before the carriages had collapsed back on to the track, ammunition and petrol exploded, creating a dazzling fireworks display that included great jagged fans of flame and clouds of oily, black smoke. The carriages, including those carrying the German machine-gun crews, then rolled over sideways and went crashing down into the fields. The engine, already lying in the field under the SAS troops, pouring clouds of hissing, scalding steam, suddenly exploded into a scorching ball of fire that set fire to the branches of the nearest trees.

Even as the few surviving enemy troops were fleeing up into the woods at the other side of the track, ignoring the demented screaming of their burning, dying comrades, the SAS jeeps stopped firing, rolled across the track and continued south as fast as they possibly could, losing themselves in a darkness illuminated by the flames of the burning train.

Again, when they drove on, the SAS men came into no direct contact with German foot patrols or armoured columns. Indeed, they were beginning to believe that they were on a wasted journey when they reached the edge of the Forest of Chantillon. There, the jeep out on point stopped and its lights went off. Seeing this, Greaves told his own driver, Neil Moffatt, to do the same. When Moffatt had done so, Greaves used a hand signal to tell the rest of the column to follow suit.

Eventually, when the column was silent and still, hidden in moonlit darkness, Lorrimer came running back from his jeep, still out on point, to report that there was a German radar station in a clearing just beyond the trees.

Even as he was speaking, a number of German machine-guns opened fire on the jeeps.

The SAS gunners returned the fire with their Vickers as the drivers throttled the engines and drove the jeeps to opposite sides of the road, practically burying their armoured bumpers in the tall hedgerows. From there, though unable to see where the German fire was coming from, the gunners sprayed the undergrowth ahead, tearing it to shreds, as if devastated by a hellish tornado.

'Enemy still unseen,' Lorrimer, still out front, conveyed to Greaves over the S-phone. 'We're still firing blind and without adequate protection. We could get chopped to pieces.'

'Everyone withdraw!' Greaves snapped into the open line. 'Stop when I say so.'

The Tail-end Charlie jeep instantly went into reverse, screeched into a three-point turn in the narrow lane and headed back the way it had come, leaving a swirling cloud of dust behind it. The other jeeps did the same, one after the other, until they were all heading back around the first bend in the road, about a mile away. Now second-to-last in line, Greaves waited until he knew that the final jeep, containing Lorrimer, Jacko and Rich, was safely around the bend and out of sight, before he snapped 'Stop!' into the S-phone. The jeeps then all screeched to a halt, still in a column but facing back the way they had come. At another instruction from Greaves, they drove closer to one another, until they were bunched dangerously close together. Greaves only permitted this because he intended going back to attack the Germans before they had the chance to pursue him.

'The Chantillon radar station,' he said to Harry-boy and their driver, Neil Moffatt. 'It's not clearly marked on the map, but there's a separate reference to it.'

'Terrific,' Harry-boy said sarcastically.

'Jesus,' Neil added. 'That means we're close to the front. Those Krauts must have mistaken us for the advance guard of the US 3rd Army.'

'Very likely,' Greaves told him. He thought for a moment, studying the map, then shrugged, grinned in an oddly shy manner, and said: 'Well, if they're already worried, let's give them something real to worry about.'

On instructions conveyed by Greaves on the S-phone, one man remained in each jeep, manning a Vickers, while the others climbed down, carrying their personal and some heavy weapons, and clambered through or over the hedges, depending on the density of the foliage, to make their way as silently as possible along the edge of the field, back to the vicinity of the radar station.

It was well before dawn, so the morning was still dark, but in the moonlight the SAS men could clearly see the bunker-shaped buildings of the radar station. The whole area was surrounded by barbed wire and machine-guns posts, and the station was dominated by a central control tower etched like a black finger against the pale moon.

'Piece of piss,' Jacko whispered. 'That control tower's as visible as my hard-on when I'm having a shower.'

'Modest as always,' Rich replied. 'So how the hell do we get to it?'

'The three-inch mortar,' Lorrimer told him, then made the same recommendation to Greaves over the S-phone.

'Agreed,' the captain said. 'But before we blow the tower, I think we should call up reinforcements to enable us to put out the whole radar station when the tower is down.'

'Right, boss. Captain Callaghan?'

'Yes. Get in touch with him. Once we know they're on the way, we'll blow the control tower. That should encourage some of the Krauts to evacuate and leave us less to tackle when the CO and his men get here. Agreed, Sergeant?'

'I'm with you all the way, boss.' Using his S-phone, Lorrimer conveyed Greaves's instructions to Corporal Jim Almonds. When the signaller had conveyed the message by Morse code via the No. 11 radio set and received coded confirmation back, Lorrimer called up the mortar crew.

The two men emerged from the moonlit darkness

of the lane, quickly embedded the metal base plate in the earth near the hedgerow, set up the mortar, made a visual estimation of the alignment and awaited the signal to fire. When Lorrimer, at a nod from Greaves, dropped his raised right hand, the first shell was fired.

The minor explosion of the firing mortar was followed almost immediately by the much louder noise of the exploding shell, which tore up soil and loose gravel in a cloud of smoke just short of the radar station's control tower. Instantly, without knowing where they were firing, the German sentries opened up with their machine-guns, spraying a wide arc of fire over the road around the bend, well out of range, and out of the sight, of the SAS column. Nevertheless, the combined noise of the exploding mortar and machine-guns was deafening.

Having used the first mortar shot purely as a visual reference, the mortar crew adjusted the calibration and fired a second shell. It exploded with a mighty roar just beyond the control tower, showering it in a downfall of swirling soil and loose gravel, before obscuring it in billowing clouds of smoke.

Splitting the difference between the first and second visual sightings, the mortar crew fired their third shell and were gratified to see the tower take a direct hit. Its pagoda-style wooden roof was blown off entirely, the struts beneath it split and buckled, then the whole of the top half blew apart, the machine-gun crew spilling out and screaming dreadfully as they fell to earth. A fourth and fifth mortar shell, fired one right after the other, virtually demolished the tower and made it collapse, sending crimson sparks showering up from the blazing wood to illuminate the dark, moonlit sky.

Even as this was happening, the gates of the radar station were opening to let heavily armed, helmeted German troops race out, some sheltering to the left of the lane, others to the right. On both sides they advanced, firing blindly from the hip, but with a potentially devastating amount of fire-power.

'*Retreat!*' Greaves bawled into his S-phone.

Instantly, the SAS men on the ground returned to their jeeps and, now facing away from the tower, were driven away from the German troops and out of range in a matter of seconds. However, under telephoned instructions from Greaves, they kept going for thirty minutes until they reached the next village. Knowing that the Germans would not follow them this far, but would return to the radar station, either to evacuate or regroup for a defensive action, the SAS men disembarked from the jeeps and relaxed with cigarettes and drinks of cold water from their flasks, waiting for Callaghan to arrive with the reinforcements.

The CO's column of seven jeeps arrived at the village just before first light. Noting that Greaves's men were lolling about the village square at dawn, inviting the curiosity of the surprised, sleepy villagers and clearly enjoying their cold breakfast, Callaghan grinned broadly as he approached his second in command.

'I thought you men were having a hard time,' he said, 'but this looks like a party.'

'Not quite,' Greaves replied good-humouredly. 'What we have along the road is a German radar station that's lost its control tower but still has a bunch of crack troops defending it. I suspect that the loss of the tower will encourage them to evacuate, but I say we should go and attack while we still have the advantage.'

'If we do, we must do it right now,' Callaghan insisted, 'before they move out.'

'Ready, willing and able.'

The two groups of jeeps moved out of the village and, as quickly as the lane would allow, headed back to the radar station. The flames of the destroyed control tower had flickered out by the time they reached their destination, but it was now light enough to see the lazily rising smoke from the smouldering wreckage around the sharp curve in the lane. Not knowing what lay around that bend, but assuming that the German troops would have retreated back into the barbed-wire enclosure of the radar station, some of the SAS men jumped down from the jeeps, leaving a driver and one gunner in each vehicle. Splitting into two groups, one on either side of the road, both hugging the hedgerows, they marched quietly, cautiously around the bend with their personal weapons at the ready.

As Greaves had suspected, the Germans had

retreated from the lane, back into the barbed-wire compound, and were evacuating the radar station, via the rear gate, in troop trucks, jeeps and armoured cars and on foot, under the protection of gunners whose machine-guns were aimed in the opposite direction, towards the bend and the SAS troops it was concealing.

'If we advance any further,' Lorrimer whispered to Callaghan and Greaves. 'We'll be chopped to pieces.'

'A few mortar shells should do the job nicely,' Callaghan suggested with a devilish smile. 'What say you, Dirk?'

'Absolute agreement, old boy,' Greaves replied. 'Lob 'em in and let's go.'

While the bulk of the men knelt on each side of the road, hugging the hedgerows, the mortar team went just around the bend, where they set up the mortar. Their immediate priority was the machine-gun crews defending the main gate, one on either side; their second was the other machine-gun crews along the front barbed-wire fence. This time, having already ascertained the correct calibrations from their attack on the control tower, they were able to drop their first mortar shells almost directly on the gate, between the machine-gun teams on either side. The resultant blast not only split the night's silence with a deafening roar, but blew the barrier of the gatehouse to pieces and showered both machine-gun emplacements with debris from the building, and with soil and gravel.

Unharmed, the German machine-gunners on either side of the barrier opened fire ferociously, turning the road in front of the SAS mortar crew, as well as the hedges on either side of them, into a tornado of leaves, branches and dust. Undeterred, the mortar crew made adjustments to their line of fire and fired two more shells, one to the left, one to the right, tearing up the ground just in front of one gun emplacement and blowing another up entirely. Beyond curtains of swirling smoke, they could just make out Germans screaming and writhing spectrally in the chaos.

'Very nice,' Callaghan murmured. 'But not quite enough. I want those other gun positions destroyed before the men are asked to advance. Sergeant?'

'Yes, boss,' Lorrimer said. Disappearing around the bend, he returned a few minutes later and said: 'Keep your fingers crossed, boss.'

Callaghan and Greaves's position in the road just about allowed them to see around the bend without exposing themselves to enemy fire. Their ears came into play when they heard three mortar shells exploding, one after the other in quick succession. Then, when they witnessed the exploding gun emplacements, and heard the enemy soldiers screaming as they somersaulted and crashed back down to earth, they had seen enough to let them simultaneously call out: 'Attack!'

Naturally courageous, but unerringly cautious, the SAS men advanced at the crouch around the bend, hugging their respective hedgerows at both sides of the road. Then, seeing that the Germans' front gun emplacements had indeed been demolished, they released themselves from their constraints and raced pell-mell towards the demolished main gates. Isolated bursts of rifle and machine-gun fire from inside the radar station cut some of them down, but as the majority of the Germans were fleeing through the rear gate, most of the SAS managed to surge into the compound at the front.

Once the foot soldiers were inside, the drivers of the jeeps gunned the engines and raced around the bend with the gunners all set to fire. This the gunners did the second they saw their first targets inside the breached compound, adding the savage roar of the twin Vickers to the already deafening cacophony of assault rifles and sub-machine-guns. Thus, while the majority of the Germans had already made their escape, those still inside the compound, some on foot, others in trucks, were cut down in a hail of bullets.

Five minutes later, the mopping up had been completed and the compound was littered with dead bodies. Smoke wreathed the scene of devastation. After checking who was dead and who merely wounded, the SAS picked up their own dead, who numbered five, placed them in the back seats of their jeeps and drove away from the hellish scene, back to the forward operating base.

Once back at the FOB, they arranged for the dead and wounded to be transferred by truck to the nearest

Allied airfield; then they all followed breakfast with a long, much-needed sleep. For they knew that by nightfall they would be on the move again, looking for more targets.

11

'I have to confess to being pleased with our progress so far,' Captain Callaghan told Greaves as they watched the Bedford QL trucks rumble out of the FOB, taking more SAS dead away for burial and the wounded to the nearest field hospital, for treatment there or to be casualty-evacuated to England. 'It's astonishing, when you think of it, just how much territory we've covered between us and how many Germans and targets we've managed to knock out during this first fortnight. I can hardly believe it, but it's certainly encouraging.'

'Good for the men's morale as well,' Greaves reminded him.

'Of course.' Glancing about him in the growing light, Callaghan saw that most of the men had finished breakfast and were already creeping into the lean-tos or LUPs for a well-earned kip after the latest of their successful night raids. 'I wonder how the Maquis group's getting on. We haven't heard a peep out of them.'

'Extraordinary,' Greaves said. For the past two weeks, ever since that first night a month ago when they had split up into three separate groups, sending the Maquis out on their own, they hadn't received a single message from André. To all intents and purposes, the resistance fighters had disappeared like a puff of smoke.

It had been an extraordinary two weeks for more than one reason. In that hectic time, C Squadron had criss-crossed central France relentlessly, always travelling by night, to engage the enemy directly, blow up railway lines, radar stations and communications cables, attack passing trains and troop convoys, and in general cause a great deal of mayhem. In doing so, they had seen a France less welcoming than the one they had experienced during their first, daylight forays across the attractive, mostly liberated countryside. Instead, in the course of their night raids, as the Allies pushed the Germans back towards their own border and the SAS had moved ever closer to the receding front, they had seen the real devastation caused during the occupation and by the retreating Germans since then: whole villages razed to the ground by shelling; churches gutted by fire, with blackened corpses still lying amid their ruins; captured enemy soldiers hanging from trees and lampposts; the bloated, scorched, dismembered carcasses of cows, sheep and horses caught in the cross-fire of battles or misguided bombing raids; rubble, dust and, everywhere, dead soldiers and civilians. During their first two weeks of night raids, the SAS had seen it all.

During that time, also, the war of liberation had continued. The British 2nd Army had advanced 250 miles from the Seine to Antwerp in one week; the 1st Canadian Army had freed Rouen and pushed on to the Somme at Abbeville; Nice and Monaco had been occupied by the Allied forces, who had pushed back the German 19th Army; and General Patton's 3rd Army had reached the north-west edge of Sombernon, on the last leg of its relentless advance to Dijon. The SAS raids in that area were still designed to aid Patton's advance and had so far been very successful.

'Successful though we've been,' Greaves said, 'we've had heavy casualties and I'm worried about our depleted numbers. We're down to half the men and jeeps we had two weeks ago; and according to HQ, we won't be getting any more after the next resup.'

'No problem,' Callaghan replied, grinning broadly. 'Come with me. I've something to show you. It won't take long.'

'I haven't had my morning's sleep yet,' Greaves reminded his fellow captain.

'You can catch up on that later.'

He led Greaves to his jeep and they drove out of the FOB and along the winding lane they had taken so often on their night raids of the past fortnight. Now, in broad daylight, the countryside looked very pretty, with the bright-green, gently undulating hills covered with trees and the occasional white-roofed farmhouse silhouetted against the blue September sky, with its fleecy clouds. This time, however, instead of following the road, Callaghan took a very narrow turning, no more than a dirt track, that led them across a cultivated field and into dense woods.

Eventually, when the trees had become more numerous, cutting down the light, they emerged into a sunlit clearing where, to his surprise, Greaves saw another camp of lean-tos and bell tents concealed cunningly in the trees. As most of the men were wearing Denison smocks, dispatch rider's breeches, motorcycle boots and red berets with the winged-dagger badge, he knew they were members of the SAS.

'D Squadron,' Callaghan explained, pulling up in the middle of the camp, between a row of bell tents and a larger, open-ended tent obviously serving as an HQ. The latter was presently occupied by two officers seated on folding chairs at a trestle-table strewn with maps and papers. 'They parachuted in about a month before us, but in the area of Le Mans. They fought their way from there to Fontainebleau, then moved south to here. I think we can do something about our depleted numbers by joining up with them. So let's meet the CO.'

As they walked across the clearing to the HQ tent, Greaves had a good look around him and was impressed by what he saw: dumps of stores, tents made from khaki parachutes draped between the branches, and brushwood barriers protecting the main exits. Those rude shelters, he realized, would be next to impossible to detect except at the shortest range; and inside, he noticed, they were furnished comfortably with proper camp-beds, folding chairs, small trestle-tables containing hand basins, lamps and hexamine stoves. Very well equipped indeed, Greaves thought. He also noticed that most of the men were bearded and that their berets were beginning to fade. Clearly, they had been out and about a lot.

In the HQ tent the officers, both SAS captains, were still seated at the overburdened trestle-table. Though it was only ten in the morning, one of them, Captain Wilfred 'Will' Lazenby, whom Greaves knew from the SAS camp in Fairford, was filling two glasses with whisky. He looked up when Callaghan and Greaves entered.

'Ah!' he exclaimed. 'We'll need two more glasses.'

'At this time of the morning?' Callaghan asked with mock severity.

Lazenby merely grinned. 'This is D Squadron, not C,' he said. 'We're not softies here. Pull up a chair, Paddy. You, too, Dirk.'

Callaghan and Greaves shook hands with Lazenby, who indicated the other officer with a lazy wave of his free hand. 'Captain Julian Crittenden,' he said. 'A good officer with a mouthful of a name, so just call him Jules.' Greaves shook hands with Crittenden, then pulled up a chair beside Callaghan and accepted the glass of whisky offered by Lazenby. They all raised their glasses in a mock toast, then took the first sip.

'Wonderful!' Lazenby exclaimed softly, reverently. 'This is better than breakfast.'

'Not bad at all,' Callaghan told him. 'You don't go short of anything here, I see.'

'Judging by the look of this place,' Greaves added, 'you've been here some time and are well supplied.'

'Our brief was to avoid engagement with the enemy and instead remain in hiding and concentrate on building up supply dumps in the forest, to be used by the advancing Allies when required. In order to do this we secured an old civilian lorry and used it to transfer the stores from the DZ to various caches scattered widely around the area. Though we did indeed build up a lot of dumps for the advancing troops, we also amassed considerable quantities of food, petrol and ammunition for ourselves – so, yes, we're well stocked and equipped. Now, what have *you* been up to, gentlemen?'

Callaghan summarized the past fortnight's activities, then said: 'So both our SAS groups did extremely well. Unfortunately, we can't tell you how the Maquis group got on as they disappeared and haven't been in touch. Not one radio message.'

'Possibly wiped out by Jerry,' Greaves suggested.

'No, they weren't,' Lazenby said, surprising them both. 'You're talking about the group led by André Flaubert, I take it?'

'Yes.'

'We've been in close contact with that group for the past fortnight,' Lazenby informed them. 'They're presently located at Aignay-le-Duc, about fifteen miles to the south, and they go out daily on hit-and-run raids.'

'By "daily" do you mean during the day?' asked Callaghan.

'Yes. Sometimes at night as well, but mostly during

the day. I think they just go when the mood takes them – or when their intelligence informs them of a good target.'

'When you say you've been in close contact,' said Greaves, 'does that mean you're working with them?'

'No. What it means is that we visit them almost every day for information, but otherwise let them do things their own way, which, let's face it, isn't our way.'

'Although the partisans are undoubtedly an enthusiastic bunch,' Crittenden clarified, 'we've found that the difference between our respective methods makes close co-operation difficult. It's therefore better to maintain no more than a loose liaison with them. Isn't that what you found?'

Callaghan sighed and took another sip of whisky. 'Yes. I just wish they'd told us where they were and what they were up to.'

'That's not Flaubert's way. He likes to go his own way.'

'Which is energetic, but completely undisciplined.'

'Quite so, Paddy. And his girlfriend, who has a sweet face, likes to slit German throats.'

'And shoot them in the back of the head,' Greaves informed him.

Lazenby and Crittenden grinned. 'The abrupt dispatch of unhelpful prisoners,' the latter said. 'I think that's a less crude way of putting it.'

Greaves nodded and smiled sardonically. 'Much more tasteful,' he said.

'Are you still in concealment and supplying the dumps?' Callaghan asked.

'No. All that ended last week, when we were told to embark on aggressive patrolling. So a few days ago we began our first offensive moves against Jerry, destroying a number of vehicles, attacking a small post on the main road, blowing up railway lines and bringing down electric pylons with Lewes bombs.'

'God bless Jock Lewes,' Callaghan said and meant it, recalling his late friend with real affection. Lieutenant John Steel Lewes, No. 8 Commando and one of the founder members of the SAS, had created many of the early SAS training methods, invented the highly effective, portable Lewes bomb, and was killed during the raid on Nofilia, in Libya, in December 1941 – shot by an Italian Savoya SM Sparviero light bomber that attacked his LRDG Chevrolet truck. Lewes was now revered by the whole regiment, including Callaghan, who had been on the raid against El Agheila at the same time and marched out of the desert with the other survivors, including Dirk Greaves and David Stirling. He would never forget those raids as long as he lived. He would always miss Lewes.

'God bless Lewes indeed,' Lazenby said. 'Anyway, our activities were pretty successful – certainly enough to encourage a number of countermoves by the Krauts. In fact, they picketed the road between Auberive and Aubepierre and, according to Maquis intelligence, are now beating the forest north of this base, vainly trying to find us.'

'They'll get here eventually,' Callaghan said, 'so you'd better move on.'

'Yes, I suppose so,' Lazenby replied, sighing, 'though I *do* like it here.'

'Since you're going to have to move anyway,' Callaghan said, seeing his chance and taking it, 'why not double your strength by combining with us?'

'Double *your* strength, you mean!'

Callaghan grinned. 'I admit, our numbers have been badly reduced by our recent activities and that after the final drop tomorrow night we won't be receiving any new men – so, yes, you're right, we need you to make up for our losses.' He spread his hands in a gesture of helplessness. 'But why not? What's good for us is good for you. Combined, we'll be twice as good as we are now, so it's well worth doing.'

'And where do you suggest we move to?' Lazenby asked.

'Even further south,' Callaghan replied. 'To the southernmost tip of the forest, well away from those Germans advancing from the north. Down near Aignay-le-Duc.'

'An area you know well,' Lazenby said.

'All to the good, Will.'

'And precisely where André Flaubert's Maquis are located.'

'That won't hurt us either. You never know when we'll need them.'

Lazenby glanced at Crittenden, who stared back thoughtfully, then gave him a nod. Turning back to

Callaghan and Greaves, Lazenby raised his glass in another toast. 'All right, gentlemen, it's a deal. Let's drink to it.'

They touched glasses, toasting their forthcoming, unpredictable liaison.

'Who dares wins,' Captain Greaves said.

12

The move to Aignay-le-Duc was made two days later, D and C Squadrons travelling separately under cover of darkness. Like the previous hide of D Squadron, the new base was located in dense undergrowth, with the bell tents in a clearing hidden under a natural arch of trees and the lean-tos practically woven into the foliage to make them invisible from the air and difficult to see even at close quarters. Callaghan was thrilled by the new hide, though he expressed his concern that the absence of good paths might cause the new jeep tracks to be noticed.

'We have an effective but extraordinarily tedious way of preventing that,' Captain Lazenby replied.

'Oh?' Callaghan asked. 'What's that?'

'When a jeep is either leaving or returning to the camp, its two gunners have to walk for about half a mile behind it, covering the tyre tracks with vegetation. That means the jeeps arrive and depart very slowly, but at least it works.'

'My gunners will go mad when I tell them that,' Callaghan replied.

'They're probably mad already.'

Once the new hide had been completed, Callaghan sent a coded message on the radio, asking for a resup at 2200 hours that evening and giving details of the chosen DZ. As this drop was to include the last of his personnel replacements, a mere six men, he asked Lazenby to take him on a visit to the Maquis camp, which was in another part of the forest, about five miles away.

'Even our combined numbers are dangerously low,' Callaghan explained, 'so we might have to call on the Maquis, whether or not we like it. So let's all be sociable.'

Callaghan and Greaves drove with Lazenby, cruising in broad daylight through a landscape seemingly untouched by war and devoid of soldiers, friendly or otherwise. The day was bright and cold, and an autumn breeze was blowing. The softly rolling fields, as yet unharvested, and broken up by darker green hedgerows, forest and the occasional glittering stream, reminded all three officers of rural England, particularly Gloucestershire, where the regiment was presently based. Nevertheless, though no other soul or vehicles could be seen, all three officers had 9mm Sten guns resting across their laps, ready for use.

In the event, nothing happened and since the journey was so short and they were cruising at an average speed of forty miles per hour, they arrived at the Maquis camp in about ten minutes. Like the SAS camp, it was secreted in a clearing deep in the forest and had its tents and lean-tos carefully camouflaged with foliage. What surprised Callaghan and Greaves most, however, was the size of the supply dump they could see at the far edge of the clearing and the ammunition dump not far from it. They were even more surprised to see sandbagged gun emplacements bristling with Bofors anti-aircraft guns and even six-pounders. The Maquis had not had all that equipment when they split from the SAS two and a half weeks ago. In fact, they had had practically nothing.

After climbing out of the jeep, the three SAS officers were escorted by a man wearing a plain grey suit and a black beret, and carrying an American M1 carbine, to the largest tent in the camp. Inside, they found André seated in a canvas-covered folding chair with maps spread out on the trestle-table in front of him. Maxine was behind him, wearing an old British Army tunic with black sweater and trousers. A black beret perched jauntily on her thick, black hair, above her ivory-coloured face, made her look even more beautiful than normal. An M1 carbine was slung across her back and bandoliers of ammunition criss-crossed her slim, curvaceous body. When she looked up, she recognized the Englishmen, but did not smile at them. André, by contrast, grinned broadly and raised his right hand in greeting.

'Ah! My old friends, Captains Callaghan and Greaves! It is good to see you again. Please, be seated,' he said in English.

The three officers took chairs on the other side of the table, all aware that André was enjoying his role as commander and host. Before anyone could speak, he clapped his hands and asked Maxine to fetch the bottle of vermouth and five glasses. When she did so, taking them from a small cupboard on the floor of the tent, André poured everyone drinks and passed the glasses around.

'To General de Gaulle!' he said, holding up his glass. 'To the liberation of Paris!'

'To the King,' Callaghan rejoindered sardonically. They all drank, then Callaghan said in French: 'We wondered what had happened to you, André. We were a bit concerned.'

The Maquis leader just shrugged. 'Why should you be concerned? You asked us to go out on raids against the Germans and that's what we did. It is what we have *always* done.'

'But you didn't keep in touch,' Greaves said.

André shrugged again. 'I didn't think, Captain. We were too busy doing what we do best. What would we call you for?'

'We were supposed to be having a loose liaison.'

'That term means nothing to me. I only know that we have our own ways of doing things and that unfortunately you do not always approve of them. We like to do things as we have always done them and I decided that we do not need the assistance of the British Army – not even the SAS.'

'So why have you come here?' Maxine asked.

'For a pleasant reunion,' Callaghan replied without pause, 'and to find out just what you've been doing.'

'We have been doing what *you've* been doing,' Maxine replied without a smile. 'Blowing up bridges, railway lines and communications cables, stealing weapons and supplies, and, of course, killing Germans.'

'Yes,' Callaghan said. 'You're very good at that.'

'Count yourselves lucky that we are,' Maxine replied, her lovely brown eyes flashing a challenge.

'I noticed a lot of supplies and weapons outside. You didn't have those when you left us. Where did you get them?'

'From German convoys and trains. We don't attack and flee back into the woods as you do. When we attack, we finish what we start, killing all the German guards and taking their weapons and the supplies. So we kill for a purpose.'

Callaghan smiled. 'You're obviously well organized.'

André nodded. 'We are. Now we even operate our own stretch of railway line through this territory. It runs between two local stations taken over by us when we got rid of the Germans who were there. That railway line is invaluable, enabling us to bring in the kind of big guns we could not have had otherwise.'

'Yes,' Captain Lazenby said, 'we noticed when we came in. The Bofors and the six-pounders. They were taken off the Germans?'

'From German trains, yes. Probably stolen from the British.'

'No doubt,' Greaves said.

'So what have you *really* come here for?' the relentless Maxine asked.

'Because of our depleted strength,' Callaghan replied candidly, 'we've joined our forces with Captain Lazenby's D Squadron. Because the Germans were beating the forest north of his hide and would eventually have found it, we decided to move as far south as possible – to Aignay-le-Duc, which is where we are camped now.'

'This is our territory, Captain.'

'We can't go elsewhere and must remain here at least until General Patton's 3rd Army reaches Dijon.'

'As you are here to help liberate us, Captain, I can hardly tell you to leave,' André said generously. 'Besides, apart from not wishing to work your way, we are grateful for what you have done in France. Therefore, if there is any way we can help . . .'

That was precisely what Callaghan wanted to hear. 'We appreciate that you find it difficult to take orders from us,' he said, 'but have come here to ask you to keep the loose liaison open should we need to work, if not exactly together, then relatively closely, in the near future.'

'Agreed.'

'We would also appreciate it if you would include us in any local intelligence that you feel may be of benefit to us.'

'Agreed.'

Callaghan finished off his drink and placed his glass on the table. The others did the same, then Callaghan smiled, stood up and reached across the table to shake the Frenchman's hand. 'Thank you, André.'

'My pleasure,' André said in English.

Maxine just nodded solemnly as the three SAS officers stood up, left the tent, clambered into their jeep and headed back the way they had come, all aware that they would not get any sleep that day because they had to prepare for the resup drop that night.

The drop took place as scheduled in a field approximately 800 yards long and about three miles from the hide. As usual, a heavily armed SAS guard surrounded the field, facing out towards any possible advancing enemy forces. And as before, two more groups of SAS troopers were spaced well apart in lines that faced each other across the long leg of the L-shaped DZ, which was illuminated with three red lights and one white. Greaves stood at the end of the short leg of the L, flashing clearance to land with his Morse lamp while Corporal Jim Almonds used his S-phone as a homing beacon and for direct communication with the incoming aircraft's pilot.

The night was particularly dark, with heavy clouds obscuring the moon and stars, and an unseasonably fierce wind was blowing. The aircraft being used this time was a Douglas C-47 Dakota, powered by two Pratt & Whitney R-1830 1200-hp engines. Shortly after it had banked and made its first low-altitude run over the DZ, four white parachutes billowed out over each of the many crates it had dropped.

The crates floated down and thudded into the soft, grassy earth even as the Dakota was disappearing in the dark sky to circle around and come back for its second run.

Knowing that the second drop would be the descent of the six SAS paratroopers, the men on the ground were particularly quick to run into the middle of the DZ to remove the crates and canisters, then clear the parachutes and other debris, including wood from smashed crates, from the area. They were already heaving the crates and canisters, all unopened since there were no jeeps, up into the Bedford QL trucks as the Dakota returned and the white parachutes of the paratroopers blossomed high in the ink-black sky.

The many men humping the crates and canisters into the trucks had been replaced at the DZ by a smaller group of men whose function was simply to welcome the six new arrivals, help them out of their parachute harnesses and then guide them to the jeeps that would take them back to the hide. Those men, expecting to see six parachutes billowing out high above them, were therefore shocked to see only five. Not knowing what was happening, they waited tensely on both sides of the DZ, watching the white parachutes float down out of a sky so dark that they couldn't even see the paratroopers.

Even as they were looking up, they all heard a thud on the ground just outside the DZ. Assuming that one of the paratrooper's leg bags had broken loose and crashed to earth, the watching men were not too concerned, remaining where they were until the chutes had collapsed to the ground and started whipping like great flags as the rolling paratroopers tried to tug the cords tight. Instantly, the welcoming teams rushed into the DZ to help the new arrivals.

'Shit!' the first paratrooper freed said in an anguished whisper. 'Oh, shit!'

'What?' Jacko asked, being the first out on the field. 'You're down, mate! Safe and sound! In one piece! Welcome to France!'

'Miller went down!' the man said in a choked voice, his breathing heavy and tortured. 'I'm convinced he went down. he was right in front of me, but when I went out I couldn't see his chute. I don't think it opened. Oh, shit, where *is* he?'

'Don't worry, we'll find him,' Jacko said, thinking: Only five parachutes. Five out of six. 'Now get out of your harness.' As the man was struggling to do so, being tugged sideways by the wind-whipped parachute on the end of his cords, Jacko turned to the rest of the welcoming party and bawled: 'Miller! Where's Miller? *Look for Miller!*'

Galvanized into action by the anxiety in Jacko's voice, the men, including the newly arrived paratroopers, started calling out the missing man's name and scattered across the DZ to find him. When, after about ten minutes, they had failed either to elicit a response from Miller or to find him in person, they made their way back to the trucks. However, just as they were climbing up into them,

Rich's voice called out of the far side of the DZ: 'Over here!'

Immediately, the men, including the new arrivals, rushed back across the field to where they could see Rich frantically waving. When they reached him, they found Lance-Corporal Ron Miller at his feet, smashed into the soft earth and looking like a crimson jelly. There was no opened parachute near him.

'I've examined him,' Rich said, sounding shaky. 'Poor sod didn't have a prayer. One end of his static line looks singed and tattered. My guess is that acid somehow ate through it in the Dakota and his chute didn't even pull out of its pack. In other words, because some penguin back in England was careless in packing the poor bugger's chute, he went out of that Dakota without it. It's still right there in his backpack, tucked up nice and neat. Christ, don't even *talk* to me!'

As the Welshman turned away from the mangled corpse, the other men muttered various curses against the lazy bastard back in England whose carelessness had cost Miller his life.

Jacko brutally brought them back to reality by bawling: 'Don't just fucking stand there! Go and fetch a stretcher and get this body out of here. We haven't got all night!' Shocked back to their senses, four of the men raced off for a stretcher, always carried in one of the Bedfords for a tragic event such as this, while the others removed their small spades from their webbing and proceeded to scoop the soft soil out from under the dead paratrooper.

'Don't talk to me!' Rich repeated in a tone of voice that did not remotely resemble his own. 'Those lazy, murderous bastards!'

Jacko walked up to the Welshman and placed his hand on his broad shoulder, to gently, sympathetically, shake him.

'Yeah,' Jacko said. 'Right. But forget it, Rich. Fuck it. It's just one of them things.'

'Fucking penguins!' Rich exploded, venting his rage at those who packed the parachutes back in England and often did it carelessly, either out of exhaustion or, as the SAS would have it, out of pure laziness or indifference. 'Fuck 'em all!'

'Know just what you mean, mate,' said Jacko as comfortingly as he could.

A few minutes later, the four men who had run off returned with a stretcher, picked the bloody, sagging body of Lance-Corporal Miller up out of the hole created by his fall and the subsequent digging of the SAS troopers, rolled it on to the stretcher, then humped it back across the dark field to the waiting Bedford. Within minutes, the crater had been filled in by the other men and covered with loose foliage to render it invisible to prying eyes. Shortly after that, the trucks and jeeps moved out in single file, away from the DZ, heading back to the hide in the forest.

Lance-Corporal Miller, who had never fought his war, was buried with full military honours in the tiny churchyard of Aignay-le-Duc the following day.

13

Six hours after the ill-fated paratrooper had been buried, and two hours after last light, the combined C and D Squadrons commenced serious operations against the enemy, with separate patrols going out on all the main roads through the Forest of Châtillon. Determined this time to be as aggressive as possible, the group led by Captain Greaves, but with Sergeant Lorrimer's jeep out on point, parked, spaced well apart, on both sides of a road marked on their maps as a major MSR and waited patiently in the darkness to ambush the first German convoys that came along.

They did not have a long wait. The first German vehicles to pass, only thirty minutes later, were three canvas-topped supply trucks travelling at no more than thirty miles per hour with dimmed headlights. Greaves waited until the German column had drawn parallel to his own hidden line of parked vehicles, then gave the signal to open fire.

The savage roar of the combined twin Vickers was followed instantly by the smashing of the glass in the German trucks' windscreens and the demented whine of ricocheting .303-inch bullets. The first truck immediately careered off the road with a screeching of brakes and plunged nose first into the ditch at the far side. The middle car, which must have been loaded with ammunition, exploded with a deafening roar and became a ball of fire shuddering to a halt, into which the third truck then crashed.

As the dreadful screaming of the men in the cabin of the blazing truck rose briefly even above the harsh chatter of the Vickers, the flames from the burning vehicle, which were extraordinarily violent and of a dazzling whiteness, swept back to engulf the cabin of the truck that had smashed into it, producing more dreadful cries from the men trapped there. The SAS men not manning the machine-guns emptied their 9mm Sten guns and tommy-guns into the drivers' cabins to put them out of their misery, and as the men stopped screaming the canvas top of the third truck burst into flames. Within seconds, this fresh blaze had ignited the ammunition in that truck and it, too, exploded with a mighty roar, turning into a ball of white fire and billowing black smoke.

'Move out!' Greaves bawled into his S-phone.

Before any Germans who might have been following the first three trucks could pursue them, the SAS jeeps reversed on screeching tyres, then headed back into the forest by the same narrow track that had taken them to the MSR. Half an hour later they were again parked by the side of the MSR, but now ten miles east of their previous location, waiting for another convoy to pass. This time their victims were a convoy of ten German motor-cycle troops, all on powerful bikes, wearing heavy leather coats and steel helmets, with

semi-automatic rifles slung across their backs. When
the Vickers roared into action, the motor-cyclists were
briefly caught in a dazzling web of phosphorescent
green, blue and crimson lines created by the hail of
mixed incendiary, tracer and armour-piercing bullets,
which gave them no time to escape. Chopped to pieces
even before the other SAS troops had opened fire
with their personal weapons, the Germans either
fell off their wildly careering motor-cycles or were
incinerated when their petrol tanks were pierced and
exploded into flames. Within seconds, a nightmarish
spectacle had unfolded, accompanied by deafening
explosions and demented screams.

'Move out!' Greaves bawled into his S-phone.

Again the SAS jeeps reversed hurriedly, turned
around and roared back the way they had come.
Their third stop, forty minutes later, just before
midnight, was ten miles further along the MSR,
where it ran between the old market town of
Auxerre on the River Yonne and Avallon, further
south. Knowing that the Germans were beginning to
evacuate the captured towns and villages of this area
as Allied forces swept south from liberated Paris and
Patton's 3rd Army closed in on Dijon from the east,
Callaghan was confident that sooner or later more
German columns would come along the MSR, fleeing
from Auxerre.

This turned out to be true, though they had to wait
in the darkness for nearly two hours. Meanwhile
the moonlit sky directly above them filled up with

an awesome number of Allied aircraft – Fortresses and Liberators of the US 8th and 9th Air Forces; RAF Handley-Page Halifaxes and Lancasters of RAF Bomber Command; and a protective umbrella of US Thunderbolts and RAF Spitfire fighters – all heading south-east. Minutes later, the muffled thunder of distant bombing could be heard and the dark sky beyond Dijon was fitfully illuminated by fans of silvery-white light where the bombs were exploding.

'That's the area between Dijon and Belfort,' Greaves told Lorrimer through the S-phone. 'Patton must be preparing to make his final push to Dijon.'

'Which means Jerry will soon be swarming all over this place,' Lorrimer replied.

'Let's hope so, Sarge.'

Eventually, about two in the morning, as the immense Allied fleet of aircraft passed overhead and the distant muffled pounding continued, Greaves's expectations were fulfilled when an unusually large German convoy of what looked like troop trucks with dipped headlights came along the road from the direction of Auxerre, heading south to avoid Dijon. Realizing that he could well have a major fire-fight on his hands, but that the proximity of the German convoy made it too late to contact the other SAS men and tell them to make a tactical withdrawal, Greaves again waited until the passing convoy was parallel with his own hidden jeeps before slapping Jacko on the shoulder and bawling: 'Open fire!'

The combined roaring of Jacko and Rich's twin

Vickers was the signal for the machine-gunners in the other SAS jeeps to open fire too, covering the passing convoy in the customary web of phosphorescent green, blue and crimson lines. The bedlam of the machine-guns was followed instantly by the shattering of windscreens, the popping of exploding tyres, the screeching of skidding tyres and brakes, then frantic bawling in German and the screams of wounded men. A couple of the trucks careered sideways and ploughed nose first into the ditch; two or three more crashed into each other as some braked unexpectedly; and the petrol tank of one of them was peppered with .303-inch bullets and exploded, engulfing the driver's cabin in a sheet of searing white flame that set fire to the men inside, who filled the air with their fearsome screams.

As German troops jumped out of the rear of the stalled trucks, unslinging their weapons even as their boots hit the ground, the SAS men not manning the machine-guns opened fire with Sten guns, tommy-guns and .303 Lee-Enfields, increasing the already deafening roar and cutting many of the Germans down before they could work out exactly where the fire was coming from.

Hearing the roar of a fighter plane and the chatter of its guns directly above him, even in the bedlam of the SAS attack, Greaves glanced up and saw a lone USAF Thunderbolt swooping down over the German column. The fighter's guns stitched parallel lines of spitting dust and gravel along the road, running right up to the first of the stalled German trucks, then tore through the trucks with a murderous fusillade that chopped the canvas covers to shreds and exposed the men screaming and dying inside.

As more of the Germans frantically tried to escape from the trucks, the Thunderbolt swept up and away to circle round before coming back for a second dive. Meanwhile, the SAS men continued the American's deadly handiwork by chopping down more of the Germans with their personal weapons while the twin Vickers continued to rake the trucks, peppering more petrol tanks and causing more deafening explosions of dazzling white flame and billowing black smoke.

Less than two minutes later the Thunderbolt swooped back down over the column with all its guns chattering noisily, again strafing the stalled, besieged convoy mercilessly. This time, however, the Germans returned the fire with a hail of bullets from an uncovered anti-aircraft gun and when the Thunderbolt had made its devastating run over the column and was ascending again, it was hit and left a trail of smoke behind it. High in the sky, it went into a spin and managed to level out long enough for the pilot to bale out. As his white parachute billowed like a flower in the dark sky, the Thunderbolt went out of control, going first into a spin, then into a nose dive, leaving a wavering smoke signature behind it as it plunged into the ground far away and exploded in a fan of silvery light. The parachute continued to drift gently to earth and had soon disappeared beyond a dark line of silhouetted trees to the east of Auxerre.

'Pull out!' Greaves bawled into his S-phone.

With the German trucks either destroyed completely or damaged beyond repair, and the enemy troops severely depleted, Greaves could see little point in remaining by the side of the road long enough to let the dazed survivors of the raid get their senses back and launch a counter-attack. Instead, as before, the SAS jeeps screeched into reverse, then turned away and raced back into the forest, using a secondary road that led them in a wide arc around Auxerre and on to Châtillon, some forty miles north of Dijon.

They had been driving for about half an hour when Jacko, who insisted on standing behind his twin Vickers in the lead jeep, driven by Sergeant Lorrimer, said: 'There's someone on the road straight ahead and he's waving at us, obviously wanting us to stop.'

'Is he armed?' Lorrimer asked, not sharing Jacko's more expansive view out of the jeep and straining to see through the darkness.

'No,' Jacko replied, though he cocked the Vickers all the same, 'but he might have armed friends in the trees at either side of the road. He's still frantically waving, though.' However, as the jeep drew closer to that dark figure on the road, Jacko spotted the flying jacket the man was wearing.

'Unless he's wearing stolen clothes, I think he's an American pilot,' he said.

'That would make sense,' Lorrimer replied. 'The pilot of that Thunderbolt came down in this general vicinity. We'll slow down until we can check, but keep your fingers on the triggers of those K guns and your eyes peeled for any movement on either side of the road.'

'Right, boss, will do.'

'Slowing down to check identity of possible downed US pilot,' Lorrimer told Greaves, in the jeep behind him, on his S-phone. 'If he checks out, we'll pick him up.'

'Confirmed,' Greaves replied. 'Over and out.'

Lorrimer slowed down and eventually stopped right in front of the man in the road. The other jeeps came to a stop behind him and the machine-gunners each covered his own side of the tree-lined road. The man was stocky and brown-haired, and his flying jacket, Lorrimer noticed, was slightly singed, though he was grinning broadly as he held his hands in the air.

'Don't shoot!' he shouted melodramatically. 'Cap'n Oliver Ladd of the US 8th Air Force. You guys shot up that German convoy back near Auxerre?'

'Correct,' Lorrimer said.

The pilot lowered his hands to spread them in the air, palms up, his grin still wide. 'Well, I was flying the Thunderbolt that shot that convoy up, helping you guys out. You might've seen me bale out.'

'We did,' Lorrimer said, jerking his left thumb to indicate that the American should take the seat beside him. 'Hop in, Captain.'

'Call me "Olly",' said the pilot, positively beaming as he climbed in beside Sergeant Lorrimer, waved to Jacko and Rich, and then at the jeeps lined up behind them, before settling into his seat. Starting up the jeep and moving forward again, Sergeant Lorrimer introduced Captain Ladd to Jacko and Rich, then said: 'So where did you land, Olly?'

Ladd waved his right hand to indicate the field they were just leaving behind them. 'Over in that cow pasture,' he said with a lazy drawl. 'Ankle-deep in mud, but otherwise OK. I buried the chute over there.'

'What's the accent?'

'Fort Worth, Texas. A Texan born and bred.'

Using the S-phone, Lorrimer called back to Greaves and gave him Ladd's details, then clipped the phone back to his chest webbing and asked: 'You were part of that fleet of aircraft heading beyond Dijon?'

'Right,' Ladd replied. 'We were going to bomb and strafe the hell out of the area between there and Belfort.'

'In support of General Patton's 3rd Army?'

'You got it, friend.'

'Does that mean the final push on Dijon has begun?'

'Correct. It's all over but for the singing, Sarge. At least in this area. You guys have done a really fine job of keeping Jerry distracted.'

'And we're not finished yet,' Lorrimer told him.

'You mind if I stick with you guys for a while?'

'I don't think you've much choice.'

206

'You SAS?'

'That's right, Captain.'

'We've heard an awful lot about you guys and all of it good.'

'That's nice,' Lorrimer said.

'So where are you going next?' the American asked.

Lorrimer shrugged. 'We don't know. We just drive around until we find something. Tonight we've been hitting the MSR at ten or fifteen-mile intervals. We did a fair bit of damage.'

'Well, I don't know if this is of interest or not, but when I parachuted into that field, I nearly fell on the Frog farmer who owns it. When I asked him if the area was safe, he told me no, that there was a German headquarters in a farm near Châtillon. An enthusiastic old buzzard, well down on the Krauts and well up on weaponry, he told me he thought that it might be a good target for some men with mortars or big guns. I notice you've got mortars back there, so it might be worth checking out.'

'Indeed it might,' Lorrimer replied. Unclipping the S-phone, he called back to Greaves and passed on Ladd's information. Greaves agreed that nothing would be lost in reconnoitring the area, so they changed direction accordingly and headed for Châtillon. It was just before dawn when, at a roadside farmhouse not far from the town, they stopped to seek further information.

Covered by the Vickers of Jacko and Rich, as well

as those in the second jeep, but with Lorrimer's Sten gun at the ready just in case, the sergeant and Greaves walked up the path to the farmhouse, carefully looked in through both front windows, one man at each, and saw the farmer and his wife, the latter still in her nightdress, sitting at the kitchen table, eating a breakfast of fried eggs and crusty rolls.

The two SAS men converged on the front door, which Lorrimer hammered on with his clenched fist. When the farmer's flushed, well-fed face appeared at the left-hand window, his gaze sleepily curious at this early hour, Greaves stepped away from the door to let himself be seen. Eventually, satisfied that they were British, the farmer opened the door, greeted them in French, then switched to passable English for the rest of the conversation.

'Yes, Captain,' he said, automatically addressing the man with senior rank. 'What can I do for you?'

'Do you know of a nearby farm being used as a German headquarters?'

The farmer nodded. 'I believe one is being so used, but unfortunately I do not know which one.' He smiled and scratched his pink, blue-veined nose. 'But maybe I can find out for you. Step inside, *messieurs*.'

Captain Greaves and Lorrimer followed the farmer into what appeared to be his living-room. It contained mildewed sofas and soft chairs, a tremendous amount of clutter, and a row of recently killed rabbits, strung up by their hind feet on a string that ran above the fireplace. Greaves shivered, but Lorrimer just grinned.

'I will ring the Mayor,' the farmer told them, as if it was a perfectly normal thing to do at that time of the morning. 'If anyone knows where the Germans are staying, he'll be the one. As the Mayor he has to liaise with them, so surely he'll know.'

He dialled a number, waited for what seemed like a long time, then bid someone good morning, possibly the Mayor's wife or child, and asked for the Mayor. After another lengthy pause, the farmer bid the dignitary good morning, explained that he had some British soldiers in his farmhouse and added that they wanted to know which local farm the Germans were presently using as their headquarters. He listened carefully, then thanked the Mayor for his information and put the phone down.

'He was most obliging, since he is grateful to the British,' he said. 'Unfortunately, he told me that the farm recently used as a German headquarters has since been evacuated. He also told me to inform you that because of the last Allied bombing raid and the imminent advance of General Patton, the main garrison of Châtillon is being relieved by Panzer Grenadiers from Montbard. He would not be averse to the idea of your men attacking them and getting rid of them for good.'

'How many are there?' Greaves asked, hardly able to believe he was receiving valuable local intelligence in this casual manner, but noticing the amused grin on Lorrimer's face.

'Approximately 150 Germans with twenty trucks in the precincts of the château. However, more are expected tomorrow. Perhaps you could wait for them.'

'Perhaps we could,' Greaves said. 'What's the most convenient way into the town?'

'Turn left at my front gate, then follow the road around to the aerodrome. There are no planes there, so it is rarely guarded and will give you easy access to the town. All of the Germans, I believe, are in the château, so you should get there unmolested.'

'Thank you, *monsieur*. You've been very helpful.'

After returning to his jeep, Greaves directed the column to the aerodrome, which they reached in less than ten minutes. As the farmer had stated, the aerodrome was completely deserted and they were able to drive across the airstrip and enter the town by a side road. The first people to see them, some farmworkers, men and women, looked up in surprise as they drove past.

Continuing through the town, they emerged at the other side without encountering a single German and found themselves at a dried-up river bed, which was marked on their map and ran to the foot of the hill on which the château stood. When they reached the hill, Greaves ordered the column to stop and wait for him, then turned to Lorrimer and simply said: 'Bring a rope.' When Lorrimer had obligingly slung a knotted abseiling rope with a steel grappling hook at the end over his right shoulder, he and Greaves clambered up the steep slope until they came to the rear wall of the château.

Lorrimer unwound the rope and threw it up the side of the thirty-foot-high wall, until the hook had caught on the sharp-edged brick. After checking that it would hold by tugging vigorously and repeatedly at it, he placed his feet on the lower brickwork, leant well back and began expertly to scale the sheer wall, reaching the top in no time at all. He then threw the end of the knotted rope back down and Greaves made the same arduous, dangerous climb.

During their ascent the two men were watched by many amazed townspeople, from the upper windows of the tall houses surrounding the château. Once on top of the wall, precariously balanced on the narrow ledge that ran around it, they were able to look down into the courtyard and take note of the number of men and vehicles there, as well as the nature of the heavy weapons spread out around them. But not for very long, for within seconds, they had been spotted by some of the German soldiers in the courtyard and warning shouts were followed almost instantly by a fusillade of rifle fire that sent bullets ricocheting noisily about them, chipping off splinters of stone and creating blinding clouds of dust that billowed up from around their feet.

'Let's get back down,' Greaves said.

'No argument, boss.'

One after the other, the two men abseiled back down the wall as bullets ricocheted off the inside ledge on which they had been standing moments before. Just as the second to descend, Sergeant Lorrimer, reached the ground, half a dozen helmeted German troops ran out of the opened back gate of the château, firing sub-machine-guns on the move. Instantly, the SAS men in the jeeps below the hill opened up with their Vickers, firing in an arc that kicked up the dirt all around the Germans and then made most of them convulse frantically amid clouds of dust in the seconds before they died. The few who survived were backing into the rear gateway, still firing on the move, as Lorrimer and Greaves ran back down the slope and climbed hurriedly into their respective jeeps. As the vehicles roared away from the hill, the Vickers in the last jeep, fired by Jacko and Rich, kept the Germans in the gateway pinned down to let the convoy race out of range.

'Gee, you guys are really something!' Olly Ladd exclaimed, grinning excitedly. 'I mean, scaling that goddam wall! I'd heard you guys were something special and now I believe it.'

'It's all in a day's work,' Lorrimer replied as he sped away from the château. 'And the day isn't over yet.'

Indeed, it wasn't. As they turned off along a track that led back into the forest, they saw a convoy of four trucks heading for Châtillon on a road running parallel to their own. Standing up to use a hand signal, Greaves, hoping to catch the Germans at the next junction, indicated that the jeeps should turn around and drive back the way they had come.

Unfortunately, they were too late to intercept the Germans. The sudden, shocking sound of massed rifle fire indicated that the Germans had been stopped by André Flaubert and his fellow Maquisards further along the Châtillon road.

'Keep going!' Greaves ordered with another hand signal.

To the delight of Olly Ladd, the SAS jeeps continued to race along the narrow track until they were approaching the broader road used as an MSR. Before actually getting there, the jeeps slowed down and crept along in low gear, trying to make as little noise as possible. Given the bedlam being created by the combined fire of the Germans and the Maquis, this was not too difficult and soon the SAS were close enough to get a good view of the two warring sides.

The Maquisards had set up a roadblock of fallen trees and foliage. Now they were firing along the road at the Germans hiding behind their four blocked trucks, which they had parked across the road for their own protection. As the Germans had their backs to the SAS jeeps and could not hear their quiet approach because of the clamorous gunfire, the SAS men were able to drive to a distance within the firing range of their personal weapons and open up with those, as well as with the more powerful mounted Vickers.

Two of the trucks, their petrol tanks riddled by .303-inch bullets, exploded into flames, instantly killing some of the Germans kneeling behind them and setting two others on fire. As the burning Germans ran about yelling dementedly, only to be cut down by a merciful hail of SAS bullets, the combined might of the various SAS guns sent a murderous fusillade into the backs of the other Germans. Shocked, the few left turned around in a vain attempt to fire back. As they did so, the Maquisards used the respite to clamber over their makeshirt barricade and advance along the road, firing on the move, thus catching the last of the Germans in a deadly cross-fire.

A few minutes later the SAS men and the Maquisards were standing over the dead bodies of the German troops sprawled bloodily across the road, behind and between their four trucks, two of which were still blazing and filling the air with boiling, black smoke. The battle was over.

Later that afternoon, after they had had a good sleep, every officer, NCO and other soldier in C and D Squadrons reunited at their hide in the forest near Aignay-le-Duc, drove to André Flaubert's camp five miles away and celebrated their joint victory with a typically lengthy French lunch of excellent local dishes, wine and calvados. Even the normally suspicious Maxine was in good spirits and looked lovelier than ever. In the course of the lunch, provided by the Maquis from their bountiful supply dump, the bearded, dirty men from both sides treated each other with respect and, under the influence of too much wine, repeatedly toasted one another and formed maudlin friendships that were unlikely to last much past dawn.

André, now looking more favourably upon the SAS, agreed with the officers, including D Squadron's Captain Lazenby, that the combined SAS and Maquis should attack Châtillon at dawn the next day, while the German relief was still going on. He also agreed to supply five hundred men if the SAS would give them enough petrol for their trucks. When Callaghan said that this would be arranged, the men drank another toast to victory and the party continued, not breaking up until last light when everyone was very drunk.

When they woke at first light to commence the raid that would finally chase the Germans out of the area and pave the way for the last push of General Patton's 3rd Army, nearly all the SAS men were suffering from excruciating hangovers. Nevertheless, they knew that this was to be a decisive battle.

14

It was just after dawn and the light was still pearly grey when the first group of SAS troops, commanded by Captain Greaves, crossed the deserted aerodrome and occupied the Montbard–Dijon crossroads. Once there, buffeted by a sharp wind and showered with stinging dust, they began setting up a defensive perimeter that included a 3-inch mortar and a Bren gun, both behind sandbagged gun emplacements, and a team of men armed with .303-inch Lee-Enfield bolt-action rifles, 9mm Sten guns and tommy-guns, lying in shallow scrapes at strategic points at the side of each of the four roads, all near the junction and each other.

'Where the hell are the Maquis?' Greaves asked anxiously, knowing that at that moment the rest of the SAS men were reliably taking up their own positions in Châtillon and around the château, but feeling nervous because the resistance fighters had not shown up at the RV near the SAS's forest hide.

'Probably still sleeping it off,' Captain Lazenby said sardonically, knowing the Maquis well. 'Either that or our proud little friend André, and his mistrustful Maxine, have changed their minds and decided to let us go it alone.'

'That would be a right bloody help,' Greaves

muttered softly. 'Anyway, you'd best be on your way to set up that mortar.'

'Right,' Lazenby said.

Leaving Greaves and his men to complete their defensive perimeter around the junction, Lazenby and the other half of the group, consisting of a foot patrol following a jeep carrying a second mortar, went along the road to find a position that would allow the weapon to attack the north face of the château. Having found such a position on the wooded lower slopes south of the château, he called a halt and climbed down from the jeep, followed by his two-man mortar team. While the rest of the men prepared their personal weapons, the two in charge of the mortar dug a shallow scrape, placed the steel base plate in it, supported it with a couple of shells in tightly packed soil and gravel, then fixed the mortar to the base plate and piled a total of forty-eight bombs beside it, in readiness for action. The first shot fired by that weapon would be the signal for the others to begin the attack.

While Greaves's men were taking control of the junction and Lazenby was settling in with his mortar and assault teams south of the château, Callaghan was moving another forty men by jeep into the town, where, under the curious, hopeful gaze of the townspeople, most of whom were emerging silently from their homes to look on, they occupied all the main junctions leading into the market square.

'Where are the bloody Maquis?' Callaghan growled,

glancing anxiously up and down the various streets running into the square and seeing only more curious inhabitants.

'Buggered if I know,' Lorrimer replied. 'Whether they turn up or not is anybody's guess.'

'I'll kill that bloody André if he doesn't show,' Callaghan said, displaying a flash of the anger for which he was well known and which had often got him into trouble in the past. 'With my bare hands!'

'I'd like to be here to see it,' Lorrimer replied, grinning, though secretly just as anxious, 'but I've got to go and cut those military telephone cables.'

'Yes, you do that, Sarge.'

Taking two of the jeeps and their three-man teams, with Jacko and Rich manning the twin Vickers guns in his own vehicle, Sergeant Lorrimer drove to the Troyes–Chaumont crossroads. There he asked for one man from each vehicle to climb the telegraph poles and cut the cables with their wire-cutters. One of the 'volunteers' was Jacko. As he and Corporal Reg Seekings from the second jeep were cutting the wires, the other two men, Rich and Corporal Benny Bennett, remained standing at the mounted guns in their respective jeeps, scanning the Troyes and Chaumont roads for signs of advancing enemy convoys.

There was no sign of the Germans.

The Maquis did not materialize either.

South of the château, Lazenby checked his wrist-watch and waited for the second hand to move to

0700 hours. He raised his right hand, concentrating on the hand creeping round the dial, and then, at exactly 0700 hours, dropped his hand to his side.

At this signal, the first mortar bomb was dropped into the tube and fired immediately. A muffled thump was followed by a cloud of smoke from the tube, then, mere seconds later, by a much louder explosion that brutally shattered the morning's silence as the bomb erupted near the top of the slope, just in front of the northern wall of the château, hurling up a spectacular storm of soil and gravel, but leaving the wall untouched.

The instant that single explosion was heard some of the SAS men from Callaghan's group in the square advanced up the road towards the front of the château, preparing to engage with the German troops they knew would come down eventually, either to attack or to escape. At that same moment Lorrimer's team were kicking the chopped military communications cables to the side of the roads at the Troyes–Chaumont crossroads. This done, they climbed back into their jeeps to take up positions behind the Vickers guns and, if necessary, either prevent the German soldiers in the town from escaping this way or stop reinforcements from entering the town in support of their comrades.

'Where the hell are those bloody Maquis?' Sergeant Lorrimer asked rhetorically as the second mortar bomb fired by Lazenby's team exploded on the northern slope of the château, followed almost immediately by a third and a fourth. By the time the third shell had exploded, the mortar team had ascertained the correct calibration and were pleased to see a great chunk of the wall spewing outwards in a billowing cloud of stones, dust and pulverized cement.

Other bombs lobbed off in quick succession completely devastated the northern wall, provoking a fusillade of small-arms fire from along its ramparts. Simultaneously, the front gates of the south side opened and a horde of steel-helmeted Panzer troops raced out and marched down the road to take command of the town, unaware that the SAS were already in position on both sides of the road leading into the market square.

When the enemy troops were within range, the SAS men opened fire with their combined .303-inch Lee-Enfields, 9mm Sten guns, tommy-guns and two bipod-mounted Bren guns. They were followed immediately by a succession of bombs from another 3-inch mortar.

Around and between the advancing Panzer troops the earth became a violent convulsion of erupting soil and gravel, flying stones, spitting, swirling dust and smoke as the exploding bombs and rain of bullets took their toll. Some of the Germans did, however, emerge from the hellish murk and noise to hurl 'potato-mashers'. Exploding at both sides of the road, the grenades tore three of the SAS men to shreds, seriously wounded another and left half a dozen more temporarily dazed. This was enough to enable the rest of the Panzer troops to rush down the hill, hurling more potato-mashers and firing their Schmeissers on the move, forcing the SAS to make a tactical retreat back towards the town.

Fifteen minutes into the battle, a column of about thirty German trucks containing the relief party arrived at the river bridge near Greaves's position on the Montbard–Dijon crossroads. Though his jeep, manned by Harry-boy Turnball and Neil Moffatt, was in the middle of the road, Greaves let the Germans approach to within twenty yards before he gave the order to open fire.

The instant the twin Vickers roared into action, the 3-inch mortar and Bren gun in the sandbagged gun positions opened up as well, followed by the machine-guns of the other SAS jeeps and the personal weapons of the men in the shallow scrapes by the sides of the roads that converged at the junction.

This combined fire-power was devastating, tearing the first trucks in the German convoy to shreds, making the first two skid in opposite directions across the road, and then igniting the ammunition in the third, fourth and fifth. The subsequent explosions were awesome to behold, throwing up loose gravel, soil and debris in great mushrooms that sent back to earth a rain of blazing pieces of canvas, scorched, buckled metal, glistening shards of glass from the broken windscreens, scraps of uniform and dismembered limbs. The German troops who survived this and managed to spill out of the back of the remaining trucks were caught in a savage cross-fire of mixed incendiary, tracer and armour-piercing bullets that resembled a brilliant pyrotechnic display. Amid that bizarrely beautiful spectacle the Germans shuddered, jerked spasmodically, twisted into grotesque shapes, screamed horribly, dropped to the ground and expired.

As most of their comrades were dying in the hail of bullets, a motor-cycle with a sidecar carrying an armed trooper broke away from the end of the convoy and raced off in a cloud of dust, travelling in a broad arc that brought it around to one of the roads leading to the Troyes–Chaumont crossroads. Before noticing the SAS men placed there, the motor-cyclist turned on to the road and headed straight for the bridge leading to the junction.

'Get those bastards!' Lorrimer bawled.

The combined Vickers of the two jeeps at the crossroads roared into action as the motor-cycle came up over the slight hump of the picturesque stone bridge that spanned the river running past the town. The startled motor-cyclist just had time to catch a glimpse of the SAS jeeps facing him before he was almost chopped in half by a fusillade from the two machine-guns and lost control of his machine. Even as the bike was careering towards the side of the bridge, the desperate passenger instinctively let off a short burst from a Schmeisser. Short it surely was – because at that precise moment another hail of .303-inch bullets turned the sidecar into a hell of

222

flying wood chips and dust even as the machine flew off the side of the bridge, sailed through the air and then plunged into the river, the driver and passenger both flying out even further before also splashing into the water.

The steel helmet of the passenger bounced against the bank, then rolled down into the river. Water eddied around the wrecked motor-cycle as it sank out of sight.

The bodies of the motor-cyclist and his passenger sank briefly and then bobbed up again, letting the stunned SAS men see, as the latter turned in the swirling water, a skein of long, golden hair spreading out in the bloody water.

'Oh, shit!' Jacko exclaimed. 'It was a bleedin' woman.'

'Bleeding now all right,' said Rich, often soft-hearted yet just as often coldly pragmatic. 'Bleeding and dead.'

The sounds of battle reverberated through the streets of the town behind them – rattling Brens, roaring Vickers, whining and ricocheting bullets, the distant thump of mortars, followed by noisier explosions – making them all glance back in that direction.

'Sounds hot back there,' Lorrimer said.

It was. By this time, Captain Greaves, knowing that no more German reinforcements would be arriving, had led his men away from the appalling carnage at the Montbard–Dijon crossroads and back into the town square to lend support to Callaghan's group. Once there, Greaves took a Bren for himself and, balancing it precariously on the nearest wall, 'hosepiped' the advancing Panzer troops with crimson tracer. As he was doing so, the gun jammed.

Cursing to himself, Greaves tried releasing the mechanism and, glancing up, saw Olly Ladd joyfully firing a 9mm Sten gun from the hip, raking it from left to right to give himself the widest possible arc of fire. Even as some of the advancing Panzer troops were cut down by the American's fire, a German bullet blew the top of his head off, making him drop the Sten gun and jerk violently sideways, almost backwards. Then he walked a few yards, like some ghastly apparition, his exposed brains lifted up on a rising tide of blood as his knees gradually gave way beneath him. Eventually, blood still spurting from his shattered head, he collapsed, slid down the wall of a house, fell sideways and rolled on to his back. A Frenchman took hold of the pilot's ankles and dragged him into the hallway of the house, no doubt thinking he was still alive and could be saved.

Greaves could hear shooting from the far side of the square, as well as firing from behind the château, so he knew that Callaghan and Lazenby were still engaged. Glancing across the square, he saw the rest of Callaghan's men firing on the move as they retreated back down the slope leading up to the front of the château. Other men were doing the same in the other streets leading back into the square.

Suddenly, to Greaves's surprise and amusement, after the brutality of Ladd's death, a pretty French girl with long, jet-black hair and wearing a vivid blue, figure-hugging, low-cut dress, leaned out the top window of her house and gave the V sign to the embattled SAS men. Some of the SAS men actually stopped firing long enough to wave back and either cheer or wolf-whistle. Then they went back to attacking the Germans.

Shaking his head in amusement, Greaves returned to the task of unjamming his Bren gun, managed to free it, then rested the barrel on the wall and began firing again at the four Germans he saw advancing down one of the side streets. All of them were bowled over like skittles, leaving the street clear for the moment.

Just then, Callaghan and his team came backwards into the square, crouched low and firing on the move. Greaves gave them cover by firing his Bren at the Panzer troops swarming down the slope from the château. He was aided in this by the SAS troops grouped around him and soon Callaghan was right there beside him. Callaghan stopped firing his Sten gun, straightened up, removed his red beret from his head with a flourish and wiped sweat from his dust-smeared forehead.

'Those bloody Panzer boys don't give up easily,' he said. Placing his beret back on his head and carefully adjusting its position, he continued: 'Got to hand it to them: they're damn persistent. Still fighting their way down from the château. On the other hand, they're so confused about what's happening that they've started mortaring their own side. Any sign of the French?'

'No,' Greaves replied.

'Then I think we'd better get out of here and give ourselves time to reconsider the situation and, perhaps, find out just what happened to them.'

'I agree. Shall I give the signal to withdraw?'

'Please do.'

As Lazenby's mortar fired yet again from the wooded slopes on the northern side of the château, Greaves marched boldly into the middle of the square, waved to the girl in the upstairs window, then fired two Very lights into the air, signalling that the various SAS groups scattered around the town and the château should withdraw. Then, waving one last time to the French girl, he and the other men, including Callaghan and Lorrimer, piled back into their jeeps and raced out of town, back to the forest. There they hoped to tuck into a well-earned breakfast and, more importantly, receive an explanation regarding the missing Maquis.

15

They didn't make it as far as the hide – for breakfast or anything else. As his own jeep had been knocked out during the battle in Châtillon, Captain Callaghan had decided to march back on foot with seven of his men. On his way back across the formerly deserted aerodrome, he met André and Maxine marching across the airstrip with nearly eighty of the promised five hundred Maquisards strung out in loose file formation behind them. Almost exploding, the volatile Callaghan hurried up to the Maquis leader and screamed: 'Where the hell were you?'

André gave his familiar carefree shrug. 'It was not my fault,' he explained. 'I was up an hour before dawn to go looking for the other Maquisards, who I thought were in a separate camp in the forest. But they had moved on without telling me . . .'

'Bloody typical!' Callaghan interjected.

'. . . and so I had to return to my own camp and prepare my own men.'

'This lot?' Callaghan said, waving his free hand to indicate the eighty-odd men and women pressing up behind André and Maxine.

'Yes. However, when I told them that the other four hundred would not be coming with us, they decided to have a meeting to see if they should still come. Naturally, this took time and . . .'

'They decided to have a bloody meeting?' Callaghan bawled. 'We're fighting a war here!'

'*We're* fighting a war!' Maxine exploded with a ferocity to match Callaghan's. 'And we're doing it our way.'

'And your way means promising to help us, only to leave us stranded?'

'We work by democratic rule. If anyone disagrees with a plan, it must be discussed.'

'And in this case,' André added, 'the loss of the other four hundred Maquisards made some of my men think this battle would lead to too many casualties.'

'So you left us to get on with it on our own!'

'No!' Maxine snapped. 'Even though we all agreed that the battle would be too costly, in the end we voted to come, not only because we had already committed ourselves to you, but also because we wanted to minimize your losses. You should be grateful, not angry, Captain.'

In fact, Callaghan was so angry that he had to turn away from them and take deep, even breaths to control himself. One of those who had decided to come with him on foot was Sergeant Bob Tappman and when Callaghan saw his sly grin, it helped him cool down and act more diplomatically.

'All right,' he said, turning back to André and Maxine, 'I'll accept that. I'm sorry I got a bit annoyed, but I'm sure you understand. We left a lot of dead SAS men back there and it still isn't finished.'

'I understand, Captain,' André said, then shrugged again. 'So let's finish it.'

'I'm worried about the Germans killing off any wounded SAS men that they find, so I want to go straight back. If I call Captain Greaves, already back at the hide, and ask him to return and give us support, will you undertake to help my small group mount another attack right now?'

'Yes.'

'Good.'

Callaghan immediately removed his lightweight S-phone from its aluminium box strapped to his chest webbing and used it to contact Greaves, who had just arrived back in the hide. When the situation was explained to Greaves, he agreed to forget breakfast and return immediately to the town with his men, hopefully to meet up with Callaghan's group in the market square. Satisfied, Callaghan replaced the S-phone, then, gripping his Sten gun in his right hand, waved the weapon above his head and bawled: 'Move out!'

With the eighty well-armed Maquisards behind them, the nine SAS men from the three destroyed jeeps marched resolutely back to the town, crossing the low, humpback bridge over the river and then entering a street that led them directly down to the market square. As the SAS men entered that street, the Maquis were splitting up into six separate groups and circling the small town to enable each group to tackle a separate street. Going down the street he had chosen, Callaghan ordered his men to press themselves against the walls of the houses, hug the doorways, and move as quickly and as quietly as possible from one doorway to the next, so minimizing the chance of being hit by German snipers.

In fact, they managed to get down nearly all the way to the market square without interference. When close enough to see the square itself, they noted that it was filled with Panzer troops who were clearly regrouping to defend those clambering into trucks, preparing to flee the town. There was also a German armoured car in the square.

During the previous engagement, Harry-boy Turnball had removed a bazooka from a dead SAS trooper. Now, using hand signals, Callaghan indicated that he should set it up, aim for the armoured car, and fire at Callaghan's order, which would also be the signal for the rest of the men to attack with personal weapons and hand-grenades. Harry-boy duly dropped to one knee, adjusted the bazooka on his right shoulder, let himself be steadied by his friend Neil Moffatt, then squinted along the sight. At another hand signal from Callaghan he fired the bazooka.

The backblast punched Harry-boy backwards and the flying shell left a smoke signature that ran straight from Harry-boy to the armoured car. The Panzer troops had heard the backblast and were starting to look around just as the shell made a direct hit and the armoured car blew up with a deafening roar, filling the air with debris and bowling over some of the Germans. Instantly, before the other Panzer troops had realized what was happening, the SAS men spreading along both sides of the street around Harry-boy opened fire with their Sten guns, tommy-guns and .303-inch Lee-Enfield bolt-action rifles, cutting down the Germans they could see framed by the walls at the end of the street. At practically the same time, the sound of firing came from the other streets where the Maquis were using the same tactics.

'They're scattering!' Callaghan bawled. 'Watch out for the corners!'

While the German troop trucks started rumbling out of the square into what they thought were safe streets, the Panzer troops attempted to give them cover by dividing into teams that took one corner each of a street. From there they attacked the SAS or Maquis by leaning in and out to fire short bursts from their sub-machine-guns. Callaghan's group returned this fire by hugging the doorways and ducking in and out in a similar manner, also firing savage bursts that hit very few Panzer troops but at least ensured that they could not move up the street.

After ten minutes of this, just as Callaghan was wondering how to break the deadlock and get his men on the move, Lorrimer's jeep came racing down the narrow street with Jacko and Rich already firing their deadly twin Vickers at opposite corners. Their sustained fire was enough to devastate the corner walls, fill the air with flying cement and dust, and keep the Germans on both sides pinned down until the jeep was racing out past the street corners and into the square. As it did so, the two gunners swung their weapons in tight arcs and kept firing, massacring the Germans huddled behind the walls.

Cheering, Callaghan's men leapt out from the doorways and raced down behind the jeep towards the square. As they emerged from the street, they saw other SAS jeeps racing into the square from the other side-streets, with the gunners firing their Vickers at the Germans huddling at the corners. Those jeeps were followed by hordes of Maquisards, who were cheering and firing their weapons at the same time.

Racing at the crouch across the square towards where Greaves's jeep was screeching to a halt, Callaghan heard explosions from different directions just outside the town. Glancing back over his shoulder as he ran, he saw ugly clouds of smoke billowing up beyond the surrounding houses, from what appeared to be the vicinity of the outlying crossroads. Callaghan then reached Greaves's jeep and dropped down beside him.

'I posted jeep ambushes on all the main roads leading out of the town,' Greaves explained, 'to stop the German trucks from leaving. Sounds like they succeeded.'

Callaghan glanced over the roofs and saw the columns of smoke on all sides – clearly the product of bazookas and Lewes bombs. 'I think you're right,' he told Greaves. No sooner had he spoken than the sound of Sten guns, tommy-guns and Lee-Enfield rifles came from the nearby streets. 'The Germans who escaped from the trucks must be retreating back into the town, pursued by our men,' he said. 'In some of the streets they'll be trapped between the men pursuing them and the Maquis or SAS troops down here. But some of the streets are unprotected, as are the narrow lanes connecting them, so I think we'll have to get the men to spread out and clear the whole town in a close-combat mop-up.'

'I don't think you have to tell them that,' Greaves replied, leaning sideways and peering around the front of the jeep. 'They seem to be doing that already.'

Callaghan saw immediately that this was true. With most of the Germans already cleared from the market square, even the SAS gunners manning the mounted Vickers were jumping down off the jeeps, carrying their personal weapons at the ready, and chasing the rest of the Germans into the streets leading out of the square. Once in that maze of narrow streets and criss-crossing lanes, close combat between small groups or individuals became unavoidable.

Jacko, Rich, Harry-boy and Neil were operating as an extremely efficient four-man team, each protecting the other as they clambered over the low walls dividing the backyards of houses, taking pot-shots at the Germans trying to escape by doing likewise.

The Germans were being trapped in a pincer movement, with the SAS and the Maquis closing in on all sides. Jacko knew just how frightened they must be, and why they could not afford to surrender, when, from his vantage-point on top of a wall, he saw three of them trapped in a pretty, tree-lined cul-de-sac. Backed up against a white-painted wall by a group of resistance fighters, including the sharpshooting Maxine, the Panzer troops had no choice but to drop their weapons and surrender. In fact, one of them had scarcely managed to get his hands above his head before he was chopped down by a combined blast from two Maquis carbines. Even as he convulsed, was slammed back into the wall, then slid down it like a punctured balloon, his two companions were turning away to face the wall with their hands high. Without hesitation, Maxine stepped up to them, raised what looked like a Luger in her right hand, and blew the back of both men's heads off. She and her fellow Maquisards were already running back out of the cul-de-sac to find more Germans as the last two were collapsing, leaving a trail of bright-red blood on the pretty white wall.

Instinctively understanding that Maquis justice had been bred from years of torment and torture of the French by the Germans, Jacko ignored what he had seen and clambered over another wall, following Rich, Harry-boy and Neil. After climbing over the last wall in the row of back gardens, he dropped down beside his mates, glanced left and right along the narrow, winding lane, then followed them along it until reaching another street. Leading out of town and into the square, it had fights going on at both ends, with a mixture of SAS and Maquisards showing no mercy to the Germans trying to battle their way out in one of two directions.

Out of range of both groups of Germans, Jacko and the others raced across the street, explored another narrow, dark lane and emerged on to the parallel street just as a group of about thirty German troops, all on bicycles, were coming up the hill in the hope of getting out of town. Instantly, the SAS men dropped back into the shelter of the narrow lane, but only three of them made it before the first of the Germans had let their bicycles fall to the ground, swung their Schmeissers up and fired a frantic burst.

Jacko was piling into Rick and Neil behind the shelter of the wall when he heard a truly dreadful sound from just behind him. Disentangling himself from his two mates, who were already swinging their weapons up to fire, he glanced back and saw Harry-boy writhing on the ground, screaming hideously and clawing dementedly at the blood-soaked area around his groin. His clothing there was tattered from the many bullets that had torn through it and there appeared to be nothing left between his legs except a hash of torn flesh.

Deeply shocked for the first time in years, Jacko tried to block out his mate's dreadful screams and instead gave his anger free rein as he fired off a sustained, savage burst that sent bullets ricocheting noisily off the bicycles and caused their riders to topple over like skittles.

'Kill me! Kill me! Kill me!' Harry-boy suddenly started screaming as he slithered over the ground, clawing frantically at his bloody groin. 'Ah, Jesus! Oh, God!'

Mercifully, a burst from a German sub-machine-gun kicked the dirt up around him, then stitched right over him, blowing off most of his head and punching his body full of holes. He shuddered violently while the bullets were stitching him, then froze and went quiet.

Outraged, Jacko fired another ferocious burst from his Sten gun, then hurled a 36 hand-grenade. It landed in the midst of a group of five Germans who had leapt back on their bicycles and were attempting to escape up the hill. The explosion sent men and bicycles flying, the former hitting the ground like charred, shredded dolls and the bicycles buckling and, in one instance, falling to pieces, with a wheel spinning away down the hill towards the square. Jacko's grenade was quickly followed by a similar device thrown by Rich, then by a stolen German potato-masher hurled by Neil. The three grenades went off almost simultaneously, causing an ear-splitting cacophony and wreaking havoc among the dazed, bloodied Germans. Even as those untouched were running away in both directions, leaving their bicycles behind, Jacko, Rich and Neil were mercilessly cutting them down in a sustained hail of bullets. The few who actually managed to escape were then finished off by the SAS men and Maquisards taking control of both ends of the street.

While this was happening, Greaves and Lorrimer were leading a foot patrol round the east side of Châtillon, where the only firing that could be heard was taking place behind them in the town itself. Nevertheless, isolated groups of Germans were to be seen everywhere and Greaves's group soon found themselves following four escaping Panzer troops over the crest of a low hill and into a copse of beech trees. When the Germans stopped to study a map of the area, arguing in a whisper among themselves, the SAS men all opened fire at once, swiftly dispatching the Germans with a fusillade that peppered their backs before they could even turn around.

Marching in a large arc that would ensure they would not be found by any Germans who might have seen them entering the trees, Greaves's men emerged by a lock in the Seine, which partly encircled the town and château. Crossing the lock and walking along the side of the tow-path, hugging the hedgerows, well away from the exposed space by the river, they saw two more Panzer troops zigzagging at the crouch across a graveyard. Lorrimer, carrying a .303-inch Lee-Enfield, picked both Germans off with two well-placed shots, then the group moved on.

After walking for another five minutes they found themselves in the garden of a farmhouse beside a narrow lane which, they now realized, curved down in the direction of the Troyes–Chaumont crossroads. Clambering over the wall in the garden and inching carefully around the blind bend, they were surprised to see that German machine-gun posts had been established on each side of the Troyes road. Clearly they had been left there by an optimistic officer who had hoped to give protection to his fellow Panzer troops when they fled the city. Equally clearly, that officer had not returned and the machine-gun crew did not know that the few of their comrades still left alive were trapped in the streets and lanes of the town.

The crew manning the guns, all wearing greatcoats and steel helmets, had their backs turned to the SAS men. Unable to think of what to do other than shoot the Germans in the back, in cold blood, Greaves and the others, not turned murderous with rage by witnessing the dreadful death of Harry-boy Turnball, decided to wait it out in the garden, assuming the Germans would leave eventually. When, after another thirty minutes, it became clear that the Germans were not likely to move for some time, Lorrimer boldly clambered back over the wall of the farm, hammered on the door of the farmhouse and, when the startled farmer's wife came out, charmed bread, cheese and a bottle of wine from her. Despite being forced to keep their eyes glued to the Germans below, the men enjoyed their light lunch enormously.

'Bloody good, that was,' Lorrimer said. 'But we can't sit here all day drinking wine and waiting for those bastards down there to leave. What say you, boss?'

'They're not going to surrender,' Greaves said, 'and I still don't like the idea of shooting them in the back.'

'We're not shooting them in the back in cold blood,' Lorrimer insisted. 'There's a battle going on and we've got to get rid of them somehow. Short of standing up and announcing our presence, giving them time to shoot us, I say shoot them now.'

'Actually,' Corporal Jim Almonds said, 'we'll only have to shoot one of them in the back. Once we do that, the others will turn around to face us and we can fire with clear consciences.'

'Our signaller is a pragmatist,' Lorrimer said, 'and I agree with him, boss.'

'Right,' Greaves said. 'Let's do it.'

'So who shoots the first man in the back?' Lorrimer asked.

'Let's toss for it,' Almonds suggested.

Impressed more every second by the normally reticent signaller, Greaves nodded and pulled a French franc from his pocket. After tossing it two or three times, with each man choosing heads or tails and candidates for the task gradually being eliminated, the loser turned out to be Lorrimer. As the sergeant was the best single-shot rifleman in C Squadron, he suspected that he had been fitted up by Greaves and told him so.

'What a low thing to think of me,' the captain replied with a mischievous grin. 'Now get on with it, Sergeant.'

Impatient to be getting back to town where, as the greatly diminished firing indicated, the mopping-up was nearly finished, Lorrimer wasted no more time and, taking careful aim with his Lee-Enfield, squeezed the trigger.

The single shot split the silence and the German in Lorrimer's sights jerked forward violently and fell on his face. Instantly galvanized into action, the other members of the gun crew swung their machine-guns and personal weapons round to aim up the hill. They were doing so as the rest of Greaves's group unleashed a fusillade down on them and had the pleasure of seeing some of the Germans jerk sideways or backwards, collapsing across their weapons.

Their pleasure was short-lived. Suddenly, Schmeissers and Spandaus roared from behind the hedgerow at the far side of, and lower down, the lane, sending bullets ricocheting noisily off the ground around the SAS men. Those bullets soon found their target, chopping down Sergeant Riley and Corporal Seekings, both of whom died instantly.

'I've been hit!' Corporal Almonds bawled, dropping his Lee-Enfield, staggering back a little, and clutching his bloody left upper arm. 'Fuck!'

'Over the wall!' Greaves yelled, shocked to learn so brutally that another large group of Germans had been camping in the field at the other side of the high hedgerow. Firing his Sten gun from the hip, he made his way backwards to the low stone wall bordering the farmer's garden, screaming as he went: 'Bug out! Withdraw! Over the wall!'

By now, the narrow, high-banked lane had become a virtual death-trap, with Schmeisser bullets whining between and around the SAS men, soon claiming another one of their number.

'Lance-Corporal Taggart down!' Lorrimer shouted into his S-phone, hoping that someone in the town would hear him and send reinforcements. 'Sergeant Riley and Corporal Seekings down! We're withdrawing right now!'

A Schmeisser bullet ricocheted off the S-phone container and went winging off into the blue, though its impact was enough to propel Lorrimer backwards into the wall, where he turned around and began clambering up the stones. He had just dropped down the other side when the man beside him, Trooper Phil Bellamy, grunted as if punched, then jerked forward and flopped face down on the grass with an enormous red stain spreading over the back of his bullet-riddled Denison smock. Knowing he was dead, Lorrimer saw no sense in picking him up and instead followed the others across the garden to the farmhouse as bullets continued to buzz angrily about them. More bullets were zipping off the white walls of the farmhouse, peppering it with ugly holes, as the SAS men kicked the front door open and rushed inside.

Waving and shouting apologies to the startled woman who had fed them, they ran straight through the living-room and kitchen, then out through the back door. Once outside, with the house between them and the Germans, they scrambled down the bank of the canal, then made their way back along the tow-path to the lock. Crossing the lock again, they headed towards Châtillon, thinking they were safe. But suddenly, in the middle of a ploughed field below the château, they heard the sound of a single Spandau.

Lorrimer yelped briefly and folded double.

'Damn!' he muttered, sitting up again and clutching his bloody left leg. 'I've been hit in the thigh.'

As two of the men poured a fusillade of sub-machine-gun fire in the direction from which they thought the Spandau was firing, Greaves swiftly knelt beside his sergeant, gave his bloody wound a cursory examination and said: 'It's just a flesh wound, my old mate, so you've no need to worry. I'll . . .'

He was cut off in mid sentence by the distant but unmistakable roaring of 9mm Sten guns. Abruptly the Spandau went silent. A few seconds later a green flare burst in the sky over where the men had suspected the Spandau was located. Greaves turned back to Lorrimer.

'Our boys,' he said. 'They've put the Spandau out of action.' Even as he spoke, the sounds of a vicious fire-fight exploded in the distance, in the direction of the Troyes–Chaumont crossroads. The battle raged for some time, then gradually faded away. When the last shot had been fired, another green flare exploded above the area of the intersection, indicating that the SAS were in control.

Indeed, green flares were exploding all over town and there were no more shots.

Châtillon was now in the hands of the SAS and the Maquis.

'Still,' Greaves said to Lorrimer, 'there might be the odd Kraut about, determined not to give in, so we'd better be careful. Do you think you can make it back to the town or shall I send someone back for you?'

'As long as I'm breathing I can make it,' Lorrimer replied in a defiant tone. 'I can crawl on my belly.'

'We'll all be doing that,' Greaves said.

This was true. In order to avoid any remaining German snipers, Greaves and the rest of his men, including the wounded sergeant, wriggled on their bellies along the furrows of the ploughed field until they reached a stretch of 'dead' ground which, being hollow, would shield them from gunfire. Once there, Lorrimer, weakened by loss of blood, let Greaves temporarily bandage his wound while two of the other men advanced at the crouch to recce what was in front of them. They returned a couple of minutes later to confirm that the town had been taken and that the only men in front of them were SAS and Maquis. Two of the former would be coming up any minute with a stretcher for Lorrimer.

In fact it was Callaghan who appeared in a jeep with Jacko, Rich and Neil, all of whom were distraught at the horrible death of their friend Harry-boy Turnball. Behind that jeep, however, was another jeep carrying a medic, two stretcher bearers and a stretcher. Lorrimer was rolled on to the stretcher, humped into the jeep and then driven back to the town, where the grateful

Mayor had offered his large house as an emergency medical post.

Setting up a temporary command post in the post office in the market square, the three SAS officers, Callaghan, Greaves and Lazenby, conferred with André Flaubert and Maxine, to learn that between them the SAS and the Maquis had killed over a hundred Germans and wounded many more. They had also destroyed many German vehicles, including armoured cars, jeeps, motor-cycles and bicycles. The battle for Châtillon was over.

That evening, when the SAS men returned to their woodland hide, they heard over the No. 11 wireless set that General Patton's 3rd Army had taken Dijon earlier in the day.

There was no longer any need for night raids – or any other kind of raids – in that particular area. The SAS, with the help of the Maquis, had completed their task.

16

The SAS had picked up an inaccurate report about the fall of Dijon. In fact, it was French troops who liberated Dijon on 11 September 1944. On the same day the first waves of General Patch's 7th Army, having advanced 350 miles in slightly less than a month, made contact with General Patton's US 3rd Army at Sombernon, west of Dijon. Later that day, Patton and a contingent of his men made the short journey to Dijon, where they met up with the French and secured the city.

SAS operations in France, Belgium, the Netherlands and Germany continued right up until the unconditional surrender of the Germans on 4 May 1945. During that time the SAS killed approximately 2000 of the enemy, wounded over 7000, captured more than another 7000, and even negotiated the surrender of a further 18,000. In a total of 164 raids they also destroyed 700 vehicles and seven trains, derailed a further thirty-three trains and cut numerous railway lines. Last but not least, they reported many bombing targets to the Allies and otherwise supplied them with a wealth of invaluable intelligence.

The price paid for these achievements was 330 reported casualties, including the deaths of many French civilians and Maquisards, who were tortured and shot for assisting the SAS. So successful were the SAS in harassing the Germans that Hitler ordered captured SAS men to be tortured and then put to death. The exact number of SAS dead has never been revealed.

The SAS was officially disbanded in October 1945. A month later the SAS Regimental Association was formed. Then, in 1947, the War Office established a Territorial Army raiding unit which was attached to the Rifle Brigade, a unit that merged with the Artists Rifles, the latter raised in 1859 as a volunteer battalion and known in 1947 as 21 SAS (Artists). In 1950, Brigadier Mike 'Mad Mike' Calvert, a Chindit and SAS commander during World War Two, was called upon for a solution to the Malayan Emergency and suggested the creation of a special military force able to operate independently for long periods in the jungle. His recommendation led to the formation of the Malaya Scouts and a detachment from 21 SAS (Artists) soon joined them. Following the initial success of the Malaya Scouts, 22 SAS was formed out of them in 1952.

The Group's HQ was located in the Duke of York's Barracks, London, and the regimental base was Bradbury Lines, Merebrooke Camp, Malvern, Worcestershire, where it remained until 1960, when it was moved to Hereford.

Many of the Originals who had been founder members of L Detachment, SAS Brigade, in 1941 and fought in north-west Europe, went on to fight more major campaigns in Malaya, Borneo, Oman and Aden throughout the 1950s and '60s. Some were killed in action, others wounded so badly that they could not serve again, and yet others, when the inexorable passage of time rendered them too old for active duty, went on to become drill instructors and teachers at the Training Wing, Counter Revolutionary Warfare Wing, Demolitions Wing or 264 SAS Signals at Bradbury Lines and, later, Stirling Lines, Hereford; or intelligence officers and strategists at Operations Research Wing or Operations Planning and Intelligence, known as 'the Kremlin'.

The lessons learnt by the Originals, and the tactics and skills developed as a consequence of those lessons during their first forays into the North African desert with the Long Range Desert Group and, later, during their many day and night raids against the Germans in Europe, stood them in good stead in the future and were constantly revised to accommodate new kinds of warfare and the introduction of more sophisticated weapons and technical equipment, particularly in the areas of communications and surveillance. It was therefore no accident that, after the North African campaigns and the battles in north-west Europe, the SAS should find themselves being used over the years for sabotage, intelligence-gathering missions, 'hearts-and-minds' campaigns, long-range reconnaissance, clandestine insertion, Counter Insurgency (COIN) and Counter Revolutionary Warfare (CRW) in locations as diverse as the Far East, the

Middle East, Northern Ireland, the Falkland Islands, and Iraq.

At least once a year the SAS Originals of World War Two – some retired from the regiment, others scattered throughout its many wings and camps, and yet others, mostly officers, returned to their original units – would have a reunion at which they would fondly reminisce about what most of them believed were, if not the most spectacular, then certainly the most romantic days of the SAS: the early years in North Africa and north-west Europe.

During such boozy, noisy reunions, the Originals, their numbers diminishing annually through death from both 'natural' and 'unnatural' causes, would mock their own heroic or foolish acts and make jokes about old mates. They always made a point, however, of never mentioning the names of those who had failed to return. Those names were taboo.

And yet the dead were not forgotten. The names of those who died in action were inscribed on plaques originally attached to the base of the Regimental Clock Tower at Bradbury Lines. For this reason, 'beating the clock' became SAS slang for staying alive. When the new barracks block, Stirling Lines, was complete in 1960, the plaques were resited outside the Regimental Chapel, but by now the term was well and truly established in SAS parlance.

Even though the names of the dead were rarely, if ever, heard among the SAS, they lived on in the collective memory of the regiment. They were part of SAS history and duly honoured in silence.